Tom Holt was born in London in 1961. At Oxford he studied bar billiards, ancient Greek agriculture and the care and feeding of small, temperamental Japanese motor-cycle engines; interests which led him, perhaps inevitably, to qualify as a solicitor and emigrate to Somerset, where he specialised in death and taxes for seven years before going straight in 1995. Now a full-time writer, he lives in Chard, Somerset, with his wife, one daughter and the unmistakable scent of blood, wafting in on the breeze from the local meat-packing plant. For more information about Tom Holt visit www.tom-holt.com

To find out more about other Orbit authors register for the free monthly newsletter at www.orbitbooks.net

TOM HOLT

Dead Funny

Contains

Flying Dutch and
Faust Among Equals

www.orbitbooks.net

ORBIT

This omnibus edition © Tom and Kim Holt 2000
Reprinted 2002, 2003, 2004 (twice), 2005, 2006, 2008, 2009

Flying Dutch
First published in Great Britain in 1991 by Orbit
Copyright © Tom Holt 1991

Faust Among Equals
First published in Great Britain in 1994 by Orbit
Copyright © Kim Holt 1994

The moral right of the author has been asserted.

A CIP catalogue record for this book
is available from the British Library.

ISBN 978-1-84149-025-0

Printed and bound in Great Britain by
CPI Mackays, Chatham, ME5 8TD

Papers used by Orbit are natural, renewable and recyclable
products sourced from well-managed forests and certified
in accordance with the rules of the Forest Stewardship Council.

Mixed Sources
Product group from well-managed
forests and other controlled sources
www.fsc.org Cert no. SGS-COC-004081
© 1996 Forest Stewardship Council
FSC

Orbit
An imprint of
Little, Brown Book Group
100 Victoria Embankment
London EC4Y 0DY

An Hachette UK Company
www.hachette.co.uk

www.orbitbooks.net

CONTENTS

FLYING DUTCH

To Malcolm

CHAPTER ONE

It's always a little startling to hear your name in a public place, and Vanderdecker froze. The beer in his glass didn't, and the froth splashed his nose. He put the glass down and listened.

'The story of the Flying Dutchman . . .' the man opposite had said. Slowly, so as not to be seen to be staring, Vanderdecker looked round. His profession had trained him to take in all the information he needed to enable him to form a judgement in one swift glance, and what he saw was a plump young man wearing a corduroy jacket and a pink shirt with a white collar. Trousers slightly too tight. Round, steel-rimmed spectacles. Talking at a girl at least seven years his junior. American. Vanderdecker wasn't much taken with what he saw, but he listened anyway.

'Most people think,' said the plump young man, 'that Wagner invented the story of the Flying Dutchman. Not true.'

'Really?' said the girl.

'Absolutely,' the plump young man confirmed. 'The legend

can be traced back to the early seventeenth century. My own theory is that it represents some misconstrued recollection of the Dutch fleet in the Medway.'

'Where is the Medway, exactly?' asked the girl, but the plump young man hadn't heard her. He was looking through her, as if she were a ghost, to the distant but irresistible vision of his own cleverness.

Vanderdecker knew exactly where the Medway was, and frowned. He disliked being referred to as a legend, even in his own lifetime. But the plump young man hadn't finished yet.

'The version used by Wagner – I say used, but of course the Master tailored it to his own uses – tells of a Dutch captain who once tried to double the Cape of Good Hope in the teeth of a furious gale, and swore he would accomplish the feat even if it took him all eternity.'

'You don't say,' said the girl.

'No sooner had the fateful oath left his lips,' he continued, 'when Satan heard the oath and condemned the wretched blasphemer to sail the seas until the Day of Judgement, without aim and without hope of release, until he could find a woman who would be faithful until death. Once every seven years the Devil allows him on shore to seek such a woman; and it is on one such occasion . . .'

'I always thought,' said the girl, 'that the Flying Dutchman was a steam train.'

This had the effect on the plump young man that sugar has on a full tank of petrol. He stopped talking and made a request that Vanderdecker, for his part, would have found it difficult to grant.

'Pardon me?' he asked.

'Or was that the Flying Scotsman?' said the girl, realising that the joke needed explanation before an American could understand it. She might as well have been speaking in Latvian for all the effect she had, however, and again a moment of bewilderment the plump man started off again with the details of the Daland-Senta plot from Wagner's opera. At this point, Vanderdecker let his attention drift back to his pint of beer, for he loathed the story. He had seriously considered taking legal action when the opera was first presented, but the problems of proving who he was would have been insurmountable.

By an odd coincidence, although not even Vanderdecker was aware of it, the plump young man was Vanderdecker's great-great-great-great-great-great-great-grandson; the final product of an evolutionary process which had started with a fleeting encounter with a barmaid in New England in 1674. And there was proof, if proof were needed, that the version of the story that Junior had just gone through was nothing but a pack of lies, for Vanderdecker had been off and away without waiting to see if the barmaid in question would be faithful until a mild cold, let alone death. He was younger then, of course – a stripling of one hundred and sixteen – and still obsessed with wild notions of having a good time every once in a while. Nowadays, on the rare occasions when he met them, he looked upon barmaids simply as people who were paid to sell him alcoholic beverages.

The girl looked at her watch for the third time in four minutes and said that they had better be getting along or they would be late for the curtain. Her companion said there was no hurry, he hadn't finished telling her the plot. She replied that she would just have to muddle through, somehow or other. Vanderdecker got the impression that she wasn't enjoying herself very much.

They got up and left, leaving the Flying Dutchman staring at his glass and wondering why, when so many things had remained basically the same through the centuries, the human race had chosen to muck about with beer quite so much. In his young days they slung some malt in a bucket, added boiling water, and then went away and forgot about it for a week or so. The result of this laissez-faire attitude was incomparably preferable to the modern version, he seemed to remember – or was that just another aspect of getting old? Not that he was getting old, of course; no such luck. He looked and felt exactly the way he did in 1585 – which was more, he reflected, than you could say for Dover Castle.

Melancholy reflections on the subject of beer led him to even more melancholy reflections concerning the great web of being, and in particular his part in it, which had been so much more protracted than anybody else's. Not more significant, to the best of his knowledge. His role in history was rather like that of lettuce in the average salad; it achieves no useful purpose, but there's always a lot of it. But this was by no means a new train of thought, and he knew how to cope with it by now. He finished his drink and went to the bar for another.

As he stood at the bar and fumbled in his pocket for money, he tried playing the old 'I-remember-when' game which had entertained him briefly about a century ago and which now only irritated him. I remember when money was real money, he said to himself, when it was made of solid silver and had lots of Latin on it. I remember when you could have bought all the beer in Bavaria, plus sale tax and carriage, for the price of half a pint of this. I even remember flared trousers. That dates me.

As he sat down to his drink, he tried to think of something that wouldn't set him thinking about how incredibly long he had lived, just for a change. He tired to think of what he was going to do next. But that, of course, wouldn't take him very long, because he knew exactly what he was going to do next. He was going to get pathetically drunk, crawl back to his hotel, and wake up with a splitting head next morning which would leave him in no fit state to go flogging round Hatton Garden selling gold bars. After he had sold the gold bars, he would traipse through the bookshops and buy up enough reading matter to keep him from going stark raving mad for the next seven years. Then he would do the rest of his shopping, which would only leave him just enough time to get pathetically drunk again before slouching back to Bridport and his bloody ship and his bloody, bloody shipmates. It wasn't that he didn't want to find a woman who would be true until death; he simply didn't have the time.

He was following the first part of this programme with almost religious diligence when, several hours later, the plump man and the girl came back for a last drink. Vanderdecker hoped that they would enjoy it, since it might make up for an otherwise completely wasted evening witnessing that puerile burlesque of his life story. For his part, as usual, Vanderdecker had come to terms with modern beer, and was rather better adjusted to the world in general. He no longer cared if he appeared to be staring. Staring was fun – at any rate, it was considerably more entertaining than what he had been doing for the last seven years – and a good long stare might help clear his head.

'The costumes,' said the girl after a long silence, 'were quite pretty.'

Her companion gave her the sort of look that should have been reserved for a tourist who goes to Rome just to look at the gas works. 'What did you think,' he asked – with obvious restraint – 'of the music?'

'I got used to it,' she replied, 'after a bit. Like a dripping tap,' she added.

That seemed to wrap it up, so far as the plump young man was concerned.

'Is that the time?' he said without looking at his watch. 'I must go or I'll miss the last train.'

'Must you?' said the girl. 'Oh well, never mind. I think I'll just finish my drink.'

'See you tomorrow, then,' said the plump man. 'Perhaps we can make a start on the July figures.'

Shortly afterwards, he wasn't there any more. Vanderdecker, however, continued to stare. If the girl was aware of this, she gave no sign of it. She was reading her programme. Presumably, Vanderdecker imagined, the summary of the plot.

The injustice of it made him suddenly angry, although he recognised in his soul that it was too late to do anything about it now. He finished his drink and stood up to go. His route to the door and the street led him past the girl's table and as he passed over the top of her bowed head he heard himself speak.

'All that stuff,' he said, 'about angels and faithful until death is rubbish. It was the smell.'

The girl looked up sharply, and just as Vanderdecker was going through the door she caught a glimpse of his face. Somewhere in the back of her mind she had a vague, indefinable, inchoate feeling that she had seen him somewhere before.

'I remember,' said the stranger, 'when money was real money.'

'That's right, mate,' said his new friend. 'Pounds, shillings and pence.'

'And testoons,' said the stranger, 'and groats and placks and angels and ryals and ducats and louis d'or and louis d'argent . . .'

'You what?'

'And nobles of course,' continued the stranger. 'I remember when you could get pissed as a rat, have a really good blow-out in a bakehouse, see the bear-baiting, and still have change out of a noble.'

The landlord turned his head very slightly. Drunks were no problem, but loonies he could do without.

'What are you talking about?' asked the stranger's new friend, in a tone of voice that suggested that their friendship might soon end as rapidly as it had begun.

'Before your time,' explained the stranger, twirling his beer round in its glass to revive the flagging head. 'Can't expect you to remember nobles.'

'Are you taking the . . .'

'No,' said the stranger. 'Are you?'

Twenty years of keeping a pub in this particular district of Southampton had given the landlord a virtually supernatural instinct for the outbreak of a fight. Unfortunately he was at the other end of the bar, and before he could intervene the stranger's new friend had hit the stranger in the face, very hard.

'Christ almighty,' said the stranger's new friend. There was blood streaming from his lacerated knuckles, and the stranger was grinning.

'Go on,' he said, 'hit me again.'

Before this invitation could be accepted, strong and practiced hands had taken up both parties and put them out in the street. For his part the stranger landed awkwardly, staggered, lost his footing and fell extremely heavily against a parking meter. The parking meter broke, but not so the stranger. He simply gathered himself carefully to his feet, looked around, and set off in search of another pub he remembered in this part of town. When he got there, however, it was boarded up. It had been closed for the last seven years, ever since a party of Royal Marines had started a fight with a man they thought was trying to be funny, and which had ended with five very confused Marines receiving treatment for fractured hands and feet.

At this stage, of course, the Dow Jones was still buoyant, the Hang Tseng had never had it so good, the FT was climbing like a deranged convolvulus, futures were trading as if there was no tomorrow, and the only currency that wasn't performing too well was the Confederate dollar.

In an alleyway in the centre of Cadiz, a rather disreputable-looking cat was stalking an empty crisp packet.

Just as the cat had resolved to pounce, a puff of wind caught the crisp packet and blew it into the middle of the highway, along which an articulated lorry full of cans of tomatoes was travelling. The cat saw this, but decided to pursue its quarry nevertheless. He had been stalking it for over half an hour and he was damned if he was going to let it slip through his paws now.

The lorry driver, to his credit, did his best to brake, but the momentum of a heavily laden Mercedes lorry is not an easy thing to dissipate quickly. There was a thud, and the cat was sent flying across the road. The lorry-driver continued on his way, and soon put the incident out of his mind.

The cat wearily got to its feet and looked around for the crisp packet, but it was nowhere to be seen. At that moment an English tourist came running across to inspect the damage. The tourist was female and fond of cats.

When she saw the cat get up, she couldn't believe her eyes. She had seen the poor animal being run over by the lorry – it must have been killed. But it hadn't been. She came closer, and it was then that the smell hit her. She reeled back, with both hands over her face, and groped her way out of the alley.

The cat was used to such reactions, but that didn't make them any more pleasant. He sulked for at least ten minutes, until a discarded fruit juice carton caught his eye and he settled his mind to the serious business of hunting. In a very, very long life he had learned how to get his priorities right.

On her way back home to Maida Vale on the tube, the girl who had seen the Flying Dutchman was bored, for she had forgotten to bring a book with her to read on the journey. Not that she had ever doubted for one split second that she was coming home tonight – perish the thought! It had been simple forgetfulness, and the tedium of having nothing to entertain herself with but the posters and her opera programme was a fitting punishment.

After a random sample, she decided that the opera programme was marginally less dire than the posters, and she read the synopsis of the plot again. A modern version of the story, she decided, with the Dutchman doomed to spend the rest of time going round and round the Circle Line with nothing to read but vilely-phrased propaganda from the employment agencies, might have some possibilities, but by and large the whole idea was not so much tragic but silly. The daftest part, she reckoned, was the idea that Satan could get you just for expressing a determination to get round a traffic hazard – if that rule still applied, she said to herself, then you wouldn't be able to set tyre to pavement on the Chiswick Roundabout for souls in torment. Or perhaps the rule did still apply. It would explain the way some people drove.

The train stopped at Paddington, opened its doors, and sat very still. In the corner of the carriage there was a tramp with wild white hair and very distressing shoes, fast asleep with his head almost between his knees, but otherwise she was alone. The girl abandoned the legend of the Flying Dutchman and turned her thoughts toward the great web of being, with particular reference to her own part in it. I am an accountant, she said to herself, working mainly in banking. Why is it that, whenever I remember this fact, I want to scream?

Perhaps, she considered, the Dutchman story wasn't so silly after all. Perhaps Satan did hover unseen in the ether waiting to pounce on ill-considered sayings. She had only said one very stupid thing in her life – 'I want to be an accountant' – but of the various explanations for her present condition to which she had given consideration before, the Satan theory was as good as any. Was there such a person as Satan, by the way? Why not? Satan was no more incredible a concept than Mr Peters, the senior partner, and he undoubtedly existed. All one would have to do to make the gentleman in horns conceivable would be to get him out of those stuffy medieval clothes into a nice three-piece suit, and convert the Fires of Hell into a microwave. You could possibly get a Government grant for that.

The girl recognised that her train of thought was becoming alarmingly metaphysical, but when you are stuck in Paddington station at a quarter to midnight with nothing to read, you can afford to indulge flights of fancy. Plato would have loved the Bakerloo Line.

I may not be Dutch, she said to herself, but I'm positive I would hate to live for ever. She remembered that week in the middle of the summer holidays when she was young, that one, inevitable week when the joy of not being at school had worn off and the dread of going back to school had not yet taken hold. That week when there was no longer anything to do, when everyone else had gone off with their parents to Jersey, when there was nothing on the television except Wimbledon, and cousin Marian from Swansea came to stay. That week that was free of all the pressures of doing the things you hated doing, devoid of all the pleasures of doing the things you liked doing, that week that lasted at least a month and probably longer. No crime a human being could commit, however terrible, could merit a punishment as dreadful as another of those weeks of killing time. Perhaps she should stop thinking along these lines, before she found out just exactly how shallow her mind really was.

It was then she remembered hearing a voice somewhere above her head at some stage during the evening, which had said that the angels and the love interest were all rubbish, but that the smell had been the real reason – or words to that effect. It was peculiar, to say the least, that her brain should seek to filter out this scrap of jetsam from the rubbish that her memory was sorting and discarding; her mind, she reckoned, was like the little grill thing over the plug-hole which catches fragments of cauliflower and pasta shells when the washing up bowl is emptied. She was reckoning thus when sleep finally caught her out, and she slept through Warwick Avenue and only just woke up in time to scramble out of the train at Maida Vale and walk home the long way.

There is one pub in Southampton which it is impossible to get yourself thrown out of no matter what you do or say, and there the newcomer ran into someone he knew very well.

At first they tried to avoid each other, since it was three days yet before they had to go back to the ship, and then they would be together again, inseparable, for another seven years. But this plan broke down when the newcomer realised that he had run out of money.

'Antonius,' said the newcomer to his friend in Dutch, 'lend me a fiver till payday.'

Antonius felt in the pocket of his shirt and found a five pound note, which he gave to his companion. His companion's name, for the record, was Johannes, and he and Antonius had been born in the same village south of Antwerp over four hundred and thirty years before. Barring shore leaves like this, they had been out of each other's company for a period exceeding eight hours exactly once in four hundred and seventeen of those years, when Johannes' mother had suspected that her son had caught the plague and locked him up in the barn for a few days.

Neither of them would have chosen to have it this way, since they didn't get on very well and never had. Johannes was a short, noisy man with a hairy face and hairy arms, who liked drinking a lot and falling over. What Antonius liked doing best was standing quite still, unfocussing his eyes, and thinking of nothing at all. Each of them found the other remarkably uncongenial, and the only point on which they were united and could talk for more than three minutes without losing their temper with each other was their dislike of everyone else on board the ship, and in particular Captain Vanderdecker.

'After all,' said Johannes, a few minutes later, as they sat in a corner of the bar under the dartboard and drank their beer, 'he was the one got us into this in the first place.'

'That's right,' replied Antonius. 'All his fault.'

A dart bounced out of treble fifteen and point first onto Antonius' brown, bald head. He extracted it and handed it back to its owner.

'What the hell did he want to go drinking that stuff for in the first place?' Johannes continued, picking a grain of chalk dust out of his beer as he spoke. 'He should have known it would end up all wrong.'

'He just didn't think,' Antonius agreed. 'No consideration for others.'

'And then dropping it,' said Johannes bitterly, 'into the beer-barrel.'

'Typical,' said Antonius. It was a word he was very fond of and saved for special occasions. He didn't want to wear it out by overuse.

'This beer,' said Johannes, unconsciously echoing his captain, 'grows on you after a bit. You could get used to it.'

'It's got a taste, though,' Antonius asserted. 'You want another?'

'Might as well.'

So they had another, and another, and two or three more after that, and then they went outside to get some air. By now they were feeling quite relaxed, and Antonius remembered the girl who lived round the corner. They decided to go and visit her. They did this every time they came to England, just as, every time, they forgot that she had died in 1606 and that her house was now a car park. They always left a note though, saying that they were sorry to have missed her and would be sure to drop in next time. Since the building of the car park they had taken to sticking these notes behind the windscreen wipers of the parked cars, and once they had left one on the car of an avid and knowledgeable local historian, who had read it and was quite ill for months afterwards.

The plump man, who was also an accountant, although a vastly more important one than the girl, made himself a cup of lemon tea and tried to forget that he had wasted a performance of *The Flying Dutchman* at Covent Garden, with Neustadt singing Senta, on a cultural void like Jane Doland. Next to his career, he loved opera above all things and a failure to appreciate it was a crime that could not be forgiven. He opened his briefcase, switched on his calculator and put *Rienzi* on the CD player. Slowly, like the return of spring, the wound began to heal.

CHAPTER TWO

The National Lombard Bank is situated in the very heart of downtown Bridport. It is the sort of location any red-blooded bank manager would give his heart and soul for, right in the epicentre of a triangle formed by the town's most beguiling attractions – the fish and chip shop, the Post Office and the traffic lights. In summer, whole families still make the difficult journey into Bridport from the surrounding country-side to stand and watch the traffic lights performing their dazzling *son et lumiere*; and although they now have a set of lights in Charmouth – a deliberate and cynical attempt to poach the holiday trade that has introduced much bitterness into the previously friendly relationship between the two com-munities – purists insist that the Bridport set has a purer green, a rosier red, a more scintillating amber than any others this side of Dorchester.

To a Sybaritic Londoner like Jane Doland, however, the Bridport Lights meant nothing more than another hold-up on her way to a not particularly pleasant assignment, and with the poverty of spirit that is the hallmark of the city-dweller she assumed that the small throng of children gathered round them were merely waiting to cross the road. She had no street-plan of Bridport to help her find the bank, but she located it nevertheless simply by looking straight in front of her as she drove in from the roundabout. A bank, she said to herself, what fun. This is well worth missing the London premiere of *Crocodile Dundee 9* for.

The causes of momentous events are often so bewilderingly complex that even highly-trained historians are at a loss to unravel them. Men wise in their generation have gone grey, bald and ultimately senile in the great universities grappling with the origins of the English Civil War, the Peasants' Revolt and the rise of Hitler, and it is doubtful now that the truth will ever be known. In contrast, the reason why Jane Doland was in Bridport, two years (give or take a week or so) since she had gone to see *The Flying Dutchman* at the Royal Opera House, was quite remarkably simple. A decree had gone out from Caesar Augustus that all the world should be taxed, and since this particular decree had had some viciously unexpected things in it about Advance Corporation Tax, all leave was cancelled in the offices of the leading accountancy firm where Jane Doland occupied a trivial and poorly-paid position, and accountants were dispersed like dazed bacilli into the blood-stream of British commerce to sort out the affairs of the National Lombard Bank, the firm's largest and most complicated client. Since the National Lombard has more branches than all the trees in the New Forest, and the Bridport branch occupies roughly the same place in the bank's list of priorities as that assigned to Leatherhead Rovers in the Football League, its affairs were unhesitatingly entrusted to Jane Doland's skill, expertise and highly-motivated commitment.

Jane was considering this when she parked her car under a lime tree in that famous Bridport thoroughfare which some unusually imaginative soul had christened South Street. In fact the term 'nonentity' had been rattling about in her brain like a small, loose bearing all the way down the A303, and by the time she reached her destination she was in no mood to be pleasant to anybody or to appreciate anything. This would go some way towards explaining her lack of enthusiasm for the traffic lights, which happened to be at their luminescent best this not particularly fine morning.

Nevertheless, Jane said to herself as she walked through the door of the bank. When trying to cheer herself up, she never got further than nevertheless, but it was always worth giving it just one more go. As she had expected, they had looked out lots of nice accounts for her to amuse herself with, and although they were all in such a hopeless mess that Sherlock Holmes, with Theseus to help him, Einstein to handle the figures and Escoffier laying on plenty of strong black coffee, would have had a devil of a job sorting them out. Jane told herself that it is always the thought that counts. She could imagine the faces of the bank staff when the news hit them that an accountant from Moss Berwick was coming to visit them. 'Moss Berwick, eh?' she could hear them saying to each other. 'Somebody hide the July returns while I shuffle the invoices.'

After several false starts, the hour-hand of the clock on the wall in the pleasantly intimate cupboard they had set aside for her personal use crept round to one o'clock and she made her Unilateral Declaration of Lunchtime. The precious forty-five minutes that her contract of employment allowed her for rest, nourishment and the contemplation of the infinite was mostly dissipated in locating and booking into the Union Hotel, which Jane was able to tell from the public lavatories next door by the fact that the roller towel in the public lavatories worked. By not bothering to unpack, Jane was able to dash down to the bar, fail to get a drink and a sandwich before it shut, and sprint back to the bank just in time to be three minutes late for the afternoon session. The manager wasn't impressed, and one of the cashiers gave her a look that nearly stripped all the varnish off her nails. At about three-fifteen her pencil broke.

Stay with it, girl, she said to herself as the office junior came to tell her to go away because they were locking up now, you've got four more days of this. Think (she said to herself) of the Honour of the Firm. Think of old man Moss hauling himself up by his bootstraps out of the slums of nineteenth-century Liverpool, studying all the hours God sent at the Mechanics Institute to pass his examinations, qualify, meet up with old man Berwick and found the greatest accounting firm the world has ever known. She had read this stirring story in the recruitment pamphlets they had sent her when she joined, and the recollection of it never failed to arouse in her strong feelings of pure apathy. Oddly enough, the pamphlet had been curiously reticent on the subject of old man Berwick, preferring to concentrate on his more dashing colleague, and Jane often wondered where he had pulled himself up out of by his bootstraps. Harrow, probably.

A year or so back, the compilers of the same recruitment guide had been going round interviewing members of staff for the new edition, and they had asked Jane what the most satisfying, fulfilling, life-enhancing thing about working for the firm was, in her lowly opinion. She had replied, without hesitation, going home, and they hadn't included her in the guide or even the video, although she prided herself that she had the best legs in the department. Since the rest of the legs in the department belonged to Mr Shaw, Mr Peterson, Mr Ferrara and Mr Timson respectively, this was no symptom of vanity on Jane's part, merely the scrupulous accuracy and devotion to truth which marks an accountant out from his fellow creatures.

Since then, Jane had kept her opinion of her chosen career very much to herself; but, as if to compensate, she let it out of its cage pretty freely once she was alone with it. As she was now, for instance, on a cold Monday night in Bridport.

There are few excitements to compare with one's first night

in a strange new town, and despite her weariness and a deplorable urge to take her tights off and watch 'Cagney and Lacey' on the black and white portable in her room at the Union Hotel, Jane set out to immerse herself completely in the town. After all, she reckoned, she might never come here again; live this precious moment to the full, crush each ripe fruit of sensation against the palate until the appetite is cloyed in intoxicating richness.

The cinema was closed when she eventually found it, what with it being half past September, and since she had no wish to be raped, robbed or murdered she didn't go into the White Hart, the Blue Ball, the Bunch of Grapes, the Prince of Wales, the Peacock, the Catherine Wheel, the Green Dragon, the Four Horseshoes, the Hour Glass, the Half Way House, the Bird in Hand, the Bottle and Glass, the Jolly Sportsman, the Dorsetshire Yeoman, the Boot and Slipper, the Rising Sun, the Crown and Cushion, the Poulteney Arms, the Red Cross Knight, the Two Brewers, the Black Dog, the Temporary Sign, the Duke of Rochester, the Gardeners Arms or the Mississippi Riverboat Night Club. Apart from these, the only place of entertainment open to the public was the bus shelter, and that was a touch too crowded for Jane's taste. She went back to the Union Hotel, had a glass or orange juice and some fresh local boiled carpet with gravy in the dining room, and went upstairs to catch the last ten minutes of 'Cagney and Lacey', which had been cancelled and replaced with athletics from Zurich.

Isn't it fortunate, Jane reflected, that I brought a good book with me. The only thing which can stop me enjoying my book is if the proprietors of this charnel-house forget to put a shilling in the meter. She picked the book out of her suitcase, opened it where her expired Capitalcard marked the place, and began to read.

This is not the right book, she said to herself as her eye fell upon the corduroy furrows of the page. This is the book I finished reading yesterday.

You can tell of your Torments of the Damned. You can, if you wish, allude to Sisyphus and the Stone. You can wax eloquent, especially if you are a television evangelist, about what is going to happen to the fornicators and the bearers of false witness when they finally come eyeball to eyeball with the Big G. But you cannot begin to describe, not if you speak with the tongues of men and of angels, the exquisite agony of being stuck in a fleabag hotel in a shut town with a choice between watching a load of tubby East Germans putting the shot in their underwear or reading a detective story every detail of whose plot is etched on your mind.

A berserk fury came over quiet, tranquil-minded Jane Doland. She pulled on her tights, picked up her room-key and went out into the gloomy corridor. Downstairs, in what was described with cruel irony as the residents' lounge, there might be a week-old newspaper or the July 1956 issue of *Woman and Home*. Or perhaps she might find a reasonably well-written telephone directory, or even a discarded matchbox with a puzzle on the back. There is always hope, so long as life subsists. The beating of the heart and the action of the lungs are a useful prevarication, keeping all options open.

She did find a matchbox, as it happens, but all it said was 'Made in Finland, Average Contents Forty Matches', and after the third reading Jane felt that she had sucked all the value out of that one. Disconsolate, she wandered out to the reception desk. The sound of a television commentator joyfully exclaiming that Kevin Bradford from Cark-in-Cartmel had managed to avoid coming last in the six hundred metres drifted through the illuminated crack above the office door. Jane looked down and saw the hotel register. Salvation! She could read that.

It was a fascinating document. For example, Jane learned that in November 1986 Mr and Mrs Belmont from Winnipeg had stayed three nights at the Union Hotel, and although they had had breakfast, they had not had any evening meals.

Why was that, she wondered? Had they spent every last cent

on the flight, and been reduced to eating their way through all the individual portions of jam and marmalade on the breakfast table to keep body and soul together during their stay? Did they spend the evenings flitting from casino to night-club to casino, scorning the Union's prosaic cuisine? Perhaps they just didn't like the look of the menu terribly much. She could sympathise with that. And what had brought these globe-trotting Belmonts half-way across the world, uprooting them from their cosy timber-frame home among the wheatfields, beside the immeasurable vastness of the mighty lake? Had they come back in search of their heritage, or to pay their last respects to a dying relative, resolving a twenty-year-old feud in a final deathbed reconciliation? Did they feel that same restless urge that drove much-enduring Ulysses to see the cities of men and know their minds? Or had they simply got on the wrong coach?

Another thing that Jane discovered, and could well believe, was that not many people stayed at the Union Hotel, or at least not enough to fill up an optimistically large register in a hurry. This one went back nine years, to when a Mr J. Vanderdecker of Antwerp had booked in for two nights. Oddly enough, she noticed, another J. Vanderdecker (or the same man that bit older and wiser) had booked in seven years later. On neither occasion had he risked the evening meal, but he had insisted on a room with bath both times. A shy, private sort of man, Jane imagined, who would rather die than have strangers see him in his dressing gown and slippers wandering the corridors at half-past seven in the morning.

The office door started to open, and Jane dodged guiltily away from the desk. As she did so she barked her shin on a low table, on which reposed a dog-eared copy of *Shooting Times* and *Country Magazine*. She seized it, fled, read it from cover to cover, finally fell asleep and had a nightmare about a man-eating ferret.

★ ★ ★

'I spy,' said the first mate, 'with my little eye, something beginning with W.'

Nobody took any notice. Even Jan Christian Duysberg had guessed that one back in the 1740s, and he had been thirty-four years old before he realised he was left-handed.

A seagull drifted across the sky, staggered in mid-air, banked violently and flew off to the south-east. Cornelius Schumaker clipped his toenails quietly in the shade of the mast. Wilhelm Triegaart completed his seventy-ninth crossword of the trip.

For some of the crew of the sailing-ship *Verdomde* (which is Dutch for 'Damned') the second year of each seven-year term was the worst. Just as Jane Doland often felt at her most miserable on Tuesdays, because the memory of the brief freedom of the weekend had already faded without bringing Friday appreciably nearer, so it was with the more impatient of Vanderdecker's command. Others were content to take each year as it came, whiling away the time with impossible projects – Pieter Pretorius, for example, was building a scale model of the battle of Lepanto inside an empty Coca-Cola bottle, while his brother Dirk pushed back the limits of pure mathematics by calculating the overtime claim he was going to put in when the trip finally ended – while the remaining members of the crew saw no further than the next watch. By now, the only man on the ship who even bothered trying to do something about the mess they were all in was the captain himself.

Captain Vanderdecker was a great reader of the *Scientific American*. He sat in his cabin with his feet up on the map-table and a relatively recent copy of that publication on his knees, trying to do long division in his head while he shook his solar calculator violently in a vain effort to make it work. Something important to do with the half-life of radium was on the point of slipping away from him for want of the square root of 47, and if it got away this time it might take him weeks to get it back. The fact that time was not of the essence was something he tried not to think about, for fear of giving up altogether.

Vanderdecker generated artificial urgency with the same fatuous optimism that makes an eighty-year-old woman dye her hair.

Ever since 1945, Vanderdecker had been fascinated by radiation. His original wild hopes had been dashed when he and the crew had lived through an early nuclear test in the Pacific and suffered nothing worse than glowing faintly in the dark for the next week or so; but he had persisted with it with a blind, unquestioning faith ever since he had finally been forced to give up on volcanoes. Not that he approved of radiation; he had read too much about it for that. For the rest of the human race, he thought it was a bad move and likely to end in tears before bedtime. For himself and his crew, however, it offered a tiny glimmer of hope, and he could not afford to dismiss it until he had crushed every last possibility firmly into the ground.

And so he read on, disturbed only by the creaking of the rigging and the occasional thump as Sebastian van Doorning threw himself off the top of the mast onto the deck. In 1964 the poor fool had got it into his head that although one fall might not necessarily be fatal, repeated crash-landings might eventually wear a brittle patch in his invulnerable skull and offer him the ultimate discharge he so desperately wanted. At least it provided occasional work for the ship's carpenter; every time he landed so hard he went right through the deck.

'The Philosopher's Stone?' the captain read. 'Breakthrough In Plutonium Isotopes Offers Insight Into Transmutation of Matter.' Vanderdecker swallowed hard and took his feet off the table. It was probably the same old nonsense he personally had seen through in the late seventies, but there was always the possibility that there was something in it.

'It is rumored,' said the *Scientific American*, 'that experiments at Britain's Dounreay nuclear reactor will lead to a new reappraisal of some fundamental aspects of atomic theory. If recently published results by physicists Marshmain and Kellner are vindicated by the Dounreay tests, the alchemist may shortly step out of the pages of histories of the occult and into European R&D laboratories. The co-ordinator of the new programme, Professor Montalban of Oxford University . . .'

Montalban. *Montalban*, for God's sake!

Over four hundred years of existence had left Vanderdecker curiously undecided about coincidences. Sometimes he believed in them, sometimes he didn't. The name Montalban is not common, but it is not so incredibly unique that one shouldn't expect to come across it more than once in four hundred years. Its appearance on the same page as the word 'alchemist' was a little harder to explain away, and Vanderdecker had to remind himself of the monkeys with typewriters knocking out *Hamlet* before he could get himself into a properly sceptical frame of mind to read on. By then, of course, the lamp in his cabin had blown out, and rather than waste time trying to light it again with his original but clapped-out Zippo, he decided to go out on deck and let the sun do the work for once. With his finger in the fold of the magazine so as not to lose the place, he scrambled up the ladder and out of the hatch, just as Sebastian van Doorning made his ninth descent of the day.

Vanderdecker was knocked sideways and landed in a pile of coiled-up rope. As he pulled himself together, he saw his copy of the *Scientific American* being hoisted up into the air by a gust of wind and deposited neatly into the Atlantic Ocean.

'Sebastian.'

The sky-diver picked himself sheepishly off the deck. 'Yes, captain?' he said.

'If you jump off the mast ever again,' said the Flying Dutchman, 'I'll break your blasted neck.'

They didn't bother lowering the ship's boat, they just jumped; the captain was in that sort of a mood. Eventually Pieter Pretorius fished the magazine out, and they tried drying it in the sun. But it was no good; the water had washed away all the print, so that the only words still legible on the whole page were 'Montalban' and 'alchemist'. Dirk Pretorius calculated the odds against this at nine million fourteen thousand two hundred and sixty-eight to one against, something which everyone except the captain found extremely interesting.

There, Jane said to herself, is a funny thing.

Do not get the impression, just because Jane is forever talking to herself, that she is not quite right in the head, or even unusually inclined towards contemplation. It was simply that in her profession there are not many people to talk to, and if one is naturally talkative one does the best one can. It is important that this point be made early, since Jane has a lot to do in this story, and you should not be put off her just because she soliloquizes. So did Hamlet. Give the poor girl a chance.

Extremely strange, she considered, and stared at the ledger in front of her through eyes made watery by deciphering handwriting worse even than her own. Undoubtedly there has been a visit from the Cock-Up Fairy at some stage; but when, and how?

It should not have been her job to look at the ledgers recording the current accounts; but an exasperating detail in quite ordinary calculation had gone astray, and she had, just for once, become so engrossed in the abstract interest of solving it that she had stayed with it for six hours, including her lunch break. Although she was not aware of it, she was pulling off a quite amazing *tour de force* of accountancy that her superiors would never have believed her capable of.

The reason why she had gone overboard on this one was a name. It wasn't a particularly common name, you see, and she had come across it once already. The name was Vanderdecker, J.

Vanderdecker, J had a current account with the National Lombard Bank. It contained £6.42. It had contained £6.42 for well over a hundred years.

A pity, Jane said to herself, it hadn't been a deposit account. The bank staff had stared at her as if she was completely crazy when she demanded the excavation of ledgers going back almost to the dawn of time. They had protested. They had assured her that the ledgers for the period before 1970 had been incinerated years ago. They had told her that even if they hadn't been incinerated (which they had), they had been lost. Even if they hadn't been lost, they were hopelessly difficult to get at. They were in storage at the bank's central storage depot in Newcastle-under-Lyme. Even if they weren't in Newcastle-under-Lyme, they were in the cellar. There were spiders in the cellar. Big spiders. A foolhardy clerk had gone into the cellar five years ago, and all they ever found of him was his shoes.

Until computerisation, all the ledgers were handwritten, and some of the handwriting was difficult to read. Jane's eyesight had never been brilliant, and too much staring at scrawly copperplate gave her a headache. She had a headache now; not one of your everyday temple-throbbers but something drastic in the middle of her forehead. Despite this, she was managing to think.

The logical explanation of the mystery – there is always a logical explanation – was that Vanderdecker, J had opened an account in 1879, lived his normal span of years and died, leaving the sum of £6/8/4d. In the anguish of his parting (Jane had read some deathbed scenes in Victorian novels and knew that people made a meal of such things in those days) the account had been overlooked. Inertia, the banker's familiar demon, had allowed the account to drift along from year to year like an Iron Age body in a peat bog, dead but perfectly preserved, and here it was to this day. Very salutary.

The only problem was the name J. Vanderdecker in the register of the Union Hotel. Dammit, it *wasn't* a common name; and if J Vanderdecker was swanning around Bridport two years ago, and seven years before that, he couldn't have died in the early nineteen-hundreds, which was what the sensible theory demanded.

Anyone but an accountant would have told the sensible theory to stuff it and gone on with something else. But accountants are different. Legend has it that all accountants are descended from one Barnabas of Sidon, a peripheral associate of the disciples of Our Lord who had done the accounts for Joseph's carpentry business in Galilee. After receiving a severe shock at the Feeding of the Five Thousand, he had been present at the Last Supper but had missed all the fun because he was too busy adding up the bill and trying to remember who had had what. Like fish, accountants see things in a different way from people, and details which people find unimportant are their reason for existing.

Well now, said Jane to herself, what are we going to do about this? In theory, all she had to do was report her findings to the manager, who would say, Yes how interesting, have you got much more to do or will you be going soon? and then write the account off against arrears of bank charges as soon as she left the premises. Jane felt very strongly, for some reason, that this was not something that ought to happen. She had no idea why it was important, but it was.

The only other information she had about the account, apart from the name Vanderdecker, J and the sum of £6.42, was an address: Lower Brickwood Farm Cottage, Melplash, near Bridport, Dorset. It followed that if there was anything else capable of being found out about this mystery, it would have to be sought there. She would go there this evening, she resolved, and everything would be explained; there *would* be a simple explanation, and she would find it at Lower Brickwood Farm Cottage. In the meanwhile, she could get on with her proper work and put it out of her mind.

Came half-past six, and Jane was off in her W registration Ford Fiesta looking for Lower Brickwood Farm Cottage, a task marginally more difficult than finding the Holy Grail. Melplash is not on the street map of Bridport which the seeker after truth can buy at the newsagent; neither, if the truth be told, is most of Bridport itself. When it comes to Melplash, however, the stranger is definitely on his own. It is assumed that the only people who need have anything to do with Melplash are people who live there already, and of course they all know where Lower Brickwood Farm Cottage is. They have gone past it on their way to the pillar-box or the Green Man every day since they were six, and they don't know it as Lower Brickwood Farm Cottage; they know it as 'Davis's' or 'the old linney', or even, rather metaphysically, 'in over'. The postal address concerns nobody except the postman; and since he was up at half-past four this morning, he is presumably now in bed.

Jane was not one of those people who are too embarrassed to stop people and ask directions to places, but this facility wasn't a great deal of use to her. Of the six people she stopped and asked, two were retired Midlanders who had only been living in Melplash for a year or so, two were informative but completely incomprehensible, and one gave her a set of clear and concise directions which, had she followed them, would have taken Jane to Liverpool. The sixth informant was the landlord of the Green Man. He asked if she was from Pardoes and were they going to do the old place up at last? Jane remembered the name Pardoes from For Sale boards, and said yes for the sake of a quiet life.

By the time Jane got to Lower Brickwood Farm Cottage – which is, of course, about as far from Lower Brickwood Farm as you can go without leaving the parish – it was nearly dark. The directions she had been given led her down an unmetalled road to a yard containing five fallen-down corrugated-iron sheds, which looked for all the world as if they were used for storing the proceeds of plundering expeditions against the neighbouring villages. There were in addition a spectacular collection of damaged tractor tyres, a burnt-out Ford Anglia with a small tree growing through the windscreen, several discarded items of farm machinery and a derelict stone structure of great age.

Jane would probably have given up at this point, for she was unused to such scenes; but she saw a crudely-painted sign on the derelict stone structure which said 'Lower Brickwood

Farm Cottage' and decided that this must be it. She walked up to the door and, being a well-brought-up young lady, knocked. A voice in the back of her mind called her an idiot, and she tried the door instead.

It wasn't locked; indeed, it gave a couple of inches before coming to rest against something low and heavy and thereafter becoming immovable. It has previously been recorded that the book Jane Doland had been reading before she came to Bridport was a detective story, and it should be noted that Jane was a devotee of this genre of fiction. In many detective stories, the detective tries the door of the lonely house to find it open but obstructed in precisely this way. The obstruction, you can bet your sweet life, will invariably turn out to be a dead body.

The last thing Jane wanted to find was a dead body. However, the same inner voice that had called her an idiot only moments before urged her to push against the door, and when she did it opened. There was no dead body. Instead, there was a heavy snowdrift of envelopes, most of them extremely mouldy. Some of them had stamps with the head of Queen Victoria on them. All of them had come from the National Lombard Bank. Jane knelt down on a century's worth of bank statements, invitations to take out credit cards, insurance company mail-shots and encomia of National Lombard Unit Trusts, and searched her handbag for her torch.

A brief torchlight survey produced evidence that Lower Brickwood Farm Cottage had not been inhabited for many, many years by anything except small animals and birds. It was extremely unpleasant, and Jane found herself thanking Providence that she had been born with virtually no sense of smell. She picked her way tentatively across the floor to the middle of the one room that occupied the ground floor and peered round. She saw that the staircase had long since collapsed, along with large portions of the ceiling. She decided that it probably wasn't terribly safe in there.

Just as she was about to leave, she saw a small tea-chest. It too contained envelopes. Having come this far and found so little, Jane made up her mind to investigate these. With extreme distaste, she fished out a handful of them and looked at them in the torchlight. They were all addressed to J Vanderdecker, and they contained invoices.

Whoever J Vanderdecker was, he had been a good customer of Jeanes' boatyard for a very long time. Each invoice was marked 'Paid with thanks' and related to some sort of repair done to a ship. A wooden ship, evidently; many references to tar, nails, boards, ropes, lines, sailcloth, as well as a mass of nautical technical terms which Jane did not pretend to understand. The earliest invoice, which was so sodden with damp and rot that it fell to pieces in her hand, was dated 1704. The most recent one was exactly two years old. By the time her torch battery died on her, Jane had traced the invoices back in an unbroken line, from the present day to the reign of Queen Anne, at twenty-one year intervals.

Jane fumbled about in the dark looking for the door, and eventually she found it. No the front door, with all the dead bank statements; the back door, which was also unlocked. Jane suddenly felt very nervous; something was going on, and from the facts she had at her command it looked as if it was something highly peculiar. Peculiar things, her common sense told her, are usually illegal. Perhaps she didn't want to know any more after all. Perhaps she should forget all about it and go back to London.

One thing was definite, and that was that she needed a drink, quickly. From what she had seen of it, the Green Man was fractionally less unpleasant than the snake-pit in a Harrison Ford adventure movie, but it was close and the landlord might tell her something else about Lower Brickwood Farm Cottage. She went there.

'So they're selling the cottage, are they?' said the landlord. 'They'll be lucky.'

The pub was virtually empty, and Jane wondered how the

landlord made a living out of it. She looked at him and decided that he probably did a little body-snatching on the side.

'Oh yes?' she said. 'Why not?'

The landlord looked at her. 'Haven't you been up there, then?' he asked.

'Yes,' Jane said, 'just now. But even if the building's all fallen down, the site must be worth something, surely.'

The landlord looked at her again, and Jane started to feel uncomfortable. 'You sure you went there?' he said.

Jane described what she had seen, leaving nothing out except the bank statements and the invoices. 'Is that the place you mean?'

'You didn't notice the smell?'

Jane explained that she had a truly abysmal sense of smell. The landlord burst out laughing. When, after a long time, he regained a semblance of coherence, he explained. He said that the place had been deserted for as long as everyone could remember because of the worst smell in the entire world. The story went that a foreigner with a funny name had rented it for a week or so, years and years back, before anyone now in the village had been born, and that ever since he left nobody had been able to stay more than ten minutes in the place, because of the smell. Everything had been tried to get rid of it, but it persisted. An attempt to use it as a pigsty had failed when all the pigs died. After being on the books of Messrs Pardoes for fifty-two years it had been taken off the market and forgotten about.

'Didn't they tell you that, then?' he concluded.

'No,' Jane said, 'they didn't mention it.'

'And you, not being able to smell, you didn't notice it.'

'That's right.'

'Well,' said the landlord, 'if that doesn't beat cock-fighting. That'll be a pound five, for the gin and tonic.'

Jane drove back to Union Hotel and went to bed. She didn't feel the lack of something to read. She was too preoccupied with thinking.

CHAPTER
THREE

The slight misunderstanding concerning the legend of the Flying Dutchman came about like this.

In the summer of 1839, a young German musician was sitting in a cafe in Paris drinking armagnac and thinking uncharitable thoughts about the regime of King Louis Philippe. It was a hot day, armagnac is by no means non-alcoholic, and the German was fiercely Republican by temperament, so it was perhaps understandable that the intensity of his reaction to the crimes against freedom that were going on all around him led him to speak his thoughts out loud. Before he knew what he was doing he was discussing them with the man sitting at the next table.

'Kings,' said the young German, 'are an anachronistic obscenity. Mankind will never be truly free until the last king's head is impaled on the battlements of his own palace.'

If the young German had bothered to look closely at the stranger (which of course he didn't) he would have seen a neatly-dressed weatherbeaten man of absolutely average height and build, who could have been any age between a gnarled twenty-nine and a boyish forty. There was just a hint of grey in his short beard, and his eyes were as sharp as paper can be when you lick the gum on an envelope. He considered the German's statement seriously, wiped a little foam off his moustache and replied that in his experience, for what it was worth, most kings were no worse than a visit to the dentist. The young German scowled at him.

'How can you say that?' he snarled. 'Consider some of the so-called great kings of history. Look at Xerxes! Look at Barbarossa! Look at Napoleon!'

'I thought,' interrupted the stranger, 'he was an emperor.'

'Same thing,' said the young German. 'Look at Ivan the Terrible,' he continued. 'Look at Philip of Spain!'

'I did,' said the stranger, 'once.'

Something about the way he said it made the young German stop dead in his tracks and stare. It was as if he had suddenly come face to face with Michaelangelo's David, wearing a top hat and a frock coat, in the middle of the Champs Elysées. He put down his glass and looked at the stranger.

'What did you say?' he asked quietly.

'Please don't think I'm boasting,' said the stranger. 'I don't know why I mentioned it, since it isn't really relevant to what you were saying. Do please go on.'

'You *saw* Philip of Spain?'

'Just the once. At the Escurial, back in '85. I was in Madrid with nothing to do – I'd just got rid of a load of jute, you could name your own price for jute in Madrid just then, I think they use it in rope-making – and I thought I'd take a ride out to see the palace. And when I got there – took me all day, it's thirty miles if it's a step – Philip was just coming home from some visit or other. As I remember I saw the top of his head for at least twelve seconds before the guards moved me on. I could tell it was the top of *his* head because it had a crown perched on it. Sorry, you were saying?'

'How can you have *seen* Philip of Spain?' said the young German. He never doubted the stranger's word for a moment; but he needed to know, very badly indeed, how this could be possible. 'He's been dead for two hundred and fifty years.'

The stranger smiled; it was a very peculiar smile. 'It's rather a long story,' he said.

'Never mind.'

'No but really,' the stranger said. His accent was very peculiar indeed, the sort of accent that would always sound foreign, wherever he went. 'When I say long I mean long.'

'Never mind.'

'All right, then,' said the stranger. 'But don't say I didn't warn you.'

The young German nodded impatiently. The stranger took a pull at his beer and sat back in his chair.

'I was born in Antwerp,' he said, 'in 1553.' He paused. 'Aren't you going to say something?'

'No,' said the German.

'Funny,' said the stranger. 'I usually get interrupted at this point. I'll say it again. I was born in Antwerp in 1553. Fifteen fifty-three,' he repeated, as if he wished the young German would call him a liar. No such luck. He went on, '. . . And when I was fifteen my father got me a job with a merchant adventurer he owed some money to. The merchant was in the wool trade, like more people were then, and he said I could either work in the counting-house or go to sea, and since handling raw wool brings me out in a rash I chose the sea. Funny, isn't it, what decides you on your choice of career? I once knew a man who became a mercenary soldier just because he liked the long holidays. Dead before he was thirty, of course. Camp fever.

'Well, I worked hard and saved what I earned, just like you're supposed to, and before I was twenty-seven I had enough put by to take a share in a ship of my own. Not long after that I inherited some money and bought out my partners, and there

I was with my own ship, at twenty-nine. Dear God, I'm sounding like one of those advertisements for correspondence courses. Excuse me, please.

'Anyway, soon I was doing very nicely indeed, despite the wars and the Spanish taxes – the Spanish were pretty well in charge of the Netherlands then, you remember, what with the Earl of Leicester and the Duke of Parma and all that – and I was all set to retire at thirty-five when I had a stroke of bad luck. Two strokes of bad luck. The first was the bottom falling out of jute, just when I'd got a ship crammed with the stuff. I'd put every last liard I had into jute, and suddenly you couldn't give it away. I hawked it all round Spain and Portugal and people just stared at me as if I was trying to sell them tainted beer. It was amazing; one minute you had perfect strangers accosting you in the street begging you to sell them some jute, the next thing you know jute is out. I'm not even sure that I know what jute is. I'm absolutely positive I don't care.

'And then I had my second stroke of bad luck, which happened just off Cadiz. I happened to run into the celebrated Francis Drake, who was on his way to singe the King of Spain's beard. You've heard of Francis Drake? Oh good.

'When I said you couldn't give the stuff away I was exaggerating, because actually that's exactly what I did. I needed some persuasion, mind, but I think it was the way Sir Francis drew up alongside and said that if I didn't surrender my cargo he'd blow me out of the water that tipped the scale.

'Well, after that there was nothing much I could do except wait until Sir Francis had finished messing about in Cadiz harbour and go for a drink. Even that wasn't easy, what with the bombardment and so forth – one of the depressing things about licensed victuallers as a class is the way they dive for cover at the first little whiff of gunpowder – but eventually I found a tavern that wasn't actively burning down and where they were prepared to sell me fermented liquor.'

The stranger paused and looked at the bottom of his glass,

but the young German didn't take the hint. He appeared to be spellbound, and the stranger carried on with his story.

'I'd been sitting there for a while, I don't know how long, when this man came in and sat down beside me. It's odd the way people sit down beside me in liquor-shops – no disrespect intended, of course, perish the thought. Anyway, he had this huge box with him, a sort of junior crate, and he was obviously worn out with lugging it about. Tall chap, thin, nose on him like an umbrella-handle, about your age or maybe a year or two older. I thought he was Spanish, or Italian, or he could have been French at a pinch. Anyway, a Southerner. Well, he looked even more miserable than I felt, which would have made him very miserable indeed, and I remember wondering if his trunk was full of jute. Incidentally, I've often wondered what Sir Francis did with all that good stuff he took off me. I bet he had no trouble shifting it at all.

'Do excuse me, I tend to get sidetracked. This Southerner came and sat down in this tavern, and I offered to buy him a drink. He seemed offended.

'"I can afford my own drink, thank you very much," he said. "That's the least of my worries." Brittle sort of bloke, I thought, highly-strung.

'"All right then," I said. "You can buy me one."

'He looked at me, and I think he must have noticed that I was still in my sea-boots and general working clothes, because he suddenly became very much less hostile.

'"If you could tell me where I could find a ship to get me across to England," he said, "I'd buy you as many drinks as you like."

'"England!" I said. "You don't want to go there. The English are a load of thieving bastards, they'll kill you for the buttons on your doublet."

'He shook his head. "Better than being burnt alive," he said. "And that's what's going to happen to me if I stay around here much longer. I've got to get to a Protestant country double quick."

'I didn't like the sound of this, but he wasn't going to give up. "If you find me a ship that'll take me to England," he said, "I'll pay you a hundred pistoles, cash."

'To a refugee from the jute trade, this sounded too good to pass up, even if the man was clearly three sols short of a livre tournois, as we used to say when I was a boy. "What would you pay me if I could provide a ship myself, then?" I asked.

'"Think of a number," he replied, "then double it. I can afford it, rest assured."

'"Who are you, then?" I asked.

'"Does it matter?" he said.

'"No," I replied, "I'm just incurably nosy." Which is true, as it happens.

'"My name's Juan de Montalban, but I trade as Fortunatus Magnus," he said, with just a hint of pride. "You've probably heard of me."

'I mumbled something about how out of touch you get in my business, but I could see he was disappointed. It's true, though; you do lost track of things when you spend most of your life surrounded by hundreds of miles of open sea. Oh yes.

'"Well," he said, "if you must know I'm an alchemist."

'"You mean cures for headaches and things?" I said.

'"Certainly not," he replied. "I am a philosopher, and I have discovered the answer to the riddle of transmigration of the elements."

'I was startled. "Base metal into gold and all that sort of thing?" I said. He sneered slightly.

'"That's transmutation, not transmigration," he said. "Vulgar party trick, though it pays the rent, I'll grant you. I do that, too."

'Suddenly I could understand why he wanted to get out of Spain in such a hurry. Apart from being incredibly hard on heretics – and alchemists are heretics by definition – the Spanish had a peculiar horror of anything which might disrupt the nice little monopoly on gold and silver they'd been enjoying ever since Cortes came back from the Americas. Have you ever been to America? Funny place. You can't get a decent boiled egg for love nor money.

'"Be that as it may," he said, "I'll give you five thousand pistoles for a ride to Bristol. Good Spanish coin," he added, "I wouldn't try and palm you off with the home-made stuff."

'By now my natural scepticism was telling me that alchemists you meet in taverns at the end of a long, difficult day may well turn out not to be alchemists at all, particularly if they end up trying to borrow money or sell you a lump of cut-price gold; but there was something unusually convincing about him – probably the way he wasn't trying to convince me. Do you see what I'm getting at, by any chance?'

The young German nodded. He saw only too well.

'So,' continued the stranger, 'I said that if he showed up at the quay next morning with five thousand pistoles I'd take him to England with the greatest of pleasure, and then I went off to get drunk in slightly less eccentric company. I was so successful in this – getting drunk is one of the things I'm best at – that I didn't get up till quite late the next morning, and I reckoned that even if he'd kept the appointment he'd have given up and gone away long since. But when I got down to the quay at about half-past ten – I had some business to see to in the town first – there he was, looking extremely nervous and asking what the hell had kept me.

'I explained about my bad headache, but he didn't seem terribly interested. He did, however, seem extremely anxious to show me a large number of very genuine-looking gold coins, and I decided that even if he was a lunatic he was a rich lunatic, and that if he wanted to go to Bristol then I wanted to take him there, before any unscrupulous character turned up who might exploit the man's mental frailty by asking for six thousand pistoles.

'My crew were by no means overjoyed to be off again so soon, and when I told them that we were going to England they made some very wounding remarks about my intelligence. They pointed out, perfectly accurately, that Sir Francis Drake was English, and so were John Hawkins and Black Jack Norris, and that a country capable of producing such unsavoury characters was somewhere they were in no hurry to visit. In fact, so determined were they that I had to take the unprecedented step of promising to pay them before they would do any work at all.

'Their fears turned out to be absolutely groundless. Sir Francis and his fellow merrymakers were far too busy chivvying honest businessmen off Puental to bother us, and an unusually obliging wind took us right up to the mouth of the Bristol Channel.'

The stranger hesitated for a moment. 'You don't really want to hear the rest of this,' he said. 'I think it would be much better if we go back to discussing kings. Take Charlemagne, for instance. Did you know that Charlemagne didn't learn to read until he was forty?'

'Never mind Charlemagne,' said the young German. 'Go on with what you were saying.'

'I'd really much rather talk about Charlemagne,' said the stranger, 'if it's all the same to you. Believe me, I have very good reasons.'

The young German said something vulgar about Charlemagne, and the stranger shrugged and went on.

'It was then,' he said, 'that things started to go wrong. The unusually obliging wind went away again, leaving us stranded in mid-sea with nothing to do but look at the coastline of Wales, which is not something I would recommend unless you have an overwhelmingly keen interest in geology. To make matters worse, something unsavoury got into the ship's beer, and when you put twenty Dutchmen on a ship – did I mention we were mostly Dutch? Well, we were – when you put twenty Dutchmen and a *Scot* on a ship in the middle of the sea with nothing to drink but cloudy beer, then you have a recipe for unpleasantness on your hands.

'Halfway through the second day we were starting to feel more than usually thirsty, and by that evening the ship was alive with parched mariners in search of hidden caches of the right stuff. Me among them, I might add; I had an idea that the answer to the riddle of the transmigration of matter wasn't the only thing Fortunatus Magnus had in his luggage. You see, he was the only person on board who didn't seem worried about the beer crisis. When the first mate told him about it, all he said was "So what?" Suspicious, you'll agree.

'As soon as I'd got his big trunk open – it didn't take more than five or six blows with the axe – my suspicions were confirmed; there was this huge glass bottle arrangement, carefully packed with straw and about half-full of the most delicious-looking tawny-yellow liquid you ever saw in your whole life. I closed what was left of the lid of the trunk and went in search of privacy and a tankard.

'The tankard was no problem at all; but more or less the only privacy you can find on my ship is in the crow's nest, which is why I tend to spend a lot of time there. Even then, I wasn't going to take any chances, since the crow's nest is directly above the beer-barrel – we keep it permanently on deck, where everyone can see it; just knowing it's there can be a great help at times of stress – and there was a crowd of indomitable optimists gathered round it trying to fine the repulsive mess with Irish moss and fishmeal. I pulled the rope ladder up after me, uncorked the bottle, and poured myself a drink.

'It tasted odd to start with, but it had a certain something, and after the third tankard I was feeling much more relaxed and in tune with the music of the spheres. Just then the alchemist appeared on deck, looking absolutely livid, like a sort of manic cormorant. I reckoned I knew why, but by then of course I couldn't care less.

'He started yelling about how someone had broken into his trunk and stolen something of great value, and of course I was grinning all over my silly face with pleasure. Nobody was taking much notice of him apart from me, because a couple of the crew had just put another cupful of Irish moss in the beer-barrel and were peering anxiously at it to see if it would do any good. Funny stuff, Irish moss – I think it's made up of ground-up fish bones, and I haven't the faintest idea why . . . Sorry, you're right, I do tend to wander off the subject from time to time. It's probably subconscious.

'I imagine the alchemist must have lost heart, because he stopped shouting after a while and went and leaned sullenly against the rail, muttering to himself in Latin and breathing heavily through his nose. Did I mention he had a big nose? Oh, well, anyway, what with the drink and the general *stimmung*, and it was extremely wrong of me, I admit, but I suddenly felt the urge to let the alchemist know exactly what had become of his precious hoarded treasure. After all, selfishness is a major sin, and the creep hadn't offered any of us so much as a sniff of the cork. I leaned over the edge of the crow's nest, waved the flagon at him, and jeered.

'Given the quantity of its contents which I had consumed, waving the flagon was a bad move. It was, as I said, a big thing, and as soon as I lifted it up so that the alchemist could see it, I felt it slipping through my fingers. I made a desperate attempt to grab it back, but all I succeeded in doing was spilling its contents, which went soaring off into the air in a magnificent golden wave, like a sort of proof rainbow. A moment later I followed it, since I'd completely lost my balance; and that is a foolish thing to do in a crow's nest. Shall we talk about Charlemagne now? All right, please yourself.

'It's a very, very strange feeling to fall from a great height, I can tell you, and not something I would recommend to anybody who isn't employed by the Revenue. It seems to take a long time, and it isn't actually particularly frightening, even though the logical part of your mind is telling you that when you land you are definitely going to die. Of course I did land – eventually – and very unpleasant it was, too. Only I didn't die.

I didn't even break anything. I just lay there on my back feeling an utter fool, with the crew gathered round staring at me as if I'd just grown an extra ear.

'After a while I got up and walked round the deck a few times, and my loyal crew seemed to lose interest. They muttered something about some people being born lucky, looked back a couple of times to make sure I was still alive and hadn't been fooling them, and went back to the beer-barrel. The only person who seemed to want to talk to me was the alchemist, and since I had a fairly good idea of what he was likely to say I kept plenty of deck between him and myself. He was gaining on me steadily when a terrific cheer went up from the vicinity of the beer-barrel.

'I pushed my way to the front and saw the most miraculous sight. That beer was actually clearing; the Irish moss must have done the trick after all. There was a very short interval, while everyone dived for vessels of any description, and then an orgy of sploshing noises while twenty involuntary abstainers made up for lost time. I had to use all my authority as captain to get close enough to the barrel to dip a tin cup in.

'In the general excitement I had forgotten all about the alchemist, and when I emerged from the ruck round the barrel he was standing over me with a face only marginally more pleasing to the eye than Sir Francis Drake's culverins. The only thing to do, I thought, was try to jolly him along.

'"Now look," I said, "I'm sorry I pinched your beer but there's plenty for everyone now. Grab a jug and get stuck in."

'"It wasn't beer," he said.

'"Porter, then," I replied, "perry, ale, whatever. Does it matter?"

'"Yes," he said. "That was my elixir."

'"Your what?" I asked.

'"My elixir," he replied. "The philosopher's stone. The elixir of life. The living water."

'I frowned., I hate beer snobs, don't you? "All right," I said, "so it was better than ship's beer, but let's not get carried away. They say you can get a very nice pint in Bristol."

'"It wasn't beer,' he said solemnly. "It was elixir."

'Then something clicked in my brain and I remembered something. I remembered that I had just fallen out of my own crow's nest onto a deck of hard oak plants without suffering so much as a nosebleed.

'"Elixir?" I said.

'"Yes," he said. "E for Enrico, L for Lorenzo, I for Iachimo, X for Xeres, I for Iago, R for Roderigo, elixir. And you drank it."

'I felt unwell. "Is it safe?" I asked.

'He grinned. "I don't know," he said, "but it definitely works."

'"Does it?" I asked.

'"I think you just proved that," he said, "by falling out of the crow's nest. Or how would you interpret it? Luck? A sudden gust of wind? Dry rot in the deck? What do you expect if you drink the elixir of life?"'

The stranger fell silent and drew the tip of his finger round the rim of his glass. 'Anyway,' he said at last, 'that's how I came to acquire eternal life, for what it's worth. All this talk of beer has made me thirsty. Can I get you one?'

The young German replied in a small, awed voice that he would like another armagnac, and the stranger entered into an oral contract with a waiter for an armagnac and a half-litre of Stella Artois. Once the contract had been discharged to the satisfaction of both parties, the stranger continued.

'Not only me,' he said, 'my whole crew as well. You see, when I spilt the rest of the stuff in the flagon, just before my untimely descent from the crow's nest, it landed in the beer-barrel, rendering the beer free from impurities and immortalising everyone who drank it. The alchemist saw it happen, and once he had calmed down he explained it all to us. I don't think we were really convinced until he drank a half-pint of the beer and shot himself. Then we were all profoundly convinced.

Especially the first mate; it was his pistol the alchemist borrowed, and when he pressed it to his head and pulled the trigger, the barrel burst. The first mate was livid, of course, but when he tried thumping Fortunatus Magnus all he did was squash his wedding-ring. The man was completely invulnerable. So were we all. As soon as it had sunk in, we all went completely mad and started belting each other about with our swords and roaring with laughter until there wasn't anything larger than a paperknife left on the whole ship. Mind you, we had all been drinking rather heavily.

'As for Fortunatus, he cheered up very quickly. It turned out that he had been lugging this elixir of his around with him for years but had never found anyone brave enough to test it out on, and he was damned if he was going to risk it himself, since he was petrified of possible side-effects. Naturally we asked him what possible side-effects, but all he would say was that so far as he knew there weren't any but we were bound to find out sooner or later, weren't we? The only living thing he'd ever given any to, he told us, was a stray cat in Cadiz, and the contrary thing had escaped before he could do much in the way of properly-organised tests. Mind you, I don't think he had intended to drink any himself, even when he saw that it hadn't killed us outright. He just got caught up in the general spirit of adventure and wanted to justify his discovery to us. Common or garden scientific vanity. Well, there we are.

'The next morning we got a breeze that took us straight into Bristol, where Fortunatus was immediately arrested as a Spanish spy and thrown in prison. He went very quietly for an invulnerable man, but when we offered to rescue him he said no, he'd much rather go quietly, since he had a lot to think over and prison seemed as good a place as any. So we left him to it and set out to spend five thousand gold pistoles on refreshments and riotous living.

'We were all fairly well pleased with ourselves, as you can imagine, what with suddenly being made immortal and having five thousand gold pistoles. At first, we couldn't see beyond the immediate benefits, such as being able to clean up on extremely dangerous wagers involving tall buildings, loaded firearms and ravenous bears; but even after the first wave of euphoria had worn off and nobody would bet us any more, we reckoned that we had done all right for ourselves, all things considered. For example, being immortal we were incapable of starving to death, which meant a tremendous saving on food; we could drink as much as we liked without the slightest danger of damaging our health; and since we were completely immune from what was then described as the Pox . . . Anyway, we felt we had every reason to be cheerful, one way or another. My only regret was that the morning before we left Cadiz I had wasted five pistoles taking out a life assurance policy, which was no obviously of no use whatsoever.'

As the stranger stopped speaking again the young German caught sight of his face. It was a terrible sight, completely indescribable, and the young German looked away quickly. He could still see it behind his eyelids days later. He felt a sudden urge to discuss the career of Charlemagne, but before he could do this the stranger resumed his narrative.

'However,' said the stranger, 'there were side-effects. Shall I tell you about the side-effects? Do please say if you'd rather I didn't. We could talk about Gustavus Adolphus if you like.'

'Tell me,' said the young German, 'about the side effects.'

'We spent a fortnight in Bristol drinking to excess and laying up a cargo – wool, I think, and tin ore, and a bit of salt fish, definitely no jute – and then we left. We would have liked to stay longer, but we had somehow made ourselves unpopular in Bristol and most of the taverns had banned us – and that took some doing in Bristol, even then. So we set sail for Flanders, and we made good headway for a day or two, until the wind dropped again. But we didn't care; we had plenty of beer now, and no killjoy alchemist on board. It was then we noticed it.'

'Noticed what?'

'The smell. The nastiest, most sordid, least pleasant smell you ever came across in all your born days. Nothing more unlike the scent of dewy roses could ever exist this side of Plato's Republic. And the smell was coming from us.'

The stranger finished his drink and looked through the empty glass at something the young German couldn't see. The young German decided that that was probably just as well.

'After a day of frantic and hysterical washing,' continued the stranger, 'which only seemed to make it worse, one of us hit on the idea of consulting the alchemist's notebooks, which he had left behind on the ship when he got arrested. Sure enough, we found the answer, in a passage where our old buddy Fortunatus was describing his experiments on the cat in Cadiz. He had done his best to get round the problem by fiddling the recipe here and there, and he was pretty positive he had fixed it, which I suppose explains why he drank it himself after we'd done his guinea-pig work for him.'

'Well,' said the young German, 'that was fascinating. I really ought to be getting . . .'

'I really wish,' said the stranger, 'I could describe that smell for you now. Try to imagine, if you possibly can, a muck-heap on which someone has placed the decomposing bodies of three hundred and thirty-three dead foxes. Next to this muck-heap try and picture an open sewer. Not just an ordinary open sewer, mind – this one collects the effluent from an ammonia works on the way. The muck-heap is, of course, in the back yard of a cholera hospital . . . No, don't bother. Just take it from me, it was an absolute zinger of a smell.

'Anyway, it soon became painfully obvious that unless and until we found some way of toning this odour down a bit, the only place we could be was as far out in the middle of the ocean as we could possibly get. So we set sail for nowhere in particular, rationed the beer, and waited. We waited and we waited and we waited. Occasionally something would happen to relieve the monotony. A Barbary corsair would creep up on us and attempt to board us, which was good for a laugh. One of us would go for a swim, and an hour later you couldn't see the surface of the water for dead fish. Not to mention the run-in we had with what you would know as the Spanish Armada; boy, did we have some fun with them! Oh, don't get me wrong, there were the occasional highlights. But most of the time it was dead boring.

'After three months we were all so crazy with boredom and mutual loathing that we decided to blow up the ship and ourselves with it. It didn't do any good, of course. The ship blew up all right, but we didn't. We floated, and after a while the number of dead fish got so embarrassing we decided we'd better swim on a bit before we wiped out the livelihood of every fisherman in the Atlantic Ocean. After a day or so of nonchalant doggy-paddling we ran into another ship. They must have been downwind of us, because before we'd got within two hundred yards of them they'd taken to the boats and were rowing away as fast as their arms could work the oars. That sort of thing really dents your self-confidence, you can imagine. You begin to despair of making those lasting relationships with people that add the interest to life.

'Well, after we'd made the new ship comfortable – painted out the name and got it nice and squalid – we sailed on a bit longer and a bit longer still, and we came to a decision. The time had come, we decided, to try and do something about it, rather than tamely giving in. That's the way we are in Holland; every brick wall you come to has big red marks where people have been beating their heads against it. Now it so happened that when we blew the ship up I had old Fortunatus' notebooks in the pocket of my doublet, and although the ink had run in a few places they were still legible – I think he'd written them in some kind of incredibly clever new ink, and it makes you wonder why he ever bothered with turning base metals into gold when he had such a fantastically commercial proposition at his fingertips. Anyway, we read through those notebooks until we knew them by heart. We discussed them, argued about them, tried experiment after experiment, even tried reading them upside down; all totally useless, needless to say, but at least it passed the time, and although we didn't discover an antidote to the elixir we did find out some extremely interesting things along the way. Extremely interesting . . . I'm sorry, I'm wandering off again. I do tend to do that, I'm afraid. It comes of having nothing to do for long periods of time but talk; it makes you extremely wordy.

'Where was I? Oh yes. One morning, exactly seven years after we'd first drunk the elixir, we all woke up to find that the smell had actually gone. It was amazing. We were still invulnerable and immortal, of course, but at least we didn't niff quite so much, and the first thing we did was set course for the nearest land-mass, which happened to be Le Havre. We had all assumed that one of our numerous experiments had finally worked, and that we'd cracked it.

'We spent the next month getting thrown out of every tavern, inn and brothel in Le Havre, predictably enough, and we were just on the point of saying goodbye to each other and going our separate ways – as you can easily appreciate, after all that time on the ship and what with the smell and everything, we all hated each other so much you wouldn't credit it – when the first delicate whiff of the Great Pong came filtering through and we knew that we weren't home and dry after all. We spent a frantic afternoon buying up every drop of beer, every chess-set, every book and every piece of chemical apparatus that we could lay our hands on, and we got back to the ship just before a mob of extremely savage Frenchmen with handkerchiefs in front of their faces threw us into the sea.

'We were still kidding ourselves that we had found an antidote and that it had worn off, and so we carefully recreated all the experiments we had done in the last seven years, and made scrupulous notes in proper joined-up writing in a big leather-bound book. But when we'd tried everything and nothing had worked, we lost heart and spent a whole year playing shove-ha'penny all round the coast of Africa. We did land once or twice, but only for hours at a time, and there is – or was – a tribe in Madagascar that worships us as gods; pretty ceremonies, very heavy on the incense. Now then; seven years after our brief visit to Le Havre, the smell stopped again, and we scrambled into Tangier to do our shopping – we wasted a week getting there, what with contrary winds – knowing full well that we had exactly a month before we had to leave. We were right, of course. Three weeks later, the smell came back, and seven years later it went away again. That's the way the pattern works, and once we'd spent forty-nine years reading up on alchemical theory we all knew why, it was blindingly obvious.

'We were all pretty good alchemists by then, incidentally, and that's how we make our living. For eighty-three months in each seven years we turn base metal into gold, and in the remaining month we spend it. That's the problem with alchemy; it works all right, but compared with simply taking a pick and a shovel and digging the stuff out of the ground it's hopelessly inefficient. There I go again, digressing. Do please excuse me.'

There was a very, very long silence, during which the young German tried to recapture the use of his brain.

'So you've been alive since 1553?' he said at last.

'Yes,' said the stranger, 'that puts it very neatly. And also in perspective. Is there anything else you want to ask me?'

'No,' said the German. 'No, I think you've said quite enough.'

'Oh well,' said the stranger. 'I seem to have that effect on people. Not,' he went on, 'that I tend to tell my story much these days. In fact, you're the first person in over thirty years I've told it to.'

'Well . . .' the young German started to say; then he thought better of it and decided to stare horribly at the stranger, like a man in one of Hieronymus Bosch's less cheerful paintings. The stranger seemed to find the silence awkward, and to break the tension he started to speak again.

'Oh yes,' said the stranger, 'I've had some interesting experiences in my time. Well, fairly interesting. Now you mentioned Napoleon a moment ago. The only time I met Napoleon . . .'

The young German suddenly jumped up, screamed, and ran away, very fast.

Vanderdecker shook his head and went to the bar for another drink. It had been roughly the same the last time he told the story, when he had landed in Porlock and met the man who was on his way to a wedding. That, he had said to himself, is the last time; but the pleasure of talking to someone new after seven years with Antonius, Johannes, Pieter and Cornelius had gone to his head.

In case you were wondering, the young German made a moderate recovery, after two or three months of careful nursing, and went on to become the composer of such celebrated operatic masterpieces as *Lohengrin*, *Götterdämmerung* and *Parsifal*. To his dying day, on the other hand, his manner was always very slightly unsettling, particularly to strangers, and if anyone happened to mention Philip II of Spain he would burst out into maniacal laughter which could only be cured with morphine injections. Unlike Vanderdecker's earlier confidant, however, he never became addicted to narcotics, and the rather garbled version of the story which he embodied in his opera *The Flying Dutchman* can probably be attributed to nothing more serious than artistic licence or a naturally weak memory.

CHAPTER FOUR

The plump young man is now two years older and an inch and an eighth plumper, and he has become a partner in the firm of Moss Berwick. Oddly enough, there were no comets seen that evening nine weeks ago when Mr Clough and Mr Demaris told him the wonderful, wonderful news; the only possible explanation is that it was a cloudy night, and the celestial announcement was obscured by a mass of unscheduled cumulo-nimbus. These things happen, and all we can do is put up with them.

Although they had made the plump young man (whose name, for what it is worth, was Craig Ferrara) a partner, they had not seen fit to tell him about The Thing. Or at least, they had not told him what it was; they had hinted at its existence, but that was all. For his part, Craig Ferrara had been aware that it existed for some time, ever since he had been allowed access to the computer files generally known in the firm as the Naughty Bits.

Moss Berwick's computer was a wonderful thing. It lived,

nominally, in Slough; but, rather like God, it was omnipresent and of course omniscient. Unlike God, you could telephone it from any one of the firm's many offices and even, if you were a show-off like Craig Ferrara, from your car. You could ask it questions. Sometimes it would answer and sometimes not, depending on whether it wanted to. Not could, mark you; wanted to. It would take a disproportionate amount of ingenuity to think up a sensible question that the computer couldn't answer if it wanted to, up to and including John Donne's famous conversation-killers about where the lost years are and who cleft the Devil's foot – and this despite the fact that the Devil is not (as yet) a client of Moss Berwick.

But in order to ask the computer high-rolling questions like these, you have to be the right sort of person. Only someone with a Number can get at that part of the computer; all that earthworms like Jane Doland can get out of it is a lot of waffle about the Retail Price Index for March 1985. Not that Jane Doland hadn't been trying, ever since she came back from Bridport. That, although he didn't know it, was the main reason why Craig Ferrara had become a partner.

Craig Ferrara was only human, and so he would dearly have loved to find out what The Thing was. However, it had been made unequivocally clear to him by Mr Clough and Mr Demaris that he didn't really want to know; and although in law he was now a sharer of their joys, sorrows and financial commitments, he was not so stupid as to believe that a mere legal fiction made him worthy to loosen the straps of their sandals, should they ever behave so uncharacteristically as to wear such things. His relationship to The Thing was that of ignorant guardian. If any member of his department started showing an unhealthy interest in anything to do with Bridport, he was to report directly to Mr Clough and Mr Demaris, who would take the necessary action. What that action might be Mr Ferrara knew not, but he had a shrewd notion that it would be the terror of the earth.

A brief glance at the computer's call-out sheet told Mr Ferrara that Jane Doland, the girl with the tin ear, had made a large number of Bridport-related enquiries of the computer in the last few months, most of them at times of day when she could normally be relied on to be hanging from one of those Dalek's antennae things in a compartment in a Tube train. This was exactly the sort of thing Mr Ferrara had been told to keep an eye out for, and he felt a degree of pride at having immediately succeeded with the project his betters had entrusted to him. Find us a mole, Clough and Demaris had said, and here one was. For such a fiercely, passionately corporate man as Mr Ferrara, it was roughly the same as discovering insulin.

But accountants are not hasty people. They do not out with their rapiers the moment they hear rats behind the arras. Smile and smile and smile and be an accountant is the watchword. Before calling in Clough and Demaris, Mr Ferrara resolved to try one more, utterly diabolical test. He would give Doland the RPQ Motor Factors file.

The RPQ Motor Factors file, it should be explained, was where failed accountants went to die. How the affairs of a relatively straightforward small business had come to get into such a state of Byzantine complexity nobody really knew; it had just happened, like the British economy, and the more people tried to straighten it out, the more it wrapped itself round its own intestines. Just reading through the horrible thing was enough to make most young accountants run away and become wood-turners, but trying to sort it out was an infallible cure for sanity. Jane Doland was henceforth to be its custodian; furthermore, she was to be given a month to produce a balance sheet and profit-and-loss account.

Although a degree of sadism went into the decision – Ferrara could never forget that Jane Doland was the girl who didn't appreciate Wagner – it was mainly a shrewd piece of tactical planning. Anyone with a month to sort out the RPQ Motor Factors file wouldn't have time to brush their teeth, let alone ask the computer awkward questions about Bridport or The Thing. By the time Jane Doland had either succeeded or failed with RPQ, she would be so sick of sorting things out and investigating anomalies that she could safely be entrusted with the expenditure accounts of the CIA.

Mr Ferrara dictated the memo, smiled and started to hum the casting scene from *Die Freischutz*.

It is galling, to say the least, to have been to every place in the world and then not know where somewhere is. It's rather like having a doctorate in semiconductor physics and not being able to wire a plug. You begin to wonder whether it's all been worthwhile.

Vanderdecker, typically, blamed himself. Instead of frittering away his time and money on beer and scientific journals, he should have remembered that he was, first and foremost, a ship's captain and got some decent charts. Quite a few of the ones he still used had bits of Latin and sea-serpents in the margins, and he defended his retention of them by saying that: (i) he was used to them, (ii) they looked nice and (iii) in the circumstances, what the hell did it matter anyway?

Since his crew generally lacked the intellectual capacity to argue with a man who spoke in bracketed roman numerals, he had managed to have his own way on this point, but the short-sightedness of this attitude was coming home to him at last.

He had heard of Dounreay; he had an idea it was somewhere in Scotland, on the coast. That, however, was as far as his memory took him. After four hundred years of existence, one's powers of recollection become erratic. Just as when a stamp collector has been going for a year or so, he will discard all the used British definitives his elderly female relatives have been clipping off envelopes for him and start buying choicer specimens, so Vanderdecker was becoming selective in what he chose to keep in his head.

He rummaged around in his map-chest and dug out a chart

he hadn't tried yet. Unfortunately it showed Jerusalem as being at the centre of the world, and he put it back with a sigh. The next one he found was extremely non-commital on the topic of Australia, and that too was discarded. As it happened, Vanderdecker had been the first European to set foot on Australian soil. He had taken one look at it, said 'No, thank you very much' and gone to New Guinea instead. Subsequent visits had not made him review his opinion.

There was, he said to himself, only one thing for it. He would have to ask the First Mate. Not that Antonius would know the answer; but it would at least put his own ignorance in some sort of respectable context.

Antonius was playing chess with the cook on the quarter-deck. Vanderdecker saw that of Antonius' once proud black army, only the King remained. This was by no means unusual. Antonius had been playing chess for three or four hours a day for four centuries and he still hadn't won a game.

'Antonius,' he said, 'do you happen to know where Dounreay is?'

Antonius looked up irritably. His expression suggested that he had been on the point of perfecting a sequence of manoeuvres which would have resulted in victory in four moves, and that his captain's interruption had dispersed this coup to the four winds.

'No,' he said. 'Is it in Italy?'

'Thanks anyway,' said Vanderdecker.

'I know where Dounreay is,' said the cook.

Vanderdecker stared. It was remarkable that anything should surprise him any more, but this was very much out of the ordinary. The last time the cook had been deliberately helpful was when Sebastian van Doorning had gone through a brief wrist-slashing phase and the cook had lent him one of his knives.

'Do you?' Vanderdecker asked.

'Yes,' replied the cook, affronted. 'It's on the north coast of Scotland.'

Vanderdecker frowned. 'How do you know that?' he asked.

'I was born there,' said the only non-Dutch member of the crew. 'They've built a power station over it now. Typical.'

Well yes, Vanderdecker said to himself, it is rather. Miserable things tended to happen to the cook, probably because they were sure of an appreciative welcome.

'So you could tell me how to get there?' he asked. The cook shook his head.

'No way,' he said. 'I'm a cook, not a pilot. I couldn't navigate this thing if you paid me.' The cook frowned. 'That reminds me . . .' he said.

'All right, all right,' said Vanderdecker. 'But you'd recognise it if you saw it again?'

'Maybe,' said the cook, 'maybe not, how the hell should I know? Like I said, they've built a bloody fast-breeder whatsisname on top of my poor granny's wee croft, so there's probably not a lot of the old place left to see.'

'Thanks anyway,' Vanderdecker repeated, and wandered off to have a stare at the sea. It was his equivalent to beating his head repeatedly against a war.

On the other hand, he said to himself, as he let his eye roam across the grey waves, the number of nuclear power stations on the north coast of Scotland is probably fairly small. All one would have to do in order to locate it is to cruise along keeping one's eyes open for three-headed fish and luminous oysters. And God knows, we're not in any hurry. We never are.

He walked back along the deck, feeling that he had earned this month's can of Heineken. As he passed by the cook (who had finally and irretrievably checkmated the first mate, who seemed very surprised) he stopped and said thank you.

'Forget it,' growled the cook, in the tone of one who firmly believes that his request will be acted on.

'Just one more thing,' said Vanderdecker. 'How did you know they'd built a nuclear power station on your granny's wee croft?'

'I saw it last time we were there,' said the cook. "Last February, I think it was. I seem to remember it rained.'

Vanderdecker didn't say, Then why the bloody hell didn't you say so earlier. He said thank you. Then he went to have another good look at the sea.

Jane was feeling pleased with herself. Just when she had begun to think that her career was going nowhere and that she might soon be looking for another job, here she was with an important new file to look after.

Not that she was particularly fond of her career, but it did help pay the rent, and she was enough of a realist to know that it was probably the only one she was likely to have, what with the vacancy of Princess of Wales having been filled and so many O-Levels being needed for pearl-diving these days.

She knew for a fact that the RPQ Motor Factors file was something of a mixed blessing. Look at Jennifer Cartwright. Look at Stephen Parkinson. In fact, you would need binoculars if you wanted to do this, since both of them had left the firm and gone to work in Cornwall after a week or so with RPQ. A hot potato with the pin out, as Mr Peters would say.

Of course, it would mean less time to try chasing up that strange thing she had come across in Bridport, but that was no bad thing. Ever since she had got back to the sanity of London, she had been seriously doubting whether she had actually seen all those curious and inexplicable things. There is nothing like a few trips up and down the Bakerloo line to convince you that nobody can live for ever, and the fierce determination to get to the bottom of it all had waned after the first few cracks at the computer.

It stood to reason that if there was anything to find out, it would come up on the wire from Slough. Slough – figuratively speaking – was brilliant. You could ask Slough anything and the answer would be waiting for you before you had time to blink twice. But she had found nothing, which must surely mean that there was nothing to find and that the Vanderdecker non-sense must all have been a figment of her imagination.

The coffee machine was going through one of its spasmodic fits of nihilism, during which it produced cups of white powder floating on cold grey fluid, and Jane decided to have tea instead. The tea came from a device which looked like a knight's helmet, and generally tasted as if the knight hadn't washed his hair for a long time, but Jane could live with that now that her future seemed slightly more secure. It is remarkable how quickly ennui evaporates when faced with a rent demand. Her Snoopy mug filled, she return to her desk and opened the RPQ file.

She read for about half an hour, and found that she was almost enjoying it. Jane had a perverse curiosity about the people who had left the firm shortly before she had joined it. Had they still been there and she had got to know them, she would doubtless have filed them away in her mental portrait gallery under Poison Toads and that would have been that. But knowing them only from their letters and file notes, she was able to recreate them as they should have been. She knew most of their names, but some were no more than initials or references, and of course these were the truly glamorous ones. She would, for example, have loved to know more about RS/AC/5612, who had passed briefly and intriguingly through the RPQ story like a Hollywood star playing a three-minute cameo, dictating four letters and disappearing into the darkness like the sparrow in the mead-hall. She pictured him – it had to be a him – as a tall, cynical man with hollow eyes and long, sensitive hands who had eventually turned his back on accountancy, started to write the Great Novel and died of consumption. At the other extreme there was APC/JL; an old man, broken by frustration and disappointment, struggling to keep his job in the face of relentless youth and seizing on the RPQ file as his last chance to make his mark. There was a pathetic dignity in his last letter to Johnson Chance Davison, and the dying fall of his 'we thank you sincerely in anticipation of your reply' moved her almost to tears.

Jane suddenly stopped dead in her tracks. She instinctively knew that the paper in front of her was different. For a start it was handwritten, and the handwriting was erratic. It read as follows:

THE VANDERDECKER POLICY

This has nothing to do with RPQ. This is a warning, in case they do it to you too.

I found out about the Vanderdecker Policy, which is the proper name for The Thing. It's a safe bet, whoever you are, that you've found out about it too or you wouldn't have been given this file.

The Vanderdecker Policy is important. It's so important that anybody who finds out about it gets given the RPQ file. That's how important it is. Sorry if you can't read my writing, but I daren't have anybody type this out, in case they find out. That's why I've put this message here, in the RPQ file, because it's the only place nobody would ever think of looking. Except you, and you're only looking at it because they've found out that you've found out. Which is why they gave you the RPQ file.

I can't risk doing anything about the Vanderdecker Policy. I can't tell you where to look or what I've found out. I'm getting out and starting a new life a long, long way away, where they won't find me.

Whatever you do, don't let them know that you know that they know. For God's sake stay with it, for as long as you can stick it out. Someone's got to blow the whistle on it sooner or later, it just can't go on like this much longer, it all has to stop.

So just carry on, pretend you don't know they know, do something about it. If you've read this, please tear it out and burn it.

Jane looked round, then tore the sheet off the treasure tag, folded it up and stuffed it into her pocket. Her heart was beating like a pneumatic drill.

Somehow she survived the rest of the day and took the train home as normal. Every few minutes, in the intervals of looking over her shoulder for murderers, she tried telling herself that this was just some poor fool who'd finally flipped after doing too many bank reconciliation statements, but the name Vanderdecker was too big and too noisy to ignore.

She packed everything she thought she could possibly need, plus a pot of marmalade and her hot water bottle with the woolly tiger cover, into her car and drove. At the first National Lombard cash dispenser she saw, she stopped and withdrew all the money the machine would let her have. If only she'd been sensible, she told herself, and not been put off by all those idiotic white horses in their advertising campaigns, she could have had a bank that wouldn't betray her whereabouts to Slough every time she made a withdrawal.

The question was where to go, but the answer wasn't easy. She thought of her parents' house, but the thought made her shudder; her father had succumbed to National Lombard Unit Trust propaganda nine months after retiring to the Sussex coast. Surely they wouldn't do anything to hurt her parents? Better not to think about that.

Where else, then? Her sister had a National Lombard Home Loan, so that was out. Ever since she had left the world behind and taken to accountancy she had alienated all her friends by boring them to tears with accountancy stories. That only left . . .

No.

Yes, why not? It's a long way from London. Even idiots have their uses. Even obnoxious, repulsive, pathetic little gnomes. She found a call-box and fished out her diary. Fortunately, the local vandals had spared the dialling codes section and she located the code for Wick. The phone started to ring. It was answered.

'Is that you, Shirley?' she asked. Shirley said yes, it was.

Jane took a deep breath. Even when her life was quite possibly at stake, this was extremely distasteful.

'Look, Shirley,' she said – the very words were like a live worm in her mouth – 'I'm going to be up near you for a week or so, can I come and stay?'

Shirley said, 'Well, it's a bit short notice, isn't it?' Jane's fingernails were hurting the palm of her left hand. She fought herself and won.

'Look, Shirley, I'm in a call-box, I haven't got much change. Will it be all right? I'll be with you tomorrow afternoon some time. See you.'

She slammed down the receiver quickly and jumped back into the car.

Maybe being murdered would be better after all.

Fair stood the wind for Scotland, which made a pleasant change. Indeed, it was nice to be going somewhere, as opposed to just going, and Vanderdecker found the crew rather less tiresome than usual.

The first mate climbed up onto the quarter-deck. He was going to ask the captain a question. Vanderdecker could hear his brain turning over like a coffee-mill before he so much as reached the foot of the stairway.

'Captain,' said the first mate, 'we aren't going to land, are we? When we reach wherever this place is we're going to.'

'Yes,' said Vanderdecker, cruelly. As he had expected, this was beyond the first mate's understanding. Antonius stood very still for a while as the coffee-mill approached maximum revolutions.

'Yes we are,' he finally asked, 'or yes we aren't?'

'Yes we are,' Vanderdecker said. 'We're going to land.'

Antonius considered this reply and then looked at his watch, just to make sure. 'But captain,' he remonstrated, 'we can't do that, it isn't time yet.'

'So what?' Vanderdecker said, 'we aren't going to have a good time and get drunk. We're going to see if we can find that blasted alchemist.'

'But won't they just run away?'

'Possibly,' Vanderdecker admitted. 'But it's worth a shot, isn't it? If we wait another five years we may be too late. They may all have gone away anyway by then.'

'Oh,' said Antonius, relieved to have been given an explanation even if he couldn't understand it. All he needed to know in order to feel reassured was that there was a reason and that somebody was in control of it. Vanderdecker envied him.

'After all,' Vanderdecker went on, 'we've got absolutely nothing to lose, have we?'

'I don't know, do I?' said the first mate truthfully. 'That's why I asked.'

'Take it from me,' said Vanderdecker firmly, 'we've got nothing to lose. If we're lucky it could be the answer to the whole mess. If not, well, it makes a change, doesn't it?'

The first mate nodded and went away. The coffee-mill was still turning fitfully, but it would soon be still again. Vanderdecker, for his part, was beginning to have his doubts. What if the smell did drive everyone away as soon as they came within smelling distance of the plant? And presumably it wasn't going to be all that easy getting to see Montalban even if he was till there. He knew that all self-respecting governments are less than happy about the thought of members of the public tripping lightly round nuclear power stations, or even coming near them in a disconcerting manner. Now there was something about the sailing ship *Verdomde* that many people found highly disconcerting, and although its crew were invulnerable, the ship wasn't. Not that he felt any great sentimental attachment to his command – far from it; he hated every timber in its nasty, clinker-built frame – but if the *Verdomde* got blown out of the water by some over-excitable patrol boat, they might have problems in finding another one; or at least one sufficiently primitive that it ran on wind and not oil. Oil is hard to come by when you spend all your time in the middle of the ocean and smell perfectly horrible.

Vanderdecker was still busy worrying himself to death (so to speak) with these and other misgivings when the look-out sighted Duncansby Head. This was Vanderdecker's cue to get out his charts and his sextant, since there were other perils to navigation in these waters besides patrol-boats; for one thing there were rocks, and also sandbanks, eccentric and malicious tides and sundry other hazards to navigation. It was refreshing to be doing some real sailing again, and the Flying Dutchman's mind soon became far too full with getting there to contain any worries about what he was going to do as and when he succeeded in this aim.

'If I remember right,' said the captain to the first mate, 'there's a little cove around here somewhere that we can hide up in.'

It was getting dark, and Vanderdecker was worried about shoals. They hadn't progressed very far with their inch-by-inch search for Dounreay, but progress was necessarily slow because of the need to keep out of sight. Now a good skipper can plot a course that keeps him from being seen from the shore; or he can hug the coastline in such a way as to render himself almost invisible from the open sea. But not both at the same time. As it turned out, the *Verdomde* was seen by several ships and a fair number of landsmen, but none of them took any notice. They naturally assumed that the fishfinger people were filming yet another commercial, and carried on with their everyday tasks.

Vanderdecker found the cove in the end, just before it became too dark to see anything at all, and the anchor slithered down and hit the water with its usual dull splosh. The crew settled down to sleep, but Vanderdecker was too restless to join them. Somewhere out there he might find the answer to his problem, and although common sense told him that the power station was not something he was likely to overlook, he felt an urge to get off the ship and go and have a look about. He licked his finger to reassure himself that the wind was still out to sea, lowered the boat, and rowed ashore.

A brisk climb brought him to the top of the low, shallow cliff, and he walked down the slope on the other side. To his dismay, he saw a building with lights in the windows, and the wind was changing. No good at all. He set off briskly in the other direction.

How it happened was always a mystery to him. One minute he was walking along the tarmac road, the next minute a car came round the sharp bend, failed to stop, and slammed into him. He went over the bonnet, bounced on the roof, and slid over the hatchback rear end to the ground. The car screeched to a halt (and why the devil couldn't you have done that in the first place, said the Flying Dutchman under his breath), the door flew open, and the driver came running towards him. Vanderdecker groaned. Whoever this road-hog was, he was going to get the shock of his life just as soon as he next breathed in. Served him right, too.

It wasn't a he, it was a she. Very much a she, bending over him and looking extremely worried.

'Oh God,' she said, 'are you all right?'

Vanderdecker stared in disbelief. Even he could smell it, and he had long since stopped noticing the smell, except when it was at its most virulent. For some reason, contact with dry land tended to make it even more rank and offensive than usual. But this girl didn't seem to have noticed, or else she was being quite incredibly polite.

'I'm fine,' Vanderdecker said, and stood up to prove it. 'Look, no broken bones or anything. You may have shortened the life-expectancy of my trousers a bit but . . .'

A horrible thought struck him. He had forgotten to change. He was wearing his old, comfortable clothes, which were very old and very comfortable indeed. The girl seemed to be having enough difficulty in coming to terms with his invulnerability. As soon as she saw he was dressed in sixteenth century seafaring clothes, she would probably have hysterics.

Fortunately it was dark, too dark to see anything but silhouettes. Vanderdecker dusted himself off and started to back away. But he wanted to know, very much, why this girl couldn't smell the smell.

'Are you sure you're all right?'

'Positive,' he said. 'Sorry to have frightened you. My own silly fault.'

'Can I give you a lift anywhere?' the girl persisted. Vanderdecker remembered that they have funny little lights inside cars that switch themselves on when you open the door. He refused politely and said that he was nearly there. She didn't ask where, thank God.

'I still can't understand how you aren't hurt,' said the girl.

'Luck,' replied the Flying Dutchman. 'Fool's luck. Look, can I ask you a question?'

'Yes,' said the girl doubtfully.

'Can you smell anything?'

'*Smell* anything?'

'That's right,' Vanderdecker said. He hadn't meant to ask, it had just slipped out. But now that it had, he might as well know the answer.

'No,' said the girl. 'But I've got a really rotten sense of smell, so I'm not the best person to ask.'

'I see,' Vanderdecker said. 'Sorry, I thought I could smell something. Can you tell me the way to Dounreay nuclear power station, by any chance?'

'I'm sorry,' said the girl, and Vanderdecker could tell she was staring at him despite the darkness. 'I don't come from around here, actually. I've got a map in the car . . .'

Vanderdecker remembered the little light. 'That's all right,' he said. 'Well, I mustn't keep you. Bye.' A moment later and the darkness had swallowed him.

Jane Doland stared a little more, realised that such an act was futile, and got back into the car. She still had twenty-odd miles to go, and it was late. She had missed her way at Lybster, or had it been Thurso, just before she had got behind the milk-tanker that was behind the tractor which had been trying to overtake the JCB ever since Melvich, and she knew that her obnoxious cousin Shirley went to bed at about half-past six. As she drove, she tried to work out what was really unsettling her; believe it or not, it wasn't the fact that she had just run into a fellow human being at forty miles an hour, or even the remarkable lack of effect the collision had had on her victim. It was the vague but definite notion that she had met him before. Not seen him, heard him, a long time ago.

An hour later, she pulled up in front of Cousin Shirley's bungalow in the picturesque but extremely windy village of Mey, put on the handbrake and flopped. She needed a moment to pull herself together before meeting her least favourite kinswoman again. She had hoped that when Shirley married the burnt-out advertising executive and went off with him to Caithness to keep goats and weave lumpy sweaters that they would never meet again this side of the grave. She remembered something from an A-Level English set book about something or other that made vile things precious, but she couldn't remember what the something was and let it slip by.

She was just bracing herself to go in and have done with it when the door of the car opened. She looked round, expecting to see Shirley, but it wasn't Shirley. Perhaps you are now in a position to judge the significance of the fact that she would far rather have seen Shirley than the person she actually saw.

'Jane Doland?' said the mystery door-opener. A tall, fat man with grey hair and a face that did nothing to reassure her. She looked round quickly at the passenger door, but that had been opened too.

'My name is Clough,' said the door-opener, 'and this is my partner Mr Demaris. We want to talk to you about Bridport.'

* * *

The cat arched its back by way of acknowledgement to the sun, and curled up to go to sleep. It had had a long day chasing cockroaches in the shunting yard, and if it didn't get forty winks now and again it was no good for anything. The live rail was pleasantly warm against its head, and the sleepers were firm under its spine. An agreeable place to sleep.

The 16.40 from Madrid is an express, and it doesn't usually stop before Cadiz. It stopped all right this time, though. It stopped so much that all the carriages jumped the rail and didn't stop slithering until they reached the foot of the embankment. It was a miracle nobody was seriously hurt.

The cat took it in its stride, the way cats do. It wasn't in the least nonplussed by waking up to find an express train running over its head, and when the last sprocket had bounced off its ear and gone spinning away into the air it got up, licked its paws and set out to find somewhere a bit less noisy. On the way it caught a large brown rat, which offered remarkably little resistance. It just curled up in a ball and squeaked once or twice. That had happened a lot in the last four hundred years, and the cat found that it took all the fun out of hunting.

Three days later, some men in gas masks lured it into a cage with a saucer of milk and some catnip and took it away to a large building with lots of clean white paintwork and scientific equipment. It was dull there, but the food was good and you didn't have to chase it if you didn't want to. The men in gas-masks tried to get the cat to play some very silly games with funny lights and big metal cylinders that went round and round, but after a while they gave up. A day or so after that, they put the cat in a basket, took it to the airport and put it on a flight to Inverness.

Everyone was amazed that a man could exist and survive to maturity who would willingly marry Cousin Shirley; but since the idiot groom proposed to take her off to the northernmost tip of Scotland as soon as he had finished getting the rice and

the confetti out of his hair, everyone kept extremely quiet –
Aunt Diana, in fact, attributes the arthritis in her fingers
to keeping them crossed throughout the six months of the
engagement. On the other hand, it seemed to everyone that
Julian was a nice young man once you got used to him, and it
really wasn't fair, and they ought to tell him. But they didn't.
Shirley was a sullen bride, and when Julian fumbled putting
the ring on her finger she clicked her tongue so loudly that
her mother thought all would yet be lost. But the service
proceeded to its tragic close, and Shirley went away. To judge
by the wedding presents she received – a tin opener from her
parents, a reel of cotton from Jane, three paper-clips from Paul,
Jenny and the twins, a paper bag from Uncle Stephen – it
seemed likely that contact would not be maintained between
the newly-weds and the rest of the House of Doland. Distance,
however, is a great healer, and everybody remembered to send
Julian a card on his birthday.

Jane had, obviously, never been to see Mr and Mrs Regan in
their new home-cum-workshop only a long mortar-shot from
the romantic Castle of Mey, but she could guess what it would
be like inside. Miserable. It was.

Cousin Shirley's greeting to Jane and the two senior partners
of Moss Berwick was nothing if not characteristic.

'You're late,' she said. 'Wipe your feet.'

Mr Demaris was a tall man in his late forties with the face
of a debauched matinée idol. He had charm, which on this
occasion thoroughly failed to have any effect. His partner Mr
Clough, just as tall but alarmingly fat, thatched with a sleek
mat of senatorial grey hair and blessed with a voice that they
could probably hear in Inverness, also had charm. Astoundingly, Cousin Shirley seemed to like him, for she gave him a
pleasant smile. The three were permitted to enter.

Jane noticed that Julian, who was sitting by the fireside
weaving something, had changed since the wedding, in roughly
the same way as a slug changes when you drop it in a jar of

salt. In another year, Jane reckoned, you would be able to see right through him. His reason for giving up a thriving career in advertising in order to make primitive garments out of goats' wool had not been a desire to test the theory that a fool and his money are soon parted, but a feeling that the pace of life in the rat-race was wearing him out. Lord, what fools these mortals be.

Jane considered, just for a moment, throwing herself on Julian's protection and asking him to send the nasty men away, but a glance at her cousin-in-law disillusioned her. His reaction to the intrusion of two startling strangers into his living room was to say hello and go on weaving. Mr Clough sat down in the least uncomfortable chair, Mr Demaris leaned against the mantelpiece, and Jane subsided onto the footstool. She noticed that Cousin Shirley had left the room, and thanked heaven for small mercies.

If Jane had expected an awkward silence she was wrong. Men who charge over three hundred pounds an hour for their time are rarely silent for longer than it takes to breathe in.

'You weren't at the office today, then,' said Mr Clough.

'No,' said Jane. 'I had some holiday coming.'

'That's fair enough,' said Mr Demaris. 'Next time, though, perhaps you should clear it with Craig Ferrara first.'

'You didn't come all this way,' said Jane shakily, 'to tell me that. Or were you just passing?'

Cousin Shirley was back in the room again. She had brought Mr Clough a cup of tea. Just the one cup. She hadn't stirred it, and the milk lay about a quarter of an inch under the surface like a grey cloud.

'We're flying back to London tonight,' said Mr Demaris. 'We'll give you a lift, if you like.'

'That's very kind,' Jane said, 'but I don't want to put you out in any way.'

There was a shuffling noise and Cousin Shirley was with them again. She was offering Mr Clough a plate of very hard biscuits. He took one without looking down at the plate, popped it into his large mouth and said, 'You've done well on the Bridport matter, but I think we should work together on it from now on.' Then he reached out, took another biscuit, and smashed the one already in his mouth into powder with one movement of his powerful jaws.

'I do think that would be best,' said Mr Demaris, 'don't you? Don't get me wrong, we're very impressed with how you've handled it, but this is something where we have to be very careful, don't you think?'

Jane had intended to fight, but her willpower had melted like a candle in a microwave. 'How did you find me?' she asked.

'Right then,' said Mr Clough, standing up and smiling, 'now that's settled we'd better be on our way. Thank you for the tea, Mrs Regan, and we'll be in touch about that other matter in due course.'

This remark jerked Jane out of her comatose state. 'What other matter?'

Cousin Shirley gave her a look of pure scorn. 'Mr Clough is our accountant,' she said.

'We're thinking of making the business into a limited company,' said Julian unexpectedly. 'But George thinks we should wait another year, because of the tax implications.'

That, as far as Jane was concerned, was that. She went quietly.

Mr Clough explained it to her on the drive to the airport. It was very simple. Moss Berwick were the accountants for the advertising agency where Julian had worked, and since the agency was such an important client, Mr Clough had acted for them personally; at least, he let his subordinates do the work but personally attended the more important lunches. When Julian had decided to get out of advertising and into authentic knitwear, he had mentioned this fact to Mr Clough over the nouvelle cuisine. Mr Clough, whose greed for clients was pathological, immediately appointed himself accountant to the projected enterprise, obtained a cheque for a thousand pounds on account of initial costs, and handed the matter on to the YTS girl. Accordingly, when Mr Clough turned up on the doorstep half an hour before Jane's arrival and started talking loudly about rollover relief and Section Thirty elections, Julian and Shirley hadn't been at all surprised. They simply handed him a cheque for another thousand pounds and believed everything he told them, the way people do when they talk with their professional advisers.

'So now what?' Jane said.

'Mr Gleeson will explain,' said Mr Demaris.

Jane stared and was incapable of speech. Mr Gleeson was the senior partner. Mr Gleeson, it was widely rumoured, did the accounts for God. In fact, so the story went, it was Mr Gleeson who first gave God the idea of organising the Kingdom of Heaven into a properly integrated group of holding companies. The idea of actually talking to him was more than Jane's mind could hold.

'Really?' she said.

'He's waiting for us at the airport,' said Mr Clough.

While Jane's mind did another series of forward rolls, Mr Demaris was considering something. 'I've heard people say,' he said, 'that you've got no sense of smell. Is that true?'

Jane admitted that her sense of smell was none too good. Mr Clough looked at Mr Demaris.

'I think it's about time we reviewed your salary,' he said.

CHAPTER
FIVE

'Can I speak,' Vanderdecker shouted, 'to Professor Montalban?'

In a long life, reflected the Flying Dutchman, I have come across many bloody silly ideas, but two of them are in a class of their own for pure untainted idiocy. One was the Court of King Ludwig of Bavaria, and the other is the privatised British telephone service.

A long way away, definitely in another continent and quite probably in another dimension, a little voice asked him to repeat the name.

'Montalban,' he said. 'M for Mouse . . .'

The lovely part of it was that he was standing in a telephone kiosk within sight of the gates of the power station he was telephoning. If he was to shout just a little bit louder they'd be able to hear him without using the phone at all.

'Who's calling, please?' said the voice.

'My name's Vanderdecker,' Vanderdecker said.

'I'm sorry,' said the voice, 'I didn't quite . . .'

'*VANDERDECKER* . . . Oh I'm sorry, I didn't mean to shout, it's not a very good line . . . Oh I see. When do you expect him back?'

'Professor Montalban has gone to Geneva,' said the voice, 'we don't expect him back for a week or so. Will you hold?'

'No, no,' said the Flying Dutchman, 'that's fine, have you got a number for him in . . .'

'Could you speak up, please?' the voice said, 'it's rather a poor line.'

'Have you got a number where I can reach the professor in Geneva?' Vanderdecker enunciated. The voice said no, she didn't, could she take a message? Vanderdecker thanked her and hung up.

Even on his antiquated maps, Geneva was clearly marked as being a long way from the sea. Not from water, but from the sea. All in all, it would be foolish to risk trying to reach him there. Vanderdecker pressed the little lever, but no change came cascading down into the tray marked Returned Coins. There would be nothing for it, he said to himself, but to put out to sea for a while until the good professor came back.

For above the seven thousandth time, Vanderdecker assured himself that the alchemist would be as keen to see him as he was to see the alchemist. If Montalban was even remotely concerned with the same field of research as he had been in the reign of His Most Catholic Majesty Philip II, it stood to reason that he would welcome a chance to examine his very first human guinea pigs. His reading of scientific journals had taught him a lot about the way scientists think. They like to have plenty of data. Vanderdecker had a ship full of data; noisome, foul-smelling data, it was true, but . . .

At this point, a thought entered into Vanderdecker's mind. During the short time it stayed there, it made its presence felt in more or less the same way a hand grenade would assert itself in a glassworks.

If Montalban had drunk exactly the same stuff as he had,

presumably Montalban had been subject to exactly the same side-effects. Yet here the alchemist apparently was, spending a week here, a fortnight there, completely surrounded by human beings. It was by no means unlikely that he had gone to Geneva in an aeroplane, and that while there he would stay in a hotel. If he was able to do these things, it necessarily followed that he didn't smell. How was this?

In Caithness, many of the postmen still ride bicycles. If without any warning they get downwind of a member of the crew of the sailing ship *Verdomde*, they tend to ride these bicycles into trees. The sound of a postman's head making contact with a Scots pine brought Vanderdecker out of his reverie. He was being antisocial again. Time to move on.

While he had been away, the crew had passed the time by going for a swim in the sea. Complete immersion in seawater did nothing to impede the communication of the smell, but it did make you feel better. Now the water around Dounreay has been declared completely safe by NIREX, which may be taken to mean that it's about as safe as a gavotte in a minefield; but from the point of view of Vanderdecker's crew, this was a point in its favour. They could bathe in it with a clean conscience if it was polluted already.

By some strange accident of chance, it was Antonius, the first mate, who noticed it first; and this in spite of the fact that the odds against Antonius noticing anything at any given time are so astronomical as to be beyond calculation. The next person to notice it was Sebastian van Doorning. He only noticed it because after his ninth attempt to drown himself he was so short of breath that he was inhaling air like a vacuum-pump. Then Pieter and Dirk Pretorius noticed it, and they pointed it out to Jan Christian Duysberg. He in turn mentioned it to Wilhelm Triegaart, who told him that he was imagining things. In short, by the time Vanderdecker returned, everyone was aware of it. They all decided to tell their captain at the same time.

'Hold on, will you?' Vanderdecker said. There was a brief but total silence, and then everyone started talking again.

'Quiet!' A man who has just spent five minutes talking into a British Telecom payphone is not afraid to raise his voice. 'Sebastian,' he said, choosing someone at random, 'can you please tell me what's going on?'

'It's the smell, captain,' replied the spokesman. 'It's gone.'

Vanderdecker stared. Then he sniffed so violently that he almost dislocated his windpipe.

'When did this happen?' he asked quietly.

'Must have been when we were all swimming in the water, captain,' Sebastian said.

'You don't say.' Vanderdecker closed his eyes, buried his nose in Antonius's doublet and concentrated. There was still a whiff of it there, but it was very faint. 'This water here?'

'That's right,' several voices assured him. Others urged him to try it for himself. They didn't want to be rude, they said, but he smelt awful.

Vanderdecker needed no second invitation. He pulled off his shirt and trousers and jumped into the sea.

'I do believe you're right,' he said, a quarter of an hour later. They were back on board ship again by this stage. The ship itself was as bad as ever, but what could you expect? 'It's definitely still there, but it's faded a hell of a lot.'

'What d'you think's happened?' asked the first mate anxiously. 'What's going on?'

Vanderdecker had a shrewd idea that it wasn't a coincidence. He didn't know much about these things, but it stood to reason that the sea next to a power station absorbs quite a fair amount of any escaping vapours or things of that sort. Until a few days ago, Professor Montalban had been doing experiments inside that very same power station. If that's a coincidence, Vanderdecker said to himself, then I'm not a Dutchman.

An hour later, it had worn off. The cloud of avaricious gulls which had formed over the ship suddenly evaporated. The fumes from Wilhelm Triegaart's repulsive pipe were once again the sweetest-smelling things on the ship. Because he had had his immersion later than the others, Vanderdecker was slightly more wholesome than they were; only slightly. He would still have been barred from any fashionable sewer as a health hazard.

Vanderdecker said, 'Get me all the empty barrels you can find. Then fill them up in the sea where you lot were all having your swim.'

Antonius, who was a conscientious man, felt it his duty to point out to Vanderdecker that you can't drink seawater. Vanderdecker ignored him politely. He was thinking again.

It no longer matters, he said to himself. Geneva can be on top of the Alps for all I care – if we can keep ourselves from smelling for just a couple of days, we could make it to Geneva and go see Montalban.

While we're on the subject of coincidences, how else would you account for the fact that the Dow Jones' second biggest slide in twenty years started that same afternoon?

The most direct route by sea from Dounreay to Geneva, so to speak, is straight down the North Sea and into the Channel. Vanderdecker, however, was extremely unhappy about going anywhere near the Channel now that it was so depressingly full of ships. He made for Den Helder.

Yet another of these wretched coincidences; MV *Erdkrieger*, the flagship of the environmentalist pressure group Green Machine, left Den Helder at exactly the same time on the same day that Vanderdecker left Scotland. It was headed for Dounreay. Its progress was slightly impeded by its cargo of six thousand tons of slightly wilted flowers, contributed by Green Machine's Dutch militant sister organisation Unilateral Tulip, which the *Erdkrieger*'s crew intended to use to block the effluent outlets of the newly-built Fifth Generation Reactor whose construction and installation Professor Montalban (better known in environmentalist circles as the Great Satan) was presently supervising. As a result, the *Erdkrieger* was not her usual nippy self. She was going about as fast as, for example, a sixteenth century merchantman under full sail.

'Now then,' said Mr Gleeson, 'the Vanderdecker Policy.'

Mr Gleeson was not what Jane had expected, but then she shouldn't have expected him to be; not if she'd thought about it for a moment. What she should have expected was an extra-ordinary man; and for all his shortcomings, he was certainly that.

He was short; maybe half an inch shorter than Jane, who was a quintessential size 12. He was round but not fat, and his head had hair in more or less the same way a mountain has grass – sparse and short and harassed-looking. He had bright, quick, precise eyes and a smile that told you that he would make jokes but not laugh at yours. As to ninety per cent of him he looked like somebody's nice uncle. The other ten per cent, you felt, was probably pure barracuda.

'I don't know,' said Mr Gleeson, 'how much you've found out for yourself, so I'd better start at the beginning. Would you like something before we start? Cup of tea? Gin and tonic? Sherry?'

Jane had never been in Mr Gleeson's office before, and she didn't feel at all comfortable. It was an unsettling place – just comfortable enough to make you start to feel at home, and just businesslike enough to make you suddenly realise that you weren't. Jane had the perception to understand that this effect was deliberate.

'No, thank you,' she said. Her mouth was like emery paper.

Mr Gleeson reclined in his chair and looked at his finger-nails for a moment. 'The Vanderdecker Policy,' he said, 'is the single most important secret in the world. I don't want to worry you unduly, but when you leave this office tonight you'll be taking with you enough information to wipe out every major financial institution and destabilise every economy in the world. I just thought you ought to know that. You can keep a secret, can't you?'

Jane mumbled that she could. Mr Gleeson nodded. He accepted her word on this point. He was a good judge of character, and could read people.

'Actually,' he continued, 'the risk involved in telling you this is minimal, because if you leaked it to anybody they wouldn't believe you. I'm not sure they'd even believe me. Or the President of the United States, for that matter. When you actually come face to face with the true story, it's so completely incredible that you could publish it in the *Investor's Chronicle* and it wouldn't make a blind bit of difference. What we've been trying to cover up, ever since long before you were born, is not what the secret is but that it exists. And mainly, of course, we're trying to deal with the actual problem, so that by the time it does get out – it will one day, it must, there's no stopping it – we'll have solved it and that will be that. Now then.'

Mr Gleeson scratched his ear slowly and gently, as if this was a very delicate and difficult feat to perform and required all his concentration. Then he leaned forward.

'So that you can understand what I'm going to say,' he continued, 'I'd better just fill you in on the history of this firm's most important client. You don't need me to tell you that that's the National Lombard Bank. It's a very old bank; in fact it's the oldest bank of all. To be honest with you, nobody knows exactly when it was founded; it started off as a large number of silver pennies in a sock belonging to an Italian merchant who was too fat to go to the Crusades in person, but was alive to the fantastic commercial opportunity they presented. These silver pennies bred so many other silver pennies during the Siege of Jerusalem that the sock was too small to contain them all, and the Italian merchant, or his grandson or whoever it was, built a bank instead and kept them in that. Spiritually, however, the whole organisation remained a sock, and a sock it is to this day. Remember that, and you'll understand a lot about how banks work.

'For reasons best known to itself, the sock left Lombardy early in the fourteenth century and migrated to the cities of the Hanseatic League, where it went to live with some people called Fugger. They were kind to the sock and fed it lots of silver pennies, until almost all the silver pennies in the world were either in the sock permanently or else indefeasibly linked to it by a series of binding legal agreements. The more people tried to take money out of the sock, the more money ended up in there, and although everyone complained bitterly about this state of affairs, none of them realised that the only way to break the vicious circle was not to take money out of the sock in the first place. Even now,' said Mr Gleeson, 'the lesson has not been learned which is why the economic infrastructure of the developed nations is completely up the pictures.'

'Anyway,' continued Mr Gleeson, 'the Fuggers were industrious men, and they weren't content to let the sock do all the work. They were forever trying to think up new ideas for getting even more silver pennies from people, and one of them hit on a very simple but extremely effective concept. It was basically a form of gambling, and it went something like this.

'The Fuggers would think of something that was extremely unlikely to happen, and then they would persuade someone to wager them money that it would. Now the proper term for this arrangement is a sucker bet, but the Fuggers wanted to find a respectable name for it, so they called it Insurance. It caught on, just as they knew it would, and soon it became so respectable that they were able to get people to make a new bet every year, and they called this sort of bet a premium. But although everyone was soon convinced that the bets were totally respectable, the Fuggers were perfectionists and wanted to make absolutely sure, so they took to writing the bets out on extremely long pieces of parchment, frequently in Latin. This practice survives to this day; we call them policies, and usually they're so completely and utterly respectable that it takes a couple of trained lawyers to understand what they mean.'

Jane nodded instinctively, for she had just renewed her car insurance. Mr Gleeson went on.

'Well,' he said, 'if we can just fast-forward for a bit, the House of Fugger became Fugger and Company, which in turn became the Lombard National Bank, which turned into the National Lombard Bank plc. The name has changed, but the sock remains the same. In fact, you would be forgiven for thinking that the sock is the only truly immortal entity in the world. You would be wrong.'

Mr Gleeson paused and opened the top drawer of his desk, from which he extracted a packet of digestive biscuits. He offered one to Jane, who refused, and then ate one himself. Once he had cleared his mouth of crumbs, he continued.

'Back we go to the sixteenth century. We are in Cadiz, one of the most important seaports in the world. If you are tired of Cadiz, you are tired of life and so on. Naturally, there is a Fugger office in the High Street, offering low-interest overdrafts, mortgages (the word mortgage literally means "dead hand", which I find terribly evocative, don't you?), bottomry loans, whatever they were, and the inevitable life insurance. It is a Thursday.

'Into the Fugger office walks a relatively prosperous sea captain in his early thirties. He has become rather concerned about the risks involved in his profession now that the seas are full of English pirates, and he wants to take out some insurance on his ship. This is perfectly natural, because his ship is his living, and if somebody puts a culverin ball through its bows, our sea-captain will be out of a job.

'The manager of this particular Fugger office is well versed in the basic tenets of his trade, and the fundamental rule of insurance is, Don't take bad risks – that, by the way, is what an insurer calls a sucker bet when you offer it to him. There is a severe risk that what the sea-captain fears so much will actually come to pass. Therefore, regretfully, the manager has to refuse to insure the ship. But he is nothing if not a tryer; it hurts him severely if someone walk out of his office without making at least a small bet, and so he suggests to the sea-captain that he might do worse than take out a little life insurance.'

Again Mr Gleeson paused, and Jane noticed to her amazement that he was quivering slightly. Mr Gleeson must have noticed her noticing, for he smiled.

'This is the good bit,' he said, 'don't go away. I remember when I was told it. By rights, of course, I should never have been told it at all. You see, the story is handed down from generation to generation of managing directors of the House of Fugger or whatever they're calling it this week. Fortunately, the managing directors of the bank had always died in their beds with plenty of notice from the medical authorities, and so there was always time to pass the story on. The way I got to hear it was extremely fortuitous, a complete break with tradition, you might say. You see, I was at Oxford with the son of the then managing director, and I was staying with the family one long vacation. We all went out rough shooting and there was a terrible accident, the old man got shot. No time to get a doctor, he just rolled over and with his dying breath blurted the whole horrible thing out. I happened to be there, and so of course I heard it. I wasn't even qualified then, but of course I became the bank's chief auditor on the spot, just as my friend became the next managing director, because of what we had heard. You see, the system is that the whole board knows there's a secret, but only the MD knows what the secret is. I've introduced the same system at Moss Berwick, but it doesn't seem to have worked so well there.'

'So what is the secret, exactly?' Jane asked.

'I'm coming to that,' said the senior partner. 'I was just trying to put it off for as long as possible, because it's so . . . so silly, I suppose is what you'd have to call it, if you were going to be savagely honest. I've lived with this for thirty years, my entire life and phenomenal successes in my career are built around it and I've never ever told anyone before.'

Jane looked him in the eye. She was sorry for him. 'Go on,' she said.

'Thank you,' said Mr Gleeson. He was probably quite nice when you got to know him, should you live that long. 'The policy that the manager sold Captain Vanderdecker – the sea-captain's name was Vanderdecker – was a perfectly standard policy specially designed to meet the needs, or rather the gullibility, of sea-captains. You had the choice of paying regular premiums or a single lump-sum premium – the sea-captains found it difficult to pay regular premiums in those days, you see, because they rarely knew where they'd be at any given time from one year's end to the next – and in return you got an assured sum on death. It wasn't exactly a fortune, but it would tide your nearest and dearest over until the plague or the Inquisition finally finished her off, and since there was no income tax in those days it was guaranteed tax free.

'The sting in the tail was this. Because sea-captaining was such a risky job in those days, it was a virtual certainty that the policyholder wouldn't make sixty years of age. This is where the sucker-bet part of it comes in. Because of this actuarial semi-certainty, the policy contains the proviso that the sum assured – the payout – will increase by fifty per cent compound for every year that the life assured – the sucker – survives over the age of seventy-five. Seventy-*five*, mark you; those Fuggers were taking no chances. It made a marvellous selling point, and the age limitation only appeared in very tiny script on the back of the policy, just underneath the seal where you wouldn't think of looking. They sold tens of thousands of those policies, and for every one sucker that made seventy-six, there were nine hundred and ninety-nine that didn't.

Mr Gleeson stopped talking and sat very still for a while, so still that Jane was afraid to interrupt him. It is very quiet indeed in a soundproofed office on the fifteenth floor of an office block at two in the morning.

'Talking of sucker bets,' Mr Gleeson finally said, 'this one was the best of the lot. You see, Captain Vanderdecker didn't die. He just went on living. Nobody knows why – there are all sorts of far-fetched stories which I won't bore you with, because your credulity must be strained to breaking-point already. The fact remains that Vanderdecker didn't die. He is still alive, over four hundred years later. Please bear in mind the fact that the interest is compound. We tried to calculate once what it must be now, but we couldn't. There is, quite literally, not that much money in the whole world.

'So, you see, if Vanderdecker dies, the whole thing will go into reverse. All the money which has gone into the sock – and that's every penny there is – will have to come out again, and it will all go to Mr Vanderdecker's estate. This is of course impossible, and so the bank would have to default – it would have to welch on a sucker bet. And that would be that. End of civilisation as we know it. You know as well as I do that the economies of the major economic powers are so volatile that the markets collapse every time the Mayor of Accrington gets a bad cold. The faintest hint that the National Lombard was about to go down and you wouldn't be able to get five yards down Wall Street without being hit by a freefalling market-maker. And that is the basic story behind the Vanderdecker Policy.'

That same long, deafening silence came back again, until Jane could bear it no longer.

'But surely,' Jane said, 'if Vanderdecker is going to live for ever, he'll never die and the problem will never arise.'

Mr Gleeson smiled. 'Who said he was going to live for ever?' he replied. 'All we know is that he hasn't died yet. It's scientifically impossible for a man to live for ever. Logically, he must die eventually. And every year he doesn't die, the problem gets inexpressibly worse. You see the trouble we're in. We can't afford for him to die, any more than we can afford for him to live any longer. Fifty per cent compound. Think about that for a moment, will you?'

Jane thought about it. She shuddered. 'So where is he now?' she asked.

'We don't know,' said Mr Gleeson. 'We lost track of him in the 1630s, and then he kept turning up again. He turns up once every seven years or so, and then he vanishes off the face of the earth.'

Suddenly Jane remembered something. 'You mean like the Flying Dutchman?' she said.

'Vanderdecker is the Flying Dutchman,' said Mr Gleeson. 'The very same.'

'I see,' Jane said, as if this suddenly made everything crystal clear. 'So where does Bridport come in?'

'I was coming to that,' said Mr Gleeson, 'just as soon as I'd given you time to digest what I've just told you. Obviously you've got a remarkable digestion. Or you think I'm as mad as a hatter. Bridport comes in because that's where Vanderdecker was last recorded in this country. He opened an account at the bank's Bridport branch in 1890-something. I believe you found it.'

'I did,' Jane confirmed. 'Why on earth haven't you closed it?'

'Easy,' replied Mr Gleeson, 'we can't close it without either his instructions or sight of his death certificate. Rules are rules.'

Jane was astounded. The last thing she had expected was integrity. 'But what about bank charges?' she said. 'Couldn't you just write it off against those?'

'No bank charges in eighteen ninety-thing,' replied Gleeson. 'It wouldn't be right. There would be an anomaly which would have to be noted in the accounts. As the bank's auditor, I would have to insist on it.'

'I see,' Jane said again. 'I didn't realise the rules were so strict.'

'All we can do,' said Mr Gleeson, 'is keep very quiet about it. The only people who know the significance of that account are me, the chairman of the bank, and now you. Obviously the local manager doesn't know. And if anyone finds out apart from us, of course, we hound them to insanity and have them locked up in a mental hospital.'

'That's within the rules, is it?'

'I've read them very carefully,' Mr Gleeson replied, 'no mention of it anywhere. Therefore it stands to reason it must be legitimate.'

'In that case,' Jane said slowly, 'why haven't I . . .'

'Because,' replied Mr Gleeson, 'you have no sense of smell.'

For the third time, Jane asserted that she saw. She lacked conviction.

'Let me explain,' said Mr Gleeson. 'There's one other thing we know about the Flying Dutchman. He smells. Awful. You've heard of the *Marie Celeste*?'

Jane said that she had.

'National Lombard were part of the syndicate insuring her, so it carried out its own investigation. It found the only survivor.'

'Ah.'

'Well might you say Ah,' replied Mr Gleeson. 'As soon as the managing director found out what was going on, he cleared everyone else out of the way and spoke to the man personally, just before he died of acute bewilderment. He reported how they were all sitting there minding their own business when this old-fashioned sailing ship came alongside. There was this smell, the survivor said. It was so bad, he said, everyone jumped into the sea and was drowned. Except him. The old-fashioned ship picked him up just before he was about to drown and took him on board. He was on the ship for three weeks before it dropped him off. He described the smell in detail; that bit of the report runs to four hundred and seventy-nine pages, so you can see it made quite an impression.

Anyway, it turned out that the name of the ship's captain was Vanderdecker. Since the name is not common and the survivor said the whole crew were in sixteenth-century costume, it's a fair assumption that it was him. There have been other incidents since which corroborate the story, but the names won't mean anything to you because they happened in remote places and the bank managed to cover them up in time. It is an undoubted fact that Vanderdecker smells so horrible that nobody in the world can bear to be in his presence for more than a few seconds at a time. This,' said Mr Gleeson, 'is where you come in.'

'I see,' Jane said, for the fourth time.

'What we want you to do,' said Mr Gleeson, 'is find Vanderdecker and reason with him. Tell him he can't take it with him. Negotiate with him to surrender the policy in return for an annuity – a million pounds a year for life or some such figure. It'd be worth it, the bank can afford it. You'd be on commission, naturally.'

'But how do I find him?' Jane said. 'If it was possible, surely you'd have done it by now.'

'We haven't dared try,' Mr Gleeson replied. 'In order to find Vanderdecker, we'd have to let too many people in on too much of the secret. Far too risky. Sucker bet. Only someone like you can do it, because you know already. And you only know because I've told you, and I've only told you because you have no sense of smell. Do you follow me?'

'I think so,' Jane said, 'more or less. Actually, I might have a lead already.' And she told him about Lower Brickwood Farm Cottage, and the invoices. When she had finished, Mr Gleeson nodded and smiled, a you-can-call-me-Bill sort of smile that he usually reserved for Prime Ministers.

'Will you help us, then?' he said. 'If you succeed, you can name your own fee.'

'Well . . .' Jane hesitated, genuinely doubtful. If she accepted the job, she would have to find some way of coming to terms with what she had just been told, and that would not be easy, not by a long way. On the other hand, and bearing in mind all the material circumstances, with particular regard to the section of the rules which said nothing at all about locking people up in lunatic asylums, she felt she didn't have much choice.

'Yes,' she said.

Mr Gleeson grinned at her. 'That's the spirit,' he said. 'May the Sock be with you.'

CHAPTER SIX

'Cheer up, for God's sake,' said the other man in Quincy's, with his mouth full, 'you're putting me off my asparagus quiche.'

His companion scowled at the little cardboard square under his glass. For reasons which it would be counterproductive to rehearse, he knew that the jolly little cartoon on the beermat of a Viking warrior drinking lager was completely inaccurate, but that wasn't the thing that was upsetting him.

'I don't want to cheer up,' he said. 'Cheerfulness would be very strange behaviour just now, don't you think?'

Suspense is a legitimate literary device only if responsibly handled. Know, then, that the other man's name is Gerald.

'You always were a gloomy sod,' said Gerald, his jaws temporarily free, 'even when we were kids. You had this knack of always looking on the black side. And what good does it do? Tell me that.'

'It enables me,' said Gerald's friend, 'to harmonise with my karma. My karma is presently as much fun as a traffic-jam on

88

the M6. Therefore I am gloomy. If I were to cheer up now, I could suffer severe spiritual damage.'

'Funny you should mention the M6,' Gerald replied. 'I was three hours – three whole hours out of my life – getting between Junctions Four and Five the other day. And you know what caused it all? Changing the light bulb in one of those street-lamp things. Pathetic, I call it, absolutely bloody pathetic.'

'Tell me all about the M6,' Gerald's friend said savagely. 'I'm sure it's incredibly relevant to my getting the sack.'

'You have not got the sack,' Gerald said. 'How many times have I got to tell you? You've been moved sideways, that's all. It happens to everyone. I got moved sideways last year, and it's been the making of me.'

'Gerald,' said his friend, 'how long have we known each other?'

Gerald's friend thought for a moment. 'Good question that,' he said. He put down his fork and began to count on his fingers. 'Let me think. Seventy-three, was it? Seventeen years. My God, how time flies!'

'I've known you for seventeen years?'

'Looks like it.'

'Why?'

Gerald frowned. 'What do you mean?' he said.

'Why?' said his friend angrily. 'I mean, what has been the point? Seventeen years we've been meeting regularly, sending each other postcards from Santorini, inviting each other to parties, having lunch; you'd think it would count for something. You'd think it would go some way towards creating some sort of mutual understanding. And now you sit there, drinking a glass of wine which I paid for, and tell me that getting transferred from Current Affairs to Sport is a sideways move.'

'Well it is,' said Gerald. He had grown so used to this sort of thing that he took no notice whatsoever. 'More people watch sport than current affairs, it's a known fact. Call it promotion.

Will you be able to get me seats for Wimbledon, do you think?'

'What's Wimbledon?' asked his friend.

Gerald frowned. He didn't mind Danny trying to be amusing, but blasphemy was another matter. 'Doesn't matter if it's behind a pillar or anything like that,' he said. 'It's the being there that really counts.'

Danny Bennet ignored him. 'Anything but Sport,' he said, 'I could have taken in my stride. "Songs of Praise." "Bob's Full House." "Antiques Roadshow." Take any shape but this and my firm nerves shall never tremble. Sport, no. At Sport I draw the line.'

'You never did like games much,' Gerald reflected, as he cornered a radish in the folds of his lettuce-leaf. 'Remember the lengths you used to go to just to get off games at school? You just never had any moral fibre, I guess. It's been a problem with you all through life. If only they'd made you play rugger at school, we'd be having less of these theatricals now, I bet.'

'Have you ever tried killing yourself, Gerald? You'd enjoy it.'

'If I were in your shoes,' Gerald continued, 'I'd be over the moon. Plenty of open air. Good clean fun. What the viewer really wants, too; I mean, quite frankly, who gives a toss about politics anyway? Come to think of it, maybe you could do something about the way they always put the cricket highlights on at about half past three in the morning. I'm not as young as I was, I need my eight hours. And it's all very well saying tape it, but I can never set the timer right. I always seem to end up with half an hour of some cult movie in German, which is no use at all when I come in from a hard day at the office. My mother can do it, of course, but then she understands machines. She tapes the Australian soaps, which I call a perverse use of advanced technology.'

'Isn't it time,' Danny said, 'that you were getting back?'

Gerald glanced at his watch and swore. 'You're right,' he said, 'doesn't time fly? Look, I hate to rush off when you're having a life crisis like this, but the dollar's been very iffy all week and God knows what it'll get up to if I'm not there to hold its hand. You must come to dinner. Amanda's finally worked out a way of doing crème brulée in the microwave, you'll love it. Thanks for the drink.' He scooped up the remaining contents of his plate in his fingers, jammed the mixture into his mouth, and departed.

With Gerald mercifully out of the way, Danny was able to enjoy his misery properly. He savoured it. He rolled it round his palate. He experienced its unique bouquet. It is not every day that a living legend gets put out with the empty bottles and the discarded packaging; in fact, it would make a marvellous fly-on-the-wall documentary. For someone else.

Perhaps, Danny said to himself, I am taking it rather too hard. Perhaps they were right, and I was getting a bit set in my ways in current affairs. Perhaps it will be an exciting challenge producing televised snooker in Warrington. Perhaps the world is just a flat plate spinning on a stick balanced on the nose of the Great Conjuror, and my fortunes are so insignificant as to be unworthy of consideration. Perhaps I should pack it all in and go work for the satellite people.

In the three years since his story (the details of which are not relevant hereto) Danny had often considered leaving the BBC and signing on under the Jolly Roger, but only when he was in no fit state to make important decisions. He had come as close as typing his letter of resignation on that day which shall live in infamy when they told him that they had no use for his searing revelations of corruption in the sewage disposal department of a major West Midlands borough, provisionally entitled 'Orduregate'. That same letter had been typed and stamped when 'Countdown to Doomsday', his mordant exposé of the threat posed by a popular brand of furniture polish to the ozone layer, had ended up on the cutting room floor; while a third edition brushed the lip of the postbox after the top floor suspended filming of the script which would have unmasked a hitherto-respected chiropodist in Lutterworth as the Butcher of

Clermont-Ferrand. But he had never done it. The final Columbus-like step off the edge of the world and through the doors of the South Bank Studios was not for him, and he knew it.

The fourth edition of his resignation letter, therefore, remained unwritten, and when he left Quincy's he returned to the studios and went to see the man who was going to tell him everything he needed to know about sports broadcasting in twenty-five minutes.

'The main thing,' said the expert, 'is to turn up on the right day at the right place and keep the sound recordists out of the bar. Leave everything else to the cameramen, and you'll do all right. That's it.'

Is it like this, Danny asked himself, in death's other kingdom? 'That's it, is it?' he said.

'Yes,' said the expert. 'Apart from the commentators, of course. They're a real pain in the backside, but there's absolutely nothing you can do about them, so don't let it worry you. It's basically a question of hanging on and not letting it get to you.'

'Even if they say "Well, Terry, it's a funny old game"?'

'That, my son,' said the expert, 'will be the least of your worries.' He paused and looked at Danny curiously. 'Aren't you that bloke who did the thing about the buried treasure?'

'That's right,' Danny said. The expert grinned.

'I saw that,' he said. 'Load of old cobblers. You're lucky you've still got a job after a stunt like that.'

'Oh yes?' Danny said.

'Listen,' said the expert. 'I've been in this game a long time. The average viewer doesn't want all that. No goals. No big girls. No car-chases. We're living in the age of the video now, just you remember that and you won't go far wrong.'

'Thank you,' Danny said, 'for all your help.'

Now that he knew everything there was to know about producing sports programmes, he felt that he was ready to take on his first assignment. He was wrong.

'For God's sake,' he exclaimed. 'You can't be serious.'

'Someone's got to do it,' he was told.

'They said that about Monte Cassino.'

'What,' came the reply, 'is Monte Cassino?'

'Be reasonable,' Danny urged. 'Quite apart from the fact that it's a fate worse than death, it must be a highly difficult technical assignment. Stands to reason. I've got no experience whatsoever. I'll have no end of problems.'

'That's right, you will. But you'll cope.'

'I don't want to cope,' Danny blathered, 'I'm a perfectionist.'

'And look where it's got you.'

Danny paused, but only because he had spoken all the breath out of his lungs. As he breathed in, a terrible thought struck him.

'This is deliberate,' he said. 'Of course, why didn't I realise it before? You've given this to me just so as I can cock it up and you can fire me.'

'You and your conspiracy theories.'

'Stuff conspiracy theories,' Danny snapped, 'this is my career at stake. You can't do this to me. I have friends.'

'Name one.'

Put like that, it wasn't easy. The life pattern of a television producer is not conducive to the forming of friendships. The only one he could come up with was Gerald, and he probably wouldn't count for much.

'Contacts, then,' Danny said. 'I have contacts. All I'd have to do to get my own show on Channel 4 is snap my fingers.'

'All *I'd* have to do to get a show on Channel 4 is snap my fingers,' his interlocutor pointed out reasonably. 'Look, stop being such a pain about it and go and film some yachts. You'll like it once you get there. They tell me the trick is not to lean backwards too far or you'll fall off the boat.'

'What boat?'

'You have to film it from a boat,' he was informed. 'That's how you film boats. They tell me.'

Danny fumed, like a cigarette discarded on flame-proof

furniture fabric, and then said, 'All right, you win. Where do I have to go?'

On the other side of the desk a very faint grin started to form, and out of it came the word 'Bridport.'

'Bridport? Where the bloody hell is Bridport?'

'Bridport,' said the context of the grin, 'is where the Bridport Old Ships Race starts from. Beyond that, I must confess I know very little. Mandy in the front office has an atlas, ask her.'

Mandy in the front office did indeed have an atlas, which was so up to date that it showed all the principal towns in the Belgian Congo. It also showed Bridport.

'You going there, are you?' she asked.

'No,' Danny replied, 'I just needed reassuring it was still there.' He sighed and went to sort out his briefcase.

Aboard the protest ship *Erdkrieger*, all was not well.

'Woher,' someone said, 'kommt der Gerucht?'

Someone else asked what the hell that was supposed to mean, and a third party translated for her.

'Where's the smell coming from?'

'That's the trouble,' remarked the second party from behind her handkerchief, 'with being on a goddamn multilingual ship.'

Wherever the smell was coming from, it was not pleasant. Some of the ship's company compared it to a Zellophan-papierfabrik; others got halfway through saying Exkremente-verarbeitungswerk before the vapours got into their lungs and reduced them to spluttering hulks.

'Sewage farm,' explained the translator.

'I guessed.'

In any event, it was a horrible smell, and horrible smells out in the middle of the sea can only mean one thing to the crew of an environmental patrol vessel.

'We'd better get those guys, whoever they are,' said the imperfect linguist. 'You fetch the handcuffs and I'll go connect up the fire hoses.'

The translator, a short, weatherbeaten New Zealander, refused to budge. She was happy where she was. It might be cramped and wet and full of discarded foodstuffs, but it was out of the way of the terrible breeze that was carrying the Geruch in from wherever it originated. Her companion started off full of scorn, but came back rather quickly.

'Jesus,' she said, 'it smells really awful.'

The captain, a tall, blond German, was going round issuing gas masks. They helped, but not all that much; they had only been designed to cope with relatively minor environmental pollution, such as mustard gas. Nevertheless, their morale value at least was sufficient to enable the imperfect linguist and a few other diehards to scramble out of hard cover and take stock of the situation.

Through the misted eyepieces of their masks, they could dimly make out a ship creaking slowly towards them across the whale-road. It was slow, and it was unnaturally quiet. But the imperfect linguist, whose name was Martha and who came from Bethlehem, Pa., knew what that signified.

'This is something big,' she said to the New Zealander.

'Is it?'

'I read about it,' she replied. 'There's some new kinds of waste so volatile they daren't put them on conventional ships because of the danger of combustion; you know, sparks from the electrics, that kind of thing. So they use these sail-powered ships.'

'I never heard that.'

'Well you wouldn't, would you,' Martha said. 'It's secret.'

That made sense, and the New Zealander scurried off to tell the captain, whom she eventually found inside one of the lifeboats, with a tarpaulin over his head.

The captain's appeal for volunteers was truly a call for heroes, for the mission that was proposed called for selfless dedication to the cause. It demanded the sort of sacrifice that ought once and for all to sort out who were the real friends of the earth and who were the ones who just dropped in now and then for a cup of coffee and a chat. So rigorous was this selection process that the result was two people only. As the outboard motor of the dinghy finally fired and propelled the frail craft towards the poison ship, the New Zealander set her jaw and tried to think of the rain forests. It wasn't easy.

'For Chrissakes, Jo, you nearly had us over,' remarked her fellow martyr, as they bounced off a rather bumptious wave. 'This isn't Indianapolis, throttle back a bit.'

Jo throttled right back while Martha checked the handcuffs with which they were going to chain themselves to the side of the poison ship. Deep down in the unregenerate parts of her brain, there was a tiny hope that the handcuffs would fall to bits and they could go back to the *Erdkrieger* with honour.

'They seem to be taking it very calmly,' she muttered as they came within fifty yards of their target.

'You what?'

'They seem to be taking it very calmly!' Martha yelled. Jo shrugged. By and large, she was thinking to herself, she was regretting that she hadn't become a dentist like her family wanted her to. Dentists also have their part to play in the Great Society, and they don't have to chain themselves to extremely smelly ships.

'If they turn the hoses on us,' Martha continued, 'just try and kinda roll with it.'

'They don't look like they've got any hoses, Martha,' Jo replied. 'Looks a bit on the primitive side to me.'

'That's just a front,' Martha replied confidently. She had been in this game long enough to know that all the masks of the enemy are fundamentally weird.

'Are those cannons sticking out the side?' Jo asked.

'Could be,' Martha said. 'They sure look like cannons. Probably the pipes they pump the stuff out of, though.'

At last they could make out a human being on the ship. Two human beings, two human beings leaning against the rail looking mildly interested. They seemed entirely oblivious to the smell.

Martha seized the grappling-hook while Jo swung the tiller. There didn't seem an awful lot you could get a handcuff round on the gleaming oak sides of the ship, but she owed it to herself to try.

'Hello there,' said a voice from above her head. 'Are you lost?'

Martha blinked. 'Are we what?'

'Lost,' repeated the voice.

'Don't try that one with me, buster,' Martha said. 'We're coming alongside, and don't bother trying to stop us.'

The taller of the two men gazed at her with a puzzled expression. 'Do you really want to come alongside?' he said.

'Yes.'

'Takes all sorts,' replied the taller man. 'Shall I drop you a line?'

Martha was about to say something, but Jo explained that it was also a seafaring term. 'He wants to lower us a rope,' she whispered.

'What?'

'He wants to lower us a bloody rope!' Jo shouted.

'That's right,' said the man on the ship, 'I want to lower you a rope. If you'd like me to, that is. I'm not bothered one way or the other.'

Martha only had a few seconds to decide whether this was simple or duplex treachery. She decided on duplex.

'Lower away, sucker,' she replied. 'See if I care.'

'Your friend isn't very polite, is she?' said the man on the ship. He threw a rope to them, and Martha grabbed it and made it fast. Together, she and Jo hauled themselves level with the ship. With the best will in the world, there was nothing – absolutely nothing – to handcuff themselves to short of the rail that ran round the side of the ship. Martha thought of acid rain and the whales, and started to scramble up the rope.

'Hold on,' said the man on the ship, 'it's wet, you'll slip.'

He was right.

Several other men had joined him now. There was sniggering. But no hoses. Martha was not enjoying herself. She was at home with hoses, she knew where they were coming from. But nobody seemed to be taking her seriously.

'Come on, Jo,' she panted as she hauled herself up into the dinghy again and seized the rope. She was feeling angry, frustrated, humiliated and above all wet, and a little voice in the back of her mind was saying that it really was about time the whales learned to look after themselves, or what the hell was the point of evolution, anyway? She dismissed it with the contempt it deserved. 'Scared, are you?'

'No,' Jo replied. 'I'm going up the ladder.'

'What ladder?'

'The one they've just lowered,' Jo replied, and stepped out of the dinghy.

Vanderdecker had just managed to say the 'What can I do' part of 'What can I do for you?' when the smaller of the two visitors deftly and entirely unexpectedly manacled herself to the ship's rail. The second – rather unwillingly, Vanderdecker felt – followed suit.

'Is something the matter?' he asked.

On the bridge of the *Erdkrieger*, the captain observed the scene aboard the poison ship and felt ashamed in his Teutonic heart. His Kameradinen had dared to go where he had been afraid to go, and that was not good enough. He proposed the motion – it was a fundamentally democratic ship – that they lower the other boats, and that they jump to it.

'Why,' Vanderdecker was asking, 'have you two ladies chained yourselves to the rail of my ship? Sorry if that sounds nosy, but . . .'

'Because,' Martha replied, 'we are sisters of our mother Earth.'

There was a brief silence, and then the first mate spoke.

'Captain,' he said, 'if they're her sisters, how can she be their mother?'

Vanderdecker smiled patiently at his first mate. 'Not now, Antonius,' he said. 'I'll explain later. Environmentalists?'

'That's right,' Martha said. 'So . . .'

'So why are you chained to the railings of my ship? Practice?'

Martha sneered, although Vanderdecker couldn't see because of the gas mask. 'Don't act innocent with me. We know what you've got on this ship.'

'What have I got on this ship?' Vanderdecker said. 'Go on, you'll never guess.'

'Extremely hazardous toxic chemical waste,' came the reply, in chorus. Vanderdecker shook his head.

'No,' he replied, 'you're wrong there. Apart from a few tins of supermarket lager we got in Bridport last time, that is. It's true what they say, you get what you pay for. I'm sorry,' he said, noting a certain hostility. 'You were guessing what I've got on this ship.'

'If there's no toxic waste on this ship,' said Jo sardonically, 'how do you explain the smell?'

Vanderdecker shrugged and turned to the first mate. 'All right,' he said, 'which one of you forgot to buy the soap?'

'Very funny,' Martha snarled. 'We know you've got that filth on board, and we're not unchaining ourselves until you turn back to where you came from.'

'I promise,' Vanderdecker said solemnly, 'there's not so much as a thimbleful of toxic waste on board. You can look for yourselves if you like.'

Martha laughed. 'What, and unchain ourselves? You'd really like that, wouldn't you?'

Vanderdecker frowned irritably. 'Look, miss,' he said, 'if you think I'm getting any sort of thrill out of seeing two females in wetsuits and gasmasks chained to a railing, you're working the wrong pitch. Try Amsterdam. And if you're so damned nosy as to want to go poking about looking for seeping oildrums, then be my guest. If not, then please excuse me, I've got a ship to run.'

The two women stood firm and scowled at him. Just then, Sebastian drew his attention to the other four dinghies making their way across from the *Erdkrieger*.

Their arrival solved what could have developed into a very tedious situation. Once the raiding party had been over the *Verdomde* inch by inch, molesting the ship's stores with Geiger counters and sticking litmus paper into the beer barrel, they had to admit that it was clean as a whistle. But smelly, nevertheless.

'Tact,' said Vanderdecker in German to his opposite number from the *Erdkrieger*, 'is clearly not your strong suit. I admit we aren't all lavender bags and rosewater, but we have been at sea for rather a long time.'

'But this ship,' said the German. 'It's so peculiar. Why are you sailing in a galleon?'

'Living archaeology,' Vanderdecker replied. 'We're reconstructing Magellan's circumnavigation of the world.'

As he said this, Vanderdecker was conscious of a puzzled noise behind him. It was the first mate.

'So that's what we're doing, is it?' he said. 'I was beginning to wonder.'

The smile reappeared on Vanderdecker's face. Over the centuries it had worn little tracks for itself, and its passage was smooth and effortless.

'That's right, Antonius,' he said. 'I'll explain later.'

'Who was Magellan, captain?'

'Later!' Just for a split second, the smile was disrupted; then it smoothed itself back. 'We're doing it in aid of the rain forests,' he said to the German, to whom this remark, astonishingly, made sense.

'Oh,' he said. 'That's very good. Sorry to have bothered you.'

'Not at all,' Vanderdecker replied. 'I mean, we're on the same side, aren't we? All Greens together, so to speak.'

The captain nodded enthusiastically, so that the hose of his gasmask clunked on his muscular stomach. Vanderdecker winced, but imperceptibly.

'So,' he asked, as casually as he could, 'where are you off to then?'

'Dounreay,' said the German cheerfully. 'We're going to sabotage the nuclear power plant.'

'Jolly good,' said Vanderdecker. 'But isn't that a bit counter-productive? Blowing up a nuclear plant?'

'Who said anything about blowing it up?' said the German. 'We're going to stuff tulips up the drainpipes.'

'What a perfectly splendid idea,' Vanderdecker said, through his Antonius smile. 'Very best of luck to you. Got enough?'

'Enough what?'

'Tulips.'

'Ja, ja, we have Uberfluss of tulips.' He waved proudly at the distant profile of the *Erdkrieger*. 'Our whole ship,' he said, 'is full of tulips.'

'Isn't that nice,' Vanderdecker said, afraid for a moment that the corners of his Antonius smile would meet round the back of his neck and unzip his face. Then an idea occurred to him. 'If you're going to Dounreay,' he said, 'you could do me a small favour.'

'Certainly,' said the German.

'Have you,' Vanderdecker said, 'got any paint?'

'Ja, naturlich. Uberfluss of paint.'

'Red aerosol paint?'

'Ja,' said the German. 'Humbrol.'

'Then,' said Vanderdecker, 'I don't suppose you could see your way to painting a little message for me on the walls some-where. I'll write it down for you if you like.'

Thus it was that when Martha, Jo and the German were finally bundled off in vans by the Sutherland and Caithness Con-stabulary, they left behind them a crudely-inscribed but extremely visible message on the perimeter wall of Dounreay power station.

ALL THAT GLITTERS IS NOT GOLD, it read. YOU SMELL, MONTALBAN. YOURS, VANDERDECKER.

CHAPTER
SEVEN

Gerald – you remember Gerald – was puzzled. He
squashed the plastic cup in his hand into a spiky ball and
dropped it in the waste-paper basket, where it bounced off a
heap of shareholders' circulars and rolled onto the floor under
his swivel chair.

Actually, Gerald wasn't the only person in the City of
London that morning who was seriously puzzled, and we only
single him out because we have already been introduced to
him and know what a level-headed sort of fellow he usually is.
If Gerald can't understand it, it must be odd.

It was. Something extremely unpleasant was happening to
the dollar, and Gerald didn't like it. His relationship with
the dollar was rather like Heathcliffe's relationship with
Cathy, although which of them was which at any given moment it
was generally difficult to decide. But if something bothered the
dollar, it bothered Gerald. It was like telepathy.

At the next desk, Adrian was getting into an awful tangle
with the Deutschmark, while Imogen had washed her hands of

the yen and was having a quiet sit down and a cup of lemon tea. In fact, virtually all the occupants of the glass tower that housed Marshall Price Butterworth were behaving like ants whose queen has just died; there was a great deal of activity and absolutely no unified purpose. And over the whole organisation hung the dreadful possibility that if this went on much longer they were all going to have to miss lunch. It was as bad as that.

Black Thursday, as it has since come to be known, started in the usual way. The breakdown of Middle East peace talks took some of the shine off oil and vague fears on Wall Street about the possibility of the restoration of the Jacobites caused the pound to fall two cents in early trading, but good figures from the banking and insurance sector helped the FTSE to perk up a bit, and only the lost, violent souls whose business it was to follow the vertiginous progress of the Hang Seng were having anything but a perfectly average day. Then it happened. Somewhere in the ether through which the faxes hurtled invisible the notion was spawned that something too ghastly for words was about to happen to the National Lombard Bank. Nobody knew where it came from, but such instances of parthenogenesis are so commonplace in the Square Mile that nobody ever bothers to ask. Consult anyone who has had anything to do with the markets since they introduced the new technology and they will tell you that all such rumours originate with a little man who lives in a converted railway carriage in Alaska and phones them through to the newspaper seller at Liverpool Street station. It may not be true, but it provides a much-needed focal point for baffled indignation.

Once the rumour had started, it grew. Nobody believed a word of it, of course – nobody ever does – but as custodians of the trust of countless small investors they saw it as their duty to wipe as many millions off the price of everything as they possibly could, and so the process was set in ineluctable motion. In the short time it takes for a message to bridge the

Atlantic on fibre-optic wings the rumour had hit New York, and from there it moved on, faster than light and considerably faster than thought, to Tokyo, Hong Kong, Sydney, Paris, Geneva and all the other financial capitals of the world. So swift was its development and transmission that within two hours of its immaculate conception it was prompting market-makers in the Solomon Islands to get out of cowrie shells and knocking the bottom out of the reindeer futures market in Lapland.

Gerald took another long, unfriendly look at the screen, scratched his ear with his left index finger, and decided to take an early lunch. The dollar, he decided, was only doing it to attract attention to itself, and if he ignored it then it would stop playing up and return to normal. It was not, perhaps, the view that Keynes or Adam Smith would have taken, but it made about as much sense as anything else. He picked up his personal organiser, scribbled a note saying 'Sell' on his scratch pad to remind him when he came back, and tottered off to the Wine Vaults.

All the time in the world, said Vanderdecker to himself through teeth clenched tight as masonry, we've got all the time in the world, so let's not get all over-excited about a little puff of wind in the North Sea.

The gale howling through the shredded canvas of the mainsail was so loud that Vanderdecker was compelled to stop talking to himself and shout to himself instead. All around the *Verdomde*, waves as high as towers were forming and collapsing, like those speeded up films which show you a rosebud forming, flowering and withering away. The rain meanwhile was lashing horizontally into his eyes, so that even if it hadn't already been as dark as midnight he wouldn't have been able to see anything anyway. Nothing unusual, he screamed at his subconscious mind. Normal business hazard. Slight electric storm in the North Sea.

Out of the tiny corner of his eye which was still operational,

Vanderdecker noticed something, and he edged out from under the insufficient shelter of the beer-barrel. 'Sebastian!' he yelled, 'pack it in, will you? This is neither the time nor the place.'

As soon as the first bolt of lightning had split the velvet sky, Sebastian had hurried on deck with a great lump of magnetic iron ore in his hands. He kept it specially for thunderstorms, and although he had so far failed to attract a single skyborne volt with it there was always a first time. Up to a point, Vanderdecker admired the man's ingenuity, to say nothing of his tenacity, but he wasn't in the mood for a swim if a baffled thunderbolt went straight down through the soles of Sebastian's invulnerable feet and reduced the *Verdomde* to woodshavings.

'Take in all sail!' Vanderdecker shouted, but nobody was listening, as usual. That's what's wrong with this bloody ship, mused its captain as a wave broke over the side and tried to pull all his hair out, too much bloody apathy. Nobody cares if all the sails get ripped into dusters. So what? We weren't going anywhere anyway. Only this time they were going somewhere; they were going to Geneva to see Professor Montalban, with five barrels of radioactive deodorant safely lashed down in the hold. The one time I want to get somewhere, I run into the worst storm in fifty years. Tremendous!

Just then there was a horrible rending sound; timber, grievously maltreated, giving way. The yard arm of the mainsail had cracked under the pressure of a freak gust, and its own weight was dragging it down on a hinge of splintered wood. Down it came with shattering force on the back of Sebastian van Doorning's head, crushing him onto the deck like a swatted cranefly. Old instincts die hard; before he knew it, Vanderdecker sprang forward and knelt over his fallen crewman, shielding his crumpled body from the violence of the storm.

'Is that you, skipper?'

'It's all right,' Vanderdecker said, as Sebastian's large eyes slowly opened. 'You're going to be all right.'

'Am I?'

'Yes,' Vanderdecker promised.

'Oh, for crying out loud,' Sebastian exclaimed, picked himself up, and shuffled away through the driving rain, muttering something about it just not being fair. Vanderdecker shook his head and retreated back to the cover of the beer-barrel.

When, eventually, the storm had blown itself out, Vanderdecker hadn't the faintest idea where they were. By a miracle – or sheer force of habit – the ship had stayed in one piece, but only just. The sails were in tatters, the mainmast was completely useless, and the whole structure of the vessel had been so badly knocked about that it was patently obvious that major repairs would be needed just to keep her afloat. Just my luck, Vanderdecker raged in the silence of his mind, just my perishing luck.

Ironically, there was now no wind whatsoever; the ship sat there like a rubber duck in a bath all the rest of the day, and when darkness fell the stars were clear and bright in a cloudless sky. With their help, Vanderdecker worked out more or less where he was and then faced up to an agonising decision.

The first mate's report on the damage forced him to admit that a change of plan was inevitable; unless it was patched up pretty damn quick, the ship would be going nowhere except down. And there was only one place, in the whole wide world, that the ship could be patched up. No alternative. Pity the place was such a dump, but still.

Vanderdecker called the crew together on deck and told them. We are no longer going to Geneva; instead, we are going to Bridport. As the all-too-familiar chorus of groans, complaints, accusations and other going-to-Bridport noises reached its crescendo, Vanderdecker walked away and opened the last can of Stella Artois. He needed it.

Man's reach must exceed man's grasp, or what's a heaven for? For twenty years Marion Price had dreamed of a nice little cleaning job at a chicken-plucking factory somewhere, and here she still was, running the tourist information office in Bridport.

Every year, when the clouds close in and Aeolus lets slip the sack wherein the four winds are pent, about a hundred thousand miserable-looking holiday-makers with children dangling from their wrists traipse in from West Bay and demand to be informed as to what there is to do in Bridport when it's wet. To this question, there is only one answer. It rarely satisfies. Nothing shall come of nothing; speak again. Sorry, ladies and gentlemen, but that's all there is to it. There is absolutely nothing to do in this man's town in the rainy season except grow your hair.

You don't put it like that, of course. You suggest that they go and take a look at the Bridport Museum, or the Rural Crafts Exhibition, or the Working Water Mill. You draw them little plans on the backs of envelopes to show them how to get there. They stand there, dripping, and stare at you, as if you were keeping from them the secret of the location of King Solomon's Mines, and finally they take a few Glorious Dorset leaflets and go away. On your way home in the evening, you retrieve the Glorious Dorset leaflets from the litter bin on the corner and reflect on the vanity of human wishes.

Some of them, however, refuse to go away until you come up with something that sounds at least bearable, and these poor fools are generally advised to go and visit Jeanes' Boatyard. As a cure for optimism, Jeanes' Boatyard, which is open to the public from 10 till 3 Mondays to Fridays all year round, has few rivals. In the interests of research, Marion has been there once. Never again. There is a hackneyed quip about such-and-such being as interesting as watching paint dry. The paint-drying shop is the highlight of a visit to Jeanes' Boatyard.

Here is Marion Price, and she is talking to a pair of hopeless, incorrigible, dyed-in-the-wool optimists and their seven-year-old offspring.

'Boatyard?' says the male optimist.

'The oldest working boatyard in Dorset,' replies the tape recording that lives inside Marion Price's larynx. 'Boats are built there as they have been for the last five hundred years. Traditional crafts are lovingly kept alive by master shipwright Walter Jeanes and his two sons, Wayne and Jason. Nowhere else in Dorset can you more perfectly recapture the splendours of Britain's age-old maritime heritage. A wide range of refreshments and souvenirs are also available.' And the very best of luck to you, my gullible friends. Why don't you just go back home to Redditch and redecorate the spare room?

A long silence. Jean-Paul Sartre would have savoured it. 'How do we get there, then?' says the female optimist.

'Let me draw you a map.' Nimble, practised cartographer's fingers that have long since sublimated the last dregs of guilt draw a plan of the most direct route. The optimists depart. The rain falls. Time passes.

Jane Doland, being properly brought-up, wiped her feet before walking into the tourist information office. It was her last hope; she had tried the phone book, the post office and the hotel desk. If they couldn't tell her here, she would give up and go back to her room.

'Excuse me,' she said, 'can you tell me where I might find Jeanes' Boatyard?'

'Certainly.' The woman behind the desk smiled at her. Thank God. It was wonderful to find someone actually helpful in this dismal place. 'Shall I draw you a map?'

'If you wouldn't mind,' said Jane. 'I always forget directions, in one ear and out the other. Is it far?'

'Oh no,' said the woman behind the desk, drawing busily without seeming to look at the paper, like one of those machines in hospitals that draw charts of people's heartbeats. 'Have you been to Bridport before?' she asked. Jane said yes, once.

'It's a lovely little town, isn't it?' said the woman behind the desk. 'Some people just keep coming back time and time again.'

Very true, Jane reflected, you don't know how true that is. 'This boatyard,' she asked, 'is it very . . . well, old?'

'Yes, indeed,' the woman replied brightly. 'Boats are built there as they have been for the last five hundred years.'

'As old as that?' Jane asked. 'That's quite a record, isn't it? Well, thank you very much.' She looked at the map. 'Which way is north?' she inquired. The woman pointed, and smiled again. Clearly she enjoyed her work. Just now, Jane envied her that.

As she waded through the puddles in South Street, Jane cast her mind over the events of the past week, starting with the slump on the markets. As soon as she had seen the report of the attempted sabotage at Dounreay and what had been painted on the wall there, she had set off for the North of Scotland as quickly as she could. It was no problem getting to see the protesters who had done the painting; she simply called the Inverness office of Moss Berwick and they fixed it, using their contacts with the lawyers who were defending them. It had not been an easy interview. None of the Germans spoke A-level German, only proper German (which is a quite different language) and all of them were clearly confused as to why they should be talking to an accountant when they were facing criminal damage charges. But the story had slowly co-agulated there in the lawyer's interview room, and when all was said and done, it didn't get anyone terribly much further forward. All that Jane could say for certain was that one place that the Flying Dutchman was likely *not* to be was the North of Scotland, since he had just left there.

She arrived at West Bay at the same time as a television van, and the sight of it made her heart stop. For a terrible moment, she thought that the van might be there for the same reason as she was – after all, the link between the couple of sentences in the newspaper about goings-on at Dounreay and the dramatic slide on the world markets had yet to be sorted out; had some sharp-nosed ferret of an investigative journalist found out about the Vanderdecker policy? But the little mayfly of terror was soon gone as Jane remembered what she had heard on the car radio about some idiot boat-race at West Bay in the next day or so, and she dismissed it from her mind.

It was, she admitted to herself as she parked in front of the boatyard, a long shot, a hunch – or, if you preferred English to the language of the talking pictures, a very silly idea. It had started as she sat on the flight back from Inverness, trying to think of good reasons why she shouldn't follow the Montalban lead. This had not been easy; it was, after all, the logical next step, to go to Geneva, find this Montalban, dream up some pretext for talking to him, and find out what he knew. But for some reason best known to herself – natural diffidence, probably, with a large slice of embarrassment and laziness thrown in – she didn't want to go to Geneva. Her mind had been floating on the meniscus of this problem when she saw a paragraph on the back page of someone else's newspaper about terrible storms in the North Sea. It occurred to her that Vanderdecker would be somewhere in the North Sea at this precise moment, on his way to wherever he was going when he met the *Erdkrieger* (Holland, probably; after all, he was Dutch) and that he might have got caught up in this storm. With unaccustomed boorishness she leaned forward and studied the other person's newspaper, and saw that the storm (the worst for fifty years, so they reckoned) had been off the Dutch coast. Well then, she said, Vanderdecker's ship is very old and probably very fragile. If he's been out in that, he may well need repairs. And where does he come to get his boat fixed? Bridport, of course. A long shot. A hunch. A very silly idea. We shall see.

'Sorry,' said the sound recordist. 'I didn't see you there.'

Danny Bennet looked at the sleeve of his suede jacket, then at the sound recordist, and said something very quietly which nobody was supposed to hear. His debut in the field of sports coverage was not going well, mainly because he hadn't the faintest idea of what was going on.

It was still raining outside, and from that point of view the inside of the scanner van was as good a place to be as any. It was dry, there was a Thermos of at least luke-warm coffee, and no cameramen. That, however, was about it as far as the attractions of the venue went. On the other hand, there were the monitors, and Danny didn't like them at all.

So far as he could make out, his job was to direct operations in such a way that the viewer at home got the best possible view of the proceedings from the best possible angles. In order to manage this, Danny had to make sure that the little motor boats with his camera crews in them were in the right place at the right time. Since he hadn't the faintest idea where they were, this was of course impossible. All he could see were the pictures on the screens. There was another minor difficulty to face up to; he was entirely ignorant of the rules of old ship racing, which meant that he didn't have a clue what the pictures on the screens were supposed to look like. Racing, as far as he understood it, meant a number of competitors trying to go faster than each other; but all the old ships went quite remarkably slowly. This was confusing, like a boxing match between two pacifists. There was no way of knowing whether he was doing it right or not.

Usually in these situations the wise thing to do was to leave it all to the cameramen and not get under their feet. Cameramen have invariably done it all before and know precisely what they are supposed to be doing; their Aatens would be glued to the centre of the action all the time, and all the producer would have to do is sit in the van and stay awake. Unfortunately, this was the first year that the BBC had seen fit to televise this stirring maritime spectacle, and so everyone was as ignorant as he was. For the first time in his television career, cameramen were asking him things instead of telling him. It should have been a moment to savour. It wasn't.

At least he had the radios. He could shout into them. It didn't improve matters – in fact it seemed to make them worse – but it make him feel better.

'Chris,' he yelled, 'can you hear me, Chris?'

Chris replied that he could hear him perfectly well, thank you.

'Chris,' Danny said, 'what the hell am I meant to do with this close-up of a seagull you're giving me? This isn't bloody "Naturewatch", you know.'

Not unreasonably, Chris asked what he should be filming instead, and Danny was at a loss for a reply. Then he had an inspiration.

'Chris,' he yelled, 'use your bloody common sense, will you? This is supposed to be a boat race, right?' Then he switched to another frequency quickly, before Chris had a chance to argue.

'Don't let's play silly buggers, Terry,' he was saying now, glorying in this marvellous new formula he had found, 'this is meant to be a boat race, okay? Just use your common sense and get on with it.' Click. 'Derek, can I just remind you we're supposed to be filming a boat race here?' It was as easy as that.

Then a horrible thought struck him. Perhaps it wasn't meant to be a boat race, or at least not yet. He pulled off his earphones and leant back to talk to the man from the brewery which was sponsoring the event, and who seemed to know more about it than anybody else. 'Excuse me,' he asked, 'have they started yet?'

The brewer shook his head. 'Not for five minutes,' he said. 'Everyone's just getting into position.'

'Oh.' Danny drove his fingernails into the palm of his hand. 'What's the starting signal, then?'

'They fire off a cannon,' said the brewer. 'From that big white yacht.'

'I see,' Danny said. 'Which big white yacht?'

The brewer shrugged. 'The starter's yacht, naturally. Shouldn't you have a camera on it, by the way?'

Danny cast a frantic eye over his bank of monitors. No big white yacht. 'Haven't I?' he said.

'No.'

Danny grabbed the headphones and jammed them on. 'Terry!' he shouted. 'Stop arsing about and get a shot of the starter's yacht. Don't you realise they'll be starting in five minutes?' Then he switched frequencies as quickly as a rattle-snake. Miraculously, a big white yacht appeared on one of the monitors. It worked!

Danny turned back and smiled at the brewer. 'Amateurs!' he explained. The brewer looked at him but said nothing.

'Chris,' Danny was off again, 'I can see the seagull, pack it in, will you – Dear God, what's that?'

On one of the monitors there was the most remarkable ship Danny had ever seen. It wasn't just another reconstruction of a tea-clipper or overgrown yacht; it was a whacking great galleon, like a pirate ship or something left over from the Armada Year. It was extraordinary.

'Phil,' Danny bellowed, 'zoom in, I want a closer look. What is that?'

Phil did what he was told, and Danny could see little men in funny costumes running up and down rope ladders. The ship looked like it was in a bad way; its sails were in rags, and some of the wooden bar things the sails were supposed to hang down from were broken off or dangling precariously from frayed ropes. Surely they weren't proposing to enter it in the race?

Danny was aware of someone sitting beside him. It was the brewer. He was staring.

'Odd,' he said. 'I don't remember that being on the list of competitors.'

Danny stared too; there was something magnetic about this very old-looking old ship. He tried to think if any film companies were releasing spoof swashbucklers this year, and were trying to crash the race to get coverage. But the ship didn't look as if it was trying to attract attention to itself; if a ship can have an expression, it was looking more embarrassed than anything else, as if it had come to the party wearing the wrong thing. Which it had, at that.

'Phil,' Danny said, 'get in closer.'

'All right then,' Vanderdecker shouted, 'if any of you bloody intellectuals think you can do any better, you're welcome to try. Come on, then, who's going first?' Total silence. 'Right then, let's have a bit less of it from now on.'

Righteous indignation is a useful thing; it was galvanising Vanderdecker into an uncharacteristically assertive display of authority at a time when, left to himself, he would be curled up in his cabin wishing it would all go away. But, because the crew were all muttering about him and calling him names behind his back, in spite of the fact that he had managed a quite spectacular feat of seamanship in just getting his shattered ship this far, here he was, doing his best. It probably wasn't going to be good enough, but that was just too bad.

They had started shipping water badly just off the Isle of Wight, and soon after that it was clear to Vanderdecker that he was going to have to be very clever and even more lucky to get this miserable remnant of a sailing-ship to Bridport in one piece. There would be no time to lie up and sidle into their usual sheltered and discreet cove under cover of darkness; they were going to have to go in in broad daylight, and the hell with it. That's if they could get that far. For the last six hours it had been touch and go, and Vanderdecker had amazed himself with his own brilliant resourcefulness and skill in managing to cope. Nobody else was impressed, of course; they all seemed convinced that it had been his fault to start with. But that couldn't be helped.

Vanderdecker had groaned out loud when he saw all the ships in West Bay; there was no way they could make themselves inconspicuous now. So far they hadn't been intercepted, but it couldn't last. He had considered not using the deodorising water from Dounreay, so that the smell would keep them at bay, but he recognised that that would cause more problems than it would solve. Better to get it over with.

Danny Bennet got up from his place in front of the monitors. He felt that peculiar tingling at the base of his skull that meant 'story'.

'Julian,' he said, 'I'm just popping out for a minute. Film the race for me, will you?'

Julian said something, but Danny chose not to hear it. Partial deafness ran in his family. The brewer got up too.

'Are you going to have a look at that ship?' he said.

'Yes,' Danny replied. 'Coming?'

The brewer nodded. 'They aren't on the list of competitors,' he said. 'My company is very strict about things like that. For all I know, it could be demonstrators or something.'

Danny jumped down from the van and called to a camera-man who was sitting on a packing-case reading a newspaper. They hired a boat and set out to take a closer look.

For the record, Julian filmed the race, and he did it very well. Remarkably well, considering that he had only dropped in to take orders for pizzas. Even D.W. Griffiths had to start somewhere.

'Right then,' said the Flying Dutchman, 'gather round, let's get a few things straight before we go in to land.'

It wasn't a particularly brilliant speech – not in the same league as King Henry's address at Harfleur or something by Churchill – and it got the reception it deserved. Vanderdecker wasn't in the least surprised.

'You will have noticed,' he continued, 'that the bay is full of boats. What you may have overlooked is the fact that most of them are sailing-boats, not motor-boats. I think we've been lucky, and pitched up in the middle of some sort of yacht-race or regatta or something, so if we act naturally and mind our own business, perhaps nobody will take any notice of us. Meanwhile, it's quite important that we should get this ship over to Jeanes' Boatyard in the next half hour, because if we don't we're all going for a swim. Got that?'

A rhetorical question. With an exquisitely fine mixture of apathy and contempt the crew of the *Verdomde* slouched back to their positions and got on with their work. They were going to make it, but only just.

'Captain,' Vanderdecker turned round to see the first mate behind him, looking worried.

'Not now, Antonius,' Vanderdecker said.

'But Captain . . .'

'Please,' Vanderdecker said, as gently as he could, 'I know you mean well, but just now . . .'

'Captain,' Antonius said, 'there's a boat coming alongside.'

Vanderdecker stared at him for a moment in horror. 'What?'

'I said there's a boat . . .'

'Where?'

Antonius pointed proudly at the boat, which was about thirty yards away and closing fast. 'There,' he said, as if he was pointing out a new star in the Crab Nebula. 'I saw it just now.'

'Oh God,' Vanderdecker muttered, 'not now, we haven't got time.'

'Haven't we?' Antonius said. Vanderdecker had almost forgotten he was still there. 'Time for what?'

'That's bloody marvellous,' Vanderdecker went on, mainly to himself. 'We've got to get rid of him somehow, and quickly.'

Antonius beamed. 'Leave it to me, skipper,' he said, and disappeared down the companionway before his commanding officer could stop him. He was heading towards the gun deck, where the ship's entirely authentic sixteenth-century culverins were lined up. Vanderdecker called after him but he didn't seem to hear. He had thought this one up all by himself. It was his big chance.

'Fire!' he shouted down the hatch.

'You what?'

'Fire!' repeated the first mate impatiently, 'and less lip off you.'

'Please yourself,' said the voice, and a moment later there was the unique sound of an entirely authentic but hopelessly corroded sixteenth-century culverin blowing itself to shrapnel, followed by disappointed oaths from Sebastian van Doorning.

In the bay, the competitors in the Bridport Old Ships Race jumped to their positions and cast off. The motor-boat, which contained Danny Bennet, a representative of a leading brewery, a cameraman, the boat's owner, thirty thousand pounds worth of camera equipment and a roundshot from an entirely authentic sixteenth-century culverin, sank. As the water closed over Danny's head, he suddenly remembered that he had forgotten something. Swimming lessons.

'You've got to do something,' the brewer said. 'I'm telling you, they shot a cannon at us. They were trying to kill us.'

The coastguard smiled a sort of 'well-yes-quite-possibly smile'. 'What exactly happened, then?' he asked.

The brewer shuddered and pulled the blanket closer round his shoulders. 'I went out with the producer in a launch – he wanted a close-up of the ship, and I wanted to see their entry form. They weren't on the list of competitors. We came in alongside and bang! They shot at us.'

'Shot at you,' repeated the coastguard. 'With a cannon.'

'With a cannon, yes.' The brewer had the feeling that his word was being doubted. 'They shot a hole in the boat and we sank. We swam back to shore.'

'I see,' said the coastguard. 'And which ship exactly was that?'

The brewer scowled. 'The galleon,' he said. 'The Tudor galleon.'

'Excuse me,' said the coastguard, 'but there isn't a Tudor galleon anywhere on the schedule.'

'Exactly,' said the brewer.

'Exactly what, sir?'

'Look,' said the brewer, who had not expected Socrates, 'you ask the rest of them, they'll say exactly the same thing.'

'I might just do that, sir,' said the coastguard. And he did.

The cameraman said that he'd heard a bang, sure. What he wanted to know was who hired that perishing boat in the first place, when it was obvious that the man driving it was as pissed as a rat. He must have been, or he wouldn't have run into that buoy. The buoy we collided with. Just before we sank.

The owner of the boat said that he had almost certainly heard a bang, and he would be sueing the BBC for every penny they'd got. It was definitely the last time he hired his boat out to film people. They should have warned him that all that electrical gear was liable to blow up when it got water on it. Some people have no consideration for others. They just don't think.

Danny Bennet didn't say anything. He wasn't there. He was on the deck of the *Verdomde*, drinking a can of Skol and thinking 'Oh no, not again.'

CHAPTER EIGHT

Never a particularly dressy man, Vanderdecker had not taken much trouble choosing an appropriate outfit to visit Jeanes' Boatyard. He hadn't even stopped to consider whether his shirt went with his trousers; he'd just flung open the lid of his sea-chest and grabbed. As a result, he was wearing a good, solid herringbone overcoat which had blossomed on the loom when George V was on the throne, a pair of flared slacks, a coarse Venetian doublet from the early seventeenth century, and Hush Puppies.

Jane Doland, on the other hand, didn't share this lilies-of-the-field attitude to clothing. By nature and inclination she was very much a baggy pullover and pleated skirt person, but she had realised quite early on that accountants are not as other women are; that it stands as an edict in destiny that unless you wear a suit nobody will believe you can add up. She therefore affected the imitation Austin Reed look, and wore her light grey dogtooth check as if it had broad arrows running down the sleeves.

Most people who frequent Jeanes' Boatyard either buy their clothes in the army supplies shop or find them in the corners of fields. As a result, both callers at the yard looked rather out of place.

The problem of dealing with the House of Jeanes had been a constant source of worry to Vanderdecker for longer than he could remember. Usually he only went there once every generation, so there was no danger of being recognised and rebuked for not being dead yet; on the other hand, there was the equally difficult job of explaining himself from scratch every time he called. By now the words flowed out of his head without conscious thought; but the worry was still present, like a submerged rock.

The speech, as perfected over the centuries, went like this:

'Mr Jeanes? My name's Vanderdecker, I wonder if you can help me. I have this very old ship, and it needs some work doing on it.'

So far, so good. Mr Jeanes is expecting, at the worst, something that was last a tree in the 1940s. He says something non-committal, like 'Oh.' Although it was completely wasted on him, Vanderdecker had over the years acquired enough research material to write a definitive study of heredity among the seafaring classes; the only part of which that had registered with his conscious mind was the fact that every Jeanes since 1716 had said 'Oh' in precisely the same way.

'Yes,' Vanderdecker now replies. 'She's down in the cove half-way to Burton at the moment. Do you think you could come out and look at her?'

The invariable reply to this suggestion is 'No.' If by some wild sport of genetics a stray proton of politeness has managed to get itself caught up in the Jeanes DNA this quarter-century, the 'No' will be coupled with a mumbled excuse concerning pressure of work, but this is not to be taken too seriously. The truth is that deep down in their collective unconscious, the members of the Jeanes tribe believe that the world outside the Yard is populated by werewolves, particularly if you venture out beyond Eype, and consequently they try to go out of the curtilage of their fastness as infrequently as possible. Once a week to the bank is plenty often enough, thank you very much.

'Right then.' Vanderdecker replies, 'I suppose I'd better bring her in. There's not a lot needs doing, actually,' he adds, 'just a general looking-over, if you could manage that.'

This rarely gets a reply from a Jeanes, and Vanderdecker goes away and comes back with a sixteenth-century galleon. This is where the fun starts.

'Here she is,' Vanderdecker will now say. Jeanes will stare out of small, ferretlike eyes and say nothing. We have reached the unsolicited explanations stage, the trickiest part of the whole undertaking. The knack to it is not to look as if you have anything to explain, and it is best achieved by seeming to boast. The preferred gambit is something like 'bet you haven't worked on anything like *this* before?'

A flicker of a Jeanes eyebrow will communicate 'no', and we're away. We explain that the *Verdomde* is either: (a) a film prop; or (b) a rich man's toy; or (c) part of a ten-year project by the University of Chicopee Falls History Faculty to prove that Columbus was a liar; or (d) the entire naval strength of Monte Carlo; or (e) a fishfingers advertisement; depending on what this particular Jeanes is likely to believe. From then on, it's just a matter of waiting for the work to be done and parting with an extremely large sum of money at the end of it.

The presence of so many Old Ships in West Bay dictated that it was rich man's toy time once again, and Vanderdecker quietly rehearsed some patter about how he had been all set to wipe the eyes of those cocky Australian so-and-so's with their fibre-glass hulls when the storm hit him, and now look at her. It wasn't perfect, but it ought to do well enough to get him out of here in one piece. Another consistent feature of the House of Jeanes throughout the ages is a notable lack of intelligence, which probably explains why they are still in the boat-building business after all these years.

With that characteristic shrug of the shoulders that you see so much of among fighter pilots and professional lion-hunters, Vanderdecker walked towards the yard entrance and put his hand on the gate. As he did so, he saw a face that he recognised. Not an everyday occurrence for the Flying Dutchman.

The last time he had seen it had been in Scotland, on the A9 near Dounreay. The time before that, his memory rather irrelevantly informed him, was in a pub in Covent Garden. I never forget a face, lied his memory smugly, but he wasn't listening.

The girl was staring, and Vanderdecker's heart froze. It wasn't a friendly stare. For a part of a second that only a scientist could accurately quantify there was silence and stillness. Then, very softly, the girl spoke.

'You're standing,' she said, 'on my foot.'

Many years ago now, when he had still been a force to be reckoned with in the jute business, Vanderdecker had been condemned to death. He couldn't remember the details – something about exceeding the permitted tariff in a Hanseatic League town in election year – but he could remember the flood of relief when the jailer came into his cell on what he had been led to believe was going to be his last morning on earth and told him that the sentence had been commuted to a seventy-groschen fine. Ironic, really, when you thought of what was going to happen to him a few years later; but the feeling had been just like coming up after being underwater for rather too long. The same sensation caught Vanderdecker somewhere in the windpipe, while his brain registered the apparent fact that the girl hadn't recognised him after all. When his respiratory system started working again, he apologised and lifted his foot.

'Sorry,' he said, 'how clumsy of me.'

'That's all right,' said the girl slowly. She was looking at him again, and as soon as her eyes met his, Vanderdecker realised how he would have reacted if on that cold morning in the 1540s the jailer had gone on to wink and say, 'Sorry, son, I was just kidding.'

The logical thing to do, said a part of Vanderdecker's mind that was still functioning, is to get out of here quickly. Vanderdecker noted this advice but took no steps to act on it. He was looking at the girl's face. A nice face, if you like them slightly on the round side. Some words bubbled up into his mouth, like nitrogen into the brain of a diver with the bends.

'Is this Jeanes' Boatyard?' he asked.

'I hope so,' said the girl. 'I've been looking for it all morning.'

She had noticed the doublet. Perhaps, suggested the voice of optimism, she's thinking what an idiot I look. Perhaps not.

Had Vanderdecker been able to get inside Jane's mind, he would have seen a brief replay of her sixth-form History of Art classes, and heard the words 'I've seen that shirt somewhere before.' Jane didn't know it, but she had, in a painting by Tiepolo. A hint to people who are contemplating living for ever; never have your portrait painted, even if it only costs a couple of soldini, because there is always the risk that centuries later the scruffy-looking artist who did the painting will have turned into an Old Master and be studied in good schools.

Come to that, said Jane to herself, I've seen that face before; but where? Meanwhile, her voice started to work, out of pure reflex.

'They gave me a map at the tourist information place, but it can't be very accurate. Or maybe it's just that I'm hopeless with maps.'

'Me too,' Vanderdecker lied. 'Let's see.'

Jane fished the folded glorious Dorset leaflet out of her bag, and the two of them examined Mrs Price's cartography with exaggerated diligence.

'If that's the Post Office over there,' Jane started to say; then something fell neatly into the right place in her mind. The clothes he's wearing, she said to herself, come from different periods. He looks like a tramp who's robbed a theatrical costumier. Jeanes' Boatyard. Different periods of history. Surely not . . .

'Well,' the man was saying, 'if that's the Red Lion, then that over there must be north. Try turning the map the other way up and then we'll see.'

Jane thought for a moment. It was worth a try.

'So that's the Red Lion,' she said. 'I wonder what was there before.'

'A butcher's shop,' Vanderdecker replied. Then he lifted his head and stared at her.

'And when would that have been?' Jane said. Her voice was quiet, slightly triumphant, and more than a little bit frightened. The Red Lion had been built, according to the smugly-worded inn sign, in 1778.

'Before your time,' Vanderdecker replied.

'But not yours.'

'No', said the Flying Dutchman. 'Not a lot is. Have you been looking for me?'

'Yes,' Jane replied sheepishly.

'Then,' Vanderdecker said through a weak smile, 'you've made a pretty lousy job of it. This is the third time we've met. Small world, isn't it?'

Jane seemed to shrink back from even this tiny display of aggression, and Vanderdecker suddenly felt a great compacted mass of fear sliding away from him. It was like having your ears syringed; you could perceive so much more without it. Jane said nothing for a long time, and then looked at him.

'I imagine,' she said carefully, 'that someone in your position would think so.' She felt that she ought to add 'Mr Vanderdecker' at the end of the sentence, but that would be too much like a detective story. She waited for a reply.

'Too right,' he replied, and the smile began to solidify, like wax dropped on a polished table. 'Small and extremely boring.' He paused and took a deep breath. 'Just to make sure we're not talking at cross purposes, do you know who I am?'

'I think so,' she said. 'I think you're Julius Vanderdecker.'

For some reason, he had expected her to say 'The Flying Dutchman.' It was a nickname he had always hated – Dutchman yes, perfectly true, but why 'Flying', for pity's sake? – and the fact that she used his proper name was somehow rather touching.

'And you've been looking for me?' he asked.

'That's right.'

'I see.' His face seemed to relax, as he said. 'Will you just bear with me while I go and see about my ship? Then we can go and have a drink and talk about it.'

'Fine,' Jane said. Very matter-of-fact. Very civilised. Noel Coward saying it's a fair cop, but do let's be *adult* about it. 'Mind if I come too?'

'Be my guest,' Vanderdecker said. 'You can watch a master liar at work, if you don't mind being an accomplice.'

'Doesn't worry me,' Jane replied. 'I'm an accountant.'

Very slowly and cautiously, Danny Bennett peeled back the blanket from over his head and looked about him. He was not one of those shallow people who judge by first impressions; he needed more data before he could responsibly start to scream.

A man in a threadbare woollen doublet, patched hose and a baseball cap walked past him and gave him a friendly smile, which Danny did his best to return. The curiously-dressed one started to climb the rigging of the ship. After a long climb he reached the unrailed wooden platform (was that the crow's nest, or was that the little thing like a bran-tub at the very top? Briefly, Danny regretted not reading the *Hornblower* book his grandmother had given him when he was twelve); then he waved, took a deep breath, and jumped.

Danny's eyes instinctively closed; the tiny muscles of his eyelids were perfectly capable to taking that sort of decision without referring back to the central authority between his ears. As soon as his conscious mind had reasserted its authority he looked for a broken mush of flesh and bone-splinters. Instead, he saw the badly-dressed man picking himself up off the deck, apparently unharmed, and shouting to someone else. Someone else was also dressed like one of those comic relief characters in *The Merchant of Venice* whose names Danny could never remember, except that he had a Dire Straits tee-shirt instead of a doublet, and a baselard and dusack hung from his broad leather belt. A production of *The Merchant of Venice* at the Barbican, he decided.

'Hey!' shouted the sky-diver, 'I want a word with you.'

The heavily-armed man turned his head. 'You talking to me?' he said.

'Too right I'm talking to you.' The sky-diver pointed to one of the many tears in his doublet. 'Look at that.'

'I'm looking,' replied the other man. 'What about it?'

'That's your fault,' said the sky-diver angrily.

'Really?' The other man didn't seem impressed. 'How do you make that out?'

'Look,' said the sky-diver, 'you're meant to be the carpenter on this ship, it's down to you to make sure there's no nails sticking up where people can tear their clothes on them every time they take a jump.'

The other man laughed scornfully. 'Listen,' he said, 'if you didn't keep on jumping, I wouldn't have to keep on fixing the damned planking, so there wouldn't be any nails. Would there?' And he thrust his head at the sky-diver, until their noses were almost touching. For some reason Danny was reminded of the Sistine Chapel, except that that had been fingers, not noses.

'Don't give me any of that crap,' said the sky-diver. 'I've had it up to here with your shoddy workmanship, and . . .'

'Are you,' said the armed man quietly and furiously, 'calling me a bad carpenter?'

'Yes.'

With a movement of the arm so swift that Danny only saw the arc it described in the air, the carpenter whipped out his dusack and brought it down with sickening force on the sky-diver's head. This time, Danny's eyelids stayed where they were. So, incredibly, did the sky-diver's brains. Just then, another of these peculiar people came hurrying up. He too was dressed in a thought-provoking manner, but Danny didn't even bother to analyse it.

'Cut it out, you two,' said the third party. 'Can't you see we've got visitors?'

The two combatants turned round and smiled sheepishly at Danny, who reciprocated. 'It's all right,' the third party called out, 'they're just kidding about, same as usual.'

It was the 'as usual' that really worried Danny. He could feel his mouth open and his chin melt into his neck; always a bad sign.

'That's fine,' he said. 'Don't mind me.'

The three of them looked at him for a moment. Then they walked over to him. He tried to shrink back, but he was already tight up against a large coil of rope and there was no scope for further withdrawals.

'I'm Danny Bennett,' he said, 'I'm with BBC sports.'

This remark had slightly less effect than an air rifle in an artillery duel, and Danny wished he hadn't said anything. The three peculiar people looked at each other. Then one of them extended a large hairy-backed hand, which Danny took. The skin on its palm felt like coarse-grain sandpaper.

'Pleased to meet you,' said the third party, the one who had broken up the fight. 'I'm Antonius, this' – indicating the sky-diver – 'is Sebastian, and this' – the homicidal maniac with the big sword – 'is Jan.'

Danny smiled, a sort of railway-buffet-tea smile. He felt he would be able to remember the names.

'So,' said Antonius. He was leaning forward, with his hands on his knees. 'Sorry about your little boat.'

'My boat?' Danny asked.

'Your little boat,' said Antonius. 'We sank it, remember?'

'Oh,' said Danny, 'that boat. Yes. No hard feelings.'

Antonius smiled warmly. He was obviously a man who gave due credit for magnanimity when it came to sunk boats. 'Tele-vision,' he said.

Danny nodded, and then said, 'What?'

'You're with television,' Antonius said, 'aren't you?'

Danny nodded again, deeply relieved. For a while he had thought he was among pagans.

'Television,' Antonius went on, 'is a wonderful invention. We all watch it when we're on shore leave. "Coronation Street".'

'I beg your pardon?' Danny said.

'"Coronation Street",' repeated Antonius. 'That's television. We like that.'

'Really?' Danny narrowed his eyes, as if trying to see a single cell without bothering with a microscope. He felt that the conversation was drifting away from him again.

'Of course,' Antonius went on, 'we find it hard following the plot.'

'I know what you mean,' Danny started to say, but Antonius carried on over him, like a steamroller over a shrivelled apple. 'You see, we only get to see it once every seven years, and a lot changes.'

'Oh I don't know,' Danny said. 'Why every seven years?'

'We spend a lot of time at sea,' said Sebastian, 'don't we, Antonius?'

'That's right,' Antonius confirmed, 'because of the smell.'

Danny saw Sebastian kick Antonius on the shin, and for a moment he expected swords to start flying. But instead Antonius looked sheepish and said, 'Of the sea. We love the smell of the sea, we Dutch. It's in our blood.'

Whatever's in your blood at this precise moment, Danny thought, it's sure as hell not seawater. However, he kept this comment to himself.

'No,' said Antonius, 'I dunno what we used to do before there was television. We played the flute a lot more than we do now, of course, and danced galliards and went to bear-baiting, but you can get sick of that sort of thing, can't you?'

'Yes,' Danny said. It was a good, non-commital thing to say, in the circumstances.

'The skipper, of course,' Antonius went on, 'he's got his alchemy. Apple?'

'I'm sorry?'

'Would you like an apple?'

'No thanks.'

'Please yourself. The skipper, he's never happier than when he's got his nose in some alchemy book or other. Can't see what he sees in it. Tried to read one myself once. No pictures. Just funny little line drawings. But he seems to like it, and I suppose it's better than ships in bottles. You ever tried that?'

'No,' Danny confessed.

'Don't bother,' said Antonius sagely, 'Waste of time. At least there's something at the end of the day with alchemy, so they reckon.'

'Is there?' Danny said.

'Course there is,' Antonius replied. 'But it wouldn't suit me, not all that reading and stuff you've got to do. It's all right when you're stuck in the middle of the sea, maybe, but the skipper doesn't stop there. He even does it on shore leave. I remember one time in New Amsterdam . . .'

'New York,' Sebastian interrupted him. 'They call it New York now.'

'Do they?' Antonius looked surprised. 'What a daft name. New York, then. Miserable place, that. You ever been there?'

'Yes,' Danny said.

'Do they still have that law where you can't get a drink anywhere?'

'How do you mean?' Danny asked.

'You can't get a drink in New Amsterdam,' Antonius explained, 'It's against the law. Same in the whole of America, come to think of it.'

'Hang on,' said Danny. 'When was this?'

'Year or so back,' Antonius said, 'when we were last there. Didn't they have that law there when you went?'

'No,' Danny said. 'No, they didn't.'

'Anyway,' Antonius went on, 'there we all were, shore leave coming up, everyone as dry as the bottom of a parrot's cage, and where does the Skip take us in to? New bloody Amsterdam, just so's he could go and look something up about alchemy in a library there. We were not pleased, I can tell you. I mean, what would you have thought?'

Danny shuddered very slightly. If he tried very hard, perhaps he could nudge what he had just heard into some dark, damp corner of his mind where his subconscious could hide it and build a protective layer of mother-of-pearl over it until it wasn't quite so uncomfortable any more. 'I'd have been livid,' he said.

'We were,' Antonius went on. 'Sick as parrots, the lot of us. And then there was that other time, when we all had to go to Easter Island to see Halley's Comet. That was all to do with alchemy, he said. Something about magnetism. There is nothing, absolutely nothing, to drink on Easter Island except water. Mind you, the skipper's completely nuts on Halley's Comet. Never misses it.'

That word 'never' was a problem, Danny thought. Do what we may, we will not get the mother-of-pearl to stick on that one.

'Really?'

'Obsessive, I call it,' said Antonius, disgustedly, 'I mean, comets are all right, but once you've seen one, you've seen them all, and Halley's Comet's just another comet, right? But to hear the skipper talk, you'd think it was free beer and Christmas all rolled into one. Every time it pops up, there's no talking to him for weeks. Not unless you want your head bitten off, I mean. God knows I don't mind a man having a hobby, but there's such a thing as taking it too far.'

Danny glanced at Sebastian out of the corner of his eye, just in case there was a clue to be gleaned there. After all, it was possible that Antonius was the sole loony on this ship and that everyone else was reasonably sane. But Sebastian only looked bored.

'What was all that you were saying about alchemy?' Danny asked Antonius. 'About your captain, and it being a hobby of his?'

'Oh, he's serious enough about it,' Antonius replied. 'You interested in that sort of thing, then?'

'Yes,' Danny said. 'Not that I'm an expert or anything, but . . .'

'Pity you missed the captain, then,' said Antonius. 'Tell you what, though, you could have a word with old Cornelius. He's not alchemy mad like the skipper, but he helps him a lot with the actual cooking of the stuff. He could show you the crucible and all that, if you like.'

Cornelius, it turned out, was only too happy to show the visitor the crucible, perhaps because the alternative was playing chess with Antonius. He led the way down to the rear gun-deck. There were no guns on the rear gun-deck; instead, there was a large stone basin with a sort of stove arrangement under it backing onto a bulkhead, with five or six shelves behind it. Half of these shelves had small, dark jars with handwritten Latin labels, while the other half contained books. Some of the books looked very old, but most of them were shiny new paperbacks, and when Danny glanced at the spines he saw that they were scientific textbooks. Because he had spent his science lessons daydreaming of scooping the big Board of Governors corruption scandal for the school magazine, Danny couldn't tell whether they were really as high-powered as their titles suggested, but he was prepared to bet that 'Elements of Quantum Mechanics' wasn't in his local library, and neither were 'Properties of Fissile Materials' or 'Sub-Atomic Particle Dynamics'. Unless Fissile was rotten proof-reading for fossil, that was something nuclear, while Atomic spoke for itself. Nuclear! Suddenly, very far off, Danny began to see a chink of light.

'So you do a bit of this yourself, then, do you?' Cornelius' voice broke in on his reverie. It was a loud voice, rather jolly, filtered through a lot of facial hair.

'A little bit,' said Danny cautiously. 'Quantum mechanics, fissile properties, that sort of thing.'

'Huh.' Cornelius was not impressed, apparently. 'All that modern crap the skipper's so hot on. Boring. Give me the old ways any time.'

'Good, are they?' Danny asked. Cornelius grinned.

'Good?' he chuckled. 'Watch this.'

He produced a Zippo from the battered leather pouch that hung from his sword-belt and opened the stove door. Then he messed about with a few of the jars. 'Don't tell the skipper,' he said, 'he gets all snotty if I use his gear. But I've done it lots of times, it's like falling off a log.'

'Dangerous, you mean?'

'Easy,' said Cornelius. 'You got anything metal on you?'

Danny had a sudden flashback to a children's party when he was six. There had been a conjuror, and he had ended up with a lot of coloured flags being pulled out of his ears. He pulled himself together and reached in his pocket for his car keys. 'Will these do?' he said.

'Fine,' replied Cornelius. He took them and tossed them into the crucible before Danny could stop him. There was a flash of white light and a faint humming noise, like the sound you hear when you stand under an electric pylon.

'Takes about thirty seconds to do all the way through,' Cornelius said. 'Beats your fission into a cocked hat, if you ask me.'

Thirty seconds later, Cornelius reached under the stove and produced what looked like a solid gold ladle. With this he extracted the car keys from the crucible and held them under Danny's nose. They were glowing with the same blue light, and they seemed to have been turned into pure gold. Pure gold car keys. It reminded Danny of the time Gerald had taken him round the Stock Exchange.

'There you go,' Cornelius said, and tipped them out onto Danny's hand. 'Don't worry, they aren't hot or anything.'

Danny winced, but he could feel nothing. The blue light faded away. The keys felt unnaturally cold and heavy. Solid gold. What did solid gold feel like?

'Impressive, huh?' said Cornelius.

'Very,' Danny said. He stared at his car keys. In his mind, a strange and terrible alchemy of his own was taking place. All this meaningless garbage was turning into a story; a story about unlicensed, clandestine nuclear experiments on a weird ship manned by lunatics. Story. Story. Story. If only he could get off this dreadful ship and get to a telephone, he would be through with even the distant threat of sports reporting for ever and ever. Until then, however, there was investigative journalism to be done.

'Tell me something,' he said as casually as possible. What was that man's name? The arch-fiend of the nuclear lobby, the man behind all those goings-on at Dounreay. There had been a protest, he remembered.

'What?'

'Do you know someone, a guy called Montalban? Professor Montalban? He's into all this alchemy, isn't he?'

Cornelius' face split into a huge laugh. 'Too right I know Montalban,' he said. 'He's the one who got us into this mess to start with.' Then something seemed to register inside Cornelius' head. He looked at Danny again; eyes not friendly, not friendly at all. 'How come you know Montalban?' he said.

Fortune, it has often been observed, favours the brave. At that particular crucial moment, two boats were approaching the *Verdomde*. On one, coming in to the starboard side, was Vanderdecker and Jane Doland. On the other side was a small motor-boat, containing a couple of stray newspaper photographers who thought the ship looked pretty and reckoned some of the glossies might be able to use a photograph. Because the bulk of the *Verdomde* was between them, of course, neither could see the other.

Danny spotted the motor-boat through an open gunport.

On the one hand, he said to himself, I cannot swim. Never mind.

'Where do you think you're going?' Cornelius roared at him, and tried to grab his arm; but it was too late. Danny had already squeezed his slight shoulders through the gunport. A moment later he was in the water, bawling for help and thrashing about like a wounded shark. The motor-boat picked him up just before he drowned.

The first thing he saw when his eyes opened was a camera-bag with lots of lenses and rolls of film in it. 'Press?' he gasped.

'Well, sort of,' said one of his rescuers. 'Freelance. Does it really matter, in the circumstances?'

Swing low, sweet chariot, said Danny's soul inside him. 'Listen . . .' he said.

CHAPTER NINE

'There you go,' said Mrs Clarke, 'I've brought you a nice cup of coffee. Don't let it get cold.'

She put the cup down on the table, next to the other two cups. They were all full of cold coffee, with that pale off-white scum on the top that right-thinking people find so offputting.

'Thank you,' said the man at the table without looking up. He reached out, located a cup by touch, lifted it to his mouth and drank half of its contents. It was one of the cold ones, but he didn't seem to notice. Mrs Clarke shuddered and went away. Although she was not a religious woman, she knew where people who let hot drinks go cold went when they died. Back in front of her typewriter she shook her head sadly and wished, not for the first time, that she'd taken the job at the plastics factory instead.

Had Professor Montalban, who had recently returned from Geneva, realised how much pain he was inflicting on his secretary, he would have taken care to drink the hot coffee. He was by no means a callous person. Just now, however, his powers of concentration were directed elsewhere. His mind was centred on a small area of the table, which contained a foolscap pad, three pencils (sharpened at both ends), a calculator and ten or fifteen books, all open. He had a headache, but that was not a problem. He had had the same headache for three hundred and forty-two years, and he knew it was caused by eyestrain. Because of the elixir, it was impossible for his eyesight to deteriorate, however much he abused it, but it didn't stop him getting headaches. He also knew that the optician in Cornmarket Street could fix him up in ten minutes with something that would cure his headache for ever. It was just a question of finding the time. Tomorrow, perhaps, or the next day.

Ironic, really, time was one thing that Professor Montalban had plenty of. Genius he most certainly lacked; he didn't even have that little spark of intuition that the scientist so desperately needs if he is ever going to get anywhere. He was nothing more than a competent and careful follower of the proper scientific procedures. But, because he had plenty of time, this didn't matter. He could do everything by a process of elimination. This may sound haphazard, but the true test of any scientific method is results, and Montalban's results were quite astoundingly spectacular, if you chose to look at them that way. Every major scientific discovery from gravity to the electric toothbrush was based on the work of Professor Montalban. Every breakthrough, every quantum leap, ever new departure he had either initiated or, more usually, carried through himself to the verge of publication. In every case, someone had come in at the last moment and stolen all the credit, but that was what the professor wanted. He had reasons of his own for not wanting to make himself conspicuous.

Suppose a Neolithic cave-dweller had wanted to put some shelves up in his cave. All he has is a tree. What he must do is invent the refinement of metals, the saw, the plane, the chisel, the drill, the screwdriver, the screw, the rawlplug, sandpaper, polyurethane varnish, the spirit level, the carpenter's pencil and, finally, the marble-look Formica veneer, and then he can set to work. Nothing intellectually taxing about it all, but it takes a lot of time.

Professor Montalban had not set out to discover electricity, nuclear fission, or the circulation of the blood, just as the caveman has no great urge to pioneer the Stanley knife: they were just tiresome and necessary stages in the quest for the final overriding objective, in the same way as modern mathematics is a by-product of Richard the Lion-Heart's desire to recapture Jerusalem. Professor Montalban's objective was, in his eyes at least, infinitely more important than the little side-shows on the way, such as splitting the atom: Professor Montalban was searching for the Ultimate Deodorant.

That had not always been the objective. When he was young, he had been more interested in the secret of eternal life and the transmigration of elements, which was how he had got into this mess in the first place. He now regarded his earlier ambitions in the way the managing director of a major multinational might review his childish intention to be an engine-driver. If he had any philosophy of life, it was that everything happens by accident, and that at any given time, ninety-nine-point-nine-five per cent of the human race are a confounded nuisance.

He worked on, as he had been doing for so many years, until his headache became so insistent that he could concentrate no longer; and by that time, of course, the optician had shut up shop and gone home. So the professor put on his jacket and took a stroll round the college yard to clear his head. It was a cool evening, and if Montalban hadn't been so engrossed in a fallacy he had detected in the theory of Brownian motion he would probably have enjoyed the sunset. As it was, he wandered into the college bar without thinking and sat down at one of the badly-scarred chipboard tables in front of the television. He didn't take any notice of what was on the screen – a sports programme of some sort – and let his thoughts wander back to the interplay of random particles. Then he became aware of somebody yelling something loudly in the very furthest part of his mind.

'Look!' it was yelling. Professor Montalban looked. On the screen, in the far corner of the picture but unmistakable, he saw something he recognised. It was a ship.

'And?' Jane asked.

'And,' Vanderdecker said, 'that's about it, really. I have had other experiences, but none of them germane to the point at issue. Which reminds me.'

'Yes?'

Vanderdecker smiled, and lifted his glass to his lips. 'What is the point at issue? Why were you looking for me?'

Despite the recent reform in British licensing laws, the only place you can get a drink at half-past three in the afternoon in West Bay is the Rockcliffe Inn. It is hard to imagine a thirst powerful enough to drive a person into the Rockcliffe Inn. It can therefore be taken as read that Vanderdecker was not smiling at his beer, which was thick, cloudy and infested with little white specks that reminded him of the stuff you find in the corners of your eyes after a long sleep.

'Because of the insurance policy,' Jane said.

Vanderdecker looked up. 'What insurance policy?' he asked.

'The Vanderdecker policy,' Jane said.

'Don't let's be all cryptic,' Vanderdecker replied, 'not when the beer's so foul. If you want to be cryptic, I demand Stella Artois at the very least.'

'Who's Stella Artois?'

'Barbarian.'

'Sorry.'

'Stella Artois,' said Vanderdecker, 'is a brand of beer. I'm sorry, that was very rude of me. I shouldn't have called you a barbarian just because you've never heard of it. Are you sure you've never heard of it?'

'Yes,' Jane replied. 'I don't like beer very much, I'm afraid.'

'Then you are a barbarian. What's the Vanderdecker policy? Go on, it's your turn.'

'Your life insurance policy,' said Jane. 'With the House of Fugger.'

Vanderdecker was just about to object when two tiny leads connected in his memory. 'My life insurance policy?' he repeated.

'That's right.'

'Oh.' He frowned. 'That's all?'

'Yes.'

Vanderdecker put down his glass. 'After four hundred and fifty years,' he said, 'you want to sell me life insurance. Don't you people ever give up?'

But Jane was shaking her head. 'We don't want to sell you any life insurance,' she said, 'we want to buy it.'

As she stared at him, a tiny germen of a thought thrust a green blade through its shell in the back paddock of her mind. It was an extraordinary thought, but it was there.

'Why?' Vanderdecker said.

Jane said, 'Surely that's obvious,' but her heart wasn't in it. She could feel an enormous, colossal wave of laughter welling up inside her. Her entire body wasn't big enough to contain it. Meanwhile, Vanderdecker was talking.

'Are we talking about the same thing?' he was saying. 'I remember taking out a policy with the Fuggers, sure, but that was years ago. Hundreds of years ago, come to that. I haven't paid a premium for centuries; I mean, what was the point?'

'But you've still got the policy?' Jane could feel the laughter crashing against her teeth like the Severn Bore, but she kept it back.

'I don't know,' Vanderdecker said. 'I'm hopeless with things like that. Hang on, though.' He paused, and felt in the pocket of his overcoat. 'I usually put important documents in here,' he said, and he pulled out a big sealskin envelope. 'Not that I have all that many important documents, after all this time. Let's see.' He lifted the flap and started to rummage about. 'What's this? Alchemical notes, that's not it. Birth certificate, passport, the receipt for my electric razor, book of matches from Maxim's, what's this?' He peered at a curled yellow scrap of paper. 'No, that's not it. Ah, we're in luck. Is this it?' He fished out a folded sheet of vellum with the remains of a crumbled seal attached to it.

'I don't know,' Jane said. 'I can't read it.'

'Can't you?' Vanderdecker glanced at the tiny, illegible sixteenth-century script. 'I suppose you can't,' he said, 'it's in Latin. Yes, this is it. Is it important?'

'Have you ever read it?' Jane said. Of course, she realised, she shouldn't be doing this. She should have got hold of it and destroyed it, and so saved the world. But the pressure of the laughter against the sides of her skull was too much for her; she had to let him in on the joke.

'To be honest with you,' Vanderdecker said, 'no, I haven't. I can't be doing with all that legal-financial mumbo-jumbo.'

'You should,' Jane said.

Vanderdecker looked at her. His face had a tired, harassed look, as if this was starting to turn into a problem. 'Let me guess,' he said. 'You're after me for four hundred and fifty years unpaid premiums. Well, you can forget that, because I just don't have that sort of money.'

That was too much for Jane; she started to laugh. She laughed so much that the afternoon barmaid of the Rockcliffe Inn withdrew her attention from the Australian soap opera she was watching on the bartop portable and stared at her for at least three seconds. She laughed so much that her body ached with the strain, and her lungs nearly collapsed. Vanderdecker raised an eyebrow.

'What's so funny?' he said.

With a Herculean effort Jane stopped laughing, just for a moment. 'Read it,' she said. 'Read it now.'

'If it'll stop you making that extraordinary noise,' said the Flying Dutchman, and started to read. When he had finished, he looked up and said, 'I still don't get it.' Fortunately, Jane was incapable of further laughter.

'I'm sorry,' she said.

'So you should be,' Vanderdecker said, 'it's very embarrassing. You've no idea how conspicuous it makes me feel. Do please try and keep a hold of yourself.' He folded the policy up and put it away again, along with the birth certificate and the receipt for his electric razor.

'Are you from the insurance company?' he asked.

'Yes,' Jane said. 'It's a bank now, of course, as well as an insurance company. And I'm not actually with them; I'm an accountant.'

'So you said.'

'So I did.' Jane wiped the tears from her eyes with a corner of her handkerchief.

'Do you know,' Vanderdecker said, 'you remind me of someone.'

'Do I?'

'Yes.' Vanderdecker looked faintly embarrassed, as if he didn't want to say what he was saying. 'Someone I used to know, years back. In fact,' he mumbled, 'that was her address on the piece of paper you saw just now. She must have been dead for three hundred years now.'

'Go on,' Jane said.

'Greta,' said the Flying Dutchman, 'from Schiedam. There's nothing to tell, actually. We met at a dance and just seemed to hit it off. I told her a joke, I remember – actually, it wasn't a joke as such, just something that had happened to me that she thought was funny – and she laughed so much she spilt wine all down my trouser leg. Anyway, it turned out that she was leaving for Bruges the next day, and it was the last day of my shore leave. She gave me her address. I wrote to her, seven years later, and seven years after that I picked up her reply from the poste restante in Nijmegen. Apparently she'd met this man, and perhaps he wasn't the most wonderfully exciting human being there had ever been but by all accounts he was going to be very big in worsteds one day, and of course she would always think of me as a very dear friend. Undoubtedly for the best,' he went on, 'things being as they are. Still.'

'And I remind you of her?' Jane asked.

'Only because you laugh so damned much,' replied Vanderdecker austerely.

'I see,' Jane replied. 'Can I get you another drink?'

Vanderdecker swirled the white specks round in the bottom of his glass. 'Yes,' he said. 'Only this time I'll try the mild.'

'Is that good?'

'No,' he said.

Shortly afterwards, Jane came back with the drinks. 'If it's nasty,' she said, 'why do you drink it?'

'Because it's there,' Vanderdecker replied. 'What's so special about my life policy, then? Do try not to laugh when you tell me.'

Jane took a deep breath. She was, she realised, gambling with the financial stability of the entire free world. On the other hand, it didn't seem like that, and the strange man had turned out not to be all that strange after all. 'Before I tell you,' she said, 'do you mind if I ask you something?'

'Be my guest,' Vanderdecker replied.

'Mr Vanderdecker,' she asked, 'what exactly do you want out of life?'

Vanderdecker smiled; that is, there was an initial movement at the corners of his mouth that developed into a ripple just under his nose and ended up with a full display of straight, white teeth. 'What a peculiar question!' he said.

'Yes,' Jane admitted, 'and as a rule I'm not into this soul-searching stuff. But you see, it is quite important.'

Vanderdecker was surprised. 'Is it?'

'Yes, actually,' Jane said, 'it is.'

'Well then,' Vanderdecker said, composing himself and looking grave, 'The way I see it is this. After all this time, and bearing in mind the things I've told you about, I would have thought it was more a question of what the hell it is life wants out of me. Blood?'

'I see,' Jane said. If she'd had a notebook, she would probably have written it down. 'So you've never had any urge to rule the world, or anything like that?'

'What, me?' Vanderdecker said. 'No, I can't say I have. It would be nice to change some things naturally.'

Jane leaned forward and looked serious. 'Such as?'

Vanderdecker considered. 'I don't know,' he said, 'now you come to mention it. I can't actually think of anything that even remotely matters. You get such a wonderful sense of perspective at my age.'

'You look about thirty-three.'

'Thirty-five,' Vanderdecker replied. 'And you flatter me. Aren't we getting a bit sidetracked, or is this all relevant?'

'It's sort of relevant,' Jane said. 'So you would say that you're a relatively balanced, well-adjusted person?'

'Perhaps,' said the Flying Dutchman. 'When you consider that I've lived for over four hundred and fifty years, and seven-eighths of those years have been mind-numbingly boring, I think I've coped reasonably well. What do you think?'

'I think,' said Jane with conviction, 'that I'd have gone stark staring mad in the early fifteen-sixties.'

'I tried that,' Vanderdecker reminisced. 'It lasted about eight hours. You can't go mad running a ship, which is what I do most of the time. You simply don't get an opportunity. Just when you're starting to work up a good thick fuzz of melancholia, someone puts his head round the door to tell you that the cook and the bosun are fighting again, or that some idiot's lost the sextant, or we appear to be sixty leagues off the Cape of Good Hope and weren't we meant to be going to Florida? There's all sorts of things I was always meaning to get around to – learning to play the flute, calculating the square root of nought, going mad – but I just didn't have the time. After a while you give up and get on with things.'

'But don't you ever feel . . .' Jane searched for the right words, only to find that she'd forgotten to bring them. 'Don't you feel sort of different? Important? Marked out by Destiny?'

'Me?' Vanderdecker said, surprised. 'No. Why should I?'

'I'd have thought you might,' Jane said. 'What with being immortal.'

'That's not what it feels like,' Vanderdecker said. 'May I put it bluntly?'

'Please do.'

'It's hard to feel special or important,' he said, staring at the table in front of him, 'let alone marked out by Destiny, when you smell quite as bad as I usually do. I trust I make myself clear.'

'Perfectly,' Jane said.

'Good.' Vanderdecker lifted his head and grinned. 'Do I get to hear your story now? About this life policy of mine.'

'If you like,' Jane said.

'Fire away.'

So she told him.

'Look,' Danny said to the telephone, 'what you obviously fail to grasp is . . .'

The pips went, and Danny fumbled desperately in his trouser pocket for more small change. What he found was five pennies, a washer and a French coin with the head of Charles de Gaulle on it which he had somehow acquired at Gatwick Airport. He made a quick decision and shoved the French coin into the slot. Remarkably enough, it worked.

'What you obviously . . .' he said. The voice interrupted him.

'No, Danny,' it said. 'What *you* fail to grasp is that you're supposed to be filming a boat race. Anything not germane to high-speed navigation is therefore off limits. Keep that principle firmly before your eyes and you won't go far wrong.'

Danny dragged air into his lungs, which were tight with anger. He forced the same air out through his larynx, but he sublimated the anger into determination.

'All right,' he said. 'You leave me with no alternative.'

'You're going to film the race?'

'I am not going to film the race,' Danny said. 'I am going to telephone Fay Parker at the *Guardian*.'

Coming from a man with five pennies and a washer in his pocket, this was clearly an idle threat. But of course the voice didn't know that, and just for once it said nothing.

'And you know what I'm going to tell her?' Danny went on. 'I'm going to tell her the truth about the Amethyst case.'

The voice wasn't a voice at all any more. It was just a silence.

'I'm going to tell her,' said Danny to the silence, 'that the person who recommended to the Cabinet Office that the Amethyst documentary should be banned wasn't the Prime Minister or the Home Secretary or even the Minister of Defence. It was the head of BBC Current Affairs, who wanted it banned so that he could get himself hailed as a martyr to the cause of press freedom and then nobody would dare sack him on the grounds of gross incompetence. Do you think she could use a story like that?'

The silence carried on being a silence, and Danny was terribly afraid that Charles de Gaulle would run out before it became a voice again. 'Well?' he said.

'Bastard,' said the voice.

Danny glowed with pleasure. 'Thanks,' he said, just as the pips went.

'Really?' said Vanderdecker.

'Cross my heart and hope to die,' Jane replied, rather tactlessly. 'That's why I was looking for you.'

'Oh,' Vanderdecker said. 'Do you know, that's rather a disappointment.'

'Is it?' Jane queried. 'Why?'

Vanderdecker scratched his ear. 'Hard to say, really,' he replied. 'I suppose it's just that I've been half expecting people to be looking for me for a long time now, and for other reasons.'

'That's a bit paranoid, isn't it?'

'Maybe,' said Vanderdecker, shrugging his shoulders. 'I just had this notion that what I was doing – being alive after so long and all that – was – well, *wrong*, somehow, and that sooner or later somebody was going to find out and tell me to stop doing it. Act your age, Vanderdecker, that sort of thing. And since I couldn't stop even if I wanted to, I wasn't keen to be found. I have this feeling that somehow or other I'm breaking the rules, and that's not my style at all.'

'What sort of rules?'

'The rules,' Vanderdecker said. 'Maybe you don't understand; let me try and explain. Do you remember the first time you went abroad?'

Jane shuddered. 'Vividly.'

'Do you remember that awful feeling of guilt,' Vanderdecker said, 'that you felt – I assume you felt – as if you were breaking all sorts of local laws and violating all sorts of local customs without knowing it, and sooner or later one of those policemen in hats like cheeseboxes was going to arrest you?'

'Yes,' Jane replied. 'That's a natural feeling, I guess, from being a stranger in someone else's country.'

'Well then,' Vanderdecker said, 'that's how I feel all the time. I'm a stranger everywhere except on a ship in the middle of the sea. I don't think I've broken any laws – I don't think just being alive is actually illegal anywhere, except maybe in some parts of South-East Asia – but the thought of all the embarrassment if anyone ever asked who I was or what I was doing . . . Do you see what I'm driving at? It means that I can't give a truthful answer to virtually any question I'm likely to be asked, for fear of being thought crazy or rude. It gets to you after a while, let me assure you. And of course there's the smell.'

'Yes,' Jane said. 'I could see that would be a problem.'

'It is,' Vanderdecker assured her. 'Decidedly.'

'If we could just get back to what I was saying,' Jane suggested tentatively. 'About your life policy.'

'You want me . . .'

'No.' Jane couldn't understand why she was so definite about this. '*They* want you to sign it away. Assign it back to them, actually, but it amounts to the same thing.'

'I see,' said the Flying Dutchman. 'Why should I?'

Jane couldn't think of a single reason. Not good.

'Excuse me for muddled thinking here,' Vanderdecker went on, 'because I haven't even started to consider all the ramifications of this yet, but why the hell should I?'

'Well,' Jane said feebly, 'it's not going to do you any good, is it?'

'That,' said Vanderdecker, 'if you'll pardon me saying so, goes for all life policies. Correct me if I'm wrong, but the prerequisite for collecting on the blasted things is being dead, and I remember hearing something somewhere about not being able to take it with you.'

'Exactly.'

'Exactly what?' said Vanderdecker, confused.

'You can't take it with you,' Jane said. 'So it's no good to you. On the other hand, it's putting the financial stability of Europe in jeopardy.'

'So what's so wonderful about the financial stability of Europe?' Vanderdecker said.

Jane felt that she could explain this, being an accountant: but while she was deciding where to start, Vanderdecker continued with what he was saying.

'Let me put it this way,' he said. 'If what you say is true, I'm in a position to tell all the money men in the world what to do. I have the power, the actual and useable power, to introduce a little bit of common sense into the economic system of the developed nations. In other words, I could save the world.'

'Do you want to?' Jane asked.

Vanderdecker considered for a moment. 'No,' he said.

'Why not?' Jane asked. 'Sounds like a good idea to me.'

'No it doesn't,' replied the Flying Dutchman. 'That's why you were asking me about whether I'd ever suffered from megalomania or a desire to rule things. To which the answer is still no. I mean, it's all very fine and splendid to think that I could sort out interest rates and conquer inflation and send the rich empty away and all that, but that's not me at all. Damn it, I couldn't even understand the jute market back in the fifteen-eighties. I'd just make things even worse than they are now.'

'So why not do what they want?' Jane said. 'It would make things easier for you as well.'

'Would it?'

'It could,' Jane said. 'All you'd have to do is think of the right price.'

'Go on.'

'Something like,' Jane said, 'an index-linked annuity starting at two million pounds a year, plus all the co-operation and protection you need. Passports, nationality papers, a new ship, bits of paper signed by presidents and prime ministers to shove under the noses of customs men and coastguards. Everything necessary to make life easy for you. No more of this skulking about, hiding, getting your ship fixed up by Jeanes of Bridport because there's nowhere else you dare go to. You could demand anything at all. A new identity. No questions asked. You could even start enjoying life. You wouldn't have to spend all your time in the middle of the sea, come to that.'

'What about the smell?'

'Demand that they build you a special massively air-conditioned bunker in the heights of the Pyrenees. A hundred special bunkers, one in every country. Real Howard Hughes stuff. That really wouldn't be a problem.'

Vanderdecker thought for a moment, then grinned. 'That's

very kind of you, and I appreciate the offer, but no thanks. I think we'll just leave matters as they are.'

Jane felt as though someone had just pumped sand in her ears. 'Why?' she said.

'I don't know,' Vanderdecker confessed. 'Instinct, mainly. Look,' he said, putting his chin between his hands, 'I remember reading somewhere about these tramps, people who'd been living rough for years and years, who finally were persuaded to come in out of the wind and the rain into a nice clean hostel. Clean clothes, beds, hot food. After a week or so, they all started sleeping on the floor, wearing the same clothes all the time and eating the scraps out of the dustbins. The staff couldn't understand it at all, but the tramps just couldn't trust the beds and the clothes and the food; they reckoned they must be some sort of trap and they wanted nothing to do with it. You get that way after a while.'

'I see,' Jane said. 'So I've failed, have I?'

'Looks like it,' Vanderdecker said. 'Sorry.'

Jane considered for a moment. 'How about as a personal favour to me?' she asked. Vanderdecker stared at her.

'Come again?' he said.

'As a personal favour,' she said, 'to help me out of a jam.'

'But . . .' Vanderdecker's voice trailed away, and he looked at her. Perhaps he saw something he hadn't seen for a long time. 'You mean, just because I like you or something?'

'Just,' Jane said, 'because you're a nice person. Like letting someone through in a stream of traffic, or giving up your seat in the Underground.'

'I hadn't looked at it from that angle,' Vanderdecker admitted.

'Try it.'

Vanderdecker drew in a deep breath. 'Did I mention,' he said, 'about my adventures in the real estate business?'

'No,' Jane said. 'Are they relevant?'

'Fairly relevant, yes.'

'Oh,' Jane said. 'Fire away, then.'

'Right.' Vanderdecker leaned back in his chair and closed his eyes. 'Many years ago,' he said, 'many years ago even by my standards, I bought some land in America. Don't know why; it was cheap, I had some capital for once, I thought I'd invest it. My idea was to build a little place out in the middle of nowhere but next to the sea, where I and my crew could be sure of some privacy and a glass or two of beer when we came in to land. That sort of thing. Anyway, before I could start building, I met this man in a pub who was down on his luck. He was Dutch, too, and I felt sorry for him. He had a dreadful story to tell, about how he'd been chased out of Holland because of his religious beliefs, forced to sell his farm and his stock and come out to the New World and start all over again, and how he hadn't got anywhere like the right price for his property back home and the fare out here had taken up a large slice of that because all the carriers were profiteers, and on top of all that the weevils had got into the seed-corn and three of his cows had got the murrain and how he was going to afford enough land in America to support a wife and three children he really didn't know. So I asked him how much he had and he told me and I offered to sell him my land for exactly that much. It was very cheap indeed, and he accepted like a shot. And I did it because I'm a nice chap, and of course it didn't matter a hell of a lot to me, considering how I was fixed.'

'And?'

'And what I sold him was the island of Manhattan,' said Vanderdecker, sadly. 'Error of judgement, wouldn't you say?'

Jane didn't say anything.

'Of course,' Vanderdecker went on, 'I wasn't to know that then. You never do. But that's the thing about eternal life; you have to live with your mistakes, don't you? Like when I met the Spanish Armada.'

'You met the Spanish Armada?'

'Pure fluke,' Vanderdecker said. 'It was just after the coming of the Great Smell, and we were lying off Gravelines, becalmed.

Suddenly the sea is covered with Spanish ships. Marvellous. Then all the Spaniards become aware of the Great Smell, and before their commanders can stop them they're all casting off and making for the open sea with their hands over their noses. Result; they lose the weather-gauge and get shot to bits by my old jute-trading contact Francis Drake. Or what about Charles the Second?'

'Charles the Second,' Jane said.

'Exactly,' said Vanderdecker. 'There I was in this pub, having a quiet drink, when this tall man with a moustache asks me if he can hitch a lift as far as France. No problem. Cromwell didn't think so, but I didn't know that, of course. Dunkirk, there's another instance of exactly the same thing. If those German cruisers hadn't come downwind of me at exactly that moment, just as all those little boats were zooming across the Channel with no escort whatsoever . . . You see the point I'm trying to make. I keep having these drastic effects on history. I don't try to. I don't even want to. I hate myself for it afterwards, but it keeps happening. You asked me if I thought I had a special destiny. I know I don't, it's just coincidence. Not coincidence, even; pure, calculable probability. If one man stays around long enough, just by his being there, important things are bound to happen to him or because of him sooner or later. Now there's nothing I can do to stop it, but I'm damned if I'm going to do it on purpose. It was bad enough that time with Napoleon . . .'

'Napoleon?' Jane asked.

Vanderdecker scowled at her. 'Who do you think was the idiot who picked up a passenger on Elba in 1815?' he said. 'I met this man in a pub. "Where are you headed for?" he asks. "France," I tell him. "What a coincidence," he says, "so am I." Why is it, by the way, that they always want to go to bloody France? I tell a lie, though; Garibaldi wanted to go to Italy. Anyway, I've got to face the fact that history to me is little more than a horrible reminder of my own interference. Even now, I can't listen to the Skye Boat Song without cringing.'

Jane's eyebrows may have twitched up an extra quarter inch, but she said nothing. It was a good throwaway line, and she didn't want to know the details.

'You should write your autobiography,' she suggested.

'I did, once,' Vanderdecker said. 'It was very boring, very boring indeed. Lots of descriptions of sea-travel, with comments on licensed victualling through the ages. The hell with it. I'm sorry, but I don't think I can help you.'

'Oh well,' said Jane. 'It was nice meeting you, anyway.'

'So what are you going to do?' Vanderdecker said.

'Do?' Jane frowned. 'I don't know. Does it matter?'

'To me,' said Vanderdecker, 'yes. I mean, you aren't the sort of person who bears grudges, are you? I mean, you know a lot about me now; what I do, where I get my boat fixed, all that.'

'I see what you mean,' Jane said. 'No, you needn't worry on that score.'

'I believe you,' Vanderdecker said. 'And what are you going to do?'

'Good question,' Jane said. 'You see, I don't exactly relish the prospect of telling my boss that I didn't manage it after all.'

Vanderdecker thought for a minute. 'Am I right in thinking,' he said slowly, 'that you said you have no sense of smell?'

'Rotten sense of smell, at any rate,' Jane said.

'Well, then,' said the Flying Dutchman, 'would you like a lift anywhere?'

'Anywhere, where?'

'Anywhere,' Vanderdecker replied. 'I can assure you that my ship is entirely free of etchings.'

'Etchings?' Jane asked and then said, 'Oh I see,' quickly and reflected that it was one way of putting it. 'I don't know,' she said. 'I mean, you said yourself, it's quite boring being at sea for seven years at a time.'

Vanderdecker smiled. 'Ah yes,' he said, 'but is it as boring as being an accountant?'

Jane thought hard. 'Nothing,' she said, 'could possibly be as boring as being an accountant. What was he like?'

'Who?'

'Bonnie Prince Charlie,' Jane said.

'Oh, him,' Vanderdecker replied. 'Just like all the others, really.'

He stood up and went to the bar for another drink, just as the barman put the towels over the pump handles.

Not for the first time, Danny was stuck for the right word. As a result, he was feeling frustrated, and he gripped the telephone receiver so tightly that it creaked slightly.

'You've got to look at it,' he repeated, '*globally*.'

'You what?'

'Take the *global* view,' Danny urged. 'Perspective-wise.'

'You do realise I haven't the faintest idea what you're talking about?'

The slender umbilical cord connecting Danny to his self-control snapped. 'What I'm talking about,' he said, 'is the biggest story since Westlands. And you're prepared to jeopardise it for the sake of the cost of hiring a boat.'

'What was Westlands?'

Danny made a noise at the back of his throat not unlike an Irish linen sheet being torn into thin strips. 'Don't play silly buggers with me,' he said. 'God, what a way to run a television network! Don't you understand, all I want to do is hire a bloody boat and go and shoot some pictures.'

'I understand that, yes. What I don't understand is why. That's where our communications interface appears to have broken down.'

'But don't you . . .' Danny paused for a moment, and an idea sprouted in his mind like the first pure, simple snow-drop of spring. 'Stuff you, then,' he said.

'Sorry?'

'You will be,' Danny retorted, slammed the received down and retrieved his phonecard from the jaws of the machine. It was pathetically simple, he said to himself. I'll hire a boat myself. With my own money. Or, to be precise, put it on expenses. Alexander the Great, unable to untie the Gordian Knot, sliced through it with his sword. Similarly, Danny had reached the point where nothing was going to get between him and the story. When the time came for a documentary to be made about the making of this documentary, the actor portraying him would have plenty to work with in this scene. He strode out of the telephone booth and went in search of a boat.

It wasn't much of a boat, when he found it, but then again, by modern standards neither was the *Golden Hinde*. It would do the job. He herded his camera crew onto it, indicated to the mariner in charge that it was time to go, and sat back to prepare himself.

About half an hour later, the mariner leaned across and said, 'You sure it was here?'

'Yes.'

'Well,' said the mariner, with the authority of a pope, 'it isn't here now.'

'Then it must have moved,' Danny said. 'I suggest you look for it.'

'Where?'

'I don't know,' Danny snapped, 'use your bloody imagination.'

The mariner shrugged and fiddled with his engine. The camera crew exchanged glances of a variety unique to members of a powerful trade union who are on overtime and are getting wet. Among such specialised social units, language ceases to be necessary after a while.

Three quarters of an hour later, the mariner suggested that that just left West Bay. He said it in such a way as to suggest that West Bay was so unlikely a place to expect to find a ship that only a complete imbecile would bother looking, but Danny was too wrapped up in his own destiny to notice.

By sheer coincidence, Danny's boat entered West Bay just as the *Verdomde* was leaving it. The *Verdomde* wasn't the only one, at that; on shore, there was a sudden and unprecedented scrambling for cars and dropping of car keys. People were getting out in a hurry, because of the smell.

Jane, for reasons which will not need to be explained, couldn't smell the smell; but everyone else could, including Vanderdecker. The effects of the enchanted seawater of Dounreay had worn off, about five minutes after the *Verdomde* had been declared seaworthy and money had changed hands, and thankfully the wind was in the right direction, at least for the purposes of navigation. Although Vanderdecker was extremely unhappy about setting off in broad daylight, he knew that he had no alternative except to take the chance. He might be conspicuous if he went, but he was going to be a great deal more so if he stayed. Once, in Puerto Rico, they had called out the fire brigade and turned the hoses on him, and that sort of experience leaves its mark on a man's psyche.

In later years, Jane often asked herself why she stayed on the ship. Occasionally she tried to tell herself that she hadn't yet given up hope of accomplishing her mission, but that was pure self-deception. Insofar as there was any rational explanation, it could only be that she couldn't stand the thought of the adventure ending. In her own defence, she could argue that she only had a five-hundredth of a second to decide, and even the clearest brains are likely to be pushed to make momentous decisions in the time it takes for the shutter of a camera to fall. Anyway, she said, 'Can I come with you?' and Vanderdecker had agreed. At least, she assumed he agreed. Perhaps he hadn't heard her, being too busy giving orders to the crew. At any rate, she stayed.

Danny saw the ship about one second before he smelt the smell, but it must be borne in mind that he had a cold. Everyone else smelt the smell first. Then they told Danny about it, just in case he hadn't noticed it for himself. They suggested that the smell was extremely unpleasant and that it might be prudent to go away. They expanded on this point. They threatened to put Danny in the sea. Finally they ignored him He shrieked at them for a while, but quite soon the sound of the ship's engine being revved to death was so loud that he was quite inaudible.

'That boat,' Jane said.

'What boat?' Vanderdecker said. 'Not now, Sebastian. Take it off.'

Sebastian van Doorning untied the anchor chain from his leg and went back to his post, muttering.

'You were saying,' said Vanderdecker, 'about a boat.' The Flying Dutchman had that harassed look again. It suited him by now, rather as a Savile Row three-piece with Jermyn Street socks suits its wearer. It looked right on him, somehow.

'I thought I recognised the man,' said Jane.

'Which man?' asked Vanderdecker.

'The man on the boat,' said Jane.

'Which boat?'

'Oh,' said Jane, 'never mind. Where are we going?'

'The long-term itinerary,' said Vanderdecker 'we can discuss later. Right now, would the statement "Out to sea" satisfy you?'

'No.'

'Tough,' said Vanderdecker. 'You see, the drill is to get as far out of the usual sea-lanes as possible before anyone sees us. Getting out of the usual sea-lanes in the English Channel isn't easy, what with all the ships. Therefore we tend to postpone the thinking part of it indefinitely.'

'Right.'

Vanderdecker deliberately slowed his brain down and thought for a moment. 'What are you doing here?' he asked.

'Well . . .' said Jane, lucidly.

'Don't get me wrong,' he went on, 'it's not that you're not welcome, far from it. It's just that we aren't scheduled to land again until the mid 1990s. If you have anything urgent lined up for the first part of the decade, now is the time to say.'

Jane hadn't thought of it like that. 'You mean you're just sort of going on?'

Vanderdecker nodded. 'It's what we do best,' he said.

'But what you were telling me,' she said. 'Montalban, the nuclear power station, all that. Aren't you going to follow it up?'

'Maybe it's not so important after all,' said Vanderdecker. 'I expect Montalban can wait another five years; he's waited long enough, God knows. That's something you learn when you're a sea captain, not to rush into things.'

'I think you should follow it up,' Jane said.

'Yes,' said Vanderdecker, 'perhaps I should. You sound just like my mother.'

Jane was startled. 'Do I?' she said.

'As far as I can remember,' replied the Flying Dutchman, 'yes. Why don't you take that job with the wool merchant? Don't you think it's about time you settled down and started making something of your life? You really ought to write to your uncle, Cornelius. I think that's what made me go to sea in the first place.'

'Oh.' Jane felt deflated. 'I'm sorry.'

Vanderdecker smiled sheepishly. 'So am I; I didn't mean to be nasty. It's just that I'm a trifle flustered, just like usual when I have to sail this blasted ship. You'd think that after all this time it would be second nature, but it isn't, quite. I reckon that if I had my time over again, I'd be a civil servant, something like that. Quiet. No need to be assertive or display qualities of leadership.'

Jane giggled. 'You'd hate it,' she said.

'Would I?' Vanderdecker shrugged. 'You seem to know an awful lot about me all of a sudden.'

Jane let that one go, and said, 'If you don't mind, I'll come along for the ride.'

'It'll be very boring for you if we don't go chasing Montalban.'

'Not half so boring,' said Jane firmly, 'as being an accountant.'

'That's a job,' said Vanderdecker, 'that I've always fancied. It was different in my day, of course. No computers, just little brass counters and exchequer boards. If you got bored with doing the quarterly returns, you could rope in another accountant and play draughts. Should I really follow up the Montalban angle?'

Jane considered. To her surprise, she was not influenced by personal motives in her choice of advice.

'I think you should, really,' she said. 'After all, that sea-water . . .'

'You're right,' said Vanderdecker, 'of course, there's just one problem.'

Jane looked at him. 'What's that?' she asked.

'The problem is,' said Vanderdecker, 'that I can't go on land for another five years. Because of the smell. Doesn't that rather hinder my freedom of movement?'

Jane smiled. 'Doesn't hinder mine, though, does it?'

'True,' said Vanderdecker, 'but of questionable relevance. What's it got to do with you?'

Jane felt exasperated. 'Let me spell it out for you,' she said. 'Watch my lips.'

'With pleasure.'

Jane ignored that. 'I will find Montalban, and pass on a message from you. If you want me to, that is.'

'Would you really?' Vanderdecker said. 'That would be a very great help to us. We'd appreciate that.'

'Right,' Jane said.

'And then,' Vanderdecker went on, 'we could meet up somewhere later, and you could tell me what he said.'

'Right,' Jane said.

'If you're absolutely sure.'

'Sure I'm sure,' Jane said. 'What's the message?'

Vanderdecker didn't reply. Instead he knelt down and picked up a short length of rusty chain.

'This ship is getting very untidy,' he said. 'Look at this, junk everywhere. I'm not a naturally finicky person, but after a while it does get to you a bit. The Flying Dutchman I can just about handle. The Flying Dustman, no.'

'What's the message?' Jane repeated.

'Are you really sure?'

'Really *really* sure. What's the message?'

Vanderdecker hesitated, then smiled broadly. 'Right,' he said. 'Listen carefully . . .'

CHAPTER
TEN

'What I need,' Danny said, 'is a helicopter.'

The voice at the other end of the telephone wire told him what, in its opinion, Danny really needed. It was not a helicopter.

'If I had a helicopter,' said Danny, mentally pigeonholing the recommendation, 'I could fly over the ship and the lads wouldn't be exposed to the waste fumes. That way, there'd be no problems from the health and safety at work angle. I take it that's what you're worried about.'

'To a certain extent, yes,' said the voice. 'Mostly, though, I'm worried about having a producer who's as crazy as a jaybird loose in Dorset. I think it's probably about time you came home and did "Playschool" for a bit, just till you're feeling better.'

'Look,' Danny hissed, 'you remember our deal, right? About a certain cover-up? I don't want to have to remind you . . .'

'Funny you should mention that,' said the voice. 'I've been chatting to a couple of other people over lunch, and I think you'll find they remember it rather differently. In fact, they seem to think you had quite a lot to do with that . . . What did you call it?'

Danny felt his knees weaken. 'You *bastard*,' he whispered. 'You wouldn't dare stitch me up like that. I've got memos . . .'

'So have I,' said the voice, casually. 'Very good ones, too. I wrote them myself, just now. I think it's time you came home.'

Suddenly Danny noticed that the hair on the back of his neck was beginning to rise. 'Just a moment,' he said. Then his phonecard ran out.

The phonecard revolution, like the French, American and Russian revolutions, is a phased phenomenon. In Phase One, they scrapped all the coin-boxes and replaced them with card-boxes. In Phase Two, whenever that comes about, they will start providing outlets where you can buy phonecards. We may not see it, nor our children, nor yet our children's children, but that is really beside the point. Every revolution causes some passing inconvenience to the individual. Ask Louis XVI and Marie Antoinette.

As he wandered through the streets (or rather street) of West Bay in search of an open Post Office, Danny was thinking hard. So there was going to be a cover-up, was there? A cover-up of the original cover-up. But what was this cover-up really covering up for? Not the original cover-up, surely; that was already well and truly covered, and nobody in his right mind would risk blowing the cover for anything so trivial as the cost of a few hours' helicopter hire. The only possible explanation was that this rather obvious warning to lay off was designed to get him off the story he was on; in other words, it was a sublimated or double-bluff cover-up. Despite his natural feelings of anxiety, Danny couldn't help licking his lips. It was the sort of situation he had been born to revel in, and revel in it he would, just as soon as he could get somewhere where he could sit down and get all the complications straight in his mind with the aid of a few charts and Venn diagrams. Then he would see about helicopters.

He found the camera crew in the Rockcliffe Inn, which had opened again shortly after Jane and Vanderdecker had left. Soon it would close again.

'Right,' said Danny briskly, 'drink up, we'd better get on with it while there's still some light left.'

They ignored him, but he was used to that. He changed a five-pound note, found the telephone in the corner of the pool room, and called a number in Shepherd's Bush.

'Dear God,' said the voice at the other end, 'not you again. Do you ever do anything besides call people up on the phone?'

'Yes,' Danny replied. 'From time to time I make television programmes. That's when establishment lackeys aren't trying to muzzle me, that is. Lately, that's tended to happen rather a lot, which means I have to spend more time telephoning. Cause and effect, really.'

'Are you calling me an establishment lackey?'

'Yes.'

'Another one who gets his vocabulary from the Argos catalogue. Look, I couldn't care less what you think of me. I get called ruder things on "Points of View". But if you think I'm going to put up with you wandering round seaside resorts spending the Corporation's money on your idiotic persecution fantasies, then you're a bigger fool than I took you for. And that, believe me, would be difficult.'

'Cirencester,' said Danny.

There was a pause. 'What did you say?'

'I said Cirencester,' Danny said.

'I thought you said Cirencester,' replied the voice, 'I was just giving you a chance to pretend you'd said something else.'

'And what's wrong with me saying Cirencester?' Danny asked politely.

'Nothing, given the right context,' said the voice smoothly. 'In a conversation about Cotswold towns, nothing could be more natural. In the present case, though, a less charitable man than myself might take it as proof that you've finally gone completely doolally.'

The pips went, but Danny was ready for them. He shoved in another pound coin. 'I said Cirencester because I know you know what it means,' he said.

'Thank you,' said the voice, 'that's the nicest thing anyone's ever said about me. What are you gibbering on about?'

'About the Cirencester Group,' said Danny, trying to sound cool and failing. 'About your being a member of it.'

There was another pause. A long one, this time. 'So?' said the voice. 'What of it?'

'I was thinking,' Danny said, 'just now, when you were trying to muzzle me. I thought, why is this man trying to muzzle me? Then it hit me, right between the eyes. Cirencester. It's not you that's trying to muzzle me, it's the whole bloody lot of you. The Group.'

'What possible connection is there between a select private literary society and you not making very silly documentaries?'

'I like that,' Danny said. 'Select private literary society. On that scale of values, the Third Reich was a bowls club. I know what you lot get up to in that neo-Georgian manor house on the Tetbury road.'

It must be pointed out at this juncture that Danny hadn't the faintest idea what went on there, although this was not for want of very strenuous trying. But the silence at the other end of the wire made it obvious that he had hit on something here. The effect of his previous threat had been pleasant, but this was incomparably better.

'What was it you said you wanted?' asked the voice.

'A helicopter.'

'Any particular make?'

Danny was taken aback. 'How do you mean?' he asked.

'Gazelle? Lynx? Sea King? I believe Sea Kings are very comfortable.'

'That sounds fine,' said Danny. 'So I can hire one then, can I?'

'Wouldn't hear of it,' said the voice. 'I'll order you one myself. Much quicker that way.'

'Oh.' Danny frowned with surprise. 'That's very kind of you.'

'Not at all,' said the voice, 'no trouble whatsoever. What's the use of having a desk with six phones if you never use them? Where do you want to be picked up from?'

'Wherever suits you,' Danny said, not to be outdone. 'I don't know where the nearest airfield is, but . . .'

'Airfields!' said the voice, forcefully, 'who needs them? Go down to the beach and I'll get someone to pick you up there. Give me half an hour.'

The line went dead. Danny pocketed his remaining change and went to the bar for a drink, just as the towels went back over the pump-handles.

Cornelius and Sebastian rowed Jane ashore in the skiff. They had to land her at a rather remote spot for fear of making themselves conspicuous, and the walk to the road over rocky and troublesome country was not to Jane's liking, since she was feeling tired enough already. She had packed quite a lot into this one day already without gratuitous exercise.

It was all very well saying she would find Montalban, as if all she had to do was look him up in Thompson's Local under Alchemists. It was all very well saying that once she had found him she would pass on Vanderdecker's message. The reality might be somewhat trickier. And was he back from Geneva yet?

As she finally joined the road, she was nearly blown off it by the downblast of the blades of an enormous helicopter that roared by apparently only inches over her head. She said something very unladylike to it as it went past, but it was very unlikely that it heard her, what with the noise of the rotor blades and all. Probably just as well.

After a long walk she reached West Bay, unlocked her car and took her shoes off. Then she wrote down Vanderdecker's message on the back of an envelope, just to make sure she didn't forget it. Montalban. Who did she know who might know where to find him?

Oddly enough, it was just conceivable that Peter might know. There was not a lot, when all was said and done, that Peter did know. He wasn't particularly well up in female psychology, that was certain, and she had her doubts if he had a firm grasp of the basics of tying his own shoelaces, but he was a scientist. Scientist. He lived in a little white box in north central Oxford and did research into semiconductors, whatever they were. All she knew about them was that they had nothing to do with buses or orchestras.

That seemed to be a likely place to start off her enquiries, then. All she needed to do now was to locate his telephone number. This should be marginally easier than finding the source of the Nile, always supposing that she had remembered to bring her address book.

She found a telephone box and tried Directory Enquiries instead. Then she called Peter's number, which was engaged. Enough of this, she said to herself. Food.

By far the best way to get something to eat in West Bay is to go to Bridport, where they will gladly sell you a sandwich if you show them enough respect. Jane discovered this eventually, and over her sandwich and a cup of pale brown oil in the Cherry Tree cafe she considered her next move. Phone Peter, get Montalban's co-ordinates, go there, see him, deliver the message, be back home in time for the afternoon repeat of 'Neighbours'. It could be that simple. On the other hand, it might be a lot harder, and it would be wise to give some thought to possible complications. But Jane's mind was starting to wander, and she found herself thinking about something quite other.

What would it have been like to spend four hundred years on a boat? The same boat? The same small, rather uncomfortable and inconvenient boat? Would she have liked it? A lot would depend, she decided, on the company. It was hard to imagine anyone, however brilliantly entertaining, that you could cheerfully spend the post-Renaissance era cooped up on a boat with without going stark raving mad, but from what little she had seen of the Flying Dutchman's crew, it wasn't very likely that they had helped much in keeping Vanderdecker from losing his grip on sanity. And yet he had managed it, somehow. Remarkable, in itself. A fairly remarkable person, in a woolly, harassed sort of way. Or had he done something rather similar to what she and everyone else did in order to keep themselves going through a generally dull and bleak existence? Accountancy, in a way, is rather like sailing endlessly round the world, in that it offers few bright spots and those widely separated by broad, blue expanses of tedium. In order to get across those, you try not to think about them. You think about the weekend instead. Now in Vanderdecker's case, the bright spots came once every seven years rather than seven days, but once one had got used to it the principle was probably the same. Jane shuddered. It was depressingly similar to he own situation, only worse.

At least all Vanderdecker had to do was find Montalban, reverse the alchemical process and render himself marginally less smelly, and he would be fine. In order for her to get out of her own vicious circle, she was going to have to do something immeasurably more clever, like win on the Premium Bonds or marry a millionaire. Vanderdecker, once he was adequately sanitised and had come to a grown-up understanding with the House of Fugger, would be able to live out the rest of Time in peace and luxury. She hadn't even got around to organising her pension scheme yet. Some people, she said to herself, have all the luck. And if I had been able to persuade him to come to that grown-up understanding with the Sock, perhaps I'd be out of it and free too. But she let that thought go. If the Flying Dutchman did decide to cash in his policy, then good luck to him. He'd earned it, in a way, and she wasn't going to be the one to bounce him into anything.

Jane dragged her mind back from its reverie and considered the crust of the sandwich and the gritty residue of her cup of coffee. That more or less wrapped up the nutritional side of things for the time being. It was time to try phoning Peter again.

'Hello, Peter,' Jane said. 'Where can I find Professor Montalban?'

'Hello, Jane' said a rather surprised voice; rather as one would expect Rip Van Winkle to sound if someone had woken him up in the early 1830s and asked him the time of the next bus to San Bernardino. 'Is that you?'

'Yes,' said Jane. 'Montalban. Where?'

'*Professor* Montalban?'

'No, Archbishop Montalban. Where can I find him?'

'It's been ages since I heard from you,' Peter said. 'How have you been keeping, anyway?'

Jane wanted to scream, but it was one of those phone-boxes that aren't closed in. 'I've been keeping nicely, thank you Peter. I put it down to the formaldehyde face-packs. Professor Montalban. What's his address? Where does he live? You do know, don't you?'

'No.'

Then why the hell didn't you say so, you furry-brained clown? 'You don't?'

'No,' Peter said. 'Sorry.'

'That's a pity, Peter, really it is. You have no idea how great a pity that is.'

'I could always look it up, I suppose.'

'Could you?'

'Oh yes.'

Give me strength, dear God. Not the strength to move mountains, perhaps; just enough to see me through the rest of this telephone call. 'What in, Peter?'

'Well, the faculty directory, of course.'

Of course. How silly of me not to have known. That sound

you can hear is me slapping my wrist. 'And do you have a copy of it handy, Peter?'

'Naturally.' Peter sounded a trifle offended. 'It's right here on my desk now.'

'That's good, Peter, I think we're getting somewhere at last. How would it be if you opened it at the letter M.' She counted five under her breath, to give him time. 'You there yet, Peter?'

'Yes.'

'Montalban, Peter. At a guess I'd say it was somewhere between Mellish and Moore. Any luck?'

'Hold on, I've dropped it. Ah yes, here we are. Montalban. You want his address, you said?'

'That's right,' Jane said cheerfully. 'You must be a mind reader.'

'Well,' Peter said, 'It's . . .'

'Hold on,' Jane squawked. 'I've got to get a pencil.'

The pips went. Just in time, Jane crammed a pound coin into the slot, then unearthed a pencil and the back of an envelope. 'Ready,' she said. 'Fire away.'

'It's Greathead Manor, High Norton, near Cirencester.'

'Thank you.'

'Gloucestershire.'

'Oh, *that* Cirencester. Do you know if he's back from Geneva? He is? Well, thanks a lot, Peter. How's the thesis coming along, then?'

'Not very well, I'm afraid,' Peter said. 'I keep having to go back and change the beginning.'

'Very difficult things, beginnings,' Jane said. 'Almost as difficult as middles and ends, in my experience. Stay with it, Peter. Remember Robert the Bruce and the spider. It's been lovely talking to you, must dash, bye.'

She retrieved her car, adjusted the rear-view mirror, put on her seat-belt and pulled out the choke. According to her AA book, you could get to Cirencester by way of the M4 and a number of other reputable main roads, and although it was her experience that road-maps generally tend to speak with forked tongue, particularly when dealing with the location of motorway service stations, it was certainly worth a try. As she turned the ignition key, something moved her to look out of the window and take one last glance at the little town of Bridport, where so much of such consequence had happened; the initial discovery at the bank, the visitor's book in the hotel, the curious ruined cottage, culminating in the dramatic meeting outside the boatyard and her irrational, as yet undissected decision to involve herself deeper still in this improbable but magnetic adventure. The sun gleamed on the windows of the Town Hall, and the traffic lights seemed to wink at her like old friends. Perhaps she would come back again one day, perhaps not. Perhaps she would never pass this way again, and this was to be the last time.

'Yippee!' she said aloud, and let out the clutch.

The cat woke up, uncurled its tail, and decided it would be nice to go for a walk. It got about three feet and discovered there were bars in the way.

Pleasant enough bars, as bars go. Quite probably there for its own good, to keep it from wandering too far and falling the short distance to the floor. If there were wolves about, it might keep them out for at least thirty seconds, provided they were not too hungry. The cat considered all these possibilities and rejected them. It yowled.

At the other end of the room, a man was playing a tall, elegant musical instrument, something halfway between a spinet and a harpsichord. It must be noted that he was doing so absolutely soundlessly, unless you counted the clattering of the keys under his rapidly-moving fingertips.

Hearing the yowl, he lifted his head and looked at the cage. He put down the lid of the musical instrument and walked across the room, stopping about halfway to pick up a dead mouse by the tail from a cardboard box of the kind that cream cakes come in.

'Here, pussy,' he said, in a rather embarrassed voice, for he was not used to addressing cats, small children or any of the other forms of sentient life who have to be spoken to in a silly voice. In truth, he wasn't accustomed to talking to anyone who didn't have a first-class honours degree, and it showed. 'Pretty pussy like a nice mouse, then?'

Pretty pussy yowled, and the man dropped the mouse down through the bars of the cage. The cat ducked and thereby avoided being hit on the head; it didn't look particularly grateful for the kind thought either. The man made a selection of cooing noises and poked a finger at the cat, apparently by way of a friendly gesture. The cat appreciated that all right; it bit it, hard. The man winced slightly and withdrew the finger. It was undamaged. Heartened by this minor reprisal, the cat ate the mouse. The man stepped back and looked at his watch. Five minutes later, he stepped out of the room and called up the elegant Queen Anne staircase.

'Mrs Carmody!' he said. 'Could you come through into the study for a moment?'

A tall, grey-haired woman appeared in the doorway. She was wearing an apron over a fiendishly expensive Ralph Lauren original, and her hands were covered in flour.

'Well?' she said.

'Mrs Carmody,' asked the man. 'Does that cat smell?'

The woman sniffed carefully. 'No,' she said. 'Should it?'

'No,' said the man. 'Thank you, you've been most helpful.'

The cat looked at them both in astonishment, but they took no notice. The woman asked when she should expect the guests.

'I think they said about half-past six,' said the man.

'Then they'll have to wait,' the woman said firmly. 'You can't expect me to produce malt loaf out of thin air, you know.'

The man bowed his head, acknowledging his fault, then

turned and sat down again at the spinet and began to play, as quietly as before. After about ten minutes, the telephone rang and someone read out the results of an experiment involving platinum isotopes. The man thanked him, said goodbye and put the receiver down.

Half an hour later, the man summoned Mrs Carmody again. 'Now does it smell?' he asked.

'No,' she said.

'Excellent,' said the man. 'You don't mind helping me like this, do you?'

Mrs Carmody thought for a moment. 'No,' she said. Then the man thanked her again and she left.

What the cat thought about all this is neither here nor there.

'Excuse me,' Danny asked, 'but aren't we going the wrong way?'

The pilot leaned back and grinned reassuringly. Obviously he couldn't her a word, what with the roar of the engines and the earphones he was wearing. But he was going the wrong way.

'You see,' Danny shouted, 'we're going inland, and we should be going out to sea.'

The pilot removed on earphone. 'You what?' he shouted.

'Inland!' Danny shouted. The pilot nodded.

'Yes!' he shouted back.

'No!' Danny replied. 'Wrong way. Should be going out to sea.'

The pilot shook his head firmly. 'No,' he replied. 'Inland. Much better. Right way.'

All right, Danny muttered under his breath, even if you're hell-bent on going the wrong way there's no need to talk like a Red Indian. He shook his own head equally firmly and shrieked back, 'No. *Wrong* way. We want to go out *there*!'

He pointed at the English Channel but the pilot didn't even bother to look. He had put his earphone back on and was busily flying the helicopter. Danny tapped him on the shoulder.

'What is it?' shouted the pilot, irritably, like a man who can take a joke if necessary but who'd really rather not have to prove it every five minutes. 'You'll have to speak up,' he added.

'We are going the wrong way,' Danny yelled slowly – it's not easy yelling slowly, but Danny managed it somehow – 'we should be going out to sea.'

Equally slowly, the pilot yelled back, 'No we shouldn't. Please sit down and stop talking.'

Then he leaned forward and switched on the wireless set; full volume, so that it would be audible above the ear-splitting noise.

'The Financial Times One Hundred Share index,' said the wireless, 'closed at nine hundred and seventy-six point eight; that's a slight fall of two points on yesterday's close. Government stocks were also down on the day, following a late flurry of activity shortly before the close of trading. The Dow Jones . . .'

The pilot grunted happily, switched off the wireless and leaned back. For the first time, Danny noticed that he was wearing rather a natty lightweight grey suit and a shirt with a button-down collar under his flying jacket. 'Now,' he said, 'what were you saying?'

'Nothing,' Danny replied, 'nothing at all.' He sat down, looked out of the window and tried to remember the little geography he had learned at school.

Leigh Delamere service station is unquestionably the Xanadu of the M4. Bring us, it seems to say, your weary and oppressed, your travel-sick children, your knackered and your bored stiff, and we will make them a strong cup of tea and a plate of scrambled eggs. If only it had a cinema and some rudimentary form of democratic government, no-one with any sense would ever want to leave.

As she felt the vigour of the tea flowing through her bloodstream like fire, Jane began to take stock of her situation. It was all very well saying 'I will arise and go now and deliver

Vanderdecker's message to Professor Montalban,' but there were imponderables. He might not be in. He might not wish to see her. She might not be able to find High Norton, let alone Greathead Manor. There might be danger, or at least profound embarrassment. In other words, she summed up, why am I doing this?

Good question, Jane girl, very good question indeed. As usual when faced with a thorny problem, Jane wondered what her mother would say. That was relatively easy to extrapolate; are you sure you're eating properly, Jane dear? Jane finished the last mouthful of her jam doughnut, and her conscience was clear. Yes.

Unfortunately, that left the original good question largely unanswered. Why are you doing this, Jane dear, and is it really terribly sensible? What are your employers going to say? Do you still have employers? What will become of you, you reckless, feckless child?

I used to be a bored accountant, she said, until I discovered Bridport. Then I got caught up in the destiny of mankind, and I became a sort of knight-errant for the Sock. Quite by chance. I tracked down the wholly improbable person I was sent to find, and I offered him the deal I was sent to offer him. He turned it down. I should now report back to my superiors and get back to doing some accounts. Except that my superiors have turned out to be rather spooky people, and I've got myself into such a mess now that it doesn't seem terribly prudent to go back. Don't ask me how this happened; it was none of my doing, and I suspect that I'm not cut out for this sort of thing, but it wouldn't do to think too closely about it for fear of suddenly going completely mad. Besides, I don't really want to be an accountant any more.

I am therefore going to a place called High Norton to see a very old alchemist and give him a rude message. What then? If I do all right, and whatever Captain Vanderdecker has up his sleeve works out, what then? When I suddenly decided to be on

Vanderdecker's team, what was going on inside my silly little head?

Well, Jane said to herself, Captain Vanderdecker has lots and lots of money, in a rather peculiar way. If he manages to get what he wants from Professor Montalban, no doubt he could be persuaded to express his immense gratitude in fiscal terms. Then Jane can live happily ever after and won't have to go to work ever again. Provided that Vanderdecker really exists, of course, and this whole thing isn't the result of an injudicious bed-time cheese sandwich. And if it is, why then, we'll wake up and go to work as usual. Fine.

But that's not the reason, is it? Jane frowned at the space where the doughnut had been, and was forced to confess that it wasn't. So what the hell was? Could it possibly be Captain Vanderdecker's grey eyes? We consider this point, said Jane hurriedly to ourselves, only out of thoroughness and to dismiss it. Captain Vanderdecker is very old, he spends all his time on a ship in the middle of the sea, and by his own admission smells.

Ah yes, said the inner Jane, but if he didn't smell he wouldn't have to spend all his time in the middle of the sea. Don't get me wrong, it added hurriedly, I'm not suggesting there's anything in the grey eyes hypothesis as such, I'm just suggesting that it can't be rejected as easily as all that. Are you doing all this because you want to help Captain Vanderdecker out of his predicament? Be truthful, and write on one side of the paper only. Yes, of course that's part of the reason; but grey eyes needn't enter into that at all. Then why did you bring them up in the first place?

Let's leave the eyes on one side for a moment, as they say in the anatomy labs. Did you suddenly make up your mind to be a heroine because it seemed the right thing to do? Yes, mother, I did, of that I am sure. And because I hate being an accountant, and it seemed like a good idea at the time, and there might be good money in it. Because I wanted to.

Because it means that, whatever happens next, I will be a

different Jane ever after, the sort of Jane who does that sort of thing. As for the realities of her situation, we will take a chance on the ravens feeding her. Talking of which, where is she going to sleep tonight? Even new Janes have to sleep and put on clean underwear in the mornings, and she is down to her last change of intimate garments. I may sympathise with Captain Vanderdecker, but I'm damned if I'm going to end up smelling like him.

But the voice of the new Jane had an answer to that, and told her that she would sleep in a hotel in Cirencester and first thing in the morning she would buy herself new underwear in the Cirencester branch of Marks and Spencer. Then she would go and see Montalban, and after that, who could say?

Feeling rather surprised and slightly frightened, Jane thanked her new avatar for its guidance and finished her tea. Whatever it was that had got into her seemed like it was going to stay there for some time, and on the whole she wasn't sorry.

'Mrs Carmody,' the man said, 'is everything ready?' The elegant woman nodded. 'Please be so kind as to bring it through, then, we mustn't keep our guests waiting.'

Shortly afterwards, Mrs Carmody wheeled in an old-fashioned trolley with a porcelain cake-stand and a silver tea-set on it. The man thanked her and asked her yet again for her opinion of the cat.

'No,' she said.

'Thank you so much,' said the man. 'Would you just ask Harvey to show them in?'

The man inspected the cake-stand and tried a slice of the malt loaf. It passed muster. Then he closed the lid of the spinet and leaned against it, waiting for his guests to arrive.

The helicopter pilot was the first to enter. He had taken off his flying jacket and he came into the room backwards; not out of diffidence or perversity, but so that he could keep the muzzle of his gun pointed at Danny's navel. Danny came next, and after him the camera crew. The co-pilot of the helicopter brought up the rear; he resembled the pilot very closely, except that his suit was navy blue and his gun was of a different make.

'Do sit yourselves down, gentlemen,' said Professor Montalban. 'There should be enough chairs for you all. I'm sorry you had such a long wait, but apparently the malt loaf took rather a long time to rise.'

Danny, who had spent the last hour and a half in the cellar listening to the opinions of the camera crew, was not impressed. He hated malt loaf anyway. The barrel of the pilot's gun suggested that he should sit down.

'Thank you. Harvey, Neville, please help our guests to some tea and cake,' said the Professor. The pilot gave him a severe look and picked up a plate, while the co-pilot took charge of a cup and saucer with his free hand. The Professor poured the tea and selected a slice of the malt loaf, and the two armed men delivered them to Danny, who accepted them with all the good grace he could muster, which was not much. Then Harvey and Neville repeated the same routine for the head cameraman, the assistant cameraman and the sound recordist. It all took a very long time, and more than a little tea ended up in the saucer.

When he judged that the polite thing had been done, the Professor introduced himself. 'My name,' he said, 'is Montalban. This is Harvey,' he said, indicating the pilot, 'and this is Neville.'

That, it seemed, was all the explanation that Danny was going to get, at least until the Professor had cleared his mouth of malt loaf. Danny waited, urging himself to stay calm and not do anything that could be construed as hostile or threatening. That wasn't too hard, in the circumstances; a Mongol horseman would find it difficult to make a threatening gesture with a cup in one hand and a plate in the other. He would also be hard put to it to eat the cake or drink the tea.

'And this,' said the Professor at last, 'is my personal assistant, Mrs Carmody. I trust you had a reasonable journey here.'

Danny nodded cautiously. His arms were aching from

holding up the teacup and the plate, but Harvey's gun was still pointed at him.

'Mr Bennett,' went on the Professor, 'I must apologise for troubling you like this, but to a certain extent you did bring it on yourself. You see,' he explained, 'you did mention that you knew something about Cirencester.'

Danny's hand wobbled, spilling tea. 'Cirencester?'

'Exactly. And Harvey here felt that he had no option but to bring that fact to my attention.'

This time, Danny dropped his cup. '*Harvey!*' he exclaimed.

'That's right, Danny,' said Harvey sheepishly. 'We meet at last.'

Now that he came to think about it, of course, Danny never had met his superior in the flesh, however many telephone conversations they had shared. Nor had he ever asked what the H stood for. He had invariably asked the switchboard for Mr Beardsley, and prefaced his remarks with 'Look . . .' It only went to show.

'I thought you were probably only bluffing,' Harvey went on, 'but you can't be too careful, and maybe you had finally managed to nose out something important, instead of all that crap about the Milk Marketing Board. So . . .'

'Look,' Danny said, probably out of sheer habit, 'just what is going on?'

'You should know,' said Harvey, grinning. 'You're the ace investigative producer, you started it.'

'For crying out loud . . . Harvey,' said Danny, 'put that bloody thing away and explain what all this is about. Are you trying to muzzle my story, or what?'

'What story?' Harvey asked. 'Oh, that load of old cock about nuclear dumping; no, not at all, but you were the one who dragged Cirencester into it, remember.'

'Actually,' said the Professor.

Harvey turned his head and looked at him. 'What?' he said.

'I'm sorry, Harvey,' said the Professor apologetically, 'there wasn't time to brief you in full. It was Mr Bennett's film of the Old Ships Race that made it necessary to bring him here.'

'Now wait a minute,' Harvey said, and Danny saw that he wasn't taking any notice of him any more. To be precise, the gun was pointing at the floor. Similarly, Neville had one hand full with a rather sticky slice of malt loaf, and was using the other to hold his plate under his chin to catch the crumbs. It was now or never, Danny decided. He sprang.

There was suddenly a great deal of movement, and we shall do our best to cover it sector by sector. Then we will join up the various parts to form a concerted picture.

The cat woke up, arched its back, and started to sharpen its claws on the piece of chair-leg thoughtfully provided for that purpose.

The assistant cameraman hit Neville with a small padded footstool. Neville dropped his plate and fell over, and the assistant cameraman sat on him and removed his gun from his inside front pocket.

Mrs Carmody lunged for the trolley, retrieved the cake-stand and carried it out of harm's way. A slice of malt loaf toppled off it into the carpet and was ground into the pile by Danny's heel; but that comes later.

Danny grabbed Harvey's wrist and tried to bring it down on his knee to jar the gun out of his hand. Unfortunately, Danny wasn't nearly as strong as he thought he was, and a rather undignified tussle followed, during the course of which Danny slithered on the slice of malt loaf, lost his balance and fell over. In doing so, he nearly dislocated Harvey's wrist, to which he was still clinging, and jolted his trigger finger, firing the gun. The bullet hit Professor Montalban just above the heart.

Danny, sitting on the floor surrounded by the wreckage of a chair, stared in horror and relaxed his grip on Harvey's arm. Suddenly everyone was looking at the Professor, who did something very unexpected. He didn't fall over.

'Please, Mr Bennett,' he said, removing a flattened bullet

from the lapel of his jacket for all the world as if it were a poppy on the day after Armistice Sunday, 'I must ask you to be more careful. There could have been an accident, you know.'

Harvey expressed himself rather more vigorously, and placed the barrel of his gun in Danny's ear. Gradually, everyone resumed their place, and the cat went back to sleep.

'Perhaps,' said the Professor, 'I had better explain.'

CHAPTER
ELEVEN

'Not now, Sebastian,' said Vanderdecker, and instinctively ducked. The sound of an invulnerable Dutchman hitting oak planks suggested that Sebastian hadn't heard him in time.

It's quite a distinctive sound, and to tell the truth Vanderdecker was heartily sick of it. Day in, day out, the same monotonous clunking. Had he thought about it earlier, Vanderdecker reflected, he could have turned it to some useful purpose. For example, he could have trained Sebastian to make his futile leaps every hour on the hour, and then it wouldn't matter quite so much when he forgot to wind his watch.

Too late now, however, to make a bad lifetime's work good. With the sort of deftness that only comes with long practice, he put the irritating thought out of his mind and wondered how Jane was getting on. Had she succeeded in tracking the alchemist down yet? She had thought it would be quite easy, and perhaps it would be; after all, the name Montalban seemed to be familiar to other people beside himself these days. There was the lunatic the crew had fished out of the sea and shown the alchemical plant to, for example; apparently, he'd come up with the same name all of his own accord. Certainly Jane had heard of him. So maybe all she'd have to do would be to look him up in the telephone book. Why didn't I ever think of that?

So let's suppose she's actually managed to deliver the message. What if Montalban wasn't interested? What if he didn't come? Come to that, what if he hadn't actually discovered an antidote to the Smell? That didn't bear thinking about; nor was it logical. If he was able to pass freely in normal human society, it stood to reason that he'd come up with something that dealt with the problem, even if it was only exceptionally pungent pipe tobacco. Except that they had all tried that, and it was a washout like everything else; and since Matthias had got to like the horrible stuff, there was something else they had all had to learn to put up with.

Now if there's one other thing we have all had to learn, Vanderdecker said to himself as he leaned on the rail and watched the seagulls veering away in shocked disgust, it's tolerance. With the exceptions of needled beer and country and western music, we've learned to tolerate pretty well everything on the surface of the earth. We don't mind being spat at, shot at, hosed down with water-cannon, exorcised and thrown out of Berni Inns. We can handle Sebastian's suicide attempts, Cornelius's snoring, Johannes's toenail-clipping, Pieter Pretorius's whistling, Antonius's conversation and chessplaying, pretty well everything about the cook, with nothing more than a resigned shrug and a little therapeutic muttering. In a world which still hasn't grown out of killing people for adhering to the wrong religion, political party or football team, this is no small achievement. A bit like Buddhism, Vanderdecker considered, without all that sitting about and humming.

And after all this time, what else would we do? Vanderdecker blew his nose thoughtfully, for this was something he had managed to keep from reflecting on for several centuries. What would it be like *not* being on this ship, or for that matter not being at all? The second part of that enquiry he could dismiss at once; it's impossible to imagine not being at all, and probably just as well. But suppose we can somehow get shot of the smell, what would we do?

The Flying Dutchman smiled. It's typical, of course, he said to himself, that I saw 'we'; after so many years of all being in the same boat, we poor fools share a collective consciousness that you don't get anywhere else in the animal kingdom. True, we all dislike each other intensely, or tell ourselves that we do: but the arm probably hates the hand, and no doubt the toes say cutting things about the ankle behind its back. We are the creations, as well as the victims, of our common experience. I can't see us ever splitting up, or admitting anyone else to our society. Particularly not the latter; by the time we'd all grown used to the newcomer's own particular habits, he or she would long since have died of old age.

But that's what I've tried to do, Vanderdecker contradicted himself, by enlisting Jane as an ally. Well, someone had to do the job; we can't and she was prepared to, so don't knock it. On the other hand, it was no end of a pleasant change to say more than three words together to someone I hadn't been through the War of the Spanish Succession with. But what about when the novelty wore off? It's different talking to Antonius; in our various conversations over the years, we must have used every conceivable combination of the few thousand words that make up his simian vocabulary. I can predict exactly what Antonius will say in any given situation, and I have got through the phase of wanting to push him in the sea every time he opens his mouth. Nothing he can say can do more than mildly bewilder me. That's a rather comforting thought, in a way, and to a greater or lesser extent it goes for everyone else on the ship. Why throw all that away and jeopardise a unique relationship, just for the chance of a chat or two with someone who'll be dead and gone in another seventy-odd years? Seventy years, after all, is no time at all; it took Antonius longer than that to do his last jigsaw puzzle.

'Captain.' Talk of the Devil. 'I've been thinking.'

'Good for you, Antonius. How do you like it?'

Antonius looked at him. 'Like what, captain?'

'Thinking.'

The great brows furrowed, the massive boom of the beam-engine slowly began to move. 'How do you mean, captain?'

'Nothing, Antonius,' Vanderdecker said. 'Forget I spoke. What were you going to say?'

'Well,' said the first mate diffidently, 'me and the lads were asking ourselves, what's going to happen? If that Montalban actually has invented something. I mean, what do we all do then?'

Out of the mouths of babes and sucklings, muttered the Flying Dutchman to himself, not to mention idiots. 'That's a very good question, Antonius,' he replied, 'a very good question indeed.'

'Is it?' Antonius looked pleased. 'Well, what *is* going to happen, then?'

'Has it occurred to you,' Vanderdecker said, 'that I don't know?'

'No,' Antonius replied, and Vanderdecker believed him. He discovered a lump in his throat that hadn't been there before. 'I mean,' said Antonius, 'it isn't going to change things, is it?'

'Certain things, yes,' Vanderdecker said.

'Oh.' Antonius's face crumbled. 'How do you mean?'

'For a start,' Vanderdecker said, 'more shore leave. Less getting thrown out of pubs. That sort of thing.'

Antonius's eyes lit up. 'I'd like that,' he said.

'Would you?'

'Yes.'

'Good.'

Antonius leaned forward on the rail, and Vanderdecker could hear him imagining what it would be like not to be thrown out of pubs. 'Antonius,' he said.

'Yes, captain?'

'Do you like . . . Well, all this?'

'All what, captain?'

Vanderdecker made a vague, half-hearted attempt at a gesture. 'All this being stuck on a ship in the middle of the sea and everything.'

'I suppose so,' Antonius replied, 'I mean, it helps pass the time, doesn't it?'

'Yes,' Vanderdecker said, 'I suppose it does. Do you know, I'd never looked at it like that before.'

'Like what, captain?'

'Like you just said.'

Antonius turned his head, surprised. 'Hadn't you?' he asked.

'No,' Vanderdecker replied. 'Not exactly like that. Well, thanks a lot, Antonius, you've been a great help.' Spurred on by a sudden instinct, Vanderdecker put his hand in the pocket of his reefer jacket. 'Have an apple?'

'Thanks, captain.' Antonius took the apple and studied it carefully, as if weighing up whether to eat it now or wait till it grew into a tree. 'I like apples, for a change.'

'That's what they're there for,' Vanderdecker said, and hurried away before the first mate could ask him to enlarge on his last remark. On his way to his cabin, he met Sebastian.

'Hello there, Sebastian,' he said, 'how's things?'

Sebastian frowned. 'How do you mean?' he said.

Vanderdecker smiled. 'You know,' he said. 'How are you getting on?'

'Same as usual, I suppose.' Sebastian's eyes narrowed. 'What are you getting at, skip?' he asked suspiciously.

'Nothing, nothing,' Vanderdecker reassured him. 'How have the suicide attempts been going lately? Making any headway?'

'No,' Sebastian replied.

'Never mind,' he said. 'Stick with it, I'm sure you'll get there eventually. Not that I want you to, of course. Mind how you go.' Then he slipped past and leaped up the steps to his cabin two at a time. Sebastian stared after him, tapped his head twice, and got on with his work.

Had Danny Bennett been there, he would have sympathised. As it was, he was back down in the cellar, after an entirely fruitless interview with the Professor.

Once the Professor had gleaned from him that he didn't actually know the first thing about the Cirencester Group (beyond the fact that it existed and a few fairly fundamental conjectures that a moderately intelligent laboratory rat could work out for itself in about three minutes) he had explained the dilemma he was in. Quite illegally, he had kidnapped a BBC producer and imprisoned him, by force of arms, in a damp cellar with an alleged rat. All he had managed to achieve by this was to reveal to his captive rather more about the deadly secret organisation he had discovered than he knew already. So now either Danny must join the conspiracy and work for it in some undefined but lucrative capacity, or else . . . well, there wasn't really an else, since even Danny could see that Montalban wasn't going to order his cold-blooded execution; and here he was, taking up house-room and needing to be fed and provided with clean laundry. It was all most aggravating, and if Danny hadn't been in a hurry to get out of there and start filming, he would have quite fancied the idea of staying put for a good long time and making as much of a nuisance of himself as he possibly could.

He was sitting on the floor thinking this over when Neville, the stockbroker who moonlighted as second murderer, appeared. He was holding his gun, as before, and also a large, scruffy cat. He seemed put out about something.

'Here you are, then,' said Neville, releasing the cat. 'I hope you're satisfied.'

Danny stared. 'What are you doing?' he said. Although he didn't know much about torture, he knew that it often happened to prisoners of diabolical conspiracies, and furthermore he didn't like cats.

'You said there were mice in this cellar,' Neville explained. 'So I was told to bring the cat down here. Satisfied?'

'Oh,' Danny said. 'I see. Thanks,' he added, belatedly. But by that time Neville had gone, leaving the cat.

The cat roamed around for a bit, scratched at the door, mewed querulously, and then went to sleep. It didn't seem interested in mice, and who could blame it? Danny, being of liberal views, was firmly opposed to racial and sexual stereotyping, and the principle presumably applied to species, too.

And that was it, for about half an hour. Then there were footsteps on the cellar stairs again, which Danny hoped had something to do with food. He looked round at his camera crew. They were all fast asleep, just like the cat.

The door opened, and a girl came in. Behind her was Harvey and Harvey's gun.

'In there,' Harvey grunted superfluously. The girl gave him an unfriendly look and stepped in.

It was fairly dark in the cellar, and that would explain why Jane, in normal circumstances a careful person, trod on the cat's tail. The cat woke up, screeched, and moved. So did Jane. She jumped about three feet in the air, lost her balance, and fell against Harvey. For his part, Harvey reacted according to the instincts of generations of chivalrous ancestors and caught her, in doing so dropping the gun. Please follow what happens next carefully.

The gun fell on the stone floor, landed on its exposed hammer, and went off, shooting the cat. Danny, hearing the shot, dived for cover, only to find that there wasn't any. Harvey tried to let go of Jane, but Jane refused to be let go of and grabbed his ears, thereby rendering him helpless for a long enough period of time for Danny to wriggle over, grab the gun with his least trussed hand, and try and cover Harvey with it. Unfortunately, he was too trussed to be able to cover the right person, and Jane, observing yet another perfect stranger pointing a gun at her, shrieked and let go of Harvey's ears. Harvey stayed exactly where he was. He had had enough of all this fooling about with guns and locked cellars, and was going on strike.

'Right then, Harvey,' Danny said, 'the game's up.'

'Oh for crying out loud,' Harvey replied, for he hated clichés. Danny, however, had seen far more spy films than were good for him, and felt sure that he knew what should come next. 'Freeze,' he snarled. He enjoyed snarling it, and the fact that he was still pointing the gun at the wrong person was neither here nor there.

The recent spate of moving about had woken up the camera crew, who opened their eyes, took in what was going on, and started voicing their opinion that it was about time, too. Jane, feeling rather left out, introduced herself.

'I'm Jane Doland,' she said, 'I'm with Moss Berwick, accountants. Who are you, please?'

'Danny Bennett, BBC Current Affairs,' Danny replied. 'Pleased to meet you.' He wriggled his weight onto the funny bone of his left elbow and brought the gun level with Harvey's lemon socks. That would have to do.

'Can we go now, do you think?' Jane asked.

Danny thought for a moment. 'Yes,' he said.

'Oh good,' Jane replied. 'Come on, then.'

Danny remembered something. 'Perhaps you could untie me,' he suggested.

Jane looked at the ropes, and then at her fingernails. She was not a vain person, but they did take an awfully long time to grow if you broke them, and the ropes looked rather solid. 'I'm hopeless with knots,' she said. 'Perhaps Mr . . .'

'Harvey,' Danny said.

'. . . Would do it instead. Please?'

Harvey nodded. 'Hold on,' Danny said, 'not so fast.' He was secretly pleased to have an opportunity to say that, too, although because of the angle his body was at he didn't have enough breath to spare to be able to snarl it. 'Here, you take the gun and cover him.'

With a tremendous effort, he handed Jane the gun, which was heavy and rather oily. She didn't take to it much. Harvey untied the knots, and Danny got up.

'Here,' protested the sound recordist, 'what about us?'

Harvey untied them, too, until everyone was completely back to normal and the gathering resembled nothing so much as an unsuccessful drinks party. '*Now* can we go, please?' Jane said. But Danny had noticed something else.

'Hey,' he said. 'That cat.'

'Which cat?'

'The cat you trod on. It's still alive.'

Jane frowned at him. 'I only trod on its tail,' she said.

'Yes,' Danny replied, 'but when the gun went off just now, I'm sure the bullet hit it.' He stooped down and picked something up.

'Look,' Jane said, 'I'm sure this is all very interesting, but shouldn't we be getting along?'

'The bullet,' Danny said, displaying it on the palm of his hand. 'This bullet hit that cat.'

'Really? How interesting.'

'Look at it, will you?'

When people are being tiresome, Jane's mother always told her, it's usually easiest just to agree. She looked at the bullet. Its nose had been flattened, as if it had hit a wall or something.

'Maybe it hit the wall,' Jane suggested.

'No,' Danny said, 'it definitely hit the cat. Like the cat's . . . invulnerable, or something.' Like the Professor was, in fact, he remembered.

Jane remembered where they were. 'It probably is,' she said. 'Look, I promise I'll explain, but I really do think we ought to be going. Otherwise . . .' She recollected that she was holding the gun, and she turned and jabbed Harvey with it. 'Move,' she said firmly.

Now this is all very well; but what about the sound of the shot? Didn't Neville come running as soon as he heard it, with

Montalban at his heels clutching a battle-axe and Mrs Carmody bringing up the rear with ropes and chloroform? Not quite. Neville, it seems, was outside checking the oil and tyres of his car when the gun went off, and didn't hear it. Professor Montalban heard it, but took it for a door slamming and dismissed it from his mind. What Mrs Carmody made of it is not known, but since no action on her part is recorded, we can forget all about her. Mrs Carmody is supremely unimportant.

So when Jane pushed Harvey up the stairs back into the scullery, there was no-one waiting for her. There was no-one in the hallway, either.

She asked Harvey to open the front door and go through it, and then she followed him. All clear so far. Then she caught sight of Neville, bending over the open bonnet of his car and wiping the dipstick on a piece of paper towel. She cleared her throat.

'Excuse me,' she said.

Neville looked up and saw the gun. He registered faint surprise.

'Would you please put your hands up?' Jane asked. 'Thanks.'

No-one asked him to, but Danny went and relieved Neville of his gun, which he found wedged rather inextricably in Neville's jacket pocket. The hammer had got caught up in the lining, and he had rather a job getting it out. Danny felt ever so slightly foolish.

'Right,' he said. 'Now let's get out of here.'

'What a perfectly splendid idea,' Jane said, 'why didn't I think of that? My car's just down the drive.' She prodded Harvey again, but he refused to move.

'You don't need me for anything now, do you?' he said.

'Look, chum,' Danny snarled, but Jane pointed out that there wouldn't actually be room for all of them plus Harvey as well in her car without someone getting in the boot, and then she thanked Harvey for his help and said good-bye, firmly. Harvey smiled thinly and walked back to the house.

'What the hell did you do that for?' Danny asked furiously.

'Oh do be quiet,' Jane replied. 'And put that thing away.'

Danny looked terribly hurt and Jane felt embarrassed at being so uncharacteristically rude. It wasn't like her at all, but he really was getting on her nerves.

'And anyway,' Danny said, 'where are we going? Shouldn't we hold them here until the police come?'

Jane's guilt evaporated. 'Blow the police,' she replied sternly. 'We don't want to go bothering them, do we?'

Danny looked at her. 'Why not?'

'Because . . .' Because if Montalban is arrested and sent to prison it will complicate things terribly, but I can't possibly explain all that now. 'Oh never mind,' she said. 'Are you coming or aren't you?'

'We're coming,' said the sound recordist. 'Can you give us a lift to the nearest station?'

They were still standing there when the door of the house opened and the Professor came out, followed by his two sheepish-looking henchmen. They all had their hands in the air, which made them look like plain-clothes morris dancers.

'Hold it right there,' Danny snapped, and waved his gun. Even if nobody else was going to take this seriously, he was. They ignored him. It wasn't fair.

'Miss Doland,' said the Professor, 'before you go, would you like some tea?'

'Tea?'

'Or coffee,' said the Professor. 'And if you could spare the time, there is a message I'd be grateful if you would take to Mr Vanderdecker.'

Jane frowned. 'I thought you couldn't make any sense of what I told you,' she said.

'I looked up some old records,' the Professor replied. 'So, if it wouldn't put you out too much . . .'

'Thank you,' Jane said, putting her gun in her pocket as if it were a powder compact. 'Two sugars, please.'

CHAPTER
TWELVE

'This,' said the Professor, 'is my computer.'

Danny, balancing his gun and a plate on his knee while he ate a sticky bun, looked up. Montalban was pointing at the harpsichord.

'Of course,' the Professor went on, 'it's rather an old-fashioned design. In particular, it has no screen; instead it prints out simultaneously.' He picked up what Jane had taken to be the sheet music and pointed to it. 'You see,' he said, 'when I first invented the computer in seventeen – sixteen ninety-four, the nearest approximation to a letter-free system of abstract notation was written music, and I adapted the principle for my own purposes. Minims, crotchets and quavers each have their own quantitative value in Base Seven, and as it happens it's an extremely powerful and flexible system: much better than the binary systems that I used in the first commercial models. Since I'd got used to it over the years, I never bothered to transcribe all my data resources into the new computer languages that have since been developed; I've simply tinkered with my original design as and when I needed to. So now my system is entirely sufficient for my needs, with the added advantage that nobody else in the world can understand it. Complete secrecy and immunity from the attention of . . . Hackers, I think they're called.'

'That's right,' Jane said. 'That's very impressive.'

'Is it?' The Professor was mildly surprised. 'I certainly don't aim to impress. For virtually the whole of my working life, I've sought to do the opposite; to keep out of the limelight, so to speak. Absolutely essential, if I'm to be able to get on with my work in peace and quiet. Which is why I formed the Cirencester Group.'

'Ah,' said Danny.

'I originally founded it,' Montalban said, 'in seventeen – when was it, now? It was just after the collapse of the South Sea Company. Have some more tea, and I'll tell you about that.'

The tea was cold, but nobody mentioned it. Danny had put his plate and gun on the floor by now, and was taking notes.

'The South Sea Bubble,' said the Professor, 'was my doing. I needed an economic collapse, you see.'

'You needed one?' Danny said.

'Does that make me sound terribly selfish?' the Professor said. 'Well, perhaps I am. In order to get the resources I required, I had to get control of large financial and mercantile institutions. The best way to get control is to buy when prices are cheap, following a slump. I couldn't afford to wait for a slump, so I created one. First I built up a bubble and then I pricked it. It wasn't hard; I engineered certain changes in the national economy, by introducing new technology and new industrial processes. I put the capital I had built up by the practice of alchemy into the bubble, and the bubble grew; then I pricked it, as I said. The computer was invaluable, of course.'

'I see,' Jane said. 'And then?'

'And then I got on with my work, and left all that side of things to the computer. I had programmed it to handle the economies of the developed nations, and that's what it did. That, in fact, is what it still does.'

This time it was Neville's turn to look shocked. 'You never told me,' he said.

'I know,' said the Professor, 'and I do apologise. But if you'd known, I'm afraid you couldn't have resisted the chance to make very substantial sums of money for yourself. Instead, you have helped me, and by so doing merely made substantial sums of money. I think you have been reasonably treated, all in all.'

'Just a moment,' Jane said. 'This work of yours. What exactly is it?'

'Very simple,' said the Professor. 'You asked me if I smelled. I do not. That is my work.'

'But you don't,' Jane said. 'Have you finished, then?'

'Nearly,' the Professor said, 'but not quite. I discovered that the elixir which Captain Vanderdecker and I both drank fundamentally altered our molecular structures. The change was similar to the effect of bombardment with intense radiation – we had become, if you like, isotopes of ourselves. I hope I'm not being too technical.'

'You are a bit,' Jane said, 'but please go on.'

'Thank you. Recently, about sixty years ago, I discovered that intense radiation bombardment can partially reverse the effects of the elixir. Since then, I have been trying to construct a sufficiently powerful atomic generator to provide enough radiation for my purposes. Hence, I'm afraid, the nuclear industry. I must apologise for it, but there was no other way.'

'Quite,' Jane said, rather unsympathetically. 'Go on, please.'

'Basically,' said the Professor, 'if you put a person who has drunk elixir into the very heart of an atomic reaction, it adjusts the molecular structure. It loosens them up and jiggles them about. But the sort of jiggling I want – jiggling out the smell without jiggling the whole thing out of existence – isn't easy, and I haven't quite got it right yet. The obvious difficulty was that radiation is dangerous, and I wasn't keen on experimenting on myself; nor, for that matter, on anyone else, not even Captain Vanderdecker – even though he got me into this situation in the first place. But then I remembered the cat who had drunk the elixir when I first tested it out, and eventually I tracked it down and acquired it. After some experiments at Dounreay in Scotland, I found that the smell could be temporarily suppressed by prolonged exposure to intense radiation of a certain type; a bit like the modern process of food irradiation. The longest period it's lasted so far is a month, and soon Percy and I will have to go back for another dose.'

'Percy?'

Montalban flushed slightly. 'I call my cat Percy,' he said, 'short for Parsifal. The Holy Innocent, you see.'

Jane didn't see, but wasn't too bothered. She asked the Professor to continue.

'And that,' he said, 'is my work. That is all that concerns me. The Cirencester Group, which has operated from here ever since I first built the house, comprises all the people whose assistance I require – bankers, financiers, public relations people, industrialists, heads of Government agencies . . .'

'Hold on,' said Danny, whose pen had just run out. 'Now, then. What came after bankers?'

'. . . And, of course, the most important of them all, the Controller of Radio Three. Without these people . . .'

Danny had dropped his new pen. 'What did you just say?'

'Radio Three,' said the Professor. 'Without him, the whole system would break down, obviously. Now . . .'

'Why?' Danny demanded.

'I'm sorry,' Montalban said, 'I thought I had explained all that. I said my computer used a system based on musical notation. Now, to all intents and purposes, it *is* musical notation. You can sit down at the piano and play one of my programmes with no difficulty at all, and usually (may I say, in all modesty) with great pleasure. In fact, I'd be prepared to wager that you know a great many of my programmes by heart. Of course, I wrote them all under several *noms-de-plume* . . .'

'Such as?' Danny asked.

'Bartok,' replied the Professor, 'Mendelssohn, Sibelius, Chopin, Mozart, Elgar, Delius, Handel, Ravel, Schubert, Jelly Roll Morton . . .'

Danny's mouth fell open. 'You did?'

'Yes indeed.'

'I don't believe it.'

The Professor smiled. 'You're prepared to believe that I invented the computer and the electric light, but not that I wrote the *Eroica* or *Rhapsody in Blue* – which is, as it happens, little more than a simple word-processing programme. Ah well, they say a prophet is never honoured in his own country. Let me give you a demonstration.'

The Professor got up and walked over to the rather impressive stereo system. He selected a compact disc and fed it into the machine.

'What's sixty-six,' he asked Danny, 'multiplied by the square root of nineteen, divided by five and squared?'

Danny started counting on his fingers and then gave up. 'I don't know,' he said.

'Here is a pocket calculator,' said the Professor. 'You work it out on your machine, while I do it on mine.'

Danny started pressing buttons, while Montalban played a short snatch from Handel's *Messiah*. Then he switched off the stereo and said, 'Nine hundred and eighty-four point nine five nine nine seven. Am I right?'

'Yes,' Danny confirmed. The Professor nodded.

'As you can tell by the date of the composition,' he said, 'that was one of my first programmes, a simple calculating system. Catchy, though.'

Danny handed the calculator back in stunned silence, and the Professor went on.

'Hence,' he said, 'the need to be able to dictate what is

played on Radio Three at certain times; it's my way of programming a number of other computers running my musical language in strategic positions all over the world. The consequences of the wrong thing being played at the wrong time can be catastrophic. For instance, the recent stock market slump was the result of some foolish person deciding to broadcast "The Ride of the Valkyries" at half-past five on a Friday afternoon. I didn't compose that, by the way, but by pure chance it's perfectly intelligible to one of my computers as an urgent command to sell short-dated Government stocks. I'm only thankful it wasn't the overture to *HMS Pinafore*.'

There was a very long silence, disturbed only by the assistant cameraman humming 'I Did It My Way', during which the Professor drank the rest of his tea. Then Jane rallied the remaining shreds of her mental forces and asked a question.

'So where does that leave us?'

'That depends,' said the Professor, 'on you. If you and your friends would be happy to forget all about what I've just told you, I can continue with my work until it's finished; after that, I intend to retire and keep bees. If you refuse, of course, I shall have to do my best to carry on regardless. No doubt you will broadcast your discovery to the world, and although I will naturally use all my considerable influence and power to prevent you, you may possibly be believed, and then the world will have to make up its mind what it wants to do with me. I cannot be killed, or even bruised. I can do incalculable damage before I'm got rid of – all I have to do to cause an immediate recession is to pick up the telephone and ask the BBC to play 'Sergeant Pepper's Lonely Hearts Club Band' at three-fifteen tomorrow afternoon. It will take hundreds of years of poverty and darkness to dismantle the structures that I have built, and the immediate result of my overthrow – for want of a better word – will be the destruction of the economies of the free world . . .'

'Not you as well,' Jane said.

'I beg your pardon?'

'Nothing,' Jane said wearily. 'Go on.'

But the Professor was interested. 'You said not me as well,' he said. 'Can I take it that you know about the Vanderdecker policy?'

'Yes,' said Jane. 'Do you?'

'Most certainly,' said the Professor. 'It's one of my most worrying problems.'

'One of your problems?' Jane repeated.

'Assuredly,' Montalban replied. 'You see, one of the first things I did after the South Sea Bubble collapsed was to buy up the Lombard National Bank.'

Danny Bennett felt better. He had found a television.

Although no umbilical cord connected him to the instrument, he could feel its reviving power soaking into him, like the sun on Patmos only without the risk of sunburn. Admittedly, there was nothing on except 'The Magic Roundabout' but that was better than no telly at all. As he sat and communed with his medium, an idea was germinating inside his brain, its roots cracking the thin, tight shell and groping forcefully for moisture and minerals. He could give the story to someone else.

Rather out of character? Very much so. A bit like Neil Armstrong saying to Buzz Aldrin, 'You do it, I think I'll stay in and do the ironing,' but the fact remains that Danny was seriously considering it. For all his Bafta-lust, he knew that this was a story that had to be made, and if he couldn't make it himself, he had no option but to give it to someone else. But who?

There was Moira Urquhart; no, not really. Danny would gladly have given his jewel to the common enemy of man, but not this story to Moira. She lacked vision. She would probably try and work cuddly animals into it, and that would clutter up its flawless symmetry. Moira worked cuddly animals into everything, even ninety-second clips for 'Newsnight' about the European Monetary System. Not Moira, then.

Or there was Paul. Let Paul do it. Good old Paul. The Cirencester Group would really love that, because that way the story could break once and for all and nobody would take the slightest bit of notice. Such was Paul's skill at grabbing the attention of the viewer that if he told you your ears were on fire you'd be so bored with the topic you wouldn't bother putting them out. Not Paul.

Which meant it would have to be Diana; a pity but there it was. Just then, Danny noticed that Zebedee and Dougal had yielded place to the news, and there was Diana on the screen, surrounded by fallen masonry, telling the folks back home about the situation in Lebanon. Since Danny didn't have the Beirut phone-book and had little confidence in Lebanese Directory Enquiries, that ruled her out. Not Diana either. Not, apparently, anybody.

He stood up and switched the television off. There must be something he could do, but he had no idea what it was.

'Hello, Danny,' said a voice behind him, and there was Jane, holding a cup of tea and a Viennese finger. 'Would you like a cup?'

'No.' Danny said. 'Look, when are we going to get out of here?'

'I don't know,' Jane replied. 'Nobody seems to have given it any thought.'

'We can't stay here for the rest of our lives,' Danny said.

'You wouldn't have thought so, would you?' Jane answered. 'But I don't think we're in any position to leave without permission.'

'Permission!' Danny snapped. 'Haven't you still got that gun, then?'

'Yes,' Jane admitted, 'but what does that solve? Even if I were to shoot Professor Montalban, all that would achieve would be a hole in his cardigan. Not that I think he'd try and stop us just walking out – not by force, I mean – but he did drop very strong hints that if we make nuisances of ourselves it'll be Sergeant Pepper time, and personally I don't want to take responsibility for that.'

'So, what's happening?' Danny said. 'I mean, we can't just sit here. Surely someone's planning to do something.'

Jane sipped some tea and sat down on a chaise longue. 'From what I can gather,' Jane said, 'we've really got to wait for Vanderdecker to show up. He's the only person I can think of who's got any sort of hold over the Professor.'

Danny frowned. 'How do you mean?'

'Well,' Jane said, 'first, it looks like when Montalban got off Vanderdecker's ship all those hundreds of years ago, he left some of his notebooks behind, with all sorts of calculations and results in them that he hasn't been able to reproduce since. I think Vanderdecker's still got them, and that's a start, isn't it?'

'Possibly.'

'And then,' Jane went on, 'there's the Vanderdecker policy. If anyone ever finds out about that, then bang goes the National Lombard Bank, and with it Montalban's research funding.'

'But that's not really a threat,' Danny said, 'given that that would achieve exactly the same result as Sergeant Pepper, which is what I imagine we're trying to prevent. Also,' he added, 'I don't think all that much of your first angle, either.'

'You don't?'

'Try this as a threat. "Montalban," you say, "give up your whole research project or we won't let you have your notes on a small part of it back." Breathtaking. He's got us all stuffed. Even I can't do anything.'

Jane forbore to comment on that one. 'Oh well,' she said, 'never mind. Have you actually asked yourself what's so utterly terrible about Montalban's conspiracy, or whatever it is?'

Danny stared. 'Are you serious?' he said. 'It's a *conspiracy*. It's a fundamental threat to the liberty of the free world. It's . . .'

'It's the way things have been run for the last three hundred odd years,' Jane said thoughtfully. 'True, I never liked it much myself, but I don't think the fact that it's an organised scheme by a really quite pleasant old Spanish gentleman in Cirencester, rather than the accumulated megalomania and negligence of generations of world statesmen, makes it any the more terrible, do you? I mean, Montalban isn't planning to overthrow democracy or annexe the Sudetenland, he's just trying to get rid of a smell. Will it really be so awful if he succeeds?'

'But . . .' Danny spluttered. He knew exactly why it was so pernicious and so wrong, but he couldn't quite find the words. 'But he's just one man, one selfish individual, and he's controlling the lives of millions and millions of people. You can't do that. It's not right.'

'I see,' Jane said. 'So if we have third world poverty and nuclear weapons and East–West hostility and economic depressions, but all brought about by means of the democratic process, then that's all right, but if just one man is responsible then it's tyranny. Sorry, I never did history at school, I don't understand these things.'

'Don't be stupid,' Danny said, 'you entirely fail to grasp . . .'

'Very likely,' Jane said sweetly. 'But before you found out about Montalban, you would have given your life to defend the fundamental basics of our society and our way of life against the Montalbans of this world; the status quo, you'd probably call it. And now it turns out to be all his doing, you suddenly realise it's evil and it's got to go. Please explain.'

Danny glared at her and drew in a deep breath. 'So you're on his side now, are you? I see.'

Jane shook her head. 'I'm not on anybody's side. You make it sound like hockey matches at school. I don't care at all whether Montalban gets rid of his smell or not – or rather, I do; I think it must be rather awful to smell, and besides, if he finds a cure for it then Vanderdecker will be cured too, and I . . . well, I like him. And I also don't want to see some sort of dreadful Wall Street Crash, and everybody jumping out of windows the length and breadth of King William Street, because that isn't going to help anyone, now is it? Whereas –' Jane suddenly realised that she'd used the word 'whereas' in conversation, and didn't know whether to feel ashamed or proud – 'whereas if everybody's sensible and we all act like grown-ups, we can all sort things out and everyone can have what they want.'

'Can they?'

'I don't see why not,' Jane replied. 'Vanderdecker can swap the Vanderdecker Policy for the antidote to the smell and a cash lump sum, he can give the Professor his recipe back, the Professor can wind up his various businesses – he just wants to retire and keep bees when he's finished his work, so perhaps he could put it all into some sort of gigantic trust fund for the Ethiopians or something like that. And perhaps we'll insist that he finds a substitute for atomic power and a replacement for petrol and things – to judge by his track record, he shouldn't have any trouble with that – and . . .'

'And everybody will live happily ever after?'

'Yes,' Jane said. 'And why not?'

'So you fancy this Vanderdecker, do you?'

It was Jane's turn to stare. 'What did you say?'

'Well,' Danny said, 'it's obvious, isn't it? You're prepared to sell the whole of Western civilisation down the river for a man who's old enough to be your great-great-great-great- . . .'

Jane got up and brushed crumbs of Viennese finger off her skirt. 'Good morning, Mr Bennett,' she said.

'Where are you going?'

'To ask Harvey and Neville to tie you up and put you back in the cellar,' she said. 'With the rat.'

'Mouse.'

'Rat,' Jane said firmly, and left.

Although she wouldn't admit it to herself, Danny's suggestion had made Jane very cross indeed, and she felt that she needed some fresh air. She walked out through the front door and round the back of the house, where there was a huge lawn, and sort of thing the early Edwardians used to play cricket on.

Suddenly she looked up. There was a clattering noise. A helicopter was coming down to land. Jane groaned from the soles of her feet upwards. Now what?

And then she was aware of something – very horrible and unfamiliar, but extremely faint and far away. It was a smell; a smell so pungent and horrible that even she could smell it.

The helicopter hovered for a moment over the immaculate turf and flopped down like a tired seagull. Out of it jumped a man in a gas mask. He was running for all he was worth, but another man – Sebastian, the suicidal maniac – was after him, caught up with him and brought him to the ground with a low tackle. The man in the gas mask seemed to give up and tried to bury his head under his body.

Then someone else jumped out of the helicopter; and Jane, who was able to ignore the smell, ran to meet him.

'Hello,' she said, 'what on earth are you doing here?'

Vanderdecker was looking surprised. 'Did you just kiss me?' he said, as if a nun had stopped him in the street and sprayed whipped cream in his ear from one of those aerosol cans.

'Yes,' Jane said. 'You need a bath, mister.'

'This is very forward of you,' Vanderdecker said. 'Usually I never kiss people I haven't known for at least three hundred and fifty years.'

'We'll go into all that later,' Jane said, feeling suddenly foolish. 'Look, what *are* you doing here? What's going on?'

'There's trouble,' Vanderdecker said.

'Yes,' Jane said, 'but . . .'

'No,' said the Flying Dutchman, 'a different sort of trouble. Where's Montalban?'

'In there,' Jane said, pointing to the house. 'Where did you get the helicopter from?'

'Well,' Vanderdecker said, 'there was this destroyer, and when we sailed up alongside, all the crew ran to the side and jumped off into the water. Luckily we managed to fish out one of the helicopter pilots and intimidate him into bringing us here. Have you ever been in one of those things? They're awful. Like being inside a Kenwood mixer.'

'What did you do to him?'

'Well,' Vanderdecker said, 'Sebastian threatened him.'

'With a gun?'

'No,' said Vanderdecker, 'with a sock.'

'A sock?'

'Yes,' said Vanderdecker. 'One of the socks he was wearing. Threatened to take it off and put it inside the fellow's gas mask. After that he was extremely co-operative. Look, I've got to see Montalban.'

'But how did you know where to come?' Jane demanded.

'Simple,' said Vanderdecker, 'I phoned Directory Enquiries. Isn't that what you did?'

'I think he's in his study,' Jane said. 'Follow me.'

CHAPTER
THIRTEEN

'O h,' Montalban said. 'Oh, that is most unfortunate. Would
you care for some more tea?'

'Not just now, thanks,' said the Flying Dutchman. 'Have
you got official notice yet?'

'Let me see.' The Professor stood up and walked over to an elegant Jacobean chair in the corner of the room. He pressed a knob
on the carved side, and a telex printer appeared through the seat.

'Ah yes,' said the Professor. 'It's just come through this minute.
You were right. Dear me, this is most regrettable.'

'Regrettable!' Jane said. 'Isn't that putting it rather mildly? I
mean, the Dounreay nuclear power station is about to blow up
and take half of Northern Europe with it, and you say . . .'

'Extremely regrettable, yes,' said the Professor. 'Unfortunately,
the telex doesn't give details. Perhaps I should telephone somebody.'

'Good idea,' said Vanderdecker. 'You go and do that.'

The Professor wandered away, and Jane turned to Vanderdecker. Her face was white.

'It was lucky we were there,' Vanderdecker said. 'We were

just sailing along the Bristol Channel, minding our own business, when we happened to bump into the *Erdkrieger* again – you remember, that nuclear protest ship I told you about, with all those terribly earnest young people on it. They'd just come from Dounreay, and they were seriously worried. They'd seen this sort of glow on the water, and they didn't like it one little bit. They'd tried to radio in to warn everyone, but of course nobody believes a word they say on that particular subject. So I asked them exactly what they'd seen, and when they explained I guessed that there'd been some awful accident. And then we saw the destroyer, which was following the *Erdkrieger*, and the rest you know.'

'But . . .' Jane started to say.

'Sorry?'

'I mean,' Jane said, 'no offence, but what can you do?'

Vanderdecker raised an eyebrow. 'I would have thought that was obvious,' he said. 'After all, we are the only people in the world who can do anything – that's if anything can be done, that is. But the Professor can tell us that.'

'You mean because you can't be killed?'

'Exactly,' Vanderdecker said. 'Everything always comes in handy sometime, as my grandmother used to say when she stored away little bits of string, and in our case, it's invulnerability. Well, so far as we know we're invulnerable, but I don't remember the elixir coming with label saying "Invulnerability or your money back; this does not affect your statutory rights." Remains to be seen, really, now doesn't it? That's why I brought Sebastian with me.'

'But you *mustn't*,' Jane burst out. 'Not if it's dangerous.'

Vanderdecker stared at her, and then began to laugh. He laughed for a very long time, although he seemed to realise that it wasn't going down well with Jane; he couldn't seem to help it. He was still laughing when the Professor came back in.

'Most regrettable,' said Montalban gravely. 'I blame myself, of course.'

Jane scowled at him. 'You mean it's your fault?' she snapped.

'I suppose so,' said the Professor. 'If I had never developed nuclear fission, this could never have happened. Ah well.'

'What's happening?' Vanderdecker asked. 'Was I right?'

'Absolutely,' said the Professor. 'You were entirely correct in your diagnosis. I never knew you were a scientist.'

'It's been a long time, hasn't it?' Vanderdecker replied. 'And you never wrote. But what are they doing?'

'They've evacuated the area,' said the Professor, 'and they're clearing the north of Scotland. But I don't think there will be time. And ideally, one would prefer to evacuate Europe, if one wanted to be on the safe side.'

'Would one really?' said Jane. 'How regrettable!'

'You shut up,' said Vanderdecker, 'you aren't helping. Look, Montalban, is there still time to do anything? Has the situation become critical?'

'I'm afraid so,' said the Professor. In his hand, entirely forgotten, was a stone cold crumpet. He had been carrying it about with him for at least twenty minutes, and the once-molten butter had solidified into a translucent yellow film. 'Although in theory the fire in the main chamber could still be controlled, no human being could survive in there for more than five minutes, even with protective clothing. You see, my latest modifications . . .'

'But the fire could still be put out?' Vanderdecker said. 'How?'

'Indeed,' said the Professor, 'how? No fire-fighting equipment could be taken in there; it would simply melt.'

Vanderdecker smiled. 'Aren't you forgetting something?'

'Very probably,' said the Professor. 'What?'

'I'll give you three guesses,' Vanderdecker replied. 'What's the one thing in the whole world that cannot be destroyed?'

The Professor thought for a moment, remembered the crumpet, and took a dainty bite off the rim of it; there was a crunching sound, as if he was eating a clay pigeon. Then he suddenly beamed. 'My dear fellow,' he said, 'you are of course perfectly correct. How remarkably intelligent of you! But,' he added, 'there would be a certain amount of risk. For all I know . . .'

'Yes, well,' Vanderdecker said. 'Anyway, don't you think we ought to be going?'

'Of course,' said the Professor. 'Yes. Shall we take your helicopter or mine?'

'Whichever you prefer,' said Vanderdecker. 'Look, I hate to hurry you, but . . .'

'Of course. I'll just get a few things. My instruments, and perhaps a flask of coffee . . .'

'No coffee,' said the Flying Dutchman. 'No rich tea biscuits, no drop scones, no Dundee cake. Let's just get a move on, and then we can all have tea.' The Professor, slightly startled, hurried away.

'We'll drop by the ship and pick up the rest of the crew,' Vanderdecker way saying. 'I hope his helicopter's big enough.'

'Just what are you going to do?' Jane demanded.

'Put the fire out,' Vanderdecker replied, 'what do you think? I'm not going all that way to a blazing nuclear reactor just to roast jacket potatoes.'

'But you can't,' Jane said.

'Very probably,' Vanderdecker said – how could he be so calm about it all? – 'but it's worth a go, and I've got nothing else planned.'

'You bloody fool,' Jane screamed, 'you'll get killed!'

'Now then,' said the Flying Dutchman, 'don't let Sebastian hear you talking like that. I don't want to raise the poor lad's hopes.'

'I don't believe it,' Jane said, and realised that she was getting over-excited. An over-excited accountant, like the University of Hull, is a contradiction in terms. Nevertheless. 'You actually want to get killed, don't you?' she exclaimed, and then was silent, mainly because she had unexpectedly run out of breath.

Vanderdecker grinned at her. 'Yes,' he said, 'more than anything else in the whole world. In my position, wouldn't you?'

His eyes met hers, and she seemed to see four hundred years of pointless, agonising existence staring out at her; four hundred years of weeks without weekends, without Bank Holidays, without two weeks in the summer in Tuscany, without Christmas, without birthdays, without even coming home in the evening and kicking off your shoes and watching a good film, just millions of identical days full of nothing at all. She sat down and said nothing else, until long after the helicopter had roared away into the distance. The she started to cry, messily, until her mascara ran down all over her cheeks.

Vanderdecker was not usually given to counting his blessings – not because he was an unusually gloomy person; it was just that he had tried it once, and it had taken him precisely two seconds.

However, he said to himself as the helicopter whirred through a cloud-cluttered sky towards Scotland, there is undoubtedly one thing I can be grateful for; I haven't had to spend the last four hundred odd years in one of these horrible things. Compared to this airborne food processor, the *Verdomde* is entirely first-class accommodation.

The journey had not been devoid of incident. For example, he had been so wrapped up in his thoughts that he hadn't noticed Sebastian sneakily opening the door and jumping out as they soared over the Lake District; in fact, had he not yelled out 'Geronimo!' as he launched himself into the air, they probably wouldn't have noticed his departure, and it would have taken even longer to find him than it did. When at last they managed to locate him, after several tedious fly-pasts of Lake Coniston, he was lodged head-first in the trunk of a hollow tree, and they had to use axes to get him loose.

There was also the smell. Although they were high up in the

sky, their passing gave rise to a wave of seething discomfort and discontent on the ground below, and they had had to skirt round the edges of large towns and cities to avoid mass panic. Even then, an RAF Hercules with which they had briefly shared a few hundred thousand cubic feet of airspace had nearly flown into the Pennines.

But none of these trivial excitements was sufficient to keep the Flying Dutchman from brooding. He was faced, he realised, with a dilemma, a conflict of interests. On the one hand, there was a possibility that his wearisome and unduly extended lifespan would soon be terminated, and although he prided himself on being, in the circumstances, a reasonably well-balanced and sane individual, that would unquestionably be no bad thing. Life had become one long sherry-party, and it was high time he made his excuses and left. But, the problem was the great problem of tedious sherry parties. Just as you can see a way of getting out without actually having to knot tablecloths together and scramble out of a window, you meet someone you actually wouldn't mind talking to – and then, just as you're getting to know them and they're telling you all about whatever it is, it's time to leave and the hostess is coming round prising glasses out of people's hands and switching off the music.

The problem with human life, when it goes on for rather longer than it should do, is boredom. When it's boring and there's nothing to do, it's no fun. Just now, however, Vanderdecker had an uneasy feeling that his life was rather less boring than it had been for quite a number of centuries, and he could fairly certainly attribute the lack of tedium to the influence of that confounded accountant.

He looked out of the helicopter window at Stirling Castle – he had left a hat there in 1742, but they had probably disposed of it by now – and tried to marshal his thoughts. Love? Love was a concept with which he was no longer comfortable. At his age, it did not do to take anything too seriously, and the depressing thing about love was the seriousness which had to go with it, just as these days you couldn't seem to get jumbo sausage and chips in a pub without a salad being thrown in as well. Supposing that a closer acquaintance with Jane Doland could make his life tolerable – that was by no means definitely established, and required the further presupposition that Jane Doland was interested in making his life tolerable, which was as certain as the total abolition of income tax – supposing all that, it remained to be said that Jane Doland would die in sixty-odd years time (a mere Sunday afternoon in Vanderdecker's personal timescale) and then he would be right back where he was, sailing round the world, very smelly, with Johannes and Sebastian and Wilhelmus and the lads. Bugger that for a game of soldiers.

That reminded him: the smell. Even if, by some unaccountable perversity in her nature, Jane were to wish to keep him company, what with the smell and all, that could only be done on board ship, and it surely wasn't reasonable to expect Jane to come and live on the *Verdomde* for the rest of her life. And even if she did, would even her unusually stimulating presence be enough to make life on board that floating tomb anything but insufferable? Be realistic, Vanderdecker. Of course not.

Then hey ho for death by radiation. But try as he might, he could not persuade his intransigent and pig-headed soul to accept the force of these arguments. He needed some final compelling reason, and try as he might, finding one proved to be as difficult as recovering something he had put in a safe place so as not to lose it five years ago. The idea that he was doing all this to save the population of Northern Europe from certain death was a pretty one to bounce about in the abandoned ball-park of his mind, but he had to admit that he couldn't find it in him to regard the Big Sleep with quite the same degree of naked hostility as most of his fellow-creatures. There was also the horrid possibility – quite a strong one, if one calculated the mathematical probability of it – that as soon as he and his fellow non-scientists started fooling about with the works of a nuclear reactor, the whole thing would go off pop, drawing a line under Northern Europe but leaving him and his colleagues with no worse effects than profound guilt. That wouldn't solve anything, now, would it?

The Professor had spent most of the journey with a calculator and a small portable Yamaha organ (to him, interchangeable), fussing over some ingenious calculations or other. Now he had put them away and was nibbling at a rock-cake. It was hard to know whether he was frightened, vacant or just hungry. Vanderdecker caught his eye, and over the roar of the rotor-blades, they had their first sustained conversation for many centuries.

'Well then, Montalban,' said Vanderdecker, with as much good fellowship as he could muster, 'what have you been getting up to since I saw you last?'

The Professor looked at him. 'My work . . .' he said.

'Yes,' Vanderdecker replied, 'but apart from that.'

'Apart from my work?'

'Yes,' Vanderdecker said. 'In your spare time, I mean. Hobbies, interesting people, good films, that sort of thing.'

'I'm afraid I've always been too busy to spare any time for amusements,' said the Professor, and his tone of voice made it clear that he didn't really understand the concepts that Vanderdecker was proposing to discuss, rather as Vanderdecker himself would have felt if someone had buttonholed him for a serious discussion about the forthcoming world tiddlywinks championship.

'You mean you've been too busy?'

'Yes.'

'Working?'

'Yes.'

'I see.' Vanderdecker didn't see at all. For all his sufferings, he had at least had a couple of days off every seven years. He wondered if there was any point in continuing with this conversation, since despite a vague foundation of shared experience he doubted whether he had much in common with his old acquaintance.

'I suppose,' the Professor said uneasily, 'I owe you and your crew an apology.'

Vanderdecker sighed and shook his head. 'Forget it,' he said. 'Two hundred years ago, I might have wanted to break your silly neck for you, but even grudges wear out in time, like Swiss watches. Besides, it was my fault as much as yours.'

'That's very gentlemanly of you,' said the Professor. 'I don't suppose I would have taken such a reasonable view had I been in your position.'

'Think nothing of it,' Vanderdecker said. 'Besides, you are in our position. Well, sort of.' He turned his head and looked out of the window. Sheep. Not exactly enthralling.

'Actually,' the Professor continued, 'there was one thing.'

'Yes?'

'Your life insurance policy,' he said nervously. 'have you considered . . . ?'

'Oh yes,' Vanderdecker remembered, 'that. What about it?'

'Well,' said the Professor, 'as you may be aware. I happen to own the bank that has the risk, and it occurred to me . . . If anything – well, unfortunate, should happen at the power station . . .'

'I see,' Vanderdecker said, trying to keep himself from grinning. 'Yes, of course, there'd have to be a pay-out, wouldn't there? A bit awkward for you, I suppose. Still, that's the insurance business for you.'

'What I was wandering,' said the Professor, 'was who would be entitled to the proceeds? I don't suppose you've made a will, by any chance.'

'No,' said Vanderdecker with restraint. 'I haven't. Rather irresponsible of me, I know, but it really did seem a trifle unnecessary. Well, it's a bit late now, isn't it? Besides, I never could be doing with lawyers. Did you ever meet a lawyer whose life you would willingly have saved in the event of fire? Not me.'

'In which case,' went on the Professor, 'since you have no next of kin and no testamentary heirs, your estate will presumably revert to the public treasury of whichever country you happen to be a citizen of. Would that be Holland, do you know?'

'Search me,' Vanderdecker confessed. 'I'd leave that to the experts, if I were you. I see what you mean about making a will, actually, although I still maintain that forty quid spent on deciding what's going to happen after you're dead is a waste of good beer money. Still, it's not really any of my business, now is it? I mean, I'm not going to be here to see the fun, so what the hell do I care whether the Dutch government or the Lombard government . . .'

'There isn't a Lombard government any more,' said the Professor.

'Isn't there?' Vanderdecker said. 'Oh. Don't mind me, I only read the sports pages. The Italian government, then, who gives a damn? Jolly good luck to them, and I hope they don't fritter it all away on battleships.'

'If you *really* don't care,' said the Professor cautiously, 'then might I suggest that you assign the policy back to the bank? It would save a lot of difficulties, you know. With the economy of the world and everything.'

'Can I do that?' Vanderdecker asked curiously. 'Just say who I want to have it?'

'Very easily,' said the Professor. 'All you would have to do is fill in the little panel on the back of the policy document. Unless you've done so already, of course.'

'I don't know,' Vanderdecker confessed, and he started to rummage about in his wallet again. This time he found a ticket stub for the first night of *Aida* (slept), a library ticket ('Jesus,' Vanderdecker said, 'there'll be some fines to pay on that'), a membership card for White's Coffee House and a white five-pound note before he unearthed the document itself.

'Where's this panel you were talking about?' he said, scanning the vellum carefully. The Professor pointed. It was blank.

'Just here?' he said.

'That's right,' said the Professor.

'And I just fill it in, do I?'

'Precisely, my dear fellow.'

'Got a pen?'

The Professor produced one from his jacket pocket.

'Something to rest on?'

'Here,' the Professor said impatiently, and thrust a book of mathematical tables at him. Vanderdecker thanked him, wrote something in the panel, and signed his name with a flourish. The Professor peered over his shoulder and then stared at Vanderdecker in disbelief. Although the Flying Dutchman's handwriting was usually about as intelligible as Linear A hastily written with his left hand by a drunken scribe, the Professor could clearly see that Vanderdecker had inserted 'Jane Doland' in the Benefit of Policy panel.

'Now then,' Vanderdecker said, 'we'd better put this in a safe place, hadn't we? It's just as well you reminded me, or I'd have had it in my wallet when we went into the power station, and I don't imagine it would have lasted very long in there. When I think how I've been lugging this thing round with me all these years, it's a wonder it's survived this long.' He thought for a moment, and then put it back in his wallet and went forward to have a word with the pilot.

'That's fine,' Vanderdecker said, as he sat down again beside the Professor. 'I explained to the pilot that if I didn't come back he was to post it to Jane, care of Moss Berwick. I don't actually know her address, but I expect it'll reach her there all right. I mean, if you can't trust an accountant, who can you trust?'

'But . . .' spluttered the Professor.

'It was a good thing you mentioned it, you know,' said the Flying Dutchman happily. 'To be honest with you – and this is of course in the strictest confidence – I think Miss Doland is getting rather fed up with her career in accountancy and wouldn't mind spreading her wings a bit. A nice little legacy might come in very handy, I imagine, although I assume she'll have to pay tax on it. Oh I forgot, she's an accountant, they know about that sort of thing. That's all right, then.'

'Do you realise,' said the Professor, 'what you've just done?'

'Yes,' Vanderdecker said.

'No you don't.'

'Actually,' Vanderdecker said through a big smile. 'I do. I've entrusted the economic future of the free world – when I was a boy, the free world was anything Philip of Spain hadn't got his paws on yet, and precious little there was of it too; shows how things don't change much, doesn't it? On balance, though, I think Philip was a better bet than you, if you don't mind me saying so. At least he had interests outside his work. I think he collected the bones of saints, or was that Louis the Ninth? – the economic future of the free world, as I was saying, and all that sort of thing, to a singularly clear-headed and conscientious person, who will be able to look after it much better than either of us. No offence intended, Professor, but you've got rather too much of a vested interest for my liking. And most of all you don't have any hobbies; workaholic, I think they call it now. I never could stand workaholics. We must be nearly there by now.'

Montalban quivered slightly, and then sat back on his hard vinyl-covered seat, breathing heavily. 'You're mad,' he said.

'Sergeant Pepper to you,' Vanderdecker replied affably. 'Also, nuts. Is that Suilven I can see down there? Can't be far now. I'm really rather looking forward to this.'

Below them, the coastal mountains of Caithness ranged up into a bleak, wet sky. The first mate, who had slept soundly ever since the helicopter's rendezvous, with the *Verdomde*, woke up, stretched his arms and said, 'Are we nearly there yet?'

'Nearly,' Vanderdecker said. 'I can't see the sea.'

'Big deal,' grumbled the first mate.

'True,' Vanderdecker said. 'But after it's over I'll buy you a pint. How does that grab you?'

'Thanks, skip,' said the first mate eagerly. 'What exactly is it we're going to do?'

'We're going to put out the fire,' Vanderdecker said.

'Oh.' The first mate frowned. 'Why?'

'Why not?'

'Oh.' The first mate thought about it, and could see no objection. 'And then you'll buy me a pint?'

'If humanly possible, yes.'

'Suits me,' said the first mate. Then he went back to sleep.

Danny Bennett peered through the perspex window of his helicopter and wiped away the little patch of view-obscuring condensation that his breath had formed on it. A BAFTA award, certainly, but probably posthumous. It looked decidedly hairy down there.

It hadn't exactly been easy getting here. Even after he had managed to persuade Neville, the helicopter-flying stockbroker sidekick of megalomaniac academic Professor Montalban, to pilot the spare chopper – the gun had helped, of course, but he had still had to work at it – there had been the problem of persuading the camera crew to participate in the biggest scoop since Watergate. They had been rather less easy to persuade, since they were under the impression that possession of a valid union card made them bulletproof, and he had had to resort to bribery. In fact, he had pledged the Corporation's credit to a quite disastrous extent – tuppence on a colour licence would only just cover it – and had Harvey not backed him up and said he would square it with the Director-General the whole thing would have fallen through. Harvey, clearly, was so overjoyed at the thought of Danny Bennett flying to certain death that he was ready to break the habit of a lifetime and agree to authorise expenditure.

Still, here they were and there was the story, unfolding itself in vivid sheets of orange flame below them. On Danny's knee rested a quite exquisite Meissen geiger counter, borrowed from Montalban's study, and at the moment the needle was still a millimetre or so clear of the red zone. Probably far enough. Danny communicated with the pilot, and told the cameraman to roll 'em.

Danny peered out through the perspex once again. Vander-decker's helicopter had touched down about half a mile away, just outside the red zone – pity he hadn't been able to get an interview with him, but there it was – and the small party had scrambled out of it and started to trudge towards the distinctly unfriendly-looking power station complex. Even as he wittered frenetically into his pocket tape recorder, Danny's eyes were fixed on his targets, as he expected them at any moment to dissolve into little whiffs of gamma particles (Danny's knowledge of nuclear physics was mainly drawn from reruns of Buck Rogers). He glanced across at the cameraman to make sure that the Aaten was pointing where it should. It was. Would the radiation cock up the film? Well, too late to worry about that now. Better by far to have filmed and lost then never to have filmed at all.

'They're approaching the main entrance now,' he muttered into his pocket memo, his voice as high and agitated as a racing commentator's. 'They haven't been burned to death yet, but surely it can only be a matter of time. And who can doubt that the question on their lips – if they still have lips at this moment, of course – is, what reforms to the nuclear power station inspectorate can the Government propose now if they are to retain any credibility whatsoever in the eyes of the nation? Did anyone in Downing Street know that this was likely to happen? Was there a cover . . . ?'

Before he could say 'up', there was a deafening roar, and the helicopter was jolted by a violent gust of air as the front part of the power station collapsed in a cloud of smoke and yellow flames. The Meissen geigercounter started to play 'Lilliburlero', which was presumably its quaint, Augustan way of signifying danger. Danny stared but there was nothing to see, just swirling clouds of smoke. He turned away and told Neville to take the chopper out of there fast.

'Did you get all that?' he asked the cameraman breathlessly. The cameraman looked at him.

'Oh sod it,' he said, 'forgot to take the lens cap off. Only kidding,' he added quickly, as Danny's face twisted into a mask of rage and his hand moved to the butt of the gun. 'Can't you take a joke all of a sudden?'

'No.' Danny snapped. 'That's my award you've got in that thing, so for Christ's sake stop farting around.' The strains of 'Lilliburlero' had died away, and the elegant needle was back out of the red zone. 'Right, Neville,' he shouted at the front of the helicopter, 'let's go back and have another look.'

Neville shook his head. 'No can do,' he shouted back. 'No fuel. Sorry.'

Danny swore. 'What do you mean, no fuel?'

Neville pointed at what Danny assumed was the fuel gauge, although for all he knew it could be the tape deck, and shrugged.

'You clown!' Danny shouted. 'The story of the decade and you choose this moment to run out of petrol.'

'It's not petrol,' said Neville, 'it's aviation fuel.'

'I don't care if it's methylated spirits,' Danny yelled. 'Go somewhere where we can get some more and be quick about it.'

Neville consulted a map. 'Inverness,' he said.

Danny, who had been to Inverness, shuddered, but there was nothing he could do. 'All right,' he said, 'but get on with it.'

As the helicopter turned, Danny peered frantically out of the back window, and could just see the bright glow of a burning power station through a miasma of black clouds.

'Don't go away,' he said, 'we'll be right back after the break.'

★ ★ ★

Just another day at Broadcasting House. In the rather battered and uncomfortable suite assigned to the lost sheep who run Radio Three, a harassed-looking man in what had been, thirty years ago, quite an expensive tweed jacket told the listening public that they had just been listening to a sonata by Berg. Long ago, when the jacket had been new and the world had been young and not quite such a miserable place, someone out there might have cared.

The harassed-looking man announced Schubert's 'Unfinished Symphony', took off his earphones and fumbled in his pocket for his packet of peppermints. All gone. Damn.

'George.'

The door of the studio had opened – a curious event during working hours. Had someone lost his way looking for the lavatory? No, for the stranger had spoken his name. George turned his head.

'News flash, George. We interrupt this programme, and all that.'

'Fancy,' George said. 'The last time I did one of these was poor dear President Kennedy. What's up this time?'

'Nuclear power station in Scotland's blown up,' he was informed. George raised an eyebrow.

'Well, now,' he said, 'how dreadful.'

'Indeed.'

'I mean,' George said, 'we'll have to reorganise the whole afternoon schedule. After all,' he explained, 'I'm sure there'll be lots and lots of these little bulletins as the long day wears on, and that'll make it impossible to play the Bartok. Can't play Bartok with holes in it, it's not right.'

'Well absolutely.'

'I'm glad you agree,' George replied. 'Have they come up with a revised schedule?'

'No, George, they haven't,' he was told. 'I imagine they've been too busy playing at being journalists to give any thought to anything so important.'

'Now, now,' George said, frowning, 'there's no call for sarcasm. You'd better leave it all to me, and I'll just have to cobble something together.'

'That's fine, then,' said George's interlocutor. 'I'll leave it all up to you. Let no one say you didn't stay calm and do your bit in the crisis.'

'Thank you.'

'Like the orchestra on the *Titanic*.'

'Thank you.'

'Don't mention it.' The door closed, and George thought for a moment. In the background the music played, but the only effect it had on George was to inspire the reflection that the 'Unfinished Symphony' would be used to it by now, and he could safely take it off in a moment to read the news flash. What could he think of for an impromptu programme with interruptions?

From a purely aesthetic point of view, it would be appropriate at this stage to describe the interior of the power station in which Vanderdecker, Montalban, the crew of the *Verdomde*, and a cat of indeterminate breed are just now wandering about. However, there is such a thing as the Official Secrets Act, and authors don't like prison food. Take Oscar Wilde, for example.

'What,' Vanderdecker asked as he opened a curtain door leading to a certain room in a building, 'did you have to bring that cat for?'

'Guinea-pig,' replied Montalban through the charred wisps of fabric that had once been a handkerchief held in front of his nose. The first mate frowned.

'What, to catch one, you mean?'

Montalban stopped in his tracks and turned round. 'To catch one of what?' he asked.

'A guinea-pig,' replied the first mate. 'Is that why you brought the cat?'

Montalban smiled. 'No, no, you don't quite seem to follow,' he said. 'The cat is a guinea-pig.'

'No it's not,' the first mate replied, 'it's a cat.'

'That's right,' Vanderdecker said hastily, 'it's a cat, isn't it, Montalban? Are you still wearing your reading glasses?'

'The cat,' said Montalban slowly, 'is here to perform the function of a guinea-pig.'

The first mate's frown remained as constant as the Northern Star. 'You mean, running round inside a little wheel or something?'

'Yes,' replied the Professor; he was a quick learner. 'If necessary.'

'I see,' said the first mate, and added, 'Why?'

'Because,' explained the Professor, and reached into his pocket for another handkerchief. Unfortunately, there wasn't one. Nor was there a pocket. There wasn't, in fact, a fibre of cloth among the whole party; just hot but invulnerable flesh.

'Stuffy in here, isn't it?' said Wilhelmus. 'Can't we open a window?'

'Not really,' Vanderdecker said. 'A bit counterproductive, that would be. Look, isn't it about time we started doing something, instead of just wandering about like this?'

'If you'll just bear with me a little longer,' the Professor said, 'I hope to be in a position to make a final assessment of the extent of the problem facing us.'

A large and jagged slab of masonry dislodged itself from the roof and fell heavily onto the precise spot Sebastian would have been standing on if Vanderdecker hadn't rather unceremoniously moved him. Sebastian scowled and muttered something under his breath.

'Right, then,' said the Flying Dutchman positively. Deep inside he could feel himself starting to get angry. The last time he had been angry was many years ago, when, thanks to a series of accidents and coincidences, he had wandered into the middle of the Battle of Trafalgar just as the French were on the point of victory, and a cannonball from a French ship of the line had smashed a hole in the *Verdomde*'s last barrel of Indian Pale Ale. The Flying Dutchman had felt guilty about what happened next ever since, and the sight of Nelson's Column always made him feel slightly ill.

'Where are you going?' Montalban asked.

'Never you mind,' Vanderdecker replied. 'Just lend me that cat for a moment, will you, and then you can go away and have a nice cup of tea or something. Cornelius, Sebastian, you follow me. The rest of you stay here.'

Montalban handed over the cat, which was growling slightly, and watched helplessly as the Flying Dutchman stalked off through a door whose existence is not explicitly acknowledged. The door closed, and a moment later flew open again as the room beyond it blew up.

'Now *now*, Sebastian,' roared a voice from the heart of the flames.

'Oh dear,' Montalban said. 'I really don't think he should have gone in there.'

The other members of the crew tried to peer through the cloud of smoke, flame and debris, but it was impervious to sight. They could, however, hear loud banging noises.

'Antonius, Johannes, Wilhelmus, Pieter, Dirk, Jan Christian! Over here, quick as you like!' came a thunderous command. 'Cornelius, grab the cat!'

Montalban was left standing alone in the middle of a burning room. He didn't like it much. It was unnerving, what with the falling masonry and everything, and he hadn't had a rock cake in five hours.

'Wait for me,' he said.

Jane had always hated Ceefax. It wasn't just the way the blasted thing played 'That's Entertainment' on the electronic organ at you while listing the latest casualties in the Mexican earthquake; it wasn't even the mule-like persistence with which it kept giving you a recipe for chicken à la king when you wanted the weather forecast. It was the little numbers at the top of the screen that really made Jane want to scream. She was alone in the house, and there were no neighbours close enough to be disturbed. She screamed.

Then she pulled herself together again and pressed some buttons on the remote control. Back to the index. Yes. Fine. Stay with it. News Update – 351. Key in 351. Today's recipe is Tournedos Rossini. Eeeeeeeeek!

Try the other channel, said a little voice inside Jane's head. It'll be just as bad, but the recipe may be different. She tried the other channel and found the index number for News Update. She pressed the necessary buttons. She got the Australian Football results.

A person could make a fortune, she decided, reinventing the carrier pigeon. Or smoke signals. Craftily, she went back to the main index and keyed in the code for the recipe. There was a flicker of coloured light, the television sang 'I Did It My Way' and she got the Australian Football results. Melbourne, it seemed, was having a good run this season. Come on, you reds.

Perhaps, Jane reflected, it won't be on the news at all. What if Harvey and his colleagues have organised a total news blackout? Was that why he had driven away in such a hurry just after the helicopters took off? Jane was a child of the media age, and there lurked in the back of her mind the instinctive belief that if a thing wasn't on the news, it couldn't really have happened after all. So if Harvey could keep it off the air, perhaps the whole thing could unhappen, like a film projector with the film in backwards. No. Unlikely.

Jane put down the remote control and wandered over to the window. Outside it was raining, that slow, gentle, extremely wet Cotswold rain that once used to turn watermills and was somehow or other connected with the rise of the wool trade. History had never been her best subject at school, and the wool trade had been the armpit of History as far as she was concerned, and so she found it hard to remember the details. What could rain possibly have to do with wool? Did it make the ground so soggy that you couldn't keep cows because of foot-rot, so you had to keep sheep instead? Was rain connected with the wool trade at all? Had there ever been a wool trade? Yes, because she had met someone who had been involved in it. The Wool Trade, the Hanseatic League, the Spanish Netherlands, all that bit between Richard the Lion-Heart and Charles I, in the margins of which she had drawn little racing-cars. Strange, to think that one man could have seen all that.

There was that song, she remembered. We joined the Navy to see the world, and what did we see? We saw the sea. And the Atlantic isn't romantic and the Pacific isn't terrific and the Black Sea isn't what it's cracked up to be. The poor man. It must have been awful for him.

One thing in history that had registered with her was Robert the Bruce and the spider, because she was terrified of spiders. Back to the Ceefax, then, and let's have one more go. Carefully, Jane selected the required index numbers for the Australian Football results and keyed them in. She got the Australian Football results, while the unseen orchestra played 'They Call The Wind Maria'.

Like St Paul on the road to Damascus, Jane suddenly understood. Nobody else did, but she understood. Standing there in her stockinged feet in a sitting room outside Cirencester, Jane Doland had single-handedly solved one of the most inscrutable mysteries of the twentieth century. She knew why they played background music to Ceefax, and the principle by which it was selected.

All she needed to find now was the Professor's decoder, but that wasn't going to be easy. Given Montalban's love of camou-flage, it could be anything; the Georgian tea service, the Dresden shepherdess, the ormulu clock, the little black box labelled 'Decoder' . . .

With trembling hands, she plugged it in and switched it on. As the television set launched into 'Thank Heaven For Little Girls', there was a buzzing noise from the box, a whistling, a hissing, and then a mechanical Dalek voice started to speak.

'Melbourne,' said the voice, 'sixteen. Perth nil.'

'Damn,' said Jane, and in a sudden access of fury she snatched up the remote control and dashed it to the floor. There was a snowstorm of coloured lights on the screen, and the news headlines appeared.

Jane peered at them. Latest on Dounreay crisis. Evacuation proceeding in orderly fashion. No cause for alarm as yet. Questions in the House. So that was how Harvey was handling it. How terribly unimaginative of him.

Then she caught the subdued muttering of the Dalek in the black box. It was urging the world to buy. Buy equities, it was saying. Buy gilts. Buy municipal bonds. Buy short-dated government stocks. Buy breweries, industrials, communications, chemicals, entertainments, even unit trusts. Buy.

Jane's jaw dropped, and then she picked up the remote control, made a wish, and threw it at the wall. She got the City News. So that's how it's done.

Share prices, she discovered, were going through the roof. FT All Share Index reaches all time peak. Dow Jones explodes in buying frenzy. Hang Seng hangs loose. What, Jane asked, is going on?

The decoder wasn't much help this time: it just kept on repeating its command to buy. Buy Czarist government securities. Buy South Sea Company five per cent Unsecured Loan Stock. A fat lot of help the decoder was being. Jane shrugged and went to look for a wireless.

She eventually found a portable in the kitchen and tuned it to Radio Three. We apologise for the continued interruption to the scheduled programme, it was saying, owing to the Dounreay crisis. Meanwhile, we continue with our impromptu Gilbert and Sullivan medley, and now let's hear 'Three Little

Maids From School' from the D'Oyly Carte company's 1956 recording of *The Mikado*.

The decoder raised its voice to a hysterical scream, conjured the world in the bowels of Christ to buy De Lorean 25p Ordinary Shares, and blew up. Jane shook her head several times, switched off the radio and the television, and went to the kitchen for a cup of tea.

The cat was having a thoroughly rotten time. It was hot, there were no mice, and slabs of pre-stressed concrete kept falling on its head. On the other hand, it had managed to get away from those lunatics with the silly names.

In that ineffably feline way cats have, it arched its back, stretched, flexed its claws and started to stroll quietly, a cat walking by itself. Four centuries of existence had taught it a sort of unthinking optimism. Although the odds against it seemed long, there might be mice somewhere, or birds, or even a decomposing chicken carcass. In this room here, for instance.

In the room there was a table, and on the table was a square white thing which the cat failed to recognise as a computer console. Made of the very latest space-age materials, it had not yet melted. It had been designed to withstand extremes of temperature which would long since have carbonised diamonds. This was necessary, because this was no ordinary playing-video-games computer, but the main instrument panel for the whole complex. Anything that was still capable of working inside this inferno was operated from here.

But the cat wasn't to know that. To the cat, it looked like a nice place to curl up and sleep. With a delicate little hop, the cat jumped onto the table and made its way to the centre of the console, its velvet-padded paws resting ever so lightly on the many labelled keys. The cat turned round three times, lay down and went to sleep.

★ ★ ★

'Sebastian!' Vanderdecker yelled. 'Over there, to your left.'

Sebastian looked round and saw the little patch of flame which was evidently distressing his commander. He stamped on it until it went out.

They had been at it for hours, and they weren't making much headway. It was a big building, and most of it was on fire, and it takes time to beat out flames with nothing but your bare hands and feet. Meanwhile the needle on the Professor's geiger counter (this one was enclosed in a Fabergé egg) was slowly creeping higher. Not galloping, just creeping. Not galloping yet.

'Look, Montalban,' Vanderdecker gasped, 'are we getting anywhere or not? This is not a time for conventional politeness.'

'I'm afraid not,' the Professor said. 'The fire is too widespread. There just isn't time to put it out this way.'

Vanderdecker nodded. 'So?'

'Well,' Montalban replied, 'there doesn't seem to be very much point in our staying here, does there?'

Vanderdecker shook his head vigorously. 'The hell with you,' he said. 'There has to be something we can do.' He jumped on a patch of fire, more to relieve his feelings than for any other motive.

'Unfortunately . . .' The Professor was suddenly quiet. The Fabergé egg started to tinkle out 'The Blue Danube'. 'Oh dear,' he muttered sadly.

'Now what?'

'Situation critical,' Montalban replied. 'Such a pity.'

'All right, all right,' Vanderdecker shouted, 'why don't you do something for a change instead of going all to pieces like that?' And he looked round for somebody to shout at. Just then, the first mate came up.

'Skip,' he said. 'I've lost the cat.'

'The what?'

'The cat. The guinea-pig. Whatever.'

'Really?' Vanderdecker growled. 'What a bloody cataclysm!

All right, let's go and look for the perishing cat. I'm getting bored just standing here.'

The first mate said that he had last seen it over there, so they went that way. And, in due course, they arrived at the door of the room with the computer console on it.

'What's in here?' Vanderdecker asked, curiously. 'It doesn't seem as badly damaged as the rest of it all.'

'It's the computer room,' Montalban replied. 'Everything in here is the state of the art in heat-resistance technology . . . Shoo!'

'Bless you,' Vanderdecker said instinctively, but the Professor wasn't sneezing. He was getting the cat off the console.

'That explains it,' he said. 'That dratted animal has pressed all the wrong buttons.' Montalban typed frantically for a moment, but the needle on the Fabergé egg continued to rise and 'The Blue Danube' was getting faster and faster. 'It's switched off most of the failsafe mechanisms,' Montalban explained crossly. 'You *naughty* boy!' he said. The cat looked at him.

'So that's it, is it?' Vanderdecker asked. 'There really is nothing we can do?'

'We could leave,' the professor suggested, 'before the entire complex blows up, with a force approximately nine hundred times that of the Hiroshima and Nagasaki bombs put together. I think in the circumstances that leaving would be extremely prudent.'

'Fine,' Vanderdecker said. 'You just shove off, then. I think I'll stay here for a bit.' He kicked the table.

'Well, goodbye then,' Montalban said, 'it was so nice to have seen you again. Do drop in if ever you happen to be passing.'

The Fabergé egg had stopped playing 'The Blue Danube' and struck up 'The Minute Waltz'. Montalban dropped it, screamed, and fled.

'Here, Captain,' said Sebastian. Vanderdecker turned round and looked at him. He was standing by a small door like a safe-deposit box with a lurid black and red skull and crossbones stencilled on it. 'Pirates?' he suggested.

'Very possibly, Sebastian,' said the Flying Dutchman, 'very possibly.'

'Good,' Sebastian said. 'I always loved pirates,' then he opened the door and walked in. There was a searing flash of blue light, and the world was blotted out.

Half an hour later, Sebastian got up. He looked around, pinched himself, and swore.

'All right then,' he said to the sky, which was visible through a large hole in the ceiling. 'I give up. Forget it. You win.'

He realised he was still holding the handle of the door. The rest of the door was nowhere to be seen. Then he noticed something else. He sniffed.

'Hello,' said the voice from under the fallen lump of ceiling. 'Is anybody there?'

'Is that you captain?'

'Yes. Sebastian?'

'Captain,' Sebastian said, and his voice was rather shaky, 'I don't think I smell any more. Do you think I smell, skip?'

'I don't know, Sebastian. I'm not sure. Perhaps if you got this slab of concrete off me, I might be able to give you a considered opinion.'

Sebastian thought for a moment, and then went to get the others. This took time, as some of them were similarly covered in architecture, but eventually they were all assembled and together they heaved Vanderdecker out from under the slab.

'Thanks,' he said, brushing dust off himself. 'You're right, Sebastian, you don't. Has anyone seen my egg?'

'Which egg?'

'The shiny stone egg that plays tunes, Antonius.'

'Oh,' said the first mate, 'that egg. Here you are.'

'Thank you.' Vanderdecker looked at it for a moment. 'Well,' he said, 'fancy that. Maybe it's just broken.' He shook it vigorously. The needle stayed resolutely on Normal.

'In fact,' Vanderdecker said, 'none of us do.'

'Do what, skip?'

'Smell, Antonius. The smell would seem to have disappeared. Isn't that jolly?'

There was a ripple of whispering, and the crew of the *Verdomde* sniffed at each other. Then they started to cheer.

All except Antonius, the first mate. He would have cheered, but something was puzzling him. As always, when he was puzzled he consulted his captain.

'Skipper,' he said, 'why don't we smell anymore?'

'That,' Vanderdecker replied, 'is the thousand moidore question. Why indeed? I can only imagine . . .'

'Yes?' Antonius said, his eyes alight with anticipation. Vanderdecker didn't reply. He was frowning too.

'Well anyway,' he said. 'I owe you a pint.'

'Why, skipper?'

'I promised I'd buy you a . . .'

'No,' said Antonius, 'not that. Why have we stopped smelling?'

'I don't know,' Vanderdecker confessed. 'I really don't. Nor do I know why the power station has stopped burning and the radioactivity has dropped down to its normal ambient level. I'd ask the professor, only he isn't here. It's a real mystery, if you ask me.'

'Oh.' Antonius's face had caved in. 'You *sure* you don't know?'

Vanderdecker suddenly felt terribly guilty. 'Of course,' he said. 'I'm only guessing, but purely off the top of my head it would just be that we took the full black of the explosion when Sebastian inadvertently opened some sort of pressure lock and triggered off the nuclear reaction, and that all the radiation crashing into our systems carried out some sort of molecular change that counteracted the molecular change that took place when we drank the elixir in the first place. Meanwhile, the sheer force of the explosion, which must have used up all the available oxygen inside the place, just snuffed out the flames and furthermore triggered off some sort of chain reaction which somehow or other reprocesses away all the loose radiation which had escaped previously. And here we all are. Do you see what I'm getting at?'

'No,' said Antonius happily. 'But if that's what you say happened, that's good enough for me and the lads. Isn't it, lads?'

The lads, of course, hadn't been listening. They were too busy cheering and yelling and generally not smelling horrible to listen to anything. But Vanderdecker had thought of something; what if the reaction had indeed reversed the effects of the elixir? And they were now all mortal again?

'I wonder,' he said to himself.

'What's that, skipper?' Antonius asked, and Vanderdecker pigeonholed the immortality question. He was just starting to realise what life without the 'smell' could possibly mean. So maybe he wasn't immortal any longer. Maybe. There was no need to put it to the test immediately, now was there?

'I was wondering,' Vanderdecker said, 'where we can get a pint or so of beer in these parts.'

'And some clothes, skip,' Antonius said. 'We haven't got any. They got burnt,' he explained.

'So they did,' replied the Flying Dutchman. 'We'd better get some more, hadn't we?'

'Good idea, skip,' Antonius said. 'Where?'

Vanderdecker smiled. 'Tell you what, Antonius,' he said. 'You think of something.'

'Me?'

'Yes, you.'

'Oh.' Antonius considered. 'I don't know,' he said.

'Don't you?' said the Flying Dutchman. 'Sorry, I thought you were just going to volunteer to walk over to the nearest evacuated village, break a few windows, and come back with some clothes for us. Wasn't that what you were just going to suggest?'

'No,' Antonius replied truthfully.

'Well,' Vanderdecker said, 'what do you think of it, as a suggestion? You can be honest with me if you think it's no good.'

'I'll give it a shot, skipper,' Antonius said. 'Which way to the village?'

CHAPTER
FOURTEEN

'No,' said Mrs Mackay firmly. 'Go away'.

'Now look,' said the policeman, 'you really will have to leave now, Mrs Mackay. It's just not safe to stay here.'

Mrs Mackay considered this for a moment. 'Have you been listening to my daughter in Edinburgh?' she asked suspiciously. 'Catriona?'

'I didn't know you had a daughter in Edinburgh, Mrs Mackay.'

'A likely story.' Mrs Mackay sniffed. 'She doesn't really want me to go and live with them – not that I would, let me tell you, not if I were starving in the gutter. It's this house she's after, of course; well, you can just tell her that if she thinks she's going to lure me out of my own house where I was born and then put me in a home in Edinburgh . . .'

'Now look . . .'

'And you should be ashamed of yourself,' Mrs Mackay went on, 'conniving with the likes of her. Call yourself a policeman? Go away!'

She slammed the door, and the policeman closed his eyes

and counted to ten. Would it really matter terribly much, said a voice under his cap, if the silly old bag did get burnt to death in a radiation storm?

'Mrs Mackay,' he shouted through the letter box. 'Now I've wasted enough time as it is, so unless you open this door . . .'

Just then, a party of naked men walked past.

'Unless you open this door, I'm going to have to break it down, do you understand me? So wouldn't it be much better all round if . . .'

'Excuse me,' said one of the naked men. He had a cat under his arm.

'One moment sir,' said the policeman, not looking round. 'Mrs Mackay . . .' Then something connected in his brain. He turned round and stared.

'Have you seen a man with no clothes on wandering about looking lost?' asked the naked man. 'You see, we sent him to find some clothes, but he really shouldn't be out on his own, he's not terribly bright. He's about five foot four, black hair . . .'

'Dark brown,' interrupted another naked man.

'Thank you, Sebastian, dark brown hair, thick beard, blue eyes – I think they're blue but to tell you the truth I never was very interested, so I may be wrong.'

The policeman rubbed his eyes and forehead. 'Are you from the rigs?' he asked.

'I beg your pardon?'

'The oil rigs.'

'No,' said the naked man, 'no, we're not from the oil rigs. I would imagine they were all evacuated some time ago. I take it you haven't seen him.'

The policeman nodded. It seemed to use up most of his available strength.

'Oh well,' said the naked man, 'thanks anyway. Oh, and by the way, the crisis is over, you can bring everyone back now, it's safe.'

'Safe?'

'Yes,' said the naked man, 'look.' He held up a blue egg-shaped pebble and pointed to it. 'There, see,' he said, 'back to normal residual radiation levels.' He walked over to Mrs Mackay's letter-box, lifted the flap, and shouted through it, 'It's all right now, you don't have to go, panic's over.'

'Are you a doctor?' said Mrs Mackay's voice on the other side of the door.

'No,' said the naked man. 'My name is Vanderdecker.' An idea seemed to occur to him, and he said, 'Do you by any chance have any men's clothes we could borrow? There are fourteen of us.'

The policeman started to protest, but the effort was too much for him. He sat down on the step and looked carefully at the soles of his shoes.

'Fourteen?' said Mrs Mackay. 'Are you the Salvation Army?'

'Not really,' Vanderdecker replied. 'but we would be very grateful if . . .'

'Go away,' said Mrs Mackay.

'All right, then,' said Vanderdecker, 'be like that.'

He came away from the door, and one of the naked men whispered something in his ear. He nodded and approached the policeman.

'Excuse me,' he said. The policeman looked up. 'Now then,' he went on, 'am I right in thinking that you're a police officer?'

The policeman thought hard and then nodded. Vanderdecker smiled.

'That's good,' he said. The policeman thanked him. 'Now,' Vanderdecker continued, 'my friends and I are just going to break into that shop over there.' He pointed to the small, stone-built house across the narrow main street. There was a sign by the gate that read Local handicrafts and tweeds. 'But,' Vanderdecker went on, 'please don't think that we're looting, because we're not. It's just that we lost all our clothes in the power station and we're beginning to feel a bit conspicuous. So that'll be all right with you, now won't it?'

The policeman said that he supposed so. Vanderdecker smiled again. It was a friendly, comforting sort of smile, implying that here was someone who knew what he was doing. The policeman was grateful.

'Right, that's marvellous,' he said. 'And when the proprietor gets back, will you please ask him to send the bill to Professor Montalban, Greathead Manor, near Cirencester, Gloucestershire? Have you got that? Perhaps you'd better write it down.'

The policeman wrote it down in his notebook and looked up at Vanderdecker, as if asking for his approval. Vanderdecker nodded and turned to walk away. Then he checked himself, and said, 'Oh, by the way.'

'Yes, sir?' said the policeman.

'We don't smell funny, do we?'

'No, sir,' said the policeman.

'You're sure about that?'

'Positive, sir.'

'Absolutely sure? You haven't got a cold or anything?'

'No, sir.'

'And you're not just being polite, are you? We won't be offended, you know, if . . .'

The policeman shook his head vigorously, then sat down on the step again, buried his face in his hands and started to hum softly. He looked rather tired, and it had been a long week, what with the power station blowing up and his grandmother dying and his wife insisting on a trial separation.

'Fine,' Vanderdecker said. 'Now, Sebastian, Jan Christian, find a stone or a lump of wood, something we can use as a battering ram. Dirk, will you just hold this cat for me? Watch out, it scratches if you're not careful. Come along now, we haven't got all day.'

About twenty minutes later, Vanderdecker and the crew of the *Verdomde* came out of the craft shop. They were all wearing more or less identical clothes – Shetland wool pullovers, hairy tweed jackets, caps and kilts – except that where all the others' pullovers had a design of little white sheep on them, Vanderdecker's had a single black and white panda, like some sort of military badge of rank.

'Now,' Vanderdecker said, 'all we've got to do is find Antonius.'

'Easier said than done,' Sebastian muttered. He had wanted the panda, and he was blatantly sulking.

'True,' Vanderdecker admitted. 'But all we've got to do is imagine we're idiots too, and then we can sort of reconstruct his thought processes.'

Just then, Antonius himself appeared. He was wearing a quiet grey suit under a dufflecoat. He stared.

'Hello, skip,' he said. 'I went back to the power station but you'd all gone. Why are you all wearing those funny . . . ?'

'Hello, Antonius,' Vanderdecker said briskly. 'Right, now let's all go and have that drink, shall we?' He sighed and walked over to where the policeman was still sitting.

'Excuse me,' he said.

The policeman opened his eyes and shuddered.

'Sorry to bother you again,' Vanderdecker said, 'but can you by any chance tell us where we can get a drink around here?'

The policeman pointed down the street to a building labelled Hotel. Vanderdecker thanked him. 'Maybe you'd like to join us,' he added. 'You look like you could use a drink.'

'No!' said the policeman forcefully. 'Never again.' Then he got up and started to run. Vanderdecker shrugged.

'Be like that,' he said. 'Now then, the drinks are on me.'

The crew of the *Verdomde* hastened away up the street, leaving it entirely deserted. For about five minutes, there was perfect peace and quiet, except for the distant sound of a hotel door being smashed in, and after that, the complete and utter tranquility for which the Highlands of Scotland are so famous. Then there was a clattering, roaring noise as a helicopter swung down low over the village, hovered for a moment, and soared off in the direction of Dounreay Power Station.

Very, very carefully, Professor Montalban picked himself up off the ground and applied his mind.

Being a scientist, he went about things in a systematic and methodical way. He therefore started with his head – yes, that was still there, and it seemed to be functioning properly – then his arms, then his trunk, legs and feet. All present and correct. Good.

Good but extremely surprising. The force of the explosion had been so enormous that he had been certain, in the tenth of a microsecond available for contemplation of the matter, that nothing on earth could possibly have survived it. Well, it only went to show how dangerous it was to jump to purely intuitive conclusions.

Another strange thing was the way the building was still intact. Mostly intact. The huge steel girder that he seemed to remember falling on his head suggested that bits of it had indeed come loose, but what did you expect from modern builders? Nobody seemed to take a pride in their work any more.

Oh, the Professor said to himself, for a cup of tea and a slice of home-made Victoria sponge.

He removed the cinders from his eyes and looked carefully about him. No fire. No smoke. No signs of anything much out of the ordinary. Most peculiar. He wandered away in the direction of the computer room. The sudden violent explosion was puzzling him, and he had a theory he wanted to put to the test.

As I thought, he told himself smugly, examining the wreckage of the plutonium cell. It was his own design, completely revolutionary and top secret; it was also, now, broken. But he didn't mind that.

The question that had been bothering him was what had

made the plutonium go off pop like that, and here, it seemed, was the answer. One of the idiots from the ship had opened the door and gone in. There had been nothing between him (or to be precise, the smell) and the plutonium itself. The plutonium had, in combination with the unique carbon compounds found only in the gases comprising the smell, undergone a rapid chemical reaction and evolved into a completely harmless isotope of itself. Now, since to every action there is an equal and opposite reaction (one of his more felicitous sayings, he always thought), it stood to reason that something had happened to the smell-bearer.

Montalban looked round; there was nothing, not a scrap of bone or a fragment of charred scalp. Nothing. They had obviously just disintegrated, turned back into clouds of carbon, hydrogen and oxygen. Kaput.

Oh dear, said Montalban to himself. He was thinking of the Vanderdecker policy. How terribly awkward.

'Our next programme here on Radio Three,' said the horribly plummy voice Jane had got sick of listening to, 'is Wagner's opera *Die Fliegende Hollander*, broadcast in the 1956 Deutsche Gramophon recording with . . .'

It turned out to be a coincidence, of course. Jane had found the Professor's spare decoder in the bathroom (easily done; she just carried the portable radio around the house and waited until something talked back; in this case, the toilet-roll cover) and all it could make of Wagner's early masterpiece was a jumble of incoherent sounds, with the occasional random word, such as Hippopotamus and Canasta, rising above the noise. She switched them both off, tried Ceefax one more time (Adelaide 6, Darwin 5), and gave the whole thing up as a dead loss.

The longer she waited, her reason told her, the better; so far, no clouds of radioactive dust or great searing flashes of heat had interrupted the calm of a wet Cotswold day, which argued that Dounreay hadn't blown up, or at least not yet. But – Jane couldn't help herself thinking, although God knows it wasn't a particularly nice way to think – that wasn't really the point, now was it? When all was said and done, she wasn't all that bothered about Dounreay and the fate of the North of England, or Europe. Not that she had anything against them, of course; but what she was really worrying about was what had happened to one man.

Crazy. Just suppose he did come back; what then? The best way to get rid of the yearning for something, she had always found, was to imagine what it would be like if the dream came true. Once you imagined that, you usually found that you didn't want the happy ending after all, not at any price, and the technique was particularly sound, in her experience, when it came to men. In the past, when she had felt that dreadful, cloying, having-eaten-too-much-Black-Forest-gateau feeling about someone, she conjured up a vision of living with him, ironing for him, holding things and getting sworn at when he put up kitchen shelves. But in this case, for some reason, it didn't seem to work. Perhaps it was because what she was feeling now wasn't anything like eating too much cake; it was more a sort of understanding of what her life had been about all these years. It had simply been Fate's rather cack-handed way of making sure she was there at the right time in the right place to meet Julius Vanderdecker, the Flying Dutchman. And why, Miss Doland, was that such a good idea? Because. No other reason, just because. If he had been handsome or charming or generally wonderful in some other obvious way, it wouldn't be the same thing at all; because when the wonderfulness had worn off, there wouldn't be anything left except a lot of real life. What Jane liked about Vanderdecker was the way she liked him.

Anyway, Miss Doland, your Vanderdecker is quite probably not coming back, so there. And that, after all, was what he wanted; there was no getting away from the fact. Apparently he doesn't think I'm worth staying around for, and who can blame him? Pull yourself together and have something to eat.

Jane was half-way through a cold chicken salad when the sound of rotor-blades outside the house made her heart explode inside her. Dumping her knife and fork she sprinted out of the door, quite forgetting that she wasn't wearing any shoes until she set foot on the gravel path.

But only one man got out of the helicopter; one man she'd seen before, and who wasn't quite the same, somehow.

'Professor!' she screamed. 'What's happened?'

The Professor ducked under the rotor-blades and walked towards her. He was looking at her rather strangely, but she was too preoccupied to notice.

'Ah,' said the Professor. 'Miss Doland. I'm glad you're still . . .'

'Is he all right?'

'He?' The Professor raised an eyebrow.

'Vanderdecker,' Jane howled. 'Is he all . . . ?'

'Alas,' said the Professor, 'I fear not. A great loss. But I feel sure that . . .'

Jane seemed to deflate, like a balloon, and if it hadn't been for her clothes holding her together she would probably have melted onto the ground, like a collapsing candle. The Professor smiled sympathetically and said, 'There, there.'

'Were you there when it . . . ?'

'Not exactly,' Montalban replied, 'but I feel there can be no doubt in the matter. There was quite simply nothing left. It was what he wanted, you know, and he has unquestionably saved the lives of thousands, if not . . .'

'Oh go to hell,' Jane snapped. 'It's all your bloody fault, anyway.'

Montalban's avuncular air seemed to wobble slightly, like the picture when a pigeon sits on the aerial. 'May I remind you that were it not for my elixir, he would probably have died in the 1570s. I don't think that he . . .'

But Jane wasn't listening. Which was a pity, the Professor

thought, as there really was something rather important they should be taking about. Although he understood pretty well everything else in the universe, from the nature of matter to the music of the spheres, the Professor, as he would have been the first to admit, had never known what to make of women. He shrugged his shoulders slightly, smiled again, and went in search of Eccles cakes.

Jane slowly started to compose herself. This is probably how jellyfish feel, she told herself, no bones. They manage, so I suppose I shall have to manage too. A nuisance, but there it is. Back to work tomorrow morning, and that's the end of your holiday. As she started towards the house, the helicopter pilot ran up to her and put something in her hand.

'Here,' he said, 'this is for you. The other one who smelt so horrible said to give it to you. I don't know what it's all about, but the Professor there was mad keen to get his hands on it. Lucky I was flying the chopper, or I think he'd have tried to grab it off me.'

Jane stared at the worn brown wallet the pilot had handed her. She recognised it, and she could feel something tearing at her insides, doing all sorts of damage to nerves and muscles. She thanked him and walked away.

The policy; she remembered now. He had wanted her to have the policy, keep it safe for him. Well yes, but what good was that now, to anybody? She opened the wallet and found the hard, folded vellum sheet, and breathing was suddenly rather difficult. Under the porch light, she opened it out and looked at it, and her eye fell on the coupon on the back. She read her name, and the signature under it, and that was enough to finish her off. But not, strangely, enough to stop her running after the helicopter pilot and having a word with him.

Inside the house, the Professor was talking on the telephone, his mouth full of Eccles cake. He had been busy; so many people to notify, governments to inform, evacuations to call off, that sort of thing. Now he needed to attend to his own affairs, which were shortly going to be in a rather terrible mess.

He heard the door slam, and put the phone down, ignoring the Minister at the other end of the line. He could wait; Miss Doland couldn't. It was vital that they had a quiet chat immediately.

'Miss Doland,' he called out, 'are you there?'

'Yes,' Jane said, walking into the room. 'I expect you want to have a word with me. Oh, you've got another gun, how nice for you. I'm just going to finish my salad.'

She walked into the kitchen, ignoring the menacing barrel of the Colt .38 that was trained on her, and smothered her lettuce with salad cream. After a few mouthfuls, she became aware that she was not alone.

'Do you mind?' she said. 'It's terribly rude to threaten to kill people while they're eating.'

'Miss Doland,' said the Professor, 'this time I'm afraid I have to be serious. Unless you hand me that policy document immediately, I shall have no option but to shoot you.' He cocked the hammer of the pistol and waited for a reaction. All he got was the sound of crunching radish.

'Wouldn't do that if I were you,' Jane said.

'I'm afraid my patience has run out, Miss Doland,' said the Professor grimly. 'This time . . .'

'You're missing the point,' said Jane, and pointed a half gnawed drumstick at him. 'If you shoot me, it'll cost you a great deal of money.'

'What?'

'Stands to reason,' Jane said, opening a jar of beetroot. 'Now I'm not a lawyer – God forbid – but if I die, I believe the proceeds of the policy will form part of my estate. All clear so far? Good. Now, since I haven't made a will, all my property passes on my death to my next of kin, which will probably be my parents. If you kill them, it'll pass to theirs. I have a large family, Professor Montalban, and if you go around knocking them all off, somebody is going to notice sooner or later and put you away for the rest of your life. Given your rather peculiar circumstances, that all adds up to a hell of a lot of porridge. Have a pickled walnut, they're excellent.'

'No thank you,' said the Professor, 'they give me indigestion. You're overlooking the fact that nobody but you and I know about the assignment of the policy, or even that it exists.'

'Don't count on it,' Jane said through a mouthful of pickled walnut. 'I mean, there's the helicopter pilot, for one.'

'The helicopter pilot?'

'The one who gave me the policy. Nice man. He wrote down the policy number and everything. I also wrote a short letter to my parents enclosing full details, which he said he'd post for me when he got to Yeovilton. He should be nearly there by now. I'm afraid you're stuffed, Professor. Talking of which, have an olive.'

'I do not want an olive, Miss Doland.'

'More fool you, then,' Jane replied. 'It's at times like these you need an olive in order to make sense of things. But I suppose you've been stuffing your face with cakes and biscuits; they're very bad for you, you know.'

The Professor sighed and put the revolver down on the worktop. Then he put the kettle on.

'That's bad for you too, you know,' Jane told him. 'Think of what all that tannin is doing to the lining of your stomach.'

'Academic, Miss Doland,' said the Professor. 'Purely academic. You forget that . . .'

'Hold on,' Jane said, laying down her fork. 'I know you are, and so was he. But you survived.'

'He was nearer the blast than I was,' the Professor said.

'Running away, were you?'

'Yes.' The Professor didn't seem particularly proud of himself.

'Perhaps,' Jane said, 'we could do a deal.'

A tiny part of her, which had been taken by surprise by what her lips had just said, protested; but the rest of her shut it up.

Why else, she thought, had he given her the policy? Might as well get it over with.

'Certainly,' the Professor said quietly. 'What had you in mind?'

'Well, for a start,' Jane said. 'About the rain forests . . .'

Simon Courtenay felt in his pocket for his keys, and then realised that he didn't need them. The door of his hotel was open; and not just ajar, or even standing wide. It was unconditionally open, what was left of it.

He swore. Ever since he had sold his house in Surbiton to buy the Highland hotel of his escapist fantasies, he had been waiting for the moment when the very peculiar natives of this area finally lost control and went berserk. He had often noticed them out of the corner of his eye, staring at him and muttering in Gaelic, but he had hoped that they would refrain from actual violence and damage to property. Well, he should have known better.

From the bar came the sound of drunken singing, and the sound of smashing glass. He considered whether he should call the police, but then remembered that they would be Scottish too, and likely to join in and help their countrymen. It was up to him. He picked up a chair-leg – for some reason there were a lot of chair-legs lying about his premises tonight, very few of them with chairs attached – and walked into the bar.

'We are sailing, We are sailing, Home again, Across the sea,' sang the drunkards in kilts lying around the gutted bar. They each had their own personal bottle of his very expensive and select stock of malt whiskies, except for one who was spilling a lot of beer in the attempt to find his own mouth. Pissed as rats, the lot of them. Disgusting.

'We are sailing, Stormy waters, To be . . .'

'That will do,' Simon said, in his very best stiff-upper-lip manner. 'Out, the lot of you.'

The man with the beer looked at his watch – a pity that his watch should be on the wrist of the hand he was holding the glass in – and said, 'Hell's teeth, is that the time already?' in an accent that Simon couldn't exactly place, but which certainly wasn't Scottish.

'Hang on,' said the man with beer all over his kilt, 'it's only ten-fifteen. Drinking up time,' he added. 'Gimme another pint of Guinness, and have one yourself.'

'If you don't all clear out of here in one minute,' Simon said, 'I'm calling the police.'

'Bloody British licensing laws,' grumbled one of the other drunks. 'God, what a country.'

'Come on,' said the beer-drinker, 'let's be going, I think we've outstayed our . . . Christ, is that the time? Look,' he said to Simon, 'is there a telephone here anywhere?'

Simon pointed to an overturned bookcase. 'Under there,' he said grimly.

The man grinned sheepishly. ''Fraid we've made rather a mess,' he said. 'Sorry about that, but we've just saved the world, you see, and I promised Antonius a drink afterwards.'

'Really,' said Simon. 'James Bond, are you?'

'No,' said the beer-drinker. 'Vanderdecker. Julius Vander-decker.'

'And you've just saved the . . .'

'Scout's honour. Now, let me just make a quick call, and . . .'

Just then, there was the sound of rotor-blades overhead, making the whole building shake. It seemed to go on for a very long time and Simon couldn't bear it, not on top of everything else. He sat down on an overturned Space Invaders machine and started to cry.

Meanwhile, Vanderdecker was yelling into the telephone.

'Jane? Oh, it's you. Is Jane there? She hasn't gone? Yes, it's me. Yes of course I'm alive, they don't have telephones in . . . Well get her, then. Thank you . . . Jane? It's me. Sorry if I've dragged you out of bed or . . . Yes it's *me* and I'm *not* . . . You what? Say that again? Oh, oh that's nice. Look, I've just got to find a helicopter and . . . Hang on, won't be a minute. Yes?' he added, turning to see who had tapped him on the shoulder. He registered something and turned back to the telephone. 'It's all right,' he said, 'it's that telly bloke, you know, Danny something. Bennett? Yes, that's it. God knows what he's doing here.' He turned away from the receiver again. 'Hey, have you got a . . . oh, that's yours outside, is it? Could you get them to turn the bloody thing off, I'm trying to make a call here . . . You still there? Good. Listen, Danny's got a helicopter, we'll be with you soon. Yes, yes, you too. No, there are people listening. Right, see you then.'

He put down the receiver, and stood up.

'I've been looking for you,' Danny said.

'Have you?'

'I thought you were dead.'

'Sorry?'

'I thought you were . . .'

'You'll have to speak up.'

'I THOUGHT you were DEAD.'

Vanderdecker laughed, very loudly. 'You too,' he said. 'Fat chance! Come on, let's be going.' He turned and looked round the room. 'You lot,' he said, 'this bloke's giving us all a lift to Cirencester.'

'Why do we want to go to Cirencester?' asked Pieter Pretorius. 'I've been there, it's a dump.'

'That was in 1647,' Vanderdecker said, 'you'll probably like it now. Come on, all of you who're coming.'

There was some grumbling, but the crew slowly picked themselves up and started to troop out. Danny noticed something.

'Hey,' he said, 'you don't smell any more.'

'Thank you,' said Vanderdecker, 'that's the nicest thing anyone's ever said to me. Well,' he added, remembering, 'almost. Look, do me a favour, will you?'

'Sure,' Danny replied, 'what?'

Vanderdecker pointed to Simon and said, 'Write this bloke a cheque. A thousand ought to cover it.'

'A thousand pounds!' Danny exclaimed. 'Now hang on . . .'

'Oh it's all right,' Vanderdecker said, 'I'll pay you back when we get to Cirencester. I have an idea I'll have a great deal of money when we get to Cirencester. Pieter, grab the cat.'

Danny shrugged and wrote out a cheque for a thousand pounds, which he handed to Simon, who stared at it. He was still staring at it a quarter of an hour later, when the helicopter had gone away again and he was alone in a wrecked bar with a lot of broken chairs, a cheque for a thousand pounds and a geiger counter in the shape of a Fabergé egg.

CHAPTER
FIFTEEN

Inside the helicopter, the party was still going on. It was a bit cramped, and it swayed about rather more (considered objectively) that the hotel in Dounreay, but it was the considered view of the crew of the *Verdomde* that while there was moonlight and laughter and Scotch and romance, they might as well face the music and get pathetically drunk. It wasn't every day, after all, that you escape from a four-hundred-odd-year-old curse.

'Here,' Sebastian was saying to a bulkhead, 'you remember that time in Nijmegen?'

'That wasn't Nijmegen,' Pieter replied, 'that was Antwerp.'

'No it wasn't,' Sebastian retorted. 'Antwerp was when you and me and Wilhelmus got com-*pletely* ratted and went round smashing up all the watchmakers' shops.'

'Exactly,' Pieter said, nodding vigorously, 'that was Antwerp, not Nijmegen.'

'That's what I just said.'

'You said Nijmegen.'

'Hold on,' Wilhelmus interrupted. 'Nijmegen – *Nijmegen* was when we nicked that old girl's donkey and Jan Van Hoosemyr . . .'

'*I know*,' said Sebastian angrily. 'That's what I was trying to say. That was Nijmegen. Antwerp was when we smashed in all the watchmakers' . . .'

'But you just said . . .'

The camera crew looked at each other.

'Reminds me of that time in Tripoli,' said the cameraman.

In fact, the only sober Dutchman on board the helicopter was Vanderdecker, and he was beginning to wonder if sobriety and a clear head were a good idea after all. Danny was trying to interview him, and he was finding it rather wearing.

'So when did you first suspect,' Danny was saying, 'that there had been a cover-up?'

Vanderdecker yanked his mind back to what Danny was saying. 'Cover-up?' he said. 'Oh, sorry, I was miles away. What cover-up?'

'*The* cover-up,' Danny snapped. 'When did you first become aware of it?'

'Just now,' Vanderdecker said, 'when you mentioned it. Shows what a good cover-up it was, doesn't it?'

Danny ground his teeth. 'We'll do that bit again,' he said, and would the tape back. 'Look, will you please try and concentrate on what I'm saying?'

'Sorry,' Vanderdecker said, and realised that since Danny was being kind enough to give him a lift to Cirencester, he ought to say something at least. 'You mean *that* cover-up.'

Danny's hairs bristled. 'You mean there was more than one?'

Vanderdecker laughed. 'You bet,' he said.

'Such as?'

'Where do I start?' Vanderdecker said. 'I mean, we are talking yesterday's witness here.' He leaned forward conspiratorily. 'For example,' he whispered. 'I bet you still think Columbus discovered America.'

Danny couldn't believe his ears. 'And didn't he?'

Vanderdecker smiled cynically. 'Don't you believe it,' he said. 'The Portuguese landed in what is now Florida seventy years before Columbus left Spain. But there was this . . .'

'Cover-up?'

'Exactly,' Vanderdecker said. 'On the tip of my tongue it was, yes, cover-up.'

'Why?'

'Merchandising,' Vanderdecker said. 'I mean, just think for a moment, will you? Think of all the spin-offs from discovering a new continent. America cart bumper stickers, America doublets, the official America cuddly bison; no, as soon as the Portuguese realised what they'd got hold of, they saw that unless they got the franchising side of it sorted out before the story broke, there was going to be absolute chaos, marketing-wise. So they sat on it while the lawyers sorted out the contractual basis. And you know what lawyers are like; by the time they'd got down to a preliminary draft joint venture agreement, Columbus had landed and the whole thing was up the spout.'

Danny's brain reeled. 'How do you know all that?' he said. 'That was before your time, wasn't it?'

'Or take the Gunpowder Plot,' Vanderdecker said quickly. 'I could tell you a thing about that, make no mistake.'

'Go on,' said Danny, changing tapes. 'I always thought . . .'

'I mean,' Vanderdecker went on, 'Guido Fawkes was set up. He was the biggest fall guy of all time. You won't find anything about it down at the Public Records Office, but there was big money involved there all right. Oh yes.'

'So?'

'So it was only a conspiracy by Buckingham and Salisbury to get hold of the biggest monopoly of them all. I mean the big one. None of your fooling about with Rhenish wine this time; I'm talking . . .' He stopped, and searched for the right word. '. . . Megagroats.'

'What was it?'

Vanderdecker looked over his shoulder. 'Milk,' he hissed. 'They were after the milk monopoly. They were going to set up this holding corporation – like the East India Company or something like that – with themselves as the money-men behind it; and this company was going to have the exclusive right to buy all the milk in England and sell it to the ultimate consumer.'

'You mean,' Danny croaked, 'like the Milk Marketing Board?'

'Keep your voice down, will you? Yes, just like the Milk Marketing Board. So now do you see why Guido had to take the fall?'

'I see,' Danny whispered. 'My God, that explains . . . But why did they want to blow up King James?'

Vanderdecker sneered. 'They didn't want to blow up the King,' he said. 'If they'd wanted rid of Big Jim, do you think they'd have gone about it like that? Gunpowder, treason and plot? Don't be so naive. Look, just ask yourself this. Why was it that shortly after Guido did the November-the-Fifth bit, the price of clotted cream rose by a factor of seventy-four point six per cent in most of Southern England.

Danny whistled. 'That much?'

'That's where they went wrong, of course,' Vanderdecker said. 'Too much too soon, you see. And when Hampden and Pym found out . . .'

'You mean the Civil War?'

'Do yourself a favour,' Vanderdecker said. 'Take a look at the Putney Debates; you know, towards the end of the War, when all the Parliamentary leaders sat down and tried to make up a new constitution. Is there one mention, one solitary word said about an overall dairy strategy for the 1660s? Nothing. Don't you find that just a little bit surprising?'

Danny's mouth hung open like a dislocated letterbox. 'So the Restoration . . .'

'You've got it,' Vanderdecker said. 'All that stuff with the oak tree was just a blind. And then, when you get on to the Glorious Revolution, and after that the Jacobites, it suddenly starts to fall into place. After all, why do you think they called George III Farmer George? He was as sane as . . .' Vanderdecker considered for a moment, '. . . as you are, but . . . Anyway, there's the story for you, if you really do want something big.'

Vanderdecker's mouth felt dry with so much talking, and he turned away in search of whisky, but Danny grabbed him by the arm.

'Listen,' he said, 'you've got to tell me. Was the Milk Marketing Board behind the Kennedy assassination?'

Vanderdecker raised an eyebrow. 'You what?' he said.

'The assassination of President Kennedy. Was it them?'

'Don't be ridiculous,' Vanderdecker said. 'That was Lee Harvey Oswald.' He leaned over, plucked a bottle of Famous Grouse from Pieter's hand and took a long drink. Danny narrowed his eyes. Was Vanderdecker telling the truth? Or was he in on it too?

Below the helicopter Cirencester flickered dimly, and Vanderdecker wiped the spilt whisky out of his beard. The next hour or so was going to be interesting, and he felt that it was probably just as well that he had stayed relatively sober after all. He glanced across at Danny, who was drawing complicated diagrams on the blank pages at the back of his diary, using one of those pens you get from Smiths which has four different colours in it. He was happy, the poor fool.

The crew were singing again:

'We've been together now for four hundred and eighty years,' they sang,

'And it don't seem a day too much.

'There ain't a captain sailing on the sea

'That we'd swap for our dear old dutch . . .'

Vanderdecker winced. He hadn't thought about that side of it – he hadn't really thought about any side of it, if he was going to be honest with himself, the implications of getting rid of the smell at last. What was going to happen now? In the end, every community and grouping of human beings (except, of course, the Rolling Stones) drifts apart and goes its separate ways. There was nothing to keep them together now, and God knows, they'd all been getting on each other's nerves. But actually saying goodbye – goodbye after so many years . . .

'Hey,' Sebastian protested, 'give it back.'

'Sorry,' Vanderdecker said, and handed the bottle back.

'Some people,' he said. 'That's how we all got into this mess in the first place, remember, you nicking somebody else's bottle. You'd have thought you'd have learned your lesson.'

'Still,' Vanderdecker said, 'it's been fun, hasn't it?'

'No,' Sebastian replied. 'It's been lousy.'

'But we've had some laughs, haven't we?' Vanderdecker said. 'A few good times along the way.'

'When?'

'Well . . .' Vanderdecker shrugged. 'Forget it,' he said. 'What have you done with the cat, by the way?'

'What cat?'

'Montalban's cat.'

'Oh,' said Sebastian, 'that cat. It's over there, on the life-jackets, having forty winks. I spilt some whisky, and it lapped it up.'

'Fine,' Vanderdecker said. He rubbed his face with both hands, and tried to think of what he should do next. For over four hundred years he had been doing all the thinking, and he was just starting to get a tiny bit tired of it. Another day, new problems, more of the same old rubbish; and Captain Vanderdecker standing on the quarter-deck trying to cope with it, with his usual flair. Let Julius do it – that was what his mother used to say, all those many, many years ago: 'Don't trouble yourself with that, dear; let Julius do it. Julius, put that away and . . .'

The helicopter had stopped flying and was just whirring, hovering tentatively above the grass. Then, with a rather talentless lurch, it pitched down. Suddenly, Vanderdecker didn't want to leave; he wanted to stay right here and let someone else do the coping with things for a change. No chance of that.

'Hey, skip.' Not you again, Antonius; go away, I died en route, somewhere in the clouds over Smethwick, go ask Danny Bennett or someone. 'Is this where we get out?'

'That's right,' Vanderdecker said wearily. 'Right, lads, show a leg, we're here. Sebastian, bring the cat.'

'Why do I always have to . . .' The rest of the complaint was drowned out with noise as the helicopter door opened, and Vanderdecker (lead-from-the-front Vanderdecker) dropped out onto the grass. Perhaps he was just feeling tired, but he forgot to duck and the rotor-blade hit him just below the ear. Danny, who happened to be watching, started to scream, but there was nothing to scream about; the Dutchman staggered, swore loudly in Dutch, rubbed his neck and went on his way.

'Well,' he said to Sebastian, 'that's one thing proved anyway.'

'What?' said Sebastian. 'You never look where you're going.'

Vanderdecker laughed mirthlessly, shrugged and walked towards the house. Then he noticed a smallish human figure racing across the grass towards him. He narrowed his brows and wondered what was going on.

'Julius!' said the small human figure, and crashed into him like a dodgem car, jolting him almost as much as the rotor-blade.

'Sorry,' he said automatically, and helped the small figure to its feet. The small figure was Jane, and Jane had wrapped her arms around him. He remembered.

'Hello, Jane,' he said.

'Julius, you're safe!' Jane gasped; but there was already a tiny note of doubt, an inflection so slight you would need high-quality scientific apparatus or ears like a bat to register it, but there nevertheless.

'I think we should have a quiet talk,' Vanderdecker said, prising her off gently. 'There's just a few things I've got to do first, and then . . .'

'Julius?' The inflection was rather more obvious now. Vanderdecker closed off certain parts of his mind, which were getting in the way, and nodded.

'Won't be long,' he said. 'I've just got a couple of things to see to first, then I'm all yours.' There was something in his voice which belied the words he uttered, and Jane let go of him. She felt all hollow, like an egg with its yolk blown out.

'Such as,' Vanderdecker went on, 'booting a certain professor up the backside. Did you get the policy?'

'Yes,' Jane said. 'I did. Thank you.'

'What for? Oh, I see, yes, well. Where is it now?'

'I gave it to the pilot who brought the Professor back,' Jane said. 'He's going to post it to my father as soon as he gets to . . .'

'Very sensible.' Vanderdecker said, nodding. 'Perhaps you could just 'phone your father and ask him to send it to my place in Bridport.'

'*Bridport?*' Jane gasped.

'Yes,' Vanderdecker said, 'the fallen-down old dump where you said you found all the bank statements. It'll be safe there.'

Jane was about to say something, but she had forgotten what it was. Couldn't have been important. 'Right,' she said. 'I'll just go and do that, then.'

'Thanks,' Vanderdecker said. 'Now, then.' He walked off quickly towards the house.

The Flying Dutchman was, when circumstances permitted, a man of his word; and when he said he was going to boot a professor up the backside, he stood by it.

'Ouch!' said Montalban, startled. 'My dear fellow, what . . .'

Vanderdecker kicked him again, harder. One of his better ideas, he said to himself. He tried it again, but missed this time and put his foot through a complex piece of scientific equipment disguised as a glass-fronted cabinet full of netsuke. Although he didn't know it, lights flickered in Montreal, Jodrell Bank and Geneva.

'Captain,' said the Professor, backing away while still trying to remain dignified, 'what has come over you?'

'Getting me into this mess,' said Vanderdecker, 'I can put up with. Causing me to sail round the world for nearly five hundred years I can take in my stride. Pissing off and leaving me under a ceiling and coming back here and stuffing yourself with macaroons is a bit too much, don't you think?' He aimed another kick at the Professor; it glanced off the bunch of keys in his trouser pocket and wasted its force in empty air, making Vanderdecker totter slightly. He regained his balance and his composure at about the same moment.

'Well,' he said, 'anyway, there we are. You will be delighted to know that that gimcrack Friday-afternoon job of a power station of yours is now safe again, absolutely no thanks to you. And you owe me and my lads for a complete set of clothes each. All right?'

'Yes, most certainly,' said Montalban. 'My dear fellow, I am delighted to see you all in one piece. I . . .'

'I bet you are,' Vanderdecker said furiously. 'Because if I hadn't been, it'd have cost you plenty. Well, let me tell you that . . .'

'And even more delighted,' said the Professor, with all the smoothness he could manage, 'to note that the treatment worked.'

Vanderdecker started. '*Treatment?*'

'Indeed,' said the Professor. 'Just as I had hoped. The radiation charge has eliminated the smell entirely. My experiments are vindicated. You must be very pleased.'

And grateful, his tone implied. So grateful, in fact, that you really ought to do me a little favour in return. Vanderdecker caught the implication like Rodney Marsh fielding a large, slow football. 'If you think,' he said, 'I'm going to sign over that bloody policy after what you just did to me . . .'

'And what was that?'

'Leaving me there,' Vanderdecker roared. 'Other things too, but just now, mostly that.'

'My dear fellow,' Montalban said. 'I imagined you were –

well, dead, to put it bluntly. I could see no sign of you; I feared that you and your companions had been simply atomised by the force of the blast. There was nothing I could do, I came away; my presence was needed here . . .'

Vanderdecker growled softly, but his indignation was leaking away like oil from a fractured sump. The Professor smiled kindly.

'And so,' he said, 'everything has worked out for the best. You have no idea how much pleasure this moment gives me. The unpleasant side-effect of my elixir has successfully been counteracted. My work is over . . .'

The words froze on his lips, and Vanderdecker stared at him as he quietly repeated the words.

'Montalban?' Vanderdecker asked. 'Are you all right?'

The Professor stood there like a dead Christmas tree for a moment and then grabbed Vanderdecker fiercely by the shoulders. 'Vanderdecker,' he shouted, 'did you hear what I just said? My work is *over*! I've finished! I don't have to do it any more, it's finished.'

Vanderdecker stepped back, wondering if the kick had affected the Professor's brain. 'Well,' he said, 'that's wonderful for you, I'm sure. Maybe now you can have a lie-in at weekends, read the paper, that sort of . . .'

Montalban filled his lungs and let out the loudest, least dignified whoop ever heard outside a Navajo encampment. 'It's over!' he screamed. 'Yippee! No more work! No more work!' He danced – literally danced – round the room, kicking things as he went.

'Look, Professor,' Vanderdecker said, 'I'm delighted for you, of course, but could we just have a quick chat about my policy? Then you can dance about all you like, but . . .'

'The policy?' Montalban stopped dead, turned round and stared Vanderdecker in the face. 'You can *stuff* your policy!' he squealed. 'That's it, you can *stuff* it! I don't care any more, I'm free.'

Something rather improbable fell into place in Vander-decker's mind, like the tumblers of a combination lock. 'Professor,' he said, 'are you trying to tell me you don't *like* being a scientist?'

'My dear fellow,' gibbered the Professor, 'I hate it. I hate it, do you hear? It's horrible. It *stinks*. I've always hated it, even when I was a boy and my mother said I was wasting my time composing madrigals and I should grow up and learn alchemy like my father. I've always hated it, and . . . and I've had to do it for *five hundred years*! My God,' said Montalban savagely, 'you think you're hard done by, do you, sailing round the world with nothing to do all day? You don't know you're born. Imagine, just imagine what I've had to put up with. I'd have changed places with you like a shot. Day after day after day in a foul, stinking laboratory, fiddling with sulphate of this and nitrate of that, doing equations and square roots and . . . and now I'm free. I don't have to do it any more. No more electrons. No more law of the conservation of matter. No more Brownian motion. Dear God, Vanderdecker, you can't imagine how thoroughly depressing it all was, the endless, endless difficulties, five hundred years of them – having to do it all *myself*; nobody – absolutely nobody – to help, all up to me, all that bloody, bloody *work*! I hate . . . *work*!'

'Oh good,' Vanderdecker said, calmly, 'you won't have to do that any more.'

'No,' said the Professor, quietly, grinning, 'no, I won't. I need a drink. Will you join me?'

'And the policy?' Vanderdecker said.

'Oh, sod the policy,' Montalban replied. 'Now that that's all done with, I don't need the bank any more. Just so long as I never have to do another day's work in my life, the bank can go bust for all I care and jolly good luck to it. Let someone else sort something out, just for once.'

'I know how you feel,' Vanderdecker said gently, 'believe me.'

'Thirsty?'

Vanderdecker nodded. 'That too. Look, I've just got to go and deal with something and then I'll be right back.'

'You'd better hurry,' said the Professor, pouring whisky into a big glass, 'because I'm not going to wait for you. Tea!' he sneered. 'The devil with tea! I don't have to keep a clear head any more, I can get as pissed as a mouse.'

'Rat.'

'Precisely, my dear fellow, as a rat. Hurry back!'

'I might just do that,' Vanderdecker said, and he ran off into the gardens again.

Some time later a car – more than a car; the biggest Mercedes you ever saw – pulled up outside the front door. It was full of accountants.

Mr Gleeson got out. He rang the doorbell. After a long, long time a drunken man in a kilt answered it. In the background, someone was playing 'My Very Good Friend The Milkman Says' on the harpsichord.

'What do you want?' he asked.

'Miss Doland,' said Mr Gleeson.

The man in the kilt sniggered. 'You're not the only one,' he said. He was slurring his words slightly.

'Just get her,' said Mr Gleeson. As befits a high-rolling accountant, Mr Gleeson had authority and presence. He was used to being obeyed.

'Piss off,' said the man in the kilt, and slammed the door.

Mr Gleeson was surprised. According to the latest charging-rate guidelines, it costs at least fifteen pounds plus VAT to slam a door in the face of an accountant of partner status. He rang the bell again.

'I said piss off,' said a voice through the letter-box.

Mr Gleeson muttered something in a low voice, and two other accountants rang the doorbell for him. This is known as the art of delegation.

Eventually the door opened again.

'Sorry about that. Can I help you?'

This time it was a man in a kilt with a beard. He seemed rational enough, and Mr Gleeson stepped forward. Far away in the distance, a nightingale sang.

'My name's Gleeson,' he said. 'Moss Berwick, accountants. Where's Miss Doland?'

'She's inside,' said the man with the beard, 'but you don't want to see her. You want to see me. My name's Vanderdecker.'

For a moment, Mr Gleeson simply stood and stared. Then he pulled himself together. 'We have to talk,' he said.

Vanderdecker shook his head. 'Perhaps you may have to talk, I don't know,' he said. 'If it's some sort of obsession you have, maybe a psychiatrist could help. I knew a man once . . .'

'Please,' said Mr Gleeson. 'This is no time for flippancy. Have you any idea what is happening on the markets?'

'Heavy falls in jute futures?'

'We must talk,' said Mr Gleeson.

'We are talking,' Vanderdecker replied. Gleeson drew in a deep breath and started to walk past Vanderdecker into the house. But the Flying Dutchman put the palm of his hand on Mr Gleeson's shirt front and shoved. There was a ripple of amazement among the other accountants. Vanderdecker smiled. 'So what's happening on the markets?' he said.

'Massive rises,' said Gleeson. 'The situation has got completely out of hand. It is imperative that we . . .'

'Hold on a minute,' Vanderdecker said, and he stepped back into the hallway, called out, 'Sebastian! Make him stop that bloody row, will you?' and turned to face Mr Gleeson again. Muted grumbling in the background, and the harpsichord music ceased.

'Sorry about that,' said the Flying Dutchman, 'but I think you'll find everything will be back to normal on your beloved markets in a few minutes. The Professor's got completely ratted and he's started playing things on the harpsichord, forgetting that it's a computer too. You don't understand a word of that, but what the hell, you're only a glorified book-keeper. Clerks, we called them in my day. Used to shave the tops of their heads and talk Latin at you. I see you shave your head too, or is that just premature hair loss?'

'All right,' said Mr Gleeson, 'that's enough from you. Where is Miss . . . ?'

But before he could say any more, Vanderdecker had grabbed him by various parts of his clothing, lifted him off the ground and tossed him into a flower-bed.

'Now listen,' Vanderdecker said, 'the lot of you. The phrase "under new management" springs immediately to mind; also, "the King is dead; long live the King." If in future you wish to see Miss Doland, you will have to make an appointment. Miss Doland has left the accountancy profession and has gone into banking. She is now the proprietor of the First Lombard Bank.'

There was a very long silence – if the accountants had had their stopwatches running, about twelve hundred pounds worth, plus VAT – and then Mr Gleeson said, 'You what?'

'Miss Doland,' Vanderdecker said, 'has exchanged entitlements as sole beneficiary by assignment of what I believe you meatheads call the Vanderdecker Policy for a fifty-one per cent shareholding in Quicksilver Limited, which is – I hope I'm getting all this right, it's not exactly my field, you know – which I believe is the holding company which owns the First Lombard Bank, Lombard Assurance, Lombard Unit Trusts plc, and all sorts of other money sort of things with the word Lombard in them. The remaining forty-nine per cent goes to me. We've just had a very pleasant half-hour with the previous owner signing stock transfer forms while drinking apple brandy and singing 'Lilliburlero' in Dutch. If any of you people fancy dropping by at about eleven-thirty tomorrow morning, you can help out with the Capital Gains Tax. For now, though, you will kindly shove off before I set the cat on you. Goodnight.'

The door slammed again, and there was the sound of a chain going on. Mr Gleeson picked himself up, brushed leaf-mould off his trousers and lifted the flap of the letterbox.

'Doland,' he shouted, 'you're fired!' Then he got into the car and drove off.

As the receding-Mercedes noises faded away, the door opened again, just a crack.

'Has he gone?' said a small female voice.

'Yes,' Vanderdecker said.

'Really?'

'Really and truly.'

Vanderdecker closed the door. 'But it beats me,' he said, 'why you're afraid of him. Them, come to that. Glorified, over-fed book-keepers.'

'I don't know,' Jane replied. 'Habit, probably. You know, I used to have these daydreams. The letter would come saying that my long-lost aunt in Australia had died leaving me a million pounds, and then I'd go into Mr Peters' office and say, "Peters, you're a jerk, you can stick your job . . ." But even if she had . . .'

'Who?'

'My aunt in Australia.'

'You have an aunt in Australia?'

'No.'

'Sorry,' Vanderdecker said, 'forget it, carry on with what you were saying.'

'Even,' Jane said, 'if I'd had one and she had, I still wouldn't have.'

'Because of habit?'

'Habit of mind,' Jane replied. 'Subservience, innate atavistic feudal mentality. You don't go telling your liege-lord he can stick his job even if you're leaving to join the Second Crusade. Purely theoretical, anyway.'

'Not now,' Vanderdecker said. 'You are in exactly that position, thanks to my foresight in taking out life insurance all those years ago – my mother wouldn't half be surprised, by the way, she always said I was a fool when it came to money – and yet you denied yourself a moment's extreme pleasure because of habit of mind. Strange behaviour.'

'Oh, I'm just chicken,' Jane said. 'Anyway, thanks for dealing with it for me. You did it very well.'

'Did I?' Vanderdecker said. 'Call it beginner's luck.'

They were standing in the hall. From the drawing-room came drinking noises. 'Well, then . . .' Jane said.

'Well what?'

'Oh, I don't know, Julius . . .'

'Do you know,' Vanderdecker said. 'I can't get used to people calling me that again. That Bennett bloke keeps calling me Julius, and I don't know what to make of it. Only person ever called me Julius was my mother. Dad called me son, my master when I was a 'prentice used to refer to me as "hey, you", and then I was captain or skipper for the next four hundred odd years. Being Julius again is a bit unsettling, really. I never liked the name, anyway.'

'Didn't you?'

'No.'

'Do you have another name? A second name, or something?'

'Yes.'

'What?'

'Albert.'

That seemed to kill the conversation for a moment. Then Vanderdecker said, 'You don't like the name Albert, do you?'

'Well,' Jane said, 'not really.'

'Nor me. Good old Dutch name, of course, been in my family for generations. I think it means Elf-beard, which is quite incredibly helpful. Well, too late to do anything about it now, I suppose.'

'Yes.'

There was nothing in particular keeping them in the hall,

but neither of them moved. Eventually Jane asked: 'So what are you going to do next?'

Vanderdecker raised an eyebrow. 'Next?'

'Well, yes, I mean, you aren't going to stay here drinking with Professor Montalban for the rest of time, now are you?'

Vanderdecker considered. 'Probably not,' he said. 'On the other hand, I feel like a bit of a holiday.'

'A holiday from what?'

'From whatever I've got to do next, I suppose.'

'Look,' Jane said sharply, 'you haven't got to do anything next. Or ever.' But Vanderdecker shook his head.

'It's not as easy as that,' he said. 'I really wish it was, but it isn't. It's them.' He nodded his head towards the drawing-room door. Jane stared at him for a moment.

'What, them?' she said. 'Johannes and Antonius and Sebastian and . . .'

'I'm afraid so, yes.'

'But what have they got to do with it?'

Vanderdecker smiled, but not for the reasons that usually make people smile. 'I'm their captain,' he said. 'I'm responsible for them.'

Jane stared. 'You're joking,' she said. 'I thought you couldn't stand the sight of each other. I thought that after all those years cooped up on that little ship . . .'

'Yes,' Vanderdecker replied, 'and no. Yes, we get on each other's nerves to a quite extraordinary extent, and we can't even relieve the tension with murder or other forms of violence. On the other hand, I'm their captain. I do all the thinking for them. I've had to, for the last four centuries. They've completely forgotten how to do it for themselves. So, okay, maybe we don't have to go back on that boring bloody ship ever again; but I can't leave them. It'd be impossible.'

'Why?'

Vanderdecker was silent for what seemed like an immensely

long time, then turned to Jane, looked her in the eye and said, 'Habit.'

'I see.'

'Set in our ways,' Vanderdecker amplified. 'Old dogs and new tricks.'

'Fine,' Jane replied. 'Well, it was very nice meeting you.'

'Likewise.'

'Perhaps we'll bump into each other again one day.'

'Bound to,' Vanderdecker said. 'Board meetings, that sort of thing. So what are you going to do now?'

Jane shrugged. 'I don't know,' she said. 'I think I'll have a holiday too. Only . . .' Only it won't be the same, not now. You see, Mr Vanderdecker, this freedom you've given me is a fraud. Maybe now I'm free of Mr Gleeson and accountancy and all that horrible nonsense, but I can't be free of you, not ever. Every man I see in the street, I'll look twice at him to see if it's you. But she smiled instead, and left the sentence unfinished.

'Actually,' Vanderdecker said, 'I'd had this idea of getting a new ship.'

'What?'

'A new ship,' Vanderdecker repeated. 'Only not called the *Verdomde* this time. Something a bit more cheerful. And big. Huge. One of those oil tankers, maybe, or a second-hand aircraft carrier. Only we'd have the whole thing gutted and we'd fit it out like an enormous floating country-club. A separate floor for each of us, with automated and computerised everything. Complete luxury. We could just sail around, landing where we like and when we like, just generally having a good time. I mean,' Vanderdecker's voice sounded a trifle strained, 'I think we're all a bit too old to settle down now. Don't you think?'

'You know best,' Jane said. 'Well, I think that's a splendid idea. I really do. Have you put it to them yet?'

'No, not yet. I thought I'd like your opinion first.'

'Yes, you do that,' Jane said. 'And now let's have a drink, shall we?'

They went into the drawing room. The first thing they saw was Professor Montalban, lying on the sofa fast asleep. Snoring.

'Had a drop too much,' Sebastian explained unnecessarily. 'Not used to it.'

'Fair enough,' Vanderdecker said. 'Now listen, you lot. I've been thinking . . .'

And he explained the idea of the oil-tanker. It was well-received, particularly by Antonius, who had been wondering what was going to happen next. They all had a drink to celebrate. They drank the whisky, the wine, the gin, the brandy, the cherry brandy, the rest of the apple brandy and the sherry. At this point, Danny and the camera crew passed out, leaving Jane, the Flying Dutchman and the crew to drink the vermouth, the Tia Maria, the ouzo, the port, the bourbon, the vodka, the bacardi, the schnapps and the ginger-beer shandy.

'That seems to be the lot,' Vanderdecker said, disappointed. 'And not a drop of beer in the whole place.'

'What's this, Skip?' Antonius asked, holding up a cut-glass decanter. There was no label on it, but it was a pleasant dark golden colour.

'Where did you find that, Antonius?' Vanderdecker asked.

'In this little cabinet thing.'

Vanderdecker sniffed it. 'Smells like rum,' he said. 'Anyone fancy a drop of rum?'

Everyone, it transpired, fancied a drop of rum. It must have been good rum, because it made them all feel very sleepy.

When they woke up, everyone had headaches, Jane included. From the kitchen came the smell of frying bacon, which made them all feel sick. Slowly, Vanderdecker lifted himself to his feet, looked around to see if he could see where he'd left his head the previous evening, and went into the kitchen to kill whoever was making that horrible smell.

It was Montalban, wearing a striped pinny, frying bacon. He had also made a big pot of coffee, of which Vanderdecker consumed a large quantity straight from the spout.

'Why aren't you as ill as the rest of us?' he asked the Professor.

'I never get hangovers,' said the Professor.

Vanderdecker scowled. 'Clean living, huh?'

'No,' the Professor replied. 'I have a little recipe.'

'Gimme.'

The Professor grinned and pointed to a half-full jug on the worktop. 'There's tomato juice and raw egg,' he said, 'and mercury and nitric acid and white lead and heavy water. And Worcester sauce,' he added, 'to taste.'

Vanderdecker had some and felt much better. 'Thanks,' he said. 'It was the rum that did it.'

'Rum?'

'Vicious stuff, rum,' Vanderdecker said. 'Does horrible things to you.'

'I haven't got any rum,' Montalban said.

'Not now you haven't.'

Montalban was looking at him. 'No, I never keep any in the house,' he said. 'Are you sure it was rum?'

'Well,' Vanderdecker said, 'there wasn't a label on the decanter but it tasted like rum. I think.'

'Which decanter?'

'In a little glass-fronted cabinet thing, by the telephone table,' Vanderdecker said. 'Maybe it was calvados, come to think of it, except calvados always gives me heartburn and heartburn was about the only thing I wasn't suffering from when I woke up just now.'

Montalban was staring now, but not at the bacon, which was burning. 'Large cut-glass decanter in a small glass-fronted cabinet,' he said.

'That's right. Sorry, was it special or something? We just weren't noticing . . .'

'That wasn't rum, I'm afraid,' Montalban said. 'That was elixir.'

Vanderdecker's eyes grew very round and his hands fell to his sides. 'You what?' he said.

'Elixir,' Montalban said.

'Oh *SHIT*,' Vanderdecker replied. 'Not again.'

'I'm afraid so,' said the Professor, 'yes.'

Vanderdecker's spine seemed to melt, and he slithered against the worktop, knocking over a glass jar of pearl barley. 'you stupid . . .'

'It's not my fault,' Montalban protested nervously. 'For Heaven's sake, I'd have thought you and your friends would have learned your lesson by now, really . . .'

Vanderdecker straightened up, turned his head to the wall and started to bang it furiously on the corner of some shelf units. 'Not you,' he said, 'me. Antonius. No, me. Oh hell!'

'It's not,' Montalban said, 'exactly the same elixir as . . . well, as last time.'

Vanderdecker stopped pounding his head against the shelves and looked at him. 'It isn't?'

'Well,' said the Professor, 'it's basically the same, but I did make certain changes to the molecular . . .'

He stopped short, because Vanderdecker's hands round his windpipe made talking difficult. 'Does it make you smell?' Vanderdecker snarled. Montalban said nothing in reply – not for want of trying – but his lips made the necessary movements to shape 'No.'

'You sure?' Montalban nodded vigorously, and Vanderdecker let him go.

'But,' he added, as soon as he had breath enough to do so, 'it does have side-effects.'

'It does?'

'I fear so.'

Vanderdecker groaned. 'Go on,' he said, 'tell me.'

'You understand,' Montalban said, first making sure that he had the bulk of a chest freezer between himself and his interlocutor, 'that my data is based on necessarily perfunctory and incomplete tests, confined entirely to non-human animal subjects, and that what I say is on a completely without prejudice basis?'

'Tell me.'

'You really must understand that none of this has been proved to the high standards . . .'

'Tell me,' Vanderdecker said.

'It makes you go bright green.'

'Green?'

Montalban nodded again. 'Green,' he confirmed, 'and you shine in the dark. There is also an eerie humming noise. Additional limbs are sometimes (although not invariably) acquired, depending on the individual subject's metabolism and whether or not he is a vertebrate to begin with. Also,' Montalban added quickly as Vanderdecker picked up a biscuit-barrel and drew back his arm, 'the effects are strictly temporary.'

'You what?'

'The phenomena I have just described,' Montalban said, 'are exhibited in the short term only, for no more than a few weeks at a time. They do, however, recur; like malaria, I suppose, although on a fascinatingly regular basis.'

'How often?'

Montalban shrugged non-committally, and Vanderdecker threw the biscuit-barrel at him. While he was reeling and picking smashed pottery and Bath Olivers out of his hair, Vanderdecker had time to find a spaghetti-jar and flourish it threateningly.

'My best estimate,' Montalban said, 'at the present time is that the symptoms manifest themselves on average for two one-month periods in each calendar year. But I should stress,' he said, ignoring the spaghetti jar, 'that this is based on observation of a small nest of field-voles, two of which escaped, and the tests only cover a three-year period, which is by any standards . . .'

'Why?'

'My housekeeper,' Montalban admitted, 'is terrified of mice. Green luminous mice especially. So I had to get rid of them. Since they were immortal and invulnerable . . .'

'That bit still works, does it?'

'Most certainly, yes,' said the Professor. 'Since they were immortal and invulnerable and I couldn't keep them around the house, they are now manning a small space-station in orbit three hundred thousand kilometres above the surface of Mars, providing invaluable data on . . .'

'I see,' Vanderdecker said. 'Green luminous and noisy, and perhaps an extra arm or two. What happens with the arms, by the way?'

'The additional limbs,' said the Professor, 'are also temporary.'

'You mean they fall off?'

'Yes.'

'Moult? Pine needles off a Christmas tree job? That sort of thing?'

'Roughly, yes.'

'I see,' Vanderdecker said. 'So I'll need a pair of trousers with a detachable third leg, will I? As opposed to spending the rest of history going around like a human Manx emblem. Well, let me tell you . . .'

Suddenly Vanderdecker fell silent and he lowered the spaghetti jar, spilling its contents. He furrowed his brows and then started to grin.

'Montalban,' he said at last, 'that's marvellous.'

'Is it?' Montalban raised an eyebrow. 'Well, I'm delighted that . . .'

'Don't you see?' Vanderdecker said, 'Jane drank some too. A stiff double, approximately. Don't you see, she's going to live for ever too. She's going to be one of us! Montalban – oh, look, just stay there, will you?'

He dumped the spaghetti jar in the sink and rushed through into the drawing room. There, Jane was sitting crouched on the edge of a settee, moaning slightly. With one movement Vanderdecker lifted her up in the air, kissed her noisily on the lips and said, 'Guess what?'

'Ouch,' Jane replied.

'You're going to go bright green and luminous, hum slightly, and grow an extra arm,' he said cheerfully. 'What do you think of that?'

'I think I already did,' Jane replied. 'Will you please put me down before my head falls off?'

'Sorry,' Vanderdecker said. 'Now, listen to this. No, better still, have some of the Professor's mercury soup and then listen.'

So Jane went, had some mercury soup, and listened. While Vanderdecker was explaining to her, and inducing Montalban with occasional prods from a rolling-pin to corroborate his narrative, he began to wonder whether Jane would in fact be pleased. He had no idea; all he knew was that he was pleased, very pleased indeed.

'So there you are,' he finished up. 'What do you think?'

Oddly enough, the only thing that passed through Jane's mind for several minutes was the phrase 'Death is a tax holiday', which she remembered from her tax-planning lectures.

'Jane? What do you think?'

'Death is a tax holiday,' she said.

'I beg your pardon?'

'For the year of death,' Jane said, 'personal allowances against income tax are granted for the full year, regardless of the point in the tax year at which death occurs. There is no requirement to apportion unused allowances. Thus death can be said to be a tax holiday.'

'What?'

'Sorry,' Jane said. 'I was miles away. So I'm going to live for ever, am I?'

'Yes.'

'Ah. Yes, I thought that was what you said. I . . .'

'Jane.' Vanderdecker grabbed her by the shoulders. 'Would you like some advice?'

'Yes please.'

'Don't think about it,' Vanderdecker said. 'It's not a good idea to think about it, believe you me.'

'Oh,' Jane said. 'Right, okay then.'

'Secondly,' Vanderdecker said, and then he turned to the Professor. 'Go away.'

'I'm sorry?' the Professor asked.

'I said go away. *Vamos*.'

'Certainly, my dear fellow, certainly.'

'Now then.' Vanderdecker put on a serious expression and looked Jane squarely in the eye. 'Miss Doland,' he said, 'since we are . . .'

'All in the same boat?' Jane suggested.

'Precisely,' Vanderdecker said. 'Since we've both been accidentally lumbered with a common misfortune . . . Look, do you see what I'm getting at, because this is rather tricky to put into words.'

'Yes,' Jane said.

'Yes, you see what I'm getting at, or yes, you . . . ?'

'Both,' Jane replied.

'And,' Jane continued, 'some sort of through dining-room in a sort of light Wedgwood blue, with . . .'

'Jane.'

'Sorry.'

'That's fine. Now . . .'

'And a dressing room,' Jane added quickly. 'I've always wanted a separate dressing-room. In a sort of pinky . . .'

'Absolutely,' Vanderdecker said. 'Can you play the harpsichord?'

'No.'

'Pity,' Vanderdecker said, 'because it's years since I learnt, and they've put extra pedals and things on now.'

'Couldn't we have a stereo instead?'

'A harpsichord linked to the computer,' Vanderdecker explained. 'To control the markets, whatever the hell they are.'

'Oh yes,' Jane said. 'God, you're efficient, aren't you? I'd forgotten all about . . .'

'Habit,' Vanderdecker said. 'I've got into the habit of looking after people, remember, making sure they don't get into messes or start fighting each other. While I'm at it, I might as well use the Professor's computer, since he's obviously washed his hands of the whole affair.'

Just then the kitchen door opened, and there was Sebastian. He was looking pleased with himself.

'Hey, skip,' he said, 'it's all fixed.'

'I know,' Vanderdecker said.

'What?'

'Oh, sorry,' Vanderdecker said. 'What's fixed, Sebastian?'

'The ship.'

'What ship?'

'The supertanker,' Sebastian said. 'We've booked one.'

Vanderdecker stared. 'You've booked one?'

'That's right, yes,' Sebastian said. 'We tried Harland and Wolf first, but they thought we were playing silly buggers and put the phone down. So then we tried this Korean firm, Kamamoto-something, Pieter wrote the name down, and they said they had an ex-demo tanker going cheap, low mileage, taxed till April, metallic grey with headrests, and when would we like to take delivery? So we said, can you run it over to Bristol, and they said would Thursday be all right, so we said fine . . .'

Vanderdecker smiled. 'Sebastian,' he said.

'Yes?'

'Ten out of ten for initiative,' said the Flying Dutchman, 'but let's say four out of ten for judgement. They were having you on.'

'You what?'

'Pulling your leg,' Vanderdecker said. 'Playing games. Being funny. Laughing up their sleeves.'

'How do you know?'

Vanderdecker widened the smile slightly. 'Trust me,' he said. 'I know. Why don't you just let me . . .'

Sebastian shrugged his shoulders. 'Be like that,' he said, offended. 'We were only trying . . .'

'Yes,' Vanderdecker said. 'You always are. Very. Go away and count something, there's a good lad.'

Sebastian drifted off, and Vanderdecker turned to Jane. 'You see?' he said. Jane nodded.

'And you still want to come?'

'Yes please.'

Fourteen months later, at half-past four in the morning, the biggest supertanker ever built slithered into the cold grey water of the North Sea and set off on its maiden voyage.

Curiously enough, there were no celebrations to mark the launching of this magnificent vessel (named, for sound fiscal reasons, *Lombard Venturer ID*); no crowd, no band playing, not even a small Babycham cracked against her awe-inspiring bows. Only one camera-crew filmed her departure, and that was because the owners hadn't the heart to refuse Danny Bennett a scoop to make up for the damage that the failure of his latest documentary 'Close The Creamery Door, Lads, There's Blood Inside', had done to his career.

This desire for privacy was understandable, because the owners weren't looking their best.

'I still say it suits you,' Vanderdecker said.

'People will think I'm seasick,' Jane replied.

'Let them,' Vanderdecker said. He glanced down at the instrument console before him; a cross between a huge computer keyboard, the flight deck of an airliner and a Yamaha organ. 'I wonder how you drive this thing.'

'I lent Antonius the manual,' Jane said. 'He asked me what gyroscopic means.'

'Oh well,' Vanderdecker said, and shrugged, 'never mind. It beats hauling in all those ropes, at any rate. Where shall we go first?'

'Reykjavik.'

'Why Reykjavik?'

'Because we have all the time in the world,' Jane answered, 'and I want to save the good bits till later.'

'Good thinking,' Vanderdecker said. 'I can see you're getting the hang of this.'

Through the tinted, double-glazed window they watched the coast receding into the distance. Just briefly, Jane felt her old life slipping away from her, and wondered if she ought to regret it. She was entering into a new timescale entirely now, and the next time she came back to England, perhaps everyone she knew there would be dead. But that was a very big thought, and there wasn't enough room in her head for it; all the available space was taken up with a calm, deliberate pleasure.

'Another nice thing about this ship,' Vanderdecker said, 'is not having to take it to Bridport to be fixed every time something goes wrong with it. God, I hate Bridport.'

'I gathered,' Jane said. 'It can't have been nice having to spend so many of your shore-leaves there.'

'True,' said the Flying Dutchman. 'Mind you, if you go somewhere often enough, you're bound to get sort of attached to it after a time. Even,' he added, 'Bridport.'

'Is that true?'

'No.' Vanderdecker admitted. 'Every time I went there, it had changed, ever so slightly, for the worse. A new carpark here, a fish shop turned into an estate agent there. I really thought it had bottomed out in 1837, but they hadn't built the bus station then.'

'So is it fun,' Jane queried, 'watching history unfold itself? Being a witness to the long march of Everyman? I suppose it's like being a God, really, except that usually you're powerless to intervene.'

'What long words Miss Doland is using,' Vanderdecker replied. 'It's not a bit like that. Hell, you don't notice, it's too gradual; it would be like claiming that the turning of the earth made you dizzy. I don't even feel particularly different, to be honest with you. I think I stopped feeling different when I turned nineteen and stopped growing, and since then I've always been the same. It'd be another matter if I'd gone to sleep and then woken up hundreds of years later, but . . . I guess going on a hovercraft must be like that.'

'Haven't you ever?'

'What, been on a hovercraft? No fear. Those things are dangerous.'

Jane giggled. 'But Julius,' she said, 'you're invulnerable and immortal, nothing's dangerous to you. You can't be afraid of hovercraft.'

'Want to bet?'

Jane smiled, and shook her head. Would she be like him in four hundred years or so, or would he always keep this start on her?

'Nice of the Professor to come and see us off, wasn't it?' she said.

'I suppose so.'

'Do you think he ever will get round to finding an antidote?'

Vanderdecker grinned. 'Eventually,' he said, 'maybe. Where's the hurry?'

'There isn't one.'

In the distance, the environmentalist action ship *Erdkrieger* changed course sharply. The ship's Geiger counter had suddenly started bleeping furiously and playing 'Jerusalem' and someone had suggested that the huge ship on the skyline might have something to do with it.

They launched a dinghy and set out to investigate. Business had been slack lately, what with the new initiative (nobody knew where it had started) to phase out nuclear power worldwide, and for once there was no shortage of volunteers.

'Ahoy!' shouted the captain of the *Erdkrieger*. 'You there on the tanker!'

He raised his binoculars and recognised a familiar face.

'Fancy meeting you again,' Vanderdecker replied through the loud-hailer. 'How's saving the world going?'

'Sehr gut,' the German replied. 'Is your ship making the radiation?'

'That's not radiation,' Vanderdecker replied, 'not as such. Completely harmless.'

'If that's so,' said the German, 'why are you bright green and glowing slightly?'

'Too much Limberger cheese,' Vanderdecker shouted back. 'Come on, you know me. I'm a Friend of the Earth too, you know. Me and the Earth are like *that*.'

'Okay,' said the German. 'Sorry to have troubled you. Auf wiedersehen!'

'Auf wiedersehen!' Vanderdecker called back, and added 'idiot' under his breath. He left the bridge and went below to the library. Jane was in the drawing-room, comparing carpet samples. At the moment, she was dead set on a sort of beigy-pink with a faint texture in the pile. As he thought of it, Vanderdecker shuddered, ever so slightly, until he remembered that carpets wear out, eventually, even the best of them. He'd just have to outlive the bugger.

As he walked down the ladder, Vanderdecker paused and looked out over the sea. Very big, the sea, an awful lot of it, like history, or life. The hell with it.

'Skip,' said a voice from above his head. 'You got a moment?'

Vanderdecker sighed. 'Of course I have, Antonius.' He climbed the ladder again.

'Skip,' Antonius said. 'I can't find the mainmast.'

'There isn't one.'

'No mainmast?'

'No mainmast. Propellers instead.'

Antonius reflected for a moment. 'Skip,' he said.

'Yes?'

'How do you get the sail to stay up on a propellor?'

'You don't,' Vanderdecker said. 'It sits in the water and goes round and round.'

Antonius frowned. 'And they call that progress,' he sneered.

Vanderdecker smiled at him, nodded, and went below again, banging his head on a low girder as he did so. I'll get used to it, he thought, in time.

And so he did. And they all lived happily. Ever after.

FAUST AMONG
EQUALS

For
KEN FUNNELL
and
Mike Hughes, Dave Little, Peter Wolf, Arthur Harvey,
Ed Howard *et al.*

And all charcoal burners, everywhere

CHAPTER ONE

The Laughing Cod in downtown Hlidarend is rated as one of north-east Iceland's premier restaurants. Or one of north-east Iceland's restaurants. In practice, it amounts to the same thing.

On the three hundred and sixty-four days each year when the Laughing Cod isn't being a restaurant, you can still walk in to the bar and order a coffee; and this is precisely what the Most Wanted Man in History did.

Six of the seven regulars turned and stared at him as he did so; the seventh, Wall-Eyed Bjorn, just carried on complaining about herring quotas.

Torsten Christianssen, the ever-popular proprietor of the Cod, poured the coffee, waited for it to settle, and leant back against the cash register, soaking in the thrill of a new experience.

'Just passing through, are you?' he asked after a while.

The newcomer looked up. 'You could say that,' he replied, with only the very faintest trace of an unfamiliar accent. 'Could you fix me a toasted sandwich, while you're at it?'

'Sure,' Torsten said. 'Coming right up.' He withdrew into the kitchen, wondering what the hell he was doing. It was theoretically possible to get a toasted sandwich in the Cod, but you needed references from two doctors and a justice of the peace before your application could even be considered.

When the stranger had eaten his sandwich, drunk his coffee and spent about forty-five seconds studying the framed photograph of Einar Sigfussen's record grayling on the wall opposite, he stood up and asked for the bill.

'The what?'

'The bill,' repeated the stranger. 'Please.'

'Oh, yes, right. Coming right up. Anybody here got a pencil or something?'

There was a brief, stunned silence, which was resolved when the stranger unclipped one from his top pocket and handed it over. Torsten took it as if it was red hot, and tentatively pressed the top.

'How do you spell coffee?' he asked.

The stranger told him; then took the paper from his hands, glanced at it, and fished a banknote out of his shirt pocket. A ten-thousand kroner note.

'Hey,' said Torsten, when God's marvellous gift of speech had been restored to him. 'You got anything smaller?'

The stranger looked at him, took back the note and put it down on the counter. Then he smiled at it.

It began to shrink.

You couldn't say how it did it; it just gradually occupied less and less space, until eventually it was about the size of a postage stamp. The stranger picked it up, blew on it, and passed it back across the counter.

'Is that better?' he asked.

On the other side of Death, there is a tunnel, leading to an archway. Then the road forks, and this is the point at which you find out whether the ethical system you've been following all these years was the right one after all.

If you've backed the Betamax version, you'll come at last to a rather impressive black stone gateway. There is no name or street number, but the chances are that you'll have guessed where you are anyway. However, by way of a heavy hint, the gateway bears the celebrated inscription:

ABANDON HOPE ALL YE WHO ENTER HERE

– or so your Michelin Guide would have you believe. It's very possible that it still does, but you can no longer see for yourself, because the whole of the architrave of the gateway is now covered with a huge banner, on which is painted the legend:

UNDER NEW MANAGEMENT

– and when you get up really close, you can see that it actually says:

UNDER *entirely* NEW MANAGEMENT

– just to ram the point well and truly home. At this juncture, you will be met by your guide, who will escort you to the ticket office (where you can also purchase guide books, souvenir pencils and locally-made coconut ice). The Michelin Guide doesn't mention that; but if you think about it, how would they know, anyway?

Once you've passed the ticket office, your tour will take you all round the justly celebrated architectural gems that comprise the inner courtyard, with the exception of the Council Chamber, which is not yet open to the public. This is a pity because apart from the Michelangelo floor (remember where we are) the Chamber houses three late Veroneses, a rather fine set of Dürer engravings and, naturally, the finest collection of works by Hieronymus Bosch in the universe. They are, of course, all portraits, such as may be found in the boardroom of any long-established corporate body.

On the day in question, the Council was in session, and had been for sixteen hours. The Council members (or Board of Directors, as we must call them now) each sat under his, her or its respective portrait, each one looking just the same as he/she/it had when Ronnie Bosch had painted them six hundred years previously; except that they were all wearing, somewhat self-consciously, identical red T-shirts with the words:

HAVIN' A DAMNED GOOD TIME

printed on them in big white letters.

'I still reckon we haven't thought this thing through properly,' said the Production Director stubbornly. He'd opposed the whole idea of a management buy-out from the start, and had only come in with the rest of the consortium under considerable pressure.

'Listen, Harry,' replied the Sales Director, lashing his tail irritably. 'We know what you think, so you stick to keeping the ovens going and we'll all get along just fine. You leave the management side to the grown-ups, okay?' For the record, he'd been the one applying the pressure, with a pitchfork, in the small of the Production Director's back.

'Actually,' interrupted the Admin Director wearily, 'Harry has got a point there, of sorts. I mean, it's one thing getting the blasted franchise. Keeping it's a different crock of entrails entirely.'

The Sales Director scowled, displaying a wide selection of unlikely components. 'All you can do is make problems,' he complained. 'We're running a *business* now, people. I suggest we all remember that, okay?'

'Sure.' The Finance Director nodded what, for the sake of argument, we shall call his head. 'We all know that, Steve, you've told us often enough. I'd just like to remind you that if those bloody inspectors catch us breaking the terms of the franchise, they'll have us out of here like the proverbial pea through a trumpet. Is that what you want?'

The Sales Director groaned theatrically and paused for a moment to scratch his nose (the one growing up out of his navel, not the one sprouting between his eyebrows). 'Look, Norman,' he said, 'there's ways round all that stuff, you know that as well as I do. All it takes is a little . . .'

The Finance Director shook what he had recently nodded. 'And there's such a thing as being too bloody clever for your own good, Steve. You'd do well to remember that.' He rubbed the bridge of his beak with a thoughtful claw, and continued; 'If they think we're not fulfilling the public service part of the deal . . .'

'But we are.'

'I'm not so sure.'

'Neither am I,' interrupted the Production Director. 'Take the perjury business, for instance. We could have got in serious schtuck with that.'

'I hadn't heard about any perjury stuff,' murmured the Finance Director, tapping the edge of the table with his offside front wing. 'Sounds interesting.'

The Production Director grinned unpleasantly, even for him. 'I'll bet,' he said. 'Look, in the franchise agreement it says, clause nine, sub-para three, all perjurers shall be broken on the wheel, right?'

'Right,' agreed the Finance Director. 'Standard procedure, it's what we've been doing for years. So?'

'So this dangerous clown here only had the whole department cleared out and fifty roulette tables put in. If I hadn't found out about three days before the last random check . . .'

'I still don't know what you're getting so uptight about,' growled the Sales Director. 'A wheel's a wheel, right? And I can guarantee the whole lot of them were broke by the time . . .'

He subsided under the glare of the Finance Director's six

beady red eyes, and took a sudden interest in the pencil on the table in front of him.

'That,' said the Finance Director, 'is definitely going too far. As,' he added sharply, 'is this idea of changing the name of the place to Netherglades Theme Park. How the hell am I meant to explain that to the inspectors, Steve? A smear campaign by the printers?'

The Sales Director sniffed – quite an achievement, considering. 'Come on,' he said. 'Even a bunch of blinkered, concrete-brained civil servants is going to realise the importance of image in a business like this. You honestly believe the punters are going to be able to relate to the image we've got at the moment? I mean, would you fork out good money if you thought you were going to get your lungs ripped out with a blunt meathook?'

'But that's the business we're in, Steve.'

The Sales Director waved an impatient talon. 'So are an awful lot of people, Norman, that's not the point. The point is, you can torture the punters and roast them alive and coop them up in confined spaces indefinitely and flay them on spits and they'll still fall over themselves to give you money, just so long as you can convince them it's fun. That's what the holiday industry's all about, Norman. Just so long as your image is okay . . .'

'I think we'll have to agree to disagree on this one for the time being,' said the Finance Director smoothly. 'I mean, there's obviously good arguments on both sides. Yes, we have to watch our backs as far as the inspectors are concerned. On the other hand, we've got a bloody good compliance record as far as everything else is concerned. Like, you know, waiting lists cut, catering costs reduced by half, maintenance schedules improved, security as good as ever . . .'

There was a soft cough from his left. If the Head of Security had had a head, he'd have shaken it.

'To a certain extent, yes,' he muttered.

The Finance Director turned round sharply, and his horns twitched; a sure sign of impending trouble.

'What do you mean, a certain extent?' he demanded. 'Look, either nobody's escaped or . . .'

'I was coming to that.'

As the echo of the report died away, a faint breeze dissipated the remaining wisps of smoke, revealing that (against all the odds) the Vampire King was still on his feet.

'Hmm,' he croaked. 'I'm not sure how many points you score for that.'

On the other side of the valley, Kurt 'Mad Dog' Lundqvist blinked, swore quietly under his breath, and reached into his top pocket for another silver bullet. Nothing. Just a compass, a pearl-handled switchblade and a roll of peppermints.

'Oh-*kay*,' he called out. 'You want to do this the hard way, that's fine by me.'

A few minutes later they were facing each other, *mano a mano* in the sand. Lundqvist could see that the Vampire King was sweating now, his face more than usually drawn, his teeth protruding just a telltale smidgen more. All the King could see was the flash of the noon sun on Lundqvist's mirror Ray-Bans.

'Not like you to miss the heart at four hundred yards, Kurt,' muttered the King. It was intended as a taunt, but Lundqvist accepted it as a statement of fact; which, of course, it was.

'It's this goddamn awful rifle,' he replied. 'Comes of trying to do two jobs at once, I guess. You ready?'

The King backed away. 'How do you mean, two jobs, exactly?'

'I promised the guys at *Terminator Monthly* I'd do a write-up on the new McMillan .30. Nothing like actually testing the bugger in the field, I always say. Ready yet?'

The Vampire King looked round. He was six hundred years old, completely invulnerable to anything except silver bullets and fire-hardened yew, with the strength in his hideously attenuated body of nine rogue elephants. He was also shit scared.

'We don't have to do this, you know,' he mumbled. 'We can just walk away, and . . .'

Lundqvist shook his head; a tiny, precise movement. The peak of his cap came up level with the King's third nipple. He tested the balance of the mallet in his right hand.

'Sorry, Vlad,' he said. 'A contract's a contract. Nothing personal.'

Maybe the King's mistake was to try and rush him, or maybe he didn't make a mistake at all. When you've met your match, that's it; no shame, no dishonour, just the natural course of events. In any case, there was a short blur of activity, a thud, the hollow sound of mallet-head on stake. And that was that.

As six vindictive centuries caught up with the Vampire King, he raised his head one last time and tried to give Lundqvist the stare. All that happened was that he got the stare back, with interest.

'Just tell me, Kurt,' he croaked with the last of his breath. 'Why the hell do you do it?'

'The money, Vlad. So long.'

When it was all finally over, Lundqvist got to his feet, wiped the stake off on a patch of couch grass and stuck it back in his belt. There were times, he realised, when the job did get to him, although he found it hard to admit it to himself. Not the danger, of course, or the incessant conflict with hideous and unnatural monsters, or the mind-bending horrors he came face to face with every day of his life. Certainly not the killing. When a man is tired of killing, he's tired of life.

No, Lundqvist said to himself as he tucked the vampire's severed head under his arm, shouldered the rifle and started the long walk back to the jeep, I guess what really bothers me most is the lack of excitement.

The Most Wanted Man in History, wishing to get from Iceland to Holland and having no transport of his own, had hitched a lift. Nothing unusual in that, except that he'd hitched it off an airliner.

Since there's virtually nowhere in Iceland where you can put down a 747 without breaking bits off it, the fugitive had left it hovering about four feet off the ground, on a cushion of pink cloud. With a little grunt of effort, he jumped up, caught the pilot's door, wrenched it open and swung inside the cabin.

'Hi,' he said cheerfully. 'Thanks for stopping.'

The pilot looked at him, eyes rimed over with incredulous terror. What he wanted to say was, Who are you, what's happening, have you the faintest idea what's going to happen to me when the federal aviation boys found out I dumped my plane in a volcanic desert just because some guy stuck his thumb out. What actually came out was, 'I can take you as far as Schiphol if that's any good to you.'

'Schiphol's fine,' replied the fugitive, dropping his rucksack on the floor and flopping into the wireless operator's chair. 'Thanks a lot.'

Without the pilot's having to do anything, the engines roared, the idiot lights on the console flickered into angry, bewildered life, and the pink cloud slowly floated up to around about ten thousand feet. Normal service will be resumed as soon as possible.

The wireless operator and the co-pilot took an early lunch.

'Going far?' the pilot asked, as the plane resumed its flight. He was dimly aware of a heavy, oppressive force lying across large areas of his mind like a sleeping cat on the knees of an impatient visitor, blanking off those parts of his brain that might want to raise such issues as what in God's name is going on here. Dimly aware, however, butters no parsnips.

'Just bumming around, really,' the fugitive replied. 'And Amsterdam's as good a place as any for that, as far as I'm concerned.'

Another thought that was hammering vainly on the locked

door of the pilot's consciousness was, Hang on, why am I taking this nerd to Amsterdam when this flight's supposed to be going to Geneva? It hammered and hammered and hammered, and nobody came.

'Very much a fun place, Amsterdam, from what I've heard,' the pilot's voice agreed. 'Not that I've been there for, oh, fifteen years, I suppose. Not to stop, anyway. Been travelling long?'

Flight AR675, Flight AR675, come in please, urgent, come in, please, yammered the radio. Sundry captives in the coal cellar of the pilot's mind tried using a big chunk of basic survival instinct as a battering ram, but all they did was hurt their shoulders.

'I move about,' replied the fugitive, looking out of the window at the North Sea. 'Born under a wandering star, that sort of thing.'

Flight AR675, Flight AR675, what the fuck do you think you're doing up there? Are your instruments shot, or what?

The pilot turned to his passenger. 'Should I answer that, do you think? They seem rather uptight about something.'

'I shouldn't bother,' the fugitive replied. 'They'll call back later if it's important.'

'I guess so.' The pilot leant forward and twiddled a dial on the console. The voice of Oslo air traffic control was abruptly replaced by Radio Oseberg's Music Through The Night. By virtue of some sort of ghastly air bubble in the stream of probability, they were playing 'Riders In The Sky'.

'Do you know,' said the pilot after a while, 'something tells me that if we carry on this course much longer we'll be violating Swedish airspace. Do you think they'll mind?'

'I don't think so,' replied the fugitive firmly. 'Nice people, the Swedes.'

– At which point, two massively-armed Saab Viggens were scrambled out of Birka and screamed like stainless steel banshees north-east on a direct interception course –

'Very expensive country, though,' the pilot was saying. 'I had to buy a pair of shoes there once, and do you know how much they cost? Just ordinary black lace-up walking shoes, nothing fancy . . .'

'You don't say.'

'And coffee's absolutely astronomical, of course. Not so bad in the little back-street cafes and things, of course, but in the hotels . . .'

Ernidentified ercraft, ernidentified ercraft, here is calling the Svensk er force. Turn beck immediately or down you will be shot. Repeat, down you will be . . .

'Would you like me to talk to them?' suggested the fugitive.

'Gosh, would you mind? That's extremely kind of you.'

'No problem.'

The pilot of Gamma Delta Alpha Five Three Nine set his jaw, repeated the message one last time for luck, and programmed the weapons systems. First, a five-round burst from the twin twenty-mil Oerlikons, then a couple of heat-seekers, and then back home in time for a quick beer before the press conferences.

Calling Gamma Delta Alpha Five Three Nine, come in please.

The pilot was a relatively humane man, but he couldn't help just the tiniest twinge of disappointment, deep down in the nastier bits of his repressed psyche. *Receiving you, ernidentified ercraft. Turn beck immediately or . . .*

The radio crackled. *Yes, thanks*, it said. *Do you know your flies are undone?*

Proof, if proof were needed, that technology has outgrown the ability of Mankind to control it. At the end of the day, even a really first-class piece of state-of-the-art hardware needs a human to steer it, and that human must inevitably be subject to fundamental human instinctive behaviour; such as, for example, quickly glancing down to check his zip. But in the third of a second that takes, a modern class one fighter bomber can get seriously out of hand . . .

'Good Lord,' exclaimed the pilot of the 747, 'that fighter nearly crashed into that other fighter. Whoops!'

'Butterfingers,' agreed the fugitive.

'I do hope they'll be all right.'

'I expect so. Marvellous things, ejector seats.'

'You wouldn't get me in one of those things without one.'

The fugitive craned his neck slightly to look at the sea. 'Expensive pieces of kit, these modern warplanes, I expect.'

'Very.'

'Waterproof?'

'I assume so.'

'That's all right, then.'

Lundqvist strode into the tiny branch sheriff's office in Las Monedas and banged the bell until it broke. Then he shouted.

The deputy on duty doubled as the postmaster, the trading standards officer, the funeral director, one of the town's two chartered accountants and the blacksmith's assistant. It was therefore several minutes before he was able to answer.

'The reward on these two,' snapped Lundqvist. 'In cash. And I want a receipt.'

The deputy looked up at the two severed heads and quickly ran a mental scan through his various portfolios to ascertain which one was relevant. It was easy enough to narrow the field down to two alternatives; and relatives bringing loved ones to the Las Monedas funeral parlour generally tended to have rather more of the bits.

'Hold on,' he said. From under the desk he produced a receipt book and a blue cap with red facings marked *FEDERALES*. It was entirely the wrong uniform, of course, but this was the sticks. You had to make do with what you could get.

'Vampires,' said Lundqvist, patiently (by his standards, at least). 'This one's Vlad the Indefinitely Respawned, and this one' – he broke off and glanced at the label hanging from the left ear – 'this one here is Count Bors Vilassanyi. I've got the ISBN* details somewhere, if that's any help.'

'Just a moment,' replied the deputy, thumbing through a loose-leaf binder. 'Vlad, Vlad – there's a lot of Vlads isn't there? – ah, right, here you go. Vlad the Indefinitely Respawned. Hey, Category Three, not bad. What did you say the other one was?'

'Count Bors Vilassanyi. Two 's's in Vilassanyi.'

'Sorry, doesn't seem to be here.'

'Try the supplement.'

'Yes, right. No, not in here either.'

'Okay, try looking under zombies.'

'Right – yes, here we are. Category Four A.' The deputy frowned. 'Sorry,' he said, 'but we don't keep that much cash in the office.'

'Bank's still open.'

'Or the country, come to that. You could try America, just up the road and turn left; they might be able to help.'

Lundqvist sighed. 'Fuck that,' he said. 'I guess I'll just have to take a cheque.'

'I'll need to see your licence and some proof of identity.'

Lundqvist growled ominously. 'Here's the licence.'

'Thanks, that all seems to be in order. How about this proof of identity?'

With no apparent exertion whatsoever, Lundqvist picked the deputy up one-handed by the lapels, held him about two inches from the tip of his nose and treated him to a long, special stare.

'Is that okay?'

'That'll do nicely, Mr Lundqvist.'

There was a brief interval while the deputy laboriously wrote out a cheque, during which time Lundqvist amused himself by shuffling through the file of Wanted posters on the desk. Since

_____

*International Supernatural Beings Number

they were a trifle behind the times at Las Monedas, the file read more like Lundqvist's curriculum vitae. Sorry. Curriculum mortis.

Theodore 'Fangs' Lupo – March 1992, Guatemala. Trouble getting his pelt over the border, Lundqvist recalled, because of the endangered species by-products regulations. Ironic, since it was largely due to his efforts that werewolves were endangered in the first place.

Rameses IV – July 1992, Cairo. One of the few contracts that had given any real degree of job satisfaction. Amazing what these new hi-tech wallpaper pastes could do with three-thousand-year-old papyrus bandages.

Aldazor, Lord High Marshal of the Infernal Hosts – August 1992, Akron, Ohio. A miserable job, that, and he was still getting letters from the Vatican legal department about infringement of copyright. Copyright bullshit. Show me a priest who uses bell, book and 20mm recoilless rifle, and then sue me.

With a sigh, Lundqvist flicked through the rest of the file. Nothing but the commonplace, the routine, the uninspiring, the run-of-the-mill. For a man who had got into this line of work purely for the adrenaline rush of living on the edge, he was spending far too much time pottering about in the epicentre.

And then . . .

He stopped.

He turned back.

Wow!

'Hey,' he said. 'How long's this one been out? Don't remember seeing it before.'

The deputy looked up over the rims of his spectacles. They had belonged to his great-grandfather, and it was a moot point as to whether the myopia that ran in his family was cause or effect.

'Oh, that one,' he replied. 'That's new. A man delivered it specially.'

'When?'

The deputy thought for a moment. 'Three days ago,' he said. 'Maybe four. It was the day Little Pepe's mule cast a shoe and Miguel sent the telegram to San Felipe.'

'Thanks.' With a swift movement, Lundqvist snapped open the file, removed the flyer, and snapped the file shut. 'I think I'll just borrow this for a while,' he said. 'You don't mind, do you?'

Before the deputy could answer, Lundqvist had folded the flyer away, snatched his cheque and hurried out.

In the cantina, over a triple hot chilli and a jug of coarse red, Lundqvist studied the flyer in detail.

WANTED

and then a space; and in big, old-fashioned letters:

PAST OR
PRESENT

(they keep that typeface specially for wanted posters); and then a blurred photograph; but the face was already familiar. More than that; it had been an unshiftable grape-pip behind the dental plate of Lundqvist's professional pride for more years than he cared to remember. And then the name, and the aliases. The Most Wanted Man in History.

And then the reward. There were so many noughts it looked like the string of bubbles left behind by a swimming otter.

Lundqvist nodded gravely, finished his chilli and lit a cigar. Yes, the challenge. Yes, the adrenaline rush. Yes, the chance to settle a really big old score.

And yes – yes, indeed – the money.

CHAPTER TWO

'That's fine,' said the fugitive. 'You can drop me here.'
The pilot looked at him.

'Thanks,' added the fugitive significantly, 'for the lift. I'll be seeing you. Goodbye.'

The airliner obligingly stopped. Around its wingtips, the wind howled. Below, the sea groped for the plane's belly with ephemeral talons of spray. Two seagulls flew straight into the tailplane and knocked themselves out cold.

'It was a pleasure,' replied the pilot. 'See you around.'

The cabin door opened – it shouldn't have; it was pressurised, and if it opened under pressure the entire contents of the cabin would be sucked up and spat out – and the fugitive picked up his rucksack, waved politely, and walked down a flight of nothing into thin air.

The fugitive watched the airliner fade into a dot on the horizon, then strolled across the wavetops to the fishing boat which he'd selected as the best way to make an inconspicuous entry into Holland.

'Hi,' he said in fluent Dutch as two fishermen came running with lifebelts. 'If we crack on a bit we can be home by nightfall.'

You can feel a right fool, frozen in the act of throwing a life-belt to a perfectly dry stranger in chinos, sleeveless shirt and straw hat. The fishermen paused, searching their sparse but functional vocabulary for something appropriate.

'We haven't finished fishing yet.'

The fugitive smiled. 'Don't you believe it,' he said.

He clicked his fingers, and the mechanical net-winders began to purr. As the nets cleared the water, there was a distressing sound of groaning hemp. A couple of rivets popped in the crane.

'That ought to do for one day,' the fugitive went on, indicating the painfully overladen nets. 'Right then. Chop chop, busy busy.'

The elder fisherman, who had seen some pretty weird things in his time and been told about a hell of a lot more, removed his cap, turned it round and put it back on his head. It was the first time he'd removed it in thirty-two years, funerals included.

'How did you do that?' he asked.

'Entropy.'

The fisherman's old, shrewd eyes met the fugitive's and for a moment there was a flicker of recognition; not of the man, but of the phenomenon. Forty years at sea and you learn the wisdom of taking the other man's word for it.

'Fair enough,' he said. 'Thanks. Where do you want to go?'

'Amsterdam.'

'I can take you to Ijmuiden,' replied the fisherman, 'and then you can get the bus.'

'That's fine.'

The fugitive wandered astern, lay down on a coil of rope, tilted his hat over his eyes and went to sleep.

The younger fisherman turned to his colleague.

'Dad,' he said.

'Yes,' replied his father. 'I know. Don't worry about it.'

'But you don't know what I was going to—'

'I can guess, son.' The elder fisherman prodded a heaving net with the toe of his boot. He was old, even for a fisherman, but not so old that he could remember the last time a Vollendam trawler had come home laden down to the bows with a record catch of coelacanth.

Coelacanth. An extinct species. You could name your own price. In fact, given the quantity now slopping about on the deck wondering where all the water had suddenly gone, you could cut out the middleman and open an international chain of Vollendam Fried Coelacanth restaurants.

According to the latest edition of the *Red Guide to Hell*, finding suitable accommodation during your stay should not present a problem.

For business travellers and those tourists who can afford the prices, the Hell Sheraton, the Inn on the Pit and the Hellton all offer the usual five-star facilities and enjoy a convenient central location. Tourists of more modest means can expect a warm welcome and high standards of cleanliness and service at the Mephisto, the Casa 666 and the Elysium Palace. Students and others on a fixed budget are recommended to try one of the many friendly, family-run *auberges* and guest-houses outside the old town of Los Diablos, particularly in the suburbs of Beverley Hells and Hellywood.

There is, however, one thing that all these fine establishments have in common. To put it as nicely as possible, they don't provide you with a late key. Or an early key, for that matter.

Getting out of Hell is a bit like successfully defrauding the Revenue; many people will tell you they know someone who's managed it, but the name somehow eludes them. In practice, it's never happened.

Until . . .

'It's amazing,' said the Finance Director.

'Yes,' replied the Head of Security. 'Clever little sod,' he added.

They were standing in the doorway of a room on the third floor of the Hotel Dante. It was empty, except for a bed with no sheets, a hacksaw and the Visitors' Book.

'Where he got the hacksaw from,' the Head of Security said, 'I have no idea.'

He picked up the instrument in question, which promptly sniggered at him and vanished. At the same time, the rope of sheets hanging from the stump of the severed bar in the window frame retracted itself, shrugged off its knots and slipped back on to the bed. The Finance Director examined them.

'Ironed, too,' he observed. 'I call that class, don't you?'

The Head of Security scratched the back of his head. 'I still don't get it,' he remarked. 'I mean, hacksaws don't just appear, and sheets don't just tie themselves into knots. I think they called it physics when I was at school.'

The Finance Director sighed. 'If you look at the file,' he said patiently, 'you'll see he was in here for sorcery, necromancy and dabbling in the Black Arts.'

'Was he? Well I—'

'In which case,' continued the Finance Director remorselessly, 'perhaps it wasn't the most sensible idea in the history of the cosmos to set him to work in the machine shop.'

'But—'

'Bearing in mind,' the Finance Director concluded, 'that in the machine shop he'd have access to pentangles, tetragrammata, Vernier mandalas . . .'

'They're under strict orders to keep all that stuff locked away—'

'. . . Eccentric-drive sabbats, adjustable familiars, coven wrenches and all the string he could possibly want. Let's face it, we goofed.' He closed his eyes, sighed again and thought for a while. Two of the principal skills of the high-class manager are damage limitation and positive thinking.

'We'll just have to get him back, that's all,' he said. 'Which shouldn't be difficult. I've had posters sent out and we can pay the reward out of the repairs and maintenance budget. It's more a question of time.'

They left the Dante and walked slowly back up towards the Mouth via the attractive and unspoilt Usurer's Quarter, pausing only to buy some locally-produced candy floss from one of the many picturesque stalls.

It comes in three flavours: sulphur, brimstone and strawberry.

'Why?' asked the Head of Security.

'Because,' replied the Finance Director through a mouthful of sticky yellow froth, 'he was a Purchase, and we've got the auditors in next month.'

'Sorry?'

The Finance Director wiped his mouth on his sleeve, which smoked. 'A Purchase,' he repeated. 'Sold his soul to the . . . to the previous administration. There was a lot of it went on in the old days. Sort of like subsidies. Bloody awful way to run a railway in my opinion, but what the, um, thing, it was just public money, so nobody cared. Anyway, we've got stuck with the aftermath. From an accountancy point of view, it's an absolute nightmare.'

He stopped, while the Head of Security, who had foolishly chosen the strawberry, was violently sick.

'It's all a question of book-keeping, you see,' he went on, when the retching had subsided. 'Purchased souls go in the balance sheet under Fixed Assets. Subject to straight-line depreciation and writing down allowance, of course, but you've got to account for them at the end of the day. If they go missing, you're in real trouble, believe me. Since miladdo's only been here, what, five hundred years, he's still got about eighty-five per cent of his original value after allowances. That's one heck of a shortfall.'

The Head of Security frowned. Books in his experience

were not things you kept so much as threw at persistent offenders.
He groped under the sink of his memory.

'Can't you write him off?' he suggested.

The Finance Director scowled. 'Against what? Good debts?
No, we've just got to get the bastard back again. It's as simple
as that.'

'Right,' said the Head of Security. 'So you'll be wanting me
to get a squad together and—'

'No.' The Finance Director shook his head, nearly slicing
the Head of Security's scalp off in the process. 'Out of our
hands now, I'm delighted to say.'

'So what are we doing about it?'

For the first time that day, there was a faint glint of pleasure
in the Finance Director's voice, and his third eye positively
sparkled. 'I've hired a bounty hunter,' he replied. 'The best.'

He smiled, set light to the rest of his candy floss, and ran up
the steps to his office.

There are three immutable laws in the Universe. Only three.

Two of them concern death and taxes, and they have been
waived on occasions. Not so the third, which states:

NOBODY GETS TO SEE
MR VAN APPIN
WITHOUT AN APPOINTMENT.

Having played fast and loose with the other two in his time,
the fugitive (now dressed in a lightweight grey suit, smart light
tan brogues and a dove-grey tie) is going to have a crack at the
third.

'Excuse me,' said the receptionist, 'but do you have an
appointment?'

The fugitive turned round slowly and looked at her.

'That depends,' he said.

'I doubt that, sir,' the receptionist replied. If you left her tone of voice outside in the rain overnight, it'd have rust on it come morning. 'Do you have an appointment or not?'

'That depends,' said the fugitive, 'on which way round you like your Time. I personally like it arse-about-face, so I make all my appointments retrospectively. Come back about five minutes ago and I'll have got it sorted for you.'

'I'm sorry,' said the receptionist. 'Nobody sees Mr Van Appin without an—'

'He'll see me.'

'With respect, sir . . . '

The fugitive smiled, and vanished.

Almost simultaneously, he rematerialised in Mr Van Appin's office, sat down in the large leather armchair and started linking paperclips together.

'Morning, George,' said Mr Van Appin, without looking up. 'I'll be with you in two shakes.'

Although his face did not betray the fact, the fugitive was impressed. It's not everyone who's cool enough to take the sudden materialisation of an escaped soul in torment so totally in his stride.

'That's okay,' he replied. 'No hurry.'

Mr Van Appin finished annotating the document he had been studying, put it in his out tray, steepled his fingers and leant back in his chair.

'Long time no see, George,' he said, 'if you'll pardon the expression.'

'Good of you to fit me in at such short notice,' the fugitive replied. 'Look, I'm in a bit of a jam, I wondered if you could help me get it sorted out.'

The cigar box on Mr Van Appin's desk floated across the room and opened itself under the fugitive's nose. He shook his head slightly.

'I'll do my best,' Mr Van Appin said. 'Tell me all about it.'

The fugitive grinned. 'Starting where, Pete?'

Mr Van Appin considered. 'Well,' he said. 'I think we can

take all the In-the-beginning-was-the-Word stuff as read and pick up the story where you'd sold your soul to the Very Bad Person and he'd taken delivery. To be honest with you, George, I took that as being a suitable juncture to close my file and send in my bill.' Mr Van Appin frowned. 'Did you ever pay it, by the way?'

'By return,' George replied. 'Or rather, my executors did. I saw to that well in advance, believe me. I may have been facing eternal damnation, but I didn't want to get into *real* trouble.'

'Ah yes.' Mr Van Appin's brow cleared. 'I remember now. Anyway, to get back to what we were saying just a moment ago, I'd rather assumed that that was it, as far as you were concerned. Terribly sorry to lose you as a client and all that, but these things happen. In fact, the term "banged to rights" did float across my mind more than once in connection with your affairs. Nobody followed you here, did they?'

'Unlikely,' said the fugitive. 'As far as I can see they haven't the faintest idea when I am, let alone where. Listen, Peter, I want to fight this one.'

Mr Van Appin raised an eyebrow. 'Fight it, George?'

'Yeah.' The fugitive nodded. 'Call it a matter of principle.'

Mr Van Appin frowned again. 'That's expensive talk, George.'

'I've got the money.'

Mr Van Appin shrugged. 'I don't doubt that you do. Even then, I can't really hold out much prospect of success. Those soul-and-purchase contracts are the nearest things you'll ever get to watertight.'

The fugitive looked amused. 'Are they really.'

''Fraid so, George,' replied Mr Van Appin. 'I drafted them myself. And,' he added, with a wisp of nostalgia, 'I was good then. Just starting up, I was, anxious to make a name for myself. Landing a client like that, I wanted to make a good impression.'

'So you don't think it's possible?'

'I think it'll be very, very difficult,' Mr Van Appin replied.

'Mind you, I'm looking at the worst possible scenario here, you understand.'

'Playing devil's advocate, in fact.'

Mr Van Appin smiled without amusement. 'You could say that,' he said. 'Actually, I don't act for them any more. All their work's done in-house these days.'

'Really?'

Mr Van Appin nodded. 'Makes sense,' he said. 'After all, they get their pick of the entire profession down there, sooner or later.'

'Except you, Pete.'

A faint pinkness experimented with crossing Mr Van Appin's cheeks. 'Flattery will get you nowhere,' he said. 'I'm not saying it's impossible, George. Nothing's impossible. I just can't see how, that's all. Maybe I'm getting old or something.' He stopped, tapped his teeth with a pencil, and considered for a moment. 'That's a thought, actually,' he said. 'A hundred years ago I'd have accepted like a shot. Why don't you try our office then?'

(As a result of the unique nature of his practice, Mr Van Appin found it convenient to have a main branch office in every century, with sub-offices at thirty-year intervals to take over his practice each time he retired. Because of his equally unique skills, he had never been able to find a worthy partner or associate, with the result that he ran all his offices simultaneously, thereby taking the concept of overwork into a whole new dimension.)

The fugitive shook his head. 'Nah,' he said. 'I've got other business to attend to in this decade, Pete, I couldn't find the time.'

There was a long silence.

'It'll cost you, mind,' said Mr Van Appin.

'Like I said,' the fugitive replied. 'No worries.'

Mr Van Appin grinned. 'In that case,' he said, 'I'll need a copy of the original agreement, a signed affidavit from the Holy Ghost and fifty billion guilders on account.'

'I thought you'd say that,' replied the fugitive. He passed over the attaché case he'd brought in with him. Mr Van Appin raised the lid and nodded.

'Where can I call you?' he said. 'I imagine you'll need to be hard to find for a while.'

'I'll call you,' the fugitive replied. 'Better that way.'

When he'd gone, Mr Van Appin swivelled round in his chair a couple of times, chewing the end of his pencil and humming. Then he reached for the dictating machine.

'Please open a new file, Miss Duisberg,' he said. 'Client profile C, client name, Faust, that's F-A-U-S for sugar -T, George Michael. Re . . .' He paused, wound the tape back, wound it forward again. 'Re, dispute with Hell Holdings plc.'

Faust wasn't, of course, his real name.

Faust was just the German abbreviation of Faustus, which was the nickname he'd picked up as an undergraduate at Wittenberg. It means 'Lucky'.

Only goes to show how wrong you can be, doesn't it?

Out of a particularly ill-fated year (his contemporaries included Martin Luther, Matthias Corvinus and Hamlet, Prince of Denmark) Lucky George was the student people remembered as having come to the most spectacularly sticky end. So devastating was the ensuing scandal that the university authorities promptly dropped Black Arts from the university curriculum; replacing it, seamlessly, with economics. A wave of hysteria swept across Europe, and for the next two centuries, witchcraft and sorcery remained (so to speak) a burning issue on the agenda of the known world. Even Lucky George's mother stopped talking about her son, the doctor, and transferred the picture of him in his matriculation robes from the mantelpiece to the coalshed.

Lucky George was not, however, such a misnomer as all that. Nobody could deny that he had more luck than any other hundred people put together. It's just that luck comes in two varieties.

Call them flavours, if it makes it any easier.

The other scoop in George's cone, in his opinion at least, more than adequately made up for the slight downside effect he'd experienced over the soul business. All that had been a means to an end, and a very nice end it was, too. Make no mistake; Lucky George had got value for money.

Ronnie Bosch sat in his studio, stared long and hard at his drawing board, and groaned.

It was, they'd told him, all part of a concept which was definitely going to be The Future as far as Hell Holdings was concerned.

For reasons he couldn't quite grasp, but which he couldn't help but find mildly flattering, they were going to call it Euro-Bosch.

Visit, they had postulated, a land of wonder and enchantment. Meet your favourite characters from the repertoire of Europe's most imaginative artist face to... Take a ride through spectacular landscapes to see sights you'll never see anywhere else.

Sounded good, in theory; but Ronnie, faced with the prospect of creating seven hundred thousand different appropriate latex masks in time for the Grand Celebrity Opening, was asking himself whether they'd really thought it through properly before committing the funding.

For a start, he muttered to himself, scowling at a recalcitrant design and then turning it upside down (much better that way), masks really weren't going to be enough, not for some of the more *outré* designs. We're talking body suits here, and quite probably bodies as well. Dammit, about forty per cent of his best work was anatomically impossible. Which meant starting from scratch.

Yuk.

A stray pellet of inspiration struck home, and he reached for a pencil.

A mouse, he thought. A seven-foot, grinning, anthropomorphic mouse, with perky little front fangs and big hands which . . .

He shook his head, as if trying to dislodge the very idea. Broad-minded he most certainly was, but there are limits. The mere thought of it gave him the willies.

What he'd really always wanted to do, of course, was design helicopters. And parachutes, and telescopes, and wonderful ships powered by paddles driven by treadmills turned by oxen. And siege engines, and washing machines, and refrigerators, and combination tin-openers and potato-peelers, and space-saving compact disc racks, and ironing-boards that ingeniously fold away into nests of coffee tables. He would have been good at it, too. In fact, he'd invented the Swiss Army Knife before the Swiss even had an army.

Unfortunately, he'd been too successful as a commercial artist and illustrator, at a time when what the public wanted was spare-part-surgery demons and hideously teeming egg-shells. It was a bit like being a fashionable book-jacket artist, only not quite so well paid.

And then it had started coming rather too easily. Even when he shut his eyes. Particularly when he shut his eyes. Like now, for example.

How about an enormous mutant duck, with huge oval eyes and a beak the size of a tennis racket, and a hideous sort of hungry leer which made you think it was about to . . . ?

Quickly, he opened his eyes, rubbed them with the knuckles of his fists, and swallowed a heaped handful of librium.

He started to draw a cow.

Drawn-faced, travel-sore and ever so slightly out of his head with fatigue, Lundqvist pushed open the door of the American bookstore in Paris and leant both elbows heavily on the counter.

'Goethe,' he said.

'Pardon me?'

'You deaf or something? I said Goethe.'

The girl behind the counter adjusted her spectacles. 'You want a book by Goethe?' she hazarded.

'You got it.'

The girl considered. 'I think we've got one somewhere,' she said. 'We used to have, anyway. I haven't been here long.'

'Fetch.'

The girl went away; shortly afterwards she came back.

'You're sure the book you wanted was by Goethe?'

'Yes.'

'We've got this one.' She handed over a dusty paperback with the air of someone who's been asked for some pretty daffy things in their time but is still just occasionally capable of surprise. 'Is this the . . . ?'

Lundqvist glanced down at the spine. *Faust*. Parts One and Two. Complete and unabridged. A Mentor Classic. 'Yeah,' Lundqvist growled. 'Marlowe.'

The girl took a look at his hard-worn trenchcoat and the bulge under his left arm. 'That's your name, right?'

'Christopher Marlowe,' replied Lundqvist, suggesting that his patience was not unlimited. 'British sixteenth-century dramatist. Complete works. Move it.'

The girl went away again, and again came back.

'We've only got Volume One in the NEL edition,' she said. 'I can order . . .'

Lundqvist took the book, flipped it open at the list of contents and nodded. 'That's fine,' he said. 'No problem. Keep the change.'

On a bench beside the Seine, Lundqvist ripped open the paper bag in which the girl had insisted on wrapping the books, selected the Complete Works of Christopher Marlowe, and began to read.

He found it hard going. His usual reading matter tended to

be terser and less flowery ('Step three; wire up the timing device to the detonator') and he knew for a fact that large parts of Marlowe's version were heavily embroidered, fanciful or just plain wrong.

He wondered why. For a start, the jerk he'd known all these years had his faults, God knows, but even he didn't go around talking poetry all the time, like some goddamn faggot.

Eventually, however, he found what he was looking for. Having underlined it heavily in yellow marker pen and noted down the page number in his notebook, he opened the Goethe version and, after a great deal of tedious slogging through, found the passage that corroborated exactly what he'd found out in the Marlowe. Fine.

He stuck the books in his pocket and went off to buy a 55mm recoilless rifle.

The Company Secretary looked up, his hand over the mouthpiece of the receiver.

'It's *him*,' he hissed. 'What do I do?'

The Finance Director frowned. 'I'll take the call,' he said. 'You get Security to see if they can get a trace on the line.'

He lifted the telephone in front of him, took a deep breath, and said, 'Yes?'

'Hi.'

The Finance Director thought for a moment. 'It's a terribly bad line,' he said. 'You'll have to speak up.'

'Listen,' replied the voice at the other end. 'I'm giving you fair warning. No doubt you've got people on my trail. Call them off. Otherwise, you'll regret it. Got that?'

The Finance Director smiled. 'I think so,' he said. 'You're saying that unless we leave you alone, something *bad* is going to happen to us.' He paused, for effect. 'Hasn't it crossed your mind that every conceivable bad thing there is has probably happened to us already? Bearing in mind—'

The line went dead.

'No luck,' said Security. 'Not enough time. Somewhere in Europe, probably late twentieth, early twenty-first century. Otherwise . . .'

'It doesn't matter,' the Finance Director replied with a sigh. 'The chances of him doing anything silly and giving himself away are a snowflake's chance in . . . Anyway,' he went on, 'at least we're in communication. Of a sort. We'll have him, don't you worry.'

The Company Secretary stroked his chin, causing sparks. 'Excuse me if I'm barking up the wrong tree here,' he said, but wasn't that a threat he just came out with? *Otherwise, you'll regret it,* something like that?'

The Finance Director shrugged. 'Bluster,' he said.

'Ah,' replied the Company Secretary. 'For a moment there I thought it was a threat.'

'Same thing. Bluster is a threat you make when you're backed up against a wall facing certain death at the hands of overwhelmingly superior forces.'

'Ah. Like, Bluster's last stand, sort of thing?'

The Finance Director gave him a look, and he grinned sheepishly. They both knew what the Company Secretary had originally been sent down for; and it wasn't simony or stealing sheep. You'd have thought he'd have learnt his lesson by now.

'Don't worry,' the Finance Director said. 'There's no threat he can possibly pose to anyone. He's got nothing up his sleeve except his arm, take it from me.'

CHAPTER THREE

Not long afterwards, Lucky George started his reign of terror.

That's overstating the case somewhat. More a series of brisk showers of extreme aggravation.

Historians have, after exhaustive research, pinpointed what you might term the Sarajevo or Harper's Ferry of Lucky George's war against humanity. It was half past six on a Friday; the place, the centre of Amiens. The victim, a young insurance salesman whose name is not recorded. As a result, the annual wreaths are laid at the Tomb of the Unknown Soldier, although soldier is probably pushing it a bit.

The victim, hurrying to catch his bus, pauses for a moment outside a branch of the Credit Lyonnais. He fumbles in his wallet until he finds his cash dispenser card. He inserts it. He waits.

After five seconds or so (which is a long time when you're standing out in the street, painfully conscious of the ebb and flow of the French provincial bus service passing you by) the cash dispenser makes a noise. Par for the course, sure; but this isn't part of its usual repertoire.

It burps.

The victim frowns. He presses the button marked *Cancel Transaction*, and waits.

The lights flicker. The machine spells out a message.

YOUR CARD HAS BEEN RETAINED

it says. Then it flickers again.

OR RATHER, EATEN

The victim raises an eyebrow. Some last smear of the basic survival instinct spattered across the back of his mind prompts him to take a step back. The lights dance.

RATHER SALTY, I THOUGHT

This time, the victim can actually smell the danger, but it's too late. The machine is looking directly at him. In fact, it's smiling.

AND YOU CAN'T HAVE IT BACK, SO THERE

There is a fundamental and rather dangerous urge in all of us to try and cling to the jagged edge of normality, even when it's blindingly obvious that the longer you hold on, the further you're going to fall when your grip finally fails. The victim presses *Cancel Transaction* again. Bad move.

LOOK, FOUR-EYES

The victim tries to back away, but the machine is doing a very good mongoose impression. It seems to have a direct line to the victim's feet.

NOBODY TRIES TO CANCEL ME AND GETS AWAY WITH IT. YOU GOT THAT?

The victim's first thought is to apologise, but the dead hand of normality is gripping the scruff of his neck. You can't talk to these machines, he's thinking, they're just machines, they can't . . .

A stream of banknotes, glued together to form something disquietingly like a tongue, lashes out of the cash slot, flails horribly in the air, and lands on the victim's tie. Then it retracts.

TWO CAN PLAY AT THAT GAME, BUSTER

Just as the victim's nose is pressed up against the perspex screen, his chin flattened against the diagram showing the Right Way Up, the tortured fibres of the tie give way, leaving the tongue wrapped round three inches of terylene, and the victim flat on his back in the gutter. But not for long.

He scrambles to his feet. He runs. In his haste to get away, he fails to notice the patrolling gendarme and collides with him heavily. There's a short interlude, while the gendarme brushes the insurance salesman off his lapels.

'Monsieur!' There's a wildness in his eyes that commands attention, and fair enough. When a Frenchman is palpably more afraid of something that he's recently seen than a gendarme he's just knocked over, there's got to be something badly the matter. 'Monsieur, the bank just tried to kill me. It swallowed my card, and then it ate my tie.'

The gendarme has summed up the victim as mentally disturbed and is just about to render psychiatric first-aid with his truncheon when he catches sight of the banknote tongue, still thrashing about, trying to feed three inches of tie in through the cash slot. He stares.

The machine stares back. Then – there's no other way to put this – it sticks its tongue out at the policeman.

The gendarme stiffens. There are certain things you just don't do, no matter how many branches and wholly-owned subsidiary companies you've got.

It only takes him a fraction of a second to bark out the obligatory warning. The tongue extends further and waggles about. In fact, it connects with the gendarme's kepi, twists it round a couple of times, and stuffs it into the cash slot. There is another burp. A button lands on the pavement and rolls drunkenly away.

The rest is most definitely not silence. Out comes the gendarme's 9mm service automatic. Three cracks, like the breaking of a giant's leg bones. The machine goes on grinning.

It displays a derogatory message on its screen.

All this is well known, of course; you'll find it in any history book, in one version or another. What isn't so well recorded – probably because it's so very unnerving, and mankind can only take so much reality before it starts demanding that something be done about it – is the fact that when the gendarme in question received his bank statement at the end of the month, he was disturbed to find an entry recording three rounds of 125-grain full metal jacket 9mm Parabellum credited to his account on the day in question.

With interest. And, of course, basic rate tax deducted at source.

Shortly after the first reports of this contretemps had reached the Hot Seat and were dismissed as being a rather offbeat practical joke, a fax machine in Toronto grabbed a secretary by the wrist as she was feeding paper into it, hurled her across the ionosphere and dumped her down in Winnipeg, in the front office of a highly respected firm of water diviners.

To make matters worse, it was a wrong number.

Microwaves the length and breadth of Florida burst simultaneously into song until switched off, while a team of firemen in Tokyo fought for two hours to release a chat-show host from the interior of a portable television set. When the unfortunate man was eventually freed, he was found to have broken several small bones in his wrists while hammering on the inside of the glass.

In Novosibirsk, an entire warehouseful of retractable ball-point pens was destroyed by long-range artillery fire after turning into small but incredibly agile yellow snakes. The President of Venezuela appeared on national television to appeal for calm after all the office dictating machines in the country started answering back. Large parts of the centre of Perth were sealed off, leaving a handful of bemused Marines to watch the stately dance of the traffic lights over the sights of their machine-guns. In London, all the telephones refused to speak to each other for three hours, but nobody noticed. Workers on a People's Farm at an undisclosed location in Shantung province were frightened out of their wits when they reported for work only to find that the newly planted rice-paddy had spontaneously landscaped itself into an eighteen-hole golf course, complete with electric carts, clubhouse and conference facilities.

Absolutely nothing peculiar happened in Ireland at all, which was perhaps the most disconcerting part of it. No statues of the Virgin Mary moved their arms or were seen to weep tears for a period calculated to have been in excess of three hours.

In Paris, the Mona Lisa giggled.

'Okay,' said the Finance Director. 'You win. We're withdrawing our agents.'

'And about time too,' replied Lucky George. He fumbled in his pocket for a coin to feed the phone box, but could only find a small, bent washer. He smiled at it. 'Just count yourselves extremely lucky I'm a bit out of practice.'

'You won't get away with it, you know. You can hide, but you can't run.'

'Shouldn't that be the other—'

'Think about it.'

Lucky George thought about it and decided he didn't like the Finance Director's tone, with the result that back in the hastily prepared emergency rooms at Pandaemonium, the receiver gave the Finance Director's ear a big, wet kiss. The Finance Director wound his handkerchief round the earpiece and went on:

'Tell you what we'll do, George. Give yourself up, come quietly, we'll forget all about it. You can even have your old job back in the . . . We'll give you a nice cushy job in the kitchens. Now I can't say fairer than—'

The mouthpiece of the telephone popped an apple neatly into the Finance Director's mouth, and the line went dead. Lucky George hung up, smiled the phone booth back out of existence, and crossed the road to a cafe, where he ordered a beer and a toasted sandwich.

Withdrawing all their agents. Like hell they were.

He sat for a while and smoked (a process which in his case did not involve tobacco) and then reached for his glass, upended it on the table, and began a seance.

In order to conjure the spirits of the dead, you need to link up at least three pairs of hands. Although he was alone, Lucky George didn't seem to find this a problem.

'You there, Bull?'

The saucer with Lucky George's unpaid bill in it rocked backwards and forwards a couple of times. Lucky George grinned and slipped a coin under the rim . . .

Oh. You thought it was the *waiter* who took it. Sorry to have disillusioned you.

. . . Whereupon a cloud of ectoplasm materialised above the table and hovered there, refracting light. A man in a bow tie and a black waistcoat hurried up, and took its order for coffee and a slice of cheesecake.

How.

'Sheer bloody-mindedness, mostly,' replied Lucky George. 'And you?'

Not so dusty, replied the shade of Sitting Bull. *They've recently transferred me to a job in Administration.*

'Administration?' Lucky George raised an eyebrow. 'Why was that, Bully?'

Search me. The only reason I could come up with was that my name fitted. Like, you do a lot of sitting and—

'Quite so,' Lucky George replied. 'Anyway, to business. I seem to remember you owe me a favour, Bully.'

The ectoplasm shook its head violently, causing a fortuitous rainbow.

Don't make me laugh, paleface. Your people stole our lands. They wiped out the buffalo. They raped our hunting-grounds with the telegraph and the iron horse. They massacred us when we tried to fight and drove us into reservations. They destroyed our unique and vital cultural traditions and poisoned our youth with fire water and flame-grilled spicy bisonburgers. I don't seem to recall owing any favours to anyone with skin that particularly revolting shade of pinky-apricot.

Lucky George frowned. 'Short memory you've got, Bully,' he said. 'I'm amazed you've forgotten who it was advised you to invest heavily in railroad bonds and Wells Fargo Unsecured Loan Stock back in the early 1870s. Maybe I'm thinking of somebody else.'

The ectoplasm quivered slightly, like a fluorescent jelly.

Point taken. All right, what do you want?

Lucky George paused while the waiter brought the coffee. They shared the cheesecake.

'To tell you the truth, Bully,' said Lucky George, 'I find myself in a bit of a fix.'

You don't say.

'Leave heavy irony to the living, Bully, they've got a flair for it. The point is, I need a spot of help. From someone on the inside on the Other Side, if you follow me.'

You want jam on it, you do.

'Do I?' George replied mildly. He smiled at the remains of

the cheesecake, rendering it inedible under two centimetres of damson preserve. 'It's not a lot to ask. Of course, if you want the entire Sioux nation to find out about your career in bond-washing . . .'

All right, there's no need to get nasty. They've called off all their agents, just like they said.

George raised both eyebrows. 'You surprise me, Bully, you really do.'

Freelances, on the other hand, are not covered by the term 'agent'. In contract law, as no doubt you recall, no contract of agency subsists in the case of a unilateral, open-ended contract (such as the offer of a public reward) until the contracting party signifies his acceptance of the offer by actually performing the contract. The leading authority on this point is the old case of Carlill versus the Carbolic Smoke Ball Company, in which—

'I beg your pardon?'

I'm taking law at night school. No way I'm going to be just another dumb Injun all my life. I'm allergic to sun-dried buffalo and wampum gives me eczema.

'Good for you, Bully. Any particular freelance you have in mind?'

The ectoplasm began to laugh; and laughed so violently that it shook its fragile manifestation out of existence and vanished, absent-mindedly taking the rest of the cheesecake with it. Lucky George sighed.

'Oh,' he said. '*Him*. I might have guessed.'

Ask any detective, and he'll tell you that getting the initial lead is the difficult part. Once you've got something, however slight, to go on, it's just a matter of inspired perseverance. The problem is getting that initial lucky break.

Ask Kurt Lundqvist, and he'll tell you that the only way to get a break is to hit something hard. Or someone.

'Now, then,' he said, wrapping his belt round his fist. 'We could do this the hard way, or . . .'

He paused and reflected. Nah. Why confuse the issue by introducing alternatives?

'We'll do this the hard way,' he said.

Possession of a warrant card valid in all jurisdictions, temporal as well as geographical, meant that it was no problem whatsoever for Lundqvist to nip backwards and forwards in Time in the pursuit of his enquiries. This was a great help. For one thing, if a suspect sneakily died under interrogation, he could rewind back to the deceased's last lucid moment and start all over again . . .

'I've never heard of him,' whimpered the interviewee. 'Honest.'

'Listen.' Lundqvist laid aside the belt and put an arm round the subject's shoulders. 'Co-operate, why don't you? Do yourself a favour.' He paused and grinned. 'I have to say that, you know, it's in the rules. Personally, the less you talk, the more I like it.' He picked up the belt again and waggled it meaningfully under the subject's nose.

'No, but really,' the subject said. 'I honestly have never heard that name in my life before. How can I have, for Christ's sake? He won't even be born for another seven years . . .'

Nostradamus paused, and bit his lip.

'Oh shit,' he said.

'Precisely,' Lundqvist replied. 'Don't mind me, though. If you want to persist in fruitless denials for an hour or so, that's absolutely fine by me.'

Nostradamus passed the tip of his tongue across his bone-dry lips. 'All right,' he said. 'All right, I admit, I've heard of him. Doesn't mean to say I know where he is. I mean, I've heard of all sorts of people, I've heard of Elvis Presley. Doesn't follow that I know where he's hiding out.'

Lundqvist raised an eyebrow. 'Who's Elvis Presley?' he asked.

Nostradamus shrugged. 'After your time, I suppose,' he said. 'Or before. It gets a bit confusing, sometimes.'

'Yeah.' Lundqvist smiled, or at least he drew back his lips to exhibit his teeth, and clenched his fist round the belt. 'You know, it's really nice of you to be so brave about this. Most guys just crack up and start talking the moment I've tied them to the chair.' He patted his knuckles against the palm of his other hand. 'Say this for you, Nos, you've got balls. For now, anyway.'

'Hold on!' Nostradamus closed his eyes tightly, clenched his eyebrows together and grimaced alarmingly. 'Something's coming through, right now.'

'There's a coincidence.'

'I can see . . .' The prophet began to rock the chair he was tied to backwards and forwards. 'I can see a man.'

'Good start.'

'He's beating up this other man. He's got a belt round his knuckles. He's punching – Ouch!'

Lundqvist grinned sardonically. 'Yes?'

'The man's just broken his hand,' Nostradamus replied. 'God, he's in real agony, poor devil, rolling about on the floor. Hey, that really does hurt. If only I could see who it is, maybe I could warn . . .'

He stopped. Lundqvist had taken hold of his ear and was trying to unscrew it.

'Thanks for the tip,' he said. 'Now, try again.'

Well, Lundqvist decided as he washed his hands, it was a start. It was something.

He examined himself in the mirror, and then stopped for a moment to remove a last splash of something nasty from his left cuff.

A date, in the late twentieth century. Some rather peculiar events, which could only be explained by reference to (a) the supernatural, (b) the considerably aggrieved, and (c) the extremely childish. Could be; or was it just coincidence?

Not that Nostradamus was in fact the greatest seer the world had ever known, he reminded himself, as he opened the door and walked out of the washroom. If he'd been any good at all, it was a safe bet that he'd have made bloody sure he spent

Thursday March 16th, 1498 in a locked stone-walled room surrounded by armed guards.

It had been a long time since Lundqvist had last been in Amsterdam, or almost. In fact, he'd been here the previous week – May 9th to 16th, 1995 – but that was seven years ago . . .

He tried to remember if there were any warrants out for his arrest. Or was that next month? Probably, he decided with a grin, that was after he'd done whatever it was he'd come here to do.

Lucky George.

George and Lundqvist went way back (and forwards, of course). Not that he'd ever had a failure, exactly; at the end of the day, he'd served the warrant, collected the subject and delivered him, in accordance with the terms of the retainer. But even he had to admit that Lucky George hadn't come quietly. In fact, he'd come very noisily indeed, and nearly taken a substantial tranche of the fabric of reality with him. There had been moments – April 1563, for example, and December 1749, not to mention February 1255 and August 2014 – when he'd been sure that the bastard was slipping through his fingers. Likewise, just as the thing any cop dreads most of all is having his own gun used against him, he particularly resented the way George had made him look a fool in the final showdown. Even bounty-hunters have their feelings, and nobody likes being chased round the centre of a densely populated city by a seven-foot-tall scale replica of himself, brandishing an array of hopelessly anachronistic weapons and calling out for all to hear, 'Look at me, I'm a pillock!'

And they'd let him escape! The idiots!

Outside the airport he found a telephone booth with a directory in it. He skimmed through it until he found what he was looking for.

TROY, H.O.

Relieved, he made a note of the address, fed the machine some money and dialled the number.

* * *

The lady in question was, just then, having a bit of a problem at the port of Rotterdam.

She'd got as far as 'I name this ship . . .', and then dried. Buggery!

Trying not to appear conspicuous, she glanced out the corner of her eye at the big letters painted on the side. That wasn't much help; they called ships some pretty weird things these days, but even so she had a feeling that *Passengers are not allowed beyond this point* probably wasn't the damn thing's name. She'd have to mumble.

'I name this ship rhubarbrhubarbrhubarb,' she therefore said, 'and God bless all who sail in her.' Then she smiled. That was okay.

I needn't have worried, she told herself later, on her way home. The chances of anybody listening to what Miss World actually says are pretty minimal. In fact, it's reasonably safe to say that nobody takes any notice of Miss World at all, except in a fairly superficial way. Otherwise, how come she'd held the title forty-seven times under various assumed names, and nobody had ever noticed? The number of people who look at her *face* is, after all, limited; the number who remember it, more limited still.

Which was, she reflected, a pity, for them. It was a nice face, besides having been extremely useful over the years to the shipbuilding industry.

For the time being, Home was a flat in one of the terribly old, terribly beautiful houses beside the Kaisergracht. It was hellishly expensive and the stairs half killed her unless she took her heels off and walked up them in her stocking feet, but that's the price you have to pay for being sentimental. For it was in this very room, in this very building, that she and George . . . She blushed.

The building had been new then; in fact, not completely and one hundred per cent finished. No roof, for one thing. But they'd been young, and in love, and it's nice to be able to lie in each other's arms and look up at the stars. They'd been on a day trip to the seventeenth century, and had been so wrapped up in each other (literally as well as figuratively) that they'd missed the last time-warp home. Not that they'd minded terribly much about that. It had been, she remembered with a slight shudder, about four months before George's year ran out, and even then they'd both spent an awfully large proportion of the time Not Thinking About It.

Having paid off her taxi, she let herself in, slipped off her shoes, and trotted up the stairs. As she reached the second-floor landing, she started to feel that faint prickling down the back of the neck that means either a premonition of terrible danger or too little fabric softener. Since she was wearing a backless dress, she decided it was probably danger.

Unfortunately, she had a very bad attitude towards danger, mainly because when she was around, it tended to be something that happened to other people. Ninja-silent in her shoe-lessness, she crept along the landing and pushed the door of her flat with the tip of one finger.

It swung open.

She swore.

At first sight, it looked like the aftermath of a visit from an incredibly conscientious burglar – you know, one of those dreadfully pernickety perfectionist types who insist on knifing the cushions for concealed pearls and ransacking the shelves for hollowed-out books. Unless, however, he had also been an extraordinarily picky burglar, brought up on only the finest aristocratic country houses and the hunting lodges of minor royalty, it would only be reasonable to expect him to have taken something; and he hadn't.

Or rather he had. And that was something of a bitch, because it was the one thing she would really rather not have parted with, given that it was genuinely irreplaceable. A framed portrait, early sixteenth century.

She made sure that the intruder had gone, and then sat down on all that was mortal of the bed and had a good swear. While she was doing this (and doing it ever so well) a thought struck her like a Mack truck and she froze in mid-oath.

If they'd come here just to steal his picture . . .

Why would they want to steal his picture?

And who the hell were they, anyway?

From the epicentre of the mess she extracted a suitcase, a few changes of clothing and a big, heavy, silver candlestick. Then she left the flat and caught a taxi.

CHAPTER
FOUR

Having concluded his interview with Lucky George, Sitting Bull had a wash, brushed his teeth and put on his body.

For someone who'd been dead for over a century, his wardrobe was extensive and reasonably fashionable; a credit to his good taste and the lucky fact that he could put on a lot of noble savage/oppressed ethnic minority chic without actually trying. He selected one of his favourite outfits – the Mexican/Chicano adolescent streetfighter with designer scars and matching paranoid psychosis – and took the elevator down to his grave.

Not so much a grave; more a sort of pied-à-terre. It was perhaps the only grave in the entire United States that had remote-control operated hydraulic car-port doors.

Down at the Silver Dollar on Whitier Boulevard, heart of the *barrio*, is one of the best places to pick up anything that's new on the street in downtown LA; at least, that's what they say in the brochure for the Los Angeles package tour offered by Mob 18-30, the holiday company specialising in tours for militant activists. When Sitting Bull wandered in and ordered a beer, the place was empty except for two old men playing dominoes and the brewery rep. And a strangely obscure figure, sitting on a bar stool by the juke-box drinking a pineapple juice.

'Hiya, Jack,' said Sitting Bull. 'How's it going?'

'I got a cold,' replied Don Juan, heavily.

'Too bad. You want to play some pool?'

They strolled over to the pool table, and Don Juan racked up.

'How's business?' Sitting Bull asked, chalking his cue and examining it for straightness. Don Juan shrugged.

'Not so good,' he replied, 'not so bad. Still, I think maybe I did wrong to change my career direction. As a philanderer I was good. This I don't do so well.'

Sitting Bull tossed a coin and called heads, accurately. 'Maybe,' he said. 'Then again, maybe not. The way I see it, Jack, informing is good, steady work. Philandering, you're only ever as good as your last job.' He drew back his arm and shot the white against the pack with a satisfying crack. Nothing went down. 'Is there much about right now?'

'Pretty quiet, Bull, pretty quiet.' Don Juan crouched down over the table, examining the lie of the cue ball. 'You know how it is. All the guys are out of town right now. Nobody who's anybody sticks around this dumb century for June these days.' He executed a tiny, stabbing movement that sent the white ball spiralling across the cloth like a vertiginous comet. 'Things'll pick up again in July, probably. I'm okay,' he added, straightening up and noting the position of the balls with approval. 'I had a good May, so I'm not complaining.'

'Anything special?'

Don Juan nodded. 'I turned in the captain of the *Marie Celeste*,' he said. 'There's some guys in the insurance business in London who want to see him real bad, you know?' He chuckled without humour. 'This time I have the feeling he's going to disappear *completely*. Your shot.'

Sitting Bull examined the table, calculating angles of incidence and refraction. He liked his new lifestyle (deathstyle, whatever). It was lower profile, but it was worth it simply for not having to shave every day. The hair and the fingernails were a nuisance, of course, but you can't have everything.

'I heard,' he said, perhaps trying a little too hard to sound as if he was just making conversation, 'that there's something really big going down in your line right now.'

'Maybe.'

Sitting Bull addressed the cue ball, made the shot and chalked his cue. 'Yeah,' he said. 'I heard Lucky George is back on the street.'

'That's interesting.'

'I heard,' Sitting Bull continued, sizing up the chances of cannoning off the back cushion to bring the cue ball back for the seven, 'that there's a nice long price waiting for anyone with good information.'

'Could be.'

'Wish I could get me a piece of that,' said Sitting Bull to the cue ball. 'Just because you're dead doesn't mean you can't take it with you.'

He watched the cue ball drift down the baize, clip the lip of the middle pocket and run with a clatter into the remains of the pack. Too much goddamn left hand side. Don Juan clicked his tongue sympathetically and sank four balls in quick succession.

'You got anything, then?' he asked.

'Who, me?' Sitting Bull drank some beer. 'I was just interested, that's all. In case I'd missed something.'

'I wouldn't bother,' Don Juan replied. 'The latest is, they've called off all agents, what with the trouble and everything. Pity about that,' he added sideways. 'If you had got anything, I mean.'

He took his shot, but misjudged it by about an eighth of an inch. The ball quivered in the jaws of the pocket and stayed put.

'Hey,' Sitting Bull said. 'Just as well I don't, or I'd be disappointed.' He walked round the table a few times, remembering some very good advice he'd received from the Great Sky Spirit, way back in the old days. Never shoot pool with a spic, the Great Sky Spirit had said, or at least not for money. 'What would the trouble be, Jack?'

'A lot of very heavy things, Bull,' Don Juan replied, stroking his chin. 'Well, maybe not heavy. More making the administration look a complete asshole without actually breaking anything. Neat touch the man's got, you've got to hand it to him.' He looked up, his eyes catching Sitting Bull's attention like, say, a sawn-off shotgun placed two inches from one's nose. 'I like Lucky George, Bull,' he said. 'A really regular guy.'

'Absolutely.'

'Got me out of a jam more than once. I hope he makes it all the way.'

'Yeah, me too.'

'That's good.' Don Juan bent his back and cleared the rest of the table in successive shots. 'You know, maybe I am in the wrong business, Bull. Maybe I should try your line, huh?'

'What, being dead?'

Don Juan shrugged. 'It's a living,' he said. 'And you don't have to sell nobody down the river, either. I feel bad about it sometimes, Bull, I really do. Basically I'm a very sensitive person.'

'Me too. I was misunderstood.'

'You want another game?'

'Thanks, but I've gotta move.' He put his cue back in the rack. 'It's been good seeing you, Jack.'

'Yeah, you too.' Don Juan smiled thinly. 'And remember,' he added, 'if you do get to hear anything about Lucky George, nobody wants to know, right? You got that, Bull?'

'I got that, Jack. Be seeing you.'

After Sitting Bull had left the Silver Dollar, Don Juan sat for a while, staring at the dregs of his pineapple juice and ignoring the obvious glances of the barmaid. It's a wonderful thing, being retired.

Some time later, he got up and went over to the payphone.

A trapdoor opened, and four shadowy forms emerged.

So shadowy were they that the driver of the car didn't see them till too late. It would have been a nasty accident if the shadowy form actually hit by the car hadn't simply dematerialised.

'Brilliant,' muttered the leading shadowy form under his breath, as the three survivors paused in a shop doorway to regroup. 'What bloody genius put the hatch in the middle of a main road?'

They looked back at the scene of the tragedy, which was faintly illuminated by the edge of a streetlamp's penumbra.

'Stone me,' growled the Number Two form. 'It's a perishing manhole cover. How cheapskate can you get?'

'I thought I could thmell thomething while we were coming up.'

The leader shrugged. 'Ours not to reason why,' he said, with a certain deficiency of conviction. 'Right, here's what we do. We slip in, we ransack the place, we slip out again, we go home. All clear?'

'Yes.'

'Yeth.'

Try as he might, the leader couldn't help but find Number Three's speech impediment tiresome in the extreme. Sheer bias on his part, he knew; spectral warriors are considered fit for active service if they pass a number of physical and mental tests, painstakingly designed after extensive research to ascertain whether the subject is up to the demanding tasks likely to be encountered by Hell's commandos in the field. None of these tasks involved the correct pronunciation of sibilants, and quite right, too. Nevertheless . . .

'Okay,' the leader sighed. 'Synchronise your watches, people. Now . . .'

'I make it nine forty-three.'

'Nine thorty-*thickth*.'

'No, you're wrong there, Vern. I checked with the speaking clock before we left, and—'

'Now,' repeated the leader, 'according to the street map, we're in Silver Street, so King's College should be . . .'

'Your watch mutht be thatht. Hey, thkip . . .'

The leader turned slowly round. 'Yes?'

'What do you make the time, thkip? Only my watch theth—'

'Yes, but I checked it before . . .'

The leader winced. 'It doesn't matter,' he said. 'Just synchronise them, okay?'

'Yeth, but thkip, mine theth nine thorty-thickth and hith theth—'

'Yeah, skip. What does yours say?'

With a gesture of suffering fools, the leader looked at his wrist, only to see the sleeve of a black pullover and nothing else. Dammit, he'd forgotten his watch.

'Nine forty-five,' he said. 'Now, can we please get on with it?'

The brief: break into King's College, Cambridge and comb the archives to see if there was anything there which might shed some light on where Christopher Marlowe, sixteenth-century dramatist and graduate of said college, had got his information from. It was, the leader decided, absolutely typical of the bloody stupid, pointless . . .

'Shit,' observed Number Two, looking up at the gatehouse. 'It's like a damn fortress. How are we supposed to get into *that*?'

'Through the door,' replied the leader, mercilessly. 'They haven't locked up for the night yet.'

'Oh. Right.'

'That's the whole idea. We go in, we hide till everyone's gone to bed, we frisk the place and bugger off. Now, when you've quite finished . . .'

'Hey thkip, that'th pretty neat thinking.'

'Thanks, Vernon. Come on, follow me.'

Hiding till nightfall in a Cambridge college during termtime is easier said than done. Particularly if you're distinctively dressed in black trousers and pullover, black balaclava and black face-paint. Acting natural and inconspicuous takes just that bit more effort than usual. Stanislavski could have managed it, but not first time out.

'Thuck thith for a game of tholdierth,' observed Number Three eventually, after they'd been politely requested to leave the boiler room for the third time. 'I thought you thaid—'

'Well I didn't,' the leader replied. 'Just count yourselves lucky this is a university. Here, the weird is commonplace, so we should be okay. Let's go and have a drink in the bar.'

'Have they got a bar, skip?'

'They'd bloody well better have.'

They did. Huddled in a corner of the Junior Common Room over three pints of Abbot Ale, just under the dartboard, they looked totally inconspicuous.

'Real bummer, Howard getting run other like that,' observed Number Three, wiping froth from the mouth-hole of his bala-clava.

'Yes.'

'You'd have thought they'd have warned uth.'

'Yes.'

'Maketh you thick, thometimeth.'

'You are already, Vernon.'

'What, thick?'

'Yes.'

Number Three considered. 'No I'm not,' he replied, puzzled. 'I had a headache thith morning, but . . .'

The leader cleared his throat with a semblance of authority, before the whole bloody thing degenerated into farce. 'Accord-ing to the plan,' he said, 'the library is up the stairs on our left as we came in, keeping the hall doorway to our right. Got that?'

'Sure thing, skip.' Number Two finished the last of the salted peanuts. 'What is it we're looking for, exactly?'

'A lead,' replied his commanding officer, with wasted irony.

'What thort of a lead?'

'Any sort of a lead.'

'Only,' Number Three continued, 'there'th a lead coming out of the back of thith computer game thing, if that'th any help. It goeth right acroth the wall and back into the—'

'A clue. Something to go on. A material fact.'

'What sort of a material fact, skip?'

One of the minor tragedies about being a spectral warrior is the fact that, being inhuman, they can't settle down and have children. Just now, the leader felt, he had an inkling of what he was missing.

'All right,' he said. 'Listen carefully. There's this bloke called George Faustus, right?'

'You mean Lucky George.'

'You got it. Now, shortly after he was arrested – very shortly, in fact – this nerd of a playwright called Christopher Marlowe wrote a play all about him. Lots of details in it that he couldn't possibly have known unless he was privy to some pretty restricted stuff. Marlowe was a student here at the time. The idea is, perhaps there's some papers or diaries of his lying about here somewhere which might put us in the right direction. Understood?'

Number Two considered the proposition, and clearly found it counter-intuitive. 'Hey,' he said, 'that was years ago. Unless they're really, you know, untidy . . .'

'My couthin Thimon'th very untidy. He keepth all hith old electrithity billth and gath billth and water billth and—'

'Not for over four hundred years he doesn't, I bet.'

'That'th becauth he'th only thirty-thickth. Give him a chanthe.'

'No, listen,' interrupted the leader, slightly desperate. 'Marlowe's a great playwright. When you're a great playwright, they keep all your letters and papers and things. It's called research.'

'My couthin Thimon'th not a playwright.'

'Vernon.'

'Yeth?'

'Shut up.'

At twenty to twelve, the bar steward turned them out and they wandered about in the night air for a while, waiting for the college to go to sleep. At half past one, they crept noiselessly, or relatively noiselessly, to the library door, and the leader fumbled for his skeleton key.

'Keith.'

'Yes, skip?'

'Whose turn was it to bring the key?'

'Yours, skip.'

'Kick the door in, Keith.'

'Okay, skip.'

It was, they realised, a big library. Big as in huge. There were, as Number Three perceptively remarked, books everywhere.

'All right,' the leader said, raising his voice to a whimper. 'Let's make a start, anyway. Those shelves over there.'

They hadn't been at it for more than an hour, scrabbling aimlessly by the light of small dark torches, when all the lights suddenly went on. They turned, to see a small, bald man in a dressing gown bearing down on them.

'Thkip.'

'What is it now?'

'Can we do the thilent killing, thkip? It'th my turn to do the thilent killing, and you promithed.'

'It's not really appropriate right now, Vern. Next time, I give you my word.' The leader then straightened his back, smiled and said, 'Can I help you?'

The bald man stopped in his tracks for a moment. 'Who the hell are you?' he asked.

The leader thought quickly. 'Interloan,' he replied. 'We got here late, your librarian's gone home for the night, we're in a bit of a hurry, so . . .'

The words dribbled away like a test-tube of water into the Gobi desert. The bald man shook his head.

'I know who you are all right,' he said.

'Oh.' The leader frowned. 'I don't want to sound facetious, but you don't seem terribly frightened, in that case.'

The bald man snorted. 'Frightened?' he replied. 'Frightened of you? Don't make me laugh. It'd take more than a cack-handed attempt at academic espionage to frighten me.'

The leader felt a nudge at his elbow. 'What'th academic ethpio—?'

'Well,' the bald man went on, 'you can jolly well think again, because it's not here. I suppose that rat Amesbury sent you, didn't he?'

Why not? 'That's about it,' the leader said. 'Mind, we're only obeying ord—'

'Appalling! Going about trying to steal another man's research papers and you call yourselves scholars! Where's your ethics?'

'Hang on, I know that. It'th the one between Kent and Thutholk, ithn't it?'

The bald man blinked twice. 'What?'

'Ethekth.'

Just for once, the leader was glad he had Vernon along. Someone capable of saying something so completely disconcerting at a time like this was worth his weight in gold. He decided to press home the advantage.

'Right,' he said. It was his favourite word. Positive without meaning anything. 'That's enough out of you, Grandad. You tell us where it is, or it'll be the worse for you.'

'I beg your pardon?'

'He thaid . . .'

Time to get moderately heavy, the leader decided. From behind his back he produced a heavy black metal object that glinted unpleasantly in the fluorescent light of the library. It was, in fact, the remote control for opening the trapdoor, and likely to break or come loose if you so much as breathed on it, but not enough people knew that for it to be a problem. 'Show me where it is or you'll get it, understand?'

There was a pause, just long enough to set the leader wondering what he was going to do when the old man said *What are you pointing that remote control key at me for?* Then he started to back away. About bloody time too.

'You won't get away with this.'

'That's our business. Come on, move.'

Slowly, and with deadly hatred written all over him, the bald man opened a cupboard and produced a folder.

'I'll make you pay for this,' he said.

'Hey, thkip, that'th not right. I thought thith wath a library. You can take thingth out for free from a library, that'th the whole—'

'Okay,' the leader snapped, 'that'll do. Come on, move it out. Now.'

It was a close-run thing, at that. Eluding the porter and his wife's Yorkshire terrier wasn't a problem, and neither was the Yale lock on the main gate. What they hadn't bargained for was the Rugby Club, celebrating defeat at the hands of a superior Magdalene Fifteen.

'Hey skip,' Number Two panted as they fled along the High Street, hotly pursued. 'You know back there, when you said, Show me where it is or you'll get it.'

'I know.'

'But,' Number Two persisted, 'if he knew where it was, surely he'd got it already.'

The leader pulled up short, too breathless to run any further. The pack was about forty yards behind, and closing.

'Stone me, Keith, I never thought of that. Right, lads, going down.'

The trapdoor opened, just in the nick of time. For the reasons stated above, the manuscript, when it eventually reached the Hot Seat, was soggy, curled at the edges and just a little smelly. But nobody noticed.

It was Professor Ambermere's long-awaited disclosure of his researches into new material on the life and works of Christopher Marlowe, based on recently discovered manuscripts. The so-called Amsterdam Archive.

CHAPTER FIVE

Thanks to research carried out in the last twenty-odd years, it is now tolerably well known that once they reach the stage of being able to make articulate sounds, all babies, regardless of nationality, ethnic grouping or environment, make virtually the same noises.

Far from being meaningless gurgles, these noises are the only words human beings ever get to speak in their own basic, unpolluted, indigenous language, of which the myriad tongues of Mankind are mere vulgar and corrupt dialects. Within weeks of finding their voices, human infants begin the long process of soaking up the stimuli of their immediate surroundings, and by the time they reach five months old, the Old Language has been supplanted in their centres of speech by the variant they will usually speak and think in for the rest of their lives.

What they are saying, in those initial weeks of vocalisation, is, 'You *bastards*! Get me back up there *immediately*!'

The Old Language is, of course, not confined to the newly born; it is also the lingua franca of the dead, the immortal and the ineffable. And magicians, necromancers and conjurors also speak it, albeit with an accent that makes them sound like the Germans in war films. For the convenience of our readers we shall ignore this and translate simultaneously as we proceed.

'Ronnie, old mate,' said Lucky George. 'Wonderful to hear from you. How in buggery did you get my number?'

In his office in Pandaemonium, Hieronymus Bosch glanced furtively about him and cupped his hand tight round the receiver.

'Shut up and listen,' he hissed. 'I'm only doing this because I owe you one, right? Remember that. If they catch me, my life won't be worth . . .' He hesitated. 'Sorry, Freudian slip. Anyway, they'll bloody well crucify me. Look, George, they're on to you.'

'They are?'

'Believe it. I got this number from your dossier, okay? That suggests they're pretty well informed about your whereabouts, doesn't it? They got it all from your diary.'

'My diary? I've never . . .'

George stopped, blinked and then winced.

'Sod it,' he said. 'That's really aggravating, that is.'

Everyone, at some stage of their lives, keeps a diary. Now, the usual reason for doing so is to help you remember, years later, what you did in the past.

Trust Lucky George to be different from everybody else.

'Where was it?' he asked.

'Long story,' Bosch replied. 'To cut it short, though, it showed up in Amsterdam, about twenty years ago. I think you left it on a tram or something.'

'Did I?'

'Not did. Will. I think. Did you ever read it, by the way?'

'What, and find out my future? No fear. I wouldn't be able to sleep nights.'

Bosch shrugged. 'Anyway,' he said, 'never mind all that. It's showed up at last, some of our boys from the Spooks department raided some university somewhere and got hold of a copy. The rest is history, if you'll pardon the expression.'

George frowned. 'Thanks,' he said. 'Now I owe you one. Has Lundqvist seen it yet, do you know?'

'It's a reasonably safe bet,' Bosch replied. 'Of course, they've undertaken to you to call off all their people from persecuting you, so they couldn't have shown him openly. I did hear, though, that once they'd read it, they deposited it in the maximum security vault of the Credit Infernale, with fifteen armed guards and a hi-tech laser-assisted alarm system. Where Lundqvist's concerned, that's the next best thing to pinning it on the notice board in the staff canteen. He's bound to have seen it. It's also on the database, of course, which is what I'm looking at, but Lundqvist's computer-illiterate.' Bosch raised his head, glanced round once more and added, 'I have an idea they also know about Nellie, so maybe you'd better . . .'

George shook his head. 'Nah,' he said, 'that's all right, Nellie can look after herself. Well, thanks a lot, Ronnie. I won't say *Be seeing you*, but take care, be good.'

'Don't worry about it, George. Oh, George.'

'Yes'

'You didn't mind me reversing the charges, did you? Only they check the phone bills now, and—'

'No problem, Ronnie. Ciao.'

History, most aggravating of the Nine Muses, has forgotten what the favour was that Lucky George did Hieronymus Bosch all those years ago, when they were students at Wittenberg together. History's other infuriating habit, apart from forgetting things, is using all the sugar in the communal kitchen and never replacing it.

The first thing George did after replacing the receiver was to turn round, very slowly. Nothing untoward happened. Good.

Next on the agenda was getting the hell out of town, but there were a couple of things he had to see to first. First Van Appin, then Nellie. Or maybe the other way round.

He was trying to make a decision on this point on his way

downtown when a choice became unnecessary. A girl on a bicycle drew up beside him with a screech of brakes, walloped him on the back and said, 'Hello, George.'

Now then. We want this to be a civilised book. There are some authors, prurient types with the morality of paparazzi, who stoop so low as to eavesdrop on their characters' most private and personal moments and then print the whole lot, verbatim. Well, not quite; they do leave some bits out. In all the works of D.H. Lawrence, for example, the girl never once says to the man, 'Hold on a minute, my arm's gone to sleep.' Nevertheless, standards in this respect are deplorably low. It's time something was done about it.

We therefore rejoin the narrative at the moment when Helen of Troy and Lucky George have got over the emotional side of meeting again for the first time in over four hundred years, and are discussing what they should do next over coffee and pancakes.

'It's looking hairy,' George said. 'Apparently that toad Lundqvist is after me.'

Helen clicked her tongue sympathetically. 'Poor lamb,' she said, 'what a bore. Is that what all the stuff with the credit cards and the biros and the golf courses was about?'

George nodded. 'Actually,' he added, 'I quite enjoyed all that. It's been a long time, you know.'

'You always did have a childish streak.'

'Maybe.' He shrugged. 'Comes in handy. Anyway, it didn't do a blind bit of good. Sure, all the hobgoblins and so on were pulled off the street, but that's neither here nor there. The day I can't sort out a few idiots with pitchforks . . .'

Helen frowned. 'Be that as it may,' she said. 'Had you got something in mind?'

'Not really. I was thinking of keeping my head down until the lawyer's ready, playing it by the book, that sort of thing. There's no point looking for trouble, after all; I don't want to start a fight if I don't have to.'

Helen considered this as she finished her pancake. 'Somehow I don't think it's going to be as easy as that,' she said. 'Besides, if turning all the traffic lights in Milan into sunflowers isn't starting a fight, it'll probably do to be going on with. That's always been your trouble, George,' she added sternly. 'Too much of this silly artistic integrity stuff.'

By way of reply, George simply grinned. 'All this,' he said, changing the subject, 'may look to you like aggravation, but to me it's more like . . . What's the word I'm looking for?'

Helen of Troy applied her mind in the search for the appropriate word. 'Extreme danger?' she hazarded.

George shook his head. 'Fun. That's the word I'm looking for.'

'Fun?'

'Fun.'

Helen broke off a corner of bread to mop up the last of the maple syrup. 'Breaking out of Hell,' she said. 'Being hunted across the face of the earth by the most deadly contract killer history has ever known, who incidentally has a personal grudge against you. If that's your idea of the meaning of fun, I suggest you sue the compilers of your dictionary.'

George shrugged. 'I get what you're driving at,' he replied, 'in a way. On the other hand,' he said, smiling at the empty coffee pot, 'compared to what I've been doing for the last four hundred years, it's absolutely bloody hysterical.'

Helen gave him what, in a poor light, could have been mistaken for a serious look.

'And what have you been doing, George?' she demanded.

'Time.'

Funny old stuff, Time.

There is, notoriously, a lot of it about. But it is, of course, a finite resource.

This could have been a problem. Back in the dark ages, pre-ecology, the powers that be had the curious notion that they could go on pumping the stuff out indefinitely. 'Plenty more where this came from,' they reassured themselves, as they gaily sank new bore-holes and erected giant new rigs.

But they were wrong. Time, like everything else, is running out.

Not that you'd know it if you went by the commodities markets. Just now, for example, over-production has led to a serious glut. The price has, accordingly, tumbled. They're practically giving the stuff away, with free wineglasses.

This state of affairs can't last, of course, and the wiser heads are already planning for the day when the wells run dry. They're also at last grasping the nettle of what to do with all the enormous dumps of used Time which litter up the under-privileged back lots of the Sixth Dimension, slowly rotting their half-lives away and doing awful things to the environment.

This stuff, they say, can be recycled. All we need is a little more research, one tiny breakthrough.

Which is rather like saying that Death can be cured just as soon as we can find a way of making people live for ever.

'I'm sorry,' the receptionist said. 'Nobody can see Mr Van Appin without an appointment.'

The mirror sunglasses stared back at her, and she wriggled slightly.

'That's okay,' said the man in the shades. 'Seeing him is not essential. Just so long as I can kick his liver out through his ears, I'll pass up on the visual contact.'

Before she could press the panic button, Lundqvist leant over, ripped the wires out with a tiny flick of the wrist, wrapped them round a couple of pencils, and presented them to her, corsage-fashion. Then he kicked in the door.

'Kurt,' said Mr Van Appin, not looking up, 'great to see you, take a seat, I'll be with you in just a . . .'

Shit, Lundqvist thought, I'm getting slow. He'd managed

to get the drawer open two millimetres before I grabbed him.

'Help yourself to a revolver,' Mr Van Appin said. 'I usually have one myself about this time.'

Lundqvist smiled without humour, removed the revolver from the drawer and pocketed it. Then he leant forward, thrusting his chin under Van Appin's nose.

'So,' Mr Van Appin said, 'what can I do for you? Thinking of making a will, perhaps?'

Lundqvist shook his head.

'You should,' Van Appin said. 'Dodgy business like yours, I'd have said it was a very sensible precaution. Thinking of buying a house, then?'

This time, Lundqvist didn't shake his head. For variety, he shook Mr Van Appin's.

'Shall I take that,' remarked Mr Van Appin, spitting out the syllables like a boxer spitting teeth, 'as a negative?'

'Where is he?'

'Who?'

'Faust.'

Mr Van Appin smiled, his professional smile which does not mean, 'Hello, I like you, shall we be friends?' Quite the opposite, in fact.

'I'm sorry,' he said. 'Mr Faust is my client, and I cannot disclose confidential information. And,' he continued quickly, 'just in case you were contemplating being so ill-mannered as to threaten me with bodily injury, may I just remind you that I practise the law in all the major centuries simultaneously, and I include your present employers among my most valued clients. One false move out of you, and I'll have an injunction out to stop you ever having been born before you can say "chronological dysfunction".' He paused, and gave Lundqvist a patronising grin. 'In your case,' he added, 'that's probably being over-ambitious. Do you think you could manage "Jack Robinson"?'

There was a long pause.

'You think you're really smart, don't you?'

Mr Van Appin looked modest. 'In the same way that I think cold is the opposite of hot and that water is wet, yes, I do.'

'Fine.' The telephone at Mr Van Appin's elbow rang. 'Answer it, it's for you.'

For a moment, the lawyer hesitated; then he picked up the phone.

'Yes,' he said, 'Van Appin here.'

Likewise. This is Van Appin of Van Appin (Fifteenth Century) and Company. Hiya, partner, how's things your end?

Mr Van Appin blinked twice. 'Fine,' he said. 'We're doing okay. A bit different from your day, of course, we're doing more in the commercial property line and not so much of the witch-craft trials, but we make a living. What can I do for you?'

It's like this, partner. I'm speaking to you from the maternity ward here in AD 1449, where Mr Kurt Lundqvist is just about to be born.

If Mr Van Appin was thrown by this remark, he didn't let it show. 'It's a small world,' he remarked.

You can say that again, because I have Mr Kurt Lundqvist with me right now. I've tried explaining to him that he's risking setting off a really serious temporal paradox just by being here, but it's hampering me having this cheesewire round my throat, you know?

Mr Van Appin (twentieth century) nodded slowly. 'I can relate to that,' he said. 'I would most strongly advocate not making any sudden movements.'

I was working along the same lines myself. I'd also appreciate it a whole lot if you told Mr Lundqvist what he wants to know.

Mr Van Appin frowned. 'I hear what you say,' he replied. 'I'm just wondering how that would leave us from a professional ethics viewpoint.'

There was a gurgling noise from the telephone, and for a brief moment, Mr Van Appin was aware of a most curious sensation; that of vaguely remembering that he didn't in fact exist, having died many years previously. *I think we're just going to have to take a view on that one, really. Like, I think we have a serious conflict of interests situation here, and maybe it's time we took a more flexible approach vis-á-vis the strict interpretation . . .*

There was a particularly vivid flashback, which made Mr Van Appin wince sharply. It wasn't so much the physical pain, or the fear, or the horror; it was the thought of the catastrophic effects that having been unwittingly dead for five hundred years while continuing to trade would have on his tax position that decided him.

'What you're saying,' he therefore gurgled into the receiver, 'is that maybe this is an instance where we should interpret the statute in its wider sense, having regard to all the circumstances and implications of the case.'

Absolutely, partner. I would also recommend doing it quickly, because otherwise . . .

The sentence was not completed. Mr Van Appin, tearing himself away from a rather fascinating recollection of his own funeral, nodded sharply three or four times.

'Okay,' he said, 'you got it. I'll tell him right away. Oh, and by the way.'

Yes.

'You'll never guess who didn't even bother sending a wreath or anything.'

The line went dead; and, by dint of some rapid talking, Mr Van Appin narrowly avoided the sincerest form of flattery.

Lucky George came out of the phone booth, stopped, turned back and smiled at the coin slot, which promptly disgorged slightly more loose change than he'd originally fed into it. Slightly more, only because there's a limit to the amount of coins one man can conveniently carry, or one government can comfortably produce.

'Right,' he said, 'that's got that sorted. What do you fancy doing the rest of the day? If you like, we could go to the Rijksmuseum and wake up some of the paintings . . .'

Helen frowned. 'Hold on,' she said. 'When you say that's sorted . . .'

'I mean,' George replied, 'I've taken care of things. For now, anyway. Some friends of mine owe me a few favours. Things'll be okay, you'll see.'

'In that case,' Helen said, 'let's go eat. I'm hungry.'

One of George's telephone calls had been made to a small family-run Italian restaurant in Brooklyn.

Mrs Loredano had taken the call.

'Hey, Lorenzo,' she called, over the rumble of simmering pans, 'it's for you. Some guy called Buonaventura.'

There was a crash, as Mr Loredano dropped four helpings of osso bucco, two garlic breads and a side salad.

'Giorgio Buonaventura?'

'Yeah. You know him?'

'Give me the phone.'

Mrs Loredano shrugged, handed over the receiver and went for the broom.

'Larry?'

'George,' replied Mr Loredano, with slightly too much emphasis on the ecstatic happiness. 'Hey, it's been a long time. What you doing out?'

'I absconded, Larry. I got bored. How's things?'

'Fine, George, fine. Couldn't be better.'

'Business okay?'

'Well, you know, times are hard, not much money about, and then there's the overhead . . .'

'Sure.' The voice on the other end of the line hardened slightly, like a carbon deposit suddenly subjected to billions of tons of top pressure. 'Listen, Larry, I need a favour. Can you drop everything?'

'I just did.'

'Sorry?'

'Nothing. I'm just taking off my apron, George, I'll be right with you.'

'That's wonderful, Larry. Mike there too?'

'Sure,' Mr Loredano replied. 'I'll tell him to come too. Where are you?'

As George explained, Mr Loredano made notes on his order pad. After a few more cordial exchanges he replaced the phone, removed his apron and called his wife.

'Honey,' he said, 'me and Mike, we gotta go out for a while. Business.'

Mrs Loredano expressed herself, stating her opinion of this suggestion. Her husband stopped her.

'I know,' he said. 'Sure. That was George on the line.'

The penny dropped.

'We'll be back as soon as we can,' Mr Loredano assured her. 'Don't give any credit while we're away.'

He then found his business partner and explained, whereupon both men retired to the back office and changed for the journey.

'You ready, Mike?'

'Ready as I'll ever be.'

'Window open?'

'Yeah.'

'See you there, then.'

The two proprietors of La Veneziana then spread their wings, squawked a few times, and flitted out of the window. Ten minutes later they were midway across the Atlantic, slowed down by a strong headwind and driving rain from the southeast. Not bad going, nevertheless, for a pair of superficially ordinary herring gulls, particularly when you bear in mind that they'd been out of practice for four hundred years.

Mrs Loredano, meanwhile, was explaining to Mrs Steno why their respective husbands had abandoned the restaurant at the height of the mid-day rush. She knew all about it, having been let in on the secret some years ago; and besides, she believed that a good marriage is built on mutual trust. Mrs Steno, who believed that a good marriage is built on unilateral terrorism, hadn't been favoured with her husband's confidence in this regard.

Mrs Loredano explained that many years ago, before they went into the restaurant business, Larry and Mike had worked for this guy back in the old country. What as? Well, as familiars. No, not that, that's a valet, familiars are those guys who help out sorcerers and magicians. Yeah, hand them the top hat and get sawn in half, that sort of thing. And other things, too, of course. Yeah, usually it's some bimbo with no clothes on, but sometimes it's men as well. And sometimes – here Mrs Loredano took a deep breath – it's seagulls.

Seagulls? You mean like performing animals?

Yeah, only more than that, sometimes.

She explained further.

It took Mrs Steno some time to recover.

You mean, she said, Mike and Larry are *seagulls*? Yes, well, *were* seagulls, but when the guy they were working for, (pause for thought), when he *retired*, he turned them into human beings, regular guys. Even set them up in the restaurant business. A very thoughtful man, by all accounts, the guy really knew how to look after his employees.

Seagulls!

Catholic seagulls, Rosa, I absolutely guarantee that. Almost the first thing they did after getting their human bodies, they went out and got baptised. You've got absolutely nothing to worry about on that score.

Anyway, part of the deal was that if ever this Mr Buonaventura needed them again for anything, anything in the familiaring line, then of course they'd be only too pleased. A matter of honour. You've got to have respect in this life, or what have you got?

Yes, but seagulls . . .

At which, Mrs Loredano became slightly affronted. No offence intended, but she hoped Mrs Steno wasn't prejudiced in any way, because that wasn't a very nice thing to be. After all, everybody's something, if you go back far enough: Italian, Jewish, Irish, German, Chinese, seagull, Greek, whatever. Bring us your huddled masses. Had Mrs Steno taken a look at the Statue of Liberty lately, by the way?

There was a long silence.

'Sorry, Maria,' said Mrs Steno.

'That's okay, Rosa,' replied Mrs Loredano. 'Just forget it, okay?'

They went and tossed the salad.

CHAPTER
SIX

A fortuitous tail wind and a lift hitched from a passing anticyclone helped Larry and Mike make up time, and they swooped down on the Oosterdok just on two and a half hours after leaving Brooklyn.

They were only just in time.

Not that they were to know that, of course. They circled for a while, making kawk-kawk noises and generally getting used to being seagulls again. Oddly enough, what both of them found strangest was being without their watches.

'It's like riding a bicycle,' Larry observed.

'Bloody uncomfortable, yeah.'

'No, I meant—'

'And cold. And very, very tiring.'

Mike tilted his wingtips and dropped down a hundred feet or so. 'Right,' he said, 'we'd better report in, I guess. Where's the map?'

Larry looked at him. 'What map?'

'The street map.'

'I thought you had it.'

'Don't be dumb. How can I carry a goddamn street map in a seagull outfit? You think I've got pockets in the wings or something?'

Larry made no reply. He'd been putting up with Mike's logic for approximately twice as long as America had been an independent nation, and although it still occasionally had the power to make him want to scream, he had built up a sort of immunity to it; apparently, you can do the same thing with arsenic, if you take a microscopic amount each day. 'What was the address again?' he asked.

'Intersection of Keisergracht and Hartenstraat,' Mike replied. 'I guess we just fly around until we see the street names, or . . .'

He broke off and craned his head down under his wing.

'Hey,' he remarked. 'Maybe we won't have to, at that. Look.'

'That's him all right,' said Lucky George. 'I'd know him anywhere. Come on, time we weren't here.'

From their window they could see a man in mirror sunglasses and a green jacket strolling along the canal bank, with a long brown paper parcel under his arm. At a respectful distance of maybe five yards, there followed a troop of assorted demons, all unexpected heads, misplaced organs and unfashionable colours, wheeling handcarts. The carts were piled high with some very impressive-looking machinery, the specific uses of which you couldn't hope to guess if you didn't actually know (although you'd have no trouble coming up with the general idea). For the record, they were a set of the latest state-of-the-art magical effect suppressors, together with generators, transformers and other ancillary hardware, capable of neutralising supernatural forces up to thirty kilograils within a six-hundred-yard radius.

Nobody seemed to be taking the slightest bit of notice, probably because the entire procession was theoretically invisible; a wonderful new effect produced by photoelectric mimesis.

Put simply, the process works by making the subject closely resemble the viewer's most boring relative or acquaintance. The viewer is then so preoccupied with getting past without being noticed himself that he doesn't stop to look twice at the subject. The only living person in the cosmos who can't be taken in by theoretical invisibility is, of course, Lucky George; all of whose relatives have been dead for centuries, and none of whose friends are boring.

'Where?' Helen asked, hopping towards the window with one leg in and one leg out of a pair of Ann Klein slacks. 'I can't see . . .' She froze. 'Hey, that's not possible.'

George grinned. 'I know. Personally, I can see my aunt Hilda, my cousin Norman, my cousin Norman's second wife's brothers and what looks like seven enormous cappuccino machines. You make a break for it down the back stairs while I try and hold them off with a few . . .'

He stopped in mid-sentence, his face a picture of absolute bewilderment. Then he swore.

'Suppressors,' he muttered. 'Nuts. All right, we'll just have to run for it. Come on.'

(Meanwhile, the magical effect which he'd launched by way of a ranging shot and which had ricocheted off the suppressor field sang away into the upper air, bounced off a TV satellite and was broadcast into millions of homes worldwide in the form of a seven-hour-long subtitled Japanese art movie about a day in the life of a portable typewriter.)

Lundqvist looked up sharply and raised his hand.

'In there,' he snapped.

As posses went, he reckoned, they were no worse than being trapped in a lift with an independent financial adviser; second-rate press-ganged local evil spirits, reluctant to get involved and anxiously awaiting any pretext for slipping quietly away to a bar somewhere. He could handle them.

'You,' he said to the tallest demon present, 'rig up the kit and give me maximum power. The rest of you, fan out, don't let anyone or anything leave the building. And,' he added, 'remember, I've got all your serial numbers, and anyone who's not here when I get back is going to find himself in an oil lamp granting wishes so fast his hooves won't touch.'

He hitched up his trousers, unwrapped the flame-thrower, and strode towards the house.

His hand was on the doorknob when something white, wet and smelly hit him smack in the eye.

'Shot!'

Larry shrugged modestly. 'It's a gift,' he said. 'Either you got it or you haven't. Your turn.'

By this time, Lundqvist had wiped his eye carefully with his handkerchief, turned round and stared long and hard at a goat-headed electrician who'd sniggered, and put on his hat. Bugger the doorknob, he was thinking. In fact, bugger the door. He turned the dial on the back of the fuel tank to one-quarter power, pressed the pilot light switch, and . . .

And a passing seagull swooped down, gave him a nasty nip on the left index finger, and rocketed off into the sky. Lundqvist swore, dropped the flame-gun and sucked the wound.

While he was thus occupied, a second passing seagull flapped up behind him, caught the fuel throttle awkwardly in its beak and twisted it on to maximum.

The flame-gun at his feet at once erupted, making Lundqvist jump about three feet in the air and dislodge his sunglasses. By some quirk of gravity, they reached the pavement before he did (although they had quite some way further to go), just in time to be under his feet when he landed. There was a crunch, like a lorry crossing gravel.

Two seagulls met in mid-air.

'That'd better do for now,' said Larry. 'Otherwise he might start to suspect . . .'

He didn't finish what he was saying, his attention having been distracted by a fifty-foot jet of fire passing within twenty centimetres of his tail. With more speed than dignity, the sea-gulls withdrew.

Outside the back gate, meanwhile, a demon stood guard.

He had the head of a dog, the nose of a gryphon, broad bat-like red wings, a pitchfork, four feet of tail and a stammer. He was the diabolical equivalent of sixteen and a half years old, and this was the first time he'd ever done anything like this. The reason why he'd been assigned this spot was because he was too junior to be able to refuse.

'Excuse me.'

He looked up. Despite his poor eyesight (he was short-sighted, glasses made him feel self-conscious and, although he had contact-lenses, such was his biochemistry that they melted as soon as he put them in) he could see that the back door had opened and a female head had appeared round it. He swallowed hard, and tried to remember his lines.

'Huhalt,' he said, in a high, quavering voice. 'Whogugugu-goesthere, friendorfufufufufufoe?'

'Sorry, what was the choice again?'

'Fufufuf . . .'

'Friend.'

'That's all right then.' He lowered the pitchfork and stepped forward, and five seconds later was lying on his beak wonder-ing how come the house had fallen on him. Helen of Troy, for her part, was looking at a slightly bent silver candlestick and sighing.

'Okay?'

She nodded. 'George,' she said, as he came out of the house and locked the door, 'we are friends, aren't we? I mean, you and me.'

'I guess so,' he replied. 'Why?'

Helen stepped over the demon. 'I'd hate to think I'd told a lie, that's all. Which way now?'

George shrugged. 'Doesn't really matter, so long as it's

generally north-east. All I really need is a phone box. Ah, there they are. About time too,' he said, as two seagulls flopped down on to his outstretched wrist. 'What kept you?'

'We came as fast as we could,' replied Larry, wounded.

'Like hell you did,' George replied. 'What were you doing, waiting for the exchange rate to swing in your favour? Follow me.'

By dint of reckless trespassing in the gardens of perfect strangers, they came out by the Westerkirk, where George flung himself into a telephone booth, grabbed the receiver and rattled his pockets for change. Helen sat on a bench and took out her powder compact. The seagulls ate a discarded ice-cream cone.

'Right,' said George, stepping out of the booth and not bothering to gather the cascade of change that was flooding out of the coin box, 'that's all settled. Lunch?'

Larry raised his head. 'Settled, chief?'

'Settled. What we need,' he went on, leading the way, 'is either somewhere with a garden or somewhere they don't mind pets. Otherwise, you two'll have to hover overhead with a bottle of lemonade and a packet of crisps.'

Helen of Troy gave him a look. 'Settled exactly how, George? Not that I'm doubting you for a minute, of course, but . . .'

George grinned. 'I phoned a couple of old friends of mine,' he said. 'They're on their way.' He glanced up at the sky, smiled and nodded. 'My only regret is, we'll miss all the fun.'

The ability to make friends easily is a gift you're either born with or you aren't. If you've got the knack, cultivate it. It's worth having.

People who have the gift do tend to find life rather easier than the rest of us. If they want a new solenoid for the car, they get on to their friend who works in a garage. If they fancy a holiday in Portugal, they stay in the villa which belongs to a couple of friends who only go there for three weeks in July. The houses of the friends of builders tend to sprout porches and extensions like a flourishing tree.

Lucky George is to the likes of these as the Sargasso Sea is to nine square inches of pondweed.

'I can see that,' Lundqvist observed. There was a certain icy quality in his voice which would have started an Eskimo property developer rubbing his hands and applying for planning permission.

The demon who had just remarked that the fugitives would appear to have escaped shrank back and tried to look inconspicuous, something he frankly wasn't cut out for. He was unsuccessful.

'Okay,' Lundqvist went on, 'you're such a goddamn expert, go find them.' The bounty hunter growled irritably. He should, he knew, have been exercising his uniquely incisive mind on what the fugitives were likely to do next, but try as he might his thoughts kept straying off in the direction of seagulls, bird-snaring and new and savage advances in the ancient art of taxidermy. 'Jump to it,' he snapped, breaking free from his reverie. 'The trail shouldn't be hard to follow.'

With a soft whimper, the demon in question looked round and prepared to do his best. Fortunately for him, he was about eighty-five per cent nose, having been custom-designed for the torment throughout eternity of a cocaine dealer. He sniffed.

'Thad way,' he said. 'Foddow me.'

Now then.

Given the choice, a good storyteller tries to keep the early stages of his narrative relatively plain and simple – clarity begins a tome, as the old saw has it. Sometimes, though, with the best will in the world, this option just isn't available. If confusing things happen, with people dashing about hither and yon and tripping over each other's feet, the narrator has to do the best he can. At least let him try and bring the participants on stage in some vestige of order.

In possession of the field, then, Lundqvist and his highly trained and motivated associates.

Somewhere off and circling, two seagulls.

In a taxi bowling down the Leidsestraat, sincerely wishing he was somewhere else but remembering to keep a careful note of time engaged so as to facilitate drawing up his bill of costs at the end of the day, Mr Van Appin.

In another taxi speeding up the Stadholderskade, completely at a loss as to what was going on but chuffed to little mint balls at being allowed on dry land three years ahead of schedule, and looking forward to seeing his old college chum Lucky George again after all this time, one Julius Vanderdecker, otherwise known as the Flying Dutchman.

Sharing the taxi with him, two other fellow students from those dear old Wittenberg days (an inventor of parachutes and a shabbily dressed Dane with a habit of muttering to himself) and a TV reporter*, who'd asked if he could share their taxi as he had to be at an important meeting at the Anne Frank House in twenty minutes.

Down below somewhere, the management of Hell Holdings plc, roughing out the publicity campaign for Fryathon '95 and blissfully unaware of what was just around the corner.

In the gods, God.

Two seagulls swoop Stuka-like on to a traffic jam by the Stads-schouwburg and peck frantically on the window of a taxi.

'Hello, Mike, long time no see,' exclaims the designer of parachutes, winding down the window. 'What are you two doing in these . . . ?'

'Use your brains, Lenny,' mutters the Dane.

'Gee, sorry. Of course, you're from . . .' the parachute designer lowers his voice to a conspiratorial whisper they could

---

*Guess who

still probably hear in Leiden '. . . From *you know who*. Any orders from the big guy?'

'Quark, quark,' replies the seagull patiently. 'Quark. You got that?'

'You bet, Mike,' says the parachute boffin, grinning. 'Just leave it to us. Ciao.'

Two seagulls perch, a few seconds later, on the window-sill of a taxi a hundred yards further up the same jam.

'Larry, Mike, good to see you,' exclaims Mr Van Appin. 'This is really opportune, you know, 'cos I was going through the accounts and you guys still owe me for doing the lease of the restaurant.'

'Quark,' interrupts a seagull quickly. 'Quark quark quark.'

'Quark,' confirms the other seagull.

Mr Van Appin shrugs. On the one hand, he's simply not the running-about type, every minute out of the office is costing him thousands of guilders in lost fees and the course of action to which his client has apparently committed himself is extremely hazardous and liable, if it goes wrong, to have disastrous consequences both for himself and his professional advisers. On the other hand, it's a poor heart that never rejoices.

'Okay,' he says. 'Go for it.'

'Helen.'

'Mmmm?'

'Pass the maple syrup, there's a love.'

Cleaving the air like two postgraduate smart missiles, two seagulls flash down out of the sun on an increasingly ragged procession hacking its way through the back gardens of the Keisergracht.

Lundqvist sees them; and just as the penny drops and he realises that these are no ordinary herring-gulls, they bank in mid-air over the handcarts, snip lengths of wire off the suppressor machines with surgical precision in their sharp beaks, and beat it.

No point even trying a shot at this range. With a snarl, he holsters his .475 Wildey, scowls horribly at his skilled assistants, and returns to the task of cleaving a path through someone's begonias with his machete.

Three old college chums standing rather self-consciously on the banks of the Prinsengracht, wondering what they've let themselves in for.

'You ever done anything like this before, Jule?'

'Nah. What about you, Lenny?'

The designer of parachutes stroked his beard. 'Depends,' he replied. 'In 1499 I designed a contrivance for harnessing the power of the winds and the tides to operate a small, left-hand-thread ratchet screwdriver, not that there was any demand, bloody Luddites. Does that count?'

The Dane and the Dutchman looked at each other.

'Frankly,' said the Dane, 'no. Oh well, I suppose we'll all just have to learn together.'

Two seagulls flapped wearily over the rooftops and perched on the Dutchman's head.

'Quark,' they said in chorus.

'We're on, then,' said the designer of parachutes. 'Over the top, and all that.'

'You can say that again.'

'Right,' the parachute man continued, 'let the dog see the rabbit. Which one of us do you think ought to say the magic words and so forth? Any volunteers?'

The Dane mole-wrenched his mind back from recollecting what a right pain in the arse Lenny had been in the old days, and locked it back on course. 'Tell you what, Lenny,' he said, 'why don't you do it?'

'If you're sure.'

'I'm sure.'

'Jule? How about you?'

'Just get on with it, Lenny, please. And could you possibly manage to be a tiny bit less cheerful about everything, because you're giving me a migraine.'

'You always were a gloomy old sod, weren't you? All right then, here we go.'

Three old college chums, plus two seagulls, vanished.

Lundqvist lowered his field glasses, licked his lips and smiled. He didn't speak, but his lips framed the word *Gotcha!*

He was standing in a large, rather mangled gap in the front wall of a fine late seventeenth-century merchant's house facing on to the Prinsengracht – when serious guys take short cuts they don't muck about – and observing the rather awkward progress towards him of three giant, self-propelled windmills. Show-off, he said to himself.

'You,' he called to an assistant demon, 'full power to the suppressors, now.'

The demon scurried away and pulled a lever. Nothing happened.

'Excude me,' the demon said in a small, terrified voice, 'only I think sud of the wired are mithing frod the machide.'

Lundqvist stared at him for a moment, as if the demon had just leant forward and extracted all his teeth. Seagulls, he was thinking, oh *shit*.

'Try the others,' he yelled. 'Move it, quickly.'

The demons, however, were backing away, muttering. As if by telepathy, they had all suddenly started thinking, Yeah, sure, we're demons, but this is *spooky*. A few seconds later and they'd gone.

The windmills continued to advance. They were swinging their sails. Little puffs of superfluous flour drifted out on the wind and scattered like mist.

You can disconcert Kurt Lundqvist, but you can't frighten

him. It took him about a third of a second to get his head together, lose his temper, draw his gun and start firing. Bullets whistled through the sails of the windmills, melted and dropped into the canal.

Never mind, there was still the flame-thrower. A few deft twists on the fuel tap, and a billowing, wind-blown rose of red flame swept across the street and licked the brickwork of the windmills.

Complete waste of time. Goddamn, the Dutch pioneered fire regulations.

He could feel the backdraught from the sails now, as the three shadows fell across him. Time to withdraw and regroup. What would Napoleon have done under the circumstances?

Swish!

Okay, Napoleon would most probably have curled up in a ball and screamed, and likewise Hannibal and Irwin Rommel. Alexander the Great, however, would have jumped back into a shop doorway, grabbed the first thing that came to hand – in this case, a long wooden pole with a hook on the end, used for raising and lowering shutters – and *attacked*, by golly. And what was good enough for Alexander was good enough for Kurt Lundqvist.

He tucked the pole under his arm, lowered his head, and charged.

A taxi drew up at the intersection of Radhuisstraat and Prinsengracht, and a man got out. He was late for a college reunion.

'*How* much?' he demanded, shocked.

The taxi driver said it again. Muttering darkly about inflation, the passenger paid him and looked down the street.

Because, like the other Old Wittenbergers present that day, he was dead and buried, the theoretical invisibility effect cut no ice with him. He therefore saw, in the distance, a man running frantically backwards and forwards, trying to prod three windmills with what looked like a spear.

'Damn,' muttered Don Quixote de la Mancha. 'Buggers have started without me.'

Okay, thought Lundqvist, as a sail whistled past his ear and cut off a button from his sleeve, that's what Alexander would have done. Any other suggestions?

He thrust hard with the shutter pole, and had the satisfaction of connecting with a bit of winding mechanism. The pole broke.

Ulysses S. Grant. A really savvy guy. He'd have dropped the pole and run like buggery.

Also Belisarius, Cortes and the Duke of Marlborough.

The edge of a sail whirled past his head as he ran, parting his hair down the middle and making him look like a nineteenth-century curate. As he sprinted past the 'now useless suppressors his subconscious mind was thinking, *About three feet of ordinary insulated cable and I'll have you yet, you bastard*. His conscious mind was saying, *Help, help*, very loudly.

Lundqvist was a good runner. Usually, of course, he ran after people, not away from them, but the principle is pretty well the same. On the corner of Prinsengracht and Berenstraat he was able to stop, lean heavily against a wall and catch up on his breathing, secure in the knowledge that the windmills were a long way behind.

He looked up.

Those windmills, sure. The three animated monsters advancing towards him, sails slicing the air like so much salami, were probably entirely different windmills, or else the same windmills, cheating. Did it really matter? He picked up his feet and ran.

Not noticing that overhead, two seagulls were floating on a thermal, in their claws two string bags. Simultaneously they let go their payloads, said 'Quark!' and banked off.

The bags hit the pavement and burst, scattering bulbs everywhere. Ordinary everyday tulip bulbs, only recently snatched up from a stall in the flower market.

They started to grow.

Fortunately, Lundqvist still had his machete with him, and by hacking away for all he was worth, he was able to clear a path through the thicket before the horrible snapping flowers could reach down and wrap their petals round him. Gasping for air and soaked from head to foot in sticky green sap, he staggered out, only to find himself surrounded by furiously sprouting daffodils. Meanwhile, two seagulls were hovering in the still air, string bags clutched in their talons . . .

The windmills were closing. The tulips were opening a path for them, letting them through . . .

The key thing to do in situations like these is to keep your head, Lundqvist remembered, as a sail-edge grazed his collarbone. He ducked down on his hands and knees, machete between his teeth, and crawled. The sails couldn't reach him down here, neither could the carnivorous flowers. If he met an ant, at least it would be hand-to-mandible fighting, he'd have a chance.

Behind him, he heard a rumbling sound, like thunder, and the nauseating squeaking of living tissue being crushed. He cast a quick glance over his shoulder, and saw . . .

. . . A huge yellow wheel, at least twelve feet high at top dead centre, flattening a squishy path straight at him. Not a wheel. A cheese.

Lundqvist stood up. He'd had enough.

'You bastard!' he screamed. 'You fucking bastard! Can't you take *anything* seriously?'

Then he threw himself at the cheese, tripping over tulip-roots, dodging the murderous sails, soaked in sap and three-quarters blinded with pollen. As the leading edge of the cheese rushed towards him he hurled himself sideways, cannoning into a tulip stem, bouncing off the rubbery surface, being hurled like a baseball at the mountainous flank of the cheese. He thrust the machete out in front of him and screamed . . .

And found himself sitting in the gutter, a bent machete in one hand, a large slice of Edam in the other, surrounded by a crowd of bemused onlookers and wearing a baseball cap inscribed with

I ♥ AMSTERDAM

Five minutes later, a police car came and picked him up. He was later charged with obstructing the highway, disorderly conduct and fourteen breaches of the street trading regulations.

CHAPTER
SEVEN

There was, of course, only one course of action open to Lucky George after the battle of Amsterdam: retribution. Immediate, savage and on a sufficient scale to convey the magnitude of his displeasure.

Not that he minded. Not one little bit.

As soon as he had thanked his old college chums, therefore, and caught the first available flight to his next port of call, he settled down and worked all the details out in his mind. Then . . .

The first intimation that the members of all the governments of all the nations of the earth had been turned overnight into farmyard animals came from the BBC radio news, with its crack-of-dawn summary of yesterday's proceedings in Parliament. Being a radio broadcast, there was no visual confirmation; and at first the grunts, squeals, clucks, squeaks, miaows and moos were interpreted as the combined effect of atmospheric disturbance, a fault on the line somewhere and the full and free exchange of views in the most highly respected democratic forum in the world. It was only when the breakfast television pictures started to come through that anyone was able to bring himself to put a more logical interpretation on the data.

Toast-crunching news addicts were greeted with footage of the pleasant green lawn-cum-verge outside the House of Commons, where the House was dividing on the third reading of the Finance Bill. The doors opened, and what can only be described as a flock shambled out, led by an extremely old, indifferent-looking sheepdog in a full wig.

The flock divided; the goats wandering into one lobby, the sheep into the other. After the tellers had done their work with their customary speed and efficiency, the sheepdog sat up on its hind paws, waggled its tail, and proclaimed that the meeeehs had it.

Simultaneously, in Washington DC, an old grey mule opened the day's proceedings of the Senate by eating the order papers and kicking the Barker of the House with his offside rear hoof. In the Knesset building the rows of seats were empty, and the elected representatives present wheeled and banked under the ceiling as the hawks tried to catch up with the swifter but less agile doves. This was at about the time when the German parliament adjourned for Swill, oblivious of the fact that across the border in France, the nation's leaders had abandoned a crucial debate on the economy to chase a catnip mouse round the boiler room. The Japanese legislature twice narrowly missed complete annihilation; first when somebody spilt a kettle of boiling water down a crack in the floor, and second when the Peruvian foreign minister arrived in the building for a top-level meeting and nearly swept the whole lot of them up with one lick of his long, sticky tongue. The Belgian government buried the contents of the Exchequer under a tree, curled up in little nests of scraped-together leaves and went to sleep for the winter.

Perhaps the most startling manifestation of all was in Iraq, where the entire government were changed overnight into human beings.

'I suppose we ought to, really,' admitted the Marketing Director, wistfully. 'Seems a shame, though.'

'We've got to,' replied the Production Director, stifling a giggle. On the TV screen in front of him were satellite pictures of the emergency debate in the European Parliament, meeting for the first time in that august body's history on the summit of a steep cliff outside Ostend. 'I mean,' he went on, 'fun's fun, but . . .' He broke off and stuffed his tie in his mouth as a cascade of small, scuttling, furry-bodied politicians streamed off the edge of the cliff into the waves below. Further out to sea, the Council of Ministers were leaving a sinking ship.

'Not,' commented the Finance Director, with more feeling than originality, 'for the first time.' He stopped, and forcibly returned his mind to the issue in hand. 'Look,' he said, 'this has got to stop. Get the tiresome little man on the phone, somebody, and tell him to turn them back this instant.' He hesitated, turned his head back towards the screen, and caught a glimpse of the Parliament's select committee on agriculture scurrying frantically backwards and forwards to avoid a flock of ecstatic gannets. 'Well, pretty soon, anyway,' he said, his eyes glued to a close-up of the President of the Council playing hide-and-seek with a cormorant. 'By midday tomorrow at the very latest.'

'That's easy enough to say,' grumbled the Marketing Director. 'Got to find the blighter first. I don't suppose it's going to be all that easy . . .'

A telephone rang at his elbow and he picked it up.

'Got someone called Van Appin on the line,' he said a moment later, 'claims to be George's legal adviser. Anyone want to—'

The Finance Director grabbed the receiver. 'Hello, Pete?' he barked. 'What the bloody he-heliotrope does he think he's playing at? Tell him to get this mess sorted out immediately, or he's going to be in real trouble.'

At his desk, Mr Van Appin smiled. 'Excuse me,' he said, 'but I thought he was already. I mean, excuse my ignorance, but I thought everlastingly damned was about as in trouble as you could possibly get without actually working in advertising.'

The Finance Director waved his hand feebly. 'You know what I mean, Pete,' he replied. 'For pity's sake, this is going too far.' As he spoke, the image on the television screen changed, and he found himself staring at a huge, distended anaconda which had apparently just imposed one-party rule in the small South American state of Necesidad by swallowing the Social Democrats. 'All right,' he muttered wearily. 'Tell me what he wants and I'll see what I can do.'

There was a pause, then Van Appin said, 'You know what he wants, Norman. He wants to be left alone. Call off your people, leave the kid in peace.'

The Finance Director growled petulantly. 'I already did that, Pete,' he said. 'All agents returned to base, no further action. You want me to swear an affidavit or something?'

'Lundqvist.'

The Finance Director shuddered slightly. 'Not our man,' he said, as casually as he could. 'Nothing to do with us. Entirely freelance, you know that. I'll withdraw the reward if you like but that's the best I can—'

Van Appin shook his head. 'Don't act simple, Norman,' he replied irritably. 'After yesterday's little performance, I don't suppose the money's really at the forefront of his mind.'

'Not my fault. Serves your client right for teasing him. Anyway, nothing we can do about it, so if you'll just—'

'No.' Van Appin took the phone away from his ear, covered up the earpiece with the palm of his hand, and counted to ten.

'You still there, Norman?' he asked.

'Yes, still here.'

'This,' said Van Appin, 'is the deal. You give me your formal undertaking to do everything you can to get Lundqvist off my client's case, we'll let you have your politicians back. And that's our last offer.'

There was a long silence.

'And now,' burbled the television set, 'we're going over live to Danny Bennett at the United Nations building in New York, where . . .'

'Switch that bloody thing off!' shouted the Finance Director. 'Hello, Pete? Look, I'm making no promises but we'll do our very best. Now, tell your man to stop mucking about.'

'And you'll stop Lundqvist?'

'I'll put my best demons on it, Pete, right away.'

'You'd better,' Van Appin retorted. 'Remember, germs are also animals, of a sort. You want the civilised nations of the world led into the twenty-first century by a bad cold, all you have to do is try and be clever.'

The line went dead. With a long, chilly sigh the Finance Director straightened his back and turned to his colleagues.

'Get me the Captain of Spectral Warriors,' he said.

'What did you say it was called?' asked Lucky George, looking round at the thronged piazza, the buzzing crowds of cosmopolitan citizens, the emerald blue of the bay and, in the background, the dazzling white masonry of the eighth wonder of the world.

'Australia,' replied Helen. 'Have a crisp.'

'No, thank you.' Lucky George considered. 'Don't think we had it in my day,' he said. 'I suppose you're going to tell me it's Progress.'

'Well, isn't it?'

Lucky George thought for a moment. 'That or entropy,' he decided. 'You know, the older I get, the harder I find it to tell 'em apart. I still say we managed perfectly well without it, but there we are, what's done is done.' He sat down on the steps and focused on the sails of the yachts in the distance.

'This,' Helen continued, crunching, 'is Sydney.'

'I thought you said it was—'

'Sydney, Australia.'

'Ah. Sydney's its Christian name.'

'Don't be tiresome, George. You'll like it here.'

'Will I? Why?'

Helen sneezed. 'Because nobody will ever think of looking for you here, that's why.'

'Figures,' George said. 'I wouldn't, certainly. Wouldn't be seen dead, in fact.'

'Well, there you are, then.'

'Yes,' George replied thoughtfully, 'here I am. Indeed. Do they have food in Australia?'

Helen nodded. 'Absolutely. Tons of it.'

'Ah. That's something, I suppose. Let's go and investigate.'

Over the coffee, George expanded on his proposed course of action.

'The only real problem,' he said, 'is Lundqvist. The rest of them we can probably handle. By the way, did you know that this country you're so fond of is governed entirely by warthogs?'

Helen frowned. 'You're going to have to change them all back sooner or later, George. I mean, you've made your point. There's nothing to be gained by ramming it into the ground.'

'If,' George said, changing the subject, 'we could find some way of getting rid of Lundqvist once and for all, then I'd be prepared to try and negotiate. A few concessions here and there, it oughtn't to be a problem. But while that nutcase is on the loose, I really don't fancy it. Pass the ashtray.'

'I think you've got a complex about Lundqvist,' Helen replied. 'You saw how easy it was to deal with him in Amsterdam. We made him look a complete idiot. I expect he'll go back to chivvying the undead and leave us in peace.'

'Don't you believe it.' George shook his head, accidentally turning the cash register into a bottomless purse. 'In retrospect, I don't think I handled that particular encounter quite right. All we've achieved so far is to get so far up his nose that we're practically coming out of his ears. Not sensible.'

'But surely,' Helen said over the rim of her coffee cup, 'once they withdraw the reward, surely he'll just go away. I mean, he's a professional bounty-hunter, he doesn't do it for fun. If he's not going to get paid . . .'

George gave her an indulgent look. 'Bless the child,' he said, 'for her naivety and purity of spirit. If Lundqvist succeeds in delivering yours truly, I've little doubt they'll come across with the money. He knows that perfectly well. Besides, he'd carry on regardless, money or not. He doesn't like being made a fool of. Probably,' he added, 'an ingrained dislike of gilding the lily.'

'So?' Helen said. 'Any bright ideas?'

George nodded. 'Sure,' he said. 'That's why we're here. Although,' he added, looking round, 'when I said find me the most desolate, godforsaken place in the Universe, I didn't actually *mean* the most desolate, godforsaken . . .'

'Don't be silly, George. There are far worse places than this.'

'Name me one.'

'Adelaide.'

'Ah.' George raised an eyebrow. 'I take it she's Sydney's sister.'

'No, that's Victoria. You think we can just hide out, then, and wait for him to biodegrade or something?'

George shook his head. 'No such luck. No, what I had in mind was something quite different.'

He leant back in his chair, waiting for her to ask him what he had in mind. She, however, folded her arms and started telling him all about the First Fleet, Ned Kelly and Aussie Rules football. 'What I had in mind,' said George, raising his hand for silence, 'was going on the offensive. A pre-emptive strike, in fact.'

Helen picked up a crystal of coffee sugar and bit on it. 'And how are we going to do that from here, may I ask?'

A grin spread across George's face like a late-summer sunset;

or, if you prefer, an oil slick. 'We're not,' he replied. 'However, there's this bloke I know owes me a favour . . .'

Two seagulls, circling in the first light of dawn.

'Maybe,' screamed one above the hissing of the wind, 'I should just call them, check they've delivered the canned tomatoes.'

'Cool it, Mike,' screeched Larry. 'They're perfectly capable of running the joint for a few weeks without any help from us. We've just gotta concentrate on the job in hand, okay?'

Mike stared down through the quickening light at a wet green landscape. In the distance there was a hill, curiously man-made in appearance, crowned by what looked like a church tower without the church. At its foot, like a spilt plate of seafood risotto, sprawled a small, untidy town, coagulated around the ruins of a monastery.

'You're sure he's in?'

Larry turned his head and tried to endow his windlashed eyes with a look of contempt. 'He's been in his grave for a thousand years, Mike. Dead guys don't just slip out for a pizza.'

They waited for a suitable downdraught, adjusted their wing angles and swooped.

It used to say:

HIC IACET ARCTURUS
ANGLIE
REX QUONDAM REX FUTURUS

in rather wobbly capitals on a piece of broken millstone. In 1259, however, a passing blacksmith in need of a bit of something to sharpen scythes on removed the original memorial, and the spot remained unmarked until the middle of the twentieth century, when the appropriate government department replaced it with a large concrete slab bearing the suitable inscription:

NO DOGS

which is, considered all in all, perhaps the finest obituary a man can ask for.

Two seagulls dropped awkwardly out of a thermal and flumped on to a concrete slab.

'You do it,' whispered Mike. 'I'm sick of always having to be the one who gets landed with all the talking.'

'All right,' Larry said irritably. 'What do I do now?'

The seagulls looked around, and then at each other. 'Search me,' said Mike. 'Knock. Ring the bell.'

Larry thought about it for a moment, and then addressed the side of the slab with his beak. He rapped three times, and waited.

Piss off. We gave already.

The seagulls looked at each other again. The voice hadn't come from anywhere; nor, strictly speaking, had it been a voice. If it resembled anything at all from the realms of conventional experience, it was a vague recollection of hearsay.

'We aren't collecting,' Mike replied. 'We've got a message. From George Faustus.'

Never heard of the schmuck. Go mug a buzzard, there's people trying to sleep.

This time, however, the recollection was of a statement that had turned out, on closer inspection, not to have been true. A false rumour, perhaps, which proves impossible to pin down to any specific source.

'Mr Faustus says,' Larry went on, 'that if you've never heard of him, then you can't ever have lent him the fifty thousand marks, which means he doesn't have to pay you back, and sorry to have—'

All right. All right. You wait there, I'm coming.

★ ★ ★

'Really?' said Helen, impressed in spite of herself. 'He's a friend of yours too?'

George made a slight face. 'Friend is maybe an over-statement,' he said. 'We did some business together, I owe him money, he owes me a few favours. No, I guess friend is okay, on reflection, just so long as you leave out the affection side of things.'

'Gosh.' Helen dabbed powder on her nose and put the compact away. 'And did he really have a round table full of knights and a magic sword and a Holy Grail and all that?'

George nodded. 'Sure thing,' he said. 'Brilliant camouflage,' he added.

Helen looked up at him sharply. 'Camouflage?'

'Naturally. What else?' An idea struck him. 'You didn't think all that stuff was for real, did you?'

Helen nodded. 'Insofar as I believed he existed,' she added.

George laughed. 'Strictly for the customers, all that,' he said. 'Sure, Arthur was the best king Albion ever had, absolutely marvellous administrator, had the rivers running on time, that sort of thing. But you don't manage that just because you've got a few hundred idiots in steel long johns on the payroll.'

'You don't?'

''Course not.' He turned his head and smiled. Immediately, the waiter brought him the bill, which shows just how unimaginably powerful George's magical powers were. 'Think about it. If you want to conquer inflation, revitalise the moribund standing stone circle industry, eliminate racial tension between the Wee Folk and the Nixies in the Inner Toadstools and stabilise the magic ring against the deutschmark, what you need is sound fiscal policies, not a bunch of brainless pillocks on horses and an overgrown letter-opener that glows in the dark. Dammit, you don't drag a whole nation kicking and screaming into the Dark Ages without a firm grasp of the principles of revenue management, and that's what Arthur had. That,' he added, with an unwonted tang of respect in his voice, 'is why they called him the Once and Future Accountant. A reputation like that, it's something you've got to earn, believe me.'

'Oh.' There was just the tiniest hint of disappointment, disillusionment even, in Helen's voice. 'An accountant. How unspeakably romantic.'

'Yes,' George replied. 'And that's why he's just the man we need.'

Say what you like about accountants . . .

Finished?

Good.

Say what you like about accountants, for clarity of thought and an ability to get to the heart of the matter, they have few rivals. Accordingly, it took the greatest accountant in history roughly the same amount of time to grasp the proposition and reach a decision as, say, the shutter of a Leica is open when taking a picture of a moving object on a very bright day.

'Sure,' said King Arthur. 'No problem. It worked with Al Capone, so why not with this Lundqvist? Now we talk about money.'

Larry ruffled his feathers with his beak. 'I thought we just were.'

'Remuneration,' King Arthur replies. 'This sort of work I don't do for the good of my health. Especially,' he added, 'now I'm dead. Now then, I charge for my work on a time basis, with a basic hourly rate of—'

'Expense no object,' Mike interrupted with his mouth full. One good thing about being in a grave, he was thinking, always plenty of worms. Even (he reflected queazily) if you don't know where they've been.

'Expense no object,' King Arthur repeated. 'The fink owes me fifty thousand marks already, he says expense no object. He's probably planning to pay me with my own goddamn money.'

Mike swallowed the rest of his mouthful, fearful lest he'd

said the wrong thing. 'But you will do it?' he said. 'Only I'm sure—'

'Of course I'll do it,' grumbled the Once and Future King. 'Son of a bitch owes me fifty grand, naturally I'll do it, or when will I ever see my money again. That George, he sure understands economics. He's got a lawyer?'

'Van Appin of Amsterdam,' said Larry.

'Oy,' said King Arthur, impressed. 'That's one very expensive lawyer, the boy has taste. A good man, Van Appin, he acted for my Uncle Joe when he first came to this country from Arimathea. Artie, he said to me on his deathbed, if ever you're in trouble with the law, see Van Appin. A goy but a good lawyer. All right, this is what we've gotta do . . .'

It's bad enough having to do something you know is pointless, dangerous and doomed to failure. Having to order your subordinates to do it with you, when they're pointing out forcefully just how pointless, dangerous and doomed to failure it is, makes being eaten alive by ants seem like the height of Sybaritic luxury.

'It'll be a piece of cake,' muttered the Captain of Spectral Warriors, keeping his voice down. 'We go in, we nick him, we leave. No problem.'

Two pairs of coal-red eyes glowed their hostility at him in the pitch darkness of the sewer.

'You said that,' remarked Number Two, 'the last time.'

'And the time bethore.'

The Captain winced. 'That was different,' he said. 'Freak accident, that was. Nobody could've known . . .'

Somewhere in the darkness, water dripped. There are many, many strange and unexplained noises in a sewer; and Number Two, who had seen all the Mutant Turtle films, was more than usually edgy. 'Happened, though, dinnit? So, it could happen again.'

All three sat in silence, recollecting the image of that horror.

It should have been a routine job – take possession of a human body (the owner having failed to keep up the payments) and terrorise the local community with acts of demonic, hellish horror. It had, however, gone quite flamboyantly wrong . . .

'I mean,' said Number Two, breaking the silence like a rock thrown into a stagnant, scummy pool, 'double booked. Never again, I said, not if they offered me a seat on the Board. I was terrified.'

'I keep telling you,' the Captain snapped, 'they weren't real devils. The people were making a film, it was all special effects . . .'

'I know they weren't real devils,' replied Number Two with venom. 'Real devils, we'd have been all right with real devils, they'd have been in the Union. Those bastards in there, it was horrible, I've never seen the like.'

'All right, we needn't go into all that—'

'Screamin' and hauntin' and rushin' about with hideous worm-eaten faces and all that stuff. I had to sleep with the light on for weeks afterwards.'

'Well,' said the Captain firmly, 'there's no chance of that happening this time, is there? The worst that can happen to us—'

'Go and arrest Kurt Lundqvist,' Number Two interrupted relentlessly. 'Yeah. Worst that can happen to us is they scoop us up and take us home in a jam jar. Well, you can tell whoever it is who—'

'Quiet!' The Captain sat on his heels, straining for the slightest sound. It came; the signal, three knocks. 'Right, move it out. I'll go first. Stay right behind me.'

He poked his head up into the mouth of the pipe, took a deep breath (being a spectral warrior he had no lungs, but somehow it always made him feel better) and started to wriggle his way up. His two henchmen followed, grumbling on the threshold of sound as they squirmed.

A few minutes later, the Captain's head popped up through

the sink trap in Kurt Lundqvist's kitchen. Having paused to make sure the coast was clear and lever a squashed pea and a horribly limp tube of macaroni out of his path with the shaft of his ice axe, he scrambled out, looked round and hissed, 'All clear. Come on, we haven't got all damn night.'

'It'th really *yuk* down there,' snarled Number Three, hauling himself out and wiping himself against a pair of rubber gloves beside the plate rack. 'And they didn't ithue uth with protective clothing or anything. If we catch anything nathty, we could thue.'

They abseiled down from the sink to the floor. It was a long way, and en route Number Two was at pains to point out to his companions that he suffered from vertigo. By an error of judgement they all landed up in a saucer of milk left out for the cat.

'He's got a cat?' said Number Two, as he lay gasping on the rim of the saucer. 'Wouldn't have thought he's the type, somehow.'

'Wasn't in the briefing,' admitted the Captain. 'Now then, who's got the transformer? Better get ourselves back to our proper size quick, before the bloody cat wakes up.'

Pause.

'I said, who's got the transformer?'

Long pause. During this pause, if the perceived length of time passing correlates in any way to objective criteria – time as recorded by a clock, for instance – you could have built the pyramids and watched them fall down.

'Fine,' said the Captain, 'we've forgotten the transformer. Never mind. We'll just have to cope. Follow me.'

It was probably the noise made by Number Three walking into the foot of the vegetable rack and dislodging a potato that woke up the cat; either that or Number Two tripping over a grain of spilt sugar. Details are not important. What is germane to the issue is that the cat woke up, pricked up its ears and jumped out of its basket. Its tail lashed. For a cat, it had a highly developed sense of cultural integrity, and as a rule there were no mice in the house. This led to frustration, self-doubt, crises of identity and long periods of black depression, when it would sit motionless at the top of the stairs waiting to be sent to the newsagents to collect the paper in its mouth. Now at last, it seemed, the mice had arrived. Destiny called.

'Thkip.'

'Shuttup, Vern.'

'Yeth, but thkip, there'th thomething big and horrible over there watching uth.'

'It's just your imagination, Vern. Now shut up and—'

The cat sprang. It was not a classic spring; the head a trifle too low, perhaps, the forepaws not completely extended, the back not quite unflexing like a longbow at the moment of release. But it was the best the cat could do at such short notice, being out of practice and more than a little overweight, and it reckoned it would probably do. There was a thump and a squeak . . .

'Hold on, Vern, I'm coming.' The Captain drew his revolver and sprinted back, to be confronted with a nightmare mass of convulsed fur, a waking horror of green eyes and teeth like ploughshares. He stopped, raised his arms and fired three times.

Shrink a revolver, even a Smith & Wesson 686, down to 1/72 scale, and the noise it makes on firing is slightly less deafening than a grain of rice falling two inches on to a cushion. Its effect on a healthy cat is of the same order of magnitude. Chances are it didn't even notice.

Number Three was, however, making a pretty good fight of it. By virtue of his being about the size of a small spider and reasonably agile, he wasn't the easiest thing in the world to catch hold of with non-prehensile paws. Attempts to swat him were foiled by the rapidity and random nature of his movements. The deciding factor, however, was the fact that he kept yelling out blood-curdling threats in cat-language (which all demons speak fluently), which the cat couldn't help but be intimidated by.

This pantomime had been going on for quite a while when suddenly the kitchen was flooded with light, and a slipper the size of the Flatiron Building planted itself within a few millimetres of where the Captain stood, rooted to the spot.

'Fluffles,' boomed a voice high up in infinity. 'You goddamn crazy cat, what d'you think you're playing at? Gitoutavit!'

Fluffles froze in mid-swipe, horribly self-conscious, as if he'd been discovered at an all-night catnip party without his collar on. He tried to explain, but his vocal chords jammed and all that came out was, 'Mew.'

'You dumb bastard,' the boom went on, 'you've knocked over your milk. Here, it's back in your basket for you.'

A hand like the Hand of God scooped up the cat and vanished with it. The three spectral warriors crawled into the gap between the bottom of the fridge and the floor and lay there, shattered. The light went out.

'Okay,' said the Captain, five minutes or so later. 'I thought we'd had it there, lads, didn't you? Narrow scrape, I thought. Still, you've got to laugh, haven't you, or where would we all—?'

'That wath him, wathn't it?'

'Maybe,' replied the Captain. 'I'm not committing myself till we get a closer look, but provisionally . . .'

'You want *uth* to arretht *him*.'

'There may be some unforeseen technical glitches, but . . .'

'Thorgetit. I'm going home. Now.'

With which, Number Three drew himself up to his full height and walked away. Unfortunately, he went in the wrong direction.

He didn't realise this until he bumped into something, which happened to be the back of the electric plug.

A word of explanation. Lundqvist's flat was last rewired many years ago, and in places the wiring is a bit dicky. Thus, when Number Three bumped into the back of the plug, he came into contact with four millimetres of uninsulated, live, wire.

Zappo.

The immediately perceptible effect was the fridge falling over on its side, crushing the kitchen table. It did this because a six-foot-four man had suddenly materialised underneath it.

'There,' said the Captain, slightly unnerved but triumphant. 'Told you we'd cope and we did. All we had to do was bodge up a substitute transformer, and . . .'

The rest of his remarks were lost as he instantaneously went from twenty-five millimetres to six foot seven, landing up lying heavily across the remains of the pedal bin. Number Two joined them a moment later and came to rest on top of the cooker.

'Fluffles, you scumbag, what the fuck do you think you're . . . ?' The light flicked on, and the three spectral warriors turned to see Lundqvist, in a tartan wool dressing gown and slippers, standing in the doorway.

The Captain reacted well. The revolver was out of his holster and in his hand before Lundqvist could move.

'Put 'em up and keep 'em where I can see 'em. That's the way. Right, Kurt Lundqvist, I have here a warrant for your arrest, you are not obliged—'

'Thkip . . .'

'Not *now*.'

'Yeth, but I've got the warrant, it'th here in my . . . Oh, no, that'th not the warrant, that'th the tranththorm—'

'*Don't touch* . . .'

Lundqvist stood for a moment, puzzled. One moment there had been three spectral warriors draped all over his kitchen. The next moment, nothing. The cat, meanwhile, was staring reproachfully at him from over the rim of its basket with an I-told-you-but-you-wouldn't-listen expression on its face. It was as bad as being married.

Then the penny dropped.

'Okay, Fluffles,' he said, shutting the door firmly. 'This is your show now. Kill.'

It took the spectral warriors three days to escape, but in the end they made it. Their story is one of the most moving documents of courage, endurance and sheer dogged refusal to lie down and die since the escape from Colditz.

The movie rights are, incidentally, still available.

It was the Captain's idea to try and make it to the rubbish bin. Rubbish, he argued, gets chucked out sooner or later, and in the meantime there were a thousand and one places in a black plastic sack full of decaying kitchen refuse where they could hide.

The only problem, of course, was that the rubbish bin was, to all intents and purposes, a hundred and fifty stories high. King Kong might just have climbed it, with oxygen, on a good day.

Despair, gangrene of the soul, was just about to set in when Number Two noticed the onion. With a voice quivering with emotion, he explained his plan. They listened. It was a long shot, they decided, but there wasn't really any choice.

With Fluffles wandering around like a resentful tyrannosaurus, making a move from under the cooker to the vegetable rack in daylight was out of the question. As soon as night fell, however, they scrambled out, hoisted themselves up into the rack and set to work hacking a secure chamber in the side of the mouldy onion. It took them a little over eight hours, working in shifts, with nothing but their combat knives and belt-buckles to dig with. Once it was done, all they could do was climb in and wait for the onion to be noticed and thrown away.

Two days deep inside an onion is a long, long time.

Even then, it was touch and go. The hunt was still on, and despite the masking smell of the onion, Fluffles paused in his relentless prowl round the kitchen and sniffed horribly every time he passed the vegetable rack. On the evening of the second day, Lundqvist came home at a quarter to one in the morning and started to make himself a Spanish omelette. He had picked up their onion and raised the knife before he noticed anything wrong with it; and he'd stood staring at their entrance tunnel for a full two seconds before throwing the onion in the bin and selecting another one. For years afterwards, the Captain was wont to swear blind that Lundqvist must have noticed something. He could only conclude that the bounty-hunter's mind was elsewhere.

Which, in fact, it was. At that precise moment, he'd forgotten all about the spectral warriors and everything else, and was pottering around the kitchen in a stunned daze.

So would you if, returning from a hard day's work, you found lying on the mat a demand from the Revenue for over five hundred years' back taxes.

CHAPTER EIGHT

There are few experiences quite as nerve-frayingly horrible as being investigated by the Revenue. Hell (especially now that the new management team have taken over) is mild by comparison. For all his faults, the Prince of Darkness is a gentleman, or so Shakespeare would have us believe. The Inspector of Taxes, on the other hand, is an unmitigated bastard.

A week after receiving the assessment, Lundqvist was dragged out of his well-earned sleep at three in the morning by five carloads of weazel-faced young men and women in grey suits, who walked straight past him as if he wasn't there and impounded his files, records, books and bank statements. When he tried to scare them off with a 20" Remington Wingmaster they impounded that too, murmuring something about discrepancies in his claims for writing-down allowance on plant and machinery. Then they gave him a receipt and left.

When they'd gone he sat down and pulled himself together. As soon as he'd managed to overcome the feeling of having all his teeth simultaneously extracted by an army of hamsters, he got on the phone to the Duty Officer at Pandaemonium and demanded to know what they were going to do about it.

'Pardon me?' said the Duty Officer.

'Don't give me none of that crap,' Lundqvist roared. 'Get these guys off my back. Do you realise they've taken all my records back to 1456?'

'I'm terribly sorry,' the Duty Officer replied, 'but it's completely out of our hands. They're an entirely separate agency, you see. There's absolutely no way we can interfere with . . .'

Lundqvist managed to keep his temper remarkably well. Apart from formally requesting that Hell use its good offices to have the investigation suspended and formally undertaking to pull the Duty Officer's kidneys out through his nose if his papers weren't returned by five past nine the next day, he accepted the situation with a good grace and hung up. Then he burst into tears.

Business, he decided next morning, as usual. The programme for the day was to visit the Delphic Oracle and sweat out of her details of where Faust was hiding. To do this, he needed to get to the airport. Since he was short of ready cash for taxi-fares, he popped down to the cash dispenser on the corner, which took his card, informed him that his account had been frozen, and referred him to Head Office.

Ten minutes with a Sykes-Fairburn fighting-knife and the piggy-bank he kept the gas money in produced enough loose change to get him as far as the airport, where he waved his credit card at the check-in girl and demanded a seat on the first flight to Athens. The girl smiled politely and asked him to wait just a moment while she ran the routine checks on his card . . .

Fine, he thought, as he slouched disconsolate and ticketless away from the desk. I can't buy a ticket, I'll have to hijack a plane. No worries.

He was strolling up and down the observation area, casting his eye over the various airliners and deciding which one he liked the look of, when a discreet cough at his elbow made him turn.

'Excuse me, sir,' said a weazel-faced man in a grey suit, 'but if you were thinking of leaving the country, I'm afraid that's out of the question. Not until the investigation is completed, sir. We'll get a court order if necessary.'

Under normal circumstances, the next that anyone would have seen of the young man would have been his head, separated from his body, on some railings somewhere. So demoralising, however, is the cumulative effect of having the taxman after you that Lundqvist simply whimpered and walked away in the opposite direction. He found he had just enough change left for the bus-fare home.

Okay, so he couldn't leave the country. Nothing to stop him leaving the century. He phoned his usual firm of time-travel agents and asked for a reservation for the fifth century BC, first-class, non-smoking, not too near the engine.

'I'm terribly sorry, Mr Lundqvist, but we've had instructions. No credit till further notice.'

'But I've got an *account*,' Lundqvist screamed. 'Dammit, I've been travelling with you since five hundred years before you first set up in business. I've got a goddamn gold card. Doesn't loyalty count for *anything*?'

'I'm afraid your account has been suspended, sir. Court order. Injunction. Terribly sorry, but we can only help you if you can make it cash in advance.'

'Tell you what,' Lundqvist was physically shaking with rage by this point, hardly able to hold on to the receiver. 'Take me back to last Thursday and I'll pay you anything you like. My credit rating'll be fine then, I give you my word. Only for Chrissakes get me out of here.'

'Sorry, sir, but I've got my orders. If you'd care to come round to our offices with the money, we'd be only too pleased . . .'

He slammed down the phone and snarled impotently. Then

he pulled open his desk drawer, slipped something under his shoulder and walked out.

He couldn't withdraw anything from the bank, huh? We'll soon see about that.

'Stick 'em up,' he hissed across the counter. 'This is a forty-five automatic and I don't care if I use it. Fives and tens, and take it real easy.'

'Certainly, sir,' replied the cool and efficient girl behind the till. 'Please bear with me a moment while I get your money for you.' She leant back and called to someone behind the scenes. 'Yvonne, could you bring me some more fives, please? Gentleman robbing the bank.' An unseen hand passed her a wad of currency notes, which she dropped into the little perspex shuttle thing and passed over. 'Thank you for calling,' she said. 'While you're here, can I perhaps interest you in our new range of personal equity plans, specially tailored to meet your individual investment requirements and help you plan for a secure and prosperous future?'

Lundqvist had got through the door and had his hand on the door-handle of the getaway car when a discreet cough at his elbow made him freeze in his tracks.

'Excuse me, sir,' said a weazel-faced man in a grey suit, 'but I trust you're going to declare all that? Let me see.' He took the money from Lundqvist's unresisting fingers, counted it and handed it back. 'I make that fifty thousand dollars which, seeing as how it's the profits of a crime, malfeasance or illegal enterprise, is taxable at your highest applicable rates under Schedule Nine Case Six. Plus, of course, grossing up to allow for notional basic rate tax deducted at source, leaves you with . . .' The young man produced a calculator from thin air, pecked at it with a moist fingertip and nodded sagely. 'I make that a deficit of two hundred and sixty-three dollars, sir. If you'd just sign here, please.'

Dazed, Lundqvist signed the receipt, allowed himself to be relieved of the money, and fell limply into his car, where he sat for about twenty seconds until the police arrived and he had to drive like buggery to shake them off. By the time he'd done that, he'd used up all his remaining petrol and had precisely one dollar and two cents to his name.

He dumped the car and walked home.

'That's all very well,' said Lucky George, 'but I'm buggered if I'm staying here. I mean, *look* at it.'

He waved his arm in an histrionic gesture and scowled.

'I think it's very nice,' said Helen. 'A bit suburban, maybe, but—'

'Suburban!' George turned up the malignity in his scowl. 'For pity's sake, woman, the only difference between this and where I've just come from is you don't have to die to get a visa.' He threw himself into a chair and grabbed a can of beer out of the coolbag. Helen gave him a disapproving look.

'You're exaggerating a little, I think,' she said coolly. 'No little men with pitchforks, for a start. No roaring flames. No—'

'You're wrong there,' George interrupted. 'Except here they shove bits of raw meat in front of them and call it a barbie. When I was a boy in Nurnberg we had a thing, I think it was called an *oven*. Wonder if the patent's expired, because you could make an absolute fortune . . .'

'George.' In this light, George thought, with her hair curling like that in the evening breeze and exactly that tone of voice, she's just like my mother. And no, I will *not* eat up my nice parsnips. 'It's only temporary,' she went on. 'Until—'

'Temporary.' George grinned. 'I don't think so, love. This is one case where you can't simply outlive the bastards. You know what that pompous little toad of a Finance Director told me the other day? You can hide but you can't run. He was right. And,' he added, draining the last of the beer and crumpling the can in his fist, 'there's no percentage in hiding, none whatsoever. It's exactly the same porridge, only with a slightly different tin.'

Helen sighed. 'That's just culture shock, George,' she said. 'We don't have to stay in Sydney, you know. It's a huge country. There's bits of it not even properly explored yet. We could go anywhere.'

'Marvellous.' George rubbed his eyes wearily. 'We can go and live in the middle of the bloody desert. Hell may not be all fun and games, but at least they've got hot and cold running water.' He considered for a moment. 'Hot water, anyway. All the hot water you can use, free. Bit like an Aga.'

'Give it a try.'

'What, go straight, you mean?'

Helen nodded enthusiastically. 'That's right,' she said. 'We could start a sheep farm or something. It'd be fun, George, really it would. No more magic and being chased about, just you and me and—'

'A sheep farm.'

Helen frowned. 'Yes,' she said. 'For my sake, George, please.'

'You're serious?'

'Yes.'

He shrugged. 'I've heard some pretty daffy suggestions in my time,' he said, 'but this has got to be one of the daffiest. You're really saying we should set up a—'

'Yes.'

'Okay, then.' He stood up, closed his eyes for a moment, and then smiled. Positively beamed.

When he opened his eyes again, they were standing in the middle of a huge, fenceless, featureless wasteland; a wasteland covered in white, seething bodies. From the air it would have looked just like a big, manky, sheepskin rug.

'You got it,' said George. 'Now, what precisely do you *do* with the little buggers to make them grow?'

It was three months later.

Australia is an old country; very old. At a time when Paris was a soggy fen and Rome herself little more than a select new development of starter homes for Sabine commuters, the sun-bleached immensity of the Outback was already cross-hatched with a hundred thousand intricate songlines, scored on the folk memory and linking the Dreamtime to the nebulous future as directly and reliably as fibre-optic cable.

Stare at this brain-curdling immensity long enough and your eyes will play tricks on you. You'll start to imagine that, just at the destruction-test limit of vision, you can make out a tiny black dot, moving as slowly as an hourly-paid glacier, dawdling across the infinite. You might even take it for a human being.

Which it is. This is Tjakamarra, humming and mouthing his way along the line with the precision of a wire-guided missile and the sense of urgency of a holiday postcard. Around him the Ancestors, perceptible to all the senses except five, crowded in a happy, shuffling mass, passing him on from hand to hand like a parcel.

The song takes him across the flank of a long, low escarpment and to the crest of a ridge overlooking a few thousand acres of dead ground . . .

'Stone the flaming crows,' said Tjakamarra under his breath. In front of him was . . . Well, now. Yes.

A man on a quad-bike roared up out of the shadow of the crest and stopped, leaning on his handlebars.

'Can I help you?' he said. Tjakamarra stared at him.

'Sorry, mate,' he replied. 'I think we got a crossed line.'

The man with the bike raised an eyebrow. 'Really?' he said.

'Too bloody right,' Tjakamarra answered. 'How long's this lot been here?'

The man grinned. 'Not long,' he said. 'Oh, that reminds me. Is your name . . .' He dug a scrap of paper out of his pocket and consulted it. '. . . Tjakamarra?'

Tjakamarra nodded.

'Carpet Snake clan?'

'Yeah. How did you know . . . ?'

Lucky George nodded. 'Message for you from the Ancestors.

It says, "Temporary interference with reception, please do not adjust your reception, we apologise for any inconvenience, C sharp minor, F natural, A sharp with a dot, rest, G natural." That make any sense to you?'

Tjakamarra nodded, relieved. 'Yup,' he said. 'It means, turn left at the gully and watch out for low-flying aircraft.' He paused, wondering how to phrase his next question tactfully. 'What the fuckin' hell are you *doing*, anyway?'

George shrugged. 'Earning a living,' he replied.

'Any money in it?'

'It's early days yet,' George replied. 'Once it catches on we'll be laughing, you wait and see.'

Tjakamarra pursed his lips. 'Best of luck, mate,' he said guardedly. 'Well, I gotta be making tracks. You sure it was C sharp minor?'

'Pretty sure. Is it important?'

'You bet. One wrong note, I could find myself in bloody Tasmania. Much obliged.' He waved solemnly and continued on his way . . .

. . . Through a shallow valley full of sheep. And each sheep was tethered to a post, from which hung a scale and a pair of scissors. And in the middle of the valley was a big, brightly-painted notice, which said:

GEORGE'S SHEEP FARM
SHEAR YOUR OWN

The one comforting thing about Hell is knowing that it can't get any worse. Once you're there, you can't actually get in more trouble.

Unless, of course, you run the place.

'It wasn't,' grumbled the senior accounts clerk, 'like this in the old days.' He tucked three overfilled box files under his arm and scurried off down the corridor. His assistant followed on with a heavily laden trolley.

'Sodding auditors,' the senior clerk went on. 'In the old days, all we had to put up with was the Bursar. And he was one of us. You knew where you stood.'

'Better the devil you know, huh?' hazarded his assistant.

'Yeah.' The senior clerk stopped to adjust his grip on a file and plunged on. 'What they want with this lot beats me. It's just old lost souls registers.'

'We should put all this on computer,' mused his assistant. 'Then they'd be *really* lost.'

'Shut up and wheel the bloody trolley.'

It had been a long day in the suite of offices assigned to the visiting audit team, but they were damned if they were going to let anyone see it. Mr Price, Mr Vincetti, Ms Khan, Mr Kowalski and Ms Gould of Messrs Moss Berwick Flintlock had worked long and hard to secure the second most impressive prestige client in all accountancy, and they were determined to do the best job they possibly could.

'Thanks,' said Mr Kowalski. He hadn't removed his jacket, let alone loosened his tie, and he had a shrewd suspicion that his feet had melted and were seeping out through the eyes of his shoes. 'Just put them on the table over there and bring us the green purgatory chits for the last twenty-five years. There's a few anomalies here we'd better get to grips with.'

The senior clerk shuffled his feet. 'Actually,' he said.

'Yes?' Mr Kowalski raised his head. 'Any problems?'

'Might be tricky,' replied the senior clerk. 'For the whole period, like. I mean,' he added wretchedly, 'we just don't have the storage, and . . .'

'Yes?'

'It's the economy drive,' the clerk confessed. 'I mean, the furnaces have got to run on *something*, so when they said—'

'You've destroyed them?'

A look of panic flitted across the clerk's eyes. 'Some of them. I mean, I'm not sure precisely which, it's just . . .'

Mr Kowalski gave him a nasty look. Although he didn't

know it, he was running a severe risk of being the first man ever to be chucked out of Hell on the grounds of excessive unpleasantness. 'Don't worry,' he said. 'Mr Price will come with you and look for himself. I'm sure we'll find the ones we're looking for.'

Sure enough, he did. How the files in question had found their way into the roofspace, buried at the bottom of a disused sulphur tank and guarded by a fire-breathing dragon and a triple-headed dog, the senior clerk was at a loss to explain, although he mumbled something about Health and Safety and storage of bulk inflammable materials. The fire-breathing dragon didn't quite ring true there, but Mr Price was too polite to say anything. Instead he looked down about half a mile of nose and snickered.

As they trudged back to the file store, the senior clerk stopped from time to time to bang his head against the wall. 'I knew we should've shredded them,' he said. 'Bloody liability. It just goes against the grain, that's all, shredding files after all these years. I mean, this *is* Hell, it's about the only place in the sodding universe where they actually respect paperwork.'

'Hooky, was it?' enquired his assistant. 'Someone been cooking the books or something?'

The senior clerk grimaced. 'Worse than that, son,' he grunted. 'That's all the Lucky George stuff they've just asked for. If they spot that and cross-reference to the Visitor's Book, the sods'll realise he's flitted and then where'll we be?'

His assistant glanced round. From each of the dingy cells leading off the corridor came the muffled souls in various ingenious but cost-effective permutations of everlasting torment.

'Sorry,' he said. 'I thought we already were.'

His superior sniffed. 'Son,' he muttered, 'don't you believe it. That's just the stuff they give the customers.'

The third dustbin contained the end of a stale loaf, a sardine tin with a little grimy oil left in it, a rotten tomato and the carcasses of two smoked mackerel. Lundqvist sighed with relief and made himself a sandwich. The neighbourhood alley-cat gave him a poisonous look, but he ignored it.

Nobody loves you when you're down and out. Admittedly, nobody had loved Lundqvist when he was absolutely loaded, but at least he'd been able to raise the price of a hamburger whenever he felt his ribs prodding their way out of his shirt-front. Not that he was a luxurious person by any means; but there is a subtle difference between surviving on roots and grubs because you're under deep cover five hundred miles behind enemy lines, and pigging it because the Revenue have garnished every last cent you own.

The bailiffs had even seized his entire collection of Ninja throwing-knives and death-stars, despite his objection that they were tools of the trade and therefore exempt. The most lethal object left to him was a toothbrush. When you're Kurt Lundqvist, however, a toothbrush will do nicely. It's all a matter of knowing how to use it.

Once he'd finished his meal, therefore, he walked the five miles to the private airstrip on the outskirts of the city and wandered into the first helicopter charter establishment he came across.

'Hi,' he said to the youth behind the desk. 'I want a chopper, now.'

The youth looked at him, observing the dusty jacket, the slept-in trousers. 'You want a helicopter,' he said. 'Fancy.'

Before he could go on, Lundqvist had vaulted the desk, landed beside him and thrust the toothbrush handle hard into the small hollow just below the lobe of his ear.

'Yeah,' he said. 'Is that a problem?'

The youth made a low, guttural noise, like a man gargling with custard; then he raised one shaking hand and pointed.

'Keys in the ignition?'

'Yug.'

'Much obliged to you.' He hopped back over the desk and

strode quickly across the tarmac to the helicopter indicated. Nobody even tried to stop him. He jumped in and slammed the door.

A moment later he opened it again.

'Hey, you,' he shouted to a cowering mechanic. 'Which one of these goddamned levers is the handbrake?'

As he flew, Lundqvist rationalised. He'd found an ancient bar of fruit and nut chocolate in the glove box – a bit grey and fluffy, but the sudden surge in his blood sugar level made his brain roar like the engine of a drag-racer on the starting line.

If I was Lucky George, he asked himself, where would I go?

Yes, well, if I actually *was* Lucky George, I'd cut my own throat this minute, because I'd know Kurt Lundqvist was on my trail, and it's only a matter of time, and I don't want to be sentient when he finds me. That guy is completely something else . . .

So, I'd go somewhere he'd never dream of looking. Three alternatives:

(a) Somewhere with lots of people, where I'd melt away into the crowd.

(b) Somewhere so far away and godforsaken, nobody even knows it exists.

(c) I'd stay exactly where I am.

Yes. Well, (a) was a non-starter, because wherever Lucky George went, the one thing he could never be was inconspicuous. His habit of turning things into other things saw to that.

Likewise, (c). The Amsterdam authorities are famous for their ability to look the other way when expedient, but even they would have trouble overlooking armies of marauding windmills and giant attack-cheeses.

Which left (b), and very good thinking it was, too, because the chances of finding him by guesswork were very remote indeed.

He was just coming to these conclusions when the radio crackled and addressed him; peculiar in itself, since it wasn't switched on.

Hey, Kurt, my man, gimme some skin.

Lundqvist groaned. He really wasn't in the mood.

'Piss off, Bull,' he said. 'And switch that thing off before you go.'

Don't be like that, man. There's something really heavy going down, and . . .

'Later, Bull, okay? I'm busy. And besides, I still owe you a kicking for that last tip-off you gave me. Remember?'

The radio crackled nervously. *Hey, man, that wasn't my fault. How was I supposed to know . . . ?*

'Rule number one, Bull, nobody grasses up the Antichrist, even if he is moonlighting. He wasn't pleased, Bull. We had him down at the station five hours before he told us who he was. I nearly got my licence pulled over that one.'

Yeah, well, nobody's perfect. This time, I got what you want. I got George for you.

Lundqvist jammed a wedge in his adrenaline and raised an eyebrow. 'Sure, Bull,' he said. 'You and every other cheap informer between here and Delphi. Go hustle somebody else.'

No, man, I'm serious. I know where he is. Or at least, where the girl is.

'How?'

How.

'No, you clown, how do you know where the girl is? Is it just pure intuition, or have you actually seen her?'

Let's talk money first.

Lundqvist snarled. Then he took off his tie, jury-rigged the joystick and put his hands palm-downwards on the console.

What you doing, man?

'Holding a seance, Bull. And when you materialise, I'm gonna kick your ectoplasm up through your ears, okay? Now then, have you seen her or not?'

Okay, okay, cool it. The Ancestors told me.

'I'm losing patience here, Bull. If you don't come clean before I count to five, it's gonna be one sadistic beating for yes, two sadistic beatings for no . . .'

I'm telling the truth, man, I heard it from the Ancestors. Like in Australia, okay? There's all these wild dudes out there who run the songlines, and they're all in the same union with me. As soon as I heard, I thought of you, I thought . . .

'Australia?'

You got it. Place called Maralinga. They don't call it that, of course, they call it D sharp minor, F natural, B natural, G flat, but I looked it up on a map and . . .

Lundqvist grinned and untied the joystick. 'Thanks, Bull,' he said. 'I'll check it out. And maybe I'll let you off with exorcism when I see you next. And maybe not.'

The radio switched off.

CHAPTER
NINE

Danny Bennett knew for a fact that he had a Destiny, just as a dog knows it has fleas.

It was written in the stars that one day, Danny Bennett would unmask the most staggering conspiracy, lay bare the most Machiavellian cover-up, make the ultimate documentary, win the ultimate award, make the once and future awards ceremony speech. The trouble with the stars is that sometimes they can't read their own handwriting. Either that, or there was another Daniel Woodward Bernstein Bennett out there somewhere who got all his namesake's mail by mistake.

In any event, his latest staggering exposé of corruption and intrigue in the Foodstuffs Colouring and Preservatives Directorate, engagingly titled 'Offal You Can't Refuse', had made such an impression that here he was, covering the Round-Australia Land-Yacht Race for one of the top forty satellite TV companies. Promotion, you could say, if you're happy with the concept of being promoted downwards.

Media analysts tended to observe that if Isaac Newton had

followed Danny's career over the last five years, the apple would have been entirely superfluous.

He pulled in, stared blankly at five miles of featureless, arrow-straight road in front of him, and consulted the map. Even with the map held the wrong way up, the only possible conclusion was that he'd come the wrong way, and that there was nothing for it but to turn round and drive the eighty-seven miles back into Arrampagatta. The fact that by the time he got to where he was supposed to be, the race would be across the state line and heading north was tempered by the certainty that Danny wouldn't be able to recognise a land-yacht if one ran up his backside.

Which is what one promptly did.

Glancing in his rear-view mirror, all Danny could see was a whacking great sail, flolloped untidily across the back window. He frowned, opened the door and got out.

'Excuse me,' he said. He couldn't help noticing something that looked uncomfortably like a sailing ship on wheels, which seemed for all the world as if it was trying to get into the boot of his car.

'Why the hell,' said a voice from somewhere inside the canvas, 'don't you look where you're bloody well going?'

'I wasn't going,' Danny replied. 'I was parked. What is that thing?'

Out from behind the sail came about seven feet of man, topped with flashing Ray-Ban mirror sunglasses and idly passing a toothbrush from hand to hand. 'Is that your car?' he said.

'It's a hire car,' Danny replied. 'What's . . . ?'

He became aware that the handle of the toothbrush was level with his heart. Somehow, this frightened him.

'I need a lift.'

'Right,' Danny said. 'That's fine. I'm going back to Arrampa-gatta; that's about ninety miles that way, but you're welcome to—'

'No. I need to go this way. Get in and drive.'

The stranger emphasised these words by drawing the bristles of the toothbrush against the pile across the palm of his hand, and some sort of atavistic survival instinct told Danny that this was a really good opportunity to practise being scared shitless. He complied.

As he shut the door and turned the key in the ignition, he realised why. He knew the guy.

'So you're in the race,' he said, by way of a diversion.

'What race?'

'The land-yacht race,' Danny replied, looking straight ahead. 'That was a land-yacht you were riding, wasn't it?'

'Yes.'

Lundqvist! It had to be Lundqvist.

Excellence is its own best advertisement, in the covert assassination and dirty tricks business as in everything else. Build a better mantrap and the world will beat a path to your door. As a result, Lundqvist's identity and professional reputation were tolerably well known among certain circles, although nobody with a penchant for waking up two mornings in a row would ever have dreamt of trying to make any sort of fuss about it.

Now Danny had a talent; a quite staggering intuitive ability, which enabled him to see just under half the story in a blinding flash of inspiration. Once the speck of insight had found its way into his brain, he then proceeded to coat it with innumerable layers of his own brand of imaginative gibberish, but that was by the way. His most recent researches had led him to the plain fact that wherever something significant, mysterious and horrible had happened in the last fifteen years, one Kurt Lundqvist had been somewhere in the vicinity at the time – visiting his aunt, seeing his dentist, attending a conference on early church music perhaps, but *there*, nevertheless. Once you'd seen that common factor, the conclusion was obvious.

Danny Bennett knew, instinctively but conclusively, that Lundqvist was the number one torpedo for the Milk Marketing

Board. And here he was, in Danny's car, toothbrushed up and twitching with raw adrenaline, out in the middle of the Australian Outback.

'Um,' Danny said. 'Where was it you wanted to go, exactly?'

'George's Sheep Farm. Carry on along this road another seventy miles, it should be the first turning on your left. Got that?'

Danny nodded, his brain teeming all the while.

Sheep farm! What the hell would the Milk Marketing Board want with a sheep farm? Either the MMB bosses were running a covert dairy operation using cows with cotton wool stuck all over their backs, or else the whole thing was a front for something even more sinister. Part of his flesh crawled with feverish excitement. The rest just crawled.

'Funny thing,' Danny said. 'I'd got the idea the race didn't go anywhere near here.'

He didn't look round, but he could sense the lenses of the Ray-Bans scorching the side of his head. 'I'm taking a short cut,' Lundqvist said.

'A short cut. In a race.'

'Yeah.'

'Fine.'

The next hour seemed to pass very slowly. There was Lundqvist in the passenger seat, grimly munching his way through a roll of peppermints he'd found in the glove box, and there was Danny, desperately trying to suss it all out and find the little stray clue that would tie in a New South Wales sheepranch, the Watergate break-in and the Banco Ambrosiano. It was there, he knew it; just a matter of isolating one little wisp of a connection . . .

'We're here.'

Danny stood on the brake, slewing the car half round. His eyes met Lundqvist's, in roughly the same manner as a hedgehog meets an eighteen-wheel Mack truck.

'So,' Danny said. 'This is where you get out, then.'

'Yeah.' The door opened, Lundqvist grabbed his rucksack off the back seat and extracted the grotesque lengths of knee and elbow from which he appeared to be largely constructed. He slammed the door and started to walk up the long dirt track.

Discretion is the better part of valour, as the saying goes. By the same author, but not perhaps so well known, are such equally profound saws as, 'Aspirin is the spice of geography,' and, 'You can lead a horse to water but never double on three no trumps.' Danny drove on, decided to count to ten, got to seven and backed up. Then he drove on down the narrow track. On the seat beside him there now rested a loaded video camera.

Lundqvist froze in the doorway.

That statement is rather ambiguous. Since it was something like ninety in the shade, and there was enough moisture gathering in the armpits of his shirt to hold a tall ships race on, Lundqvist was by no means frozen. He was, rather, still.

Inside the big shed thing (Lundqvist was a bit vague about the proper names of agricultural buildings) a girl was counting sheep.

'Seventy-six, seventy-seven, seventy-eight, seventy-*nine* – come on, Hilda, up you get – eighty . . .'

The shear-your-own idea, Helen admitted to herself, hadn't been the tearaway spectacular success she'd hoped for. In the back of her mind, she had the notion that you needed just a bit more passing trade for a venture of that kind, and perhaps she should have realised that earlier. Still, no use crying over spilt milk (Danny Bennett would have disputed that remark, and it's as well he wasn't on hand to do so); what she did have on the credit side of the ledger was many, many sheep, and it surely wasn't beyond the wit of man to find some way of exploiting the resource.

She paused, hands on hips, and frowned. Then she cracked the small whip she held and shouted.

'Come *on*, Doris, you aren't even trying.'

Doris gave her a blank stare, said, 'Baaa,' and trotted grimly round the jump. The rest of the flock, however, did as they were told, and jumped. The face that launched a thousand sheeps, and all that jazz.

Not a bad wheeze, though she said it herself. What do you give the insomniac who's got everything? Trained performing sheep, of course.

Meanwhile, in the doorway, Lundqvist was motionless, listening. Where Helen was, it stood to reason, George couldn't be far away. All he needed to do was wait, like a cat at a mousehole, and the idiot would walk straight into his arms.

Well yes. Quite.

On the one hand, Lundqvist said to himself, quite apart from his virtually infinite resources of supernatural special effects, Lucky George has the reputation of being a crack shot, naturally gifted all-in wrestler and ex-Wittenberg fencing blue. On the other hand, I have a toothbrush.

Had a toothbrush.

A few seconds of frantic pocket-searching followed, at the end of which Lundqvist moaned softly and bumped his head three or four times against the doorpost. He'd come all this way – stolen a helicopter, hijacked an airliner, taken a series of cars and lorries without permission and finally mugged a sailplane pilot – only to leave his toothbrush somewhere between here and the entrance of the driveway. And Lucky George liable to turn up at any minute . . .

'Excuse me,' called the girl from the interior of the shed. 'Can I help you or something?'

Lundqvist stood upright. A stray pellet of inspiration had lodged in the back of his brain.

'Yes,' he said. 'I think you can.'

By the time Danny Bennett had climbed up on to the rail of the silage clamp to get a better view and got the camera on his shoulder and found the thing you pressed to make it go and the other thing you twiddled to get it in focus, he'd missed some of the best bits. He'd missed Lundqvist running like a hare out of the shed, with a flock of ravening sheep snapping at his heels and the current Miss World bringing up the rear cracking a whip and shouting, 'Go on, Doris, kill!' He'd missed Lundqvist's quite spectacular leap up into the hayloft, and the lead ewe's frantic efforts to jump up and bite his throat out. He'd missed the really good bit, where the girl had brought up a ladder and the sheep had gone swarming up it like firemen on piecework, followed by Lundqvist jumping out the other side and landing in the water butt.

What he had got, though, was Lundqvist grabbing the girl, bundling her under his arm and running like fun back up the drive, while seventeen livid sheep stood on the hay platform realising that learning to come *down* the ladder had been pencilled on the timetable for the week after next.

He hadn't the faintest idea of what was going on, of course, but that was so close to normality that it was comforting rather than otherwise. What he did recognise was bloody good television.

Familiarity is, indeed, the most powerful anaesthetic of all. To Helen of Troy, bumping about under Lundqvist's arm and trying to write *Been kidnapped. Dinner in fridge. Love, Helen xxx* on the back of a feed bill with an eyebrow pencil, being abducted was just like old times. It was, after all, what she was best at.

'You,' screamed Lundqvist, 'start the goddamn car!'

Danny, recognising that the remark was addressed to himself, started to climb down from his eyrie and then checked himself. Yes, sure, a good journalist's first duty is to cover the story, but did that involve assisting in the abduction of beauty queens by known hit-men?

'Start the fucking car,' Lundqvist reiterated, as if somehow conscious of Danny's internal debate, 'or I'll rip your nuts off with a plastic fork!'

Yes, Danny decided, it probably did. Without releasing his hold on the camera, he fumbled in his trouser pocket for the car keys.

You know how it is with keys. Shy, elusive creatures, the trouser pocket is their natural habitat and they are masters of the arts of camouflage and concealment. Their favourite ploy is to snuggle down into the folds of a crumpled pocket handkerchief and stop up the mouth of the burrow with any loose change that might be lying about. Failing that, they find a loose thread in the seam to snag themselves on, and cling like limpets. Danny's keys did both.

'Just a minute,' he called out, jiggling furiously. 'I won't keep you, I've just got to . . .'

He jiggled too hard and dropped the camera.

Five minutes of the best action sequence he'd ever been privileged to witness, spinning and twirling through the air on its way to obliteration on the rock-hard ground, twenty feet below. In that split second when he realised what had happened, Danny felt the most devastatingly acute feeling of loss that any human being could conceivably register without the top of his head coming unscrewed. It had had everything – sex, violence, action, comedy and white fluffy animals – and in one and a half seconds' time it was going to hit the deck and go splat. He launched himself into the air, stretched out a frantic arm like Michelangelo's Adam, and just managed to get the tips of his fingers round the carrying handle.

His last thought, before he hit the deck and went *splat!*, was *Phew, that was close.*

When he opened his eyes, it was dark. Then someone slowly turned up the lights.

It was just like being at the cinema.

The faint glow was coming from directly in front of him. As he stared, it seemed to resolve itself into shapes. Patterns. Letters.

YOU ARE DEAD

Danny started violently; or rather, he didn't. It was like trying to rub your eyes with a hand that's just been amputated; the brain ordered a spasm of movement, and the space where the nerves had once been sent back the message that spasms are off.

SORRY

Gosh, Danny couldn't help thinking, it's nice of them to say that. Perhaps it wasn't a hundred per cent sincere, no more than *We apologise for any delay* notices at the head of a twelve-mile tailback, but the fact that they bothered at all was reassuring, in a way. It implied that there was someone, or perhaps Someone, you could write to and complain.

DEATH IS PERFECTLY NORMAL
PLEASE DON'T WORRY

The letters flickered and faded, and it was dark again; but there was no immediate impulse towards terror, because they were playing piped music. Airport music. Supermarket music. Please-hold-the-line music. Now everybody knows that when this sort of music plays, the only possible emotion is passive boredom; and it's impossible to be passively bored and shit-scared at the same time. Danny sighed and allowed his mind to wander.

Well, I'm dead. What a bloody nuisance, here I am dead and no camera. My first really *big* scoop and there's absolutely nothing I can do about it.

Then it occurred to him that death is hardly a scoop for any journalist. It's the one story that everyone covers and nobody gets to phone in. Danny opened where his mouth had been and screamed.

Noiselessly.

And then the lights flickered again, this time resolving themselves into a ten-foot-high neon questionnaire.

PLEASE HELP US
TO HELP YOU
BY COMPLETING THIS SIMPLE FORM

Put like that, it would be churlish to refuse.

Full name: Daniel Woodward Bernstein Bennett

Date of birth: December 14th, 1959

Nationality: British

Smoking or non-smoking: non-smoking

Evening meal?

And so on. The form scrolled forward – breakfast is served in the dining area between 7.00 and 9.00, the fire escapes are situated at the end of the corridor, if you have managed to take it with you, please deposit it in the safety deposit box in the front office – and as it did so, Danny realised something.

A common factor. A link. New South Wales, a sheep station, Kurt Lundqvist.

Me!

Lundqvist! Bloody hell fire, I've been hit by a hit-man!

Danny's spiritual remains sat bolt upright, and where his eyes had once been shone with ecstatic joy. For, in a moment of transcendent knowledge such as one tends to associate with the Great Transition, Danny had suddenly realised that all his life, everything he'd fought and worked and sweated and been humiliated for, must have been worthwhile.

'Hey!' he yelled, 'this is great! I've been silenced! I must have known too much!'

And then the reaction, deadening and crushing as a piledriver. Absolute Sunday-morning-and-no-milk-left despair.

Yes, obviously he'd known too much. Obviously he'd been put out of the way, by Them, by the unseen conspirators . . .

(All rooms must be vacated by 12 noon on Judgement Day. Please do not place objects down the toilet bowl. If you would like your past life to flash before you, please dial your credit card number down to the front desk and select channel 12 on your remote control handset . . .)

Unfortunately, he hadn't the faintest idea what it was he'd known too much about.

CHAPTER
TEN

G eorge frowned. This, he couldn't help feeling, was a trifle disturbing.

Your dinner, the kidnap note had said, is in the fridge. Upon inspection, however, the fridge turned out to contain nothing but vegetables. One of the things that he'd always liked about Helen was that, unlike ninety-five per cent of the rest of her sex, she didn't confuse food with scenery. Had she chosen this moment of all moments to go to the bad? Or had she simply written 'fridge' when she meant 'freezer'?

The latter hypothesis proved to be correct, since the freezer turned out to contain two frozen pizzas and a microwave lasagne. He decided on the lasagne, turned it out of its foil container on to a plate, and smiled at it.

Then he frowned at it, to give the melted cheese on the top that distinctive browned-under-the-grill look.

Callous? Insensitive? Just like a man? These are hard thoughts, and not really applicable. It's true that there have been heroes and men of action who've gone haring off to rescue damsels on an empty stomach, but what the epics don't tell you is that their subsequent performance was considerably hampered by indigestion and heartburn. Your class hero knows this. Hercules, for example, had a double cheeseburger with fries, coleslaw and an ambrosia shake before snatching Alcestis out of the arms of the King of Death, and Sir Lancelot always insisted on a round of cucumber sandwiches with the crusts cut off before so much as looking at a dragon.

Logic, said George to himself. A spot of logic is called for here.

Who'd want to kidnap Helen of Troy? Well, yes, that's a pretty dumb question, so let's rephrase it. Apart from every red-blooded male in the world, who'd want to kidnap Helen of Troy? Easy. Lundqvist.

By way of confirmation of this working hypothesis, there was the tape in the video camera which some untidy person had left lying about by the silage clamp, right next to the corpse. George wound back the tape and sat for a few minutes, his mind turning over like Mozart in his grave during a Jonathan Miller production of *Cosi fan Tutti*. Then he suddenly scowled and snapped his fingers.

Two seagulls hopped down and perched on the top of the telly, trying to eat the aluminium trim.

'Hey,' George said, 'this isn't on, you know.'

'Quark?'

'Kidnapping people,' George explained. 'My compliments to Mr Lundqvist, and ask him if there's any particular order he wants his bones broken in.'

'Quark.'

'No.'

The seagulls flapped their wings and lifted out of the window. George played the video through once more. Then he made a phone call. *How! This is a recorded spirit message. Kindly leave your name and a medium through whom you can be contacted and I'll get back to you as soon as I can.*

He shrugged and tried a different number. When it answered, his side of the conversation went like this:

'Hello? Yes, could I have Mr Bosch, please, extension 3092? Yes, thanks, I'll hold.'

The hold facility on the switchboard played you the *Dies Irae*, as interpreted by a computer synthesizer. Eventually . . .

'Bosch here.'

'Ronnie,' said George, 'how's tricks? The project coming together at last?'

'Bloody hell, George . . .' The voice changed in pitch, though not in volume, until it became a rather heavy conspiratorial hiss. 'You really have got to stop calling me at work like this. You have no idea how *embarrassing*—'

'Yes, sorry. How's the Garden of Earthly Delights coming along, by the way?'

Bosch sighed. 'Don't ask,' he said. 'Even if we make it out of foam rubber instead of expanded polystyrene, the ninety-foot-high cracked eggshell just isn't going to stay up there, I just know it, and the sprinkler system's completely up a tree. I've got seventy-six thousand purple tubular carnivorous plants out there dying of dehydration, but do they listen?'

George tutted sympathetically. 'Par for the course, it sounds to me. Look, can you do me a quick favour?'

Bosch growled darkly. 'Depends,' he said. 'I mean, there's favours and favours. I think opening wormholes in the fabric of virtual reality for you to hide your rope ladder in probably puts us all square, don't you?'

George laughed cheerfully. 'Call those wormholes, Ron?' he said. 'I'd have been better off stashing the gear under the bed only I didn't want to hurt your feelings. I would also remind you of that time back at Wittenberg when I let you borrow my red slashed fustian doublet three weeks running when you were chasing after that barmaid with the big—'

'All right,' Bosch cut him short. 'I was younger then. Dammit, I was *alive* then. What do you want this time?'

'Just a note of where Lundqvist is right now.'
'That's *all*?'
'For now, Ron.'

Meanwhile, Lundqvist was negotiating with two seagulls.

'We got the Revenue off your back like you said,' Larry croaked, 'although we couldn't do anything about your 1986 expenses claim. I mean,' he added quickly, as Lundqvist's eyes smouldered, 'putting five thousand cubic feet of cyanide gas down as entertaining potential clients *is* going a bit too far, you've got to—'

'The hell with you,' Lundqvist snapped. 'Those particular clients were pretty peculiar people. So what? You've got to be weird to need a transtemporal security consultant in the first place.'

'Okay,' said Mike. 'But do you really expect the tax guys to believe you got through thirty-seven dozen throwing knives in one fiscal quarter. Don't you *ever* re-use them?'

A shrewd thrust from a wingtip suggested to him that this was a subject best left alone. He cleared his throat, ruffled his feathers with his beak and changed tack.

'Anyway,' he said, 'they've unfrozen your bank accounts and the bailiffs have released your goods. We've kept our side of the bargain.'

'Good,' Lundqvist replied icily. 'Now we can start talking.'

The seagulls exchanged glances. 'I thought we'd been—'

'Preliminaries,' Lundqvist said. 'Now we get to the good stuff. That is, unless your man wants to play it the hard way. Because if he does, the only thing the girl's gonna be launching from now on is oil rigs.'

Larry sighed. 'Let's hear it, then,' he said.

'Fine by me,' Lundqvist said. 'I want George, I want him here, and no tricks. You got that?'

'Quark.'

'Right. Now piss off.'

The seagulls lifted their wings and flapped noisily out through the open window. Lundqvist grinned and drew the shutters.

'Actually,' said a voice from the corner of the room, 'would you mind awfully much leaving the window? It's a bit stuffy in here.'

Lundqvist snarled.

'Please.'

'Sure. You want me to leave the window. You think I was born yesterday?'

'Not really,' Helen said, smiling. 'If you had been, you'd be all pink and small and covered in fluffy down, and you'd need feeding all the time. Talking of which, I thought we'd have dinner around sevenish.'

Lundqvist scowled. 'We'll eat when I say so,' he said. 'If I say so. You got . . . ?'

Helen ignored him. With a dainty flick of her slim wrists, she wriggled free of the handcuffs and drew a liberated finger along the top of the table next to where she was tied up. It left a furrow in the dust. She didn't say anything, but she tutted.

'I'll need some ingredients,' she went on. 'Four pounds of potatoes, a large cabbage, two pounds of parsnips . . .'

'We'll have corned beef and like it,' Lundqvist grunted.

'I doubt that,' replied Helen. 'Also some desiccated coconut, some ginger, sunflower oil – it's better for you, more polyunsaturates – and a pound of self-raising flour. You'll just have time to pop out before the shops shut.'

Lundqvist turned round slowly. Helen had slipped free of all her bonds by now. She was standing up and tying a pinny round her waist. There was a horrible look in her eye, and for a moment Lundqvist's heart stopped.

Far back, in the left luggage room of one of the most twisted psyches in the history of Creation, a woman's voice was calling; shrill, hard, cruel.

Kurt, it shrieked, *You come here this instant, you hear me? You want that I tell your father?*

But Mom . . .

Kurt Lundqvist, you tidy your room, you polish your shoes, you do your homework, you practise the violin for half an hour like Miss Horowitz told you, then maybe you can go play with your impaling-sticks.

Yes, Mom . . .

The flashback faded, as swift and terrible as it had come, leaving Lundqvist standing with his mouth open. 'You get back in the corner,' he said, 'or I'll—'

'Nonsense,' replied Helen briskly. From somewhere – God only knew where – she'd produced a feather duster and a can of furniture polish. 'Off you go. Don't forget the sunflower oil.'

Lundqvist struggled to remember. He was Kurt Lundqvist, the biggest, meanest, most savage . . .

. . . Untidiest, scruffiest kid on the whole block. *No!* The most savage . . .

'Sure,' he said weakly. 'I go out and as soon as my back's turned you're outa here and . . .'

Helen smiled. 'Don't be silly,' she said. 'First, I'm going to give this place a really good clean. Then we'll be able to see what colour the curtains are.'

She fluttered her eyelashes cruelly.

'I mean,' she said, 'if we've got to be cooped up in this smelly old place, we might as well make it as comfortable as possible.'

Lessons Learned The Hard Way Number One: Don't Kidnap Helen of Troy.

The wooden horse was basically a face-saving exercise, something to make it all look slightly more convincing to the outside world.

Within three months of Helen's arrival in Troy after her abduction by Prince Paris, there wasn't a square inch of original carpeting in the whole city. The entire workforce had been transferred from sword-tempering and arrow-sharpening to curtain-making, and King Priam had mortgaged his empire and taken out a personal loan from the First Achaean Bank to pay for new three-piece suites in every room in his gigantic palace. It wasn't Achilles or the wrath of the gods or the curse of Dardanus that did for Troy of the Hundred Gates; it was the sheer bloody havoc wrought on the Trojan economy by a determined home-maker with a Liberty catalogue and a Gold AmEx card.

The reason that the siege of Troy took so long was simple. Once King Menelaus had got used to being able to wipe his hands on the towels and smoke in the living-room again, it took the concentrated moral pressure of three continents ten years to persuade him to take her back.

CHAPTER
ELEVEN

There is only one bar in Potters Creek (population 53) but the awareness of its own monopoly hasn't led its enterprising and forward-thinking management to grow complacent. Nothing is too good for the customers (especially the beer, which wouldn't be too good for an elephant, let alone a human being) and the proprietor is constantly striving to make such improvements as his means permit. Thus, last year, he put in chairs. This year, tables.

Around the smaller of the two tables, a film crew sat, staring into the suds at the bottom of their glasses, trying to shame each other into getting in the next round.

'Reminds me of that time in Afghanistan,' said the sound recordist.

'Yeah.'

'Or that time last year in Ghana.'

'That wasn't Ghana, that was Mozambique.'

'Nah,' interrupted the assistant cameraman, 'I'm not thinking of *that* time in Ghana, I'm thinking of that *other* time in Ghana.'

The sound recordist nodded. 'Yeah,' he said. 'I was reminded of that, too.'

There was a long silence, broken only by the distant commentary of the kookaburra, and the whisper of a slight breeze in the eucalyptus.

'Let's give him till half-seven,' muttered the chief cameraman. 'Then we bugger off, right?'

His companions nodded (except the continuity girl, who'd fallen asleep). Everyone fiddled with their glasses, suddenly noticing that they were empty.

'Aidan,' said the chief cameraman at last to the junior electrician, 'go and buy the beer.' The junior electrician, who was young, poor and saving up to buy a moped, slouched to the bar.

'Sodding lousy country, this,' opined the chief cameraman. 'Bit like Paris.'

The others nodded. 'Except,' qualified the chief electrician, 'the handles on the bogs are on the left. Anyone else notice that? I did.'

'Sodding awful place, Paris,' continued the chief cameraman. 'Full of holes.'

'Yeah. Like Tangier.'

'Or Laos. Laos is full of sodding holes. Can't get a tripod level anywhere.'

Under their hands, the table moved.

Well, you know how it is with tables in bars. There are strict international specifications about precisely how much shorter one leg should be than the others. The object is to make customers spill their drinks and buy more.

'I remember we were in Cairo once,' said the chief electrician. 'Holes *and* flies. Bloody horrible place.'

'Like Valparaiso.'

'Or Genoa.'

'Venice,' said the assistant cameraman, 'is a real bog-hole. Armpit of the universe, Venice. You want to film something, a building or something, you step back to get the bugger in the frame, splash. Here, who's jogging the bloody table?'

'Not me.'

Simultaneously, the film crew lifted their elbows. The table continued to move.

'Hey,' remarked the chief electrician, breaking a nervous silence, 'this *is* like bloody Valparaiso.'

'Yeah, or Archangel.'

The table was balancing on three of its legs. With the foot of the fourth, it was pecking tentatively at the ground, like a spider at its first tap-dancing lesson. The continuity girl woke up, blinked, and went back to sleep.

Help.

'Did someone just say something?' enquired the sound recordist.

'Yeah.'

'Ah. Right.'

'The table just said Help!'

Listen, it's me. Danny Bennett. You've got to help me.

The crew looked at each other. They were, after all, a film crew, and he was a producer. Had they thought of it, they might have quoted the line about the triumph of hope over experience.

I'm dead.

The sound recordist cleared his throat.

'Not a lot we can do about that, my son,' he said. 'What you need is more like a priest or something.'

I was murdered. It was a cover-up.

The chief cameraman checked the movement of his glass to his lips and frowned.

'Jesus!' he said. 'Danny! That really *is* you, isn't it?'

It was a cover-up. I knew too much. They killed me because I knew too much.

'Too much about what?'

The table bucked like an unbroken colt, lifting all its feet off the ground and landing six inches from its original position. *I don't bloody well know, that's the whole bloody point. That's why I need help.*

The chief electrician raised an eyebrow. 'Hang about,' he said. 'If you're dead then it's all watchercallit, academic, innit? I mean, if you're dead, you're dead, doesn't matter a toss *why . . .*'

The table jumped again, landing on the chief electrician's foot.

It matters to me, Julian. Look, about seventy miles from here there's a sheep farm . . .

'So?'

Let me finish, will you? There's a sheep farm, called George's Sheep Farm. That's where I died. I want you to go and pick up a video camera, because there may be a clue . . .

'Seventy miles?'

Yes, more or less. There may be a clue . . .

The chief cameraman furrowed his brows, creating the impression of copulating hedgerows. 'You want us to go there.'

Thank you, Colin, yes. You see, there may be a clue . . .

'And we can claim the mileage?'

What?

'If we go there,' said the chief cameraman. 'We can claim the mileage, can we, off the firm?'

How the hell should I know? Look . . .

The chief cameraman looked at his colleagues. 'And it'd have to be time and a half, because by the time we get there, if it's seventy miles like you said, not to mention getting back . . .'

Look.

'It's our rest and recreation period,' the sound recordist butted in. 'If we work in R and R time, it's time and a half. Are you *sure* the firm'll pay the mileage? Mean sods, the lot of 'em, I remember once in Finland—'

I neither know nor care, you bastards. Look, I'm dead, I need your help. I always thought you were my friends . . .

The camera crew looked at each other; then they stood up and walked over to the other table.

The other table was, of course, bolted to the ground.

After a while, the hammering noise stopped, and the crew relaxed and calmed themselves with another round.

'You know what?' said the assistant cameraman, wiping foam off his lips. 'That was bloody Szechuan all over again.'

His colleagues nodded sagely. That, they felt, put it in a nutshell.

CHAPTER
TWELVE

W e have touched lightly on the subject of friendship.
The classic definition – friendship means never having to pay the full retail price for car spares – is all right as far as it goes, but there is another, more spiritual side to friendship.

A *true* friend is someone who'll lend you his Lear jet and a full tank of petrol without asking what you want it for.

'Thanks,' George shouted, above the roar of the engine.

'Any time, George, you know that. Thanks for the tip, by the way.'

'Oh, that's all right,' George yelled back. 'It works even better if you add a thimbleful of turps.' He opened the throttle, pulled back on the stick and let her have her head.

At least finding her would be easy, he said to himself. It might get a bit tricky after that, but we'll cross that bridge when we come to it.

As soon as he'd worked out his course and pointed the plane in the right direction, he leant forward and grinned at the radio; which bleeped, crackled and homed in.

. . . This is Radio Dante, I'm Danny Bennett, I'm your host for this afternoon, and later on I'll be talking to Benito Mussolini in our regular Where I Went Wrong spot. But first, this.

George twiddled a knob slightly, leant back and took the two-way control in his hand. 'Hi,' he said. 'How's tricks?'

His voice echoed over every tannoy, loudspeaker and PA in the place; and, believe it or not, there are more speakers per square metre in Hell than anywhere else in Creation. For the piped music, you see.

The Finance Director swore.

'Get him off the bloody air,' he shouted. 'Switch 'em all off or something.'

Once the nuisance had been confined to one small telephone, the Finance Director picked up the receiver and said, 'Well, what is it now?'

'I thought you said you were getting that nutcase off my back.'

'We did.'

George shook his head. 'No you didn't,' he replied. 'And he's starting to get ever so slightly up my nose. In fact, his head is wedged up my sinuses and I want something done about it. Otherwise there's going to be trouble.'

The Finance Director winced. 'We did our best,' he mumbled. 'Put our crack team on it. What more—?'

'I heard about that,' George said. 'Got stuck in an onion, so I was told. Try again. Helen walks by six o'clock your time, or I won't be responsible for the consequences.' He paused, and the Finance Director could just picture the nasty little grin flitting across his face. 'Well, actually I will be responsible for the whole lot of 'em, so think on. Over and out.'

Before the Finance Director could reply, the line went dead and almost immediately, every speaker in the Nine Rings started to play *Chicago*, until the Chief Technician pulled out all the wires.

The Head of Security held up both hands.

'No can do,' he said. 'If I ask those lads to go back out there again, I'll be going home tonight in a plastic bag. Can't you buy him off?'

'Lundqvist?' The Finance Director considered. 'Nah,' he said, 'not this time. Anyway, even if I could I don't know where he is. He's not answering his carphone and his bleeper's switched off. We'll just have to let George do his worst and then blame it on someone else.'

The Head of Security frowned. 'Who?'

'I don't know,' replied the Finance Director. 'The CIA. The nuclear power people. The Milk Marketing—'

'Which reminds me . . .'

'Anyway,' continued the Finance Director, 'we'll just have to do the best we can. I wish I'd never started this whole perishing thing now,' he added.

The Head of Security shrugged his shoulders. 'Maybe we're worrying too much,' he said. 'I mean, when it comes right down to it, he can't do anything *too* terrible, can he?'

There's a time differential between Hell and the rest of the cosmos, naturally. In Hell, however, time is told not in hours and minutes but episodes, such as half past four on a Sunday afternoon when there's nothing on the television except the Olympics, or three minutes after the bar you've just walked into closes.

One minute past six in Infernal Mean Time is, therefore, the split second between the moment when you've just let go of the china ornament that's been in your employer's family since 1868 and the point in time when it hits the lino. To match this up with Greenwich, you multiply by four, divide by six and forget to turn off the gas before leaving for a fortnight's holiday.

And that was the precise moment when . . .

'Brilliant,' said the Finance Director, between gritted fangs. 'You've got to hand it to him. For sheer brilliant simplicity . . .'

'The switchboard,' reported the Marketing Director, 'has just overloaded.'

'Oh good. Now perhaps we can hear ourselves think.'

(In the clouds above New South Wales, Lucky George felt a tug on one of the tendrils of his mind. He smiled, and four hundred thousand miles of fused fibre-optic cable running through the centre of the earth took on a new lease of life . . .)

'Malcolm!' The Finance Director waved a hand vaguely at the Duty Officer. 'Get that for me, will you?' He turned to his fellow directors. 'Let's go down to the executive lavatory for a bit. There's no phones there.'

'Basically,' he went on, when the meeting had reconvened, 'the situation is that, thanks to Lucky George and his magic bloody wand, the entire human race have all gone on holiday at precisely the same moment.' He paused and tried to take a sip from his glass of water, the meniscus of which danced like a formation flamenco team. 'This has, of course, produced complete and utter havoc in every country in the world except France, where they're used to it. The tailbacks on all major roads leading to airports and coastal resorts are causing a critical mass which is threatening to send the whole works shooting off into another dimension, and the price of a pair of Bermuda shorts has now risen to approximately twice the gross national product of the United States. Now, what are we going to do about it?'

He looked up. The room was empty.

'Come back!' he roared, and flung open the door.

He was just in time to see the Production Director and the Marketing Director, in bathing trunks, heading for the car park with a plastic bucket and spade and a large rubber ball.

And there it was. Plain as the proverbial pikestaff.

A three mile tailback of articulated lorries in the middle of the Australian Outback, it is fairly safe to say, is probably a symptom of something; apart, that is, from road works. George peered down from the cockpit of the Lear, grinned and circled away.

His second pass over the traffic jam, a few hundred feet lower, simply confirmed his diagnosis. He read the names on the sides of the lorries and that was enough. Certainty.

There were soft-furnishing lorries, DIY homecare lorries, carpet vans, lorries of all descriptions, delivering to a small, bleak wooden shed in the middle of half a million acres of wind-scoured, sand-blasted nothing. What you might call a woman's touch.

In the back yard of the shed, a team of forklifts were staggering about like exhausted dung-beetles under enormous loads of big cardboard cartons, while on the other side, a team of crack carpenters were starting work on a huge, Versailles-dwarfing extension to the shed, presumably to provide a bit of space for all the stuff to go. Two enormous industrial cement-mixers stood like hormone-stuffed dinosaurs round the back, while conveyor belts fed them unlimited supplies of cans of paint. George nodded; Helen's favourite colour, what she in her artistic way called Harvest White. Many years ago, George had made himself temporarily unpopular by pointing out that you could get exactly the same effect by painting the room in question ordinary white and smoking unfiltered cigarettes in it for twenty years.

He knew without having to look that one of the giant artics backed up out there in the desert was carrying a cargo of forty square miles of anaglypta.

With a flick of a wingtip he turned the plane round and headed off. When the curvature of the Earth had hidden him from the shed, he landed the plane, got out and whistled . . .

. . . Whereupon two seagulls drifted down out of the sky, perched on his tailplane and tried to eat it.

'Dry old place, this,' said Larry, critically. 'Gives me bad vibes, to be honest. Dunno where my next fish is coming from.'

'Yes,' George replied. 'Putting that to one side for a moment, I want you two to do something for me.'

★ ★ ★

'You're *sure* you like it?' Helen enquired. 'I mean, really *really* sure?' She observed Lundqvist carefully. 'You aren't, you know. Admit it.'

'It's fine.' Lundqvist ground the words out like flour. 'I love it. Really.'

'No.' Helen shook her head. 'You're just saying that to please me.' She leant out of the window, picked up the loudhailer and shouted, 'Excuse me!'

The wallpaper-pasting squad heard her, downed tools and signalled to the rest of the workforce, using flags and mirrors. A few minutes later, there was silence.

'Sorry to be a pest,' Helen loudspoke sweetly, 'but I'm afraid we've changed our minds again. Could we try a paleish sort of Chrysoprase White on the walls of the ballroom, please, with Crushed Eglantine on the ceilings and the Summer Caramel carpet. No, not the Axminster, the Wilton. Thank you.'

There was a moment of complete stillness; then a great deal of subvocal muttering; then an emptying and refilling of cement-mixers, a ripping-up of carpets and a cleaning of brushes, like the foreriders of a tsunami hitting the outlying coral reefs of a Pacific atoll. There was a certain practised resignation about the whole scene. Not all that surprising; it was the fifth time she'd changed her mind that morning.

'Now then,' Helen said brightly, 'if you don't like it, promise you'll say, won't you? I mean, you've got to live here too, you know.'

'Gr.'

'And, like you said, we might be here for some considerable time before George does the sensible thing and gives himself up.' She smiled warmly, like the sunrise. 'And you did very sweetly say I could tidy the place up and give it a lick of paint and so on, didn't you?'

Lundqvist nodded sadly. His 'Yeah, sure, do what you like' in this context clamoured for inclusion in the Library of Congress Index of Incredibly Unfortunate Remarks, along with such classics as 'Of course it isn't loaded', 'Let them eat cake' and 'When I leave school, I want to be a solicitor'. However, even the meanest street punk in the barrios knows that any kidnapper who values his professional credibility doesn't welch on a deal unless he wants the word to get around that he's a two-face who can't be trusted. It was just a pity he'd also told her his AmEx Gold Card number.

'Well,' Helen said, putting her feet up on a Louis Quinze fauteuil and leafing through the colour charts, 'this is cosy, don't you think?'

'Mmm.' Lundqvist nodded as if his head had just been replaced with a large log. 'You think so?'

'It's coming along, anyway,' Helen replied. 'I mean, we're not there yet, but we're beginning to see the light at the end of the . . . Oh.'

She broke off and held the colour chart up against the wall. Inside his chest, Lundqvist's heart stopped and tried to burrow its way into his intestines.

'Oh *yes*,' Helen said. 'Yes, I think I'm on to something here. What do you think?' She pointed to a small square in the middle of the page. As far as Lundqvist could tell it was exactly the same colour as the seventy-four other little boxes. 'For the ballroom, the main hall, the drawing room, the sitting room, the front stairs, the back stairs, the pantry, the scullery, the study, the loft conversion, the annexe, the loggia, the cloister, the fifth spare bedroom and the observatory? Then we can do the rest out in Orchard Haze and have the Golden Wave curtains in the back hall and the conservatory.' She paused. 'What d'you think?'

Lundqvist considered. It took him a long time.

'I think,' he said, 'it'd be very easy to escape from here right now. Very easy indeed.'

Helen raised an eyebrow. 'Oh no,' she said, 'I wouldn't *dream* of trying to escape. After all,' she added mercilessly, 'you told me not to.'

Lundqvist scowled. 'You don't want to take any notice of all that,' he said. 'That's just bluster. I mean, all you'd have to do,' he went on, pouring out a cup of coffee and passing it across the table to her, 'is, say, throw a cup of coffee in my face, run across to that door there, the one that's conveniently ajar right this very minute, and—'

'Not really,' Helen interrupted.

'Oh I think you'll find you could.'

Helen shook her head. 'Because,' she explained, 'in about thirty seconds the men are going to take that door out and make a start on the French windows.'

'French windows? In a hideout?'

'Absolutely,' Helen replied. 'Then, I thought, you'll be able to keep a good watch out to see if anybody comes up trying to rescue me. And if we put a couple of yards of old Venetian lace curtain across – I saw some in one of the catalogues, it's only ninety dollars a metre – then they couldn't see in. And of course, there's the locks.'

'Locks?'

Helen nodded. 'I told them, we want deadlocks *and* mortice locks on all the doors and windows. After all, security's the one thing you've got to have in a place like this, isn't it?'

Lundqvist choked back a whimper, with indeterminate success. Back in the second millennium BC, when the Greeks besieged Troy, things had been a whole lot different. Carpets, for example; the most expensive carpet you could get back then was little more than rush matting with ideas above its station. Velvet curtains were still over a thousand years in the future. Split-level grills and co-ordinated built-in kitchen units were nothing but a troubled oscillation in the subconscious mind of God. It had been, in other words, a very basic and primitive trial run, nothing more.

'Okay,' Lundqvist said. 'Sure, if I'm conscious it might be a bit tricky getting out of here. But if I was accidentally to slip on something and knock myself out . . .' He picked up a banana from the fruit bowl and unobtrusively started to peel it.

'Unlikely,' Helen replied with a smile. 'That's why I insisted on wall-to-wall fitted carpets.'

Lundqvist abandoned the banana. 'All right,' he said, 'point taken. Something might land on my head, though. Have you thought of that?'

Helen frowned. 'Such as what?'

'Well,' Lundqvist said, looking round, 'say a big glass ash-tray. Like this one here, for example.' He tested it in his hand for balance. 'Knock a guy out cold with no trouble at all, something like this.'

'Do you really think so?'

Lundqvist grinned at her, threw the ashtray up in the air and ducked under it. It landed on his head and broke cleanly in two.

'Thought not,' Helen said. 'If I were you, I'd put iodine or something on that cut.'

Muttering something under his breath about goddam cheapskate Taiwanese glassware, Lundqvist stood up and walked to the door.

'Hey,' he observed, as he reached for the doorhandle, 'my back's turned. Just thought I'd mention it.'

He went out, found the iodine, applied it liberally, counted up to a thousand, and went back. Helen was still there, her feet up on the sofa, reading a glossy magazine.

'There's a really good bit in this about ideas for brightening up drab mezzanines,' she said. 'Have a look.'

Lundqvist stood in the doorway and growled for a moment. Then he cleared his throat.

'Good lord,' he said. 'I left my gun right there on the coffee table, just where you could reach out and pick it up. How care-less can you—?'

With a quick movement, Helen reached out and grabbed for the gun. Her fingers closed tight around the Pachmayr grips . . .

'Okay,' Lundqvist started to say, 'you win, I'll come – what are you *doing*?'

'Catch.'

The gun flew through the air towards him. It took a considerable effort of will to suppress the instinct to catch it. There was a thud as it hit the door.

'Butterfingers,' Helen remarked tolerantly. 'Now that door'll have to be painted again. While we're at it, actually, I thought of having all the woodwork a sort of light Drowned Violet . . .'

Lundqvist closed his mouth, which had frozen open, just as his mother had warned him it would all those years ago. Nevertheless. He was as patient as he was resourceful.

'Just come wonder,' he said, without moving. 'Lucky you don't know about the *other* gun, the one hidden under that cushion you're leaning against right now.' To reinforce the statement, he smiled; a pleading, rather endearing little smile, which Helen ignored.

'Yes,' she said, her head in a pattern book. 'Isn't it?'

CHAPTER
THIRTEEN

'Come in,' said the Finance Director, 'sit down, make yourselves at home. What can I get you to drink?'

The Captain of Spectral Warriors looked round suspiciously, perched on the edge of a chair, and said that he'd quite fancy a small Babycham, if that wasn't too much trouble.

'Small Babycham coming right up,' replied the Finance Director, bustling. 'Now then, introductions. This is the Company Secretary, the Head of Security you already know, of course, and this is Harry, he's the Production Director, and Steve, who heads our Sales team. Lads, I'd like you all to meet Vince, Captain of Spectral Warriors.'

The boardroom table bobbed and sparkled with smiles and little waves. Unnerved, the Captain waved back.

'Right,' said the Finance Director. 'Here's your small, er, Babycham. Everyone else, then, the usual? Right, fine.' He clattered some bottles and whooshed a soda syphon.

'Excuse me.'

'Yes, Vince? What can we do for you? Peanuts, perhaps?

Or how about an olive? Steve, get the olives.'

'Right, coming up, won't be a—'

'Excuse me,' the Captain repeated, 'but what's all this in aid of? With respect and all that, but . . .'

The various directors nodded approvingly. Here was a man, they seemed to be saying, who comes straight to the point and no mucking about.

'Well,' said the Company Secretary, folding his wings on the table in front of him, 'basically, what we wanted to do was, well, really say thank you for all you've been doing . . .'

'Greatly appreciated . . .'

'Sterling stuff, of course, absolutely sterling . . .'

'. . . And just kind of get to know you better, with possibly a view to asking you if you've ever considered – I mean if you'd *like* to – well, join the, um, board.'

'As a director,' the Production Director explained.

'One of us.'

'Absolutely.'

'Quite.'

The Captain slowly put his glass down. 'What,' he said, 'me?'

The Directors nodded. 'Why not?' said the Head of Security. 'Just the sort of bloke we're looking for.'

'Committed.'

'Dedicated.'

'One hundred per cent, twenty-four hours a day, eight days a—'

'*Seven* days . . .'

'Oh, they did bring that in after all, did they?'

'Just a moment,' said the Captain. 'Let's just get this straight. *You* want *me* to be a Director?'

The Directors nodded.

'Oh.'

'Just as soon –' The Finance Director addressed his remarks to the wall behind the Captain's head. '– just as soon as we've cleared up this little bit of nonsense we've got on at the minute, of course. Actually, you might be able to help us there, because . . .'

A forty-watt bulb started to glow in the back of the Captain's mind. He asked, 'What little bit of nonsense?'

'This whatsisname . . .'

'Loonquest?'

'Lunkfish?'

'Lund-something. Damn, it's on the tip of—'

'No.'

The Captain stood up, his face white as a soap-ad sheet. 'Absolutely not,' he went on. 'Not after last time. Sorry, but—'

'Sit down.'

'I really don't think there's much point, because—'

'*Sit down!*'

The Captain sat down. Someone refilled his glass and the Production Director produced a bowl of cheese straws, some of which had already had the ends nibbled off. This was, after all, Hell; where all the boxes of chocolates come with the coffee creams already removed, and the detective stories in the library all have the last five pages missing.

'Obviously,' purred the Finance Director smoothly, 'a little reluctance, let's say, is only to be expected. Quite right too. Absolutely understandable, under the circumstances. We respect you for it, don't we?'

Heads nodded.

'Nevertheless.' The Finance Director slid a tumblerful of breadsticks and a plate of vol-au-vents down the table towards the Captain. 'Someone's got to do it. From each according to his abilities, and all that.'

'Very sound,' murmured the Company Secretary, and he pursed his lips judicially. 'Absolutely.'

The Captain shook his head. 'No way,' he replied, trembling slightly. 'Have you people got even the faintest notion of what it's like, three days in a damn onion? Quite apart from everything else, the smell—'

'Jolly good idea,' broke in the Production Director. 'Smashing suggestion of yours. I've ordered five tons of onions for the Adultery Wing, by the way, and we're working on the design right now. Actually, we were thinking of changing the name to the Captain Vincent Schwartzschatte Adultery Wing, just to show our application of—'

'You're all crazy,' the Captain shouted. 'There's absolutely nothing you can do that'll make me go back in there after that lunatic, nothing at all. And as for the lads . . .'

The Finance Director held up his hand. 'Fair enough,' he said. 'Point taken, say no more, subject closed. And, like we said, we respect you for it, no doubt about it. Don't we, lads?'

'Absolutely.'

'No question.'

'Utmost respect. Utmost.'

'However.' The Finance Director leant forward on to the boardroom table and fixed the Captain with a selection of his eyes. 'That does bring us on rather neatly to what we might call –' He paused, and grinned disconcertingly. '– the consolation prize. Tell him about it, Steve.'

'The other, um portfolio, you mean?'

'That's right.'

The Sales Director ruffled some papers, took off his glasses and laid them on the table beside him. 'Yes indeed,' he said. 'The other portfolio. Right, where to start?'

Spectral warriors, being entirely made up out of solidified paranoia and racial guilt, have no hearts, or toenails, or anything else. However, years of mixing with human mortals had given the Captain a pretty shrewd idea of what a heart is, and what it does under circumstances of extreme apprehension. Accordingly, when the Sales Director said the words *the other portfolio*, his notional or imaginary heart turned to water and tried to seep quietly out through his ear.

'Pretty straightforward job,' the Sales Director went on. 'Recognised punishment for swearing, blasphemy, slanderous gossip and saying nice things about one's employers with intent to procure advancement – up to the neck in a big vat full of, ah, thing. Ordure. The smelly stuff. We get it delivered, you know, fresh every day. Well, not *fresh* exactly. New. Anyway, there's the question of quality control . . .'

'Ah.'

'Vitally important, quality control,' broke in the Production Director. 'There are rigid specifications laid down in the franchise, so we can't just go around giving the clients any old—'

'As my colleague says. Well, to cut a long story short, the post is now vacant.'

The Captain swallowed hard. Vacancies simply do not occur in an immortal and ineffable workforce. In Hell, dead men's shoes means nothing more than the pairs of leather things left outside the doors of the more expensive suites for the hall-porter to clean before morning.

'What,' he asked slowly, 'happened to the previous . . . ?'

The Finance Director grinned very slightly. 'Resigned,' he said. 'Or rather, misplaced.'

'Fell in the main vat,' the Production Director explained. 'Leant over too far one morning, lost his balance, splosh. Presumably,' he added carelessly, 'the poor bugger's still in there somewhere; damn steep, slippery sides that vat's got, to stop the clients getting out, of course. Very dodgy indeed. For some reason or other, volunteers to dredge the vat to look for him were not forthcoming.'

'Fourth in six months.'

'Dirty job, but someone's got to . . .'

'Still,' repeated the Captain quietly, 'in there somewhere. With the clients. I see.'

The Production Director smiled affably. 'Sooner or later,' he said, 'the thing'll solve itself. There'll be enough of them down there – our people, I mean – to form a sort of human pyramid so they can climb out again. Some of them, anyway. Meanwhile . . .'

He left the sentence unfinished. For his part the Captain closed his eyes and thought about it for a moment. He was not a dramatically imaginative person – you can't be if you're a spectral warrior, without having severe personality problems – but he could vaguely sort of picture . . .

It wouldn't, he decided, be the shit that'd get to him in the end. It'd be the endless bloody squabbling with all the other poor bastards stuck down there as to whose turn it was to stand on whose shoulders.

He indicated with a gesture his willingness to join the Board of Directors instead.

What Sitting Bull did best was, of course, sitting. Otherwise he'd have been called Standing Bull or Bull Leaning Non-chalantly, or even Bull Getting His Head Down.

On this occasion he was sitting in the Polo Lounge of Attila's Palace, sipping a margarita before wandering into the Casino to play a few hands of blackjack and feed some coins into the slot machines. He had, after all, suddenly come into money.

'How.'

He nearly jumped out of his skin. If that had been a question rather than a greeting, the truthful reply would, of course, have been, 'By grassing up Lucky George to Kurt Lundqvist.' He turned his head, and his jaw dropped like a badly lowered drawbridge.

'I,' said the taller of the two figures looming over him, 'am Carpet Slippers, of the Cigar Store nation. This is Changes Light Bulbs, of the Hollywood nation. You must come with us.'

'What, now?'

'Now.'

'How.'

'No, *now*. With an N.'

'You mean Hnow?'

The dialectic confusion was resolved by Changes Light

Bulbs taking hold of Sitting Bull and lifting him out of his chair, an operation that Changes Light Bulbs was able to perform with the thumb and forefinger of his left hand.

'Disciplinary tribunal,' he explained.

The tribunal met in a small, rather musty teepee at the edge of one of the back lots of the Happy Hunting Grounds. When the tribunal was not sitting, the teepee was used as a combined charnel-house and offal depository. It had ambience.

'Hear ye, hear ye, disciplinary tribunal of the Combined Amerindian Nations, His Honour Judge Five Ovenproof Dishes presiding, all stand.'

'Sitting Bull, alias Consorts With Lawyers, you are charged with breach of trust, betraying a friend of the Combined Nations to the common enemy and behaviour likely to bring the Combined Nations into disrepute, how . . .'

'How.'

'. . . do you plead, guilty or not guilty?'

'Hey, not guilty. Who are you guys, anyway?'

Five Ovenproof Dishes rapped his desk with a miniature tomahawk and frowned. The prisoner at the bar wilted slightly.

Couper Ses Gorges of the Paris Apaches, for the prosecution, presented his case quickly and succinctly, whereupon the judge turned and called upon the defence.

'Your Honour.' Carpet Slippers rose to his feet and frowned. 'I am of the Cigar Store nation. My nation do not tell lies. The scumbag is as guilty as a wigwamful of rapists.'

'Hey!'

The entire court turned and gave Sitting Bull an unpleasant stare. He sat down again.

'The sentence of this court,' said Five Ovenproof Dishes, breathing heavily, 'is that you be expelled from your nation until the wind ceases to blow and the eagle lies down with the wolf. I have spoken.'

'Ah come *on*,' shouted Sitting Bull incredulously. 'This whole thing is getting hopelessly jejune. I demand to know by what right . . .'

Counsel for the Defence nutted him with an obsidian club and he resumed his seat. The judge scowled.

'For calling the court jejune,' he growled, 'the mandatory penalty is burial upright in an anthill. Perhaps you would care to rephrase . . . ?'

'Okay, not jejune.' Sitting Bull looked around, selected a big, thick legal tome (*Giggles Incessantly on Criminal Procedure*), held it over his head umbrella-fashion and rose to a wary crouch. 'Forget jejune, sorry. But really, you guys are making one big mistake here. I'm a medium, goddammit, people ask me questions, I tell 'em. It's my job. I had no choice, okay?'

There was a pause. Counsel for both parties approached the bench, and whispering ensued.

'Prisoner states that he is a medium,' intoned the judge. 'Correct?'

Sitting Bull nodded.

'Fine. Call Marshall Macluhan.'

Witness testified that, in his expert opinion, the medium was the message. The message found to be inherently unlawful. Appeal disallowed. All stand.

Twenty minutes later, Sitting Bull's suitcases were put outside the front entrance, followed shortly and at great speed by their owner. After a pause, Sitting Bull got up, dusted himself off, shooed various members of the spectral buffalo herd away from his suit covers and slouched off into the Upper Air.

As he slouched, he considered.

It was fortunate, he said to himself, that he was a fully westernised, regenerate member of the indigenous American community, free from the absurd superstitions of his ancestors; because otherwise, he'd be firmly convinced that being slung out of the Hunting Grounds would inevitably result in his being chased six times round the Sun by the Great Wolf Spirit, bitten in half and eaten. 'Absolutely just as well,' he muttered aloud. 'Crazy bunch of goddamn savages . . .'

He hesitated. He could feel hot breath on the back of his neck, soft fur rubbing his ankles, a nose as cold as Death nuzzling his ear.

'Woof.'

He turned round. Behind him, two piercing red eyes, a pair of gnarled ears laid back against a long, thin, cruel skull, jaws like scrap car compressors holding between them a yellow and blue rubber ball.

CHAPTER FOURTEEN

Slowly, with infinite pains and an almost superhuman patience, Kurt Lundqvist made his way across the main room – sorry, we must now call it the drawing-room – of the hideout, towards the corner with the loose floorboard.

They train you for this sort of thing at Ninja School, of course; crossing a dark and unfamiliar room full of hideously lethal booby-traps without waking the guards. The orthodox technique is to use the scabbard of your sword as a sort of blind man's white stick. Untold generations of Japanese silent killers have succeeded with it; or if they failed, they never came to report back. And anyway, the Japanese are a conservative people.

Lundqvist believed in progress and he had no scabbard, so he used the snapped-off aerial of the clock radio he'd received as a free gift for spending more than A\$15,000 on soft furnishings with a leading Melbourne furniture warehouse. It was tricky going, and his hand was starting to shake.

Goddammit, the place was an absolute fucking *minefield*.

Because when you buy furniture, you buy surfaces, and

every major league homemaker worth her velour crowds each surface with enough breakable ornaments to fill a ceramics museum. One false move and the air would be full of needle-sharp porcelain splinters, higher velocity and more deadly than the latest generation of anti-personnel fragmentation mines (and, of course, unlocatable with a metal detector).

Ting. The tip of the aerial tapped against something cold, hard and musical. Probably the big blue pot-pourri bowl. Lundqvist froze, then reached forward with the aerial, glacier-slow and gentle as the softest breeze. Ting. Yes. Right. At least he knew where the bugger *was*. He'd been worrying about that ever since he'd millimetred his way round the standard lamp.

Thunk. The sound of metal on walnut. Bookshelves. The end wall. He flicked gingerly and tapped against the spines of big, glossy coffee-table books (*Modern Interior Design*, *This House A Home*, *Three Thousand Lounges In Full Colour* and other similar titles). He was nearly there, and nothing dislodged or smashed. Ninjas; fuck Ninjas. By this time, even the best of those black-pyjamad loons would have fallen over the footstool and be picking Wedgewood shrapnel out of his windpipe.

Delicate probing with the aerial and the fingertips located the corner of the wall, which meant that the rest would be sheer dead reckoning. The loose floorboard, under which he'd stashed the shortband radio and the spare Glock about thirty seconds before the carpet squad had turned the place into a deep-pile killing zone, was at the point of a right angle seventy centimetres out from the corner.

Lundqvist opened his big Gerber TAC II lockknife, paused and listened. He had no reason to believe that Helen wasn't still sleeping soundly, but in this game you don't last long if you confine yourself to mere existential evidence. You have to reach out and feel for the mind of the assailant, the guard, the sentry; you have to taste sleep in the air. He recognised it – the less-than-absolute stillness which means that the other person in this house isn't standing motionless behind you with a whacking great knife – and started to cut the carpet.

The Gerber is state of the art, the nearest thing to Luke Skywalker's lightsabre ever made, but there are some materials that even Death's scythe snags on, and really expensive carpeting is one of them. As he sawed, Lundqvist could feel the exquisitely honed edge of the blade being wiped away, like spilt coffee on Formica.

His hand found the floorboard, tilted it, and burrowed, until the tip of his index finger made contact with cold, smooth plastic. Gently, quietly, he drew the package out, slit it open, and felt the radio.

'Links,' he hissed. 'Links, can you hear me? For Chrissakes, Links, this is no time for goddamn screwing around – oh, God, sorry Mrs Jotapian, is Links there, please? Links. Your *son*. Yes, sorry, *Jerome*. Thank you.'

'Hi,' crackled a voice, sounding like a PA system in an echo chamber in the quiet of the drawing-room. 'Links Jotapian here, who's this?' '

'It's Lundqvist, you bastard, and keep your voice down.'

Lucky George isn't the only one who has friends, you see. Admittedly, since Crazy Mean Bernard was dragged out of a blazing chopper somewhere in Nicaragua and vanished from the face of the earth Lundqvist only has one friend, who happens to be sixteen years old and short-sighted, but it evens the score a little bit. Like, say, a single hair cast on to the balance.

'Hiya, Mr Lundqvist,' Links yelled happily. 'How ya doing? You on a job right now?'

'Yes.' Lundqvist closed his eyes and tried to find a little scrap of patience he'd overlooked previously, clinging with limpetlike tenacity to the bottom of the jar. 'That's right, Links. That's why I want you to keep your stinking voice *down*, okay?'

'Sure thing, Mr Lundqvist. Can you tell me about it, or is it a secret?'

Not for the first time, Lundqvist found himself asking why in God's name he'd allowed himself to take on a skinny, mush-brained adolescent as an apprentice. The answer was the same as always. Teenage males being, fundamentally, weirder than a lorryload of stoned ghosts, sooner or later you'll find one who's prepared to hero-worship anybody, even Kurt Lundqvist. In Jerome Jotapian, five foot eleven of virtually unfleshed bone and hideously bezitted complexion from Pittsburgh, Lundqvist had found his Robin the Boy-Wonder. And in this life, you've got to do the best with what you can get, so when a middle-aged hit-man gets a fan letter from out of the blue (*Dear Mr Lundqvist, you don't know me, I'm sixteen years old and live in Pittsburgh Pa, I really admired your last assassination and can you help me get into this line of work, I expect to get satisfactory grades in Math and English Literature and I have my own throwing knife*) he finds it hard to resist writing back.

'I finished the correspondence course stuff you sent me, by the way,' burbled Links. 'It was good. You want me to read you a bit of it now? How about the question about what plastic explosive you'd use to blow up a Roman Catholic cardinal in a small Latin American republic? I thought a lot about that, Mr Lundqvist, and finally I figured Semtex, because—'

'Not now, Links.'

'Okay, boss. Actually, Semtex isn't the answer I finally said, but you'll see when you read what—'

'Links.' Lundqvist drew a deep breath. 'I need your help.'

'Hot damn, Mr Lundqvist! Really? You mean really *help*, in a *job*?'

'Yes.' Lundqvist's face was twisted into a hideous mask of self-contempt. 'Yes, Links, and it's very important. I'm in a bit of a jam and I need you to get me out. Look, I want you to hijack me an airliner . . .'

'Wow!' The boy's whoop of joy seemed to fill the room and large parts of the surrounding outback. 'Hey, I know how to do that, it's the part you sent me the week before last, only I think

that's in with the stuff Mom made me put down in the basement last week. You want to hold while I go see if I can find it?'

'No, Links, just stay where you are and keep your mouth
shut for a minute.' Lundqvist stopped and herded his straggling
thoughts. Talking to the boy for more than fifteen minutes was
like trying to gather up a ream of A4 paper in a Force 9 gale.
'You get the plane, right? Nothing fancy, just something with
enough legs to get to Australia and back. You take the thing to
Australia, which is where I am now, you dump it out in the
desert somewhere, you get a chopper, you come in, you get me
out of here, we split. Now, do you think you can manage that?'

There was a short pause. 'I figure so, Mr Lundqvist. You'd
better tell me where you are.'

Lundqvist told him.

'That's a long way away, Mr Lundqvist, do you think we can
do this so that I'll still be back by half-eleven? Mom doesn't
like me being out after half-eleven, you see, and—'

'You leave Mom to me,' Lundqvist interrupted, 'you just get
the plane and hurry. Before that crazy bitch spends every last
cent I own.'

'I beg your pardon, Mr Lundqvist?'

'Just do it, okay?'

A glider careened through the night air like a giant owl. The
side door slid open, and three parachutes blossomed like inbred
magnolias, drifted through the blackness and slowly folded on
to the ground.

'We're here then, are we?' enquired the first spectral warrior.
He was wearing a Hawaiian shirt and brightly coloured knee-
length shorts and carrying a suitcase.

The Captain nodded and pulled the brim of his huge straw
hat down over his eyes. 'Oh yes,' he muttered. 'We're here all
right.'

'Great,' said the first spectral warrior. 'Can you let us in on
the surprise yet? I mean, yes I know it's a *surprise* works outing,

to make it up to us for having to go after Lundqvist and all that, but . . .'

The other spectral warrior looked around him and felt the desert sand between his toes. He sighed happily.

'Who careth?' he observed. 'Jutht tho long ath we're at the theathide, it doethn't really matter where, doeth it?'

'Exactly,' said the Captain. 'Right, we'd better be making a move before it starts getting light.'

Number Two looked at him. 'Getting light?' he said.

'Spoil the surprise,' said the Captain quickly. 'Now then, the, um, *hotel* is this way. Follow me, and, er, keep the noise down.'

'Tho ath not to wake the other guethtth, you mean?'

'Something like that.'

In the darkness some way in front of them they could just make out the outline of a long, low building, something like a cross between a garage and a cowshed, only bigger.

'Thith ith the hotel?'

'Yes, and keep your voice *down*, will you? They're very fussy about—'

'Here, skip.'

'Yes?'

'Look at all these empty packing cases. Like the sort of thing furniture comes in.' An unpleasant thought crossed Number Two's mind. 'Hey, skip, you're sure this hotel's actually *finished*? I mean, you hear stories, people turning up, hotel's still being built . . .'

The Captain made a noise in the back of his throat.

'It's not exactly a hotel, chaps,' he observed in a small voice. 'It's not, um, quite that sort of holiday.'

'It's not?'

'No.'

'How d'you mean, thkip?'

'It's more . . .' The Captain paused, choosing his words with care. 'More a sort of, well, adventure holiday really.' As he spoke he unbuttoned his jacket, drew out a .44 Super Redhawk and, from sheer force of habit, spun the cylinder.

'Cor,' said Number Two. 'It's one of those paintball things, isn't it? Where you run about with paint guns pretending to shoot people. I always wanted to try one of them.'

The Captain breathed out through his nose. 'Great stuff, Keith,' he said. 'Now's your chance.'

'Doethn't look like a paint gun to me, thkip.'

'That's all you know.'

'Yeth, but thkip, thothe paint gunth, they're much bigger and bulkier than real gunth, and that lookth like a real gun to me, don't you think . . .'

'Yeah, well.' The Captain grinned nervously. 'We want to *win*, don't we?'

'Okay, skip, if you put it that way . . .'

'I do. Vern, break the window, I'll cover you.'

'What with, thkip?'

'What do you mean, what with?'

'I'th got a blanket in my luggage, thkip, if you want to uthe that. To thtop the glath from the window. That ith what you meant, ithn't it?'

'Shut up.'

Links Jotapian had one quality that made him stand out from the crowd. Well, two; but there was still a reasonable chance that he'd grow out of one of them. The other, the useful one, was a quite disproportionate quantity of beginner's luck.

The first time he did anything, he did it well. The next time, maybe not so hot, maybe even a complete and utter disaster; but the first time, no problem.

Fortunately for all involved, this was the first time he'd ever flown a helicopter.

'Depress joystick,' he read aloud, mumbling slightly because of the torch gripped between his teeth, 'while simultaneously engaging left rudder flap.' He stared hard at the control panel for a moment – why didn't they write the names of the various controls on the panel, you'd think they'd do that, there were so many little knobs and levers. He sighed, and leafed back through the instruction manual to the diagram at the end.

'Okay,' he said aloud. 'The third from the left, just down from the cigarette lighter.' He tried it. It worked. The helicopter stopped in mid-air and hung there.

He turned to the index.

Holding the stick steady with one hand, he leafed through the manual with the other. 43, 44, 45, 46 . . .

Page 47 was missing. Or at least, it was there, in part; but there had been a coupon ('Why not enter our grand spot-the-rotor-blade competition and win the holiday of a lifetime?') on page 48 which some previous reader had clipped out and sent off. All that was left of the paragraph on landing procedure was the headline.

'Nuts,' said Links, annoyed.

He'd just have to work it out from first principles.

Lundqvist froze, one leg over the window-sill, and put his hand in front of his eyes.

'That you, Links?' he shouted, but his voice was drowned by the roar of the whirring blades and the rush of the down-draught. Blinking furiously in the glare of the chopper's landing lights, he threw out his rucksack and prepared to follow it.

'Freeze!'

He turned towards the voice, and saw a dark shape silhouetted against the glare of the lights. The barrel of a large-calibre revolver flashed as it swung up on target.

'Hey, thkip. *Thkip!*'

'I said be *quiet*. Okay, nice and steady . . .'

'But thkip, it'th *him*. Lundqvitht. Let'th get out of here, thkip, the bathtard'th obviouthly following uth.'

'Look, for the last time, will you shut up? You, Lundqvist, nice and easy, throw down your—'

'Hey, skip.' Lundqvist could hear the anger in the voice above the scream of the blades. 'You knew, didn't you? You bleeding well set us up!'

'Yes, fine, later. Just now I'm busy, okay? Throw down your weapons, nice and . . .'

The helicopter landed.

There's beginner's luck and beginner's luck. In this case, it consisted of Links being very, very lucky indeed to be thrown clear of the chopper before it hit the deck and blew up.

A quick status check told Lundqvist that he was being hurled violently through the air by a shock-wave of hot air. That was all right by him; he'd been there before, he knew exactly how to roll with it when he landed. The good part about it was, once he landed he'd be back on even terms. And being on even terms was, in his experience, a very unfair advantage in his favour.

By contrast, the Captain of Spectral Warriors came round from a moment of temporary unconsciousness to find himself sprawled full length, still holding the revolver, on a green satin Chesterfield. Further investigation revealed a large piece of corrugated iron between him and the cushions of the sofa, the result of his having entered the house via the roof.

'Will you get off that sofa immediately,' said a cold, hard voice behind him. 'Look, you're getting blood all over it. Have you any idea how hard it is getting blood off satin?'

The second spectral warrior, for his part, came to rest half-way through a solid pine door; his head on one side, the rest of him on the other. He wriggled, tried to free himself.

'Oh *shit*,' he said.

And stopped, dumbfounded.

'Hey skip, *skip*!' he yelled. 'Hey, skip, you know what? The fall, it must have done something to me, it's cured my speech impediment, listen, I can say esses and everything . . .'

His colleague, lodged high in the shattered rafters, sighed wearily.

'That's because you're dead, idiot,' he explained.

'Oh. Hey, what a bummer, the first time in my life I can speak properly and I'm dead. You're sure I'm dead, Keith?'

'Believe me.'

'And that's what's cured my . . . ?'

'Dead men don't lisp, old son. Well known fact. Don't worry about it, though, they just reincarnate us back into new bodies. Any old new bodies,' he added bitterly. 'I know. I've been there.'

'You have?'

'Sure.' He indicated his own body, what was left of it. 'You think I *chose* this?' he complained. 'Arms like bloody coat-hangers, but do they listen?'

By now, Lundqvist had landed. He opened his eyes and assessed the situation.

'Help,' he said.

There was a scuffling noise down below. 'Is that you, Mr Lundqvist?'

'Yeah. Links?'

'Right here, Mr Lundqvist.'

'Marvellous. Help me out of this tree, will you?'

'Tree?'

'Yes. This tree here.'

'The thorn tree, you mean?'

'That's the one, Links. Try hurrying, will you?'

'Coming right up, Mr Lundqvist.'

Links Jotapian scrambled to his feet and looked around. Lesson Three had been all about using your initiative and improvising material out of unlikely objects found in the vicinity. He found the page and followed the relevant line with his finger.

Under combat conditions, he read, *a makeshift ladder may sometimes be improvised out of a broken segment of helicopter rotor blade, using only a Bowie knife and three feet of stout cord. Full instructions are given in Lesson Twelve . . .*

'Mr Lundqvist?'

'Yes?'

'You still there, Mr Lundqvist?'

'Reckon so, Links.'

'Do you think I'm ready for Lesson Twelve yet? Only I remember what you said about not taking the lessons out of sequence, because each one led naturally on from the previous, and . . .'

'Rules were made to be broken, Links. Right, listen carefully.'

Right. Fade out on Lundqvist, cut to . . .

. . . Two seagulls, black drifting shapes against a velvet sky, circling before coming in down on the glide and pitching on the remains of the roof.

'Anybody home?'

Helen of Troy stopped and looked up. She had been rubbing at the cushions of the Chesterfield, trying to get the blood out with half a lemon steeped in vinegar.

'Larry?'

'We're on the roof. Do you need rescuing?'

Helen considered for a moment. 'Not rescuing, no. I could use a little help in here, though.'

'Coming in.'

As the seagulls dropped down through the hole in the roof, the Captain of Spectral Warriors woke up. He had been sleeping peacefully ever since Helen had bashed him on the head with a copy of *Mrs Beeton's Everyday Cookery.*

'All right,' he said, staggering to his feet and levelling the Redhawk. 'Nobody move or I'll . . .'

The barrel of the gun became suddenly heavy, its weight augmented by a perching seagull. By the time it accidentally went off, it was pointed directly at the Captain's left foot.

'Oh my God, the *carpet*!' Helen wailed. 'Look, for pity's sake, just get out of my way before you damage anything else.'

'But . . .'

'*Out!*'

The Captain wilted. It wasn't, he decided, one of his good days. Slowly and painfully he hobbled out of the room and through the front door, and was therefore just in time to be directly under the thorn tree when Links Jotapian's makeshift ladder broke.

'You all right, Mr Lundqvist?'

'Sure, Links. I think something broke my fall . . .'

(*'You knew, didn't you, skip? You knew all along, and you pretended . . .'*

'Look, I had no choice, they threatened me . . .'

'I trusted him, Keith. When he said it was a holiday, I actually trusted him . . .'

'Hey, lads, now come on . . .'

'Keith, will you tell your friend that when I get reincarnated, I'm putting in for a transfer . . .')

'Gee, that was lucky, Mr Lundqvist. I guess I didn't use enough cord where it said bind together tightly with cord, only it didn't say exactly how much cord to use, and . . .'

'Never mind.' Lundqvist pulled himself to his feet, looked round and saw Helen framed in the doorway. 'C'mon,' he hissed, 'let's get out of here before she has the whole goddamn place done out in rose damask.'

Two or three hours later, Lucky George came by with the Transit to pick them up.

'You've been enjoying yourself, haven't you?' he observed.

Helen shrugged.

'So?' she said. 'I *like* nice furniture and things, you know that. George, don't you sometimes think it'd be fun if we had a little place of our own that I could do up and make all nice and—'

'No.'

'You could have your own little study,' she said wistfully, 'for all your books and magic stuff and things, and we could—'

'No.'

'Oh.' Helen clicked her tongue. 'Never mind,' she said, 'it was only a thought.'

'Good.'

'Anyway,' she said, producing a lighter and a can of paraffin, 'I think Lundqvist's gone off the kidnapping idea. Curious,' she went on, splashing paraffin, 'how anyone could be so *dozy* . . .'

'You missed a bit.'

'Did I? Oh yes. I mean, kidnapping *me*. After the last time and all . . .'

George nodded. 'All brains and no intelligence,' he said. 'Can I do the setting alight? You know how I love setting light to soft furnishings.'

Helen smiled fondly. 'Go on, then. Only George, the labels all said *Fire retardant* and *Specially treated for your safety and peace of mind*, do you think they'll . . . ?'

George grinned. 'If I say so,' he replied.

CHAPTER
FIFTEEN

The half-life of Time is notoriously long.

Being neck-deep in boiling shit is the mother of invention, as the chronological technicians say, and some of the things they've tried have been quite staggeringly ingenious, if futile. Sealing toxic temporal waste up in lead-lined cylinders and burying it is completely passé now; recently the trend has been towards boiling it, sending it back through hairline dimensional faults in the hope of setting up a Moebius effect, or selling it to the gullible citizens of Plato's Republic in big wooden crates marked 'Tractor Spares'. These devices have taken small deposits out of circulation; however, in the time it takes to get rid of, say, 4,000 metric tonnes this way, twice as much of the loathsome stuff has built up and is leaking merrily away into the environment, poisoning the fish and causing innocent parties all over the cosmos to seduce their great-grandmothers and be late for their own funerals.

In desperation, some authorities have been illicitly shipping it out into the future, which doesn't help exactly but at least means that it becomes somebody else's problem.

Unless something is done about it pretty soon, the boffins say, the whole unhappy mess is pretty soon going to go critical and start doing horrible things to the nature of reality. Already, they report (from the relative security of their nostalgia-lined bunkers), there are rumours of the spontaneous occurrence of the dreaded isotope Overtime.

The only possible solution is recycling. Maddeningly, however, nobody has the faintest idea how to go about it.

Nobody who's been asked, anyway.

One of the few people not worried sick about the problem is Kurt Lundqvist. His own proposal for getting rid of it (loading it into canisters and dropping it from a great height on South-East Asia) having been rejected, he dismissed the matter from his mind and turned his attention to more immediate issues.

Such as nailing Lucky George. Dawn over the outer suburbs of Aspen, Colorado, found him sitting on his porch with the remains of his fifth pint of black coffee and nothing to show for his pains but a pile of screwed up bits of paper.

He'd tried direct attack. He'd tried abduction. Dammit, what else was there?

Like a dog returning to its own vomit, his mind kept coming full circle back to the idea of hostages. Kidnap one of Lucky George's friends, his instincts shouted at him, and you have Lucky George himself, because the man lives and dies by his friends. The true professional prefers to attack the enemy through his strengths rather than his weaknesses – weaknesses are carefully guarded, strengths are taken for granted – and what George really had going for him, apart from a repertoire of largely meretricious magical effects, was a quite depressingly huge network of friends and acquaintances stretching throughout space and time, but centred on the University of Wittenberg, Class of '88.

For the twelfth time that night, Lundqvist picked up that year's UOW Yearbook and flicked through, hoping that a name would catch his eye.

Martin Luther (Theology). HRH Hamlet, Prince of Denmark (Philosophy, Politics and Economics). Hieronymus Bosch (Design Studies). Cristoforo Colombo (Geography). Leonardo da Vinci (Business Studies).

The sun rose on the Rocky Mountains; and suddenly Lundqvist had the answer. Simple. Of all the friends of Lucky George, who had ultimately achieved the most?

No contest.

He who achieves the most has the most to lose.

Mr Van Appin leant back in his chair and rubbed his chin. Right now, he was beginning to wish he'd never taken Lucky George on as a client in the first place.

Sure, there had been the good times. The patent applications. The intellectual property work. The trial itself, and then the appeal. There had been big money down along the line (it's not every client who pays in genuine functional bottomless purses), not to mention the prestige and the cachet and, of course, the travelling expenses. But you had to take the holistic view; and when the presence of Kurt Lundqvist in one's waiting room at nine o'clock on a Monday morning is taken into account, even a lawyer may be heard to speculate that money isn't everything.

Pure bullshit, of course. It is. But even the Pope has doubts sometimes.

Which reminded him. He flipped the intercom.

'Sonia,' he said. 'Ask John Paul if he wouldn't mind coming back at half-past, and show Mr Lundqvist in.'

In Mr Lundqvist came, like Death into the world; sat in the client's chair and put his feet up on the desk.

'Kurt,' said Van Appin with insincere cheerfulness, 'always a pleasure, how's business?'

'Slow,' Lundqvist growled. 'Listen. I need a lawyer.'

Van Appin quivered slightly. 'Delighted to help in any way I can,' he said. 'Matrimonial problems?' he hazarded.

'No,' Lundqvist replied, 'I need to borrow a lawyer. Not you, somebody else. You got any?'

Mr Van Appin looked at Lundqvist over his steepled hands. 'When would you be needing him?' he asked.

'1492.'

'I'll see who we've got available.'

He swivelled his chair and tapped a few keys on the keyboard. The screen flickered.

'Any particular sort of lawyer?'

'Property lawyer.' Lundqvist laughed, a sound like sandpaper on sharkskin. 'Little development project I got in mind.'

'In 1492?'

Lundqvist shrugged. 'Tax reasons,' he explained.

'Bit out of your usual line, isn't it?'

'It pays to diversify.'

'True.'

Lundqvist leant forward. 'One other thing,' he said. 'What we're talking here is utmost good faith stuff. I don't want anyone to know, you got that? Especially any of your other clients.'

'Hey, Kurt.' Mr Van Appin gestured his protest. 'I got my ethical position to think of.'

He hesitated. For some reason he was finding it hard to concentrate on anything apart from the muzzle of the .40 Glock that had suddenly appeared in Lundqvist's hand.

'Ethical,' he said slowly, 'schmethical. Hell, Kurt, what are friends for?'

Lundqvist considered for a while. 'Decoys,' he replied.

Imagine . . .

You can't, of course. It's impossible. Nobody in the plush suburb of History we call the twentieth century could possibly

conceive of the stunning, mind-stripping shock of seeing, for
the first time . . .

It is 1492. Three tiny wooden shells bob precariously on the
meniscus of a blue-grey infinity. High in the rigging, a man
turns, stares, opens his mouth to shout and closes it again.

There is, he decides, no tactful way to put this. But he's
going to do his best, anyway.

'Hey, skip!'

On the deck below, a short, weary individual looks up from
a chessboard and shouts back, 'Well?'

'Skip . . .'

'What's the matter, Hernan?'

'Skip . . .' Hernan bit his tongue. 'I spy,' he said, 'with my
little eye, something beginning with A.'

'You what?'

'With A, skip. I spy it. With my, um, little eye.' Hernan drew
in further supplies of air. 'It's a game, skip. You've got to guess
what it is I've—'

'Have you been at the applejack again? You know it's reserved for the scurvy.'

'Go on, skip, be a sport.'

'Look . . .'

'Three guesses?'

Columbus sighed. Sixty-one days he'd been cooped up on
this floating strawberry-punnet with these idiots. A lesser man,
one without his inexhaustible patience, would have blown the
ship up by now.

'Albatross.'

'No.'

'Aurora borealis.'

'No. Hey skip, you aren't even *trying* . . .'

'Okay, okay.' Columbus thought hard. When dealing with
morons, he'd learnt the hard way, the trick is to think like a
moron. This is no mean accomplishment. 'Arquebus,' he said.
'Am I right?'

Hernan lifted his eyes and gazed for two seconds at the distant coastline, the one that quite definitely wasn't India, and said to himself, Look, why me, whoever says it first is going to get lynched, they'll know soon enough without me telling them. 'You got it, skip,' he replied. 'Oh, and by the way, land ahoy.'

'What did you just say?'

'Land, skip. Ahoy. Just over there on the left.'

'What ahoy? Speak up, you're muttering.'

'Land, skip. L for laundry, A for Amer . . . I mean arquebus, N for . . .'

As Columbus jerked like a shot deer and started capering hysterically up and down the deck, Hernan leant back in the crow's nest, shrugged and found the remains of his apple. He'd been nursing it along, one nibble per day, for a fortnight, saving it for a special occasion. He looked at it and chucked it over the side.

A freak gust of wind carried up to him scraps of the conversation buzzing away below – Roderigo was saying that as soon as they got in he was going to have a roghan ghosh with spicy dall and nan bread, Diego was saying no, make mine a chicken tikka with pilau rice and spoonfuls of mango chutney. The poor fools, Hernan thought. It was going to be bad enough when the crew found out, but that was likely to be nothing compared to the embarrassment that would ensue when the news was broken to their Most Catholic Majesties back in Madrid. Well, no, ma'am, not India *as such*, in fact more like a clump of hot, scrawny little islands populated by savages with no commercially useful exports of any kind; we were thinking of calling it San Salvador.

Maybe they could just sort of hush the whole thing up. Forget about it. Pretend they got to the edge of the world, turned round and came straight back.

Nah.

Hernan shook his head sadly. Some fool would be bound to let something slip, and then where would they all be?

Anyway. Hernan leant his elbows on the rail of the crow's nest and took a long, hard look. Okay, so it wasn't up to much, but it was a new country. A new continent, maybe. And here he was, the first man ever to set eyes on it. That was something. Not much perhaps, but something.

Wrong.

Because, at the precise moment when Columbus was ordering the lads to lower a rowing boat and feverishly trying to remember the exchange rate for moidores into rupees, a small, bedraggled man in a Brooks Brothers suit and waders was dragging a rubber dinghy behind some bushes on the seashore and opening a small suitcase.

The man was one Morrie Goldman, and the suitcase contained a portable fax machine with the special digital transtemporal wave shift function.

He looked at his watch. Mr Van Appin had been very insistent that he log in the precise moment of landfall. Having dictated a note into his pocket dictaphone, he switched on the fax and started typing out the message on his laptop word processor.

Not exactly an orthodox assignment, he reflected as he typed. Whizz back through time to the late fifteenth century, go to San Salvador, arriving at such and such a time, send a fax to the Land Registry stating time of arrival, and then clear off. Not perhaps the most complex matter he'd ever handled from a legal standpoint, but the travelling expenses were going to be just out of this world.

From: Maurice Goldman, Messrs Van Appin & Co
To: The Chief Registrar, Central Land Registry
Message: Arrived 3.25 p.m. precisely. Please accept this communication as our indefeasible claim of title to the continent edged red on the plan annexed hereto and confirm registration by return of fax.

He paused for a moment. If he was discovering this place, wherever in hell it was (geography wasn't his thing), he supposed he ought to give it a name, if only to enable it to be sufficiently identified.

Newly discovered territory to be known as Goldmannia.

No. You couldn't call a country Goldmannia. It lacked that certain something.

He deleted Goldmannia and typed in Mauretania.

No. There was somewhere else called that. Try again.

He deleted Mauretania and . . .

Nice snappy name. Something that'd look good on the stamps. The United States of *something*. Life is all right in *something*. The business of *something* is business. The *something* dream. Bye bye, Miss *something* Pie.

It was on the tip of his tongue.

He typed in Lundqvistia, hit the Send button and made himself scarce.

Scroll fast forward through Time, until the monitor reads 1996, and hold. The place: the Polo Lounge, Valhalla. Christopher Columbus discovered, nursing a long, cool drink and smoking a big cigar.

Not, of course, that Valhalla's what it was. Gone are the deep leather armchairs, the inedible food, the self-effacing spectral waiters. Evening dress is no longer a prerequisite for the Carousing Hall, and people no longer glare at you if you refrain from shouting in the Fighting Room. Mead has been replaced by fiddly things in stemmed glasses in the Members Bar, and the iron-corseted Valkyrie barmaids have been quietly replaced by less statuesque, softer beings with names like Cindi, Nikki and Cheryl. Nevertheless, it still has a certain cachet, and visitors still steal the headed notepaper from the library.

'Paging Mr Columbus. Visitor for you at the front desk. Thank you.'

Columbus got up and made his languid way to the lobby, his mind still lovingly turning over the thought of next month's ground rent payment. There were those, he knew, who referred to him behind his back as the biggest slum landlord in the universe, but that was just jealousy.

'You said there was a message for me?'

'Over there, Mr Columbus, by the fountain of milk and honey.'

'Him in the mac?'

'That's him, Mr Columbus.'

'Right.'

He finished his drink, placed the empty glass on the desk and wandered over to the stranger . . .

Who served him with a Notice to Quit.

Mr Van Appin leant back in his chair and replaced the telephone.

'That was Goldman,' he said. 'Everything according to plan. Columbus should be getting the eviction papers any minute now.'

The muzzle of the .40 Glock lifted and disappeared inside Lundqvist's jacket. 'Good,' he said. 'Now then, how long'll it take to get vacant possession?'

Mr Van Appin shrugged. 'Say three to four weeks. Unless they appeal, of course. They may have grounds, I couldn't say offhand. This is pretty much a grey area so far as the law is concerned.' Perfectly safe to say that, of course; as any lawyer will tell you, the law is full of the most amazingly large and expensive grey areas, so that seen from the air it resembles nothing so much as the Confederate army camped on a shale beach on a cloudy day.

'Do it in three,' growled Lundqvist. 'I want those bastards out of there as soon as possible, you got that?'

Mr Van Appin twitched slightly. 'When you say bastards, Kurt, you mean . . .'

'The Americans,' Lundqvist replied. 'All of them.' He grinned. 'Goddamn trespassers. Get the place cleared, okay? And make sure they leave it clean and tidy when they go, because I might just have another tenant lined up.'

'Yeah?'

Lundqvist nodded. 'I was thinking,' he said, 'of going into the private prison business. Long term, violent offenders. New York. It's just a matter of putting a few extra bars on the odd window and cleaning the streets up a bit, and there we are, ready to start trading.'

Mr Van Appin made a soft, lawyerly clicking noise with his tongue. 'I don't want to sound alarmist in any way,' he said, 'but something tells me the bailiffs aren't going to find it that easy. Maybe you should just stick to raising the rent a bit. You know, gradually, a few cents per annum over say the next three hundred—'

'Vacant possession, Van Appin. And if the bailiffs have any trouble,' Lundqvist said, smiling thoughtfully, 'just let me know. I haven't done an eviction since Atlantis.'

Mr Van Appin swallowed. 'That was an eviction, huh?'

'We all have our different methods.'

'I guess so, Kurt. Only . . .'

'Just do it.'

'Okay.'

Lundqvist rose. 'A pleasure doing business with you, Van Appin,' he said, adding, 'For me, anyhow,' and left. After he'd gone, Van Appin sat quite still for well over a minute, thinking Oh shit.

His special lawyer's sixth sense was telling him that there could possibly be a bit of comeback on this one. A pity, but there it was.

Lundqvistia, he said to himself. Jesus God, what an awful name for a continent.

Not a patch, he couldn't help thinking, on Van Appin's Land, or something like that.

* * *

'George?'

'Chris! Great to hear from you. How's things?'

'Not so hot, George. In fact, I've got a bit of a problem.'

Lucky George frowned and reached for the scratch-pad that lived beside the phone. 'Fire away, Chris, tell me all about it.'

On the other end of the line, Christopher Columbus took a deep breath, said, 'Well, it's like this,' and told him. After he'd finished, George sat for a while, chewing the end of his pencil.

'You still there, George?'

'Still here, Chris. Bit awkward, isn't it?'

'Yes.'

'And the bailiffs are going in – when, did you say?'

'A week's time, George. Backed up by four million spectral warriors from the Court Office.'

'Suitcases on the pavement time, huh?'

'You could say that.'

George doodled a few wavy lines, coloured in the 'O's in *While You Were Out* and chewed his lip for a moment. Then he smiled.

'Don't worry about a thing, Chris,' he said at last. 'I think I can see what we're going to have to do, and it shouldn't be much of a problem.' He paused. 'At least, it won't be if we can get the right help.'

'Anyone I know?'

'Old friend of ours, Chris. Leave it with me, all right? It's really just a question of hydraulics.'

'*Hydraulics?*'

George nodded. 'Hydraulics, Chris. Be seeing you.'

CHAPTER
SIXTEEN

Eurobosch, the theme park to end all theme parks, was on its way. Five hundred thousand spectral construction workers laboured night and day to bring into being the most sensational leisure facility in the history of Time and Space. And all because one man dared to dream the impossible nightmare.

The man in question sat in the window of the site office, looking out over the muddy shambles and trying to discern any resemblance, however slight, to the vision of unalloyed nastiness he could see in his mind's eye. It wasn't easy.

Take, for example, the helter-skelter. This took the form of a seventy-foot-high hourglass, on which was seated a stomach-churning bird-headed demon, its feet improbably thrust into two wine-jars, meditatively nibbling on the leg of a woman taken in adultery. On paper, it had looked fine. Translated into three dimensions, it was quite another sort of nightmare.

The basic structure hadn't been a problem; you've got your reinforced steel joists, your basic chipboard panels, your sixty-by-thirty sheets of galvanised. You bung those in with a few girders braced crosswise for rigidity, everything fine so far. Next you put in your actual helter-skelter track, starting under the demon's armpit and exiting rather ingeniously through the raised rump of a sinner being hideously mauled by a nine-foot-high animated tree; no problem, the builders' merchants just happen to have a continuous spiral sheet of anodised aluminium long enough to do the job and going cheap owing to a cancelled order. It's then that the fun starts.

Bird-headed demons are, to put it bluntly, a pain. You can go for your injection-moulded propylene, but you can bet your life that the two halves won't fit flush, and for the price of just one moulding you could afford to panel the Crab Nebula in French walnut. On the other hand, you can opt for good old expanded polystyrene, just so long as you're prepared to put up with bits crumbling off in wet weather and the whole bloody thing threatening to take off in a high wind. Fibreglass would be too brittle because of the length of the adulteress's leg, and anything else is out because of the weight factor and/or the aggravation of getting the sonofabitch thing installed without all the pointy bits getting broken off. Finally you persuade the money men to lash out on the injection mouldings, only to find that the pattern makers are booked solid for the next three months and when they eventually can get around to doing it, they've quarrelled irrevocably with the moulding contractors and refuse to lift so much as a Stanley knife without fifty per cent of the contract price up front. Just when you've ironed all that out and sorted out the building inspectors and the fire inspectors and the little arsehole from the planning department who's always wittering on about not exceeding the overall permitted height, the quantity surveyor (who plays golf with the company accountant who wants to see the whole project called off) tells the board that there's a firm down the road he knows who'd do the whole job for forty per cent less, including road haulage and wiring up the psychedelic lights. The moulding contractors are by now threatening to sue for breach of contract, and quite possibly the aluminium strip (which hasn't had its three coats of primer because the painters are waiting until the sound system's wired in) has turned all grey and flaky and needs to be replaced from scratch. Finally, the Finance Director drops by on his monthly tour of inspection and says, yes, love the basic concept, but really don't you think we need it a bit more, well, *yukky*, how about a couple of skull-headed snakes slithering up and down the main uprights?

The phone rang. Ronnie Bosch, his eyes riveted to an outsize polystyrene eggshell just starting to work free from its anchor points on the side of the Ferris Wheel, groped with his left hand and picked it up.

'Bosch here,' he said.

'Ronnie.'

Bosch closed his eyes. 'You *again*,' he hissed. 'For crying out loud, George, this really isn't the best time for me right now . . .'

'Won't keep you a moment, old son. Just a little job I need some help with. Basically, all I need is . . .'

With fervour, Hieronymus Bosch told Lucky George what, in his opinion, Lucky George really needed. It was pretty farfetched, anatomically speaking, but compared with some of the feats of engineering he'd pulled off in the last few months, it would probably have been a piece of cake.

'The project getting you down, huh?'

'You could say that, George. Like, how the hell am I supposed to suspend a seven-hundred-ton plywood and fibreglass mandolin with worms crawling out of the soundbox forty feet in the air without using an overhead crane because the planners say it'd be seven feet too high for the surrounding environment?'

George laughed. 'Easy,' he said. 'Look, all I really need from you for this little job of mine is—'

'*Easy?*'

'Sure. I thought you were joking when you said you were having a problem. You built the mandolin yet?'

Bosch laughed mirthlessly. 'Not much point, really, until I've sussed out how to fly the bastard thing.'

'Great. You don't make it out of plywood, Ron, you make it out of rubber. Aluminium tube frame, reinforced rubber skin, fill the bugger with helium and you're well away. Just make sure it's securely tethered with a few steel hawsers to stop it wandering off. As I was saying . . .'

Bosch nearly dropped the phone. 'George,' he said, 'that's bloody brilliant. Hang about, though, what about the volume-to-weight ratio on the worms, because . . .'

There followed a few minutes of technical discussion; after which, Bosch drew a deep breath and said, 'What was it you said you wanted?'

'Got a pencil?'

'Yes.'

'Right, then listen. First, I want you to drill me a hole in the bottom of the Marianas Trench.'

Bosch broke the pencil lead. 'Fine,' he said. 'I just stroll out on my day off with a snorkel and a bradawl, do I? Or shall I get the YTS lad to do it?'

'Next,' George went on, 'I'll need some nice, tough, hydraulic hose.' He specified how much. 'And a steam turbine, Ron; nothing fancy, just a good, old-fashioned piece of kit to work the pump. I expect you've got something of the sort lying about in one of the engine sheds down at your place. I seem to remember there being all sorts of useful bits and pieces quietly rusting away down there. Get some of the men to give it a rub over with a wire brush, she'll be as right as rain.'

'I'm not listening, George. I mean, thanks a lot for the tip with the balloon, I definitely owe you one, but this is—'

'I think that's about it,' George said, checking the list he'd scribbled on the back of a beer mat. 'No, sorry, I tell a lie, there's just one more major bit I need. Can you rustle me up a hydraulic ram? Hold on, I'll just give you the specifications.'

'George . . .' Bosch was just about to give notice of putting the phone down when his professional curiosity got the better of him. 'George,' he asked cautiously, 'what the hell are you planning to do with all this gear?'

George told him.

Engineers are a bit like mountain-climbers; not in the sense of having bushy beards and no toes because of frostbite, but because the one thing they really can't resist is a challenge. Ask an engineer to change the washer on a leaking tap and he'll tell you to get lost. Show him a design for making water roll uphill without pressure and drive a flywheel and ask him if he thinks it might work, and before you know it he's reaching for his Vernier calipers and his slide rule, and all you've got to do is decide whether you want the flywheel in pale fawn or avocado.

'You're kidding.'

'No I'm not,' George replied. 'It's basically a very simple design. Big but simple. Do you think you can do it?'

Hieronymus Bosch hesitated, his mind a Cemetary Ridge of conflicting emotions. On the one hand, his rational sense was telling him, No way, stay well clear of this, if they ever caught you at it then bird-headed demons would be Beatrix Potter compared with what they'd do to you. Louder and more insistent was the clamour in the genes, Man the Toolmaker whispering, Yes, and come to think of it there's that old molybdenum steel acroprop left over from the second day of the Creation, all you'd have to do is stone a couple of thou. off the edge, mill it square on the top and there's your basic material . . . The temptation pounded against the sides of his better judgement; as if Eve had come sidling up to Adam with a plate of apple charlotte with double whipped cream and a glacé cherry.

'I dunno,' he said. 'I'd need to see drawings.'

'I'll fax them through now.'

'Somebody's bound to notice.'

'Just tell 'em it's for the project. Say it'll save them money.'

'You do realise it's going to be touch and go with the wall thicknesses, what with all that internal pressure.'

'Don't make me laugh, Ron. Listen . . .'

And that, of course, was that. As soon as the detailed specifications started flowing up and down the telephone lines, it was all a foregone conclusion.

'Thanks, Ron,' said Lucky George. 'Oh, one last thing, we've got a forty-eight-hour deadline. A bit tight, but you can do it.'

'George . . .'

'Anybody else, I'd be worried, Ron. Absolute confidence in you, though. I'll get those plans off to you this minute.'

'George . . .'

'Ciao.'

Having replaced the receiver, George wandered out on to the balcony and sat for a few minutes, watching the gondolas go by.

'Well?' asked Helen, joining him with the coffee. 'Any luck?'

George nodded. 'No problem,' he said. 'Ronnie's a good lad, very suggestible. Mind you,' he added, dipping his top lip in the froth, 'his end of the job's the easy bit.'

Helen frowned. 'By easy,' she said, after a moment's thought, 'you mean extremely difficult, don't you?'

'Difficult?' George shook his head. 'Piece of cake to a man with the facilities at his disposal that Ronnie's got.' He sighed. 'Good lord, if I could lay my hands on all the plant and machinery he's got to play about with, I could . . .'

Helen smiled indulgently and removed the sugar bowl, from which George had been absent-mindedly saturating his coffee for the last fifteen seconds. 'When we get married and settle down,' she said, 'I think I'll let you have a little shed, down at the bottom of the garden. You can keep all your bits and pieces in that, and then we won't have them cluttering up the house.'

Below their balcony, the olive-drab waters of the Canal Grande rubbed catlike against the piles on which the house rested. Like most houses in Venice, more or less the only thing keeping it from slithering into the lagoon was force of habit, with just a soupçon of artistic licence. George had bought it as a pied-à-eau some four hundred and sixteen years ago, and one of the many things he was looking forward to doing once this dratted Lundqvist business was out of the way was chasing up the descendants of twelve generations of tenants for quite substantial arrears of rent.

'This house you keep on about,' he said. 'It's going to be terribly inconvenient, you realise.'

'What is?'

'Having to step over my dead body every time you go through the front door.'

'Nonsense,' Helen replied. 'I'll have a little bridge built over you.'

'All right,' George said, stifling a yawn. 'If you're so dead set on having a house, what's wrong with this one?'

'What, this place?'

'Why not? It works. It does the job. It's got four walls, and I'm pretty sure I saw a roof lying about somewhere, the last time I looked.'

'Don't be silly.'

'Oh.' George shrugged. 'Anyway, that's a bit academic, really, just at the moment, what with Lundqvist still on the loose and everything. Strictly between you and me, that chap's beginning to get on my nerves.'

'You don't say.'

George nodded. 'All right, at the moment he's not posing any direct threat. Actually, I'm not particularly bothered when he is. So long as he's out in the open where I can see him, bless his little heart, I can generally deal with him without too much bother.' He frowned, and rubbed his lips with his knuckles. 'But this business of hassling my friends really isn't on. Something's got to be done about it.'

'True.' Helen gazed out over the canal, watching a pair of slightly larger than average seagulls hovering over a gondolaful of German tourists. Every few minutes, they would suddenly dive like Stukas, come up on the gondola's blind side and pass uncalled-for remarks in German directly behind the head of a member of the party. During the diversion thereby occasioned, one of them would then bite a further chunk out of the little girl's ice-cream cone. 'Easier said than done, though, don't you think? I mean, if there was a simple way of stopping the wretched man from bothering us, we'd probably have thought of it by now. It's not exactly a new problem, is it?'

'Not a simple way, no. On the other hand, simplicity isn't everything. I'd settle for fiendishly complicated like a shot, if only I could think of something.' He lifted his cup, found it empty, smiled into it and burnt his tongue on the result, thereby conclusively demonstrating that his mind wasn't on the job. 'Anyway, in the meantime we've got to do something about this Columbus thing.'

'The difficult bit.'

George grinned. 'Comparatively difficult,' he said. 'All we really need to wrap it all up is a good, dirty presidential election.'

'Turning to item five on the agenda,' said the Finance Director, 'can we start with you, please, Steve? Any new marketing initiatives in the pipeline?'

The Sales Director picked up his pencil and revolved it slowly between his claws. 'One or two balls in the air right now,' he replied. 'Something we're very keen on at the moment is the Damn-A-Friend promotion.' He turned to face the projector screen, and picked up the remote control. 'Just to remind you of the basic thinking on this one, the idea is that if you the punter can bring about the damnation of a fellow human being between the first of February and the end of May, you win a recurring dream holiday for two in the guilt complex of your choice. This one works particularly well as we've got very substantial stockpiles of guilt at the moment, and we don't seem to be getting through the stuff nearly as quickly as we used to.'

'I blame the psychiatrists,' interrupted the Personnel Director, waking from a light doze. 'Damn interfering little sods, always mucking up perfectly good personality disorders and stopping people murdering their fathers. Heaven's too good for 'em, if you ask me.'

'Thank you, Dennis. Anything else, Steve? Got anything lined up for the winter season?'

'Ants.'

The Finance Director looked at his colleague over the rim of his spectacles. 'Ants, Steve?'

The Sales Director nodded eagerly. 'That's it,' he said. 'It's like a sort of sequel, really, or maybe spin-off's the word I'm looking for.'

There was a brief moment of puzzled silence, broken by the Company Secretary.

'Oh I *see*, you mean as in "Lord of the". Nice idea.'

The Sales Director nodded his head in acknowledgement. 'Yeah,' he said. 'I mean, flies, all a bit passé for the Nineties. What I had in mind was, every time you break a commandment, you get a voucher thing. So many points, depending on which commandment and the level of breach. Then, when you've collected enough vouchers, you can cash them in for ants. And when you've got *x* amount of ants, you write in for your badge and become a Deputy Lord. Pretty neat scheme, I thought.'

'Sorry to interrupt,' broke in the Finance Director, 'but why ants particularly?'

'We've got a lot of 'em,' the Sales Director replied. 'Anyway, when you've collected enough vouchers, you automatically go through to the prize draw. Pretty straightforward really.'

'Gimmicky.'

'Yes, thank you, Harry.' The Sales Director glowered at his colleague from Production. 'Actually, I don't accept that it *is* gimmicky. Good, solid marketing ploy, year's duration to start with and we'll see how we go from there. And best of all, the raw materials aren't going to cost us a penny. Look, I'll run a few projected figures up on the screen and you can see for yourselves.'

When the slide-show finally ground to a halt, the Finance Director thanked his colleague and drew the attention of the meeting to the final scheduled item.

'Any suggestions?' he asked.

There was a silence as deep and awkward as a badly-flooded gutter. At last, the Personnel Director raised his hand.

'I've been thinking,' he said. 'Why don't we just parole the bastard?'

The Finance Director looked at him. 'Go on,' he said.

'Well,' continued Personnel, 'I think it's the obvious answer. There's no chance I can see of getting him back. Security's made no headway at all, Lundqvist's been a complete washout, and every time we even try anything, the bugger makes us all look like complete idiots. That holiday stunt . . .'

'Yes. We'll skate over that one, shall we?'

'All I'm saying is,' said Personnel, 'why not just accept the situation and put it on a regular footing by letting him out early. Formally, I mean.'

'Hang on,' said the Finance Director. 'You're not suggesting we say he's been released early on grounds of good behaviour, are you, because—'

'Quite the opposite. Since when has good behaviour been a plus mark in these parts anyway?'

The Finance Director shook his head. 'Good idea in its way, Dennis, but unfortunately not possible. Not up to us, parole. We can recommend, of course, but in the circumstances . . .'

'Oh I dunno,' interjected the Sales Director. 'Look at it this way. If the guy's basically virtuous and good and fit to be at large, naturally it stands to reason he'd want to be out of here as soon as possible. I mean, the place is simply crawling with villains, you could get into bad company. I'm all for it myself.'

'No,' said the Finance Director, 'and that's final. Well, I

think that just about wraps things up . . . No, just one more item. EuroBosch.'

A slight ripple of pleasure lapped round the boardroom table. It was the one project everyone approved of; very high-profile, very prestige, very image-enhancing, very Us. The Finance Director cleared his throat.

'Memo from H.B.,' he said. 'Apparently, he wants permission to –' The Finance Director squinted at the paper in front of him. '– to drill a hole in the bottom of the sea somewhere off America, install a steam turbine on Number Six furnace, and – you know, his handwriting is *abysmal* – and he says there's a bit of old metal rod he wants from out of the Bonded Stores. He doesn't say what he wants it for, but I for one wouldn't understand if he did. Any objections?'

Thick as autumnal leaves that strow the brooks in Vallombrosa, where the Etrurian shades high over-arched embower, the Directors shook their heads, until the boardroom resembled nothing so much as a display of car rear-window ornaments produced by the design team for *Alien*. If Ronnie wanted it, Ronnie could have it.

'That's fine, then,' said the Finance Director, initialling the pink chit. 'Same time next week?'

CHAPTER
SEVENTEEN

'**W**ho, me?'

Lucky George leant forwards slightly. A persuasive enough man at the best of times, he was giving it everything he'd got. An Arab coming up against George in this frame of mind would have found himself the bewildered owner of many cubic tons of very expensive sand.

'Yes, Lenny,' he cooed, '*you*. You've got just what it takes to be a success in politics, hasn't he, Helen? I mean, you'd vote for him, wouldn't you?'

'Like a shot,' Helen replied, not looking up from her callisthenics book. She'd just got to the bit where the heroine had wrapped her left leg round her neck, with the heel sticking in her right ear; and she wanted to find out how the hell the author was going to engineer a happy ending out of that lot.

'There, you see? The women's vote tied up, just like that. C'mon, Lennie, don't be a loser all your life. Just for once . . .'

'I dunno.' Leonardo da Vinci stroked his beard, a full-time job in itself. 'To be absolutely frank with you, George, I don't think I'm really, you know, qualified to stand. Like, you know, not eligible.'

Lucky George gestured impatiently. 'Rubbish,' he said. 'What on earth gave you that impression, Len?'

'Well,' said Leonardo, counting on his fingers, 'number one, I'm Italian. I always thought that to be president of the USA you had to be American . . .'

George laughed. 'No problem,' he said. 'We get you US citizenship first, naturally. And then, of course, you've got the Italian vote sewn up before you even start.'

'Retrospectively, even,' Helen murmured. Nobody heard her.

'Also,' Leonardo went on, 'I'm dead.'

'So?'

Leonardo waved his hands feebly. 'So I guess that's not exactly going to inspire confidence in the electorate, George. I mean, *Vote for da Vinci, he would have made a good president if only he'd lived* isn't the best sort of platform you could—'

'On the contrary,' George replied. 'Look at the Kennedys. Secret of their success, that was.'

Leonardo shrugged. 'Odd you should mention them,' he said. 'Did you know that it was really the Milk Marketing Board who were behind the—?'

'Besides,' George went on, ignoring him, 'there you are, dead, running for the White House, that's the disabled vote in the can, right from the word go. Plus, being dead, I guess that makes you a sort of minority group figure . . .'

'Being *dead*? A *minority*? You're crazy, man, there's millions of us out there.'

'Yes,' George replied, 'but not that many of you down here, that's the whole point. Being dead, you say, that really gives you an insight into the problems of the victims of bigotry. Because when you're dead, you add, every man's hand is against you. Segregation, reservations, cheap dead trash – you've got it absolutely made, Lenny, you really have. The only thing that surprises me is why you haven't stood before.'

'Better things to do with your time, probably.'

'Be quiet, Helen, you're not helping. Come on, Lenny. What have you got to lose?'

'All right.' Leonardo backed away slightly. 'But anyway, isn't it a bit academic? I mean, the election's tomorrow, there really isn't time . . .'

George smiled. 'Is that all you're worried about?' he said. 'Look. I anticipated you'd jump at the chance, so I took the precaution of registering you as a candidate . . .'

'You did what?'

'Retrospectively, of course. Easy if you know how. And before you say you haven't got time to do any campaigning, I managed to get you on the Ed Sullivan show – he's a friend of mine, it wasn't a problem – so you'll have at least fifteen minutes prime time, that ought to be enough. The trouble with most campaigns is, you see, they're too long'

'But . . .'

'Which reminds me,' said Lucky George. 'You're on air in about twenty minutes, so if I were you I'd be getting along.'

With retrospect, the pundits say, it was clear the moment the Utah results came in that it was going to be a da Vinci landslide.

By 3.20 a.m., the results were in from fourteen states. All had voted da Vinci.

By 5 a.m., it was all over.

Interviewed on the Johnny Carson show later that fateful day and asked to explain why the pollsters had once again got it completely wrong, the head of the Gallup organisation said in his defence that the election had turned on factors which couldn't have been foreseen at the time the polls were taken. Such factors as (among others):

(a) a personal endorsement of the da Vinci platform by the Mona Lisa, interviewed live on NBC five minutes before voting began.

(b) the invasion of New York by hundreds of thousands of strange, unearthly gibbering fiends threatening to burn the city down if da Vinci wasn't elected.

(c) the simultaneous withdrawal by all the other candidates, accompanied by a passionate appeal from each one to vote for da Vinci and a better America.

And if that wasn't enough, he continued, wiping his forehead with a large red silk handkerchief, there was the intrinsic merit of the da Vinci manifesto to consider. Admittedly, it had only been released hours before the election, but its basic inspired simplicity made that a plus rather than a minus. When a guy stands up and says, Listen, America, all we need do in order to stop inflation, restore full employment, revitalise the dollar, put the USA back in her rightful place as the leader of the free world and give those scumsucking Ayrabs a stomping they'll never forget is to link up every building from the Rockies to the Rio Grande with a network of steel scaffolding pipes, not forgetting to install at least ten heavy-duty cup-hooks on all roofs, gable-ends and porches at the same time, and there's no way you're going to lose. With a message like that, even Jimmy Carter could have got elected . . .

At which point, the pollster's eyes seemed to glaze over, and he sat motionless in his chair with an expression of extreme bewilderment until the ads came and covered his embarrassment.

The only other dissentient voice to be heard that day was that of a caller to a low-rent phone-in show broadcast on a small-town radio station somewhere in the back end of Iowa. Giving his name as Danny Bennett and his address as the Burning Fiery Pit, the caller claimed that the da Vinci victory was the result of gross electoral manipulation, using magic, necromancy and other forms of unconstitutional inducement, on the part of one Lucky George Faust, a fugitive from Hell with a colossal price on his head. The caller was in the middle of a confused tirade about international hit-men and plots against his life (rather peculiarly phrased in the past tense) when the workmen installing the steel girders to link the radio station building with the delicatessen next door dug through a telephone cable, cutting the caller off. Since ninety per cent of the calls to any local radio phone-in anywhere are comprised of this sort of material, none of the show's seven listeners took the slightest notice.

'Great,' said Lucky George, switching off the television. 'Now all we need are the balloons.'

Repossessing a country is not, perhaps, the most straightforward of operations. It ought to be, but it isn't.

In theory, the bailiff goes along to the head of state with the necessary paperwork and delivers it, and that should be that. What's then supposed to happen is that the population leave the country in question, taking with them all movable items (but no fixtures, fittings, mineral resources or growing plants or trees) by twelve noon of the day specified in the court order. Tenants' improvements are then set off against dilapidations, and any sum required to be paid to either party by way of adjustment is lodged with the court office pending a final decision by the arbitration officer.

In practice, though, there is always hassle and not infrequently trouble; sometimes even violence. That is why most repossessions these days are handled not by the everyday court bailiff but by a firm of specialist certificated bailiffs, of which there is one: Kurt Lundqvist Associates.

Once Lundqvist is on the job, things move fast. His record for clearing a country is thirty-nine seconds, although in fairness we ought to point out that it wasn't a particularly big country. Certainly not by the time he'd finished with it.

Lundqvist attributes his success in this line of work to forward planning, executive efficiency, a calm and reasonable attitude towards the resolution of difficulties and an absolutely fucking *enormous* satellite-mounted industrial laser, capable of vaporising a land mass down to bedrock level at the rate of three hundred and twenty-five thousand square miles per hour.

He calls it the Denver Blowtorch.

Maybe, he says, it makes a mess of buildings, infrastructure and, indeed, mountain ranges. On the positive side, it clears up unsightly litter deposits, disinfects unhygienic areas and leaves a pleasant glassy-smooth surface all ready for the new tenant to build what he likes on. After all, he argues, the first thing you do when you buy a house is strip off the wallpaper and take up the old carpets.

Right down at the bottom of the Marianas Trench, the deepest point in the whole of the ocean, there is no light whatsoever. The strange and uncanny creatures that grope out a nightmare existence down there at fifteen-tons-per-square-inch pressure are born, live and die without even rudimentary traces of eyes, although there are two schools of thought as to why. One says: no light, why bother? The other replies: if you'd ever seen one of those weird buggers they've got down there, the last thing you'd want any truck with ever again is vision.

When working on the bottom of the Trench, therefore, it's vitally important to remember to bring a torch.

'What, me, thkip? I haven't brought it. Thorry, I thought you'd got it.'

'I haven't got it. Keith, you got the torch?'

'Not me, skip. I thought Vernon was going to bring it.'

'Fine. I see.'

'You thure about that, thkip? I can't thee a thing.'

'I was speaking figuratively.'

The three spectral engineers (recently transferred at their own request from the Security division) trod slime for a moment, reviewing the situation.

'Bloody dark down here, skip.'

'All right, so it's a bit dimpsy. We'll just have to do the best we can.'

'We seem to do rather a lot of that, skip, if you don't mind me saying so.'

'It'th what we're betht at,' replied his colleague proudly. 'Muddling through.'

'Right. Now look, maybe we haven't exactly got off to a copybook start here, but so long as we all keep our heads and don't go all to pieces, this is going to be a piece of cake, all right? Or would you rather go back to playing seek and destroy with Kurt Lundqvist?'

There was a heavy silence.

'It's dogged as does it, skip, that's what I always say.'

'You bloody liar, Keith, what you always say is, "Oh my God, we're all going to die."'

'With good reason, skip, be fair.'

'Ekthcuthe me.'

'What?'

'Would thith help?'

The other two turned, and became conscious of a light. Not a wholesome, help-you-see-in-the-dark sort of light, more your ghastly livid green glow. It proceeded from the tail of a sort of flatfish thing; a flatfish, that is, such as Ronnie Bosch might have thought up on one of his gloomier days and then painted over because it gave him the willies.

'Stone me, Vern,' gasped the Captain, 'what the hell have you got there? It's awful.'

'It'th a fith, thkip, with a light in itth tail. I thought it might come in handy, thkip, inthtead of a torch . . .'

'All right, all right. You hold the, er, thing while we do the hole.'

In order to dig holes in the bottom of the deepest point in the ocean, you need a large cordless drill, an enormously long drill bit and a pressure hose to blast away millions of years of accumulated, undisturbed slime. And, of course, the chuck key for the drill.

'Right, Keith,' panted the Captain. 'Gimme the chuck key, and I'll just . . .'

'Now hold on a minute, skip, you know perfectly well you've got the . . .'

'Oh *shit!*'

'Ekthcuthe me again, Thkip, but would thith be any good?'

The other two engineers turned and stared.

Basically, it was a sort of depraved looking crab. With a most peculiarly shaped tail.

'This is bloody ridiculous,' muttered the Captain.

'Dead handy, though.'

'There's still no guarantee it'll *fit*,' the Captain grumbled. 'I mean, it might be a metric size or something . . .'

It wasn't. Nor, unlike your common or garden inanimate chuck key, did it slip out of your hand just when you're giving it that last half-turn and hide under the workbench. The Captain dabbed the trigger-button lightly, thereby confirming that all systems were operational.

'Lads,' he said quietly, just before setting drill to rock, 'don't you get the funny feeling that things are going a bit too well on this job?'

The drill screamed, and started to bite. As he guided the thing, the Captain could feel his whole body juddering and stretching as the vibrations twanged through him and out into the water all around.

'Thkip!'

'What is it?' the Captain screamed. 'You'll have to shout, I can't hear you very well because of the noise of this thing.'

'I thaid thkip!'

'Yes, I heard that bit.'

'Well, that'th all I'd thaid tho far.'

'Then carry on,' the Captain screamed above the sound of the drill, whining in the rock like a baby Tyrannosaurus with wind. 'Try and maintain the admirable standard of narrative clarity you've set yourself up till now.'

'Thorry?'

'It's all right, I was only . . .'

'It'th very hard to hear you, thkip, becauthe of the drill. Can you thpeak up a bit?'

'Yes. Get on with it.'

The spectral engineer shrugged. 'I jutht wanted to athk, thkip, why are we doing thith?'

The Captain shuddered horribly. The drill had just touched on something it couldn't cut, and the side-effects radiated out across the sea-bed, giving rise to duff seismographic readings right across the world.

'Good question,' he said, as soon as his teeth had stopped waltzing about in his mouth. 'Something to do with this Euro-Bosch thing, they told me. Apparently, he wants to tap into this lot for the fountains in the main courtyard.'

'I think,' said the other spectral engineer, 'it's for drains or something like that.'

The other two looked at him.

'Drains?'

'This hole we're digging. It's either drains or telephone wires, one or the other. Stands to reason,' the spectral engineer asserted confidently.

'You reckon?'

'Use your loaf, skip. Why else do people dig holes?'

The Captain paused, drill in hand, the light from the flatfish making strange shadows on the ocean floor. Why *do* people dig holes? he wondered.

Graves.

Mantraps.

Planting land mines.

Because they get told to, mostly.

And, of course, drains. He straightened his back and looked around. Nothing to be seen, except the solid walls of the darkness all around them.

'As simple as that?' he said at last.

'Yeah.'

'No hidden or ulterior motive?'

'Why should there be?'

The Captain shrugged and repositioned the drill bit in the hole. 'No reason,' he said. 'It just seems too, well, normal to me. Useful, too.'

The drill made contact, and there was a long interval of screeching metal, spine-jarring vibrations and Keith whistling (the latter audible despite the Captain jamming the drill on to full speed). Then something gave way, and before the Captain could call out 'I think we're through, lads', the water around them started to seethe and boil. Like the emptying of God's bath, it gurgled, whirlpooled and sucked. The drill, the three engineers and forty thousand tons of yucky black goo were swept up and swallowed whole.

The last two thoughts to pass through the Captain's mind, before the whirlpool got him and catapulted him back into the whole tedious rigmarole of temporary death and routine reincarnation, were:

Maybe we drilled a bit too deep.

Funny. I didn't remember seeing Lundqvist anywhere.

Water. Mother Nature's flexible jackhammer.

Billions of gallons of the stuff, enough to fill all the swimming pools in Beverley Hills, roaring and burping down a molybdenum steel drain towards the centre of the earth.

Ronnie Bosch was proud of that drain. Not because it was a miracle of engineering (walls only ninety thou. thick, but proofed to twenty-six tons per square inch; machined from solid out of one of the pillars used for thousands of years to support the sky until they discovered it stayed up there perfectly happily of its own accord); more because he'd managed to get it made and installed in twelve hours flat, and nobody had even troubled to ask him what he wanted it for. When you've been used to having to sign four pink chits and a green requisition every time you want your pencil sharpened, it comes as a bit of a shock.

Makes you think, really.

Anyway, down the water went until it emerged in the form of white high-velocity spray in an enormous cauldron arrangement, seated slap bang above Hell Holdings plc's very latest, state-of-the-art Number Six furnace.

Let nobody say that the management buy-out hasn't led to some pretty radical changes in the way Hell operates. Number Six furnace is one of the new regime's most impressive showpieces. By the simple expedient of converting it to oil-burning from sabbath-breaker burning, it has been possible to double calorific output and halve running costs, thereby saving enough to finance a whole new sabbath-breakers' wing equipped with the latest in microwave technology. Just to add to the ingenuity of it all, the electricity to power the microwaves comes from a steam turbine built into Number Six; resulting in further savings, which in turn pay for twenty-four-hour, round-the-clock canned laughter in the extremely unpleasant corner of the Hell complex set aside for game show hosts.

It was because of the steam turbine that Ronnie Bosch had routed the water down on to Number Six. A few surreptitious modifications here and there were enough to divert the steam from the boiler away from the turbines and up another molybdenum steel tube, bigger and better than the first, proofed to an incredible thirty-seven tons per square inch, running straight up through the earth's core and coming out in an expansion chamber several thousand feet under North America.

The rest of the design was basically very simple.

The rising steam powered a piston.

The piston went up.

And all across America, in the cool stillness of the early evening of the day before the bailiffs were due to move in, people out walking were tripping over enormous steel girders that hadn't been there an hour or so earlier, and wondering what on earth was going on.

Then they remembered. They remembered that, for reasons which at the time had seemed very cogent, they had voted into the White House a centuries-dead Italian inventor whose sole proposal to the electorate had been that every building in the USA be rigidly attached to its neighbour with bloody great steel rods.

America loves cleverness. In a land where inventors of better mousetraps really do have six-inch-deep ruts worn in the tarmac of their driveways, a man who can come up with an entirely practical plan for doing something previously thought to be impossible must inevitably become the hero of the hour, even if the thing he's able to do is something nobody would ever have dreamed of doing in the first place. Otherwise, how do you explain Mount Rushmore, or the space programme, or the atomic bomb?

Even the sceptics had to admit that it was a goddamn colossal achievement. To take just one example: between Las Vegas and the small but by no means indispensable township of Pahrump, Nevada, lie fifty miles of tyre-meltingly hot desert, scarcely improved in terms of habitability by having a range of twelve-thousand-foot razor-edged rocks fatuously named the Spring Mountains running slap bang through the middle. It's the sort of geographical entity that can only be fitted into the Christian world-view by accepting that somewhere around lunchtime on the third day of creation, He stopped for a breather and left a few bits for the Youth Opportunities lad to finish off.

Yet, within fifteen hours of the Da Vinci Act becoming law, Pahrump had been welded on to Vegas by a single continuous high-tensile steel link, with spurs off it at intervals to connect in the few outlying homesteads in the middle of the desert. In fact, the whole Sierra Nevada was covered with what looked from the air like silver varicose veins, glinting and twinkling in the dazzling desert sun and playing merry hell with satellite TV reception from Bakersfield to Redding.

Or take the vast single-span bridges connecting Immokalee, Florida with Clewiston, Sunnilands and Fort Myers, arrow-straight across the soggiest excesses of the Big Cypress Swamp; the massive iron beam supporting Riley, Oregon between Burns and Wagontire; the absurd lengths gone to in order to attach Wolf Point, Montana securely to its neighbours; or, on another plane entirely, the scintillating spider's webs of carbon steel enveloping Brooklyn, San Francisco, Chicago and similar hamlets.

A message banged out on the girders in Morse code in the northern suburbs of Seattle could, in theory, be picked up by someone with a stethoscope in San Diego or Miami or Boston, although it would probably be just as easy to telephone.

And America said to itself:

Hey, *we* did that!

Hey, *why* did we do that?

'Fine,' said Lucky George, replacing the receiver.

'Well?'

'Sounds like Lenny's side of things is tied up all right. Ronnie's part . . .' He glanced at his watch, and nodded. 'If everything's running on time, Ronnie's part should already be under way. Any word yet from Larry and Mike?'

Helen nodded. 'They called in about three minutes ago. It's all ready.'

'Good.' Lucky George pulled out the original envelope on which the whole thing had been sketched out, and ran his finger down it, checklist fashion. 'And Chris is ready to cover all the legal stuff?'

'He's waiting outside the Registry right now.'

'Martin and Julius got their people in position?'

'Standing by.'

'That's all right then.' Lucky George folded up the envelope, sat down on the sofa and put his feet up. 'I could murder a coffee if you're making one.'

Helen folded her arms and frowned. 'Hold on,' she said. 'While everyone else is hard at it, what precisely are you going to do?'

George smiled. 'Nothing,' he said. 'And everything too, of course, but only after I've had my coffee. Two sugars, please, and a digestive biscuit.'

It was, needless to say, the biggest moment in all the seventeen years of Links Jotapian's life.

'Scanners,' he commanded, 'on.'

There is a convention that people who sit in front of screens giving orders have to speak funny; it's all 'Activate thruster motors' and 'Uncouple forward connecting gear' and 'Initiating docking routine'. Anybody in the least self-conscious about sounding a complete nana wouldn't last five minutes.

'Scanning,' said one of the men in white coats. 'All functions normal for phase two initiation.'

Up above the world so high, like a death ray in the sky, the Denver Blowtorch was muttering drowsily. A few lights began to flash here and there on its titanium carapace, like the jewels with which a dragon's belly is reputedly encrusted. It bleeped, twitched in its orbit and dreamed strange dreams. Radio waves crackled off it into space like the hairs of a moulting cat.

For crying out loud, it broadcast to the barren cosmos, *there's some of us trying to sleep.*

Links consulted his watch. It was a pity that his Spyderco Combat Chronometer had chosen this day of all days to fall into the bath and get all clogged up with suds, because this was just the sort of special mission he'd bought it for ($14.95 plus postage). As it was, he'd had to rummage around in his dad's bedside drawer for his spare, the one he got free with five litres of oil at the gas station. It worked fine, sure, so far as telling the time was concerned, and all that stuff; but it wasn't black parkerised steel and it didn't have a camouflage strap with a built-in compass. Sometimes, Links reflected bitterly, Life can be so *unfair*.

'Hello, Mr Lundqvist, are you receiving me? This is Links here, Mr Lundqvist. Ready when you are, Mr Lundqvist. Mr Lundqvist?'

He was just about to try again, only louder, when the reply came in through the headphones. It took the form of an urgent request for radio silence until further notice, combined with a warning as to the anatomically complex consequences of non-compliance.

'Sorry, Mr Lundqvist,' Links replied, 'I didn't mean to speak so loud. Is that any better? Gee, I hope I haven't spoiled things, I'd feel really bad if—'

'Links.'

'Yes, Mr Lundqvist, I'm here.'

'Shut up.'

'Yes, Mr Lundqvist. Am receiving you, over and out.'

Nothing to do, apparently, except wait.

Links gazed round the operations room, his eye passing over the banks of computer consoles and the white-coated boffins behind them. So far, he hadn't got to the part in the course that dealt with stealthy waiting, but he felt confident that, with his newly acquired skills, he'd be able to work it out for himself from first principles.

Waiting. Well, for a start, you obviously didn't just sit there like a sack of potatoes. Any dumb civilian could do that. Presumably you had to wait like a coiled spring, concentrating the mind's potential energy and regulating the adrenaline flow. Probably there was one of those mystic Eastern things you could do, but that was most likely somewhere around Lesson Thirty-Six. Links focused his mind and tried to imagine the sound of two hands clapping. It had said one hand in the book, but that was obviously a misprint.

Just as he was getting the hang of it (Clap. Clap. Clap.) a light flashed on the console. Incoming message from Operative One.

'Operative One, this is Guadalahara Central,' he said

brightly. 'Guadalahara Central receiving you, come in, Operative One, over.'

'Yeah,' said the voice. 'This is Morrie Goldman here, can I talk to Mr Lundqvist, please?'

Links frowned. 'Negative, Operative One.' He paused, trying to translate what he wanted to say into commandspeak. He gave up; too difficult. 'Mr Lundqvist isn't here right now, can I take a message?'

'What? Oh, sure. Look, this is Goldman. I'm just about to go in and serve the possession notice right now. Have your guys standing by, because I have this feeling the tenants aren't going to be too happy.'

'Receiving you, Operative One. Confirm all systems are operational, awaiting clearance to proceed, over.'

'Yeah, well.' The voice hesitated. 'Just tell him I called, okay?'

'Positive. Message received and logged. Over and out.'

Morrie Goldman hung up and looked around him.

This, he felt, was as good a place as any. He walked up to the counter.

After all, he reassured himself, the man had told him to serve the papers in Washington DC. And here he was in Washington. And besides, the whole goddamn country was going to be blown to antshit a few seconds after he'd effected service, so nobody was ever likely to know even if he did goof it up.

'Hi, my name is Cindi, can I take your order, please?'

Goldman froze. The papers were already in his hand. All he had to do was hand them to somebody, say what they were and timejump out of here; simple as that. He looked at the waitress and flexed his larynx.

'Hi,' he said, 'I'll have the double cheeseburger, the vanilla shake, regular, and, um, large fries.'

'Coming right up.'

He opened his mouth to say the next bit . . .

(*This is a sealed copy of a possession order issued out of the*

Sublime Court, requiring you to surrender possession of the premises known as North America. If you are in any doubt as to the effect of this order or the likely consequences of failure to comply with the terms hereof, you should immediately seek the advice of your own legal adviser.)

. . . but the waitress had gone. She now had her back to him, and was yelling the order through to the kitchen. There was obviously more to process-serving than he'd originally anticipated.

'Hi, I'm Ayesha, are you being served?'

Goldman stared into the friendly brown eyes in front of him, closed his own, thrust the papers over the counter and said the magic words. They came out in a sort of congealed lump, like melted popcorn.

'Excuse me?' said the waitress.

The sensible thing to have done would have been to turn away quickly and run for it. Instead, Goldman made a fatal mistake. He tried to explain.

'Look,' he said, 'I'm a process-server, and . . .'

The brown eyes clouded over. 'Get outa here,' they said. 'I'm telling you, I never owned the goddamn car. I never signed *nothing*. What you come in here hassling me for?'

'No, it's not about a car,' Goldman said. 'In fact, it's not you personally, it's . . .'

'You wait there,' said the brown eyes. 'I'm gonna get the manageress.'

Goldman winced. 'No, there's no need for that,' he said. 'Look, it's perfectly in order for you to accept service, in fact service has now been effectually, um, effected, so . . .'

'Don't you give me none of that bullshit, man. I ain't signing nothing. You think I'm crazy or something?'

Meanwhile a large man in a cook's hat had materialised from somewhere out back. Was there, he enquired, some sort of a problem going on here?

'You bet there's a problem,' said the brown eyes emphatically.

'This guy here says he's a process-server, I told him, I ain't accepting no service, I ain't signing *nothing*, and he says—'

'That's all right,' said the large man. 'You just get Carla and everything's gonna be fine.'

A statement which turned out to be more accurate than he could possibly have imagined.

The building began to move . . .

It happened like this.

The water from the Marianas Trench hits the boiler over Number Six furnace, turns to steam . . .

Which passes through a series of ports into an expansion chamber in the centre of the planet, fills the chamber and starts to move upwards . . .

Bearing against the piston, which is driven with staggering force up towards the surface of the Earth, until . . .

It connects with and locates into a receiving slot on the underside of a thirteen-thousand-ton slab of kevlar-reinforced concrete directly under the biggest skyscraper in Kansas City (which is, of course, as near as makes no odds the geographical centre of the United States), whereupon . . .

The skyscraper is pushed up clear of its foundations into the air; but of course . . .

Thanks to the Da Vinci Project, it's linked with steel girders to all the neighbouring buildings, which in turn are linked to all the buildings across the entire nation, with the result that . . .

(The force being exerted on the piston is, remember, absolutely phenomenal; almost a quarter of the Pacific Ocean's been turned to steam by now and the water's still coming; and when steam expands, it's got to go somewhere; and those steel girders they've got linking up all the houses aren't rubbish, they make the Golden Gate bridge look like a cheap Taiwanese paper-clip, so . . .)

America rises.

Or at least, the buildings do. The ground stays put. The

ground, after all, now indefeasibly belongs to the Lundqvist
Trust (Holdings) Corporation, and has to be surrendered in accordance with the notice to quit. On the other hand, the buildings
are tenants' improvements, and may be removed at any time
prior to the surrender of the premises. Ask any lawyer.

A split second after the moment of lifting, of course, the
steam pressure in the cylinder blows out the gaskets; the piston
goes crashing back down to the centre of the Earth in a cloud
of burning steam; the network of girders crumples under the
strain like gossamer and falls away . . .

But not so the buildings, because for the last thirty-six hours,
all the birds in North America, under the direction of two
extremely persuasive seagulls, have been feverishly occupied
knotting helium-filled balloons to all the cup-hooks screwed
into all the roofs of all the buildings in every state in the Union;
and a micron of a second before the whole thing is due to
succumb to gravity and hit the deck, the balloons take the
strain, and . . .

America floats . . .

Some twenty feet or so above ground level. Fortuitously
it's a pretty windless day, and the birds have also tethered the
buildings together to stop them drifting too far apart. They're
now zooming from building to building (a pigeon's work is
never done) with rope-and-plank bridges, to take the place of
the sidewalks.

It goes without saying, incidentally, that the balloons are
coloured red, white and blue and have been neatly arranged to
form an appropriate pattern when viewed from above. Lucky
George got them cheap, as a job lot, surplus, after the recent
round of party conventions.

And, as a final touch, from the roof of the United Nations
building in New York, twenty thousand specially trained white
doves take off and glide in perfect formation across the city and
out over Long Island. As they fly, they spell out:

OKAY KURT SHE'S ALL YOURS

until, as they pass over Port Jefferson and turn north towards New Haven, they change formation and instead read:

ENJOY

Somewhere in the City of London a young stockbroker dashed into the firm's main office, tore off his coat and tucked his long knees under his computer terminal. Preoccupied with his own concerns, he failed to notice the deathly hush.

'Sorry I'm late, everyone,' he said generally. 'Update me, someone. Wall Street gone any higher since we opened?'

One of his colleagues turned his head and gave him a long, strange look.

'In a manner of speaking, yes,' he said.

Impossible.

On the following grounds:

(a) No labour force, however well-equipped or motivated, spectral or otherwise, could dig the tunnels, machine the parts, install the girders, blow up the balloons in so short a time. Nothing was ever built that quickly. Okay, the world was put together in seven days; but that's net working time. What the book of words glosses over is the three weeks between Day Two and Day Three, during which time He sat around twiddling his thumbs waiting for forty billion reinforced steel joists to be delivered from the foundry.

(b) There isn't enough water in the ocean, let alone the Marianas Trench, to provide enough steam to lift America; or . . .

(c) Alternatively, the design as specified would have produced so much force that not only would America have lifted, but Manhattan Island would have been shot out through the Earth's atmosphere and into orbit.

(d) In any event it's academic, because that much pressure would blow apart any cylinder small enough to fit inside the Earth's core in three seconds flat.

(e) Besides which, absolutely no way could you join all the buildings in the USA together like that; and if you could, it's completely out of the question that any steel framework built by Man could withstand the leverage you'd get under the da Vinci design.

(f) Not to mention the fact that even if you could get all those houses and factories and office blocks to go up, it'd take more than a few poxy little balloons to keep them there.

Correct. Impossible.

America swayed in the slight breeze.

Gradually, her population began to come to terms with it.

True, they were hanging out of the sky from balloons; but once the rope and plank bridges were in place, they tentatively began to venture out, not looking down, trying very hard indeed not to think about it all. Within two hours, the first rope-and-plank-bridge-theatre performers were miming the man-inside-a-box routine twenty feet above Central Park.

True, there were no fields to plough, no lumber to jack; worst of all, no roads to drive on. Take away America's cars and you take away her soul. But within an hour and a half, the first Mack airship was bobbing drunkenly across Arizona airspace, country music blaring from the cockpit, the propulsive force being provided by a propeller and five thousand rubber bands.

True, with no mean streets, there was nowhere for a man to walk down; and for the first forty minutes all the cops in all the precincts in all the states of the Union suddenly found themselves with no excuse whatsoever for not catching up with the paperwork. But there are too many rooftop chase sequences in cinematographic history for the lack of streets to be a problem for terribly long.

True, nobody had the faintest idea what was going on, or

what was all behind it, or whose fault it was or how long it was going to last. In other words, normality. The status quo.

Lucky George gritted his teeth and wondered whether, this time, he hadn't been just a trifle over-ambitious.

No trouble at all lifting America by sheer magical force. Keeping it there – child's play. Suspending the disbelief of the entire human race – piece of cake. Putting the idea of staying indoors into the mind of every man, woman and child in America – a doddle. And just as easy to do them simultaneously as one after the other.

Where perhaps he had over-extended himself slightly was in doing all this and trying to make it look as though it was possible. Hence the business with tunnels, furnaces, pistons and steel girders.

Essential, nevertheless. Where there are laws there are lawyers; and the lawyers who enforce the laws of physics are arguably the nastiest ornaments of a universally unsavoury profession. Goof around with relativity, or try having an action without an equal and opposite reaction, and the next thing you know is the usher telling you to speak up because the judge can't hear you.

Bearing in mind the number of times Lucky George had disregarded the simple instructions set out in the Universe's users' manual, he'd figured that breaking every single law in the book apart from parking in the Director of Gravity's reserved space, without at least some show of mechanical activity, would be pushing his luck just that smidgen too far.

Hence all the ironmongery. Right now, the site was swarming with feasibility assessors and reality surveyors, all scratching their heads over the fact that although according to the rules it couldn't possibly work, there was a hell of a lot of existential evidence that it did, and maybe the rules were in need of a little discreet revision. By the time they'd done their sums and could prove it was all physically impossible, there was a better than average chance that the mess would have been sorted out and America could be put unostentatiously back, some time in the early hours of the morning when all the inhabitants were asleep or watching the late, late film.

Fine. But it made things that bit harder, like trying to break into a hard-boiled egg with a lead-weighted feather. Instead of just keeping the houses in the air, for example, he was having to do it by means of all those countless millions of balloons. You could put your mind out, lifting something like that the wrong way.

Accordingly, George was rather preoccupied.

With the result that he didn't hear the soft splash of oars below the balcony. Or see the shadowy figure climb hand over hand up to the railings and silently hoist himself over.

The first he knew of it, in fact, was the feel of the muzzle of the .40 Glock in his ear, and Lundqvist's voice saying, 'Freeze.'

CHAPTER
EIGHTEEN

If there is more joy in Heaven over one sinner that repents, it's a wet Sunday afternoon in mid Wales compared with the ecstatic jubilation in Hell over one escaped sinner that gets his collar felt.

Not surprisingly, the denizens of the Inferno know how to party. Within twenty minutes of the news breaking, the management had declared a half-day's holiday, and five thousand years' worth of tormented souls had formed a whirling, tail-lashing conga that roared and billowed through the various Rings like a rattlesnake on amphetamines. Objectively speaking, what with the noise and the smoke and the crush of bodies, the epicentre of the party was quite markedly worse than the torments from which the revellers had temporarily been released; however, there's absolutely no limit to what the human spirit can endure when it sincerely believes it's enjoying itself.

Meanwhile, in the large conference room, the Board were taking counsel as to the reception to be accorded the returning guest.

'It's got to have manure in it somewhere,' insisted the Production Director. 'I may be old-fashioned and set in my ways, but . . .'

The Personnel Director shook his head emphatically. 'With respect, Mr Chairman,' he said, 'no offence, but my colleague is talking through his arse. You—'

The Finance Director frowned and lifted his index finger slightly to indicate that he required silence. 'Hold on,' he said, looking dispassionately at the Production Director's rather bizarre anatomy. 'Point taken, Dennis, and excuse me if I seem pedantic, but Harry always talks through his arse. It's the way he's made, you see, what with his head being in his tummy and all back to front . . .'

'My colleague,' said the Personnel Director frostily, 'is, if you prefer, talking nonsense. Dammit, this isn't the time for poncing about, we're looking at brimstone here, because—'

'Excuse me,' interrupted the Production Director, icier still, 'but perhaps my friend from Personnel would be kind enough to let me know where I'm supposed to get brimstone from, since he's so bloody keen on the stuff. In fact,' he added spitefully, 'perhaps he'd just tell us, briefly and in his own words, exactly what brimstone is, because I've been in this business three thousand years, imp and fiend, and the amount of your actual brimstone that I've seen around here you could fit into a very small egg-cup—'

'All right, Harry, thank—'

'And still have room for the egg.'

'Quiet!' The Finance Director raised his hand. 'Thank you both very much for your views, which are noted, but I think I can offer you all an alternative suggestion which does have quite a lot going for it.'

The Directors turned and looked at him. He smiled.

'Just to recap for a moment,' he said, leaning back slightly in his chair, 'so far we've had a bed of red-hot coals from Jerry, and Colin's forty-foot earthworm, and Steve's very innovative

Game For A Laugh concept – far be it from me, by the way,
Steve, but in my opinion there's such a thing as over the top,
even for us – and of course Terry's Moebius loop of Dame Kiri
Te Kanawa Sings Country, which we're definitely going to have
to use somewhere, but not here, I think. Plus, of course, Harry's
shitwell and Dennis's brimstone.' He paused, and flicked though
his microchip Organiser. 'While we're on the subject, Harry,
from memory I think Fiends' Provident do synthetic brimstone in fifty-kilo tubs, if that's any help to you.'

He paused and took a sip of water; then went on:

'It's all good stuff, lads, but where's the money coming from?
Just think about that for a moment, would you, because once
we've paid Lundqvist's invoice and settled the compensation
claims for all those practical jokes George pulled while still
nominally in our charge and therefore our responsibility, there'll
probably still be enough left in the Entertainments budget for
a cup of tea and a ginger nut, but nothing else. Anybody got
any thoughts on that one?'

There was silence, except for the soft fizzing of the varnish
on the boardroom table where the Sales Director had breathed
on it. The Finance Director nodded.

'Okay,' he said, 'here's a suggestion. I took the liberty,' he
went on, standing up and walking to the back of the room, 'of
bringing along a few slides to illustrate what I've got in mind.
The lights please, someone.'

The lights went out, and a few seconds later the back wall
was covered with an eye-catching, rather familiar image. The
Finance Director pointed to it with his right index claw.

'You all should know what this is by now,' he said. 'It's the
right-hand panel of the *Garden of Earthly Delights*, courtesy of
our very own artist in residence, Ron Bosch. Now, as you're all
well aware, Ron's using this as the central tableau for the main
shopping and recreation area of the theme park. Can I have the
next slide, please?'

A machine clunked softly in the background, and the image

on the screen zoomed in to show a close-up of the justly celebrated centre-piece of the panel; the bird-headed demon with a cauldron on the back of its head and its feet in two water-jugs, perched in a high-chair-cum-hourglass arrangement, daintily chewing on a human torso and legs. If Hell had a mascot, this was it; the Guinness toucan, the Esso tiger, the Andrex puppy, and Captain Beaky.

The Finance Director grinned. 'Get the picture?' he said.

There was a bemused silence.

'Frankly,' said the Production Director at last, 'but no, not really. I expect I'm being really thick here, but what's Captain Beaky got to do with getting even with Lucky George?'

'Plenty, if you agree with my proposal,' the Finance Director replied. He motioned for the next slide. 'Here,' he continued, 'we've got the design specs for the fibreglass model of Beaky we're all set to order for the Park.' He tapped the bottom left-hand corner of the screen with his pointer. 'Note particularly,' he said, 'the price. Now please don't think I'm advocating corner-cutting because I'm not, but that really is a lot of bread.'

'Too bloody right,' commented the Production Director sourly. 'I've said it before, these boys from the pattern-makers are ripping us off, and we're doing bugger-all about it.'

The Finance Director smiled. 'Maybe,' he said, 'but in this instance I don't think the pricings are excessive, because the whole point about the Beaky model is that it actually works. Moving parts, all singing, all dancing. What you do is, you put a coin in here –' He indicated the hindquarters of a soul in torment just below the high chair. '– and immediately Beaky eats the sinner, with realistic noise and odour effects and piped screams. Boschy reckons it's going to be a real moneyspinner once it's up and running, but in the meantime there's the capital costs to find. Bad news, gentlemen, bad news. On present costings, it's going to be a tight squeeze.'

There was a rustle and a ripple around the boardroom table, which the Finance Director noticed. He nodded his approval.

'I can see you're way ahead of me, gentlemen,' he said. 'I think that with a little ingenuity, we've got the whole damn flock with one small pebble. Just to make sure we're all on the same wavelength, however, I'll quickly run it past you and we'll see what happens. Instead of a fibreglass disposable sinner – $750 each according to the quotes, and we estimate he'll get through ten or twelve in a day – if we could substitute a flesh-and-blood, perpetually reusable organic sinner, not only would we save on parts but the whole sideshow's going to be one hell of a lot more authentic and appealing to the punters. What d'you reckon, gentlemen?'

After a short interval, the comments started to flow. Diabolic humour is to a large degree shaped by its environment; hence the Production Director's comment that it was the sort of thing he'd like to chew over for a while, the Personnel Manager's remark that it was the sort of design you could really get your teeth into, the Company Secretary's observation that Harry had taken the words right out of his mouth and the Senior Redcoat's warning that they shouldn't bite off more than they could chew. When the Finance Director had had about as much of this sort of thing as he could stand, he raised his finger for silence.

'Agreed, then,' he said cheerfully. 'I'll tell Lundqvist to deliver on site first thing in the morning. Thank you, gentlemen.'

'You planned the whole thing, didn't you?'

Lundqvist nodded. 'And you fell for it.'

'Well, yes.' Lucky George tried to nod, but the huge steel collar clamped round his neck precluded movement of more than a thousandth of an inch. 'If it's any satisfaction to you, Smiler, yes I did. Happy now?'

'Don't call me Smiler,' Lundqvist growled dangerously.

'Why not, Smiler?' George raised an eyebrow, about the only part of him above waist level capable of motion. 'It's your nick-name, isn't it? I mean, yes, when we were at school together you did use to ponce around the yard telling everyone that from now on you were to be known as Captain Death the Terminator, but I thought Nick Machiavelli and I had kicked that out of you by the end of third year.'

'That'll do, George.'

'Sorry, Smiler.'

Lundqvist pulled savagely on the chain attached to the collar and made no reply. For his part, he blamed his entire collection of terminal personality disorders on the way George and his gang had spent their mutual schooldays running verbal rings round him and then beating him up, just because he was small and delicate and liked setting fire to people in their sleep. He'd waited a long time to get even, and he wasn't going to be hurried or flustered.

'Here, Kurt,' George called out after a while. 'Are you sure you know where you're going?'

'Yes. Why?'

'Fine, Kurt, fine, so long as you're sure. It's just that there's no deserts in Europe, and this is a desert we're in, and I thought I'd just mention . . .'

On either side of them, sand dunes rolled away into the fold of horizon and sky. Lundqvist snickered, and turned in his saddle. 'We're going the scenic route, George,' he said. 'I felt you might like to stretch your legs one last time.'

'That was thoughtful of you, Smiler.'

'Before they're stretched for you, of course.'

'Of course.' George grinned. 'There you go again, Smiler, pulling my leg as usual. Nice sunny day, isn't it?'

'You like it?'

'Yes.'

'That's just as well, isn't it?'

'You know me, Kurt, never one to complain.' George yawned. 'Yes, like I was saying, that was good thinking on your part, getting to me through my friends. My Achilles heel, you thought to yourself, or rather, my fatal flaw, because I expect you get Achilles heel and Achilles tendon muddled up. Sneaky, of course, and despicable, putting everybody to all that trouble, but there we are. All's fair in love and law enforcement.'

'They made me give it back.'

George looked at him. 'Sorry?'

'America,' Lundqvist said, with as much bitterness in his voice as there is vermouth in the driest of dry martinis. 'They made me give it back. Not,' he added, 'as if I really wanted it for anything. In fact they're welcome to it.'

'That's all right, then,' George said. 'Fun's fun, and nobody enjoys a good stunt better than I do, but it'd have spoilt it a little bit to think of the entire USA being carbonised just because of me. I was a little bit worried about that, actually, though I don't know why. It's not as if it was me that started all this.'

Lundqvist gave the chain another vicious tug, so that George staggered and nearly ended up on the ground. But he found his feet again and started to whistle.

'Been missing the old place?'

George looked up. 'Well, to be honest with you, no. Still, there are worse places.'

Lundqvist pulled hard on the reins and stopped his horse. 'There are?' he asked.

'Sure.' George stood on one leg and rubbed his left ankle with his right heel. 'Millions of 'em. All over the place. Honestly, Smiler, your mob have about as much idea of how to go about torturing souls as my aunt's cat. Less,' he added on reflection, and accurately. 'It was on my mind for a long time to mention it to somebody, because I'm a helpful sort of chap by nature, but then I thought, nah, why bother, nobody'll thank you for it. So . . .'

Lundqvist's skin prickled as he sensed a verbal trap, but his curiosity got the better of him. 'Go on, then,' he said.

George smiled. 'One of these days,' he said, 'do yourself a favour and get a job in an office somewhere. Any office, any-place. The term soul-destroying's a bit of a cliché, but it's damned accurate. Two years in Accounts has the same effect on your average soul as two teaspoons of salt on a garden slug. Whoomph!'

Lundqvist frowned. 'You're winding me up,' he said.

'No I'm not,' George replied. 'You don't know because you've never tried it. Nice outdoor life, travel, killing interesting people, you don't know you're born. And as for all those so-called torments they've got down in the Basement there, we're talking summer holidays compared to being stuck on the end of a telephone all day being shouted at because the green forms at Central don't tally with the pink paying-in slips.'

'No.' Lundqvist shook his head slowly. 'You wait and see what we've got in store for you, and then tell me all about it.'

George mustered an expression of polite interest. 'Something fun?' he asked.

Lundqvist told him.

EuroBosch: a visitor's guide.

Enter through the Burning Cities at the northern end of the Park, buying your ticket from the four-legged owl-headed egg (who also retails a wide range of souvenir goods, postcards, plenary indulgences and Masses for the Dead). Each visitor or party is then assigned a personal fiend to act as escort and guide for your tour. It's very helpful if visitors can specify any preference for a particular fiend type well in advance; the spoon-headed monks in particular are in great demand, and are allocated on a first-come first-damned basis.

As you pass over the bridge embattled by armies, the first exciting and enjoyable activity you will come to will be the Ferris Ears. All you have to do is climb up the scaffolding to the gallows on the left of the Ears to get to your seat; you're then churned round and round inside the Ears, being narrowly missed by the huge pendant knife-blade, until you're hurled out, dizzy and terrified, through the slot at the front.

Next on the programme is the amazing free-to-enter Satanic

Bagpipe Karaoke, situated on the flat circular platform on top of the severed head. Look closely at the illustration in the brochure and you'll see a delighted visitor being led to the microphone by a bird-headed fiend with a burning torch.

Just down from the Karaoke is the popular Refreshment Area, conveniently situated in the shattered eggshell. The Refreshment Area offers a wide range of traditional infernal hot and cold dishes, light snacks and bird-headed fiends. Patrons are requested to refrain from smoking in the Refreshment Area, although residents may of course smoulder unobtrusively.

Across the boating lake from the Refreshment Area is the family favourite Lost Souls Tortured On Musical Instruments game. For a moderate admission charge, you can be crushed in a viol, rolled in a drum, strung on a harp or crucified on a lute, and the attendant dog-, rabbit- and amphibian-headed demons will be pleased to assist you in any way they can.

You may then wish to cross back over the boating lake to enjoy the unique sensation of participating in the rollicking Knight Eaten By Dogs stall; or perhaps you will prefer to spend a quarter of an hour or so simply walking about the grounds marvelling at the many varied and different species of wild fiend to be found there before embarking on a helter-skelter dash through the Horse's Skull assault course, followed by a thrilling twenty minutes with the Manta Ray Paintball Team.

Whichever of the many colon-twistingly enjoyable activities you choose to take part in on your way round EuroBosch, you should on no account miss the high spot of any visit, the all-action non-stop Captain Beaky Extravaganza, guaranteed to haunt your nightmares with feverish intensity for whatever remains of your life.

Finally, a few Dos and Don'ts to make your visit more enjoyable:

1. Please *do not feed the fiends*, except with the specially prepared human souls obtainable from the gift shop situated in the Giant Lantern. The fiends' diet is carefully regulated for

their own health and well-being, and sweets, sandwiches and gobbets of human flesh can be harmful.

2. Please do not ask to be mangled by the giant bird-headed butterflies. Their wings are extremely fragile, and you risk spoiling your own and other people's enjoyment.

3. Please take your sins home with you, or place them in the receptacles provided.

4. Only children purchased on the premises may be consumed in the Refreshment Area.

'. . . And after that,' Lundqvist was saying, 'they stuff you straight back into your skin and round you go again, over and over and over, for the rest of—'

'Sounds all right to me.'

Lundqvist lost his temper. 'No it *doesn't*,' he shouted, 'it's *horrible*, and you'll scream and howl and beg for mercy, but nobody will hear, and it'll be the same, every day for ever, and—'

'Except Thursdays.'

Lundqvist's head snapped round. 'What do you mean, Thursdays?' he spat.

'The park's shut Thursdays,' George said, 'for cleaning and maintenance. And I don't imagine your bosses will want to pay for the electricity if there's nobody there, do you? I expect the whole thing'll grind to a halt until opening time on Friday.'

'Look . . .'

'By the same token,' George went on implacably, 'I very much doubt whether the machines will be running every evening after all the visitors have gone, because that's when the little men with the oil-cans come round and do all the bearings. Mind you,' he added, 'if it's like any fun-fair I've ever been to, at least a third of the time the place is open the machines will have broken down or overheated or something, so the actual net being-chewed time is reduced by – what, something like . . .'

'All right,' Lundqvist thundered, 'it won't be absolutely incessant. It'll still hurt like buggery when it *is* working.'

'It would hurt,' George replied calmly, 'if I hadn't learnt advanced tantric yoga as a young man at college. Marvellous stuff, you know, means you can lie on beds of nails and prance about on red-hot coals for hours on end and not feel a thing. You should try it some time.'

Lundqvist was pulling handfuls of hair out of his horse's mane by now. 'Okay,' he said, 'so maybe it's not incessant and maybe it won't hurt as much as it should, but it'll be very, very boring. Or hadn't you considered that?'

George smiled beatifically. 'I come from a large family,' he replied, 'and we were for ever being visited by some cousin or other; usually middle-aged, with photographs. And you presume to talk to me about being bored.'

'Look . . .'

'Plus the tantric yoga helps with that, too. It's extremely hard to be bored when you're contemplating the vastness of Being through the sharp focus of Experience while standing aside from your Persona.' George grinned like a mantrap. 'It's a bit like twiddling your thumbs, only less exhausting physically.'

Lundqvist glanced down at his bald horse and got a grip on himself. 'You'll see,' he said, 'who has the last laugh.'

'Oh, I expect you will,' said George, 'Smiler.'

Although there was still a full week to go before the scheduled Grand Opening, the management had reckoned that it would be good business to have a few sneak previews. Potential advertisers, reps from the main holiday companies and other major clients in the making were therefore cringing and lurking their way round the Park when Lundqvist trotted through the main gate, remembering to duck so as to avoid leaving his head behind as he passed under the fish-headed monster perched over the lintel. It had been put there as a hat-check fiend, but old habits die hard.

A wave of his .40 Glock was enough to persuade the Egg that Lundqvist didn't need a ticket and didn't want any hand-made demonic fudge, and after Lundqvist had parked his horse in the horse park they passed through into the Burning Cities area. Once or twice Lundqvist nearly jumped out of his skin as they turned a corner to be confronted by a flute-headed badger or a nine-foot-high cowled lizard; George simply smiled and occasionally nodded in tacit salutation.

'Scared?'

'Shut up.' Lundqvist yanked hard on the chain, and George reeled heavily against a four-legged, Alsatian-sized wine jar, which staggered, slipped in a pool of its own spillage, and crashed to the ground, shattering into hundreds of razor-edged splinters. There was a howl of fury from a scaffolding tower overhead, followed by a forceful request that the two of them should look where they were going.

'Smiler.'

'Now what?'

'If I were you, I'd let me go now.'

Amazing, the way that Life can still find things to take our breath away, even when we think we've seen and heard it all. 'Are you out of your skull?' Lundqvist demanded. 'I wouldn't let you go now for all the napalm in Iraq.'

'Sure?'

Lundqvist grinned nastily. 'Absolutely positive.'

'Okay,' George said, and shrugged. 'On your head be it, then.'

And a few seconds later, it was.

It was a truck-sized expanded polystyrene turbot, dressed in a cardinal's hat and playing a harp, and it hit Lundqvist in the back of the head before landing directly on top of him. All that was visible of him was his hands and one toe.

'Told you,' said George.

Furtively, and with a face like thunder, Hieronymus Bosch climbed down from the crane and looked round.

'Right,' he hissed, 'that's it, that's the very last time I help you out of a jam. Understood?'

'Afternoon, Ron.'

'We are now,' Bosch went on, fumbling in his pocket for the diamond-edged hacksaw, 'finally and definitively quits. Got that?'

George nodded. 'Very good of you to help me out here, Ron,' he said. 'Always could rely on you in a crisis.'

'Well,' Bosch snapped back as the severed halves of the first handcuff hit the ground, 'in future you can rely on me not being here, understood?'

'You always were a pal, Ron,' said Lucky George, smiling. 'Well, I mustn't keep you. How are you getting on with those chains and things?'

'Huh!' Bosch winced sharply as he touched the blade of the hacksaw with the tip of his finger. It was hot, very hot indeed. 'Bloody things, they've gone and used carbon steel for these damned manacles. Don't they have any idea whatsoever of how much things cost?'

'Never mind.' George swung his arms and rolled his neck to suggest that it would be nice to move, if only eventually. 'Can't expect this lot to know things, Ron. Be seeing you.'

Once he was clear of the chains and the collar, George made for the giant lantern. He needed food, and a drink, and quite possibly a new pair of feet.

Well, he said to himself as he looked round. If I did want some new feet, this would be the place to come. Hundreds of them, and some with nothing attached at either end.

After the drink and the sandwich, of course, there would be the problem of getting out of the Park. As priorities go, however, it wasn't exactly holding pole position. He walked up the back of the oversize carving knife and swung open the door.

Then he remembered. No money. Damn.

He tried to conjure for some, and then remembered. Magic doesn't work here, because of interference from the tannoy system.

'Hi,' he said. 'You got any washing-up needs doing?'

Seven pairs and three trios of eyes turned and stared at him. 'You what?' said a voice from behind the bar.

'I said,' George repeated, sitting on a bar stool, 'any washing-up you want doing? In return for a cup of coffee, something like that.'

The barfiend cackled through its twisted beak. 'Listen, chum,' it said. 'This is Hell, right? No problem getting washing-up done here.'

'Fair enough.' George nodded. 'Plenty of unhelpful husbands, you mean. All right, then, will you take a cheque?'

The fiend scowled, and pointed with its wingtip at a notice over the fireplace, which said:

NO CREDIT
NO LOITERING
SERVICE NOT INCLUDED

'I think I've been here before,' George said. 'Well, sorry to have bothered you. See you around.'

The door through which he had just walked swung shut. Worse than that, it folded its arms. George sat down again and surreptitiously pulled a bowl of peanuts towards him. Before his fingers could close around any of the contents, they jumped out of the bowl and scurried for the ashtray.

'Where d'you come from, anyway?' demanded the fiend. 'Haven't seen you in here before, have I?'

'I'm with the preview tour,' George replied. 'Actually, I'm a bit lost.'

'Who isn't?'

'Good point.' With a deft flick of his wrist, George brushed a slower-than-average peanut into the palm of his hand and swallowed it quickly. 'Could you direct me to the main gate? The bus leaves in ten minutes, and . . .'

The fiend wrinkled its beak. 'I know who you are,' it said. 'You're that Lucky George character. Well, sunshine, this time you won't be so bleeding lucky, because . . .'

Out of the corner of his eye, George caught sight of

something nice. Niceness, like beauty, is very much in the beholder's eye, because all he'd seen was two more bird-headed monsters. But these ones were different. They were seagull-headed.

'Here,' the barfiend was saying, 'you two. Are you from Security?'

A seagull head nodded.

'Took your bloody time, didn't you? Here he is. Now get him out of here.'

George waited till they were past the Knight Eaten By Dogs and out on to the hard ice of the pond before breaking the silence.

'Like the thing said,' he muttered. 'You two took your bloody time.'

Larry shrugged. 'It's not easy, you know,' he said. 'We had to find costumes.'

'And they had people in them, too,' Mike added. 'So we had to get rid of them, and then we had to find you. And people kept stopping us and asking where the lavs are. We did our best.'

George nodded. 'No problem,' he said, 'just so long as you can find the way out. To be honest with you, I don't like it much here. Don't let Ron know I said that, by the way.'

'It's over there,' Larry said, pointing. 'Up past that big head thing with the plate on top. Better still, there's a fire escape just below the Burning Cities. We could go through that.'

George nodded. 'Where's Helen?' he asked.

'Waiting out front with the car,' Mike answered. 'She insisted on coming.'

'Quite right too. Now then, I left Lundqvist under a fish, but he's probably on the loose again by now, so we'd better get a move on.'

As they made their way up the bank away from the pond, a rabbit-headed demon shuffled up and asked them if they wanted to go on the Man-Eating Lute. They shook their heads and walked on.

'*Freeze!*'

'Oh for pity's sake,' George muttered, clicking his tongue and dodging a bullet from the .40 Glock. 'Come on, we'd better make for that thing over there.'

'Just a minute, boss, you don't want to go there, it's the—'

'Come *on*, Larry, and don't dawdle.'

'I see,' George whispered, 'what you mean.'

Larry acknowledged the remark with a tiny dip of his head. The rest of him was frozen with terror.

'It's all right really, Larry, the worst that can happen is they'll ask you to sing. What's so terrible about . . . ?'

George caught sight of the seagull's face and decided that this was a topic best left alone. He folded his arms, looked straight in front of him and set his lips in a slight smile.

Lundqvist woke up.

William Shakespeare was a great describer of sleep, referring to it as (*inter alia*) balm of hurt minds, knitter-up of the ravelled sleeve of care, great nature's second course and the season of all natures. Kurt Lundqvist, who had always taken the view that the pen may be mightier than the sword but is still no match for a twelve-gauge Remington Wingmaster with an eighteen-inch barrel loaded with Double-O buckshot, preferred to think of sleep as a right bastard, particularly when induced by an outsize expanded polystyrene fish.

It didn't help matters that the first thing he saw on opening his eyes was Links Jotapian, who said, 'Are you all right, Mr Lundqvist?'

'Yes. Get this bloody thing off me and raise the alarm.'

'Straight away, Mr Lundqvist.'

'Links.'

'Yes, Mr Lundqvist?'

'Try pushing it the other way.'

'Gosh, sorry, Mr Lundqvist, I wasn't thinking. Did it hurt?'

'Not nearly as much as what I'm going to do to you if you don't get a goddamn move on.'

'I'm doing the best I can, Mr Lundqvist.'

'Yes,' Lundqvist replied bitterly, 'you probably are.'

A few minutes later, every alarm bell in the complex was howling its head off, producing a volume of noise so great that it was almost audible over the sound-effects from the various rides. On the Karaoke stall, however, it had about as much chance as a Bic disposable against Lundqvist's Remington.

'Every time I say goodbye,' Larry was singing, 'I die a little.' He didn't carry absolute conviction, because to judge strictly by appearances he was already dead; more than that, he'd been steeped for a week in formaldehyde and inexpertly stuffed.

'He's really very good, isn't he?' hissed the other seagull under his breath. 'Mind you, he gets that from his mother.'

Larry carried on singing until the rat-headed fiend in nominal charge of the proceedings eventually took the microphone away from him and passed it on to a circular nun with light shining out through her ears. All right, so this was Hell; but there are limits. The nun started to sing 'My Way'.

'Come on,' George hissed, 'let's get out of this. I really do fancy something to eat.'

Before he could make good his escape, however, the rat-head snatched the mike away from the nun, and jabbed it into George's hand. He smiled, as if receiving a bunch of flowers from a welcoming committee, took a deepish breath and sang.

It took the rat-head less than seven seconds to realise that he'd made a serious mistake; but by then the damage was mostly done. When he tried to take the mike away from Lucky George, all he got for his pains was an expertly placed elbow in his solar plexus. Thereafter he confined his energies to switching the whole plant off at the mains and biting through the mike cable with his teeth. The difference it made was negligible.

Finally, having assured the world at large that he'd done it his way, George handed back the mike and sighed contentedly.

'Can I have another go, please?'

The rat-head gave him a look of three parts pure terror, two parts unmitigated hatred.

He shrugged. 'Pity, that,' said George. 'I was enjoying myself.'

He stepped down off the platform, weaving his way round the bodies of six or seven fiends, all curled up like woodlice with their hands clamped firmly over their ears.

'Philistines,' he remarked. 'Okay, Larry, Mike, last one to the bar gets them in.'

Three minutes or so after he'd gone, an assistant fiend with the toes and claws of a lizard crawled down the nozzle of the giant bagpipe and collapsed at rat-head's feet. He'd nearly perforated his own eardrums by sticking his claws in his ears, but that was a small price to pay.

'Stone me,' he muttered. 'That was bloody horrible, wasn't it, chief?'

'Pardon?'

'I said, that was bloody horrible, wasn't it?'

'Pardon?'

'I SAID THAT WAS BLOODY HORRIBLE, CHIEF, WASN'T IT?'

Rat-head shook himself and shuddered. 'You'll have to speak up,' he said.

Links Jotapian had found a helicopter.

We use the term loosely. What he'd in fact found was a sort of walking tree with hideous branches like dry bones and a goat's skull growing out of its left armpit; it had taken the eye of youthful enthusiasm to see that if you climbed up the thing's trunk and prodded it viciously with a penknife, it could be persuaded to whirl its branches fast enough to achieve a rotor effect. Sikorski wouldn't have approved, but no matter.

'Nothing as yet, Mr Lundqvist, over,' he reported into his two-way radio. 'Results so far are one-hundred-per-cent negative.'

'Keep looking, Links, he's down there somewhere.'

'Roger and out.' Links peered through a screen of small twigs and jabbed at the tree to go lower.

This is fun, Links said to himself, much more fun than school. I mean, compared to this, school sucks. I mean, this is, well, Life. He brushed cinders out of his eyes and lifted his feet clear to avoid the pincers of a bored-looking anthropomorphic lobster, positioned on the top of the horse's skull swimming pool area.

'Quark!'

Not, said something inside him, that it's not also a tad scary. Like, it's a very long way down, and this tree could get cramp in its branches any minute. And falling a long way is bad enough at the best of times, without taking into account some of the really weird things a guy can land on in this place.

'Quark quark!'

'Get down more, you sucker,' Links yelled into the knothole which he hoped was the tree's ear. 'And when you start feeling tired, for Chrissakes rustle a leaf or something.'

The tree wobbled. Links looked up, to see two seagulls roosting in the branches. They looked decidedly nauseous, as well they might.

'Shoo!' Links yelled, and waved his arms. 'Go lay an egg or something.'

'Quark.'

'You crazy dumb birds, you'll make this thing crash.'

'Quark.'

'Oh.'

His last thoughts, before he hit the frozen ice of the boating lake and disappeared in a cloud of ice-shards, spray and matchwood, were *Never mind, this is still better than school*. His first thoughts after the fiends had fished him out and pumped half a gallon of stagnant Styx water out of his lungs, were *On the other hand, there's a lot to be said for double geography*.

★ ★ ★

'And another thing,' said Machiavelli.

With a tremendous effort, the barfiend in the Hellza-Pop-Inn refreshment area ground his head round until he was facing his most regular customer. Sure thing, these were the Torments of Hell, and this was the spot reserved for married men who forsake their wives to go boozing every evening, and as a happily married fiend with a mortgage and three wonderful imps he reckoned those drunken bums deserved everything they got, even this; but, dammit, he was staff, not a customer, and he had to bear the brunt of it.

'All this acid rain,' Machiavelli was saying, 'and all these volcanoes and stuff, sodding up the weather. You aren't going to tell me that's all a coincidence, now are you?'

'Anything you say, Nick,' yawned the barfiend.

''Cos,' Machiavelli ground on, 'it's a matter of cold fact that on the day JFK was assassinated, the weather forecast for the whole of Texas was Mainly Dry, Some Light Cloud Clearing Early. But of course, that's what they *wanted* us all to think, because . . .'

The door opened, a man came in, sat down on a barstool and said, 'Hiya, Nick, what're you having?'

'And then,' Machiavelli went on, 'when you compare the records for seismic activity for the day of the Kennedy murder with the night of the Watergate break-in, you find that exactly the same level of activity was recorded in Chicopee Falls, Iowa, on both occasions, which makes you think.' He paused, as if trying to remember something he'd just heard, and then said, 'Dunnit?'

'Sure thing, Nick,' said the barfiend, polishing a glass. It just wasn't *fair*, he said to himself. All the inconsiderate husbands are out there in the back bar playing pool and getting pissed as rats, I'm stuck in here listening to the floorshow. They've gotta *do* something about this.

'Hiya, Nick,' the stranger repeated. 'Same again?'

Slowly, Machiavelli turned his head and stared.

'George?' he enquired.

'Been a long time, Nick,' replied Lucky George. 'I was very interested in what you were saying just now, by the way. I expect you were discussing that new book by that journalist bloke, the one who got himself killed not so long back. Bunnet or something, I think he was called.'

'What the hell are you doing here, George? I thought you'd—'

'I have, Nick, I have. And a Michelob and a toasted cheese sandwich for me,' he called through to the barfiend, 'when you've got a moment. So,' he said, turning back to Machiavelli, 'how's things with you?'

'Oh, all right,' Machiavelli replied, flushing slightly. 'They've made me a trusty now, actually.'

'Have they really,' George said. 'Well my goodness.'

'Yeah.' Machiavelli looked down. 'I got this job as a saloon bar bore.'

'And what's it like, Nick?'

'Boring.'

'Uh-huh. Anyway, I interrupted you. You were saying.'

'Was I?'

'Yes. About Bunnet's book.'

Machiavelli cringed slightly. 'Oh, that. His theory is,' he went on, without expression, eyes fixed on floor, 'that the Martians have been behind all the major political cover-ups of the post-war era, which they have stage-managed by clever manipulation of the climate. This also,' Machiavelli concluded wretchedly, 'accounts for deforestation, acid rain, the green-house effect . . .'

'I see.' George scratched his ear. 'Enjoy your work, do you?'

'Not a lot, no.'

George's beer and sandwich arrived – the latter slightly charred and served on the tines of a pitchfork – and he devoted his attention to them for a moment. Then he looked up.

'You know,' he said with his mouth full, 'funny, isn't it, the way things pan out.'

'Mmm.'

'I mean,' George said, 'think of what we were like back at school. Me the quiet, studious one. You the guy with the big ideas of everything you were going to do, big career in politics, get on the pundit circuit . . .'

Machiavelli made a noise; part agreement, part shame and part pain. Surreptitiously he bit a corner off George's sandwich.

'And yet here you are,' George went on, 'stuck in this dead-end job . . .'

'No pension to look forward to,' Machiavelli interjected.

'No fringe benefits.'

'No travel. No input into the fate of nations.'

'Bet you don't have your own reserved parking space.'

'The hours are bloody terrible, George.'

'I'll bet they are, Nick.'

Machiavelli sobbed slightly. 'It's not just the hours, George,' he snuffled, 'it's the hours and hours and *hours* of it that get me.'

'They would,' George agreed. 'I wouldn't stand for it.'

'Oh, I've got to stand,' Machiavelli replied unhappily. 'Stools are all reserved for the customers. I've worn this damn brass rail paper-thin, George, I could stick my finger through it any time I like.'

'Yes.' George blinked. 'What I meant was, I wouldn't put up with it.'

'You wouldn't?'

'Not if I were you, Nick. Not the Nick Machiavelli I used to know. By the way, seen anything of Kurt Lundqvist lately?'

Machiavelli shook his head. 'Last I heard,' he said, 'he was in business assassinating redundant gods. Good line of work to be in, I should say.'

'Yup.' George nodded. 'Good steady work.'

'Must be interesting.'

'Fascinating.'

'Lucky little sod,' said Machiavelli bitterly. 'When I think how he used to burst out blubbering every time we took his stiletto away from him.'

George sighed. 'And yet,' he said, 'look at him, and look at you. No, if I were you, Nick, I'd do something about it.'

Machiavelli looked up. There were the first ripe buds of tears sprouting at the edges of his bleared eyes. 'Yeah?' he said. 'Like what?'

George finished his sandwich and drained his glass. 'Well,' he said, 'first off, I'd start a diversion.'

'Mr Lundqvist.'

'Hi, Links.'

'He's not in here, Mr Lundqvist.'

Lundqvist looked down into the pit, narrowing his eyes. 'That so, Links?'

'I'm pretty sure of it, Mr Lundqvist.'

'You'd better come back up, then.'

Pause. 'I've got a slight problem with that, Mr Lundqvist.'

Lundqvist sighed. The term 'idiot', he decided, fitted Links Jotapian like the proverbial glove. 'I thought you might say that, Links,' he replied. 'That's why I got this rope.'

'Gee, Mr Lundqvist.'

Lundqvist unslung his rope and lowered it down into the pit. It was a very long rope, and when he'd paid it out completely and was just holding the end, he leant forward again and said, 'Got it?'

'Not yet exactly, boss.'

'Jeez, Links, how deep is this pit?'

'I think,' Links replied faintly, 'it's more sort of bottomless. Like, I am in fact still falling.'

'You are?'

'I believe so, yes, Mr Lundqvist. And Mr Lundqvist, there's all sorts of really weird things down here, like—'

'Fine.' Lundqvist stood for a moment, thinking. 'Links,' he said, 'I want you to think basic physical and mathematical theory.'

'I'm doing just that, Mr Lundqvist.'

'Okay. The universe is curved, right?'

'If you say so, skip.'

'In which case,' said Lundqvist, straightening his back and blowing the dust off his trouser knees, 'if you keep falling, then sooner or later you're gonna end up exactly where you started. The trick at that point is to grab hold of something and haul yourself clear. Is that okay with you, Links? Save me having to clamber down with ropes and things.'

'Anything you say, chief.'

'It may take some time, you realise.'

'I'm game, Mr Lundqvist.'

'Thousands of years, maybe.'

'No problem, Mr Lundqvist. I can catch up on my written coursework while I'm down here.'

'Good lad. Well, if you do get free in the next hour or so, I'll be around here somewhere.'

'Okay, Mr Lundqvist. Message received, over and out.'

And, of course, in Links' case, down as well. We down, we gone, in fact. Lundqvist stood up, stretched his cramped muscles, and walked off in the direction of the refreshment area.

'You ready, Nick?'

Machiavelli nodded grimly. Since resolving to do this thing, he'd been bought several large brandies and a double measure of the native infernal liqueur, Evil Spirit. The result was that he was bloody, bold, resolute and quite incapable of standing up on his own. Standing up was not, however, a prerequisite for what George had in mind.

'You got everything?'

'Think so, George. In fact . . .'

'Mm?'

'Looks like I got two of everything,' Machiavelli burbled. 'Looks remarkably like, acshlky, because . . .'

'That's fine, Nick,' said George firmly, 'that means you'll have a spare. Ready, you two?'

Two hovering seagulls dipped their wingtips in acknowledgement.

'Okay.' Lundqvist straightened his back, blew into the loudspeaker a couple of times to check it was working, and took a deep breath. The fires of EuroBosch glinted off his mirror sunglasses, miraculously unbroken.

Around him, six concentric circles of apprehensive fiends crouched slightly lower and wished they were somewhere else.

'OKAY, GEORGE,' Lundqvist amplified, 'I KNOW YOU'RE IN THERE. IT GOES WITHOUT SAYING I HAVE THE AREA SURROUNDED.'

Pause. No sound, except for the background screams, groans and hisses of hot iron on perpetually renewed flesh. You could have heard a twenty-foot molybdenum steel pin drop.

'GEORGE,' Lundqvist boomed, 'IT'S TIME TO CALL IT A DAY. COME OUT WITH YOUR HANDS . . .'

A figure appeared, silhouetted against the background flames, in the doorway of the refreshment area. Its hands were above its head. Lundqvist relaxed perceptibly, until he was only as tense as a steel hawser at breaking point.

'Hi,' the figure said.

The fiends edged back slightly. Sure thing, they were fiends, fiends are incapable of fear. It's just that there's no point in being bloody daft, that's all.

Lundqvist jumped up. 'C'mon, guys,' he yelled, 'what are you waiting for? Grab the sucker.'

A fiend turned its bird's head and gave him a look. 'What, us?' it cheeped.

'Yes.'

'What do you take us for, cocker bloody spaniels?'

Lundqvist glanced round the various shoulder-ornaments around him. 'Some of you,' he said, 'yes. Now get on with it.'

With a whimper, the fiends threw themselves forward and sprang at the outline in the doorway. When they were within about ten paces . . .

. . . The figure suddenly went *whoosh!* and burst into flames.

Screaming with frustrated rage, Lundqvist shoved his way through the throng of gibbering, terrified fiends and hurled himself at the human torch; who hit him quite hard in the stomach, winding him, and grinned.

'Hiya, Kurt,' he said. 'Long time no see.'

Lundqvist rubbed the ash from his eyelashes out of his eyes and gurgled. 'Machiavelli!' he howled. 'You'll burn in hell for this!'

Machiavelli shrugged a pair of incandescent shoulders. 'You really think so?' he said. 'We'll see.'

Meanwhile, Lucky George, who had spent the last ten minutes breaking open all the disposable cigarette lighters from the display pack behind the bar and emptying them over Machiavelli's head, grinned and slipped quietly away down the fire escape. Every permanent structure in the complex, by the way, has to have a fire escape, because of the building regulations. Where on earth the fire is supposed to escape to is anybody's guess.

A quick dash across the frozen lake brought George out at the foot of the Try-Your-Strength machine. A nice idea, this; you push hard against a huge lever shaped like a flute, which sends the marker on the dial of the machine up the calibrated scale. If you're strong enough, the marker hits a little bell, and assorted nightmarish fiends spring out of a trapdoor in the side of the machine and carry you off to everlasting torment. Serves you right for showing off.

A seagull floated down from the top of the machine, came in on the glide, turned into the slight breeze and dropped on to George's shoulder.

'Thanks,' George said.

'It waff noffing,' replied Mike through his badly singed beak. 'Pief of duff, onfe I'd got the matcheff lit.'

'Where is he now?'

The seagull turned its head. 'Ofer there by that horfe'f head fing,' he replied. 'No more idea of tracking than my granny'f cat.'

'Fine,' George said. 'Found the emergency exit yet?'

'Larry'f ftill looking. Af foon af he'f found it, we'll let you know.'

'Good stuff,' George replied. 'I'll go over there and make myself inconspicuous for a bit. Ciao.'

'Here, boff . . .' But George had gone, stepping quickly and silently across the scorched grass. The seagull shrugged.

'Big enuff and ugly enuff to look after himfelf,' he muttered, hopefully.

Over there turned out to be the activity described in the brochure as the ultimate in paintball games.

'That was good timing,' remarked the round-bodied, owl-headed gatefiend as George strolled in. 'Just in time for the next detail. You get the stuff from that shed over there, and they tell you what to do.'

'Thanks,' George replied.

You must remember this; a shed is but a shed, a hut is but a hut. The fundamental things apply, as time goes by. True, it was apparently constructed out of a giant mother-of-pearl pumpkin with a hole smashed in the side for a doorway, but inside it was pure Portakabin.

'What size?' demanded the attendant fiend.

'Dunno,' George replied. 'You're the man with the experienced eye, you tell me.'

'67D,' the fiend replied. 'You can change over there.'

He handed George a plastic carrier bag, and George retired into a sort of sub-shed, or cubicle, where he opened the bag and inspected the contents.

'Hey!' he said, with admiration in his voice. 'Now that's really something else.'

The bag contained a full-size replacement skin, with fitted scalp and all matching bits. He hoped very much that it was designed to be worn over one's existing skin. It was.

Sticking in the small of the skin's back was a dagger, driven in up to its hilt. There was no blade, fortuitously. George eased his way into the skin, settled his face as comfortably as possible into the mask, and stepped out of the cubicle.

'Okay,' said the attendant fiend. 'The rest of the detail are waiting outside.'

'Just going.'

'Hey.'

'Yes.'

'Forgotten something?'

'Have I?'

'In the rack,' said the fiend, pointing. 'Take your pick. Limit of three per competitor.'

From the rack, George selected a nine-inch stiletto, a Venetian-pattern cinquedea dagger and a short Flemish falchion. Then he stepped outside.

There were about thirty competitors, all dressed (to take them at face value, so to speak) in skins with knives stuck through them. Some of them were having a crafty last cigarette, others were fine-tuning their eyebrows, polishing their elbows, or just standing around tapping their feet. An eagle-headed fiend with talons for hands waved an umbrella in the air to attract their attention.

'Right, guys and girls,' it said. 'Just a few ground rules before we start. Now, we all want to have a good time, so the key thing to remember is, don't get carried away. Right?'

A few of the competitors nodded. The fiend continued.

'Now,' it said, 'the objective is, to stab as many of your fellow competitors repeatedly through the body and neck as you can within the allotted time without getting stabbed yourself. Now, for your comfort and convenience, we have to say No Head Wounds. The skins are perfectly safe under normal use, but in the past we have had a *few* problems with direct hits on the temples and the eyes. That still leaves you a hell of a lot of body surface to be going on with, and I'm sure you'll all agree that safe's better than sorry.'

A slight sussuration of background grumbling soon faded away, and the fiend continued:

'The only other thing we do insist on is, for obvious reasons, No Disembowelling. Now I realise that some of you here today will have perfectly genuine tribal, cultural or religious disembowelling traditions, and of course we respect that. So all of you are equipped with our very realistic plastic giblets, which fit neatly into the concealed pocket in the front of your skinsuits here –' The fiend demonstrated, pulling a yard of polythene colon out of his stomach and folding it away neatly. '– and you release those by simply pulling on the little blue ripcord which you'll find midway between the nipples on your skinsuit. Right, that's it, basically. Go out and have a bloody good time.'

The fiend blew a whistle, jumped sideways and curled up into a tight ball with its arms over its head. George hadn't been standing there for more than a twentieth of a second when the man who'd been on his immediate left threw away his cigarette, brandished a stagshorn-hilted Provençal hunting sword and jumped at him.

George sidestepped, landed a kick on his assailant's behind as he sailed by, and said, 'Boo!' Then he ran for it.

From the cover of an overturned table (in which a Florentine-pattern broadsword and two richly inlaid baselards were already embedded) he watched the game with growing fascination. After the first heady slugfest, which eliminated the duffers and the majority of the corporate entertainment crowd, the pace slowed down dramatically and the element of skill came to the fore.

Since there was sod-all natural cover, concealment and stalking were confined to pretending to be a hideously mangled corpse until your prospective victim had turned his back. That explained, George realised, the knife-hilt already inserted in the suit. The trick, apparently, was simply to count the number of hilts projecting out of each potential body. Two or more meant he was probably genuine. Once you'd got that far, approach with caution nevertheless, because a number of competitors (who'd clearly done this before) had taken the precaution of impaling themselves with one of their three permitted weapons before hitting the deck. Not, in George's opinion at least, strictly ethical, but presumably within the letter if not the spirit of the rules.

George was just bracing himself to step out from his hide and have a go when a body crumpled down over the side of his table and landed heavily in his lap. As it fell, its face-mask was pulled aside and George recognised the features of his lawyer, Mr Van Appin.

'Hello, Pete,' George said. 'What are you doing here?'

Mr Van Appin grimaced. 'I died,' he said.

George raised an eyebrow. 'I thought you had a special arrangement,' he said.

'I did,' Van Appin replied. 'I had a watertight agreement. Trouble is, I drafted it myself.'

George restrained a snigger. 'Bad move, that.'

'It was, rather,' the lawyer replied. 'Still, a fee's a fee, and when your best client comes to you and asks you to do a job, you don't turn round and say, Sorry, conflict of interests, try the guys down the road. That's not the way successful practices are built up, George.'

'Suppose not.'

Mr Van Appin shrugged. 'It's not so bad, actually,' he said. 'I've still got my, uh, other offices in the other centuries, so I can continue to service my existing client base, more or less, while being in a position to extend my operation to this exciting new catchment area down here. I mean, if you can't get business down here . . .'

'Pete,' George shook his head sadly. 'I think you're in for a bit of a shock if you think you're the only lawyer in these parts. I think you'll find there's rather a lot of them end up here. All of them, in fact, sooner or later.'

Mr Van Appin shrugged. 'So what?' he said. 'A little competition never did anybody any harm. So long, George.'

'Ciao, Pete.'

Mr Van Appin quivered and lay still, and George leant back against his table leg and watched for a few minutes. Two competitors had run each other through with Spanish rapiers at exactly the same moment and were arguing heatedly about who scored what.

'Excuse me.' George felt a light tap on his shoulder. He whirled round, saw a figure with no clothes on looming over him with some sort of poleaxe, and lunged with the cinquedea. The blade went through smoothly and out the other side.

'I think you're supposed to fall over or something,' George said.

'Actually,' replied the man, 'I'm just the linesman.'

'Oh.' George grinned awkwardly. 'Sorry about that.'

'No problem.' The linesman, who had just been transferred at his own request from the spectral engineers' corps, after a long and distinguished term of service as a captain of spectral warriors, shrugged and died. 'It happens to me all the time,' he said posthumously.

'Was there something?' George asked.

'I just wondered,' said the linesman, 'are you Lucky George Faust, by any chance?'

George nodded. 'Who wants to know?' he asked.

'It's just that Kurt Lundqvist's headed this way with a posse of heavily charred fiends,' the linesman replied. 'For reasons of my own which I won't bore you with, I don't fancy being around when he gets here. In fact,' the linesman added, 'things have worked out pretty damn near perfect, you killing me like that. I mean, stands to reason, even that vindictive little sod can't kill me if I'm dead already.'

'It was nothing.'

The linesman smiled, reached in his pocket and produced two credit cards, which he laid on his eyelids. 'It's cheaper this way if you're a regular customer,' he explained. 'Good luck.'

'Thanks.' George looked up and saw a seagull hovering overhead. It occurred to him that Larry wouldn't be able to recognise him in his skinsuit, so he stripped it off and dumped it.

'Hey,' said a competitor, who'd been stalking George for seven minutes with a two-foot balloch knife. 'That's cheating.'

'Nuts,' George replied, and swatted him over the head with a chair. He collapsed on the ground, muttering. The seagull perched on the edge of the table and ruffled its wing feathers with its beak.

'Sodding awful place for flying, this,' Larry remarked with his mouth full. 'Thermals in all the wrong places, because of all the fires.'

'Found it yet?'

'The emergency exit?' The seagull nodded its beak. 'Follow me.'

CHAPTER NINETEEN

There is much esoteric argument in contract killing circles about the greatest asset a hit-man can have. Some say, the new Steyr sniper's rifle with infra-red dot sights and integral sound suppressor. Others argue for a mint condition, first-issue Sykes-Fairbairn combat knife, while a significant minority gives its vote to the .50 calibre Desert Eagle with Hydrashock +P ammo and a Kassnar 'scope.

Kurt Lundqvist begs to differ. As far as he's concerned, the assassin most likely to succeed is the one who has rather more brains than can comfortably be fitted into a matchbox, all the matches having been removed. This, he realises, rules out about ninety-seven per cent of his professional colleagues, but so what? The last person to call him a reactionary elitist is now an integral part of the foundations of New York's celebrated Flatiron Building.

His sequence of thought, once he'd realised that Lucky George had slipped past him at the Hellza-Pop-Inn, was as follows:

Lucky George has escaped.

When it comes to getting away with it, Lucky George is about the best there is.

It is, therefore, pointless to try and stop Lucky George getting to the emergency exit. Far better to go directly to the emergency exit and wait for him there.

Slowly, with infinite labour, Links Jotapian drove the last crampon into the side of the pit and paused, dragging air into his creased lungs before hauling himself over the lip of the pit and on to solid ground.

Some escape, huh? First, he'd broken his fall by throwing his arms and legs out to their full extent, until the friction of his hands and feet against the toughened glass sides of the shaft had slowed him down and eventually stopped him.

Fair enough, but he couldn't stay wedged like that for ever; and as soon as he moved hand or foot, down he'd continue going.

Fortunately, however, he'd got with him his Kurt Lundqvist Limited Edition Adventurer's Kit. As a matter of cold fact, the production of this piece of merchandising hadn't been sanctioned by the man himself, which may account for the fact that the merchandiser now lives at the bottom of the Hudson River and wears concrete trainers. Nevertheless, the contents of the package (which collapses down to the size of a ballpoint pen, and is made, of course, in Korea) include such useful items as suction pads for hands and feet, crampons, a folding iceaxe, two hundred yards of gossamer-thin polymer cord (breaking point six tons) and a small rectangular key thing with no discernible purpose whatsoever.

One-handed opening of Kit, extraction of suction pad, donning of same and adhesion to the wall. It was then just a case of biffing in crampons and the long hard slog uphill. Still better than school.

'Mr Lundqvist.' The walkie-talkie was dead, squatted into a jumble of springs and wires by a collision with the shaft wall.

He dumped it – a month's waiting on tables at Baisbekian's Diner down the tubes, but one learns to be stoical under combat conditions – and applied his mind. Think like Lundqvist, and you'll know where he is.

Links cast an eye over the grounds of the Park, and concentrated. Lucky George is a pro, right? Where would a pro hide? Think Lesson Six. Answer: a pro will always try and find a crowd to mingle with, because the best camouflage is people. In fact, that's really the only reason Links could possibly imagine for their existing at all.

Various crowds dotted about the place. The queue for the Ferris Ears; no, too static. A pro tries not to remain stationary for more than five seconds in a combat zone. Therefore rule out also the milling throng waiting to go on the torture by outsize musical instruments, and the Knight Eaten By Dogs booth. There was quite a knot of people hanging about at the top of the campus, opposite the Ferris Ears, but that was also too conspicuous; the Toad Rides (up to the top of the sand dunes and back astride a giant red-spotted toad, conducted by a bear-headed fiend – fifty cents, children and perjurors half price) were closely supervised by fiends, and a pro doesn't go anywhere where there're too many guards looking at faces. There were a few passers-by waiting for Captain Beaky's next feed, but in the circumstances George probably wouldn't feel too comfortable hanging about round there. That left the paintball game.

Idiots rush in where demons fear to tread. Slowly and deliberately, Links checked his equipment. Night-stick; Smith & Wesson Model 686 in .357, loaded with Federal 160-grain jacketed hollow-points; handcuffs; ninja throwing-stars. Something else, but he couldn't remember what. Ah yes, that was it, and he had indeed remembered to put on clean underwear that morning. He pulled his balaclava down over his face and broke into a loping run.

Honest to God, his intention had been simply to find Lundqvist and help out. The thought of making the collar himself, alone and unassisted, wiping his mentor's eye and incidentally claiming the staggeringly huge reward, hadn't once cross his mind. But . . .

There he was, large as life, strolling hands in pockets towards the emergency exit, eating candy floss and with a seagull sitting on his shoulder. Lucky George, History's most wanted man. Hot *damn*!

With a cool smoothness born of countless hours of practice in front of the bathroom mirror, Links crouched, drew and assumed a perfect Weaver stance. Feeling for the bottom of the trigger, McGivern-style, he drew a fine bead on the side of George's head, took up the slack on the trigger and yelled, 'Freeze!'

George stopped, looked round at him and said, 'Me?'

'You.' Links half-closed his left eye, concentrating with all his being on the little strips of light either side of the foresight. 'One move and you're history, man.'

George raised an eyebrow. 'How do you mean?' he said.

The gyroscope inside Links' brain wobbled slightly. 'What?' he shouted.

'How do you mean, history? Do I become suddenly famous or something?'

'It means you get to be strictly past tense, man. Like, the late Lucky George, kinda thing. You get?'

'Late for what?'

'Your own funeral, sucker.' The foresight of the Smith wavered about; no matter how you try, you just can't combine repartee with marksmanship. Ask Oscar Wilde or anyone.

'Oh, I think they'd wait, don't you?' George replied. 'I mean, not much point having the wretched thing if there's nothing to bury. Mind you, if, for example, mine was at ten thirty and they'd got another one booked in at eleven fifteen, say, I can see there could be problems. Hearses double-parked, that sort of thing. Right, I'll bear that in mind.'

'Look . . .'

'On the other hand,' George continued through a mouthful of finely spun sugar, 'the same would go for weddings, wouldn't it, and think how many times the bride shows up late. Never causes a problem in the long run, though, does it? I think they make allowances for that sort of thing in the scheduling.'

'*Look* . . .'

George nodded upwards. 'There's a seagull hovering over your head with a ten-pound lead weight in its claws, had you noticed?'

Links sneered. 'You think I was born yesterday?' he said contemptuously.

George considered. 'Well,' he said, 'if you were you're pretty damn precocious, that's all I can say. I take it you're not fussed about the seagull?'

'*Look* . . .'

The lead weight fell, hitting Links on the back of the head. 'Thanks, Larry,' George called out. 'Right, can we please get on? This place is starting to get on my nerves.'

The emergency exit was just behind the Helmeted Dwarf, cunningly concealed in the gaping jaws of a twelve-foot-long polystyrene dragon. Just to ram the point home, there was also a big No Entry sign just above the dragon's head, qualified by the words *Except for Access*. After a final look round, George reached for the door handle . . .

. . . But the door swung out of its own accord, to reveal Lundqvist, standing behind his trusty .40 Glock. Before George had time to move at all, Lundqvist was through the door and the pistol's ugly snout was nuzzling his ear.

'Okay, George,' Lundqvist hissed. 'Lose the gulls. Now.'

George shrugged. 'You heard the man, guys. Go for a ride on the Lucky Dipper or something. I shan't be long.'

Mike flapped his wings and opened his beak to protest; but his bird's eye, hundreds of times more perceptive than its human equivalent, saw Lundqvist's finger move maybe a thousandth of an inch on the trigger and he subsided. 'Be seeing you, then,' he gulped, and bobbed away into the breeze. Larry remained where he was.

'You too, beakface,' Lundqvist growled.

'You'll pay for this,' the gull replied. 'One day.'

Lundqvist grinned. 'You reckon?'

Larry nodded. 'Maybe not tomorrow,' he said, 'maybe not this year. But sometime, somewhere, you'll be hanging out washing or cleaning the car, and then, *splat!* You just think about it, Lundqvist, that's all.'

With long, heavy wingbeats he dragged himself into the air, and soon was nothing but a white speck. Lundqvist let his breath go.

'You and me, George,' he said.

'You and me, Kurt. How about a nice game of backgammon?'

Lundqvist shook his head. 'Not this time, George,' he said. 'This time it's goodbye, for ever. Dead or alive, they said, remember.'

'I take it you're going for the lazy option.'

Lundqvist nodded. 'It's my back,' he said. 'Too much heavy lifting and I get shooting pains up my left side.'

George raised a quizzical eyebrow. 'Don't think dead's got a lot of significance here, Kurt,' he said, 'if you don't mind my saying so. Sort of goes with the territory, if you see what I—'

'No.' Lundqvist's grin widened. 'This thing's loaded with hollow-points filled with holy water.'

'I see,' said George. 'A water pistol.'

'Holy water,' Lundqvist repeated. 'Dead and exorcised in one shot. We call it one-stop termination. You ain't going *nowhere.*'

'How terribly clever.' George's face had on its patient, let's-humour-the-child expression, the very same one that had haunted Lundqvist's childhood nightmares. It meant, 'Kurt, I'm going to make you look an absolute plonker in front of the whole school,' and it had never once failed to deliver. Lundqvist quickly reviewed the situation in his mind and decided that for the first and last time, George was simply bluffing.

'So,' George said, 'you reckon you can just cold-bloodedly pull the trigger and blow my brains out, is that it?'

'Yup.'

The expression blossomed into a smile of tender contempt. 'Not unless you take the safety catch off first you can't,' he said.

In the split second it took Lundqvist to check, see that the safety catch was indeed off, and start squeezing off the shot, George had taken the reminder of his candy floss, stuck it up the barrel of the gun and kicked Lundqvist savagely in the nuts. With a howl that was five-per-cent pain and ninety-five-per-cent frustrated rage, Lundqvist slowly doubled up and sagged on to the ground.

'Never mind, Kurt,' said George, not unkindly, as he stepped over his fallen assailant. 'One of these days you'll get something right, just you wait and see.'

Then he stepped through the door and closed it behind him.

Thanks to his abstemious lifestyle and peak physical condition it took Lundqvist maybe a total of three minutes to recover sufficiently to haul himself up on to his feet, totter wildly and fall flat on his face, banging his forehead painfully on a sharp stone. Which only goes to show; had he ruined his health with alcohol, rich foods and dissipation he'd never have been fit enough to get beaten up in the first place.

Once he'd managed to get his legs working again, he pulled the candy-floss stick out of the muzzle of his gun, kicked open the emergency exit door, and burst through.

Circumstances alter cases. None of that hyper-cautious cat-like stealth one associates with the covert operations pro – flattening oneself against walls, darting in and out of shadows and leaping round corners in a copybook FBI crouch. As soon as he was through the door, he simply ran as fast as he could down the tunnel, firing wildly into the darkness and shouting,

'You bastard, I'm gonna rip your frigging lungs out!' at the top of his voice.

Which is why he didn't notice the pillar; not, at least, until it connected with his chin.

Thirty seconds later, Lucky George emerged from behind the pillar, prodded Lundqvist's head with his foot to make sure he was indeed fast asleep, bent down, picked up the pistol and slipped it in his pocket. A more punctilious man would have written out a receipt, but George was in a hurry.

A length of parcel string and a few Boy Scout knots later, he stood up, looked both ways along the tunnel, switched on Lundqvist's torch (which the silly man had forgotten all about in his excitement) and strolled on up the tunnel, whistling.

Four hundred yards or so later, he came to a T-junction. There were helpful signs painted on the wall, thus:

> HELL →
> ←DAMNATION
> ←ADMINISTRATION

Synonyms, George thought, but never mind. He turned left.

Three hundred yards brought him to a lift. Why walk, he said to himself, when you can ride?

The trick is, not to go down.

The doors slid open, revealing the usual selection of buttons, labelled:

> PENTHOUSE
> CENTRAL ADMIN
> ACCOUNTS
> CAFETERIA
> BOILER ROOM
> MEZZANINE
> GROUND
> HELL FIRE

DAMNATION
FILE STORE

The red light was on opposite GROUND. As for the rest; CAFETERIA sounded nice, MEZZANINE was anybody's guess, and FILE STORE sent a shiver oscillating through his central nervous system. He was about to press CAFETERIA when something inside him coughed discreetly and whispered, *Try the boiler room.*

George rationalised. Well, why not? The words conjured up a picture of a big, noisy, dark jungle of pipes and machines, the sort of place you could hide in for ages with no chance of anybody finding you; a good place to pause, regroup and work out what to do next.

George wasn't convinced. What the devil do I want to go to the boiler room for? Sounds absolutely awful. He reached out to prod CAFETERIA, but his finger froze, a few thousandths of an inch away from contact.

Try the boiler room.

The philosopher Socrates, so tradition has it, played host to an inner voice, accustomed to telling him what to do in moments of indecision. History tells us that Socrates was found guilty on trumped-up charges and executed by poison, but maybe we don't have all the facts. Maybe, a nanosecond before drinking the hemlock, Socrates asked his inner voice *What the fuck have you gone and got me into, peanut-brain?* and the inner voice explained it all in words of one syllable, allowing the great philosopher to die with a huge cocky grin frozen all over his face.

Maybe there's a coffee machine in the boiler room.

He lowered his finger and pressed the appropriate button, closing the lift door.

Blessed are the pure in heart, for they shall see God.

Blessed are the jammy bastards, for they shall see God without an appointment.

★ ★ ★

It was dark in the boiler room, as he'd predicted. It was also very quiet, and very cold. All the surfaces were thick with dust. All in all, Lucky George decided, he'd been in more convivial graves. Which was, incidentally, true.

There were pipes, just as in his mental picture, and machines. Enormous machines, painted matt black enamel with heavy solid brass fittings, very old-fashioned, high quality looking. No plastic anywhere; steel, brass and the occasional glass cover, white enamel dial, engraved brass control panel. None of the machines appeared to be switched on. The place had the look of a major vintage traction engine rally five minutes after the beer tent has opened.

George had been wandering about for perhaps ten minutes or so (not that Time seemed a particularly useful concept in a place like this, like an umbrella at the bottom of the sea) when he thought he heard a tiny, distant screaming noise, like a very small, fast lathe. He walked towards it.

It was a long walk. The place was, he realised, absolutely huge, and full of these enormous, silent pieces of hardware; each one, he noticed curiously, apparently different. He hadn't the faintest idea what any of them were. Ah, but if only he could get in here with a small crane and a fleet of big lorries, there was an absolute fortune in scrap value alone.

If wishes were pantechnicons, beggars would invest heavily in offshore roll-up unit trusts. George dismissed the thought from his mind, because the light and the noise were getting closer. Still a hell of a long way away, though. George's feet were beginning to hurt.

Scree-ee-ee-eee. Pause. *Scree-ee-yoww-ee*. Unmistakable sound of cutting metal. Someone was making something.

Screee-ee-ee

Screeeeee-ee-yowwww-eee

Screee-eeeee

'Bugger!'

A minuscule voice, ever so far away. George stopped dead in his tracks and listened, but all he could hear was the sound of the lathe, like the shriek of an hysterical elf.

Blessed are the bone idle, for they shall stand and watch other people working.

George walked on towards the noise.

Had Links Jotapian been there, instead of lying on his back sleeping the sleep of the mildly concussed, he'd have witnessed a near perfect exhibition of the art of getting out of being tied up without cutting your wrists on the string.

Having woken up, assessed the position and sworn a lot, Lundqvist used his feet to back himself up against the wall. No help there; the sides were smooth as glass, so no useful rocky outcrops to saw through the rope on.

String professionally tight, so no percentage in curling the hands up small in the hope of slipping them through.

Never mind. The seasoned campaigner anticipates this sort of thing. On the back of Lundqvist's trouser belt was a thing like a big plastic button. In fact, this was a snap-on cover, easily flicked off with the fingernails, underneath which was a tiny sliver of scalpel blade fixed lengthways into the belt on a rivet. Nothing easier than to fray the rope up against that a few times and then gently ease it apart.

Cheating? In the trade, they call it materiel superiority.

A little later Lundqvist stood up, marshalled his limbs into some semblance of discipline and trudged up the corridor. He knew without being told that he was on a hiding to nothing. He was lost, unarmed, punch-drunk and thoroughly demoralised. High time he retired, made way for all those up and coming youngsters who were the hope of the profession for the years to come.

Absolutely. Just as soon as he'd found Lucky bloody George and disembowelled him with his bare hands, he'd pack the whole thing in, buy a little bungalow somewhere and grow lupins. Until then, the idea of giving up was unthinkable. It would be like going on a round-the-world cruise knowing you'd left the oven on.

In due course he came to a lift.

> PENTHOUSE
> CENTRAL ADMIN
> ACCOUNTS
> CAFETERIA
> BOILER ROOM
> MEZZANINE
> GROUND
> HELL FIRE
> DAMNATION
> FILE STORE

A likely story. You don't get presented with the Academy of Elite Forces' coveted Gold Silencer Award three years in succession ('First of all I'd like to thank my victims, without whom . . .') unless you can recognise a supernaturally induced hologram when you see one. If the wretched thing had had TRAP over the door in three-foot-high neon letters, it couldn't have been more obvious.

On the other hand, what the hell? He walked in, pressed a button at random, and folded his arms.

Screee-eee-eeeeee-ee-clunk.

'Anybody home?'

George waited for a moment, listening to his voice echoing around the galleries of silent ironmongery until it was soaked up in the dust-insulated vastness. If there was anybody there, they were either lying in wait, too engrossed in what they were doing to hear, or listening to something on headphones.

Well, if they were lying in wait, they'd had plenty of opportunities by now. He walked on.

Scree-eee-ee-scrinklescrinklescrinkle.

'Oh sod!'

The light suddenly vanished, blocked out by the bulk of an enormous machine. Slowly, feeling his intestines practising left-hand clove hitches, George edged round the machine, and suddenly saw . . .

A workbench, illuminated by a low, brilliant lamp, throwing out the special brand of extra white, hard light that you need if you're dealing with tolerances of fractions of a millimetre. Around the bench were racks of tools – George assumed they were tools; most of them he'd never seen anything like before, even in the sort of dreams that would have had Freud under a cold shower in three seconds flat – but he knew they were tools. They had that worn, shiny, reliable look, that says *I know what I'm doing even if you don't*. Mounted in the centre of the bench was this really weird lathe; it wasn't big, but it seemed to ooze power, as if once you'd worked out how to use it you could make absolutely anything at all on it. And, George realised, it was transparent. In fact, that was where the light was coming from, not the poxy 100-watt bulb in the anglepoise. Light was seeping out from it in all directions, as through a window or the crack under a door. Light from where, you really didn't want to know.

Behind the bench was a man; short, round, wearing a brown overall and a cap with a few wisps of untidy grey hair curling out under its brim like Russian vine, his face consisting of a nosetip and a mouth huddled in the shelter of an enormous pair of thick-lensed spectacles. In one hand, he held a Vernier caliper, while with the other he was scratching his neck, just behind the ear.

'Hullo, George,' the man said. 'You found your way here all right, then.'

George nodded. Never seen this guy before in my life, he thought. Something funny here.

He glanced down at the lathe. In the jaws of the chuck he could see a tiny, er, *thing*, a component, a bit out of something;

minute, hard, shiny with the magnificent hard gleam of newly turned steel, that beautiful clarity of tone that makes polished silver look like fog. Whatever it was, it had been machined to perfection. It seemed to sing in the lathe.

'Bloody thing,' said the man.

'Problem?'

The man nodded. 'Taken too much off, haven't I? Useless. Have to start again.' He opened the chuck, lifted the thing out and tossed it contemptuously into the scrap bucket under the bench. 'Me own fault,' he said, grinning. 'In too much of a rush, as per usual.'

'Been doing it long?'

'Twenty-three years,' the man replied, 'not a big job, really.' Already, he had a new blank of material in the jaws and was winding the chuck. 'Don't suppose it'll take me much longer to turn up another one.'

'I . . .' George began, and then stopped. 'What was it?' he asked.

The man looked up from his work. 'Ratchet collar for the main inner bearing,' he replied. 'Fits on the main driveshaft, stops the auto-index from getting out of synch.'

'Ah.'

''Cos,' the man went on, smiling, 'if that gets out of sequence, your whole locator drive's up the spout, and you'll be having Wednesdays for Tuesdays and Sundays midweek.'

'Ah.'

'Yeah.' The man nodded. 'It's a good life if you don't weaken,' he added, and measured something.

'Sorry,' George said, 'am I disturbing you, because . . .'

The man shook his head. 'Glad of the company,' he replied. 'Gets a bit lonely up here, fiddlearsing about all day long. You getting on all right?'

'I suppose so. Can I hold anything, or pass you things?'

'If you like.' The man scribed a line with an invisibly thin scriber. 'Four hundred yards got to come off that,' he said.

'Should be all right so long as we go nice and steady.' He stooped down and began rummaging in a box.

'Four hundred yards.'

The man nodded. 'I know,' he said. 'Bloody fine tolerances, bugger all margin of error.'

Something clicked in George's mind. It wasn't Time that was weird here, it was Scale. Everything here was much, much bigger than it looked, but the immensity of the place created its own unique perspectives. He'd probably been standing here for five years already.

'Look at the bloody mess this place is in,' the man said, waving vaguely. 'The time I waste, looking for things. Soon as I've done this job, I've got to have a bloody good tidy-up.'

George licked his lips, which were suddenly dry. 'Excuse me asking,' he said, 'but who exactly are you?'

The man looked up. 'Me?' he said. George nodded. With a flick of his finger, the man switched on the lathe. Thousands of feet below, George just knew, the faint, scarcely perceptible noise it made was midsummer thunder.

'Well,' the man said, 'the job description is General Operative (Dilapidations).'

'I see.'

'Bit of a mouthful,' the man said.

George nodded. 'Usually abbreviated, I suppose.'

'That's the idea.'

'Right.' George took a deep breath. 'I've been wanting to meet you for a long time,' he said.

General Operative (Dilapidations), better known by the handy acronym.

Lundqvist stopped dead in his tracks. He could feel the point needle-sharp against the skin of his neck; that particularly vulnerable spot between the collar bones.

'G'day,' said the angel.

Lundqvist thought about edging backwards, but knew that

the point would follow him. Angel or no angel, this guy knew his trade.

At least, Lundqvist realised, I know where I am now.

'I thought,' he said, looking down the runway of fine blued steel that ran from his neck to the angel's hand, 'you people were supposed to be equipped with flaming swords.'

The angel gave him a look. 'Stone the crows, sport,' he said. 'What d'you think this is, a flamin' letter opener?'

'Hi, God,' said Lucky George.

'Could you just pass me that file?' God replied. 'Not that one, the little Swiss job with the red handle. Ta.'

George looked down the rack, saw something like an extra-thin hair with the appropriate coloured handle, and passed it over. God pushed his glasses back up his nose, closed one eye and swept the file feather-light over the surface of the metal.

'Bugger,' he said. 'Pressed too hard. Look, bloody great graunch-marks all over the thing. Have to stone it all off and start again.' He sighed, and reached for an atom-thin whetstone. 'I must be having one of those days,' he said.

George replaced the file in the rack. 'Dilapidations?' he asked.

The man nodded. 'That means fixing things,' he said. 'It's what I mostly do these days. You made it, they said to me, you damn well fix it when it plays up. Fair enough, I suppose. Means I can put in a few mods here and there, whenever I see something I can improve.' He pointed at the component in the chuck. 'Like this, frinstance.'

George smiled weakly. 'You did say what it was,' he said, 'but I'm afraid I've forgotten.'

'Pretty simple, really,' God replied. 'Time, right? Your basic seven-day week revolves on a central spindle. Each day is indexed into position by a lifting hand driving a ratchet, and then it's locked in place by a spring-loaded pawl locating in a groove, see? Absolutely basic design.'

George nodded helplessly. Somehow or other, he understood, vaguely.

The man shook his head. 'Bloody awful,' he said. 'Makes me ashamed every time I think of it. All it needs is for the bearing the cylinder rides on to wear a bit, and the whole thing grinds to a halt.'

'And has it?'

'Bound to. This is the third one I've had to make so far, and the bloody thing's scarcely run in.'

George stared. 'You mean the World?' he said.

'The Universe,' God replied. 'Shouldn't have components like this packing up already. Should be good for another forty billion years at least, with a bit of lube and a good clean now and again, before I've got to start replacing the bearings. Must've got it wrong somewhere, don't you think?'

George remained silent. Not for him to say, he reckoned.

'So,' God continued, rubbing his nose with the back of his hand, 'this time I'm making the bugger out of sixteen-gauge chronium carbide, and I'm going to case-harden it again before it goes back in, making sure there's no soft spots where I've cut too deep. If that doesn't do it, then stuff it.'

He increased the lathe speed slightly and the cutter screee'd across the surface, throwing out tiny specks of swarf-like powdered stars.

'Leap year,' George said.

'You got it,' the man replied. 'That's only when it gets really bad, mind you, when the whole poxy year gets out of sequence. A little bit like that, you see, it can bugger up the whole sodding thing in no time at all.'

'I suppose so.'

'No suppose about it.' Screeeee, went the lathe. Tiny flecks of ground material, so small as to float in the air, drifted down, out through the air conditioning system and onwards through the galaxy, tails burning, frightening the living daylights out of superstitious princes. 'Your Time, see, that's your major motive force. If your Time goes wrong, everything goes wrong. Bits get out of place, components get all graunched and burred up, things fall apart, the centre cannot hold . . .'

'Entropy,' said George.

'Poncy name for it, yeah.' God was silent for a moment, brooding. 'This ought to do the trick. Just have to try it and see, won't we?'

He turned up the lathe speed until the component disappeared in a white blur, and screee'd for a while. From time to time, he stopped, measured, tutted, scratched his ear, started again. The surface of the Thing was so smooth it seemed to evade eyesight, like wet soap in a bath.

'Well now, George mate,' God said, miking the component up for the tenth or eleventh time, 'I suppose we ought to be getting you back to the old hot spot in a minute.' He closed one eye and squinted through his right spectacle lens at the micrometer dial. 'Another gnat's nibble still to go,' he sighed. 'Always takes longer than you think, this last bit.'

George stayed where he was, immobilised. For the first time in his life, he didn't know what to do. Not a nice feeling, but somehow it didn't hurt. This was because he knew the man would do the right thing.

'Can't have people breaking out all over the place,' God went on. 'Shocking. Got to do something about it. Just pass me that small oilcan, the one on your left. No, the other one. Thanks.'

'So,' George said (and the trumpets all sounded for him on the other side) 'you're having a problem with Time, are you?'

The man laughed. 'You can say that again,' he said. 'Bloody old stuff. Biggest blessed nuisance in the whole set-up. Here, what d'you make that? My eyes are getting so bad, it's terrible sometimes.'

George peered. He could just about make out the dial, but no calibrations whatsoever.

'I make it point three six four,' said God.

'Yup.'

'Ta. I mean,' he went on, 'this horrible old thing's the easy bit. Take out the knackered part, turn up a new one, slap it in, job done. It's what to do with all the waste stuff that's the problem.'

George nodded. He'd worked that out for himself, although by what logical route he had no idea. 'Temporal waste,' he said. 'Nasty.'

'Diabolical.' God sighed. 'Twenty-four hours more of it every day, leaking like buggery and stinking the place out. Can't burn it, can't bury it, doesn't dissolve in anything. You're stuck with it.'

'And,' George interrupted, 'it's not as if there's an endless supply of it to start with.'

God groaned. 'Don't remind me,' he said. 'Daftest thing I ever did, making the thing run on fossil fuel. Should've known better.'

'Easy mistake to make.'

'Daft mistake to make.' God switched off the lathe and lifted out the finished part. 'It's not brilliant,' he said, 'but it'll have to do. Pass me that duster, will you?'

'In other words,' George went on, 'on the one hand you've got too much waste time, and on the other, not enough raw material.' He paused, fully aware of the awesome nature of his position. 'Doesn't that suggest something to you?' he said quietly.

God looked at him.

'Like,' he forced himself to continue, 'recycling?'

God laughed. 'Sure,' he said. 'If I could. But I can't, can I?'

This is it, George old son. So go for it. 'Yes you can,' he heard himself say. 'No trouble.'

God looked at him again, and Hell was much, much better. In Hell, they only beat you up. Reflected in the lenses of God's spectacles, George could see himself; the truth, the real thing. Could have been worse, he realised, but still not a pleasant thing to happen to anybody, the sum total of your being splashed like a fly on a windscreen.

'No trouble,' he repeated. 'It works like this.'

CHAPTER TWENTY

'Freeze!'
        Bleary eyed and thoroughly narked, Lundqvist swung the door open and slouched through.

'Knock it off, Links,' he sighed wearily, 'it's me.'

'Oh.' Links Jotapian looked down at the revolver in his hand, and then at his mentor. 'You got him, then?'

'No.'

There was a moment's silence. The faint tinkling audible to the extra-perceptive ear was the sound of shattering dreams. 'You mean you *didn't* get him?'

'Mmm. Is there a bar round here, Links? I could murder a drink.'

'But.' Links stared. 'You must have got him, Mr Lundqvist. Kurt Lundqvist always gets his fiend.'

'Not this time, son. Now be a good boy and go away.'

Jotapian's lower lip quivered ominously. 'You let him escape?' A thought occurred to him. 'I get it. So's he'll lead us to where he's got the money stashed. Sorry, Mr Lundqvist, I should've guessed.'

Lundqvist gave him a cold look. 'What money, Links? There isn't any money. The little scumbag just escaped, that's all.'

'And you're just walking away?'

'You got it.'

Links pulled himself together with an effort, and stuck out his chest, what there was of it. 'No, Mr Lundqvist. He may have gotten away from you. He ain't gonna get away from me.' He jammed his hand down on the butt of his revolver, jerked his chin up high and walked resolutely through the doorway. There was a thump.

'It opens the other way, Links,' Lundqvist said. 'To open it, you pull.'

'Okay, Mr Lundqvist.' Pause. 'Mr Lundqvist?'

'Yes?'

'You *sure* you're not coming?'

'Sure, Links.' Lundqvist sat down on a rock, pulled off his left boot and massaged his foot. The lift had been out of order and it was a very, very long way down by the stairs.

'Okay, boss,' Links said. He tried not to let too much irony creep into the word 'boss'. 'Be seeing you around, then.'

He pulled on the door, banged his nose, and was gone. For a moment Lundqvist sat motionless, thinking.

The boy was his apprentice. In his charge. His responsibility. It was hard going in there.

On the other hand . . . His roving eye lit on the sign outside the Hellza-Pop-Inn; bright enough to be coming out the other side of garish, but broadly hinting that strong liquor was kept on the premises.

The boy's never going to learn for himself if you keep him wrapped up in cotton wool all the time.

But . . .

He got up, put on his boot and pulled open the door.

'Links,' he yelled down the corridor.

'Yes, Mr Lundqvist?'

Kurt Lundqvist considered for a moment. 'When he hits you, try and roll with the punch. Sometimes it helps.'

He closed the door and went to the bar.

'I dunno,' said God, reaching for an old envelope and a stub of pencil. 'Could work, I suppose.'

George held his breath. Maybe Lucky George was the right name for him, and he'd been riding his luck all these years. But luck's rather like sponge cake; it's always better if you make it yourself.

'Tricky,' said God. 'I mean, you'd have to go a bit steady. One slip and, well . . .'

'I didn't say it was easy,' George interrupted. 'I said it was possible. There's a difference.'

God grinned. 'Just go through it again one more time,' he said, 'make sure I've got it straight in my mind.'

'Okay.' George took a deep breath. 'The problem with recycling Time,' he said, 'is that it's got History engraved all over it. You can't melt down Time without losing History. You lose History, nobody has the faintest idea who they are, or what's going on. Okay so far?'

God nodded.

'Well then,' said George, 'my idea is, you skim all the History off in thin sheets, using something like a very fine-bladed bandsaw. You've got something that can do the job?'

'Somewhere,' God replied. 'There's all sorts of bits and pieces out there. Like I said, one of these days I've got to have a really good tidy-up in here.'

'That's fine,' George said. 'So, you slice off the top three or four thousandths of an inch, leaving you with sort of tin foil stuff with all the History on. You can roll that up and store it in a fraction of the space you're using at the moment. The rest you melt down and use again. That's all there is to it.'

God took off his glasses and polished them on his sleeve.

'Still going to run out one day, though, isn't it?' he said. 'You're just putting off the problem, that's all.'

'Ah,' George replied. 'That's where the clever bit comes in, the new technology and all that. You set things up so that in future, the History foil is split off as soon as it's been processed, right? The rest of the stuff goes straight back in the melt. The history foil is then copied on to disc – it's absolutely amazing how much stuff you can get on a single disc these days – and then the foil can be melted down too. As and when you've got a moment, you can transfer the archives on to disc as well. Problem solved.'

'Hmm.'

George waited.

'Well,' God said at last, slowly unwrapping a peppermint, 'there are still problems. Like, suppose when I was cutting off the foil, my hand slipped or something and a great chunk of History got torn or buggered up.'

'Well . . .'

'Or what about when it's actually on the discs? Bits could get wiped. It happens.'

'Well . . .'

'Take a case in point,' God went on. 'The whole bit where you sell your soul to Them Buggers might get somehow lost. Think about it. We'd have to turn you loose, wouldn't we? Couldn't keep you banged up if what you did never happened. And if it's not in History, it never happened, did it?'

George opened both eyes wide. 'Do you know,' he said, 'that thought honestly never once crossed my mind.'

God laughed. 'I'll believe you,' he chuckled. 'Thousands wouldn't.'

Hard to gauge exactly how many years, or tens of years, passed in the world of mortal men while God crunched up his peppermint and drew faint, deft squiggles on the back of the envelope. George could feel time passing, just as you can feel lorries going by on the main road a mile away. Nothing to worry about, in context.

'It's a bit crude, though,' God said at last. 'It's not the way I'd have wanted to do it, really. In the first place, I mean.'

George shrugged. 'In the first place,' he said casually, 'was the Word, remember? You can only do your best with the materials available.'

God nodded his head slowly. 'Damn silly word it was, too,' he said. 'Took me a hell of a time just to get a good edge on it. Between me and you and these four walls,' he added confidentially, 'I've always reckoned the daft beggars must've spelt it wrong.'

'Get away.'

'Straight up.' God drew a few more squiggles, shrugged his shoulders and laid down the pencil. 'All right,' he said, 'I'll give it a go. Why not?'

'That's the spirit.'

'Yeah. And those bits of History we were talking about just now.'

'Yes?'

'Well.' God looked away, into the darkness of the boiler room. 'Trouble is, my old eyes aren't what they used to be. Could easily muck up quite a big bit before I knew what I'd done. And then where would we be?'

'Exactly.'

'In fact. I've got this horrible feeling that might just happen.'

'Just a feeling?'

'Virtual certainty.' God winked. 'On your way, George. I've enjoyed having a natter like this.'

'Me too.'

'Yeah.' God turned, picked up another envelope and sharpened his pencil. 'Mind how you go.'

In the darkness, Links froze. His hand tightened on the butt of his revolver.

There was something out there. He could smell the danger. Very slowly, he drew the gun and thumbed back the hammer.

A soft sound, like a footfall on a million years of dust. He opened his eyes wide, trying to make the most of each stray photon.

'Jerome?'

Inside him his heart turned to water. Suddenly the gun became heavy, far too heavy to hold. His arms sagged, as rigid as over-cooked tagliatelli.

'You there, Jerome?'

'Yes, Mom,' Links whimpered.

'Jerome Jotapian, I've been looking all over for you. What do you mean by sneaking out like that and worrying us all near to death?'

'Sorry, Mom.'

A shape loomed up in the darkness. Instinctively, Links shrank back.

'You just wait till your Pa gets home,' said Mrs Jotapian.

CHAPTER
TWENTY-ONE

'Freeze!'
　　　'Piss off.'
'Oh.'

Helen of Troy frowned. She'd been to great trouble to acquire the small, pearl-handled automatic, more trouble still to get here, and virtually infinite pains to sneak up on Lundqvist in the bar and jam the muzzle of the gun into his ear. A girl likes to be appreciated.

'You do realise,' she said huffily, 'that this is a *gun* I'm—'

'Yeah,' Lundqvist sighed, 'sure. To be precise, it's a .25 Bauer, chrome finish, early seventies at a guess, pearl grips and machine engraving on the rear of the slide. I imagine you chose it to go with your earrings.'

Helen was impressed. 'You can tell all that from feeling it in your ear?'

'Lady,' Lundqvist replied with dignity, 'I've had more pieces shoved up my ear than you've had men. The difference is, I can tell them apart in the dark.'

'Pig.'

Helen sat down on a bar stool. 'It's still a gun,' she said, 'and if you make a move, I'll pull the trigger. Understood?'

'I was way ahead of you.'

'Fine.' With her left hand, Helen grabbed a handful of peanuts from the dish on the bar and gobbled them. Seven hours since she'd last eaten, not counting the biscuits on the plane. 'So what have you done with him?'

Lundqvist laughed bitterly. 'What have *I* done with *him*? Get outa here, will you? It's been a long day.'

Helen caught her breath. 'You mean he escaped?'

Lundqvist nodded. It takes practice to nod safely with a loaded gun in your ear, but Lundqvist had the experience. 'Yeah,' he said. 'If you're buying, mine's a very large Jack Daniels, no ice. If not, get lost.'

'You're sure he escaped?'

Lundqvist allowed himself a wry smile. 'Well,' he said, 'he escaped from *me*. What became of him after that is entirely his own problem.'

'You mean he's in danger?' Helen demanded angrily. 'And you're just sitting drinking?'

'I'm trying to drink. Idiots come and shove iron in my ears, but I guess I'll have to learn to take that sort of thing in my stride.'

'Men!'

Helen finished the peanuts, then nudged a little harder with the gun. 'If you don't find him this instant, I'll shoot you.'

A look of utter contempt flitted across Lundqvist's face, wiping its feet on his eyebrows as it passed. 'I get you,' he said. 'First you'll shoot me if I don't lay off, now you'll shoot me unless I find him. Consistency's not a big thing with you, right?'

'Just shut up and get on with it.'

'Anything you say, sister. Just one more drink, and I'll be—'

'Now.' By way of reinforcing her remarks, Helen pressed what she took to be the safety catch. The net effect was to send the magazine shooting out of the bottom of the gun into the residue of Lundqvist's Jack Daniels. He fished it out, made a vulgar noise and handed it to her.

'Does this mean you won't help me?' she said.

'Yeah.'

'Please?'

Lundqvist lifted his glass to his face, noticing the thin scum of gun oil on the meniscus just in time. He sighed, and waved to the barman.

'I think you're *mean*,' said Helen, and started to cry. Everyone in the bar turned their heads and stared.

'All *right*,' Lundqvist snapped. 'Whatever you like. Just for the love of God shut up that goddamn . . .'

'Sniff.'

'. . . Sniffling.'

'And no going arresting him when we do find him?'

Lundqvist chuckled bitterly. 'Me?' he said. 'Arrest anybody? That'll be the day.'

They stopped outside the emergency exit. 'He went in there?' Helen demanded. Lundqvist nodded, sat down on the grass and started to make a daisy chain.

'Come on,' said Helen impatiently. 'What're you waiting for?'

'Lady.' Lundqvist didn't look up. 'If you want to shoot me, first draw back the slide with your left hand, holding the pistol firmly in your right. When the slide is back against the stop, let go smoothly so as not to jam the feed, and release the safety catch, which is the small lever above the back of the grip on the left hand side. Your gun is now ready to fire. Do not pull the trigger; rather, squeeze firmly but smoothly in one continuous movement. I've been in there once and that'll do me fine.'

'Chicken.'

Lundqvist nodded, pulled up a dandelion and stuck it behind his ear.

'I'll start crying again.'

'Be my guest.'

Just then, Hieronymus Bosch hurried by clutching a portable telephone, flung open the door and shot through. Close behind him, running lopsided because of the heavy toolbox he had with him and looking rather charred round the edges, was Niccolò Machiavelli. Following him at a rather longer interval came Christopher Columbus, Hamlet Prince of Denmark, Leonardo da Vinci, William Caxton, two seagulls, Don Juan, Albrecht Dürer, Julius Vanderdecker, Martin Luther, Don Quixote de la Mancha wearing odd socks, Sir Thomas Malory and others too numerous to particularise. The painter Botticelli, bringing up the rear, called out, 'Wotcher, Nellie, do me another sitting sometime?' as he dashed past. All of them were carrying big dufflebags.

The door slammed.

'I take it you don't need me any more,' Lundqvist sighed. He had finished his daisy chain, and lowered it gingerly over his head. It stuck around his ears.

'No,' Helen replied distantly. 'Thanks.'

'Glad to be of service,' said Lundqvist, and returned to the bar.

The Marketing Director of Hell Holdings plc stood back, admiring his handiwork and sucking his thumb where he'd hit it with the hammer. The notice wasn't quite straight, but nailing bits of plywood to polystyrene trees wasn't exactly his thing. Not bad for a beginner.

GALA NIGHT!!!

There is no universally accepted definition of a gala night, except that it costs more to go in. He ran his eye down the list of advertised attractions and nodded his head contentedly.

BIRD-HEADED FIENDS!!

TORMENTS OF THE DAMNED!!!
UNIMAGINABLE HORRORS!!!!
OX-ROAST AND MAMMOTH CAR BOOT SALE!!!!!

He hesitated for a moment. At the time it had seemed pretty neat, but now he actually saw it in place, perhaps it lacked a certain culminating zing. Taking a thick-nibbed marker pen from his pocket, he wrote in:

CONGA!!!!!!

at the bottom, grinned and turned to depart. Just then the tree caught fire. It burned without being consumed, predictably enough. Not so the notice, which vanished in a curl of ash.

Why couldn't the old fool use the phone like everybody else?

Imagine Time.

There is no way you possibly could; but try and picture in your mind's eye an enormous machine, with a hopper at one end and conveyer belt at the other.

Into a hopper go phenomenal quantities of the raw material. It's invisible and intangible, naturally, so they use special harmless dyes to make it easier to perceive and handle. These are burnt off in the processing.

That's us.

So if some cleverdick philosopher comes up to you and tries to tell you that Man is the measure of all things and we're working towards an ultimate purpose, take no notice. The role of humanity in the Great Design is somewhere between permitted food colouring and bar codes.

Time is a convenient if misleading term used to describe the potential energy of the impending future. It burns, and the gases produced by its combustion compress a piston in the cylinder of physics, producing the power needed to turn the year on its axis and drive the barrel-organ of the spheres. Like most internal combustion engines, its burn is depressingly inefficient; Time burns at about one-per-cent efficiency, because the future is so impure with alternative sequences of events that only a minute part of each load of raw material actually oxidises on ignition. The rest might have burnt if only things had been different.

The waste material comes out the back end, is loaded on tipper trucks and taken away for the neighbours to complain about. And boy, do they complain.

CHAPTER TWENTY-TWO

Over the years there have been many attempts to describe Hell, some more felicitous than others. Jean-Paul Sartre, for example, would have you believe that Hell is other people.

Now, then; no disrespect whatsoever to the late Mr Sartre, as fine a writer as ever honed a subordinate clause and by all accounts a very competent amateur pianist. But no. To be disagreeably pedantic, Hell isn't other people at all. Other people are never worse than bloody aggravating. Hell is *hell*.

It's a very hot, noisy, unpleasant place full of inhuman tortures and bird-headed fiends; and the moonlight walking tours, souvenir sweatshirts and conference weekends introduced by the new management have, if anything, added to the efficiency of an already superbly effective eternity-spoiling unit. Any attempt at description which omits these basic elements is inaccurate.

And EuroBosch is to Hell as Piccadilly Circus is to England; more picturesque, perhaps, if you like that sort of thing, but definitely an integral part. The same rules apply; and one of the rules is that all stories in Hell have to have an unhappy ending.

* * *

The emergency exit opened.

Helen looked up, catching her breath. For a moment she couldn't see anything. Then . . .

. . . Then she cast her mind back, involuntarily, to a moment some years ago (though it seemed like only yesterday).

'Hi,' he'd said. 'My name's George. You must be Helen.'

This strange voice, coming at her from incredibly far off. A nice voice, she remembered thinking as the particles of matter and soul that had once comprised her being were suddenly scooped back from the four corners of creation for a totally unexpected reunion. A calm, wry voice, slightly cynical but not bitter. The sort of voice . . .

Just a cotton-picking minute, she remembered thinking, I'm dead. Life and I were very adult about it all and went our separate ways long ago, no recriminations, death is never having to say you're sorry.

'Pleased to meet you,' said the voice. 'I've heard *so* much about you, and . . .'

Goddammit, she'd got her legs back. And *her* legs, too; the long, perfectly proportioned honey-coloured ones she'd had as a girl, not the varicose travesties they'd fobbed her off with in her declining years. And her arms, too, and her ears, and her lips and *everything*; the whole ensemble, in fact, all in perfect working order. No scent of mothballs, no corners chewed off by earth-dwelling invertebrates. Her hair was even combed, her nails varnished. Cerise, which wasn't really her colour, but . . .

'Yippee!' she said.

'Do you mind?' retorted the voice called George. 'Only, my head is a wee bit sensitive this morning. Would you just sign here, please?'

She'd opened her eyes, and seen – well, a big piece of paper, with black squiggles all over it. They'd had paper in her day, back around 1450 BC, but not black squiggles.

'It's just a receipt,' the voice called George had told her, 'for Mephisto here. Just to say you've got your body back and it works okay. Mephisto's a good lad, for a foul fiend, but he does love his admin. Go on, just do a squiggle or something.'

She'd found a feather in her hand, with something black and wet on the end; some sort of paint, presumably. 'You want me to paint something on the paper with this feather?'

'Yes, please.'

'All right.' She splodged, and the pen and the paper vanished. And there she was. In this sort of place, sitting on what she could only presume was a chair, looking at something which might almost have been a table. On the table was a wine bottle, wrapped in straw, with a candle shoved in its neck.

'I think I'll have the sole in butter,' said the voice called George, 'followed by the stroganoff. What about you?' The voice, she noticed, was coming out of the mouth of this man sitting opposite her. He looked nice.

'To eat,' he explained. Yes, she'd thought, definitely nice. Priorities absolutely right and everything.

Over lunch he'd explained. How he'd always wanted to meet her, Helen of Troy, and how, since he'd sold his soul to the devil for an effectively blank cheque, her having been dead for well over three thousand years wasn't the insuperable problem it might have been, and how here they were with a ticket to ride throughout Time and Space, expense no object, if she felt like coming along.

'This,' he'd said, gesturing at the environment and nearly knocking a bowl of soup out of the hands of a passing waiter, 'is the twentieth century AD. Not the best of times, in my opinion, except for the food. I come here for lunch most days, in fact.'

'This place?'

'This century. It's worth the effort just for the pasta.'

'Ah.'

'But not the wine.' He'd frowned. 'Phylloxera, in the early

part of the century. Killed off all the best varieties of grape.'

In actual fact she hadn't really taken to him all that much, not at first; he seemed a bit arrogant, seen and done everything, met everyone, been everywhere. The fact that he *had* seen and done everything, met everyone and been everywhere only made it worse. There was also the fact that he'd brought her back to life from the grave, and gratitude is always a truly poisonous start to any relationship.

On the other hand, a choice between going about with a suave, accomplished, amusing, handsome man-about-Time-and-Space who has virtually infinite magic powers, and being dead, isn't exactly something you agonise over in the small hours of the morning. And after a relatively short while, she realised that being aggravating was only one facet of the man's multiplex persona. A significant facet, to be sure; but only one. Besides, George Faustus being aggravating had a lot to recommend it, particularly when he was being aggravating to somebody else. The Pope, for instance, or Napoleon, or the head waiter at Maxim's.

She'd become quite fond of him, in fact.

Which was why, the first time he'd been foreclosed upon and dragged away to Hell by bird-headed fiends, she'd been really rather upset. She had no great desire to see it happen a second time.

Accordingly, she turned her head and looked away.

Therefore she didn't see a howling, lurching nightmare of demons, beast-, bird-, and fish-headed, loathsome random assemblies from the spares box of evolution, whooping and brandishing toasting forks, kicking and dancing their way in a phantasmagorical conga against a background of leaping red flames; and, hoisted on their shoulders, the small, motionless figure of Lucky George.

Imagine . . . There isn't enough cheese in the world, Wensleydale, Stilton and Brie, to make up a bedtime snack capable of giving rise to the sort of bad dream you'd need to picture it in your mind's bloodshot eye. A riot of tentacles, pincers and talons. A maelstrom of pitchforks, meathooks, carving knives and corkscrews. Teeth beyond the wildest opium vision of dentistry, claws beyond even Satan's chiropody. Enough scaled hides to make handbags for all the witches in eternity. Enough plastic red noses . . .

Plastic red noses? Wait a minute . . .

Kurt Lundqvist, well and truly into the bourbon and branch-water, hold the branchwater, looked up and grinned. Thanks to enough alcohol to poison Chicago, he could now see clearly that he'd in fact succeeded, and the inevitable happy ending was chiming in nicely on cue. After all, he reasoned, as another billion brain cells fizzed into mucous slime, the fact that a bunch of penny-a-day fiends made the actual collar is neither here nor there. If he hadn't chased George into the one place on the whole campus where there was no possibility whatsoever of escape, there'd have been no collar at all.

'Drinks all round,' he snarled. 'C'mon, move it.'

The barfiend favoured him with a look of pure hatred.

'It's a quarter to three,' he said. 'Unhappy hour,' he explained. 'There's no-one in the place 'cept you and—'

'Okay,' Lundqvist replied. 'So I'll have another.'

As we mentioned a moment ago, the demons danced. And as they danced, they sang:

For he's a jolly good fellow
For he's a jolly good fellow
For he's a jolly good fellow –
And so say all of us.

All stories in Hell have an unhappy ending. Unhappy for whom is at the discretion of the management.

'Three cheers,' yelled the lead demon, pulling off his rubber mask, 'for Lucky George. *Hip hip . . .*'

'Hooray!' bellowed Julius Vanderdecker, Sir Thomas More, Hieronymus Bosch and Leonardo da Vinci, through their latex mouthpieces.

'Hip hip . . .'

'Hooray!' answered Niccolò Machiavelli, Christopher Columbus, Pieter Breughel the Elder, William Caxton, two seagulls, Lorenzo de' Medici, Sir Thomas Malory, Pol de Limbourg and Andrea del Sarto.

'Hip hip . . .'

'Hooray!' shouted the rest of the friends of Lucky George, raising their burden, pink with embarrassment and smiling foolishly, shoulder-high.

The barfiend turned and scowled meaningfully.

'Hooray,' muttered Kurt Lundqvist into his glass. 'Satisfied?'

All stories in Hell have an unhappy ending. The trick is therefore to keep going, so that there can be no ending.

The procession halted, dumped their rubber masks and stood. No prizes for guessing what was expected to happen next. Nevertheless, Lenny da Vinci, master of the unnecessary remark, shouted, 'Speech!'

Lucky George looked down, smiled, and scratched his ear.

'Thanks,' he said. 'I owe you all one.'

'Any time,' chorused the friends of Lucky George; and, for the first time, Helen guessed exactly why they called him Lucky.

The procession stayed halted and continued to stand. It's at times like this that inevitably somebody says, 'First of all I want to thank my agent.'

It is to George's eternal credit that he didn't. Instead, he made a vague gesture with his left hand and smiled . . .

. . . Whereupon the biggest, shiniest yellow brick road you ever saw materialised under everyone's feet. Straight as an arrow it ran, right across the middle of the theme park, due north. It was at this point that the Production Director, who'd been watching gobsmacked from the Bridge Embattled by Armies, leant over the parapet and threw up.

'Well, quite,' said the Marketing Director, standing next to him. 'On the other hand . . .'

His colleague looked up, hurriedly wiping his face with his sleeve. 'You can't be serious,' he gasped.

The Marketing Director shrugged. 'Okay,' he said, 'integrity counts for something in this game, but we've got shareholders to consider. And what it all boils down to in the final analysis is bums on seats.'

'Not seats,' insisted the Production Director. 'Spikes.'

'Whatever.' The Marketing Director stood for a moment, his head tilted slightly to one side, visualising. 'All right, maybe it's not our idea of Hell, yours and mine. But so what? We have,' he added ingenuously, 'a duty to the public. Elitism's a thing of the past, you know. You've got to go with the mood, right?'

'No.'

'That's your final word, then, is it?'

'Yes.'

'The hell with you then,' replied the Marketing Director affably, pushing his colleague off the bridge into the leaping flames below. Then he straightened his tie, and marched purposefully away in search of Walt Disney.

'George,' said Helen.

'Mmmm?'

'Where exactly are we going?'

George looked down. Under his feet, still yellow bricks, although the procession had now diminished down to two, plus a pair of seagulls circling high overhead.

'Does it matter?'

Helen snuggled closer. 'Not really, I suppose,' she replied. 'Just so long as when we get there, there's going to be fitted carpets.'

'Maybe, love.'

'And matching curtains. Say there's going to be matching curtains, George, go on please.'

'All right,' said George, 'there'll be matching curtains. Somewhere.'

'Where?'

George thought for a moment. 'Would "over the rainbow" be sufficiently precise, do you think?'

'No.'

'Oh.' He sucked his lower lip. 'Do they really have to match?' he asked.

'Yes.'

'Couldn't they clash even slightly?'

Helen shook her head. 'George,' she said, 'I've waited for you over three thousand years, I've lied for you, stolen for you, been kidnapped for you, followed you to Hell and back, don't you think I've *earned* matching curtains?'

'Well . . .' George considered. 'Just so long as they're not pink,' he said.

'What I had in mind was more a sort of pinky peach,' Helen replied, 'to go with the loose covers, which I thought of as being something like pale apricot, with perhaps just a hint of—'

'And a shed,' he added. 'I really must insist on a shed. Somewhere I can work on the magic and that sort of thing.'

Helen laughed musically. 'If there's time,' she said. 'I shall need a lot of shelves putting up.'

The sun chose that moment to glint on Helen's hair, as golden as ripe corn; or, as George couldn't help thinking, more a sort of light honey with just a soupçon of goldy fawn.

'All right,' said George, meekly. 'Anything you say.'

Somewhere in the Sublime, God looked up from his lathe and laughed.